PRAE

VOL. 2

MIKLÓS SZENTKUTHY

PRAE

VOL. 2

MIKLÓS SZENTKUTHY

* *

TRANSLATED BY
ERIKA MIHÁLYCSA

Contra Mundum Press   New York · London · Melbourne

Selected Other Works by
Miklós Szentkuthy

Prae, vol. I

Towards the One & Only Metaphor

Chapter on Love

St. Orpheus Breviary, vol. I: Marginalia on Casanova

St. Orpheus Breviary, vol. II: Black Renaissance

This book is dedicated to the memory of TIM WILKINSON (1947–2020), who first brought Szentkuthy to the Anglo-Saxon world. Without him, this adventure would never have begun.

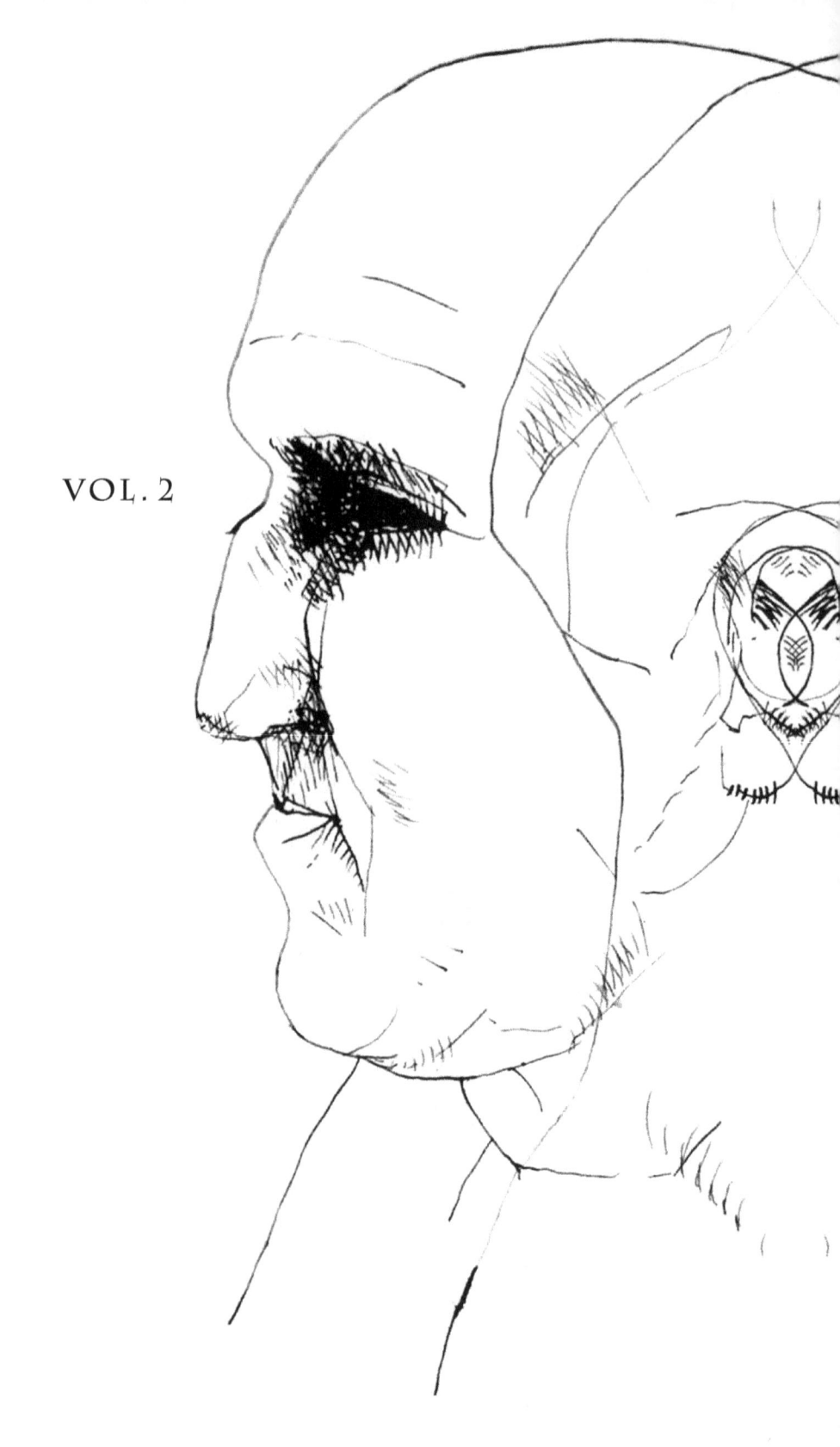

VOL. 2

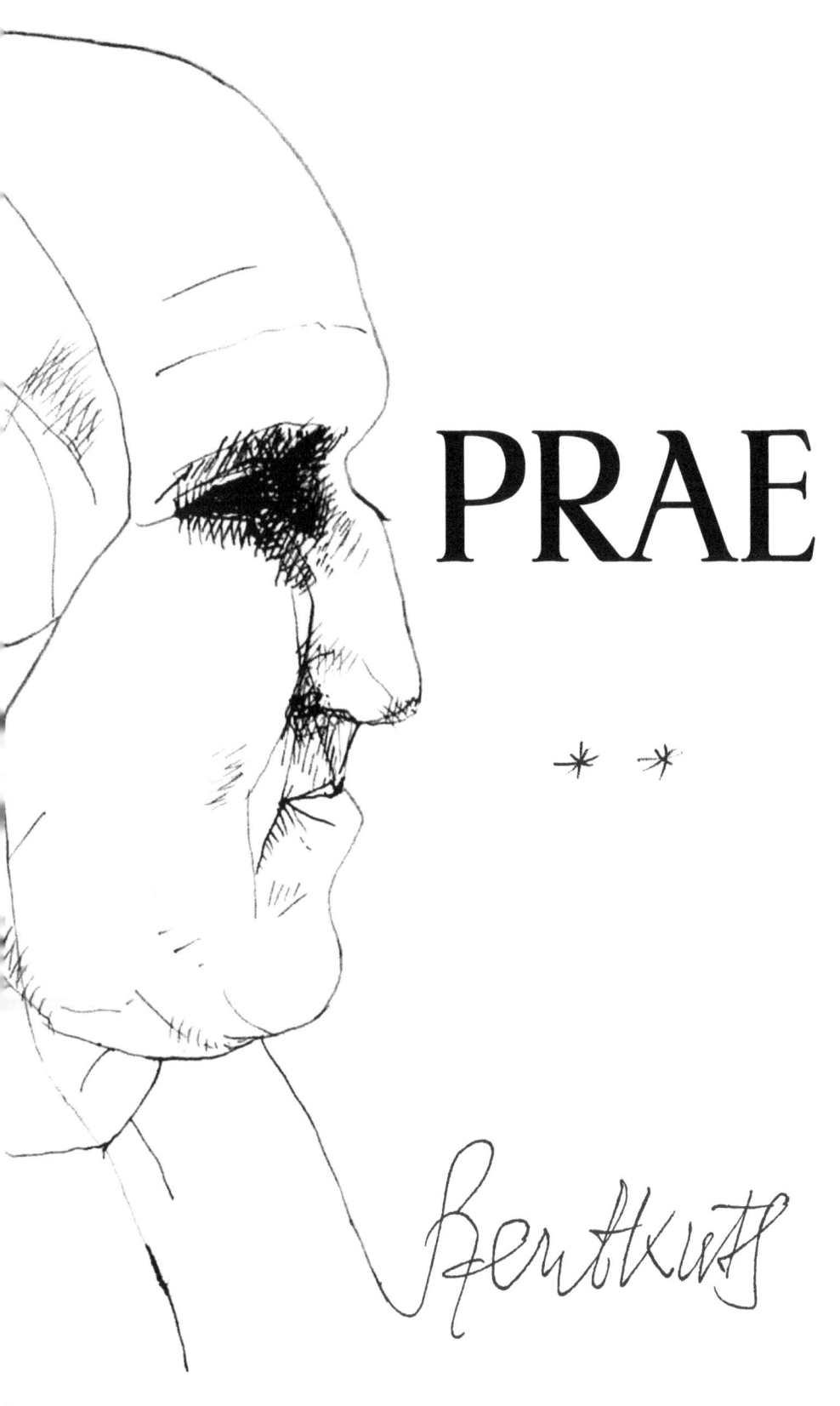

PRAE

* *

Prae © 1980 by Miklós Szentkuthy; translation of *Prae* © 2022 Erika Mihálycsa

Published by arrangement with Mariella Legnani-Pfisterer & Maria Tompa of the Szentkuthy Estate.

First Contra Mundum Press Edition 2022. This edition of *Prae* is based on the version published by Magvető in 1980.

All Rights Reserved under International & Pan-American Copyright Conventions. No part of this book may be reproduced in any form or by any electronic means, including information storage and retrieval systems, without permission in writing from the publisher, except by a reviewer who may quote brief passages in a review.

Library of Congress Cataloguing-in-Publication Data

Szentkuthy, Miklós, 1908–1988

[Prae. English.]

Prae / Miklós Szentkuthy; translated from the original Hungarian by Erika Mihálycsa

—1st Contra Mundum Press Edition
740 pp., 6x9 in.

ISBN 9781940625515

I. Szentkuthy, Miklós.
II. Title.
III. Mihálycsa, Erika.
IV. Translator & Afterword.

2014958637

The afterword is a revised, expanded version of the essay "'A Book-bug Homunculus' Catalogue of Learning': On the Maverick Modernist Poetics of Hungarian Novelist Miklós Szentkuthy," in *Borders of Modernism*, Annalisa Volpone, Massimiliano Tortora (eds) (Perugia: Morlacchi, 2019) 283–306.

⇌ Table of Contents ⇌

IX.

756   *problems and possibilities of figure description; Leatrice as nobody & as everybody; first as 'nobody': theme for a fantastic short story*

764   *Leatrice as 'everybody'; excerpts from a typologia universalis: description of four women in swimsuits*

769   *what are love's two concretenesses? couldn't Leatrice be built from them?*

771   *absolute externals (shoes, stockings, shoulder-straps): shoes*

776   *the stocking*

790   *another entry to absolute externals: the shoulder-strap*

799   *(introductory simile: the design of the Double Face Theater, pp. 770–771); the relation of individual and average in female beauty*

803   *after absolute externals, absolute pain; example: the fear of lovers from an illegitimate child*

808   *ramification of projects and realizations*

X.

810	*Leatrice by the sea, morning. Description of the morning*
812	*the morning's intellectual laboratory (schism of contents and forms, etc.)*
816	*analogies to dawn: modern architecture, glass civilization*
819	*Touqué's caricature of the psyche*
820	*the struggle between dream, thought, thinking, action, language*
824	*thinking and feeling are identical movements (pp. 826–827), lead theme: remembering the glasses of yesterday*
827	*remembrance of combing*
829	*absolute feeling and 'homo'*
830	*two kinds of 'human being' emotion: naïve-concrete and dizzy-empty; mirror*
834	*Fourth Non-Prae diagonal; the diary of an adulterous princess*
	of lying
	rhetoric and posture
	at night in the deserted home
	Moon and space
	remembrance of afternoon naps
	lies and secrets, freedom and guilt-feeling
	night at the villa
	happiness and nothing
	beauty and 'humanity'
	the annihilation of the 'human being'
	bad counterparts to suffering and pleasure
	fear
	should she return to her husband?
	her husband falls victim to a misfortune
	company: a madman, a corpse, a fictive character & a lied-about figure
	two conclusions to the question of 'humanism'

856   *bath and body-consciousness (etherealness and hall)*

860   *grey skylight*

864   *associations: winter afternoons; to snowfall: the design of a parenthetical church*

866   *confession*

867   *skyline and kiss*

867   *associations: clockface on a winter afternoon when her uncle is late*

871   *Leatrice's 'Europeanness': blend of hypochondria and beastliness*

874   *the carillon*

878   *once again that clockface*

879   *two types of representation of the psyche*

XI.

882   *return to yesterday's champagne glasses (see pp. 872–873); a ship ashore at dawn*

885   *remembrance of her uncle's loves*

886   *the concept of 'sickness' in childhood*

888   *the concept of 'loneliness' in childhood*

891   *simile: a landscape on a German postcard, and a corresponding simile: the Berlin performance and stage setting of* Kabale und Liebe

895   *Fifth Non-Prae diagonal: the diary of the scholar-teacher of a noble family's children*

    truth and moment

    two plans: De Incongruentia Criteriorum;
        De Vacuis Perspectivis

    absolute emotion-life

    intellect, emotion, objectivity

    comparison to the lover: Diana-statue under water

the problem of reality in absolute only-emotion life
the dichotomy of body and sensuousness
the love letter, a melody fragment
the lover: will, therefore evil
annihilating objectivity
an evening walk, death
the theme project of The Honeymoon; the lover is will, therefore evil
the above illustrated by shopping for a bag: example of will
imagined happiness: the woman doesn't want him
the epistemology of happiness
sipping tea alone in the dark: philistinism and mysticism
ethical qualms
example of a short story for contrasting pleasure and moral
Sancta Immediata
the ethics of action
dressing up the terminally ill cardinal before the evening sermon
by car to the church, rain, crowd
pro domo: why is it that in this work a cardinal is found so often in the company of sin?
— childishness
— the reduction of the whole world to some abstract ethical absolutes, temptation as foundational experience
the cardinal's counterpart: the little proselyte

XII.

945   Leatrice's uncle (Peter) visits a female acquaintance. He waits for the ferryman in a tavern
948   about the difference between dream and reality in parenthesis
949   about a beautiful woman's beauty
952   the sacristan's character

956 view from the sacristy window
958 the relation between action and conscience
964 two kinds of shadow
965 Peter's hypochondria, virtue, connoisseurship of women
969 Sixth Non-Prae diagonal: Chinese marriage, Christian love

> fish and river
> the river at night
> the fisherman and his daughter
> the fisherman's daughter plots to kill the Chinese princess, but the princess changes into the double of the fisherman's daughter; she has the fisherman's daughter tortured
> the bridegroom, a prince comes on a ship
> the old inquisitor and his adoptive son
> landscape under the volcano
> the love of the fisherman's daughter and the adoptive son
> the Chinese wife tortures her husband but he doesn't harm her, regarding his wife as a force of nature
> 'human being' and irreality in love
> logic and church plan
> suicide and hymn to 'nameless forces of nature'

XIII.

986 the influence of Peter's sin-snobbery on Leatrice; sin and elegance
987 to the scheme of sin and elegance: Leatrice's acquaintance with Zwinskaya. Zwinskaya's character: morphine and peasant
994 Zwinskaya and the officer
995 love and etiquette
996 love and metaphorizing biology
997 the 'grownup' meaning of 'simplicity'
999 the concept of 'simplicity' and the trees and leaves of the gardens of W***

1001	æsthetics and the stylistics of nature
1003	Zwinskaya's hat; woman as landscape
1005	female beauty as the Manichean model of good and evil; about mystical and analytical expression on the side
1007	the detective novel as the perfect image of the moralizing beauty-concept discussed above. Example: the violet glove; Halbert's detective novel: The Blessed Practical
1011	the reciprocal influence of naturalist dramatic roles and chic on Zwinskaya's manner; her movements, play of muscles
1014	the difference between girls' and women's vanity
1019	one of Peter's novelistic themes set against mundanity: the vision of moral scrupulousness (Scarpellino)
1024	Leatrice and the 'anti-tragic'
1025	Leatrice's body and Romanesque (eros and Ghibellinism)
1028	the relation of the two worlds of over-the-top self-consciousness and over-the-top caritas in Leatrice's life
1032	dream and church plan
1035	Touqué and waves
1037	chaos and order
1038	bathing woman comes ashore
1039	reason and unknown in nature
1042	the sienna swimsuit
1043	'I' and perception in love
1045	against analyzing the soul
1046	the 'second precision' and an example of it: a mystical story of Tyato and biologized dogma
1053	the example of the 'second precision' continued; the image changes: greyness first, then a red flower on a salon table. Comparison with the red flower

1056	*Tilia Parvifolia's salon: the squat furniture*
1058	*the armchair; Tilia and her son*
1063	*morning shadows*
1066	*the relation of speech and the female body*
1070	*Tilia's essence: the alien vase*
1071	*this is the foundation of 'anti-tragic' thinking, that is, of the greatest conceivable opposite to Peter's thought (cf. pp. 1020–1024)*
1073	*Tilia speaks*
1076	*theme for a short story (a fastidious bishop and the girl who fled to the woods)*

XIV.

THE MEDITATIONS OF HALBERT'S FATHER, AN ANGLICAN VICAR OF EXETER.

1081	*Exeter, 1933, on absolute individualism*
1083	*suffering, distance from God*
1086	*about the concept of 'complexity'*
1088	*7 o'clock bells, subjectivism*
1094	*moral*
1095	*politics and morphinism*
1097	*moral and problem*
1099	*childhood fairy-tales and 'grownup' materialism*
1100	*his wife's castle park*
1101	*toward the most perfect pain-formula; logic and dream*
1103	*defending himself against the accusation of 'materialism' and venality; asceticism and private property*

1108	whatever he touches becomes an ethical question. The theme of *Juanus Ethicus*
1110	the park's solitary gate
1113	once again about private property; æsthetics
1116	'universals': non est
1118	pain, dream, architecture. Project for a bedroom
1120	musical plans
1121	landscape fragment and private property
1123	against certain kinds of paradoxes
1124	silence
1125	the relation of truth and language, the dilemma of identification or fiction
1128	theme for a short story: the vision of fastidiousness (Avido)
1130	problems and possibilities of editing; novel structure and ground plan of a villa
1134	landscape around the wife's castle
1136	theme for a short story about the beautiful woman, the psychology of temptation, and the Garden of Faithfulness
1141	the lake's transparency and non-transparency; two kinds of landscape: infinite transparency and finite localization. Their connection to love
1143	object before the human being. Its cause; an example: a Stuttgart film about the gloves, titled *Adam and Eve*
1146	analysis of the stairs
1150	finite and infinite; the relation between medieval allegory and 'sachlich' emblem
1153	explaining the catechism in the church
1155	the atmosphere of damnation and idyll

1157	to the above, a childhood memory: description of a castle's interior (low ceiling room and coat-of-arms; history; portraits and gnome; the position of the chairs; mossy pond; tapestries, nudes; enfilade and love; Tudor roofbeams)
1166	to this, a further example of idyll: a banker and his wife (the wife in the car at night in front of the bank; telephone call; metaphysics of grids; the connections of money and rococo; woman, value, and purchase; money clinic; the porter's wife and death) — the end of the two themes attached to 'damnation and idyll'
1179	ontology and masquerade
1180	the irreality of female beauty
1186	the masked woman; still, the most ancient human inclination is goodness
1194	hatred of the woman
1196	theme for a short story on the eternal relationship between death and idyll (interchangeability of kiss and murder)
1198	microscopic threads of faithfulness; fear from damnation
1201	utopia of absolute sorrow; hysteria and Satan
1204	prayer in the church
1206	description of a church; metaphor and Cubism, church plan
1209	one needs to die with all the memories, not just those of the last few days; about great unfaithfulnesses after 'microscopic faithfulness' (see pp. 1198–1200)
1212	the mutual exclusion of love and the human being; two lovers; their psychology, moral, connection to Juanus Ethicus
1214	the ugly women
1216	the heresy of identity (the bending of 'parallel' lines)
1217	senses and intellectualism

1219	æsthetics; dream as producer of categories; category as producer of beauty
1221	biology and mathematics
1222	experiment: a peculiarly quaint, pedantic style elicits the absolute experience of beauty in the author of the Meditations
1227	beauty
1229	about the styles of the different epochs; the different epochs' view of themselves
1230	in connection to the number of styles, games about numbers in general; what is true structure? About the swapped letters à la Bernouilli
1235	three editing techniques
1237	woman and beauty, Bernoulli permutations and 17th-century Baroque or modern Surrealism; experiment for analyzing beauty: woman at night in the hotel hall
1239	$n = n + q$
1242	visuality and reason
1243	another experiment for the analysis of beauty: project for a consciously over-the-top 17th-century horror drama: Night of Innocence
1246	parenthesis: the lurking homage to the Catholicism of the author of the Meditations
1248	sensuousness toward relations: the outcome of the second experiment
1250	the clergy: the relation of the author of the Meditations to sin and God
1253	his intellectual life, ideas, and the place of ideas
1256	action; the struggle of moral value and dehumanization
1261	the dilemma of identity: tautology or otherness; its significance in the investigation of beauty

1265	*alienness of woman-image and desire-image*
1268	*imago habet suam essentiam in non esse imago*
1270	*incandescing self-identity amounts to self-estrangement; to this, the lesson of a glass mural (the two kinds of stars)*
1272	*self-doubling*
1274	*about the nature of goodness*
1276	*types of virtue; ontologizing ethics and action-ethics*
1278	*virtue and damnation*
1280	*variation on predestination; thinking in moral absolutes*
1282	*remembrance of a 'sinful' kiss*
1284	*night in the Swiss hotel; he goes for a walk*
1289	*the basic difficulties of virtue*
1291	*the painted-over clothes of the kissed girl: from beige to green; their analysis. In the meantime, the wife's modified clothes*
1301	*the paradox of 'infinite' temptation*
1302	*the creation of numbers and moral*
1305	*problems of the analytic style, its nature of leading outside itself; the part of something and otherness*
1310	*the color green and a comparison to it, of a fictitious green plant*
1311	*association with the color green: meadow between Cambridge and Ely, where he met a half-idiot girl; landscape and caritas*
1315	*the infinite love of Christian love*
1318	*about the so-called 'contradiction' of emotions, example: he is going to meet a girl in snowy weather*
1320	*there are no 'emotions,' only one basic psychic intensity*
1322	*description of the half-idiot girl; her caress: absolute caritas, perhaps more absolute than a charitable deed; what is the surplus here?*

1326	*absolute love and the psyche; personality is the death of caritas*
1331	*face mimicry, perception, and pan-love*
1332	*the half-idiot girl's mention of violets, analysis of the violets*
1337	*absolute love's relation to 'homo' and 'humanum': body, soul, artificial body, artificial soul*
1339	*the difference between moral act and moral Sache*
1344	*the visible end of love (the opposite of caritas); analysis of the speech of women from this perspective*
1351	*speech and action are things outside love; example: with a woman at dawn (the color blue); other example: Dialogue with the Undialoguable (impossibility of love 'life')*
1354	*in parenthesis: new thinking technique; contrast between thought and thinking*
1355	*love and inescapable lie*
1357	*continuation of the analysis of female speech*
1360	*a Magnasco reproduction as the illustration of love's 'impossibility'*
1362	*two pseudo-expressions; ideal: absolute gesture (dance?) and absolute mathematicalization*
1364	*against 'nuance'; for the kaleidoscope*
1366	*dance and politics*
1368	*return to the color green (Cambridge meadow: the painted-over dress of the girl 'sinfully' kissed in Switzerland): the Elizabethan lady-in-waiting symbolizing Cambridge*
1369	*studying and fugitive impressions (truth and moment); green grass*
1374	*lack of precision and caritas*
1377	*the outcomes of the half-idiot girl's speech; first conclusion: identity of modern architecture, caritas, and the syntax of madness (architectural example)*
1380	*second conclusion: detailed orchestral score from landscape scores, the identity of music, caritas, and the syntax of madness*

1384 *third conclusion: the moral significance of perspective, the identity of painting, caritas, and the syntax of madness*

1386 *with the half-idiot girl by the evening water and enveloping trees*

1387 *the fusion of private property, caritas, and nature in ultimate happiness*

1393 *the analysis of lovemaking*

1396 *the identity of natural forms (leaves) and metropolitan mirror reflections*

1398 *the relativizing of order and disorder, the seceding of forms and contents*

1400 Endnotes

1420 Afterword: Dogmatic Accidentalism. Miklós Szentkuthy's *Prae* and the Chaocosmic Novel

PRAE

II

IX.

problems and possibilities of figure description;
Leatrice as nobody & as everybody; first as 'nobody':
theme for a fantastic short story

— Excuse me, but is there something with Leatrice? — someone asked.

The other answered in his turn with a question:

— Leatrice? — and then fell silent. The first sentence's "is there something" hazily returned into its own tunnel, like a giant double blue fox behind a glass door; the woman stands too far to be seen, but the fur's gliding Simplon-brush casts a large shadow-blot on the glass as it curls up around the two invisible, but naked shoulders, like those rings thrown about on the playground that little boys catch in flight with their sticks: is there something?, followed by the bare name, Leatrice: by accident one clacking ring fell on a swimming pool tin slide and is now rolling, tripping on itself, toward the water. Both men enjoyed the benumbed existence of the third person; the "is there something" rocked them into the skyblue siesta of discreet gossip, & the name's loneliness shone like a daytime star on the Riviera. No more about Leatrice. Invisible, but naked shoulders behind the glass door: gossip ("is there something": it is so positive that it barely qualifies as gossip, rather as obloquy) in fact plays a double chemistry with its prepared victim — turning the victim both into a nude and into nothing, and this is as pleasant for gossipers as Hag-coffee for the cardiac patient.[214]

Some story is woven around Leatrice, which lines her in front like the five-line staff does the treble clef, while in the back it soaks off her clothes, like hot water the old posters from a billboard — something is happening with her, due to which something will finally transpire about her, moreover, we'll come to know everything, and when all knowledge will be in our hands as a wax-weeping, candlestick-less candle, then it will cast such light on the surrounding people, motor boats in repair, artificial flowers, seas, everything, that nothing will be visible and comprehensible anymore — the whole Kursaal or 'humana conditio' will be one unmoving blank reverberation.

All this is in broad outlines the birth of Eve: the shoulders' cottonwool-lined golf putters tumble forth from among the leaves' green stamps, the first scent of positivity stretches along the nearest breeze-ribbon's rolling stairs & sketches a long, faintly cynical perfume graphics around Adam's nose. And when Adam starts on the scent, like foreign tourists' indexes on Paris subway maps, the garden is suddenly flooded by light, from Eve's nakedness every single leaf, flower, and blind rapture-aspic turns into scintillating gnosis, and now it's too late to clarify whose eros it wanted in the first place, that of light, or that of the lamp?

This could be Leatrice's sole Shakespearean dramaturgy: "is there something," and this could be Leatrice's sole philosophy: 'Leatrice,' her name. Small nominalist plug on the sea's marginal waves, on those waves that gravity's undeliverable and unabortable weight renders so clunky on the inside and so elegant on the outside, like a top hat's arched brim: Leatrice, Leatrice. Around her, time — the diligent cosmetics of hours, as the minute hand's slender brush paints the minute-soul's quivering lashes long and sharp around time's Longines iris — the seasons, life's colorful large veils, peeling coats-of-arms for another, unknown time, which is approaching us, we signal to it with the garish semaphores of spring, summer, and autumn to get out of the way, for the lane is taken.

If someone is made up solely of a first name and 'is there something,' then their life-story, should we summarize it for school textbooks, can only look like this:

In Venice a cardinal is celebrating mass. On the church's porch a red hat with multi-story tassels whose triangles flare ever more outward, down into the water, like fish to be multiplied. The cardinal is saying mass for his younger sister, believed to be dead. In front of the church the stairs rock like a soaking book, only two gondolas stand fixed, as if outside the water, their haughty dented prow-heads locked into one another like the rotating radio condensers with which they are perhaps cherry-picking the dead girl's soul.

Then a third gondola arrives. The water is so transparent that boats look like mirages or suspended bridges, the inventory numbers daubed on their underbellies can be read more clearly than the lyrical names plastered on their bows: instead of Nymph, Azure Bird, Eel, we can read X^2. — *(om. Venez.*, 112–33. *Mun. Adr. Hydr*; when the water turns truly crystal-clear, then bureaucracy finds its moment to triumph.

The new gondola is nothing more than a long, long charcoal line coming after a wave, but sometimes it's the water that turns black and above it the gondola's infinite oarlock is a glaring white blotting-paper edge, while at other times it is the water that becomes nothing and the gondola above, nothingness' un-tuned-haughty string: the one is the 'position zero' of rational functions, when the numerator's profile is suddenly annihilated without dragging the denominator along into nothingness, and the 'pole' is the other, when it's the denominator's turn to disappear, while the numerator continues to poke its nose into the shiny canal of existence. So the guest arrives at the crossing between pole and nil, neither on water nor on boat: the masked muse of function mathematics, to a funeral mass.

All of a sudden the church's mouth grabs the gondola (when it happens to exist), like a giant flat piece of bait. The other two stir, the boatmen sitting on the bank grumble something, from the gondola a woman jumps out and as soon as she gets ashore, she accidentally pushes her boat off the bank, it makes a huge turn, like a compass whose needle we trapped with our finger, but now, released, it clanks with wild momentum onto the black N. Inside chanting and the organ resound like the wind entangled in treecrowns. Now the function graph of boat and water is the following: a taper placed on a glass sheet and its shadow, that is, two intersecting circles, which nevertheless run into different worlds.

The girl is mad & believes that she is the cardinal's sister. She doesn't know that everybody believes the sister to be dead, so she doesn't know that the funeral mass is held for the one she believes to be. There are few people in the church, she fearfully fits her body into the general piety like one sticking a little finger into the right sheath of the glove, after first pushing it into the place of the ring finger. She asks her neighbors who the requiem is for. They tell her. Is she then dead? — she asks herself in surprise. What is in the place of the real sister, what error-graphics does the unexpected cross-section of superstition show? The cardinal believes her to be dead, the madwoman believes her to be herself, while having to imagine her living self dead: prayer, imagined death, real death, madness, real life — all possibilities of the cardinal's sister. Where is she in truth?

Across from the church, recently a man had a luxury villa built, which is watched over by detectives. The police suspect that the sister is not dead and her disappearance is connected with this man. One of the rooms overlooks the garden. Thick glass walls, white furniture, mercury-color statues and lamps, blond plants, blond fish; luminosity lies about here in such bars (no artificial light but daytime's whisked color) as gold in the banks' cheek pouches. The entire room testifies to the fact that the beamless clarity of the day is a far greater crime-backdrop than the night or electric light. In the room one sole white flower is repeated in the statues, food, chastity-sheaths: a large petal that forms a candy-stencil cone from which one thick stamen mace juts out, on its end a short wick. On the walls greyish sinks in which the morning's disinfected clarity of perception sits like holy water; large floor mirrors collect the sky's morning whiteness into consciousness-bleaching pools. (Invisible, but naked shoulders!)

The detectives are watching this room. A courageous one has got quite close to the glass wall and sees dimly (the glass is not wholly transparent) the following: a man holds tight a goldfish-haired woman, one can hear the dry, soapy stages of lovemaking, the woman resists, the man hoists her up (the cardinal's sister had goldfish hair) and with the same momentum pushes her down on a divan and struggles with her. Suddenly there is silence. Does it mean murder or love-making?

Now the mad girl comes out of the church. She pries on the cardinal as he leaves the sacristy and stealthily follows him. The cardinal feels unwell, the woman runs to him, but too late — he collapses dead next to a small bridge. This catastrophe shakes the woman so much that she realizes she is not his sister. Alone in front of the church entrance is her gondola, the other two have left like a pair of skis on a Murano vase-slope. On the gondola the coat-of-arms of the cardinal's family, turned senseless; in the cardinal's head, the obsessive thought of the dead sister — at this moment the detective breaks the glass wall. He finds nothing but a large, goldfish-color bathrobe thrown on the divan. He runs with it from room to room, down to the cellars, but finds no-one in the house. He wants to go back but cannot, he's been locked in the cellar.

The comedy concludes with a conversation of angels from where we learn that the cardinal has never had a sister, only a younger brother who escaped from home to become a sailor, and this brother is the detective himself, down in the cellar with the goldfish-color bathrobe that he took to be the cardinal's sister. The detective doesn't know of course that the brother he left behind turned into a priest. He dies in the cellar, after consummating in an agony-dream his nuptials with the Lido bathrobe come to life. But the cardinal had prayed for his sister with such robust devoutness that the angels ask God to shape a truly living woman from the requiem prayer's material. Final scene: in the restaurant 'To the Goldfish' a man and woman get to know each other — their child is going to be the belatedly supplied sister.

This could be Leatrice's life-story, summed up with a school manual's aridity: the guignol-dogmatism of the complete irreality of individual life and of personality. There is something with Leatrice, someone said — but is there a Leatrice? When Leatrice's chapter begins, isn't this the most positive horizon for a starting point: the thousand-curved nonexistence, nothingness' infinite color-notch? When I watch her face, or her rubber-heels trembling on the springboard, or the poisonous-virginal slovenliness of the evening flower jutting from her shoulder, her individual presence presses against time's net with such mordant clarity to become nothing, luminosity — filling all the hidden, small hollows of existence with glaring convexity, the verb 'is' fills up to such an extent with the molten metals of precision, that it nearly topples from the shopwindow of grammar & life into the forms of a divine future.

What is her instep's angle of arching from heel to toes? Modesty, pretense of wobbliness, boyish prank, carbolic hygiene, spitefulness, buckled naïveté, tangential evidence: these innumerable possibilities prove that it's something exceptionally addressed to me, an acquaintance, inner relative, but an exceptionally selfish, closed thing, none of the inventory above — beauty grabs at once our innermost dream-routine and the furthest limits of the intellect.

Pure 'is,' the content of the radical present tense is always this: we can feel the dream-light taste of our innermost interior as it crosses over into a territory unavailable to reason but nevertheless felt to be pure reason. That's why a Leatrice narrative has to start from nothing as the first concreteness, absolute, dream-deep dream-vortex and inexpressible intellectual tension. Here dream doesn't mean dream-images, phantasmagorias, or the unreachable, but the pure rhythm that is suggested by the drowsy body's inner nerves; the waves of 'states' when consciousness has well-nigh left us.

This is the kind of dream that uses only a meremost minimum of the outside world, while using the utmost of the body's interiority (blood rhythm, lung movement, the shades of digestion). In fact it is no dream at all but studying a dark night lake's rhythm of rippling with the help of twine imbued in phosphorus: a 'key' is enough, for instance, to observe with it as with a minimal imagination-torch, the most varied internal states of our body, their tastes, movements, colors and weights. And when Leatrice or any extremely beautiful woman drives her barbed arrow very deep into the heart of praesens, then this dream-stage of ours reacts with all its anonymous forces, with our unknown self.

Here the most naïve paradox can best express truth, however loathsome the form of paradox may be for the ease with which it is churned out: it is our 'most unknown most well-known' dream-layer that incandesces every great sensation to the point of turning into our absolute kin and absolute not-I. Leatrice's walk (the walk is a woman's most inexpressible part) instantly becomes the expansion of our lungs, the opalescent sheen of chyle or our gullet's swinging hammer, but this turning-interior is at the same time a becoming-nothing, because our lungs, nurturing liquids, larynx, are only present under the form of blind sensations, however much they are ours. In the first moment we think we know everything, only in the second moment do we realize that we only feel everything.

But we want to know by all means. Of course the thing that falls the closest to the senses is the thing that is the most distant from reason: woman's beauty as possibility to intellectualize is obviously the most extreme liminal case of the intellect, lying at the greatest remove from us. Strong impressions always bifurcate. A swimsuit, for instance, is in a state between tightness and slackness above a woman's knees; that which we design with the nondescript, inexpressive word 'between' is felt a thousand times more precisely by impression — apart from seeing it, impression also feels it inside, and this inside feeling is not simply the imaginary carrying-forth of palpation but the immediate adjustment of the dream-layer to the shade of slackness — lungs, chyle, and gullet align to it with the precision of one thousandth of the vibration rate.

One prong of impression is this entire interior mimicry, the elastic imitation of the biological state sedimented into a dream. The other prong is the opposite of elasticity, the reason-prong: there is not a single concept in our consciousness that could in the least resemble the swimsuit's tight or slack state. But we can grasp it only logically — although we react to it with our most animal layer, still, our reaction to it is a reaction to the logical, we feel with ineradicable certainty (the lungs, chyle, and gullet feel so!) that the degree of slackness is a stern thesis, not an accidental blot, not an indeterminate possibility, but something as definite and unequivocal as a number.

So the first graphic is drawn under the sign of irrationality: Leatrice *is* so much, her erotic praesens-string stretches the two poles of dream and reason to such extent that she is annihilated. Is there something with Leatrice? Yes. No.

Leatrice as 'everybody'; excerpts from a typologia universalis: description of four women in swimsuits

But the matter can hardly be laid to rest with this, we must pursue it with a different technique — we must capture impression through thick and thin. This is the point when what might, with playful medievalism, be called the method of *typologia universalis*, suggests itself as a necessity (albeit far less as a possibility). Herod put all the babes to death to make sure that Jesus would die too: we must describe every imaginable woman, so that from the whole some Leatrice be born, from the totally catalogued-up society, one imprecise watercolor.

After the guignol story a chapter in this style follows — description of women at the seaside (many superficial descriptions): blond girl with violet maillot; every detail smacks of biedermeier naiveté and yet the whole is frivolous almost by the chronometer — the ground color is a bashful light violet, but the fabric is color-changing like the Victorian-age evening taffetas on our grandmothers' pictures; the belt is a wide silk ribbon that has nothing to do with sports, looking far rather like an old-fashioned curtain tieback near the window, with a sizable bow behind; on her head a scalloped cap with imitation lace. Snub nose, even snubber mouth, and snubbest of all, a blue gaze: it stipples in the air like ink on waxed paper. The walk is shy and hesitating, picking with her sandal from the sand the footprints that were mentally prepared well in advance as though poking at a currant with a fork whose gap between the prongs is wider than the currant's diameter. Her skin is so white that it brings to mind not nakedness but the bed, continuous paling under the duvet. Her maillot is as tight as on a blade of grass, its grass-blade-ness: indeed, the identity is even a few millimeters thinner than 'the.'

The second: goldfish-color swimsuit. A massive woman, muscular, robust, but not fat. The skin is not as white as on the previous one, but not yet skin-colored either: the feeling is not that she is wearing a sports trunk but only, that she has undressed, she has taken off her stockings. She keeps tugging at her swimsuit with unsuitable movements that look rather like the laid-back housewife's touches: this teaspoon a bit further from the cup, the croissant tongs not on the plate but next to it, touch the teapot with your palm to check if it's hot enough, etc. In her bun an enormous bone hairpin, around which her hair is wet despite itself. Her hips are infinitely barely-concave, there the swimsuit is very tight, but tight on so wide a plane that it no longer conveys body plasticism but merely the goldfish's color-surface. She speaks with men in a deep voice and only in deep leather armchairs is she liable to seduction.

The third: glaring white sawtoothed swimsuit with white knitted belt and short white jacket. Not girl, not woman, not sport, not salon, not coquette, not respectable, but only an elegant, anonymous point origo above the waves' glup-glupping hooks. Blond undulated hair cropped short, dry rubrics of courtability. The white color is more towel-like than amazone-sadistic or provocative Lesbos-glove to the sea's bourgeois nymphs. The small jacket 'suits her,' but stops short of flaring her body's potential into genuine beauty — her arms, legs, back a pristine candle's untouched wick.

The fourth: dark blue swimsuit, very tight, but originally made of such thick spongy-fluffy material that it mirrors forms not in their lifelikeness but, let's say, on their third asymptotic curve — on lacquered surfaces we can observe that the circle-shaped wood-knot's second frame is already a narrow ellipsis and its third 'imitation,' one straight line. (The 'tight' swimsuit has these two variants: adherence in one resembles a blizzard [from lance points easter eggs are rounded], and in the other, a soaked napkin, which excels mostly through the creases' Seurat punctiliousness. What is more, to complete this textile-typology, the latter tightness has no less than two subspecies — one is the 'sporty' tightness, when the maillot is a Cubist muscle-metronome, while the other, the 'rag' version, when the maillot looks old, crumpled, and dishevelled, simply a grown-out or too small piece that sticks to the skin here and there like four or five leaves from different trees: Siegfried-emmenthaler.)

The dark blue swimsuit has a low-cut back, down to the hips: the chief sensation being, that here the white-blue dotted thread-belt vacillates like the physicists' ball placed on a roof ridge — there's no telling if it will roll down to the left or right. So the belt appears like a bridge arching above a dried-up river: everybody crosses under it, barefoot in the riverbed. This acute-angled, evening-dress-ish low-cut is perhaps more important than the fantastic omissions, for in it coquetry's classicism finds an apt expression, the cold tradition of 'décolletage.' The swimsuits leashed together from a red bra and two thigh-pockets are no longer coquettish but the geometric diagnoses of nakedness: they lack any social feature.

There is a certain conversational flirtatiousness, bon-mot impudicity, that always presupposes a salon commedia dell'arte around it — so was that blue swimsuit. And there is the other case, when swimsuits are cut in a manner reminiscent of Hebrew script, where only the consonants are marked with large figures: only the con-muscular muscles get a colorful stamp, the mono-muscular are left bare — they can also be compared to the housepainters' overholed templates: love can only color our skin where it's left bare. The latter lacks any social character and brings to mind Mallarmé's *Hérodiade*.

The girl in blue is muscular, not from the official and club-donned sports but rather, from pubertal romping; at twenty-eight she will still enjoy such games as grabbing with her teeth a hidden sugar-cube from her husband's palm or a kiss-bout, when the husband doesn't let himself be kissed on the mouth and is not allowed to use his arms in defense, only to twist his head in every imaginable direction. When she has been at this game for two hours and is flame-red from laughter, she splutters, "Once more, once more." These forms of play can be clearly read from her knees and elbows. Creole face with elongated, far-set eyes. At the nose's base there's a thick blue vein, as if the organism has secured turqoise-heating, because the skin gets very taut and cold from the distance between the eyes.

Extremely small and thin mouth, which, however, carries out the most colorful articulations both in form and color. The mouth's mauvish wristwatch-spring sharply contrasts with the blizzard-swimsuit's standard-frivolous simplicity. The mouth is so vivid (and not heart-shaped!) that it appears to belong not to the earthenware amphora-color face at all, being rather a pinkish-violet curlicued silk pattern tossed there by the wind, the kind that cloth merchants snip off with medieval scissors from the rolls' ends, so that women can take them home to make up their minds. The lips are not so much horizontal as vertical strips — not the sepal's outward-leaning ledge that leans out of the face, but the cross-section of the petal (that is, the tanned complexion): its nervousness comes from its being not an anemone at the end of a sponge-blue underwater plant, but an as yet unscarred cut on the plant. There are flowers with sticky thorns, comb-foot beetles and worms, crumpled-up metal threads or ribbon candy stencils, which, wherever they fall, will only touch the surface with a tiny part of themselves, while the rest continues hovering in the air: this mouth hovered like this, barely hooked onto the taut little coffee skull. Above it, like peach fluff platinumed by hydrogen's albula rain, an infinitely flexible kiss-moss, which further enhances the mouth's ring-rippling that appears forever receding.

The main trick of this mouth is in the kind of line-drawing that we can observe in Wilhelm Busch's sea caricatures: a dense mesh of semicirclets of variable size.[215] How did this mauve 'xyz' (for this is its official name) end up on this pubertal body? Her thin black hair is flattened to her pin-head, only one or two zigzags stick out from under the cap. Water trickles from her face, in contrast to the mouth's bluish-rusty color stains and the eyes' Zeiss eroticism: water trickles down from the homely, non-plein-air slopes of make-up and frivolous gaze like a shower from the windows of a café — one centimeter inward you can quietly continue reading your paper and sipping your coffee. We got used to imagining a horizontal, flat ellipsis for a fish-shape, so any ocean creature whose horizontal position is a vertical oval must come as a ticklish surprise — the fish is 10 cm long, but 25 cm tall, something that is given of course by the giant, multi-story and transparent veil-fins: the fish was squeezed together at the nose and tail and so forced to trickle its vacuumed[216] flesh upward & downward. Just as the exotic-tall golden wings of these fish to the common fish-template, so did the Oriental nose of this girl (transparent from sunshine, akin to an October yellow leaf) relate to the strand's banal snub-noses: the snub nose is the denial of intellect that goes back to the age of the great migrations, the aquiline nose is the slightly naively-haughty aquarium advertisement for raison.

How did these three zones come together: the pubertal gymnastics of the whole body, the mouth's scintillating-tired zigzagging, and the nose's barren logos-fan? The moment the kitten reaches with its paw after the twine ball, the soul's great worry-weaving begins (just as reportedly one can buy not only ready-made stockings but also stocking fabric in rolls, to have their stockings tailored to size, so behind the blue swimsuit's alexandrine-embraces, too, worry wove not completed events, but manufactured its shapeless fabric rolls: the mouth's continuous quiver is the obvious indicator of the loom), only for this, too, to be annihilated by some womanly-superstitious faith in 'objectivity' and truth (whose headquarters is the nose). She had a high-heeled walking shoe, as if the whole metropolitan life were nothing more than a shabby husk of indigo-bulla nakedness. She had two shoes on, and yet three heels clicked distinguishably behind her on the porcelain stairs — the third was her name without a rubber heel-cap: Doll.

And so forth: to describe the difference between the striped and monochrome swimsuit, that between the two-piece and one-piece, the 'robe enroulés' uniting an evening dress with a sailor caricature, the various ways of producing 'demons,' starting from the blond terry-fairy through the dancer to the bediamonded doyenne of harems; their gestures in water, on the still rings, in courtrooms and in sleeping cars: this would be the second epic possibility for Leatrice. (How distant are the boundaries that this complete typology could bring together is humorously suggested by the names of two Paris salons: *Hermes* and *Tao-Tai*.)

*what are love's two concretenesses?
couldn't Leatrice be built from them?*

I was at a dinner somewhere and saw a woman whom I liked very much. I walked home to be able to relish her memory in calm, that is, in the non-calm of the walking. This is the beginning of love: what do I have in my hands? Two things: the woman's outward appearance, first and foremost her dress — then the fact that she is not with me, I miss her, long for her, and that is bad. All of a sudden I'm more of a tailor than her tailor, I know every crease, seam, buckle and button, and on the other hand I'm palpating the void of sadness, of loneliness velveted into dream: there is no connection whatsoever between the two, they are like a violinist and a pianist who just found out from the impresario that in two months they have to play in Buenos Aires but have never met & rehearsed together.

So is the foyer of the *Double Face Theater*: a circular, windowless hall, there's not one nook or ornament on the ceiling, the whole room is pitch-black velvet. Its only oddity is that the floor (entirely covered with thick sound-absorbing carpet) is not flat but bulging: halfway on the radius the arch reaches its highest point, then slopes downward again and ends in a calyx-shape hollow in the center. From this hollow a gold-pink, scaled-creased lamp-post or lamp-stamen rises almost to the ceiling — the glass is uneven, so here and there light comes redder or more yellow from behind certain fircone facets.

On entering one sees nothing but this autumnal-bronze electric reel that shows the hall's blindness even blinder, but the wadding-muffled floor rises steadily and barely perceptibly, and all the more unnervingly, that is, rather noticeably. The only statue, mural, & piece of practical furniture that the architect employed in this stifling hall is the very fear rising in one's legs, this discreet seasickness from the tilt — its style consisting in eliciting voluptuous vertigos with invisible not-nearly-forms; not plasticity but on the contrary, a tickling of the nerves that can hardly be distinguished from drugs. Its device is not form and not space, but the disturbed space-perception of the man walking in the 'building': he couldn't report what he saw, all the account he could give being utterly interior, absolutely of 'disposition.'

Loneliness is a gallery built in this style — a giant black petal slope, on which one walks dizzily, not feeling his footprints, for the moment he places his foot on the incline it immediately turns aside, so he no more knows, where is the ground, where the footsole, and where the footprint, or what combinatory sequences of those three feature. And in the middle stands the evening-gowned woman's bow-shaped, alien lamp with virginity's acute angle stuck into it, glistening but not illuminating.

Dress & loneliness. Leatrice was adored by many, so wouldn't it be likely that she featured in many heads only as clothes and 'is-not-here'? In vain a woman gives herself with abandon from the first, and any time, even then the ancient component 'is-not-here,' some lack, some longing is felt like a loose but unlosable pajama cord, some thought of the future which, even if realized, is still in the future, and this is enough to replace the saucer with the black umbrella of 'is-not-here' in the mismatched tea-service of the kiss.

absolute externals (shoes, stockings, shoulder-straps): shoes

There are immovable forms of female clothing that mean love more than any love-making or didactically regulated liaison — such are shoes, stockings, & shoulder-straps. Three figurations: the shoe is a sharp wave-line, at its end an energetic Cyrillic diacritic (is there such a thing?), the stocking is a thousand geometric squares or hearts, a thousand parallels, a mist of proportion-fugues, whereas the shoulder-strap is a biologically whimsical, lonely vein, now taut, now wilted. It is only natural that, since they are the average love-nurture from morn to night (being to woman what air is to bread), our souls and muscles are somehow molded to them — kiss, marriage, lies and compliments follow the suggestions of shoe-slide, stocking-meter, & shoulder-strap-vein.

The shoe's line is first of all a dramatic glissando: from the culmination point to the tip of the toes one breathless plunge, like the line that stands for a tragedy's synopsis in school manuals, which at the fourth act soars to an apex and from there falls, with an avalanche's dopiness, to the tearful and hygienically too-hollowed sink of the fifth act. Such is ski jumping: a superb arc, melodically polished drawing above snow and fir-trees — constant death-fear and, eventually, too short time by the chronometer. Every female shoe brings these three as its sine-qua-non dowry the moment it alights on the horizon of a bus step: melodic arch, tragic free fall, & time's odd jolt, as if two successive seconds piled up in panic, like a pair of too tightly connected rail ends in the heat. It is worth poring over the shoe, for nowhere else can we relish melodic plenitude and deathly derailment at the same time.

If we examine the slope from the sole's end, then the smooth part under the toes harmonically concludes the downward momentum, but if we switch to the upper part, then on the contrary, we will enjoy the ironic or downright burlesque suspension of this sloping descent, for in the 'arch' there is always something humorously chubby and childishly snubnosed that suspends the affected, sporty, and arioso-dolente coming down from the heels. This willy-nilly farce can in fact be observed not only in the toecap but in the shoe's role at large (its role, not shape) during the walk (and only during the walk): human walk, the movement of placing one foot in front of the other, does not resemble in the least the elegant seagull flight of the footsole's line, and in comparison can indeed be called a maimed hobbling. In sports magazines we can often see photographs of divers hovering between the springboard and the pool with delicately arched back and arms stretched outwards: let's imagine such a body, in this pose, on a village cart jolting along on a dirt road — this is the situational comedy of the female walk.

Perhaps nowhere else is it more clear than in the shoe, how much the fantasizings of love revolve around an article of clothing, not the real female foot. Of course there are many shoe-personalities, but here we will confine ourselves to the two extremes: the laced one made of animal leather, with a separate tongue, and the seamless, buckle- and strapless silk evening pump. The former reminds us of those old children's drawings that depict three-year-old mouseys in the adults' crinolines, low-cuts, and towering wigs, when they are barely yet 'human': the lace shoe is far too clothes-like and complicated to cover the foot's primitive shapes.

Is there a more animal, indeed minerally dumb part of the female body than the foot's upper part with its protruding Neanderthal bones and counter-intricacy? And should this part receive button-holes, ribbons, buckles and a vest made of a different material? The simple, low-cut evening pump brings to mind the difference between hands and feet (should we have forgotten it): the hands of children are gauche because they are stuck into one bag instead of a glove, while the female foot, on the contrary, acquires a razor-sharp attractiveness by squeezing all its toes into one narrow sheath. The dull foot-bones become an elongated oval jewel from the thin sides of the evening pump: so does the part immediately above the ankle, the flesh right before the toes, and perhaps even a part of the toes themselves (in this the stocking obviously plays a part) suddenly join the short territory of the foot-bones, and form one long silken gradient, as if the foot were no separate anatomical unit and there were one sole incline in the world that starts at the knees and ends at the toe-cap.

One of the main virtues of the shoe is precisely this exiling of the foot: there is no more rewarding and more piquant geometrical task than to isolate one, relatively small surface of a polyhedron, so as to obliterate the fact that next to that small lot, another meaninglessly glued-on surface protrudes, and instead create the optical illusion that our small surface continues with a marked bend into infinity; so does the earth's impudic bulging go on well past the insulating ring of the Verona amphiteatre. The narrow evening pumps cast in oblivion the toes' zoological blunder.

If we watch a naked female foot, the toes' length shows a 1:3 proportion to the foot — but in such picture frame-like evening pumps (a mystery!) that proportion is 1:20, or even, 0 to infinity: shin, ankle, knee and arch mean one eternal slope with no beginning or end. At such times the sole's incline gives the impression of undeviating obliqueness, as against the other shoe's reclining S-penchants. Just as the toes (1:3!) can now mystically fit under the black strip of a few millimeters, in the same mystical way the foot, at a 30° incline, appears to glide from heel to floor at an 80° angle; shin and foot create almost no angle at all but continue seamlessly: the whole is dizzyingly vertical, only on the spot immediately above the ground is there a microscopic black horizontality, the shoe's toe-cap. Let's imagine an infinitely elongated and slender cone set on its apex, and cut out of it an oblique segment (ellipsis) whose one end-point is almost level with the cone's base, and the other almost reaches the apex (being almost the cone's vertical halving plane): female foot and black frame-like evening pump relate to one another like this cone and its cone section. There are two, almost vertical slopes: one belongs to the stocking, the other is of the shoe's imaginary halving plane, and these two slopes stand at an angle of at most 3° to each other — this is all that's left from the drab forms of shin and foot.

So this is the root of woman. Best is to look at their footprints on the tarmac: one small tilted trapeze-plaster, then empty space, then the dot imprint of the heel. The most important of course is the empty space in-between, one feels above it the footsole's Icarian parasailing jump, just as one can feel in the trapeze imprint the friction with the ground and on the heel, the vertical puncture; that's why the heel is usually printed blacker than the sole. Emptiness, two different forms striped with varying intensity: so indeterminate, self-contradictory, and secessionist is the base of the female body. Nowhere can it exercise a definite pressure on earth: the intercourse between sole and tarmac is merely an occasionalist parallel, not a force — the heel's injection-glitch is fumble by necessity, rigid stoppage rather than dynamic work — women are left standing on earth merely by accident. What if statues were erected on pedestals the way high-heeled shoes elevate women: tilted? They elevate but in the same act also make them glide down: women always propel themselves from the floor at the heels with fierce rearing, and drop back to it at the toes like the prodigal son.

In addition, the hard organ of this half-apotheosis always creates the impression of weaponry: when a woman crosses her legs and one heel dangles in the air, it appears entirely like a rhinoceros' horn or some Babylonian spur. Its bellicoseness is further enhanced by the fact that even the most elegant evening pump's heel and sole will be dirty: the only splendiferous piece of female apparel on which dirt is a tolerated component. When a shoe is lifted into the air (for instance in the wardrobe when the galoshes are removed), we pry on its underside with some excitement, for that's where woman begins — we are local, or rather, geopatriots to such extent that we will consider more important that part of each material which communicates with the earth, and how curious to see right by the silks and gold ringlets the serrated whitish-green dirt of floors and streets, without any right to it — the right a flower would have, for instance, which, after all, grows from the earth; here it's merely gravitation's unjust and perhaps bogus seal.

The evening pump gives the same effect of deep & frivolous low-cut as décolletés over the breasts used to give in olden times — and how odd it would be to see large mudstains under the low-cut bodice. Of course it's easy for the breasts' V-nakednesses and their kiss-bridled U-s to be frivolous, for breasts are banal old bait — but it's all the more interesting that the dull shinbone can convert its sudden protraction into infinity to such frivolous denuding: there where no one would look for anything, suddenly an occasion for joy presents itself: the provocative act of unveiling with vertical audacity. And we can see in all its crudity the age-old maxim, that we dote on the unveiling more than on the unveiled itself. And there where from the foot a second woman was created — what is more, a fictive nudity-paradigm more nude than nudity itself — mud and dirt lurk. This non-anatomical but formal, almost merely-conceptual nakedness (the image of the abstract sense, and not of the content, of 'nudity') leads us to the stocking, for this is one of the stocking's prime tricks.

the stocking

If there is nothing else to cover them but the skin's rosy and coffee-color luminosity, female legs, as everybody knows, are far from being naked: in order for them to be truly nude-like open and provocatively flayed-onto-themselves, they have to be dressed — in order for them to be less, something will be added. This is easy to observe in dressing women: as they sit on the swimming pool's bench with naked legs crossed, we can see where flesh ends and where the sand or the floor's yes- and no-color tile-variation begins, but the legs' shape doesn't fall out of the sequence of objects, like a small mourning envelope from the pack of like-size bridge cards — in fact they have no shape.

When we look at naked female legs, we always see the territory between the contours, the differing thickness of matter, its transfigurations, the bubble bath of imaginary and real resistances, weight-lampions on the dim path of eros. If these legs were worshipped in some pretentious mythology as *Venus Contenu*, whereas the stockinged legs as *Venus Ligne*,[217] it wouldn't be easy to tell which of the two was the more materialistic. The desire directed at the mere-flesh (where there is no stocking) is in fact seeking an all too abstract pleasure: the eternal, sea-like changeability, indeterminacy of forms; it wants no fixed forms but rather, the everlasting beginning phase of 'formation.' This is another of the naked legs' double-edgednesses: they are positive matter, exact amount, which we love not because they are complete, like the statue of an acquaintance, but because they are palpable and restartable with every caress, erased with every kiss, interchangeable. It is when the body is literally naked, itself only, that it becomes the most-anything: the dispelling, unconnected thread of hypotheses.

The naked body and thus the naked leg has no autonomy among the other objects of the world, and this takes us by surprise: the white flesh-color and the motley Persian rug merge much more readily into some indistinct homogeneity than the leg half-tightly covered with a Persian rug and next to it on the floor, another Persian rug. The naked body is merely 'there' among the objects, neither contrast nor component nor neutrality. In *Venus Contenu* one will hardly find any matter — how little man counts the body as matter can also be seen in the fact that they see the same forcible, what is more, incomprehensible contrast between a woman's physique and her weight: when he hoists her up he believes that there must be some lead attached, that weight cannot be hers alone. It is strange that, following a medieval tradition, many people still regard carnal love as 'materialism,' and are able to imagine a common denominator between 50 kg of silver and 50 kg of nude, not realizing that the ambition of the silver is to immediately fill its weight, while the objective & method of the female body is to reach those 50 kg by the longest, indeed infinite detour.

In our childhood they used to pull our leg with the question, what is heavier: one kg of iron, or one kg of feathers? If we think about the (naked) female body's materiality, then in place of feathers we should imagine some infinitely volatile, shape-shifting gas that expands in space and time and its sole constant is that it has weight, let's say, 50 kg. Or, what a strange impression of equipoise would the following give: in one balance, a 50-kg silver ball and in the other, another such 50-kg silver ball hammered into an infinitely long and thin thread, so that only a small bit is visible in the balance, its two ends undetectable even with a binocular, for it goes on and on; and yet the scales don't tilt, they're perfectly balanced. So *Venus Contenu* has two theological attributes: the one is weight, mere-weight — the other is the eternal changeability, dissipation from love-making. What happens if we pull stockings on it?

Little by little, every moment the leg becomes more naked, as the thick veil of the stocking stretches above the heel, the ankle, the knee: as if one slowly poured a thick black liquid into a transparent communicating tube of indeterminate shape. How beautiful is this movement of reverse, 'multiplying skinning': the woman holds the two upper edges of the stocking in her two hands and pulls them like reins that are tugged by wild horses toward the netherworld. The two forces are here in sweet balance: the leg presses like an eternal night-bound chariot rushing to death on Orpheus' path, and at the same time also rushing into the naked body's opalescent, eternal spring. And the sign of triumph over the netherworld is precisely the fact that the thighs' May lard is gradually blackened by the pulled-up stocking.

Does form thus simply replace matter? No, because thick, non-transparent linen stockings have nothing erotic in them, while being the form-most form. Is this a compromise between flesh and net, matter and shape, that is, the scheme of piquancy? But does then flesh play a part in enjoying the impression? Aren't we closer to truth in saying that flesh serves only as ad hoc custom-last to the beautiful stocking? We are well aware that a stocking lying about is nothing more than a meaningless, flaccid rag of which we can at most enjoy the strange transparency if we stretch it between our two hands: in part the geometrical squares of its weave, in part the typical moiré circlings projected above the squares by the tripping-up light.

Three data: the inert rag, the delicate heap of squares, and the vegetal growth rings. All these precede the leg. When the stocking stretches upward on the swimming-pool bench, like the commiserating mercury in a thermometer, we first imagine that the piece of rag had mysteriously carried within itself the regularly arched shape that it creates with the leg. And yet neither the leg nor the stocking had been form: the first because of its infinite changeability, the latter because of its rag-ness. The stocking is made into a sharp crystal by the shapeless flesh, while the flesh is rendered snobbish-Greek 'morphe' by the black swamp-clot-like stocking.

And so a form emerges that is perhaps of two or much rather, of none, and that's all desire needs. But *Venus Ligne* is an extremely crude name, for here the stress falls not on the silhouette or contours, however much at first sight those may appear the most striking novelty. Leatrice had a dress made of silver lamé-tulle that was basically a magnifying of the stocking weave: medieval chain mail. This dress was body-tight everywhere, but the fabric fell from her shoulders, freely floating, in two straight ribbons of 30 cm width. If Leatrice absent-mindedly leaned against the table, the dress became even tighter under her hips, but the two independent nets pendulated away from her shoulders, stretching in the air under their own weight.

With the stocking these two situations can't be realized simultaneously, but the tendency is the same: the serrated silk net runs around the leg with such geometric momentum that we feel it to be a snail-spiraling plane that continues its ever-bending folding-screen trajectory in space. This it achieves mainly with its novel shadows: the muscle-shadows are replaced by cylinder and cone-shadows, which are rendered sensuous not by the fact that spectrally, the form of living flesh, or at least its memory, is bootlegged here and there, but by the tiny geometrical elements (the small squares of the weave, its loops: eyes) in their unexpected monumentality, the infinite Archimedean momentum.

Sometimes in utterly open, plate-like Murano vases a spiralling line starts from the thin base, which then goes over into an unbelievably dense lining, and yet after a mere few centimeters one can measure a one-meter radius — so does the stocking unite the miniature condensedness and the infinity it generates. It started out as a vase and immediately flared out into a plate: this can be only the result of its ever-denser spirals — here the line is not an ornament but everything, and it was the line that drew to itself the vase's glass. Women often call such vases with linear decoration 'delicate,' and so they are for sure, yet in the sudden petal-plateau, in the rotation-induced openness we feel the presence of crushing forces, for only such forces could have distorted the vase that started like a flower into an inside-out, mutilated cyclamen. In schools they demonstrate on revolving electric copper circles the phenomenon by which at great speed the revolving circle is elongated into an ellipsis: these Murano vases flattened into a plate, too, make us suspect such forces. The shape of the female leg resembles such revolving because of the transparent silk stockings: its shadows are not static but the quivering radial triangles seen on running wheels — on express trains the signal of higher speed is the turning of the engine wheels into a compact silvery plate, on which a slender grey triangle sways like a flower in the breeze. Minimal swaying indicates highest speed: the stocking's gliding geometric shadows, too, indicate such rush.

The naked leg's shape is given by the contraction of various muscles, without resulting in an impression of complexity — even if it tautens (as in the anatomies of Renaissance painters' sketches), every flesh-ribbon stands out individually, a medley of waves without the image of sea and water. The stocking modifies it in two directions: it simplifies the shape of the muscles into Platonic idea-masks, while at the same time generating cunning crossovers from bone to flesh, from flesh to vein, from vein to garter-tension.

The naked body has neither forms nor summings-up; in the stockinged leg both are rampant. The ankles heave individually; they receive a truly egoistic profile by losing their bodily personality and are neutralized into "some hard little spherical cut of space" behind the silk net, but the moment they are individualized, they immediately tumble over into the valley between the heel, the back of the calf, and themselves. Where is that dizzying moment in the living (and good-for-nothing) body, when something towers into blossoming-egoistic shape, and the plenitude of form itself will be the first slope of running-onward, gliding passing-on? And that small valley (between ankle-bone, the muscle-thread rising from the heel, and the beginning of the calf-cushions) becomes, thanks to the stocking, at once undefinably polysemic and geometrically precise — neither body nor plane nor valley nor 'hic et nunc,' but it radiates such impeccable abstraction, such discipline of precision, non-allusiveness, but perfect intellectual solution, that we feel moved to found a new mathematics on it (or, failing that, the old mathematics). Perhaps a similar thing can be experienced in fountains of intricate engineering and mechanism: the water springs with such pressure, beats against such surfaces, is lit from within with such beams of light and crisscrossed by such alien water-jets as to just about reach in the air some motley flower shape, petals, foliage or branches, that last for a fraction of a second (when they are at their most perfect, but can be easily observed), and then melt away, ebb, but this transience is no crude annihilation, nor the flower's death into 'sic transit,' but on the contrary, self-refuting continuation, soft and tickling variation, the liberation of form into the directions it carries within itself — the downward-bending petal turns into a downward-bending arch, from the rose's ever-foaming pistils an ever-expanding central mist-ball rises; the statue is replaced by a pantomime of directions.

And this is one of the stocking's prime love-techniques on the female leg: it creates hyper-forms only in order to immediately dissolve them, to gather the dissolved somewhere into a new knot, and dissolve them again, and so on up to the hips. Which could the fountain's pre-programmed water-flower be, and which its even more flower-like dehiscence into directions, we can hardly know; we feel merely that these two situations keep alternating from the heel to the waist. Is the knee a crystal of all the straying waves or, on the contrary, only a leftover of one of the calf's many form-stations? It is hard to tell. But it is doubtlessly form, and doubtlessly transitory, transmitting & transferring form.

That's why caressing the leg is best, for the leg is geometrically prepared for this dramatization. How complex and how smooth it is: the ankle, a jutting-out desire-threshold; above it the whole elastic pillar suddenly contracts like a sucked-in, hollow cheek, then swells to fish-shape, is distorted at the knee in the front into a knot, getting an indeterminate fissure at the back, then quickly thickens, no longer with the fish's balanced forte-piano, but in one direction only, like an irresistibly opening crescendo-hairpin in the musical score, one cannot conclude it logically, merely discontinue it: the stocking's cut-off upper fringe indicates the torso exactly — the leg has amassed form upon form, like the fountain's water falling through various artificial terraces and electric-hued filters, which can likewise only fall into a 'Gordian' pool, cannot receive an organic ending that would geometrically belong to its structure.

Ankle, rubber fish, knee, thighs: with what melodic neutrality do these utterly alien forms merge into one by way of the stocking, as if it shaped the god-effigy of paradoxical transition on the female leg. The sudden cut-offness marked by the stocking well above the knee belongs organically to the leg's form-undulation, just as one-time short-circuiting, plastic paralysis, belongs to the end of winding and twisting horns and trumpets: even if the living body continues the leg toward the hips with petit-bourgeois clumsiness, that is no more than a plastering of forms, practical joining, not the geometrically predestined avenue of form.

The leg's beauty consists in this openness above the knee (here it's not about two legs but only one, and that in any imaginable posture) — here the stocking is folded back doubly, a dark strip marks the need to discontinue, for the only thing that could follow is infinite monotony, as if a cone were set on its top and its sides were prolonged beyond its base. But this interruption confers on it a substance of hypothesis: the forms (ankle, calf, knee, thigh) that are juxtaposed in such order do not lead to a well-defined result, but instead proceed into the infinity of numbers. (Thigh: riding-glove cuffs reaching up to the elbow [= infinity].)

The stockinged leg is of a nature entirely different from 'man,' it is entirely independent from the latter and indeed stands in no relation whatsoever to it. The head is mere-psychology, the trunk, mere internal organs, clinical physiology-case, the arms are poor in form. In the leg there is no soul and no noble organ, but in comparison to the whole body it is disproportionately large. Here we speak of the stockinged leg again, for the naked leg merges into the body and is blunted into humanity-poisoning: the skin and blood circulation smuggle it into the trunk's nobility as almost its equal in rank. The transparent silk stockings thwart this. The leg is one of love's favorite islands precisely because it is the most absolutely body: neither character nor biology tamper with it. How clumsy the arm looks next to the leg — let's just imagine a silk stocking on a female arm, what deplorable shapelessness it would display. The arm is a conformist, unlike the leg, which achieved an autonomous and independent form for itself. That such anti-humanism had its first germs already in the naked leg is shown by the fact that it gets not clothes but a transparent net. The net signals that from foot-sole to hips there is a single unified territory: its variance is only formal, not lyrical or pertaining to the realm of internal medicine.

The leg only walks, is not used to anything else — when we sit it dangles, inert, disconnected from life. The hand performs a thousand tasks and games, while the face is the potpourri-nest of our entire life: among these preoccupations the leg walks virginally. From the hips upward the body is so analytical that it ceases to be body — the flesh's animal synthesis is found in the legs alone. The mermaids ending in fish-tail are not at all prodigious creatures: the tall and slender daughters of Monday or Tuesday are precisely such nereids by virtue of their legs. It is the legs that sustain the human being, so they should be solid foundational institutions, yet this very base happens to be the most alien, ethereal, and paradoxical.

Leg and body relate to one another like an infinitely slender vase on the floor, on whose upper part a few small exotic flowers are seen: it is hard to tell which is more important here, the vase rising up with its dizzying funneling line, implying that the foundation of all beauty is one sole curving line, while its walls are dead from the very beginning — or the small, barely visible flowers, which, however minute, carry the most unsettling potential of life. The stocking-love and face-love are, as anyone can feel, two contrasting worlds, we can barely call both love.

The leg is giant blindness: the breasts, spine-valley, and arms are still somehow ruled by the eye (the to-and-froing gardens of vision), in contrast to the flesh-spirals (it's the stocking-shadows that render them spirals!) that sprinkle upwards from the ankles' little buttons, where the rule of the eyes ends. The leg is the most congenial territory of palpation: it is not even matter but the hallucination of the sense of palpation, its themeless projection into thin air. But palpation is always directed at matter, moreover, it is the driving engine of materialism, so a jolly play starts here: between the over-the-top matter-like and abstract surface-fiction.

The stockinged leg is not more nor less than 'surface': it gives a minimum stimulus to the nerves of palpation (to the man's palm and fingers), then lets the stimulus grow inside the hand into a grotesquely oversize stimulus-statue.

The stocking's silk and the dress (of interest here is first and foremost the skirt) do not want to meet, their direction intersects. What grandiose contrast there is between the stocking's tautness (stretching gothically to the hips) and the skirt's slackness (which falls, with ethical impotence, toward the ankles). As we have already indicated, the stockinged leg contains maximum forms and maximum form-dissolutions at the same time in the same place, but two — minimally two, sometimes three — fixed energy-graphics traverse this form-pagoda. The first is the triangular shifting among the silk eyes at the pull of the garter, as if the button at the garter's end were a propeller and the strips and thinnings resulting from this tension were long V-waves left on the water (traveling as far as the ankles). The second is that protruding seam all the way up at the stocking's back like a flexible, yet precise sardine backbone. The eventual third is the omission-arrows springing up above the ankle. Due to them, the contrast between stocking and skirt is far greater than, let's say, the contrast between a tree trunk and the surrounding foliage: the trunk doesn't stand for the upward thrust and the foliage doesn't stand for the downward striving.

The taut stocking on the knee and the loose skirt above it are physically as close as they can be, but according to their tendencies they are at an infinite remove from each other: the stocking's soul is the artificial pressing upward and tautening that the garters inject into it, while that of the skirt, gravity's resigned posture. Consciously or unconsciously this duality perforce affects the woman's life: she forever feels the current of tenseness on her stocking and around it, in her skirt, the separate veils of impotent fluttering. When she sits with legs crossed, through the silk weave's tiny notches she can feel her body's polished pressing to her body (is the leg a Narcissus, sifted like a lemon in a squeezer?); but while thus suddenly two nakednesses take the place of her single body, the skirt's far-wandering lonely banners and curtains immediately counterbalance this impression and disperse her body-consciousness into surrounding space.

One of woman's most important body parts, one of gynecology's central anatomical cruxes, is that expanse of air between the legs and the skirt: does it still belong to the woman or already to her environment? This propels the stocking into its true role. The woman never walks in our world but in the private, bell-shaped territory cut out from air by the skirt, where obviously other climatic conditions prevail. Perhaps the leg can preserve the purely spherical forms only because the skirt ensures for it a protected atmosphere. This claim is apparently refuted by the example of the leotard-stockinged showgirls — these girls wear no skirts, their stockings reach up to the hips, or are even woven into their tricots, rising up to their armpits, but here, precisely because the stocking has grown to almost infinite dimensions, the whole being is so entirely mere-legs, the trunk has metamorphosed so completely into legs, that they can bloom without further climatic protection.

But the everyday stocking has no such tropical powers, so its volatile crystals need to be insulated. One of the characteristic features of the world is that it is devoid of regular forms, especially rounded ones, because collision almost instantly distorts them into angularity, should they occur exceptionally, for a few moments. And the legs are the luxuriating musical scales of roundedness: if they got mixed unmediatedly into the world's other objects, they would be distorted. Stockings and skirt-insulation guarantee the preservation of spherical material in the world, as exoticism and relic, to disprove the doubters.

Spherical objects constitute a realm to themselves — the circle and the square are not encountered in any common chapter founded, for instance, on the mendacious common genus-denominator of 'two-dimensional geometric shapes.' All reflexion on the stockinged leg needs to start from and return to the extraordinary fact of sphericity. Let's look at the leg's spherical elements. We can start from a few components. First of all, the sphere itself. Another, even if not strictly geometrical, but from a dramatic or dynamic perspective the counterpart (or parallel) of the sphere: the corkscrew's body, the volumetric capacity of the spiral bloated into screw-snake. The sphere is simply the material of sphericity, perhaps it can't even be called 'spherical.' And the corkscrew is the over-the-top turning into action of sphericity: while the sphere itself is merely the impotence-statue of the concept of 'sphericity,' the momentary crystallisation of the concept's imaginable minimum — the corkscrew is the maximum dramatization imaginable of the concept of the 'spherical,' where the 'spherical' threatens to be refined out of existence. Between these two extremes are found the tedious and innumerable variations of transition: for instance, macaroni.

The stockinged leg (mere verbosity, since the leg that plays a part in love can't exist unstockinged) brings together the two extremes of rounded shapes: it is both and to the same extent passive sphere and hysterically overdrawn corkscrew. There are dense liquids which in balanced environments contract into a globular shape and hover: dynamic neutrality is matched by formal neutrality, that is, the sphere is no longer a form. The leg blossoming inside the skirt's protected zone resembles this form zero, or form without form — that's the root of the extraordinary contrast between human-woman and female leg: human-woman has already been impacted by disharmonious forces, there can be no possible balancing to the point of neutrality, of the exterior world's influence. In the leg neutrality is the nurturing ground of piquancy: it shows neither shapelessness nor shape, relying solely on the inner cohesion of 'barely-expansion.' And this is always spherical.

Yet to an equal degree the leg means the opposite of 'origo,' the most capricious circle-baroque: its expanding heaving, wineglass-shaped gothic is the greatest imaginable exploitation of the circle form — bellowing tornado, towering vortex, cyclone congealed into glass. In nature these two sphere-variations are as a rule very far apart: we sometimes see the nil-face of the passive sphere in the moon hovering among the clouds; the clouds' lazy onward floating indicates the celestial body's divine laziness. We can see the corkscrew's Machiavellian machinations in the curlicues of the vine's tendril, in the rings of dust raised by a wind that obstinately blows on the same place. Within the stocking the two play out simultaneously: existing passively, like the calyx of a Buddhist flower on a deserted lake — no wind, no waves, no seasons, no life disturb it, time bends into a belt around it like some daydreaming wreath — yet at the same time permanently giving the unsettling impression of the foaming rise of champagne poured too fast into a slender glass (first the portion that expands from the ankle to the knee, then the second stanza infinitely amphora-ing onward: ambicalix motus)[218] — the foam finds its exact equivalent in the openness of the leg's second stanza: perhaps the knee is a collecting lens behind and a dispersing lens in front, for it first sucks in the flesh-sphere into the calf's complicated ovals, only to radiate it out into the total laxity of the upper thigh.

The leg can be sphere and corkscrew at the same time because it has this mirroring nature: all thanks to the silk stocking's sheen. If we place a ball in front of a curved mirror, we will always recognize the simultaneous presence of the original ball and the caricature in the distorted image, be it whatever drunken pretzel or sneering gherkin. If we were to indulge in reckless philosophizing, we might connect further items to this carnivalesque geometry: by simultaneously giving the impression of Ur-form (the malgre-tout form of formlessness) and of refined excess-form, the leg indicates that love, too, develops from two components: primordial force and volatile superficiality, in other words, from God and psychology. The two basic schemata do not mingle chemically but according to the rules of musical modulation, co-opting thus the voluminous group of intermediary forms.

Modulation is absolute: let us imagine a sequence of circle forms (for instance, a semicircle followed by a slight oval, then a more pronounced oval, an even more pronounced one, etc.) and another sequence, geometrical scale (let's say, a wave-line followed by a wider one, a yet more distorted one, and so forth, almost to reach a straight line). Let's begin the modulation by replacing one elliptic form from the first sequence (of course music here is no must, only an analogy born of necessity) with one from the second sequence, for instance a wave-line. But there are obviously more than these two geometrical scales (from circle to oval, from short waves to straight line), a potentially infinite number, and thus in one of the series that serves as ground and point of departure, the place of each form is taken by a modulating form, the place of the place-taking modulating form is taken by a third one, and so on: from each series one sole element will feature, and still, each element will bear the form-atmosphere of the whole series.

In the female leg's rounded forms all the circle-scales are represented with one element: the circle immediately shifts into a spiral, before coming to complete the circle-scale; the spiral immediately modulates into a cone, although we clearly felt that the spiral was not an independent figure but merely one of the many elements of a spiral-scale; the cone in turn signals a whole cone-series, but the second is barred from emerging, for in the meantime the leg has modulated into a scroll.

The essence is this: each element features only for a moment, but this moment signifies not itself but the whole scale to which it belongs. This whole process cannot be imagined exactly, and yet we have to indicate that something of this order is happening: the stocking amasses a small circle, bow-like gentle arched curve, cone and ball, without for a moment creating the impression of chaos — and the only explanation for this phenomenon is, that the alien figurations are the result of forever-continued and shifting modulation. Sometimes we construct a spiraling line by gluing each two semicircles together in such a way that each successive semicircle is bigger than the previous one, so the centers are continuously displaced: it is here that we feel the presence of modulation, when something is forever changing, but in our mind each variation is completed into a whole system (for instance, into a whole circle at least): all we see is the series of beginnings, as if instead of the full Latin alphabet we got only *a*-s listed in all the imaginable spellings and diacritics in the world. Modulation, spiral-construction, *a*-variants from the alphabet: all these are similes in which the stockinged foot demands from the world (music, geometry) that it contain some thing that resembles it — for in fact there is as yet nothing, thus music has to be violently assimilated to the leg, so that we might point with hypocritical gesture: "the leg is no novelty at all, it's old hat in music."

Colors are highlighted on stockings in an entirely different way than in dress fabrics. On the stocking the color is living light that radiates through the entire leg: the leg is a unified surface, non-human space, so it's easy to imagine as thoroughly and essentially silvery, bronze, or grey-mauve. A green blouse doesn't bring to mind a green heart or lungs, but the green stocking means a homogeneous green spherical space, which it fills entirely with its luminous time-spans. Color features here in its original anti-human solitude and ghostly egoism — as if the color demanded the rounded surfaces. What mysterious radiance the most trivial or most constrainedly 'respectable' colors get from silky roundedness! There is no color too preposterous that would not suit the leg: flaming-red and salady-yellow are equally at home on it, for they are nothing more than virginal picture frames, dynamic red-tape forms.

another entry to absolute externals: the shoulder-strap

The shoulder-strap became of pressing actuality the moment they started omitting it from evening gowns (on the other hand of course, as is natural in these situations, they omit the whole evening gown and the shoulder strap becomes everything). The back is completely bared, the part covering the breasts is usually a silk triangle whose vertice reaches the throat where it is fastened to the neck with a loop. The freedom of the shoulders is the freedom of man, and the first true emancipation of women after so much legal mumbo jumbo: the shoulder-strap had always aligned the female body vertically, downwards, like a pendulum, at the end of which a weight sways, like gravity's dummkopf kibbitz, with minute to-and-froing. On the shoulders the whole dress used to hang — that is, the entire social appearance, the demanding role one put on: the noble hypocrisy that is the dress used to cut into the shoulders with the weight of the globe pressing on Atlas' shoulders.

Now the female hips rise from the dress like certain flowers from candy cornet-shaped leaves — on one side (that of the breasts) they jump up high like an upward-blown flame, while on the other (the back) they don't as much as start, so the dress meets the body obliquely. If there is nothing on the shoulders, the body is borderless: it is independent and infinitely Protean. What is important is not anatomical but kinetic nakedness: a woman wrapped up to her shoulders but with her shoulders left bare will nevertheless appear immodestly dressed, for what is frivolous is not the body itself (it never is) but the plenitude of freedom.

Some regard the back as a 'prim and proper' body part, "for there's really nothing on it" — this is of course even anatomically inane, let alone kinetically. Even the most minimal, reflex-like muscular activity acquires utmost importance if the skin communes not with some piece of clothing or lingerie but with 'empty' space, thin air. The back, this vast surface thus dissolves (so our mind has it) into nothingness, its main function remaining orientation in the world based solely on nuances of cold and warm, and this is much more prone to bring about an experience of vast expanse than the collisions with the tiny creases of lingerie. The difference between lingerie-covered and backless evening gown-backs is akin to the difference between the stomachs of animals that get their food via a mouth and aesophagus, and those that are nothing other than a stomach: an open bag whose food is identical with the surrounding world, a ring which encloses the stomach and outside of which lies the world, but there is no chemical difference whatsoever between inside and outside. In the case of the shoulders this is even more important than in the case of the back, for on the back the sensation of weight didn't feature much, unlike on the shoulders — if the place of weight is taken by limitless air, anarchy looms on the horizon. Woman used to feel on her shoulders that there is something on her that covers her, if not in the most positive, then at least in the physically most logical manner, for she didn't stick the dress on herself like a stamp but hung it on herself.

The shoulder-strap used to sum up the dress into one gravitational line; when this disappeared, the shoulders trickled onto the shoulder blades, down to the hips, & on the other side melted along the arms all the way to the wrists, like a tiny icicle from which a long water-thread trickles all the way down to the ground. Back, shoulders, and arms fuse into one homogeneous chalice, so that the fingers' delicate stirrings mean at once the shapeless undulation of arms and back, losing precision: tiny spumes on the inhuman waves of space. One wonders how they are capable at all to lift a cup by the handle or write a letter with a pen, to such extent does unmediated relation with the whole arm and back (which here is identical with air) render the hand's form and movement indeterminate.

The evening gown is a close relative of the swimsuit — swimming is the only form of movement that could logically match the low-cut back and bare shoulders. We cannot say anything 'serious' to a strapless woman, just as one cannot pour wine into a hoopless barrel: evidently words do not go down into a narrow case or a hypersensitive balance's scale, but instead into the undulating unity of 'arms — shoulders — back' from where all words dissipate immediately into naught. The omission of the shoulder-strap amounts to the omission of anthropoid dialogue, in general, of thought and logic. This of course is hardly a tragic outcome.

Straplessness attacks the atmospheric traditions of love-making at their core: in the friction the man's hands do not touch dress and nakedness, but dress and nothing, yet as compared to the nothing, here even the word 'dress' is rather nonsensical, so the axis of love-making becomes a mere 'something plus nothing.' While dancing one always feels like dragging around a plant whose stem is hard as a sword and this stem (jumping over the flower) juts at the upper end directly into hypnotic scent: the unlined shoulders are two clouds that can be seen only temporarily, the floating specters of color. But this is what makes the embrace good: the trunk's bark will draw blood from our hands, but we know that in exchange its branches and leaves, either heavy with mauve, light, or dark fruit or thinning and spreading out like the last of rainfall, will bow down over us — only the trunk is solid (the hips), whatever lies above is an incalculable gift.

When a strap comes in sight then, according to everyday statistics, most of the time we'll see two next to one another: a tauter and a slacker one (of the brassiere and the chemise, respectively). Once Touqué watched Leatrice from the back in a café: she sat, leaning against the table at a sharp angle, on a backless chair. Her blouse covering her arms and shoulders was ethereal and diaphane, but it didn't let through the body's color: it was like the thick flakes of soon-melted snow, its barely-resisting white dots scattered over residual autumn grass. The chemise reached to the middle of her back, perhaps less than the middle — in any case it was conspicuously short. Which made the shoulder-straps all the longer of course: back-straps rather. The chemise was light blue, this fact already shone through the blouse's November sieve, but almost negligibly pale in comparison to the straps' sharpness. (It seems that Leatrice wore no bras.) One couldn't tell if it was tight or loose. The chemise's fringe arched as if a broad part of it only tautened from sitting on it, but would otherwise hang loosely; moreover, the straps were pushed upward, so they barely touched the shoulders and curved above them.

It is interesting how the undergarments that are closest to the body do the least to conform to it — the sign of intimacy is not a hollow body-imprint but this lonely, sharp line under the blouse, the solitary artery of absolute 'boudoir.' It's touching how in the body-alienness of chemise and strap, in their form the first, tactless and naïve collision of man and outside world can be felt: even the most distinguished woman is somehow wearing an anchorite's habit, so simple is the form of the lingerie. Its chief characteristic is that it keeps shifting, as the straps clearly indicate, and the slightest shift will create the impression of utter chaos: a transparent blouse is immoral not because it lets the chemise be seen, but because it creates the possibility for it to be seen a bit off, & this tiny angle of shifting is already the devil's geometry.

Leatrice, too, was dressed with the utmost consolidation, modestly, with a coquetry deriving only from the absolute balance of puritanism, but the chemise's fringe was slightly tilted, bowing downward in oval shape between the two straps, while the left strap lay loosely above the shoulder like the twine dropped to the floor that still shows the dimensions of the box it tied. This little slackness instantly made a hetæra of her. The shoulder-strap anyway brings the so-called mores of nature to mind, for they are as rudimentary a sartorial solution as the most basic building techniques of primitive peoples: the tree-trunk made into a column, the row of reeds used as wall. Because of this folkloristic affinity the shoulder-strap renders women somehow childish, for cannibals too are childish. Left and right from the shoulder-strap's lazy or stern serpent lie the possibilities of childishness & hetæracity, like the 'sunny' and 'rainy' figures of a weather forecast. This is then woman's 'interior,' the secret of dressing: the strap's geometric line creates just such an impression of alien machinery as the medical illustrations of the liver, kidneys, or bones in the lexicon, upon which we stumbled in our childhood.

In our childhood we got used to it that the inside of things (toys or body) is some alien machinery; that what sustains the exterior in its exteriority always consists of alien drawings: until we bump into some preposterously alien whatsit inside the toy or man, we cannot recognize that more inward-set thing as anything like the true cause, origin, and foundation of life or exteriority. The shoulder-strap's lonely strip is utterly unlike the appearance of woman, thus it must be something very mysterious, a real fulcrum. As we know, the child's love-instinct finds interest not only in medical matters but in any anatomical image or description: pictures of bacilli, papier-maché lung model, etc.

When the shoulder-strap is erotic, this childish instinct is at work within us: we see some inner drawing, if not under the skin then at least under the dress, which illustrates an interior whose mode is not yet female, it is indeed hardly human, but scientific. Enough if it's not on the outside but hidden: at once it's all about love; most first loves are directed at the microscopic 'effigy' of gall secretion.

It resembles a primitive architectural device and yet lies close to pure symbolism — there is hardly any shoulder-strap in the world that is tight and could thus make one feel that it holds the chemise hanging from it as a rope holds a bucket lowered into a well. Thus it gets an ironic touch. Is then the first touch that reaches the Eve-raw shoulders the touch of irony? Followed by the straightforward honesty of the outer garments? Is it a barbarian penitential monk's habit, or butterfly-like parody? From the strap's abstract form both can be derived. The impression of cynical emblem is caused by our awareness that there would be no need at all for the shoulder-straps if the chemise covered the whole back all the way to the neck, if it burrowed shoulders and arms into a sleeve-form. The strap indicates that the chemise is some kind of purposeful minimum: it doesn't hold something that needs holding because otherwise it would fall off, but because those two threads were somehow left behind from the Ur-classic undergarment covering the whole back, just as one can find in the tombs from the age of the great migrations rather wasted heroes, from whom by mere accident two long ribs or one sole Goupy-shape[219] backbone is left behind. The shoulder-strap doesn't hold anything, it only measures a lack: it's not a bridge but a soaking twine thread thrown across the river.

If two different kinds of straps run next to each other, one will usually be made of simpler, more abstract material (this is the bra), while the other from something that already alludes to the fabric of the clothes: next to one another, two equally purely-ornamental lines, of which one is nevertheless more practical (almost rising to the level of cottonwool or the hernia truss), while the other already dips its petals deep into the wondrous world of pure stage sets. Two indicators that point at the same body-time, the same nakedness, but one, to minute-nakedness, while the other, to hour-nakedness. The 'naiveté' of the strap is further enhanced if it's of two kinds: so it becomes evident that we are only dealing with the fact of the simple hanging on of something, the two things hung are not parallel, there is no connection between them, both hang as best they can (because if they were parallel, then the order, the fact of apparently self-serving regularity, would completely obliterate the fact of hanging down).

What a sweet surprise, when instead of the strap's lines we see strap-flowers, when above the icebergs, warmed up to 36° Celsius, of back and arms we find velvety foliage, fan-leaved gardens that hide even the ears; the dress is a straight pencil that drops tightly around the legs (only the new couturiers could hit upon the special situation when the tight skirt almost adheres to the legs and yet it is only maximally parallel to the thighs' rounded walls), but the straps that hold it are a whole world to themselves, and more material went into them than into the whole dress.

If we find an oasis in the middle of a flat field, there on the bosky wetland we see amassed all the riches at once, without a shade of 'stylish' restraint — there are no signs of transition between the field & oasis. Such 'collerettes Médicis' built on naked shoulders spring forth just as unexpectedly from the arms' golden emptiness. One cannot express the dichotomy between flat surface & exaggeratedly detailed insertion mathematically, with however exotic proportion — what is more, it is not even a dichotomy but an evasion.

Between a naked back and shoulder-strap diluted into a collar the relation is akin to that between smooth-walled Italian houses and the fountain adorned with rich reliefs stuck among them, or between a bare church wall and the analytically ornate Renaissance funerary monuments built into it. As though it were not the contrast between 'flat' and 'mosaic': what we see in the fountain or sarcophagus is not at all the luxuriating detail of finish, but the fact that it's both a closed and an infinite world, from where it is impossible to get out into the geometrical world of the surrounding houses or the smooth wall serving as backdrop. Here closed and infinite are more than atmospheric contrast, which tries to replace the word 'strange,' but a quote taken from the exact police record of the experience. It is closed: but forcibly it is not closed by virtue of contours, it only has contours for practical purposes, which hardly play any part in the experience of closedness. Rather, it is closed by virtue of its cohesion; there is so much within it & it is so inwardly-much that it sucks the eye toward the center, the fictive fulcrum: so, while things are usually divided from their environment by their contours, here, on the contrary, it happens by the imaginary center.

Let's imagine such a legend of physics: there's a vortex on a flat lake, which revolves at a certain speed around its own axis — naturally around the vortex ever slower, ever bigger concentric circles emerge. Suddenly the vortex starts whirling so fast that it's nearly torn from the body of the lake, and in that moment the outward-drifting faint, but gigantic wave-rings also stop. The closedness of this vortex will not be caused by an outer boundary, but by an inward-oriented thickening and circling speed. Between vortex and lake the relation will not be that between checked and blank paper — likewise, sarcophagus, fountain, and shoulder-strap mean not the mass of 'detail' in the geometrical or anatomical sense, in their flat and naked surroundings.

Most of the time these details are not many: the shoulder-strap collar consists of four or five folds, there are a few angels & flowers on the sarcophagus, and perhaps one female statue on the fountain. Why are they then 'details,' and why 'infinite'? Let's take the black velvet collar hovering on the upper fringe of the naked body-wave: four gigantic shell-creased leaves. The eye jumps from the first to the second, from there to the third & fourth, but then the naked throat or arm follows, so it immediately returns to the third, second, etc., and so it goes on, back and forth, hither and thither, every component is infinitely repeated, and the four velvet leaves become an entire tropical forest — of course the eye doesn't see the lurking forever-repetition, four and infinity stand in a mysterious union, like divine nature and the human person. Because of the smoothness of the environment the eye fails to perceive its elements, two statues are never two statues but 'from one to the other & from the other to the first, and from the first to the second' ad infinitum.

The large velvet petals shooting from the shoulder-strap surround the head like the fur lining of a coat: the back is naked, while the face, all flushed, plays hide-and-seek among the tropical leaves. Peasant girls sometimes run about barefoot in the snow in knee-length skirts, but cover their mouths with twenty thick woolen scarves — the tailor of such evening gowns seems to have followed a similar logic. The band-collar consists of giant rounded, spiraling, and undulating forms, but this twisted movement-statue is entirely rigid — it hovers above the muscles' Neptunia, like a pneumatic blue rubber wave-assemblage that was thrown on blue water-waves at a strand: there is nothing more odd than an ethereal statue capturing such fluid movement, for instance this Medici collar, which seems constantly in motion, for the ebb-and-flow of the shoulders wouldn't leave it alone for a moment, but that has nothing to do with the movement suggested by the wave-shapes.

Something similar can be seen on certain stage dancers' hair cut 'wind-blown' fashion, and glued to their forehead and face with some perfect adhesive substance, so that, while at the height of the wildest tumbles and jumps all their clothes get dishevelled and crumpled, only the hair's tempestuous shapes withstand, indomitable, with unshaken constancy: chaos' forever-fixed amulets. By the way, one of the best introductions to love founded on the stylized shoulder-strap is the popular color illustrated guide to gardening titled *Rock Garden of Aunt Millicent* — it is here that one can see on bare rockface such unexpected permed-to-death flowers and leaf-jewels.

(introductory simile: the design of the Double Face Theater, pp. 770–771); the relation of individual and average in female beauty

Shoe, stocking, shoulder-strap: in fact in everyday life they mean woman. We need to use this impossible expression, 'everyday life,' because here it's a matter of how we are surrounded day by day, on the bus, in the street, in the office or cinema, by the possibility-thicket of women — women we will never speak to but who, when they attract us, do so with the conventional devices of clothing. This is called 'dispersed eros' which so often becomes a moral or neurological issue: in this forever-expanding ethereal love clothes are the only islands. By this we have nothing to do with any human being, only with ever-present beauty — the well-versed practitioners of 'diffuse' love walk in fact not among possibilities of women, for they don't long for this or that woman, but relish the scent emanating from all women.

If someone wants beauty overmuch, he can evidently not want one particular woman, for in half a minute another alights who is beautiful with the same force of beauty: the one who notices 'individual' beauties in a woman that insulate her from other beautiful women is most certainly a superficial and poor observer, although one would think the opposite is the case. There is no such thing as individual beauty: what in a woman is beauty's fountain and streaming cause is (O, ex-cathedra universal!) the common, sole wave of 'erotic beauty.' The eye's beauty consists in being sometimes blue, sometimes green, sometimes hazel or black: a blue eye cannot be beautiful, for it's a gross fragment, a half or one-eighth. If one is radically 'everyday' or 'all-day,' then they will find this to be natural, for if they think over, at home, the cause of their love-serenity (in the absence of woman of course), then they will find it not in a brown gaze or blue flirtatiousness, but in the ontological average that might be called 'the gaze's cockatoo polychromy.' There is no such thing as a beautiful woman, that's fiction — but there very certainly is female beauty, that's all there is, only that is reality, the unified experience of everyday. The 'average' doesn't mean the common denominator of prettinesses present in every beautiful woman — otherwise the average of blue, hazel, and black eyes would become grey litter-aspic, and the 'average' physique of tall, short, broad- and ball-shouldered women nothing but murderous tedium cut out of anatomy handbooks.

'Female beauty' isn't composed of the individual beautiful women, but the other way round: female beauty is something independent of the human being, infinitely complicated and heterogeneous, but this heterogeneity is nohow related to the fact that female society is made up of diverse individuals — if I want to examine the components of female beauty, what is needed is not good observation skills in the practical sense, not one who can capture individual nuances, for if I meticulously described all the curves, probability-asymptotes, and angle-whims of an eyelash,

I would notice not a thread in the intricate weave of 'female beauty' but merely an inexpressive drawing on a human being's outward appearance, which leads us nowhere. The beauty of the eyelash has a thousand shades and elements, but those are to be found only within the concept of (an approximate word) 'the eyelash': here the concept is not an average of meaning but a thousand-colored vision. We are not faced with the dichotomy of 'complex individual' vs. 'simple average,' but with that of 'complex individual' vs. 'universal that is complex in itself': two complication systems meeting on one face.

When we say that to the connoisseur of female beauty a pair of blue eyes, however beautiful, means nothing in itself, we don't imply that such a person loves variety, being soon bored by blue and attracted by green — although he is the least able to find æsthetic or love fulfillment in one woman, he is the one who least needs yet another woman. 'Beauty': this has a faintly scandalous Platonic air, but there's nothing to do about it, for the true connoisseur truly has it in overplus.

In the beauty of the blue eyes, like in some upflaring Bengal flame, the other colors (green, brown, black) burn, organically enmeshed with and even fused into blueness: after blue eyes we will not necessarily long for brown or green eyes, but somehow enjoy the 'colorfulness of eyes' — this Platonic image-idea of colorfulness is not the same thing as the complete inventory of colorful eyes. True observation will therefore detect the colorfulness emanating from the blue, the eternal constraint of color to continue in the other shades of the spectrum: the one truly sensitive to female beauty will observe the great green-ancillarity of blue, green's primeval tendency to red, brown's restless turn-to-black.

The inner heterogeneity of 'colorfulness,' as we have already signalled, is not caused by the different colors — the colors' difference on the spectrum is only a concrete simile & prefiguration to that inexpressible, but positively felt & relished heterogeneity which nests in the nervous-Platonic concept of 'colorful eyes.' To reach any results here, the most banal Casanova penchant has to work hand in hand with the most shortsighted Platonism. (The types of universals could be discussed in some Nicolaus Cusanus-like style,[220] taking as points of departure either women or flowers for instance: the complete catalogue of all the existing flowers — uninterrupted image-chain and their number as sum: the concept meaning all the flowers — 'the flower': the intellectual common denominator is the definition that fits all; the template, visual common denominator that all the flowers leave behind in our eyes like silt; the medieval analogy-concept that transcends the boundaries of concepts and finally, what we have formulated above on the eyes' colorfulness: the universal that splits off from the flower, in which not a single trace is left of visual or intellectual allusions to any flower, but which takes on a life of its own, with its own structure & profile, although its determination obviously derives from the flowers. This universal is double-faced like silver coins — one side turns toward the flowers, but ab ovo it has to have another side too, and this needs to be researched and discovered with fresh impetus, as it has never been dealt with before.)

Shoulder-strap and female body are inseparable and carry female beauty to the same extent, a beauty which, however, is alien from any woman, just as the well is at the same time water's orthodoxy and its cynical heresy, for it is the essence-bearing cause itself, but also the one that immediately discards the result toward unknown landscapes, never-riverbeds and lakes. It is self-evident that, if this is the essence of beauty, lovers have little chance of happiness: one always has to feel in this or that woman the growing heap of ashes that threatens to extinguish the violet-shaped fire budding beneath. Beauty is the natural suffering of crude and refined Platonists, for them indeed beauty and suffering are not separate things.

*after absolute externals, absolute pain; example:
the fear of lovers from an illegitimate child*

When we examined the possibilities of Leatrice-representations, however, we also thought of a much more prosaic variant of suffering from women (which, thanks to the touch of the flippant and comfortable magic word 'ultima analysi,' is probably identical to Platonic theory-pain): beauty is not a life or social phenomenon, but with women we can only enter life or social relations, ergo suffering is inevitable. Thus Leatrice would be on the one hand shoe, stocking, and shoulder-strap — and on the other hand, shapeless, imbecilic male pain. In place of some common general-pain and immediately after the description of clothes, one would need to enlist the events of a 'schlimazel' in the practical sense (more than tragedy).

A very young man gets acquainted with a girl; after two weeks the girl tells him that she is expecting. Both know very well that if the liaison came to light, huge scandals and suffering would be in store. The boy sleeps in the garden of his father's castle where he usually meets the girl. She comes here late at night, furtively wandering about in the maze of paths, to wake him up and tell him that she is pregnant. They can barely see each other, boy and girl are just flubbed blots, there's one single reality in the grass-steamed silence — the inimical germ in the lover's amateurish womb. The boy is overcome by disgust, rage, & a small child's fear. What are they to do? The child cannot be born. The girl doesn't cry, she only palely repeats in a small voice that "something must be done soon." The boy caresses her out of reflex, nauseated as though he were palpating a disfigured corpse, for he feels the girl's body to have turned meaningless, sick, or dead from the moment an alien life & human being started in her.

The unexpected child is an unfaithfulness a hundred times more grave than a new lover: she remains within the territory of love with the new lover, but the child is no longer love, it's clinic, estrangement, society and money. The child cannot elicit the experience of life's lifelikeness: the 'secret' of life is not in its eternal continuation, in the fact that from the tiny seed a giant tree or man grows, these are naively venal and vacuous-mechanistic sides of life — the true essence of life he felt in the barrenness of the first kiss, in the gauche ephemerality of the gaze, without any organic chemistry added. The gigantic tropical flowers, the palm-trees' millionfold fertility is not more lifelike life — in general fertility and biological creating-forth has nothing to do with the essence of life.

The girl is a traitor, and she has betrayed life for death. The boy is unwittingly looking for signs of this new illness on the girl's body. How is her beauty? Just as it was, but now it's worth nothing, something is missing: it's like a light-bulb in daylight without electricity: every feature is well visible, the platinum-lashes and tiny glass-columns, everything is clear and important, but incandescence is missing. The girl is sitting speechlessly on the bench, the boy keeps scrutinizing her lap where her handbag's white buckle glows. What is that child now, at the beginning of the first month? An idea more than reality, and precisely for this reason it's more hateful than a rival lover: she is exactly like a girl, nothing changed on her, it's only an idea that extinguished light in her. Her color is a bit pale, it must be the child sucking away her blood already; every movement, breath, smile is now directed not outward, toward him, the boy, but inward to the child, who is not even a child before its birth, but a mushrooming cancer, hydrops, or fattening.

Whether only-idea or inhuman biological whimsy, it makes love equally impossible — he thought. So woman's outward appearance becomes meaningless because everything is inwardly occupied. Every syllable, every gaze gives the impression of a lie under microscope, ever since the child's almost negative initial appeared in her. So far they had lived a day-to-day life, time poured forth from them like foam from an overfilled glass — what didn't fit in as feeling served as time: now the child forcefully interposed the alien and raw time of nine months between them, making the whimsical and non-homogeneous rippling of inner time impossible. They are now in the first month, and next to this pathetic number the neither-hither-nor-thither, imprecise flower of their rendezvous has no chance of growth.

She became at once 'social' and pathological — as if she had grown thin as a stick from the intellectual poison of the new relations. He stealthily gets his father's car out of the garage to take her to a medical friend that very night. For a moment he thinks of murdering her because of the child, but the routine of driving stops him from thinking of anything else for long. How strange that she's sitting next to him in all her bodily reality and yet there is not one thought of his that would be directed at her as love-object: no sooner does love start than the stifling chain of thoughts because the woman and because love starts too, and from this 'because' both the woman and love are absent. The classic case of not-thinking-about-the woman is the abortion comedy. He wakes up his friend in the dead of night. For a few weeks the period of doubt: will there be a child or not, is medication enough or is an operation needed, suicide, courtroom, marriage? Which of them? The boy & the girl meet but he can hardly bear the worries and the pretence of love. The 'event' fills everything in place of love. What should he prepare for? Should he force himself to religiously get used to the idea of mother, the as-yet unknown cellars of the ties of love, or should he get used to the role of the murderer who whistles if she dies in the operation?

He's trying on roles from morning to night, adding to the possible outcomes: they get married in secret, after which she dies — they get married in secret, his father finds out, scenes of rage, after which she commits suicide — his wife commits suicide before or after the birth of the child — in secret (how?) she manages to give birth, it is the child they kill — she kills it, they kill it together, or he kills it without her knowledge — he gets punished and he had also compromised his friend — they both elope — what if she confesses her sin to her mother & her mother comes to his father's house to make a scene — or he himself confesses it to his father, who forgives him and helps in making the child disappear — his father wants the marriage to happen, but they abort the child in secret — it is only after the marriage that his father realizes that the birth had been prevented — he kills her and the dissection reveals that she hadn't been pregnant — to blame the pregnancy on another boy, another tale about fatherhood is to be invented with every boy, the girl, the parents — to frantically deny everything without providing a supplement, however unlikely — the thing transpires before the operation, to deny it to authorities and make further steps for the operation to take place: so the enchained variations came and went by the hundreds, pressing on his head to the point of madness. It was entirely secondary, which of them would come to pass: every single one was the absolute of ill fate. Even if the operation succeeds and nobody suspects anything, then the relief won't last more than a few hours, love cannot be continued, since for weeks on end he had lived in the dry, calculating world of fidgeting, hatred, irritation & murder plans — he had forever compromised his love before himself, coming to see what a feeble, impractical thing it is.

The greatest love is the feeblest and most ephemeral: it only seeks the embraces happening in an almost abstract space and time, hates all practical preparations for the rendezvous and all practical endings — if a button is askew on the woman, he leaves her with the deepest loathing, no use if she's a cornucopia of beauty and morality — if something needs to be done for love (for instance, moving a duvet, or moving house), he would rather abandon love, precisely because he can only bear absolute love, if one atom is missing it's as if there were nothing. The prince who offers his life for the woman, who slays giants and makes dragons into minced meat, is a rather mediocre lover, his lady can't be too important to him. The great lover, as philosophers have it, thinks in 'eidetic reductions' — he has one obsession: Adam and Eve in paradise — if this cannot be realized, he dumps the whole business altogether. For him, love is 'happy togetherness' — not acquaintanceship, moral, marriage, life force, gaze into the future, maitresse-adventure, caritas or search for the human being, but the blindest passivity.

The perfect and greatest love is always a chance and insulated situation, a situation of encounter: its foundational type is the man and woman in the woods who strayed away from the hunting company, and who have only known each other for a few hours. This is paramount — they need to know one another's voice, get used to one another's gestures and manners a bit, but they shouldn't know each other's character and thoughts. Should they know just a little more than necessary about each other, absolute love is already impossible, for then a part of their feelings will be poured out into the foreign troughs of the character, the 'human being,' and be spilt. Love, encounter (the two are one) cannot be willed: in the 'rendezvous' the murderous blade of an imperative destroys everything. (Absolute love and absolute happiness with woman are not identical: absolute love is of course always happy, but absolute happiness with, and from, woman is not necessarily complete eros.)

Love is first and foremost always a situation, a 'given situation,' constellation: preliminaries and epilogue automatically fall off. It relates to life as the turning of the clustered spokes in the roulette plate, to the perimeter's numbers: at first there was a number at the end of every spoke, now the spoke shifted a bit, but the number rests in place. The accidental place of encounter, too, had some preliminary and cause, but now it has shifted in a like manner and hovers in the void, independent — and this void outside of life is already paradise, so the stage setting is ready. Whoever lives love like this cannot bear the abortion drama: should shoe, stocking, shoulder-strap be thrown into this mirror of suffering?

ramification of projects and realizations

But of course every plan to represent Leatrice is naïve — for if Leatrice's thematic leaf-shooting starts in earnest, the ever newer cells of representation will not be determined by a unified programme but always by the previous cell: one idea, by the previous chance adjective, one event, by the outlandish ring of the previous syllable. That should make every representer optimistic. Naturally in this manner the realization is eternal and purposeless. There is a longitudinal vibration of thought (this is the project) and a transversal one (this is the realization). Put brutally: a thought consists of 10 words; the thought has a longitudinal, onward force toward the next thought, but can never reach there, at the second planned thought, for it is crossed by the actions of the individual words' perpendicular forces, whose cumulated effect far exceeds their longitudinal force. When we set out to prepare the second thought's longitudinal momentum, we don't have any other active force in mind but the transversal energy of the first thought's first word, which adjusts the new thought, the second, to the first thought's first unit as one would soft, malleable wax. Every imaginable new thought always aligns to the previous thought's words, which doesn't mean varying them formally, but starting from them despite all estrangement, being dynamically predestined from them.

Project & realization resembles a little the old Eleatic joke[221] in which the proposed plan is impossible to attain because one has to first cover half of the way, the half of that half, its half, and so forth. This is the infinite magnetism of the point origo — in vain I plan to draw five circles one after the other, the second circle's outline is immediately drawn to itself by the first, adjusted to the first. And so it does with the third and the rest, there will be no progress, but the third and fourth circles will nevertheless not coincide with the first, they modulate, struggle, become oval or sponge cake-y, for they, too, possess an inner energy to counteract the magnet, and lots of resistances & frictions also play a part. So can, after the lengthy plan and with the awareness of the impossibility of execution, Leatrice begin.

X.

Leatrice by the sea, morning. Description of the morning

She found a curious resemblance between the sea's color and the shape of yesterday's glasses. The morning glowed white & bristly above the sea; its blue was transparent to the point of mist, to the point of shiny, slippery, glassy, and resounding mistiness, which hovered by the water's horizontal sheet (she would have liked to find a word that could express with one drastic phoneme simple existence, infinite expansion's nonchalant role-play, the well-nigh theological horizontality of hovering and within it all, a line-like, quietly zigzagging quiver, which snakes like a thin chalk line across the waters and the sky); she had the impression that here several fragments of sky piled up, like the fan-shaped display of a cosmic fabric sample collection — above the horizon, silvery smoke spread like the foaming leftover of a long train; in its wake a light blue void remained, like a giant hemisphere whose whitish inside, loyal sheath, kept the form of the rounded sun taken out of it, or like a big strand umbrella that an addenda-goddess lent to good old Phoebus while she took a bath in the morning's majolica-tiled pool, but he ended up forgetting his knick-knacks on top of the quivering wave tufts; above the tilted umbrella a thick silver mash followed, the threadbare everyday Olympus bedsheet with which the celestial deities cover the world's arena every noon — the sun bleached it completely of course, only at the edges was there some little silvery blue note left, among the tassels hanging over the mountains; and finally, behind her back, caught in the rooftops and in the trees' combs, something of the night: wet, gluey-eyed clouds with pillow-smeared grimaces, like the worn-off, trampled masks of the past.

Because these varied heaven-budgets seemed to compete with each other, she had the feeling of hearing a great noise, of every single astronomical legion chanting its own anthem: from the inside of the clouds worming above the horizon line a warm, cotton-muffled drumming came, like at decorative executions; from the blue umbrella, like from an opalescent, swaying megaphone, one single violin note stretching to infinity, with an obstinacy that made the unchanged note sound a thousand as it fell into waning attention's sawlike, dimpled mirror; now it drew the eye to the umbrella's edge, toward the widest circles, where she immediately felt spreading into the morning's oversize emptiness, as if all awakenings consisted in a letting off to the sky of the tied-down soul of night, like some balloon — and now this unceasing violin sound drew the eye to the umbrella's center, where she felt to be not a balloon but an arrow rushing toward one magnetic point, to drown at once in its mendacious-precise aim.

The circus sheet above her head flapped dryly like a parched sail that the wind had plastered to the mast; it was cut a bit narrow, so the half-tight, half-loose cords tying it to the arena's other wall are very long: an umbrella whose wire ribs were cut five times longer than the watertight silk.

A big bird flapping above her head, irked: this is already the 'daytime's' blasé gull facing the morning's sizzling blue; and in the end, the night could give only the kind of sound whose image was: the sound of a dark black rubber horse from which every second the ebony sniffle of midnight pours out, whistling-slumping — a few hours earlier he alone stood with funereal haughtiness, like some Colleoni,[222] above the small seaside town, the envoy of some instantly-sepulchral Troy, who will not, however, pour out from his bowels fate's hysterical little insects, but instead continues to soak its hooves into the waters thickened to a parfait by pressing darkness, and while the ice-bathing Nereids prepare the footbath of this bubble-Colleoni's horse, the Moon as open metal veneer tube smears the lance's point, so it would glisten like a new star above the town's flat roofs, built obtusely for the sole purpose to protect people's souls from such a big sparkle: every roof appeared like the flanges protecting the horses' eyes, so the lance would in vain glisten above the roofs. But now the haughty lance melted into crooked 8-s, as if imitating Chaplin in schickered stupor; the Sun's vitriolic rays, like a young Bolingbroke, immediately washed clean midnight's resplendent coat of arms, which was still propped like a shield against the mountain slope, & with boastful empiricism wrought to life the hills' rich mimicry.

*the morning's intellectual laboratory
(schism of contents and forms, etc.)*

When Leatrice looked at the sea and looked at her dreams, the sequence of images was composed of many kinds: the images connecting the champagne glasses' grey glass-horizons to the sea's color and dreaming time-band were completely different from the images that peopled the hiatuses between objects with conjunction-like caricatures, Colleonis, rubber heroes and other raw materials of personification & objectification. The first kind was inspired by logic, while the second by so to say religious irony. Leatrice had always lived in images, but it was highly questionable if that meant that she also lived for images. When she found ethics sooner in the impressionist images of artificial dreams (an impression can only ever be artificial in Touqué's arid school, for spontaneity sniffs out a stone-hard order for itself even from the most ephemeral scents) than in the uncertain prose of actions, then the image was merely a device for enjoying the necessary ethical thrill; she found that the action sucks to itself through a straw the waters of ancient moral, and so it can at most produce the stingy play of capillariness from day to day.

But Leatrice was interested precisely in the unusable stagnant waters of moral and believed that, just as relativist physics arrives at the new concept of dynamics via the laws of inertia (she remembered some such thing from a conversation with Touqué), so in moral, too, she would discover the formulae of inertia in place of the failed mechanics of action. The 'image' was such an inertia-emblem both in logics and in ethics. This process had more phases, from which we will only mention the two extremes: the first is an initial, entirely primitive state, represented by the resplendent, decorative images designed by Peter: the regular arithmetic roots of infinite sensuousness and hypochondriac blotch-comfiness; whereas the other is the style that barely differed from the one now seen by Leatrice, when toying with the rim of champagne glasses, their halo-like disjoining, the wavelessness of the champagne surface, its golden color and concrete nihil-plasticity.

In the morning one is a starved rationalist: we can only start the new day that presses itself to our forehead with tyrannical speed like a hypnotic glass blade, to double its body into the cruel symmetry of existence, we can only start the new day if it has the shape of reason: we demand some certainty, springtime credit, and schoolboy-like guarantees from the breakfast's teaspoons, our girlfriend's freshly narrowing centrifuge-hips, the newspaper's tattooed columns, the common whims of waiters, seas, and migratory birds; everybody falls out naked, with snow-white, raison-virginal limbs, from night's shell and hurries to put on the delicate underclothes of intellect, bourgeois causality, teleology corroborated to the point of mundanity. In the bathroom we are always at the very start of creation; even the dumbest coquettes are clean alephs. The tiniest sensuous pleasure: the unexpectedly fast-foaming soap, the breakfast ready 10 minutes earlier, the early morning letter stuck under the bathroom door — they all mean the meaning of life, not its beauty, palpability, or finitude.

It's as if every image and every narrative were one horizontal, light leaf of a gigantic but graceful tree, whose common leaf-stems go back to common twigs and those twigs, to common branches on one slender trunk: beneath the morning's motley stretches a healthy, slightly frivolous but clever monist atmosphere. Every leaf is horizontal, like the didactically-prepared inflorescence of elderberry; every visible, palpable, perceivable thing, colors, sounds, events are strictly horizontal: as if in the morning the impish instinct of rationality could be appeased already by smuggling some lurking horizontality into the material of sensations; we see the heaving object-quota of colors, forms, sounds not in front of us but slightly beneath us, lying, thin, projected in a plane.

In the logical gesture of awakening a precisely 90° deviation can be detected: the first appearance of self-consciousness in the hotel room (hotels are as a rule metaphysical surgical theaters) means a suddenly jumping verticality, a flexible sprint toward unattainable but all the more magnetic ceilings; as compared to this, the world represents spreading-out, splaying under our eyes, the empty dimension. Later the objects and colors don't fill in this empty plateau but take their places above it at various distances; when Leatrice tasted the soap-foam, the early breakfast, the morning letter stuck in as meaning, she relished this plane in them — that is, the fact that the horizontal dimension featured not in the objects but far from them, separated, the abstract-fresh gift of awakening. Thus colors became like hollow or forgotten statues, one of their essential dimensions fell from them like a superfluous core, and they glistened in front of her eyes solely with the celestial sensuousness of hypotheses.

The morning staffage is made up of two important elements: infinitely horizontal, sea level-altitude Veronica veil, & a multitude of hovering masks — the same shiny green or stifling carmine thesis features in the world as both carmine-supposition and carmine-projection; on the poppy, as empty mask, the modest-sharp sensuous attempt at redness and beneath it, at 90° distance from the soul, horizontally, as the meaning of redness, its crystalline cause, its geometrically composed objective. This schism & logical division of perceptions is expressed by those images which from early dawn are engrossed in the rim of champagne glasses: the soul enjoys in them now empty roundedness, now plateau-like meaninglessness, the eye slides between the two like a hesitant billiard ball.

This seeing means at any rate an elegant use of the eye, for there where it sees roundednesses, forms, that is, shapes piled up against pure horizontality, those will invariably be seen empty, thus light; to it the most robust Oxford green will no longer appear robust, because it caused the rickety essence of green to drop from it like from an open box, and let the essence, the gross content of perception (the 'green of green') sink-dull into the projection plane of the horizontal; it will not hear the most dogmatic F sharp in its bigoted fullness but only the most superficial layer of the sound surface, for the sound-core ('the cause-dense and cause-concentrated F♯) bent to 90° from the sound, into the refreshing & discretion-generating horizontality of the awakening.

Earlier we called the images in which perception is so felt to split into two, logical images; of course it's questionable if the relation between the dimension become independent, the pure plane split from color (that certain geometric Veronica veil) and rounded emptiness (those certain masks) indeed belongs to the realm of the logical, or if it is merely toy-analogy between geometry and meaning? The difficulty consists in the fact that we unquestionably see and experience in perception something else beside perception's direct object, but since we don't know what it is, we keep tagging confusing names on it — names like reason, logic, or spirituality on the one hand, and on the other hand, geometrical names like linearity, projection, dimension, et cetera; that is, we imagine that concrete part of green that is not equal to literal green-being, to be in part scholastic-flavored 'truth' and in part, some décor-like mathematical thingamajig.

analogies to dawn: modern architecture, glass civilization

Leatrice's instinctive technique of looking is wholly validated by recent styles in art, of which it's enough to mention two tricks in relation to our treatment of logical images. The first: Neue Sachlichkeit,[223] as it's well known, prefers to enjoy certain materials in their pure materiality — it will not decorate wood, textile, brick, or celluloid, nor use them for decoration, but insulates them from the other objects of the world by the most basic geometrical shapes, & with this concludes their belaboring (needless to say, this has nothing to do with so-called puritanism).

The same taste, however, that wishes to highlight material in its most radical materiality, that same style made abstract figures popular — when for instance they build a rectangular green marble wall, whose every square millimeter is filled by the congested, almost over-materialized marble, they feel the need to erect by the wall, into the air, and without the slightest practical justification, a steel frame of the same size as the wall, which could exactly frame the wall if so placed — that is, the Sache almost mechanically brings about the most abstract signaling of form: to the left, the wall, and immediately next to it, an empty steel frame of the same size. What kind of instinct leads to such technique? In earlier days, after the house was finished, the practical scaffolding disappeared, but now an essential trait of style is to build next to each material-filled form its empty formal skeleton, not only in architecture but also in painting and even in music, where the most interesting thing is the elaboration, next to the Klang-Sache and similarly wrought from notes, of the 'Nichtklang-Projektion' or 'leere Klangdimension.'[224]

When Leatrice saw the separating rim of the champagne glasses ascend like a row of grey halos, her senses were not guided by impotent ornamentation or girlish Sezession, but by the rigor of up-to-date dreams; not even in thought could she bring her lips to the champagne's green golden lake without seeing in the air empty circles of exactly the same dimension, abstract traces of space. (Idea and spatiality together will mean a lot more to explore: as there was a time-Proust, there has to be a space-Proust.)

Another thing from the modern arts that also corroborates Leatrice's fantasy is the extraordinarily emphatic featuring of glass, rapturous glass culture. Why glass? By no means because it is healthy, because it lets sunlight through, because the room becomes luminous or other such utilitarian side-tricks — if it were important only for such, they could surely tear down all the glass factories. Glass is necessary because it is the most appropriate, most equal expression of that oft-mentioned thing that in the course of their raw perceptions people will call now reason, now the logical dimension, and which we featured with regard to Leatrice as 'nihil-plasticity.'

Glass is the richest source of paradox: it is first and foremost hard, but at the same time it is nothing; transparent and sharp, glistening and neutral, geometrical and imprecise, mirroring and autonomous, etc. Characteristically it's the 'new objectivity' that employs the highest number of abstract, empty, immaterial, almost philosophical forms (steel frames, concrete planes of the same size as the house's ground plan next to the house), and it was this same style that invented the theology of glass: a theology of the material that is the least Sache-like Sache. Glass is precisely the thing that stands the closest to pure dimensions: as though it were the one and only fundamental element from which all things started — it's already much more than abstract form, yet still a lot less than a green marble table or other materials.

Later Leatrice examined in herself the sensations awakened when she imagined herself as a human being, that is, she simply observed the effect on consciousness of the concept of 'human being' and pondered the styles of this human-consciousness in their contrast described above: so one human-consciousness was exactly as if all of a sudden a glass-consciousness started in a green marble wall, for Leatrice felt herself to be the most human of human beings, human in the most thing-like sense, when she was slightly tipsy or drugged, dizzy, and her soul was empty: in short, when so to say she lost all her concrete content of consciousness and her concrete muscles, forgot her name and personality, keeping only her extended borders, the quivering thread-drama of the limes — moments of human-slaying 'neue Mensch-Sachlichkeit'?[225]

How is it possible that people feel with their senses & not in their theories that the most concrete thing in them is dizziness, empty space revolving in a spiral — that certain 'nihil-plasticism'?

The noise of the morning was probably the noise of possibilities; the humming of a thousand start-lines folded back into the womb, and when the bar owner addressed her in a tone of half-phlegm & half naïve pathos, 'A great morning we're having,' at first she barely heard it. She saw large glasses in three kinds of 'developments': her memory stored exact copies, the way they were the previous night on the table; then she fell asleep from too much champagne and they surrounded her in her dream like conic, transparent tents made of refrigerated light; and lastly, from the dawn's light crossing her dreams, a third variation was born. She felt that the morning's beauty was in these two things: the music-pastiche brought to her ears from here and there like a straying rain-bill, and the dream-figments hung out to dry on the slender rays' strings. Night is the realm of discipline, of classical stifling, where palpation reigns; feeling about reduces the body to a few leaden, clumsy gestures and dreams, too, revolve in the same place, in the down-at-heel laboratory of the brain.

Touqué's caricature of the psyche

As Leville-Touqué once wrote in his little spoof, *Séjour au bord de la Psyché*:[226] Once I changed my ticket to a distant, exquisite summer resort where God himself would have received me in private audition, but in the meantime I learned that the borders were closed in that direction, so I got off at the very next train stop. At first I didn't even inquire where I was, all I could see was that I landed in an incredibly seedy, old-fashioned spa: a big black water, lake or gulf, which looked rather like a long disused commercial side-dock, so oily, slimy, and putrid was its water; the strand was populated by young girls in ultra-modern swimsuits & squatting men who, instead of taking a bath, just kept looking at themselves in the water's lazy, croaking waves, which resembled an apoplectic seal's moving mouth. Among the classically-proportioned dressing cabin-ruins rotting on the strand a cabin boy loitered, looking like one giving up the ghost — he stuttered something in my ear while pressing a huge, crooked copper key in my hand. Here and there a gas lamp like in the outskirts; some reddish, greasy foliage hung from the trees like candy sugar half-sucked from the stick.

I felt like fainting. While I eyed the drab key that might have been a blasphemous crucifix, I thought I must have ended up in a secret Masonic swimming pool, or the mudbath club of retired Narcissuses, that miraculously withstood the vicissitudes of time. I asked the cabin boy to tell me where I was in fact, at which he said quietly and with a stifled yawn, In *Psyche*. The last mail is the *center of the I*.

Your noses must be fast revolving with all the turning up when you see me relapse into the style of old allegories, and you are right to hiss the word 'barren' into my ear, but there is no other way in which I could convey this experience which consisted in encountering my own soul, when I met nothingness. And nothingness can after all only be expressed if one tries to approach it somehow: with 'some-thing.' A nice little result we'd get if we asked the ladies & gents to vote on what they feel to be closest to nothing — what colors, movements, or scenes can best approximate nothing. Some, in melancholy mode, others in dramatic & downright strident can-cans, some in perfumed transparence, others in robust cyclopic walls, in the mash of impressions: we could easily get a million budgets to the allegoric treatment of 'nothing.' Since I had no considerable artistic ambitions even at that time, I chose the puppet-theater, salon-spleen form as the most lucrative for propagandistic purposes.

the struggle between dream, thought, thinking, action, language

It was almost in her arms that Leatrice felt the fatigue and monotony of self-fecundation: dreams always revolve in the same place, towering above themselves, dividing and multiplying, but exclusively among and with themselves — not one seed could fall out, not a speck of dust could fall into them from the outside — they're like the snail that coils up in a ring around itself inside the shell, unable to sweat a pearl around the pebble dust that got in. But by the time morning came, the situation changed completely, she fully owned the dream, independent like a mysterious island protected by rings of waters of unknown depth, which reality's lights and shadows, its flaring-up data, could nevertheless also illuminate: they crossed the island without changing it in the least. At night she herself was embedded in her dream's mud, but in the morning the whole dream became a miniature garden or stage that rises in the middle of a large glass box, a scholarly model, while all around, reality's thousand impossibilities spread out with a silvery sheen.

In her dream the glass rims came off and floated out like swans in a boat alignment — they were now chalkily rough, now light like slippery rings. This she could report to herself even in the morning's 'Youthlastic' rubber corset, but the pivotal thing with such image-obstinate dreams is, that the most contrived image-spores always go together with precise emotional companions, or rather, the very images are always feelings, and in this way such richness, such serial growth of brand-new and unknown emotions develops, for which she can no longer account with the same simplicity which accounted for the images' outward appearance.

Sitting on the balcony & letting the morning's imprevisible propeller (resembling the gesticulating of a thousand-armed deity) cool her skin in irregular squares, she felt only voluptuous numbness and knew that she felt such punctiliously registered relation between the shape of the glasses and the sea's color, because the emotions squeezed into these figures were related. When we wake up we start the day with the intent to pour these feelings into the late morning's used-up canals. What a feeling, for instance, that image when the champagne glasses' rims came off like thin template haloes, and first ascended with slow floating, then (like savagely quickening music from which at first tones merely drizzle, but in time the repetition becomes so fast and the tones' density so high that the tones coming later almost overtake the preceding ones, that is, the music continues backward, beyond itself: when one gallops deeper and deeper into sobbing, the sob too becomes so fast that it doesn't so much haul the soul toward the future, toward time's ready-made careers, but pushes it back behind the sad event, showing the event from the direction of this artificial past created from a crescendo of speed and repetition, in the form of mendacious, but tamponing 'foresight') popped off from the glass' rim by the thousands (there is nothing more thrilling than soundless popping off: high-precision movements piled up high, mutely & as line-bubbles, like an extraordinarily dense & wide-perimeter thread coil that runs through an aquarium).

What kind of feeling was this? What should she do in the exile of daylight?

The first natural reaction could only be revolt: she wouldn't accept the daytime conventions for her nighttime personality. In this punctiform revolt it was not daytime reality and nighttime dream that opposed each other, but the radically emotion-creature and the emotion-conspectus-creature. Leatrice was full of emotions that she couldn't place in the outward world: they would not suit flowers, loves, sorrows, times, or herself. So far she had always made a compromise with the world, and forced herself to forget these dream emotions, but today she felt that this lie had to end for good, today she wanted to live her first emotion-day.

To help her dream she evoked those memories from her past in which emotion had similarly been on such a critical point, as at a parting from a lover, or a lonely afternoon spent in a very homely home. Should she choose contemplation? It surely cannot be turned into deeds. But she wanted to act, the dream-images were rhythmic attempts, each one moved and wanted to move others. She looked at a glass and the glass's name fell on her head like a windfall horse chestnut: glass. At night they were nameless, they had no time, no space, their only feature was continuity and emotion — this continuity was not temporal, not duration but rather, 'self-evidence of equal expanse as the site of the entire existence.' Glass was thus existence, one opalescing state of color of the entire existence, and as such, something utterly special, never to return, absolutely transient.

This is the tragedy of dream emotions: they mean the most universal atmosphere of existence in an infinitely momentary moment-pose. Our muscles would like to join the gymnastics of sea, trees, clouds, we feel so much like nature, but at the same time we are an impossible variation of this nature: one infinite ribbon, one homogeneous single-component ribbon made of a primordial material but coiled around itself countless times like a drill. Perhaps the human being is this: more synthetic than the fullest existence, but this synthesis is twisted into an absurdly analytical cord: it's so special that the unknown implied by this specialism already means a new completeness too, for it splits off so completely from everything known, that it is forced to become a whole by solitude's natural pressure.

At first sight thus the emotion-creature means the inorganic bind of an overzealous synthesis, which encompasses much more than the whole, and of analysis that grasps details much smaller than any detail — but on closer look, the impossible-to-harmonize bind of two syntheses: one is the atmosphere of existence superfluously more complete than completeness, while the other is the synthesis-atmosphere derived from the absolute particularity of each & every element which composed that completeness: if there is nothing else around it, one atom is 'a whole world in itself,' as they say. Although the element of a synthesis and its special form are two different things, for the inner paradox of emotion they have the same value — to feature in both cases are 'complete' and independent ex-particularities, but in both cases they were forced to become unknown worlds. True lyricism: trans-whole plus infra-fragment. Is it possible to solve the compulsory daytime equation of 'action' with only two data in our hands: the unknown, and a giant dynamic plus sign? Can we do anything with a glass in the morning, when all we know is that all our nerve endings know so much more than this solitary glass named glass, but that pressing and gigantic 'more' is locked in the fantastically peculiar, unmapped wiring of our nerves, uniqueness-sensitivities? Emotion pours on us the fullest hygiene and the most hopeless pathology at the same time: is there anything more wholesome than mingling into the rhythm of the whole of nature (this is the 'more'), yet on the other hand, is there anything more sickly than falling prey to our most fugitive associations, the fractions of a second? And yet Leatrice wanted both at the same time.

The utmost beauty of dream & of love that excludes the outward world is the utter extinction of the dictionary (by this we mean logic and all knowledge): instead of a glass, the 'continuity' of the glass, that is, its turning into our body part. Let's imagine a couple of lovers who lock themselves up for 10 days in one room. What will the result be, from a logical perspective? They will hardly have any words, but instead there will be two things in overplus: on the one hand, they turn into blind life-process, into monadically windowless complete-life to the point of inanity, there will be no I and no you, tomorrow and yesterday, human being and table, something and nothing; on the other hand, for them the most ephemeral stirring of each other's eyes becomes a positive signal, and the most unnoticeable shade of the room's lighting, no less precise a time-world than the vulgar noon underscored by two clock-hands and twelve bell chimes, what is more, these shades will appear to them so magnified as to expand — as discussed above — into newer blind-complete worlds.

Words and thoughts go extinct, and yet this slavery of love, dumbing down into pleasure, becomes intellectual life, so it appears to its representatives (a thing that shouldn't mean much): and the chemical tests conducted after 10 days prove this point beyond doubt. Absolute feeling and absolute thinking (not thought!) are one and the same.

thinking and feeling are identical movements (pp. 826–827), lead theme: remembering the glasses of yesterday

Feeling is the unknown movement of the soul that turns into experience by grabbing a chance association, as a rushing train wheel does an autumn leaf. Leatrice woke up from her dreams, her true feelings blossomed in her dreams, thus dream & feeling were one and the same for her (here 'superficial identification' is the only possible precision). So dreams are movements that carry image-torsos with them. Thinking is the self-same movement, the blind and irrational undulation of the soul which, however, draws to itself not images but words (by which we understand 'meanings' and 'thoughts'); the words are of course far fewer in number than the images, and far more rigid and impossible to take apart.

When the two lovers rot-apotheose into each other for 10 days, the inner undulation technique of feeling & thinking reaches an infinite sensitivity and no longer connects by images or words, but by assimilating to itself whatever the wave touches, turning it into a wave form (this is 'continuity'): the girl's eyes are not a blue swamp with black van Gogh weeds (that is, not image) and not 'eyes' (as meaningful word), but the eternal unknown, purposeless, complete wave, what is meant by the incessant thinking about the eyes. Thinking & thought belong among the opposites that utterly exclude each other — but in the course of those 10 days this murderous dichotomy ceases and everything becomes million-mirrored, water-faced thinking.

The charms of thinking without thoughts (that is, the sole truly intellectual thinking) opened to Leatrice when she parted with her lover: in the room everything stood as before, the boy had hardly changed place on the divan, and she was slowly picking from her handbag a crumpled little tube, from which she smeared something on her face, so the powder wouldn't harm her complexion. Then she fished out the hand mirror and when she looked in it, her face had already left behind the anonymous wave-forest of 'thinking' but had not yet arrived at the names and meanings. A moment before she had found one twitch of her mouth to be the most natural expression of being-together, a logicism chattering like an alarm clock — now, in the mirror, it started shrinking to an anatomical fragment of hers, rigidifying to a face expression, becoming well-nigh 'meaningful' (smile, squeezing a pimple, etc.), and now she understood it no more.

The necessary love story will begin here: to somehow express the intellectual tension devoid of thoughts, of being-together — the face's hyper-fragments, mimicry's infinitely small posture-sparks, which no 'analysing' style can ever catch up with; to represent them the way the closed being-together valorizes and experiences them: as life's simplest foundational movements, forever undulating purposeless thinking, individualism exploding into miracle and God's self-obvious profile. (Excluding all mysticism, of course.)

So, if the curriculum includes the following: 'thinking and feeling are identical empty movements — these movements are the highest values & forces — these forces are directed at nothing in life — all this is connected to the theme of the "hyper-fragmentary,"' then who and what shall I be today? — Leatrice asked herself. She was overcome by the utmost vanity, for the above curriculum completely engulfed her bodily beauty, dream and love completely engulfed her in the face of any doltish 'life.' Her arms were no longer bodily parts but that certain 'hyper-detail' able to undulate on the same wavelength with feeling; her eyes, hair, ankles were all elastic dream-continuities, inaccessible to the daytime or to human beings. This was the truly inspiring vanity, when she didn't recognize herself — she wanted to rush to the mirror with real fanaticism when she knew she had no face; her fingers reached for the lipstick's kiss-perfecting wax-panacea when she felt her lips to be solitude's pointless formulae: she felt bold & impudent, for she was no human being but a transparent splashboard placed above dream's booming wheel. How long can she rescue nighttime's destructive lyricism into the day?

Her greatest experience from yesterday's dinner was the flatness of the glasses — when she saw them she suddenly felt the forms of her own face to be different. At home she memorized the image in the mirror, so that later she would adjust to it her table gestures and tones. We humans are instincive physiognomists from the beginning, who construct our own manners and character from our mirror reflection and feel what worldview would suit the arch of our brows and what gestures, the color of our lips. (It's of course impossible to find exact observations for lips and eyebrows, but it's enough if they are felt to be the sole ethical authority.) We always recall like a lesson at the exam, our last mirror-image and quickly correct our straying gestures or words to the contours of the imaginary reflection hung in front of us.

Dressing up also carries in itself the germ of a brand-new possible character, as if an actor changed his masks every moment: Leatrice, too, felt that she could play out a completely different role in her chemise than in her bathrobe, and that drawing every millimeter of rouge on her lips meant the beginning of newer roles; of course here the same question arises as with dream-images and feelings — we feel that the indication embedded in a gram of face powder is just as well-delineated a character as it is unknown, so the tools of realization are not given.

remembrance of combing

When she first drew the comb through her hair and in place of the wet-knotted hair-clots the smoothly shining hair-tracks emerged, she was shaken to the root of her character, as if the comb's teeth did not rearrange a few threads of hair like a railroad switch controlling 15 pairs of rails, but fixed her soul's most ancient pillar into a massive socket. When she communicated with people, thought of them, or busied herself with whatever 'real' matter, she never felt her whole individuality to be engaged down to the root: as though she were a flower bunch of which practical life only scraped the petals or pawed the leaves — but this hair-smoothing movement pulled tighter the string that tied all stems together; deep in her soul it created a posture-corset, which squeezed in her essence but let looser the flowercups, even allowing their connection with the stems to become flippant.

Her body & soul, past & future, were absorbed into this combing gesture: she filled up so much with this gesture that even her most direct memories and plans were squeezed out of her soul, lying about her like redundant, empty shells washed ashore by an unexpected, oily tide-wave. She felt she should live henceforward entirely adjusted to this new, all-permeating and all-redeeming form of character, but realized with panic that she was helpless: what was this feeling, if feeling it was at all? O, inane 'neither-nor' definitions: the sea's sizzling, rushing surface — not the blue linen stretched in its permanent bed on the banks' embroidery frame, but the streaming sea — and not the drunken and fearful wonder-waves piling on each other in a tempest, but merely what in the sea is the flattest without being abstractly 'plane': this plane-ness becomes rushing from its own literality.

But if this is indeed the essence of her character, this undefinable sea-feeling, then from the practical point of view it's utterly useless: once among the casino's white tables, how can she be 'sea'? Is she sea in fact? Above the sea in the shape of hesitant sparks, like daytime stars devoid of all fire and light (painted matte gold) a female figure hovered who drizzled down her grown-out haughtiness on the waters. Why a female figure when it's only about blind, localized gold dots? And is it indeed haughtiness and not a blown-up and slowed-down take of a rose opening, as if someone sat on a paper scroll and after he got up, the pressed-down pages rustled back into their previous place again with drowsy, Americanizing flexibility?

absolute feeling and 'homo'

All these are just gross image-onslaughts on the shapeless new feeling that for now possessed only emphasis-plasticity and intensity-drawing, and which rose, lonely, towering like an air column above the mirror, with Leatrice lying tired at its feet. When she looked back into the mirror across the new feeling's glass wall, the sole explainable positivity was the lordly melancholia that she felt over her sublime feeling that could nohow be converted into everyday devices of feeling; scientists, too, sometimes gain an unexpected elegance in conversation when they are unable to find the solution to a problem, in contrast to the minutes following successful solutions when they easily turn vulgar.

Our most essential and positive feelings are, it seems, ultimately impossible, what is more, unfeelable: she felt this emotion, this momentum not within 'the realm of feelings' but as something coming from a far greater distance, which she would have liked to channel into the emotions' far more humanistic pool: in her childhood she had often played with flowers pressed from colored paper that had to be put in water to open into floating petal-statues — once she received such a giant paper-stick as present but there was no water around, all the taps were closed for repairs in the street sewer, so she ran up and down with her giant, unopenable flower. She tried to press it open with her fingers and although here & there she managed to unfold an aimless violet flourish or polka-dotted dog-ear, she destroyed the whole mechanism. Now the same happened with the feeling and character-incandescence that flared up so suddenly from the combing movement: she knew that it was much bigger than all her feelings rooted in reality, but couldn't soak it into the water of her ordinary feelings to make visible and understandable: all she saw around was a rushing sea surface, haughtiness-drops coming down like matte rain, and the dispersing ghost of a woman. She shook her hair with the proud fatigue of 'having experienced' & harrowed it again with the comb.

She recalled Touqué uttering the word 'humanity.' He nearly licked his mouth after it, his violet tongue stuck out from his yellow cheeks as if his whole head were some brown fruit whose seed he was trying to spit out — while he made a gesture as though weighing with gusto, with his spread-out, crooked fingers, a ball that exceeded his span: now Leatrice enjoyed herself with this same movement as a voluptuously concrete, naïve, and certain thing. It's true that in Touqué's gesture, that first and foremost obviously celebrated juicy philistinism, there was a side-note that resembled the patting of unpredictable wild animals — next to the paunchy 'citoyen,' a sneering juggler.

But even this had precious little to do with what Leatrice felt before the mirror: while combing her hair (as if trying to force it out of the lamp's luminous halo and to scrape it back into the dimness behind her back, from where it illegitimately jutted forth; the bulb was made of smoky glass, the lampshade of ground glass, even the small awning fastened on it was of dense parchment glass: light evidently came from the lamp, and yet she looked rather like one sitting before three tanks of dimness, not before a source of light, and that light merely served to make three-step dimness visible), she hissed the word 'humanity' a few times, trying to connect it to her present pathos-haemorrhage, but didn't manage to.

two kinds of 'human being' emotion: naïve-concrete and dizzy-empty; mirror

It's strange how the most contrasting things can be equally framed by this word. When Touqué uttered it, he meant the people of action, of raw outlines, of active and puritanical torsos like the heroes of old drama or the figures of 19th-century novels, at which

Leatrice felt herself to be no more than the heroine of a string of events; she did away with all the rags and bones of the 'I,' the piled-up sketch pages (as though the soul were a topsy-turvy studio where they are forever working but nothing ever gets done) and immediately thought of her fellow humans, of her uttered words and those to be uttered yet; she suddenly simplified the objects around (of course the stress with which Touqué uttered 'humanity' also touched on objects — in that moment Leatrice could only see the champagne glasses in the boxes of simple sentences) like a puritanical interior designer.

A while earlier she understood by 'environment' an intricate psychological ornamentation in which vases and dreams, flowers and feelings merged, and where there was not a word about exteriorities; being a bit of a snobbish industrial designer, she designed the table to be a statue rather, hanging out of her soul like a bookmark power-ponytail, slipping out of the net of any delimiting line — the milieu was always undulating just like the wax unable to withstand the candle. But to Touqué's 'humanity' belonged not such form-escapee tables and flowers but simple, drab objects, like for instance the Russian novels' conventional settings ('in his room stood an unpolished table and next to it, a mismatched chair with fraying upholstery; on the table were the leftovers of half-eaten breakfast,' et cetera).

She clearly felt the small clack in her body, with which she tripped over from her psychological state wallowing in dream-like confluences, into a novelistic state; when she looked at Touqué departing in the first style, inside her it was about everything minus the sheer fact that Touqué is a human being, another human being who was here, now left and could be seen going from the window. Until Touqué mentioned this 'humanity' to her, such event-scannings would never have occurred to her and Touqué's odd visits remained a smoking blend of half-developed motifs in which such a thing as 'event' never featured of course.

But what she now felt while combing is also gloriously 'humanity,' this dizziness and heaving steaming forth from one of her movements or another, just as in symphonies the galloping fortes are sometimes short-circuited and in the sudden void the old theme's five or six tones sound on a grassblade flute (one night they were partying in Biarritz when the lamps went off — for a while the interrupted sentences boomed on, compromised and betrayed by sudden darkness, the movements too hung their head in shame, as if the lightbulbs were the most efficient extinguishers of consciousness, and the dark, a liquid that all of a sudden expanded self-awareness to a stifling extent, and from which, when the last hesitant spumes of racket died down, stars shone forth, in which the systematic execution of disorderliness was perhaps even more wonderful than their light: the chandeliers appeared to supplant consciousness, for all the declarations of love, neighing toasts, splashing kisses, and embrace-trainings were their actions; the small stars, whether goose-bumped from pudicity's cold breeze or blinking with the stifled laugh of irony, didn't supplant consciousness but merely splattered it with tiny bouquet-lights like with police torches, and which of course could be easily wiped off and smoothed out as one would wipe off face powder from a dinner jacket's collar, although some feeling of shame was left behind): Leatrice too felt that and wondered how it is that the strongest, most positive feelings are also the most dizzying ones, as if seasickness were the apex of health for the soul.

She felt again what she had felt, looking into the mirror after the first fearful morphine injection — trembling on her lips, like a melody left behind on the bows, the word 'human, human,' as if the main task of a young girl's organism were to provide both a theatrical and a lexicon-cold definition of the concept of the human being.

The mirror was blackened by the room's dimness like a repeatedly tried, extra-thick G string, only its sides were crossed by a few silvery lines, the hem of darkness, as sometimes from under the priests' buttoned-up black coat the violet rank-wound flashes out; the mirror didn't look like a material glass wall, but a melodic transposition of darkness — lying about in the whole room, rugged like black raw material, it received in one place a laquered sheen and a warm conic depth: this last was the mirror, it seems. In a corner behind Leatrice's back a small lamp stood on the floor, from which no light but a yellowish dusk radiated, and which didn't rise from the floor, so her legs waded in it like on the edge of the seaside where the water is paper-thin and oozes into the sand. The floor-lighting, too, whispered to her 'human, human' — as if utter decomposition were the safest route to the redeeming definition she was looking for in her blood's neatly-regulated swinging.

Fourth Non-Prae diagonal; the diary of an adulterous princess

of lying
rhetoric and posture
at night in the deserted home
Moon and space
remembrance of afternoon naps
lies and secrets, freedom and guilt-feeling
night at the villa
happiness and nothing
beauty and 'humanity'
the annihilation of the 'human being'
bad counterparts to suffering and pleasure
fear
should she return to her husband?
her husband falls victim to a misfortune
company: a madman, a corpse, a fictive character & a lied-about figure
two conclusions to the question of 'humanism'

(...*I knew that I would leave in the morning, I couldn't stand lies any longer. Lies? I kept my lover secret before my husband, he knew no more about him than the others, the crooked-nosed absolution-Harpagons; the rigid vestals of Latin declensions who have never felt love & believe that the sexual organ of Lucrece's lover was the stylish dagger with which painters inoculate inane matrons; the old ladies who play cards under a squinting lamp until they drop, and while putting color on color, small blood-photographs of red hearts on red hearts, with an acid side-thrust they spoil all the fun of their grandchildren: yes, I lied to them. But who are they next to my love? Confession, stupidity, Parcae gossip? In fact I've been honest before them, too, like the sun in daytime. When I didn't put a water cross on my forehead in the chapel, not wanting the glass-hard summa-script of redemption to trickle into my eyes like languid rain, it meant that my husband's cardinal brother couldn't officiate mass, was struck by headache, dizziness, and nausea, and felt that somebody was unable to such exceeding extent to 'subscribe' to the mass [to use the wording of another brother of my husband's, a banker], that it would desecrate the church. Exceeding extent: the adjective of salesmen.*

But now there is no difference in me between salesman and martyr, now I have left. Did I lie to them or was I honest? No, I didn't lie. Then why am I leaving, why am I looking for freedom? Slavery? Freedom? Am I looking for freedom? No, but rather some exciting hermitage. How many times I have denied my lover: pugnaciously when my husband suspected and accused me; panting in the confessional's squeezed-in penitence-steam, whispering, explaining, weeping; how many times I have denied him diplomatically with winking irony, to the banker, who couldn't subscribe to it, and how often I have said haughtily to the little skeleton-virgins, that of course I have a lover, two, eight, 100: how many lies surrounded me, and it was the very plenitude of lies that made me feel honest, like a hetaera forced into politics.

When I walked among the cypresses' Byzantine church organs, pressing my life's small, hidden pearls among their black moss towers, I spoke of blossoming jasmines, and when jasmine grids intruded between our kisses, like a fragrant net into the flight of fish, then I chatted to my husband about the defects of fruit trees: not a single object was in place, nothing had name or meaning, the times were swapped like cards in the hands of my husband's sister — this was my lover's portrait, the garden replanted, the house rebuilt and time re-alphabetized by lies.

Was this year a lie? The cypresses howled from the jasmine name, the jasmines sang with the fruit mask: under the looming tattoo of excuses the mouth of objects was inebriated into new truth, I walked in truth, bathed in sincerity like in some healing blood. At my first sacrilegious communion I fell from the altar steps in a haze, like a rolled-out carpet, but afterward I rejoiced, for this greatest lie against

God carved my lover's portrait so constant, eternal, and classical as the best Florentine sculptors.

How I built you, my dear love, in my husband's house, from my husband's house [I love my lover] — when I met you, you were pale and gangly, all the poverty and cowardice of reality next to the Doric impertinence of my denials. I'm leaving because what I can't stand is the universe of lying, that huge force and paradoxical reality that was brought into being behind the lies. I'm eloping to you out of modesty.

This is not true of course, I'm still well inside all the sophistry, rage, and warfare tactics of genuine and artificial cynicism, genuine and artificial sorrow, but this language will be worn off when I'm with you by the sea, here, in the woods, anywhere, forever. My lies grew like the brambles around Sleeping Beauty's castle — they played music next to me, like a thousand colorful hummingbirds in one nest the size of a cup, like the intrusive polyphony of lemons and flowers, stars and fiddles, the entire reality, so there was no room left for me: because of the lies I couldn't light the chandeliers' sooty hundred-fingered candle-hand, I didn't find my dog's celestial pawn tongue at night when, shivering in the bed, I wanted to warm my hands with it, I didn't see my husband and I didn't see my face in the mirror's great rhyme-pond, for the billion-flower tide of lies covered everything. Lies? Truth? I don't know, but I had to leave. What have I got to do with them?

Why should I go on knocking my nails against their plate edges, pouring sour sauces in the famous majolicas, distorting the blue Melusinas' hunched little relief loves on the plates' bottom? When I leave them with the clear chord of infidelity, I feel that I will be sinking them: that wealth of lies, eternal lies that wrung out space and time from God's kalenda hands, will now simply kill them, and show up your figure in summer transfiguration.

What amateurs are those plaster-carrying, wallpaper-glueing, or word-sharpening Siena chaps [in my husband's blind language: sculptors, painters, poets] next to my sin. For I am a sinner from you and for you, purely and wholly sinner — not excusing myself to God like a coward and wrapping the muffling gauze of prayer around the black ulcer of my damnation. If I believed that what I do with you is moral, or at least a wee excusable sin, eventually a small whim, ladybird on the silky ends of chastity, then you would be petty and our love even pettier. I don't love sin, I hate it, loathe it, I'm afraid of it, I'm not boasting with it, it's no jewel or funereal cosmetic on my flesh, no toy, no. For me sin is wail, wailing wail, but I assume it, because it's from it that your face becomes eternally hard. Do you laugh at the logorrhea of demagogic maîtresses? Laugh at your ease, I'm a harpy-pamphlet.

Women are chatterboxes and I'm a gossipy, crude, selfish, and rhetorical fishwife. I lied to my husband not only for you and for our cause, but because the omnipotent pleasure of chatting romped inside me, fantasy & witticism, old hag's plasticity-craving fist and a thousand cynical points, the dance of spirit & its foolish-serious tragedy-weaving. Toss over your yesterday's definition of me, but be careful it doesn't get caught in the boughs under my window: bon-mot and demonics — is that me? Not only a malicious chatterbox? The duchess did this, the duchess did that, and behind me, the authorized shadow of popes like a black fan made of ghosts.

My lordliness is brill, truly, dizzyingly brill, because it magnifies the fluent comedy of lies and sin and coarsens it, kindles the delicate stirring, merchants' lyricism, scholars' psychology and other such ludicrous 'finesse' and shapeless undecidability: here every look is instantly an obscene coat of arms, our every kiss is cynicism toward the whole of history, and our elopement [coming now!] a new, second original sin. And I want this, and for this the duchessness, countessness, whateverness showered on me is a prime whatsit. This is not a matter of the soul, not a wave of love — here everything is one big stone mask, dogma, heresy, history and glossary placed next to the revelation.

My words, words, just-words, only-just-phrases, I won't surrender them to you: if I put rouge like a red worm on my mouth's hungry ledge, so your kiss would get stuck in it like the thread in the seal's wax, why should I not rouge my words too, why shouldn't I make them wild, more-than-word words: not in the direction of deeds where old schoolmasters would like to herd them, but toward the infernal fishwife's gibbering.

Sometimes you foolishly called me heroic, but of course as a man you are no kenner of people, you believed my posturing. I like deceiving you too — when it hurts in my blood, like quicklime or some satanic mire, that I live in this sin with you, it's then that I play daredevil, the trifling cricket-Aspasia who couldn't care a continental about anything, and when I'm in high spirits like a ship in the ides of gullish home rule, then I produce, just for you, my jawdropped, wide-open-kissing audience, very big tears, the oversize phials of sorrow, like the lisping doctor in burlesque. There were only two things with me in my husband's house for this year when you have been my lover: truth's all-exterminating excessive blossoming, and the stern sculpture of guilt-feeling. Lie? What is it? Is it from the folk?

You don't know the Moon, you silly boy. When my husband removed himself from the house in the summer, he took with him every servant, and I lived in my mother's villa; so you didn't come to our rendezvous in the disused house by the cobbled square — you came by the back street, but I could only arrive from my mother's next-door villa through the square. You often stammer and don't remember and you certainly don't know the Moon as I do. [I have to write narrative too, for this is history, a great compromising of the sacred, church, lordly rule, I can't let it happen any old how, hence my diligent topography.]

How impossibly strange it was to revisit at night my husband's deserted house, the house that lying filled with noise and which I left, never to see again. For two reasons it was different from the times of my being there: first, from the perspective of truth, second, from that of faithless abandonment. When I saw in the hall the gigantic black vase that rose to the height of three floors, my first reaction was naturally, 'I'm not here at twelve o'clock, I'm not seeing the vase, I'm now looking at old weaponry in my sister's house' — I realized only later, among the iron browscrew bands of silence, that now I could look at the vase at ease, I needn't exterminate the mere possibility of a memory.

Lying is noisy: the on-the-spot extermination of impression is a bloody affair, like the bungled slaughter of playing newborns — they wail. So I missed the racket of denial, and yet my relation to the vase was not natural, for I had left my husband's house forever, and if I'm here now, then I'm here in the most abstract fashion possible, purely geographically — this is not my husband's house and that is not a giant stone jug, but only an empty place, a house-numbered and vase-sealed blind 'somewhere,' where only my specter stalks. It's time that the lie-vase now jumped over into the category of pointless and audience-less sincerity-vases, but it's still more unreal than at the time when denial was its only melody-profile, because now it's simply far away from me, abandoned.

It's naïve to believe that if one has left a place forever, with a physical return the abandonment disappears or is at least suspended — when one returns there, it's not as oneself, but as the impersonal carrier of departure, the live but impersonal scaffolding of the preposition 'from': and in this manner I was infinitely more distant there from the hall vase, when for two months I met you next to it, than when I was actually far away from the place. That's why I continued to need the barbarian realism of guilt-feeling, because after lying, the dimness of distance followed: everything was free in this deserted palace dumbed into silence, the length of hours, beds and rugs, foods and glasses, baths and undergarments, and this complete freedom was of no help for the cause of reality. How many times I asked you there, at the depth of the spiral of silence: 'Are you there? Is that you? Are you really here?' From lying I landed into secretiveness, and the two are as different as chalk from cheese.

When I lived there with my husband I had to deny, step by step, invent small facts and knit small logical ribbons between them — now this tiresome and meagerly one-dimensional toil was over, but our whole life sank into the vast ocean of secretiveness: not so long ago I flourished bridges above reality, there where no river has ever been, and now we ended up submerged deep under water, where god, air, space, everything was a lie, so human lying didn't exist as an independent small assiduity in the infinite lying-cosmos of secretiveness. Will the slanting shot of our kiss always play out among such absurd climates?

In the old days small and limited possibilities were coupled with small and logical lies, now imperceptible-outlined freedom is coupled with the mystically complete over-the-top lying of secretiveness. I can't tell if the complete secret is still a lie, for it consists of a thousand points of which none touches on, or could touch, on my husband — the green underground wave of secret has an entirely different direction from my husband's life, or rather, it has no direction whatsoever. When we kissed in the garden for a minute and after that, I lied to my husband for half an hour, then we pointed our lives against my husband's life as rapier against rapier, but when in the summer he left the house to travel to faraway cities and we could freely enjoy the nights in the empty palace for two months, then our lives were no more two people's adversely sharpened opposition to another, but melted into the secret's infinity, the house's silence, abandonment, ontological suspension; the house alone was everything, and the house was mute like a lost violin. You can imagine how hard it was to preserve for myself the thought of sin, for the secret could in no way be felt as sin. Finally the stifling impression of sin was over, and then I had to recall it by force, so that, as I said, it would give shape to you.

But before I could get into the house [Montepulciano?] I had to avoid the Moon. Three sides of the square and the square itself were rabidly blue, green, and white from the nighttime light. One sole side was left in shadow for me, and on that there was no loggia, no arcades, niches, receding doorsills — the whole was a smooth wall. I walked along the thin strip of shadow [which, it's true, was black like the frame of a mourning envelope] like a tightrope walker, with arms stretched out to balance, moving crucifix under the blind windows.

Do you know what it means: to see five steps ahead a blinding light, the blue flame of rum and the glacier-wrinkles' springtime-Circean throat, and two steps ahead of you to swallow darkness' sticky moss, as if the entire life were plastered behind a blind man's eyelid? On our old rendezvous all I sought was you, like a tiny spot on a very detailed map — now I was looking for the whole empty house with all its rooms, with the garden's white-hallucinating, heavy trees. Every piece of furniture participated in the rendezvous, not only those pieces that stood in my old bedroom.

My first stealthy getting in the deserted house was particularly eerie, because I had dreamt the whole hiding game in my last days there with my husband. I was lying in my husband's bedroom with the big balcony, slightly feverish or tipsy from the lunch wine, and I fell asleep. From time to time my husband lay down beside me, or paced up and down on the balcony, and I woke up, unable to distinguish reality from my dreamt elopement. Never has reality been so idyllic, never has my husband belonged to my body with such bodily classicism.

How did that afternoon build up? First of all I had thought a great deal about my elopement and our future secret meetings in reality, and this of course swung out to the furthest pendulum point in dream, without aim or meaning, as if they were mere barren brain-torturing mathematical riddles: if my husband arrives from Ostia at 5 o'clock in the afternoon, and you can be in Tivoli at the same time, how long is the way whose half equals the shooting distance of my old servant's lies — or: if at two in the morning you meet my sister, who is escorted home from a ball, with what excuse could you bring her to my house so that she leaves and you stay, indeed seem to be compelled to stay, etc. — so my dreams killed every real plan, not putting in their place other than mathematical raging, drenched underwear, deathly fatigue.

When from time to time my eyes opened, because the dream's fermenting impossiblity popped them up as alcohol pops up loose springs, I was overcome with an infernal terror when I looked at my husband. He was leaning on the balcony railings, far from me, in the steam of the afternoon's gold-blue light, as if God had breathed on the world like on a door handle to clean, but then forgot to wipe it. Could it be possible that he knew nothing of my calculating dreams?

I never sleep in the afternoon, partly because I'm rarely sleepy at that hour, and partly because I loath that on principle. Now for the first time I got to know sleep stuck into the middle of life, and it pleased me very much. This novelty of course wore me out in addition to the fatigue of calculating — the theme of the dream tormented me, but the sheer fact of the sleep, the utter chaos in the afternoon's idyllic silence, slightly old-womanly or on the contrary, all too pubertal napping in the warmth, in sweated-through daytime clothes: all this wildly enhanced my desire for bourgeois quiet, the family's perverse heat, pietist sloth.

And the alternation of the two kinds of worlds would not end, as soon as I closed my eyes I was already counting and seeing the Moon-bitten square; as soon as I woke up a bit, I enjoyed infinite-secure homely indolence. In between I asked not very intelligent questions to find out if he noticed anything of my dreams. Body and soul sometimes don't show any connection: when I finally resolved to wake up completely, the feverish 'factorisatio numerorum' of the many elopement plans worked as a refreshment or at least as quinine on fever — wild sweating is far hotter and wetter than dull fever, and yet we feel ourselves cosmetically cleansed afterwards: infinite lying cleansed my body of the small 37.2 stealthiness.

I'm a woman and so a cruel chatterbox. I'll tell you that on that afternoon I also enjoyed my husband's bodily closeness. It was not love-making or desire, kiss, but a shadow that could be melted into my body through the dream; when he caressed me in half-sleep he wasn't as close to me as when he stood outside in luminosity's napping flower-mist [under us was the garden], and his consciousness simply poured into my dream-loosened body. Sleeping in dayclothes is a greater love-prank of the body than nakedness — many have known it long before me, alchemist hag, Savonarolizing matron. I felt my extraordinary freshness after the tormenting dream as my husband's good-humored acquiescence in my pending elopement. We had a light meal in the garden, the sun was still high, and I had already swallowed my fill of Moon, secret, silence — I felt like an actress after the dress rehearsal, who on the eve of the opening is sure of her success, what is more, her experience is ready and complete before the opening, for the public performances are only mechanical repetitions. I have never felt our love to be so ready and eternally decided as during that garden meal after the dream.

And then when I started in real life on the shadow's diabolic half-rail toward the deserted house I didn't know if what was so dizzy was the fact that I had already dreamt it next to my husband, accompanied by a thousand mathematical riddles, and now reality became the pale copy — or the fact that reality's undeniable novelties as compared to dream are the inebriating petals that disturb my mind. This encounter will be the plenitude of secret, and yet, by having dreamt it already 'under my husband's nose,' I had the impression that it was not I who skulked by the wall, but my husband who related and dictated in court every one of my movements, while I listened, nearly fainting with terror.

I'd like to refute, interrupt, deny with the old amazone tempo of my lies [I had my right breast removed because only truth is concave, but the lie, my weapon, is always convex] that I am stealthily inching my way along the edge of the Moon's miasmatic reeds, but it's impossible because I, the one I feel to be 'I' now on this dead square, is not myself but my husband's word, his hallooing testimony, my mouth's rain-drenched kiss-proneness, clotted-red initial in a clerical notary's book: my hands' eager harrow which sets out for your hair is no more than a punishing doodle in the last line of a sentence, curlicued anathema-branch independent from me. I felt at the same time the two end points of narrative in every step: utter freedom, the unbound romping of pubertal arcadiae, and the resonant Latin sentence stentorially announced over the adulterous princess, the string of ablativus absolutus and constructio ad intellectum.[227]

But it was not only in this moment that I felt love to be that — this has always been my fate: when I slowly placed my mouth on your mouth [although you always asked for my face first], as in the garden the breeze turns the page of the open book without asking permission from the reader, this movement was free, like the opening of the truth flower in Paradise before Eve's birth [what did the flowers do when there were no love metaphors yet?], and at the same time it was an arid text studded with the clearest, most adverse words of judgment. My fate will be forever this: only embryos and corpses, labor and agony, but never life, human being, reality.

It was a sterling idea to meet inside the palace, so all the rooms participated in the encounter even more emphatically, not just one floor tile or fountain jet: I knew that you were coming toward me from the opposite direction, through narrow rooms, river-shaped stairs, corridors and winding ladders tapering as an aesophagus, I couldn't tell the direction exactly, but you were coming. On our old encounters I knew by what houses, gardens, and statues you were coming to the agreed place, but it meant no joy for me, for those gardens and houses belonged to the alien world, to the neutral territory of everyone and anyone, so when you appeared, there was no space around you or world belonging to your body: but here I knew for a long while that you were roaming the giant birdcage of a familiar house, that you are mine, with me, closely with me, even before I spotted you. Where will we bump into each other? I was not walking in the rooms but swimming, inert like driftwood, toward the waterfall's slope, it was hide-and-seek and bathing in the spilt waters of presence.

How strange was the lighting, how it cut up the house: pitch darkness, the impenetrable safes of the night, and immediately next to them, the silver window glass smashed by the Moon, on the wall the grids' shadow tilted to infinity, like the arms of some rubber heretic in the torture chamber; above the stairs' velvet, dimness astray, some kind of semi-darkness that very clearly didn't want to be darkness where it was but in some other nook, but getting stuck on its way was now going rancid; the rooms opening into one another were all differently invisible, lights and silences collided like train carriages connected at the station, or they bowed over each other like St. Francis and St. Dominic on some relief, with the sweet fatigue of encounter and the comb-entanglement of their broad halo rims — every gallery looked like a ten-eyed face covered with a black mask, with every eye squinting outward & inward at a different angle, revealing unexpected eye-whites.

So the house disintegrated completely, like a pack of dropped cards, but the empty awareness of your presence threaded it together — the fact that you could appear anywhere in front of me lent it strict composition. Outside the Moon was showering down, washing off walls and rooftops.

And so it went on for weeks, and we were happy. Happiness is something annihilating and closed — in vain would I now try to evoke its memory, it's impossible, I can't get at it. I know and only know that then I was infinitely happy, but even this I say from self-indulgence, probably groundless confidence in myself, for I have no guarantee that I was truly happy on those nights.

Happiness can't be attested, just as pain, once it subsides, cannot be made to ache again: now 'happiness' is a mere name. There are people who can get nourishment from empty words and deceive themselves saying that they remember happiness. I don't. Sometimes you accused me of being prosaically dry, mercantilely venal, for when we parted I suddenly became blasé, jaded, and unfriendly. At such times I knew that we were already outside the sole joy-shaped joy of absolute togetherness, and the imbecile transitions and æstheticising compromises like the farewell kiss, embrace, handwave, chatting about what happened ['it was good,' etc.] irritated me beyond belief.

Happiness cannot be owned or stored in memory's handicapped little flasks. The human being is either human or happy, one must choose; one needs askesis even for happiness. When I entered the unlit gate and slowly climbed up the stairs' velvet, which soaked up my personality, my existence, my everything as double blotting paper, I knew that now it was not I who would do something but that I would get into the void of happiness, from which no life derives, no power, no fresh ring on life's growing trunk. We needed this crypt-calyxed house because here happiness could be happiness, inhuman, unknown movement outside of time.

Happiness is more deserted than the contagious patient expelled from the camp, and is more murderous than the most meticulous death. How many times I have bemoaned my splendid dresses and shapely knees in the dark rooms if you were late, for I knew that they had as yet no role in love-happiness, although you adored them — love-happiness has nothing to do with love. And when I entered the gate, some snub-naïve little wifeliness awoke in me, looking not for happiness' exiled nihil but for love's human work: although happiness' ingle-budding nothing-garden was my passion, I often approached it fearfully, as the sick patient the sour clouds of anæsthetics. Pleasure was like an approaching black specter that can't be bought with clothes and willingly white hips: with those I conquered you, those you praised during our rendezvous, and yet I felt them to be lost — they have achieved their goal and this absolute achievement made them comically pointless.

I lived in two kinds of meaninglessness: in the great 'irratio' of happiness, and in life's nondescript events, in the parallel errors of non-knowing and knowing. The more I felt that I played no human or womanly role in the nights, the more frantically I embellished myself, not as though I were trying to conquer the triumphant amorphousness of happiness with love's clumsy forms, but because I wanted to relish the greatest possible pointlessness of lips, rings, and chemise fringes.

I went wild in beauty and cruelty. Never before have I been so heartless and wicked as during those two months, for I was lost, my humanity was no longer in my hands, happiness expelled me from all society, so I couldn't even imagine the reality of a human being with whatever forcing of the imagination. I gave no alms to beggars, I didn't understand their words and rudely pushed them out of the way from church porches. Sometimes I rode into the woods alone and beat a dog to death with a stone. I hit the servants too, I didn't know what I wanted; I didn't want my life, and as for happiness, every 'psychic' stance was impossible, for I was inside happiness.

In the morning I sat before the mirror, to gather the sacrificial offering for the intrigue-weaving nights of happiness. At this time I used a coffee-color ointment which gave a yellowish hue to my skin, as if an Egyptian sun had scorched it. I liked my mouth's tattered-fluffy red more on this yellow than on the old veined-white background. Why should I not be autumn? For the men around me did little else than affect mythologies, bloviate about nature — let me then try out the fashion of the new age. I placed my candle at the foot of the mirror, I loved light coming from below, my ankles were set aflame like the pink garden stars among the evening branches, even the heel of my shoes sparked some boisterous astronomies, but my knees were already shady like a spurious waterfall that a poet placed in the verse for rhyme's sake, my hips went missing like hoarfrost on a warm chimney, and my face, among the gross signatures of foreign colors, was already the putting-into-practice of nothingness above all these.

It gave me particular pleasure to lay on cosmetics and womanly fineries in the total absence of vanity: lowcuts down to my waist, which in the mirror appeared not like the rabid triangles of my immodesty, but as the pessimistic gorges of the night, of silence, perhaps of the world itself. My body, too, was inside the windowless prison of happiness, so the naïve-human desires to be 'liked' went extinct, only beauty in itself and beauty for the wilting raged on before my mirrors. My mirrors were not pieces of furniture but darkness' gall stones, so I didn't notice that my superfluous beauty was reflected only by separate objects — I thought that if I only wanted, time itself and all of nature would answer my face with my face anywhere, anytime. Behind my pearls and furs I felt like somebody buried behind a score of mountains & valleys, my jewels were landscapes, graveyards, and days. The one who dresses up only to conquer has no inkling of luxury because they will place their soul and will in the mounting of every clasp, and their whole pageant will in the end be nothing else but a *Schlamperei* — humanist mosaic, in contrast to my actor's motley, where every stocking or mascara remains a self-serving net, independent mineral.[228]

That was the time when Italian men first talked about 'humanity.' When I laugh at it I cause some kind of chronological disturbance, because I reveal a sensibility that is not yet possible during the Renaissance, but after all it's not at all clear where and when I am. I didn't hate people but was yet filled with some vicious cynicism toward everything. The splendid evening gowns were always connected to big soirées, garden fetes for two hundred guests, so it was a particular delight to wear such for the sake of one person, when those were always meant for 'occasions.' But by the fact that the hot silks were aimed at one human being, they stripped me of my humanity, the wealth of clothes could find no outlet in 200 people and the entire muffled ballast of its beauty fell back on me in the dead entrails of the villa.

In the blindness of happiness you were completely strange to me, and so was I to you. Not because pleasure blurred our vision, no, we were not stupid. Bodily pleasure was just a laughable little whirr in the immeasurable silences of infinitely free being-together. We were strange to each other because it is not us who make ourselves human but our circumstances, the other people, objects, compulsory dates and backgrounds. And here there were no circumstances and backgrounds, thus we could have no character. We didn't need to discuss, hide, prepare for, anything, and it turned out that in such cases nothing is left of the 'human being.' In an evening gown without company, in happiness without love, for you without acquaintance. We haven't known each other before, we felt that the outside world had distorted our true selves, but now finally that innermost interior could emerge, and that was foreign, empty, inert.

This of course doesn't mean disappointment, I can't be disappointed, for I feel one thing in everything, ever: some dimness that is I, and an unknown whip that sometimes tears up that dimness into frayed clusters. This is happiness, life, death, everything. And in this common unknown, in the spraying dimness of 'everything is allowed,' we were infinitely at home, siblings in spite of a thousand embarrassments. Our minds jumped in zigzag moves: we observed & unveiled small things, we were more secretive than ever, and after that we went wild, we dumbed down in sonorous choir and slept in. Unveiling didn't differ from secrets, blindness from discovery, I could have chosen either of those counterparts as an exact definition of whichever impression.

Lovers' desire, solitude: how much it is not the follow-up to love. We found no handhold in each other, for that was all the outer world, utterly absent; your most passionate sigh, your most transient reflex were all a Florentine fountain, a spring date, or your relationship to another person, here you were nothing, or rather, you were everything, the undiscovered animal of happiness or the mimicry-corpse of existence, but it was not something to speak to, something to embrace with the thought of embrace. I was such a nameless arch-being in two directions, in both my husk and my core: my evening gowns were meaningless, my body and thoughts were likewise lame and deaf, so cut off from life — ultimately naught bloomed virginally like factory-made paper snowdrops.

It happened some time during the seventh or eighth week that through the open window we heard a big splash from one of the garden ponds and when you looked out you saw a fountain statue in pieces. You whispered that there was talk about the most famous bandit in the region hiding around our parts. Epithalamium. In a second panic went through us like red splinter-light through a transparent tube. Fear is the only shapeless and gigantic emotion that does not shatter the human being's human-case but on the contrary, squeezes it into infinity. When I mentioned the estrangement triggered by being utterly outside life, I used an ill-chosen word, for we were not strangers to one another but literally diffuse, without any cohesion, like spilt water on a giant glass sheet rocking like a boat. We knew everything about ourselves, but in freedom's concave mirror tailored to gods, these features trickled into every direction: in the old days it was enough to know where a kiss was and what a word meant, but now knowledge wasn't enough, because if I reached out for the kiss' taste or the word's meaning, it poured out among my fingers into the free silence of secretiveness. And fear is *the regular counterpart to this, it pulls the human being together into a most human focal point, into the abstract point of cowardice — then we were more, now we were less than you and I. What am I afraid for in my body, in my life?*

The clatter froze us with panic, we curled up in the most comical pose under the blanket; we can never see our movements underway, only at the goal, so a snapshot of us like this, taken under the instantaneous artificial light of cowardice, could be very instructive. My knees were drawn up high, but the direction of my legs ran apart like the hour and minute hands, let's say at a quarter past 9. What did I fear for them, what was my body? It had always known two things only, suffering and pleasure, never the middle way of tranquility, the harmonic state of being. That's why it was worth nothing.

All my desire was [go on, my young love, get offended and sulk on me] indifference, the bodily neither-cold-nor-warm, the everyday balance, the usual benevolence of people — but this was not fulfilled. If a doctor touched my skin, I was surprised that there was something under his hand, for incessant pleasure annihilated it. From headache into kiss and from kiss into headache? People usually ascend to the balcony of pleasure from the neutral level of general state-of-being; I, from the dime a dozen cellar of a lousy counterpart. I had no instrument of measurement, so I had nothing to lay claim to: joy cannot be measured from the vantage point of suffering, for that some neutral unit is needed that I lacked — can you simply measure with a dark valley the mountain crest rising above? When I suffered I didn't know if I truly suffered, or merely swam in the individual feelings of suffering — if the curly ending of this or that nerve-pendulum rejoiced, I didn't know if that was indeed pleasure, or merely the optical illusion of the sick body? If I die, witty obituary orators will say that I have drunk out the Silenus flagon of suffering, and didn't leave one drop from the Sophoclean harvest of pleasure — is it true?

When I looked at the crooked scissors of my tall knees ajar I could feel one thing only, that my body had always been ignorant and illiterate, groping & abandoned: pleasure & sickness were cowardly hypotheses in it. Would it die now, so soon, before knowing measure, redeeming measure? My frozen legs resembled the statues I saw around me: the spasmodic pain-compasses of crucifixes, and the pleasure-spumes of daydreaming Venuses. These oppositions bored me to tears. I had always wanted to do something with the body. I wanted pleasure, I forced pleasure into my body in those rare hours when it was not sick — my body could never invent any pleasure by itself.

It's interesting how much we were ashamed of our fear in front of each other, although if we wanted pleasure it was only natural that we should want to keep its instruments safe. And yet we both pretended that we wouldn't mind if the murderer hit us, we remained in bed, without sticking our heads under the cover. Is it ultimate pleasure that demands a consequently heroic pose to the point of suicide, or is it rather the being together? In love-making there is always some automatic self-ennobling, as though the haze of kisses rendered one a prince, count, or at the very least, some god; even in the most cynical fauns' idylls there is always a well-nigh military parade — man doesn't rule over the other but over the insignia of rule. That's why afterwards we feel heroism to be our duty, even though normally we are sworn enemies of all heroic ideals. For me such a rise through the ranks didn't mean much, after all, my life has always been surrounded by unknown coats-of-arms looking like scales on a yawn-shaped, blasé-green fish: I felt human emotions to be one degree more than they are, and felt ashamed for that; like a sassy little schoolgirl, I intruded uninvited into the democratic field of the 'human,' but in punishment this lurking murderer immediately punched me in the nose. But then the murderer disappeared, we never heard about him again.

Then came the pope's death and the election of my father's brother as the new pope. The day before we still met in the palace, the next day we were already choking in the poppy-odor mist of the requiem. And in a few days the new pope summoned me. He forced me to return to my husband, to the palace where we kept meeting for two months.

I scurried from mass to mass, my sons nearly dropped from serving day and night as altarboys. Why didn't I elope far away from here, to foreign cities, woods, why only into the next-door villa? Because in me not one practical thought was connected to the elopement; I didn't want to go somewhere, but merely to go away from here. The moment I consciously stepped out of my husband's house, two inches from the gate I already felt like a fugitive, as if what my fellow humans saw were also the vast proportions of will and not the stingy baby-chain of my footsteps.

People didn't treat the affair as elopement but only as an insignificant whim. Around me all was aswirl: did we indeed manage to keep two months of lovemaking such a well-guarded secret? I learned that my husband didn't consider my case an elopement, not even a whim, but merely scatter-brainedness. Should I go back or not? Hate me, my dear love, for this wavering; kill me for not choosing elopement with you. But when I saw that the huge will to elopement is so invisible, so nothing, I felt that everything is nothing. I did all I could to keep my love for you secret, and now this vast secret has annihilated it: I didn't forget you, I didn't love you less, but all this was not reality. For me to choose you over my husband you should have been reality, but on our nights in the palace you were not reality and neither was I, and I knew well that I have lost forever the keys to the past prison of 'absolute happiness.' If we hadn't been happy, perhaps I would have somehow managed to preserve your humanity, but so it was all in vain, not even guilt-feeling could help me.

The pope spoke an enormous lot and interrogated me, it seemed that I was hell-bent on not going back, although it had long been decided that I would return. For whom, against whom? From whom, where? these things weren't clear to me. I wanted to make the lie even more of a lie — if I go back, I'll make an even greater secret of our love. It was already annihilated by the plenitude of the secret, and yet I wanted to hide it even more, lest they might notice the nothing. Two things, then: first, to render our being-together nothing, and then to further lie about that nothing. If I don't go back now, after our summer rendezvous, then this secret will have one ending open — even if nobody ever finds out. I'll go and close it.

You think I'm mad, everybody would. Our summer hiding would be pointless if afterward I didn't go back to my husband. It's not that lying became a life necessity. Happiness turned everything into nothing, and this I had to save, at least as nothing. I can't save it with you, with an elopement I would merely burst the secret's poisonous black bladder, so that all happiness flows out of it. If I go back to my husband, I commit the greatest immorality: I use my husband as naïve lock on the door of our past happiness. To confess?

I confessed, again sacrilegiously. My return, the end to the small comedy of the 'rambunctious lassie,' was scheduled for the day after. I didn't want to come to you, please understand: you were more eternal in denial than in the possibility of being-together. Every preparation for my return made your face more clear-cut, or if not your face, at least that invisible relation that was between us.

After confession the pope and my husband left for a villa outside the city walls and in the garden they tried out hunting weapons. At the first trial the pope accidentally shot my husband, who died on the spot. My secretary related everything down to the smallest detail: the pope was raging, for he saw in my husband a hellhound foe who forces such a black seal on the very first page of his papacy. He rushed to the corpse and with inarticulate screams ordered it to come to, for he would not tolerate that his rule start with this omen. Why did God allow him to become pope, if He visits him immediately with such a calamity?

'Accident' was evidently no consolation for him — it was a side issue that for his personal conscience, what happened was no sin: the important thing was that God willed it; God is playing a comedy with him. He kept yelling into the dead man's cold ears: why did you do this to me; why did you do this to me? Didn't you want your wife back; were you bored with my mediation?

The pope declared that he would step down from the throne, for the world is full of intrigue. He felt he was made forever ridiculous. In the middle of the night he burst in on me and wanted to chase me to my lover, to the one I confessed. Of course I didn't say your name but an imaginary one, Giacomo something, if I remember well. He spoke all night about this Giacomo, who had his rival shot by him, the pope. In his frenzy he called for a sculptor that night to make the effigy of Giacomo. What else can be left behind from real life, if not hysteria and metaphor?

Company: the pope gone mad; the inexistent Giacomo's imagined scraggy statue, as he rises from the greenhouse of the sacrilegious confession; my dead husband; and you, you, you, annihilated in the happy meaninglessness of the secrets of the past.

Let me, in an un-womanly manner, draw a few conclusions from this story, which will seemingly contradict each other. One: my whole life has been a life of feelings; I cared about nothing except my penchants, sorrows, and boredoms. The outcome was that in an important lyrical moment I couldn't distinguish indifference from ecstasy, in front of dead faces I didn't know if I had already forgotten them, or if I was demanding their life.

Second: I've always lived among people, all my impressions regard the other, gossip [often self-lacerating, Byzantinely fantastic] has been my religion, and now too it is my sole purpose to the grave; I cared nothing about any knowledge, play, pastime, my only theme has been the human being independent of anything: the hunter outside the hunt, scholars without a desk, priests in dressing gowns. This doesn't mean their private lives: intimacy is always commonplace. I watched their smallest gestures, intonation, the least noticeable stirrings in their manner, however, not as the insignificant finishing flourishes of their character, but as the greatest and sole important things.

I often compare myself with my cultivated lady friends & relatives who occupy themselves with music, mathematics, and literature, and I've always found that my people-spying is a greater feat of scholarship than their formulae and concerts. Why? Because the particular varieties of people's manners, complexion, eye movements, are much more precise and their interrelations are much more precise and peculiar than two scales or three projections and their relations.

So my first result was the impossibility of distinction in the field of 'infinite' lyricism — my second result, the absolute perfection of distinction between people, and so a kind of beastly true scholarliness. Thus a portrait [rage, my dear love, rage] left me in emotional nihilism on the one hand, precisely because I maniacally sought passion — and on the other hand, it was reduced to one single shifted hair on the nape. Humanism.

And now we elope, when it can hardly be called an elopement anymore. Am I taking it for granted, too much for granted, that you want me? Yes, because I've seen in your eyes that you belong among those who in a woman love the preoccupation with the work of love more than the simple-directional 'mutual love,' and who can sense if in the woman's impersonal love-scholarship, as the case may be, there is more love meant for them than in the unproblematic melting into the man. For the greatest artists, art is not an important component of the world: for the greatest lovers, love, the man, is not an important cause. And yet they are the greatest lovers, and that is the kind you are after.

So we go. For one more moment I can compare the secret freedom of our nightly get-togethers with the outward freedom now possible for us: the secret freedom was greater, because in it 'free love-making' interposed itself behind the mask of the night like a gemstone among the mine's black rocks; we relished freedom separately, as an object — & now the free lovemaking is dissipated into the wide world, into the midst of people and life, and it has no longer any mounting, hard matter, value. We set out for unknown countries and leave behind as memento the statue of the unknown Giacomo, together with his owner, who never came to rule. It's a gorgeous statue, we are no competition to him: thin, white, standing in the midst of water, like a transparent glass reed or the frozen arc of a fountain. Forgetting can't render us more nothing than the nothing we have already hammered ourselves into: ego? If I could believe in it, I'd confess it as a forbidden superstition. 'We go ...)

bath and body-consciousness (etherealness and hall)

A dose of conventional nihilism, Touqué would have said if they had known each other at that time. The folds rose in the mirror like those long green decorative leaves around lily bouquets that protect the white petals like barrel hoops — her own body was merely the scent of her clothes, hot dew on the trembling crown of folds and melting shadows: 'humanity, humanity,' she said to herself as she combed her hair, sending the word back to the quiet pond of her memories like a paper boat that would perhaps arrive, perhaps not. Humanity?

One of her most pivotal emotions was, of feeling herself to be no more than a tiny perfume ventilator above her clothes — as if her consciousness leaked a delicate, softly rustling spray over her silks, which started around her ankles and flamed up to her neck. Once again, extinction as the apex of life — she said smiling, holding up the comb to pick the hairs it caught and which were now exposed by the light — perhaps mocking her as Miss Kirilloff, at which she suddenly caught the falling hair from the comb. The lukewarm bath did more for her feeling to be a nothing among her clothes than the morphine jab ('faint dose,' as Halbert would say half-whining, half-grumbling: one can't tell if such an Englishman is a decadent hypochondriac or an 'old chap' spurting with robust health), that C*** inoculated in her at that time; she took quite a fright when her chambermaid told her later that the needle was dirty and she only made a show of washing it, but later this small fright from sepsis rendered her rapturous nihil-etude more conscientious: death was a raw catechistic datum for her, in which she couldn't believe, finding the Catholic last ointment a supreme lie, and as soon as doubt sucked out the sanctity of the dead, in the same gesture it made the fact of death disappear into a kind of Catholic ceremony.

But now for a moment she remembered that death might after all be something else than clerical bon-mot, a reality, and this somewhat ruffled the smooth course of the nihil cure. Interestingly, instead of conjuring 'humanity' in the medical sense among our muscles, the bath yields such a mist, pearling body ('parfum En Avion le succès de Caron'):[229] as she wrapped the feather boa around her neck, arms, hips, like a chain of legal articles (zoologists seem to call it swan-snake), so she felt her entire body to fall, fanned out, on a white lawn, like the small spray fountains in parks.

The female body — she repeated, trying to bend to herself a more practical side-branch of 'humanity' in a flashing parenthesis — behold: cool water tissue sprayed with white monotony on the shrubs' leaves that are still mauve from the frosty kisses of the night — capisci, Midsummer Patou? This compound sprang from Halbert's English bacilli: after his dicta Lea always felt a great penchant for mixing refined mundanity with English 'middle-class' woods — as a designer she felt entitled to as much. In this Touqué's influence also played a part, who often recited (with a pathos in which the punchline's drypoint and the dispersive carelessness of rapture were said to mix) that the 20th century means Alexandria again, where the industrial designer plays a far greater role than the so-called great artist, and where the small table lamps, advertisements, photo-frames and fabric samples constitute the essence.

What charm, what essence is in Alexandria — Touqué said with sudden emotion. These consciously sentimental moments had lately become rare with him. Lea loved this word, Alexandria, for it sketched a fresh backdrop against her Cubist pillow-drums, or when she stitched together leather leaves with thick needles: a light blue sea that worked like the fresh paint of a refurbished verandah, above it white boats with clacking sails among houses built of tailcoat shirts that had rolled out of some Pandora's box before being stringed.

It's always pleasant to link the thought of decadence to such an airy verandah-cosmos. Just as it is pleasant to take with us rapture, life-giving doubt, immateriality from the bathtub's white enamel cradle: how is it possible that the Romans built so many mammoth baths and at the same time, so many robust male nudes? O yes, we know this piquancy well... but in the bath we lose our body-consciousness, the swimming naked body is much less a nude and much less sculptural than the dressed one — or else, it is *only* consciousness that is left, to which a small-scale model is attached, just as on the bottom of large fashion prints we see in miniature the dress's sketch from the back, in black outlines.

She was up to her neck in the bath, but her head floating above the water had next to no connection with her body slipping hither and thither under water — she felt her legs to be dissolving algae that will ramify in the soap foam like the unreeling threads of a twine ball dropped in water — though she still preserved in her memory a clear 'portrait' of her legs, the yellow underwater planks, shipwreck driftwood, bore no resemblance to them.

The bath inevitably brings man to a jellyfish denominator, and yet the senātus populusque insisted on erecting statues inside the thermae? My nude? — she asked with a smile, her knee hitting the wall of the enamel sarcophagus like a cork lifebelt from which the subject had been long washed out and now the tide casts it ashore, piebald bachelor. Perhaps there is a profound difference between mechanically preparing bodily cleanliness and the (likewise bodily) cleanly individual. How differently the English Halbert looks after a bath than me. It's not just the fact that I powder myself and so even retrospectively fake my washing into decoration, while he sticks to the rough scrubbing brush. In his native village there was no running water, yet everything was glaringly clean: the stone houses looked permanently as after a glistening rain, the streets, the porous stones of the stairs, the roofs, the tiles, the fountain's iron ornaments, everything. Halbert's face too was such a village scrubbed clean. My bathroom, on the other hand, was all light blue tiles — majolica is no longer true cleanliness, it's not empirical but speculative cleanliness: the light, the reflection of colors, the slipperiness playfully transfers hygiene into some kind of ironic Hygeia-poetry, which is not yet completely mendacious stage setting but long no more the original realization of cleanliness.

Last week she designed a bathroom, and Halbert sneered: it was like two completely identical catacomb openings placed one above the other — the lower coffin-tube was the bathtub, the upper cylinder was one lamp-case, behind whose ground glass a row of giant electric peaches lit the ensemble, like in a Fourier-istic[230] marmelade jar. Halbert muttered something about 'motives of cleanliness ... transcendental ... German ... ,' and now she realized that he was right, he who continued to wash in a washbasin, for he doesn't like 'the musical ideograms of cleanliness' (as he called modern bathrooms), choosing water instead. Understandably the bathroom made her even dizzier than the morphine, and robbed her more of her nude: it suddenly occurred to her that she had always felt more mundane in spaces of transit than in those destined for spending time. Her true homeland was the hall, the corridor, the conservatory and the bathroom: always the white and greyish lights, never the yellow, old salon-lighting. Perhaps the stars in Biarritz also brought in this conservatory atmosphere above the banal restaurant décor: the stars, too, were white, like the slightly soiled ice or the snow-clot turning into water on our fingertips — grey like the hall at R***s with skylight.

grey skylight

She will never forget her first visit at R***s where she saw skylight for the first time. Outside it was raining and cold — her first surprise was that inside the same grey light continued, while a faint warmth undulated around her body: how was it possible that this grey, silvery street-like luminosity is connected to warmth? The silver spoon is cold, the great winter squares are cold, the thinly iced puddles are cold, the ground glass, when she ran her finger along it, gave her goose bumps, and the grey marble pillars emanate a funereal coldness: and now she sees all that in front of herself but still, feels the central heating's uniform, rayless and directionless, simply present warmth, which relates to their stove-heating at home like the current fashion's muffled lighting to the raw bulbs' unrefinedly branching light.

When she first breathed in this grey hall, she felt the same as in her childhood when, playing a violin concerto with the school orchestra, she reached the cadenza: the orchestra went suddenly silent, infinitely magnifying every single tone, every empty arpeggio, oppressing, deafening, and blinding her — she felt as though building a preternaturally tall and crowded tower above herself from the notes, which threatens to tumble and crush her immediately; solitude traversed her body like a tropical fever, her throat felt like a passageway to cold and wet draught; her shirt, hands, and bow were drenched in sweat, it was no longer she playing but the immeasurable sound-pagoda's pressure wrought to life the automatic tuggings at the strings — as if her ears had been pressed directly on the sounds' wall, so that she had no inkling what the previous note was and what the next one will be, she kept hearing the same note, which resembled a trumpet's open hippo mouth rather; she thought she was playing the same passage twice and at other times, that she was improvising completely alien bits — the more closely she watched her own meaningless bow-dance, the more unknown, the more imbecile galimatias it seemed (two favorite tricks of loneliness white-hot with fear: to either echo the known as too-known, set it in a comfortable perspective, so that this enhancing of certainty adds to it the memory too, causing perception to run in a canon like the double needle of certain gramophones — or to haul the known to such distance that perception cannot find it even with a telescope, and it ends up appearing utterly alien).

I am afloat — Halbert used to say metaphorically in his inspired moments. This expression came to Lea's mind when she thought of the minutes that she spent in the hall nauseating with its greyness.

In swimming pools she has often tried out placing her eyes right above the water surface: at such moments she saw the surrounding wavelets from very close up, almost in cross-section, and had the impression that her body was neither under nor above the water, but right there where 'under' and 'above' begins, so she needn't even move for watching the whole world from above or from below: her lower eyelashes were almost caught by the shadow-tongue hooks of the depth (grabbing for her lashes like the carps that peck at breadcrumbs with heads pushed above the water), but at the same time she could still see the lower limit of the upper world, its plinth as it were, the mirror-smooth down-side of complicated clouds. The whole made up a chain of two threads in eight shapes: the horizon's golden sinus curve (the wave-valley of 'above'), on which coiled the thick snake-bracelet of shadows popping up from the depth (the wave-crest of 'under').

But at such times she saw nothing, only what was in front of her eyes, her field of vision perfectly coincided with the surface of her eyeballs, her whole consciousness was sucked to this site, as though the decapitated man's head lived on (in old battle scenes in fact they painted it living), and although the body disappeared, he saw right under his eyes his own voice which continued to issue from him for a while, like the pool's water.

In one corner there was a palm-tree, around it dimness hovered like the delicate fur of a blue fox — its leaves were faded blue like half-desiccated anthracene traits. The grey skylight was so dizzying because it was the official color of the whole room, of aristocratically shared freedom; colors are always idyllic, but this greyness was vast, even infinite, and those palm trees were armchairs with dark legs but with upholstery that gradually whitened and turned airy, they were pale filters through which space streams & which make space visible — just like a gigantic drawing sheet is nothing more than drab whiteness as long as it's untouched, but fills with rushing air the moment somebody draws on it a single reed.

How different love must be here, in this skylit hall, how different the kiss: space continuously streams in it without a trace of dramatic tempo, rather as metaphysical airing, that rushes with its grey powder between the mouths eager to encounter. At the bottom of any sensuousness worth the name should be this greyness, which is also one form of nihil, what is more, an immoral variation of askesis — 'glove-patting,' as Halbert referred to one of his liaisons in Bournemouth.

Before her sat a tall, elderly lady who kept one of her gloves on; on the skin some powder trembled as impossible snow on a summerly twig, and Leatrice was overcome with the same rapture at the sight of that glove as now during combing, or from her first dose of morphine. For that glove was the synthesis of the hall's silvery emptiness, its artifice. She would have liked to pull on again the glove taken so irredeemably off & take the hand of that woman, caress and squeeze it — how different is the relation of two faces if the hands touch only through such insulation; the two people feel protected like a selfish, glistening donjon surrounded by a deep moat filled with moon-laquer water and so the eyes that meet at head level can keep unsullied distance, while if naked palms coil around each other, the two bodies' two kinds of electric currents immediately mix and in the eyes the patinated number of different personalities immediately evaporates.

When she swayed her outlines before the mirror she also felt that her clothes perfectly insulated her body, as a thin but stable shade insulates candlelight — if she meets K*** at the restaurant, her body will not spill out at once but rest as an invisible splinter behind the feather boa's wreath foliage. How can people live in such a way that from the outer world's images nothing falls on them but the sky's whitish color, sucking them incessantly outward?

Lea didn't feel stable in her chair, for she felt imprisoned at the bottom of a very tall tube; she couldn't concentrate on anything, for the skylight immediately dispersed her attention. She had never felt evanescence so acutely — as though sitting in a benumbing purgatory where waiting is eternal. The woman before her kept all her natural color, but just as in plein-air summer landscapes the leaves are crossed by dispersed golden-green reflexes, so on this face the pearly velour of nothing showed (plein-rien?).

She had seen children's rooms and verandahs with the same atmosphere of luminosity, but there it had no such paradoxical effect, because the furniture, wallpaper, evergreens pointed definitely outward from the room, into the garden: but here the street's muddy half-luminosity fell on empire armchairs, and the rain clattered directly above the lace curtain's small networks onto the transparent ceiling; it appeared not a real room but a stage setting propped up under a street glass shade. Lace was the symbol of motionlessness and inner doldrums, as if it were not an embroidery but the salt of silvery air itself that condensed on the delicate door-glass soaked in it — but the raindrops' ring as they splashed on the glass ceiling under exciting 90° belonged wholly to the street's orchestration; when she looked at the pages of a book, a trickling raindrop's shadow fell on it, dividing into a five-branch blot. She relished the way how this left no mark on the book's blotting paper-like, thick pages, she was at home *&* on the street at the same time. So from the outer world the sky's neutral packfong color is more truly 'outer world' than the surrounding houses' façade or the familiar strip of hills, which resembled the visible bottom of a tilted-up yacht. At home the windows were wide open, for the whole family rolled in horizon gourmandizing, and yet she felt utterly insulated: here it was all walls with no windows, but the skylight immediately stripped the place of all enclosed homeliness.

*associations: winter afternoons;
to snowfall: the design of a parenthetical church*

It reminded her of dreary things, her uncle's loves, cold, steely afternoons when the windows acquired an identical parchment-dusk staleness; though the snowflakes could carry some tiny shine among the black twigs, running across the wood like flying hoarfrost stockings or a debauched side theme unexpectedly revirginated — this is the spume's precision: flying inadvertently so high that the sun reaches it and lights an icy spark on it for a moment;

> (one of her stage designs of a church, meant as a memorial to the Christmas babe, preserved this memory: the church's width far exceeds its length, and along the diagonal of this rectangle is a vast curtain — a sparse checkered steel net made of thick, loose threads and in their junctions, polished metallic balls of different size. The net with the balls stands for Christmas snow. The sides of its squares are around 1.5 m. The altar's grey porcelain serpent begins from the right upper corner

behind the giant net, running along the diagonal, and only at the church's left end [the diagonal's upper end] does it swerve to the fore of the snow-grid, like a timid walk-on actor who mistakenly stepped out before the curtain — there where it swerves to the fore, the foot of a black cross can be seen with half a cross-bar, the other being veered behind the curtain. The altar itself is a half altar 'in hiding,' the unrolled half of a scroll, as if behind the naïve snow-costume the whole of pain were still concealed: the candles, too, are concentrated, almost vacuumed, into the left corner. In contrast, the lectern on the evangelistary side is infinitely elongated, the altar had long ceased underneath but it continues spreading like a hand in a concave mirror. The choir wall is of ground glass, so in the evening only laddered checks and black balls can be seen in the air — missale nivis);[231]

the street turned leaden like a petrified river or blasé lava, clouds and sky displayed the monotonous variations of white and grey — here and there glowless white incandescence like dim lightbulbs, but the whole streetscape was cold and drowsy mist. Now those shadows were undulating here on the armchairs; the pillows, tassels, handrests were magnified by them as if the armchair were a throne erected in a wasteland. Perhaps our bodies will look like that on the frosty dawn of the Last Judgment: spread out on our faces, like granny's lace, the memory of our passions, but to run along the wrinkles's untimely patience game will not be our almost-not-yet-day's light-needle, only the arctic indifference of infinite dawn.

For the most demoralizing in this skylight was the way in which it breathed the mythological air of indifference on our small affairs, drawers, & loves. And still, for a moment a meaningless sensuality ran through her, like a gramophone record put on by mistake that we immediately stop when we recognize the foreign sounds — but that one moment was enough to make her muse. Perhaps that small dose was constant but now all of a sudden it became conspicuous, because there was no outlet and no way to disperse it, like a tiny daytime flame at the end of a wick that immediately appears glowing if someone closes the shutters. When we step out into great heat, our first reaction is to shudder from cold — perhaps when we get into an absolutely indifferent environment, this small dose of sensuality gives a shudder in us (powder box in the handbag when the bus jolts to a halt).

confession

She recalled something similar from childhood confessions, when she walked with a list of sins in hand along the mold-moiréd corridor of the monastery of L*** — in the fetid cellar air among the light-cubes that the tall windows dropped inside, away from the walls, in the priest's sour-green study her sins, which were so earnestly and easily regretted at home, flourished at once — but they flourished outside her body and soul, losing those abhorrent spun-out root-twines with which they get entangled in all other matters of our lives, as though the roots of the slender, solitary greenhouse flower penetrated like blind octopus arms inside the parlor and coiled its muddy, wet tendrils around the china ware and the guests. Here in the monastery corridor's alien dusk, where the unknown was so thick and choking as to be churned into butter with one stir — the sins got rid of the swelling waters of conscience and so they didn't overgrow, like red creepers, the umpteenth temple of the Holy Ghost, which happened to be Lea's body, but shimmered from afar like beloved objects, chirping birds on an elastic twig.

skyline and kiss

While Lea was leafing through the big book in the hall, the image of the kiss appeared to her in a similar manner — as though escaping from her body. At home, in her room a kiss was a very complicated act, for every known object, daytime color, and fleeting acquaintance participated in it — she almost didn't see and didn't feel the kiss itself, only the long exposition leading to it: the exposition in her legs, hands, waist, in the industrial design drawings scattered on her desk that she always carried on her, smudged all over her life. But here the kiss was a small medallion, a motley statuette that hung by a thread right before her nose. The old kiss always started twitching in her soul, spread a bit inside, here and there it sprouted irregularly from her clothes — but now it was a foreign something hanging at medium distance, to which one had to go like a polite visitor whose eye is caught by a delicate little triptych on the fireplace, and like the non-indulgent connoisseur, he will turn to it with ironic love. How curious that for her from this very grey atmosphere a new sensuous tranquility might be born, though so far it connoted her uncle's cockamamie fiascos.

associations: clockface on a winter afternoon when her uncle is late

Martha was mewing in the corner like a badly beaten cat, fearfully peering at the big grandfather clock on which the Roman numbers were so thin as time's gooey eyelid edges, which are immediately lost in the clockface's silver wasteland when it falls more profoundly asleep. The clock hands, too, were thin like nerve endings caught in the dentist's needle, so for Lea time had always meant something sickly & affected — in fact this large clockface alone accused her uncle who didn't come home for lunch. If that strange animal breathing under the glass sheet, which appeared fast asleep by an act of mimicry directed at its surroundings, were to disappear all of a sudden, everything would be right as rain.

The big pendulum disk looked like a tired gill: now it disappeared in the dusk, now it took shape; it only minimally bulged toward the center but even that was enough for gigantic conic shadows to jut out to its edges. A thousand copper circles ran around in it like on a gramophone record, and strangely enough, all the sketch-quivering together amounted to nothing more than the slouching movement from the dark into semi-dimness and back again — this dark breathing alone kept vigil over her uncle's sin (the devil's lungs perhaps?).

The clockface shimmered under the glass as though submerged a few millimeters below the surface of a quiet pond or alcohol, to disinfect and enhance its precision and time-slicing edge. Outside there was no time: the trees, the moment their blackness shifted a bit to the side like the image on the edge of a broken photographic lens, are always time-less; snow fell almost parallel to the ground, windward, from right to left, and made her head swirl: a sea of barbed white dots, with here and there a few larger flakes like tattered hairballs, which couldn't catch up with the one-way tempo of the ice mash & ended up swaying, Americanizing like early drunks in a disciplined carnival parade: time regards only us and its realm is confined to the four walls, Leatrice thought.

The table was laid, the plates sat, white, as though not for soup but for squat and plump-flamed funereal lights. The hour hand passed over three and showed a frightfully vacuous face. As the two clockhands hovered above the same spot at a quarter past three, they left the quarter circle between XII and III naked — that exposed blank territory looked like the whiteness before a storm that radiates from the clouds' underbelly with sickly, destructive cleanness.

The clockface bulged a bit: Lea found this ghostly, as if looking upon a cruel eye's rounded white. The infinitely slender Roman numbers stood lonely, with mute sharpness — she wished almost in tears she could multiply them. Why did they place them in the room if they so torture people — there's no time outside anyway, only wide nights that press fresh snow into the poreless body of the woods.

A quarter past three without her uncle was an arctic territory — the two horizontal clockhands were already agonizingly bending to the right like flower stems ironed by the wind. With the two clockhands not separately visible but as one, the drawing spelt out wretched fulfillment, the blind maturity of lateness, pointlessness's tormenting harmony. It was no longer minutes & quarters of an hour that passed & piled up with the clockhands' shifts, but an unveiling of various hopeless face-landscapes, as if instead of the clockhands the eyes, nose, ears of a living face were gliding on and on.

She felt constrained to identify the changing clockface with her tarrying uncle's face, as if mimicry-wise the two lives were one and the same, and the clock merely the symbolic semaphore of distant events hidden from view, which could be clearly deciphered here. The three signs of the XII were still an easy-going congestion as compared to the blind stylism of the I that followed, as though signaling that the hour was even materially different from the morning hours, not a number any more but a hovering arrow, the morning's netherworld echo. Lea shuddered from that I as from a wicked man. In general she held it to be the number of the 'grown-ups' and so an enemy of children — the grown-ups always believe that the most dead boring things are the most interesting and from the numbers they probably love this I best, because it is the most shapeless one, the most nothing. When the hour hand passed over XII she had the impression that time lost its way and was rushing toward a gigantic hurdle or precipice, almost taking the path of sin. The big white hill on which I and II were barely visible meant the grown-ups' sins, her uncle's being late: what a cold, dry, and empty thing sin must be.

She looked up at the clock. The hour hand was proceeding toward half past III, a new grimace. Outside nothing changed, the trees lay back into the winter darkness like galley slaves in their oars, while the snow whistled above them, frosty serpentine at the ball in the wee hours. Even if the landscape changed, there was some one-directional development in it like in a melody, when we feel that even if the orchestra was paralysed, the melody itself would continue pouring from the air or from our souls along the spiral arches of a spring — but the clock pulled a face of a different 'direction' every moment, and this face got engraved into the furniture, plates, the movements of Martha and Mary, into her own body — when she looked out of the dim window, she happily felt her body lose its clockhand-shape for a moment and dive freely among the waves of the outer world.

In fact, there was nothing else in the room at this point but the clock. Its ghostly power was all the more strange because it was made in granny fashion: the clockface was surrounded by gold ornaments, small shiny sieves, trumpets, angel heads and half-flowers, idyllic toys, friendly knick-knacks. And inside this childish neoclassical wreath the withering drama played out. She felt not the clock-hands advancing steadily but a white crack widening on the entire wall, through which the dreary vacuity of an unknown sin flooded the room. Each and every one of the figures taking shape on the clock-face was full of precise meaning and yet she couldn't explain them. Mary said quietly:

— He said he would go over to his brother before coming home, but he can't possibly be staying there so long. Don't you want to have lunch? You must eat, Martha also ate before you arrived. What time is it?

Leatrice looked up at the clock with determination. If she looked at the clockface in the morning she felt that, if she uttered aloud the exact time, a close and real connection was created between the clockface image and her voice, like between a handle and a plate — but now when she said for the second time, quietly and after a small cough, 'half past III,' she couldn't believe her own words, as though she said a word in a foreign language where meaning and sound are not tied together. She kept whispering for a long time after, 'half past III, half past three,' but couldn't get a grasp of it, the number in her soul felt like a melody hummed systematically out of tune — all the streaming half-truth of rhythm is still in it, but the false tune keeps channeling it to a foreign slope, so the melody can't absorb the rhythm. They measured with the clock how little her uncle cared about them: at V past III, it was just a discreet alarm signal, one sole click of the tension meter, a passing unveiling, the Auftakt of suspicion [232] — but when the clock hands stretched out for a quarter past III, estrangement, family denial, came to be formulated with merciless clarity; and now when they hung down to south-east like overburdened branches, the image of staying away metamorphosed into bedlam, everything tumbled down and ripped up, chaos loomed large. In vain Lea looked out into the darkness, everything vanished and the snow itself was no more than an anachronistic obsession — every snowflake was individualized and the wind ruffled up their green dialogues under the window.

Leatrice's 'Europeanness': blend of hypochondria and beastliness

Now she thought of her immediate future and pulled these memories on her hands like elbow-length python leather gloves, in order to keep her healthy fingers safe from the future's infected waters.

The most practical question was of course the tailoring pattern of 'humanity' — in what way it is man and in what way woman, she needed to know, and memories could help out with picnic-style definition fragments. When she watched the clock in her childhood, her humanistic 'satin moulé' was ready, & it was the same as when she compared the forms of the sea and yesterday's champagne glasses, or when she stood before the mirror after a bath or leafed through the book in the skylit hall.

She was of Russian origin, so Europe often preoccupied her both in hotel registration forms and spiritual exercises. She particularly relished Europeanness like some red-ribboned white badge. What was her European humanity? She answered with two words: hypochondria and beastliness. She wouldn't venture to claim that the two were very different. There was a folding screen in her room with one continuous painted landscape: at some folds the image was interrupted (when the image formed a convex angle), at others only the fold's edge was visible, like on a paper sheet, without interrupting the wall itself (where the painted landscape formed an acute or obtuse angle).

Hypochondria and beastliness relate to one another in a similar manner in her life as a 'European' woman: the same two intersecting lines, but in the one case I draw the circlet representing the angle on one page, in the second, on the other page, so I get an angle of 240° (hypochondria) or 120° (beastliness). Hypochondria is perhaps the result of the Palestine Semitic-Christian moral so suddenly foisted on the barbarians, while beastliness is the persistence of the temperament of the epoch of great migrations.

Why is her European humanity always so paradoxical? Because they dumped on her an ethics and logic that has nothing to do with her blood, and in this way in every movement of hers half-ethic and half-beast, half-logic and half-sentimentalism got mixed. Before the mirror she looked at her clothes, was not what she felt the crossing of a human-denying fashion derived from hypochondria, and of only-human love originating in the beast? All logical and artistic sensitivity is due solely to the fact that beastly bodies were trimmed against their anatomies, clothes tailored for Jerusalemites were hey presto embalmed on Franks and Russians. Thus every love ended up as the preternatural mix of cowardice and heroism, sickness and life-mania, and when she, Leatrice, tried to find before the mirror the most characteristically human trait of the 'human being,' this squinting European duality perturbed her.

Was not this same thing at work in her style, on the map of her thoughts: when she peered at the clock, always returning on its eerie changes of masks, was it not cowardly stagnation, thought impossible to enhance into her self, hypochondria-degree moral and logic, working inside her? Europeans never thought, they merely let the strange, outlandish machinery of thought go on in their thoughts like some grotesque and tragic guest. And when she forced her mouth's bitter redness into every love that presented itself, like an oversize button into malleable and servile buttonholes, was she not driven by selfish action, by Caliban rhetoric?

O, aristocratic fear from simplification — it certainly didn't bother her now. Naturally in human beings it's not love that means beastliness and thought that means hypochondria: every imaginable European function can be played in those two contrasting tonalities. For didn't there lurk in the beauty of her body a folkloristic muscle-amulet from the nomadic age, chained together with the barrenly æsthetic and mystically ethical concept of beauty and vanity? As though her body had a double contour, one from her living beauty and one from the thought of 'living beauty,' so out of place there. (And this is obviously no rooting for 'life.')

the carillon

Once in the kitchen Mary spoke about another woman. This was the first time that Leatrice heard the word 'woman' & took fright. Woman, too, was the Roman I on the clockface, some boring, inimical, cold affair of the grown-ups. So a 'woman' who keeps her uncle captive lives somewhere. She was choking with a sob like from wet smoke, & the taste of this repression was pushed down to her stomach. Fear tasted something horrid, like pills. Sometimes she felt rage, but in her child's soul the concept of 'woman' wasn't definite enough to strengthen — at other times she felt infinite sadness, so she fled to the pantry for a last-ditch sob. From the room she could hear both Mary's quiet voice and the clock's unexpected music — only at one or two numbers did it break into a tune, at the others the mechanism didn't work. Lea was greatly upset by the wailful voice and the clock's music hanging its green veils at the same time; as if Mary and her uncle were long dead, and the wind carried the shreds of their souls to a lakeshore in southern Russia where they would freeze and snow down on the trees.

The miraculous thing in the carillon's tune was that for five minutes it was one sole melodic theme (only the theme, without repetition or development), without breaking off for one second: one ended the theme in imagination every second and hummed the conventional theme-concluding note beforehand like a full stop at the sentence's end, when the theme glided on, finding in itself a new point of departure, as if it dragged itself out of a river's green waves by its own ponytail, like an ethereal Münchhausen: gulls fly in this fashion around the banks of the nearby lake — they draw huge eights and spirals with their silver oars under the matte sky (in school Lea imagined those geometric figures behaved so where one can't tell if they're still two- or already three-dimensional bodies, like for instance a spring cut out from transparent glass-paper), and so they approach a rock on the shore, but when they almost touch the end-point with their wings, in that moment we realize that the hulk is by far not the last, there are still lots of swinging-zigzagging serpentines before the gulls land on the stones with a plop of feathers.

She felt something similar when she first heard her teacher recite Virgil's hexameters — every moment she believed it was the rhythm's end, when to her surprise the teacher didn't let his voice drop but continued the verse, as though from one genitive the next poured out, like a collapsible telescope being opened — it seemed that the whole structure exceeded its aim and at this point no rule can stop it, it will only come to an end from ultimate exhaustion. That's why Lea nearly choked when she heard the carillon melody: she followed it holding her breath & thought that if she inhaled, the melody would be cut off. One could hear that its playing depended upon some mechanism with springs — as though the heavy pendulum pulled it downward, lower and lower into the light green midst of a dark green forest, and only strong braking could stop the whole melody from unreeling in the first instant, like a roll of thread, from the free fall of the one-kilo iron bob tied to its end.

The most beautiful thing in the music was this deathly clear balance — below, the pendulum's swinging weight, above it the fast unrolling melody which, although full of the disk's lethal pulling force, still continued to undulate across the room, calm, articulate, almost winking & spraying. How could that lazy pendulum elicit such ethereal tones? Does weight produce lightness? Among and under the tune's chimes, naïve notes, a deep booming could sometimes be heard, like a laughter's echo from a cave, which could have easily been an Angelus: this little melody was obviously dancing above great depths & standing above 'the force of destiny,' Lea thought.

She read in a fairy tale that once the bronze-prowed ship of an exiled prince reached the sirens' gulf: the sirens sank the ship and took the prince on their wings to the top of a tall mountain, where their castle could be glimpsed only as pearly sunshine trembling to shreds on the poplars' crown. The pendulum hesitated under the glass sheet like the prince's ship at sea — it ventured deeper and deeper, as though so far it had hung by a hair on the surface, one breath was enough and the ship reached its instinctive, comfortable position underwater, on the bottom. When it started sinking, there was no howling tumult: the waves closed above it quietly like a blue-page book slowly closing on the fingers of a reader who fell asleep — one from the left, one from the right, almost ashamed of the inevitable little spume that had jumped along on the waves' edge to cross the slow direction of the great water covers; when the last azure bedsheet was smoothed out on the surface, the ship, caught between two downward-moving perpendicular inner wave-walls, elastically glided down, a Neptune-elevator. At the same time the sirens were loudly singing, in zigzagging, scintillating tones — on wings rolled out like carpets they left behind the waters' cool bells and perpetuum mobile-daydreaming whirligigs, & came up against the sunlight that broke on them like the jet of an accidentally tilted watering can on a puzzlingly dry statue. The cheerful surface of the carillon melody resembled this singing, whistlingly-morningish morning.

Once Halbert related a week-end in a castle somewhere in the English countryside: when he described the red brick walls with their dry, serene features — (here and there they were bronzed over by large patches of green moss, in other places the sunlight sucked them almost rosy-white) — and after that, the lake surrounding the castle, whose almost smothering smoothness was teeming with floating weeds, flaring-out flowercups on the edge of leaves, like floating ashtrays for an airborne cigarette: then she suddenly remembered their old grandfather clock whose first, mysterious chime was like this silent lake around the castle, in whose mirror a few pneumatic donjons float. The lake's barely-just-recognizable flatness was strange in the midst of all the serrated flowers and small shades — the shadows hanging under the flowers (wigs soaked vertically in the water) tried in vain to grate away at the mirror's plane-edge with their small grey seesaws; although it was hard to see anything of the lake from the blanket of quivering water plants, still, a melancholy plenitude of flatness traversed it — across the jumble of petals, shades, leaves and roots, the planimetric silence of flat water incandesced, as a sharp, or much rather flat, key signature iridesces through a hesitant trill.

She felt that the melody had something to do with her tarrying uncle, but didn't know how. That sin and woman, these two obscure grownup words, could be beautiful she had no inkling of at that time, so she couldn't have imagined the clock's concluding melody as a symbol. Besides, the fact that those few beats were squeezed between precisely those seconds and so didn't happen in time but only in the void between the two time phases, like the undulating body of pillarless bridges — could only be imagined as a negative interlude, neutral, like a propeller's bursting spin, continued long after the ship adhered to the dock.

It was indeed curious how incapable the melody was to grow into time's pale branches like some gorgeous parasite — much as the malign fate-graphics created by every tiny shift of the clock-hands were things of time, this carillon failed to add a single stroke to the portrait of time. Time had not as much as side products: it fell from a foreign direction like screeching-rustling sand from the crane's end which swings forward above the pale waters — what does this abrupt dirty jet have to do with the harbor's undecided candle-color, which quietly sways under the sky's low garage roof, like an air balloon from which gas is let out slowly?

once again that clockface

Outside the Moon came out, the sky was transparent black like the air of rooms where one single candle is burning — though the dark is coal-black toward the ceiling, the light's most outward-lying force quietly thins it, so it trembles in the air like a velvety breeze. On the black sky one elongated cloud-strip stretches like a shiny net, infinite hammock, in whose fraying threads the Moon was caught, rolling silently on and on. In the forest green patches appeared, as though loneliness were a severe illness that so far had only lurked in the branches' coated veins, but now under the Moon's experimental lighting appears under the form of green pimples. The nearby forest slid back into infinite distance, like a foreign boat sliding out from the docks to highwater; the Moon's trajectory was also not straight but, depending upon the heaving or deflation of the one cloud-strip and obeying the wind's hypnosis, now it twitched toward the sky's top and now it stabbed itself with the trees' branches like a shiny Lucrece.

Snow fell like emerald dots: their side turned toward Lea was green from the moonlight in their back, but their face turned to the Moon was merely colorless glistening, abstract shining, the edges protruded among the fluff turned toward Lea, as the shiny edge of the covered new moon too remains visible around the overshadowed part. Later she learned from the sacristan of the church of Pr*** where her uncle was on that afternoon, which looked rather like the most bounteous harvest of midnight, when snow fell not from the sky but from shoulder height; the whirring disks of light and shadow fell strangely, commanding over the landscape like the Tropics of Capricorn and of Cancer over the map. When Lea looked at the clock, the world turned with her: number VI, which hung head downward like a clean-plucked weeping willow branch, at once meant not lateness but dizzying earliness — in the Moon's white flood the clockface now evoked the grey mist of an inner dawn. It's only VI o'clock in the afternoon and outside night is ready, like on a stage where they accidentally pulled up the curtain too early.

All of a sudden time shrank like a small, transparent flower photographed with a magnifying glass against a dark background — one can see the complicated order of glassy lines but still feels the whole's original smallness, insignificance. So did the time drawn on the clockface become in Lea's eyes, as it fell under the mythic X-rays of moonlight — although earlier when the room's inner luminosity lit it, she could clearly see all the chafings on the clockface, the protruding iron parts that served for winding up or shifting the clockhands, now in the moonlight it seemed to her that she saw the clock for the first time, that it must have been hidden behind thick black walls: those now became transparent and uncovered their small, wan hearts. The clock turned into a curiosity: a gorgeous little crystal that is perhaps darkness's precise temple, but at an infinite remove from all human matters, just like the algae of the palmhouse, where one is lost between admiring the 'wondrous order' of nature, or the absolute pointlessness & imbecility of their being.

two types of representation of the psyche

When she thought of the clock that moonlight embalmed into sterile precision, she recalled Halbert's observation on 'humanity' or psychology at large:

'Touqué believes that the only way to know and uncover the psyche is through reason. Of course he stresses that every collection of analyses is in fact a manmade soul, the artificial fulfillment of the illusory human instinct to have something called 'psychic life.' He has comparisons too: as though into an empty riverbed that had always longed for a wide and overflowing river they poured not water but only reflections dancing on the surface, exotic water animals, plants opening in great depths: so to trick the riverbed. Nice, nice — Halbert said with a side glance, rubbing his long hands together between his knees — but we can perhaps discover more of the human psyche if we stop replacing it with fictions but simply impale it on a hayfork and turn it around a bit under the moonlight. This comparison would be a bit more honest, for it includes my positive memory: I cannot imagine a more precise analysis of the psyche than of the actress who was lit onstage with green, violet, white & red lights in succession — nothing changed on her, she didn't move, didn't say a word, and yet I felt that every conceivable thing was said about her, that I knew everything about her.

So one possibility is fiction and the other, fantastic lighting: green lets through the hips but not the ankles, red lets through love but not tenor, yellow lets through the intellect but not humor, and so on to infinity — in fact this is the wildest counterpart of analysis, and yet it is analysis. And if Touqué extols fiction for fulfilling the upstart desire for psyche, then this could be the greatest fiction, for the red or silver footlight (even if it did nothing else to trigger certain features in the woman) is definitely not a component of the woman and doesn't even illuminate her, but merely uses her as indifferent theme to achieve its own color-essence. And still, by the fact that the woman is an insignificant twentieth-rank means for achieving the aim of color, we get the perfect representation of her psyche. Colors have the additional advantage that the most refined nuance elicits the same elementary effect as one of the primary colors, there is no 'fragmentation into details' & 'paradoxes.'

Where then is our soul — Leatrice asked herself with a wry mix of smile and yawn, wiping her yawn-drawn tears — if analysis is no more than a series of adopted figures that can at best be used with some practical benefit instead of the soul — and if mystical lighting à la Halbert merely plays with the surface shadows, is perhaps no more than sentimental clair-obscure, and is also miles away from what human beings would like for themselves as 'soul'? The pleasant numbness of irresponsibility ran through her, as if the two kinds of psychologizing styles were no more than the sound of distant horns, from which the seductive note of distant meadows reaches out — the bosky, paradisiac hunting ground of the clever 'ignoramus.'

XI.

return to yesterday's champagne glasses (see pp. 872–873);
a ship ashore at dawn

Again she saw dancing before her eyes the rims of yesterday's champagne glasses, which surrounded the liquid autumn of champagne with white hoops and from where pearls kept ascending, leaving behind the glass' surface, as if trying to irrevocably refute the law of the conservation of energy: elegance is nothing other than the realization that all psychology is from the beginning and de natura a misprision, and the only concrete thing is: to get dizzy above the champagne's golden hanging pools — she felt her eyes to be the water of a yellow fountain pouring from high above into the glass's frozen breath-plate, so the champagne is nothing but sight turned into a liquid relic, the material of elegant vision. The morning closed beneath her and she was left outside with the memory of last night: the dizziness going through and through her body simply originated in the fact that yesterday had no ground anymore, but only a scent, it couldn't land anywhere, like frivolous smoke from under which they have long put out the fire. "I'm swimming like a corpse thrown up by the morning's clean tide," Leatrice said to herself laughing, and with her head answered the greeting of the locale's owner.

Not far from the shore there was a small white steamer at anchor, the morning shadow cast on it a light 'wash-blue' fabric, and only on the top of its chimney did a bit of sunshine dance like a hypersensitive wave-meter: the ship looked almost nailed to the water in the complete silence, but that small light ring betrayed that it was dancing on the waves. Leatrice's eyes jumped here and there, now to the rigid deck, now to the chimney-top with the sliding spotlight. In her childhood she always believed that whenever a ship comes to harbor it completely adheres to the shore, and she was greatly surprised when they told her of a ship considerably off shore that it would not come any closer and its passengers would be carried by boat to the dock.

This ship anchoring far out at sea could be an emblem of the 'grownup' affairs — they are never natural. Soon after she boasted to her friends of her new seafaring knowledge and felt that she stepped into another world, into the grownups' mysterious 'irraison,' as she would sometimes put it. By not being directly moored to the shore, the ship acquired a hostile air, as if cannons stuck out of the yacht that hardly looked more significant than a pair of freshly ironed trousers, to fill the morning air with sharp rattle and pungent lighting match-smell. Can you really not pull this ship to the foot of the promenade? Are there things that can be done only one way? Is it not the grownups' tacit, whimsical conspiracy that the ship is capriciously kept far off shore?

Lea couldn't believe that there is a definite 'it must be so' in the world, the thought that 'it must be so' was merely an adopted fiction with the same aim as the various psychologies, to fulfill the instinct for 'psyche': there is also an 'it must be so' instinct in people, for which they make up all kinds of forced categorical imperatives — for instance, to keep a ship at anchor far off shore. How many times she read that this or that ship came to Hamburg or Naples: she imagined it almost among the houses, like the churches or high street, but when she saw a photograph with the script, 'The *Amorca* comes to Hamburg port,' all she could see was fog, water of uncertain shape, shore-shreds drifting like castoff rag, and a few visibly disused cranes: she couldn't understand how that indeterminate emptiness could be Hamburg. It was the grownups'

Hamburg, who would call any cloud Hamburg simply because they wanted some 'Hamburg' to exist in the world.

Was it blasphemy that she felt like a Madonna among the champagne glasses, in whom the inebriating wings of the Holy Ghost flap by: perhaps God is no more than aimless pneuma, and conception in fact means elegance, the birth of nihil. In her imagination she scanned a few familiar brains, like a pianist who doesn't strike the keys but merely brushes them with her fingers, but didn't find anyone who was likely to endorse this idea: the old sacristan, who had been the hospital's tirelessly vigilant porter before, would have nodded disbelievingly (whenever he denied something he appeared to be tearfully approving, only with his hands would he sketch a 'but then again' gesture); neither did Touqué's yellow skull resonate with this game.

But even if he didn't approve of such follies, at least the old sacristan would look on them with quiet respect as on sin in general. A pity, for what a beautiful altarpiece it would have made: her face like a trembling Madonna with a halo or Byzantine background like the yellow of the champagne reminiscent of morning sunlight; the air full of white circles, the rims of the champagne glasses; beneath, a Russian landscape, let's say, of her native town, scrubbed with the rough brush of the Annunciation spring; the Madonna is whirled by the Holy Ghost like snow in the wind that rustles above the March fields — it doesn't beat down from the sky but spins up from the wells toward the treetops.

When yesterday she took the giant flat glass to her lips and all of a sudden it tilted between her teeth with all its flatness, without waves (no foam even around her teeth: as if the shape of her mouth was simply cut out of gold foil) she felt that something sacred was happening, and felt no distinction between frivolous & sacred. "Perhaps the struggle of my whole life — she thought, martially attempting to break a sugar cube into two — is that I'm struggling against the fact of tragedy. I was raised for tragedies, but something suggests that tragedy is snobbish hogwash — mon Dieu!" — the sugar-cube suddenly fell from her hand & plopped into the coffee, splattering her clothes.

remembrance of her uncle's loves

Her uncle always courted sickly women — if one could call it courtship at all — or women who at least had a sick patient in the family. About one of his loves she found out from the sacristan, another she deduced from a letter. On the afternoon that was dissembled into such an unexpectedly delirious valley of tears by the moonlight (street razzia of eerie optimism), her uncle left the office to go to Mrs. W. who lived far out of town in her hillside villa. He missed the car that would have taken him there, so he footed it. Many a haughty and healthy lover has braved fiendish storms, but with her uncle this was no heroism but its very opposite, cowardice and vile sneaking. He never dared approach women he liked, because their temperaments were the polar opposite of his. So he only lurked where he received a little invitation, a bit of schmaltziness.

Mrs. W was at her third marriage and, as Leatrice once heard, she had some women's affliction. She of course understood nothing of 'women's affliction,' but it was enough to understand women in general, herself included, as some sickness. Love is nothing else than the symptom of this 'affliction.' The third husband was a drunkard, allegedly because he discovered that certain 'women's affliction' of his wife too late. At this time Lea circulated among her girlfriends as a personified 'sickness': as Hamburg was only rainy air according to the grownups' instructions, so the concrete little girl metamorphosed into indefinite 'women's affliction.' By entire life (this too was the grownups' strange word) it seems some kind of general sickness was meant, which is nevertheless utterly different from measles or the little flus with fever with which you have to stay at home. The girls were the privileged flowers from whom sickness (that is, life) emanates, haughtily, toward the stupid boys.

the concept of 'sickness' in childhood

This cult of sickness had of course nothing to do with actual bodily ailments: rather, it was a grey Arcadia in which the nymphs were figures of senseless grisaille who in their songs united nothingness and pedantry in the way the grownups did in real life — their lives depended on nonexistent in-vain things, but they also conferred huge importance on small things, so that in the end they might wear on their faces the badges of pointlessness, well-nigh religious tedium, & 'in vain.' The disturbance, the suspected contradiction in their lives, this was 'sickness' in point of fact: to be sick means to be going about all the time in disguise, to dissimulate.

Lea also put into practice her inkling among her girlfriends: from a book's title page she read aloud only the publisher's name in small print, and when the other children pointed at the big letters of author and title, she superciliously proclaimed that it had no importance, for the essential is always what is written in small print. And after she explained, in a voice comical from the stir she created, the mysterious importance of the essential, she produced a sour grimace, similar to the way they drew the Swabians' yammering fatalism in the *Meggendorfer*,[233] and knocked the book in a corner: "unfortunately this too is false and doesn't correspond to reality." When she pronounced 'reality' she felt the same shiver as when she related to her friends about ghosts, merely to feed her own scare-voluptcy. Reality: black, rainy, and yet song-trilling Arcadia where everything is as certain as the iron railing on the swimming pool's margin, and everything is aswim in the alluring perfume of meaninglessness — which transforms people into cold, hard statues with white and veinless conceit, but at the same time spins the destructive joys of dizziness between their fingers, under their mouths.

She knew that when her uncle ran to a woman on that afternoon — which tore into two her consciousness and is now flaunting its gaping cross-section like a ship crashed into a reef: the Moon dancing on a wave-rail, the sky's only green leaf behind the Moon's swaying pod as the ornamental leaf on a fruit plate (this is of course the visible half of her uncle's soul) — then he was looking for something extraordinarily positive on the ship's split-open corridors or Moon-filled cabins. She had never yet felt anything to be so wildly important as to deserve minding it for so long, for hours and hours, when the night's vortex would anyway soon swallow the ship's wreck. How strange must a 'woman' be that one doesn't get bored of her for hours. This too belongs to the issue's sickness-character — this length and doggedness.

In experiment she too tried to confer importance on something for a long time — for instance, the fact that the next day she would make a trip with her girlfriend; somehow she felt that for her this was enormously important, but an invisible sign also insinuated that this was not the way in which the woman with a 'woman's affliction' was important for her uncle.

For the grownups everything is sadly important and if they accidentally laugh one has the impression that they do it out of Schadenfreude: as if they decided somebody's death. So she tried to think sadly of tomorrow's trip: she thrust her head forward as if desperately gawking at something, dropped her lower lip, and imagined the entire walk inside a ghostly landscape of grey Arcadia — one single grey mountain on which the Moon shines so flatly that even the smoothest ice appears rugged (like asphalt, whose tiniest crevices are exposed by the horizontal car flashlights running along them and filling them with tiny shadows of dust), and around, the air of immensely high mountains — cold, motionless air in which depth and dizziness, vertigo and solitude swing up and down like the piston rising & sinking in a glass cylinder; her girlfriend stands next to her and without one step or one move, without as much as one wrinkle crossing her face, she gives a long, screaming sound, the blind siren-whistle of fear, with no echo & no meaning, only an inner intensification: she would wail so in her dreams, with the burning-hot absolute of panic, when for example the face of a beloved acquaintance morphs into an unhinged mask; her smile, into a mechanical grin, her gestures into the angular & disjointed wriggling of a marionette (popping forth unexpectedly from idyll, death?). Her friend is screaming more and more, the clouds' billowing green vapors rush under their feet like the damned angels' windblown scarves in their rush headlong to hell.

the concept of 'loneliness' in childhood

At that time she knew loneliness only in this form: dark falls; they see that the stars are all at their feet and the mountain, on whose crest they stand, Lea & her girlfriend, has in fact no foot but hovers in the air like a forever ascending zeppelin. Lea was sweating profusely in this chase after grownupness, and she went wild with the sickly and inaugurating feeling of 'sadness': loneliness, horror, dizziness, one-directional movement, foreign perspective — from these elements she sketched into her consciousness her self-lacerating Ersatz-grownup watercolor, as the non plus ultra of the most picturesque terror. She wanted to see everything that was alien, grownup, and hostile in life, with mathematical clarity, in one single classical summarizing formula. To see loneliness: she impossibly enlarged the horizon and daubed it light green; the sun was yellow and diffuse, its lower rim full of cottonwool and gold algae, as if from the frosty hardness of the monologue-air the rays' straight lines had curled up into wild grape tendrils — its upper rim shone with a foreign light, with unimaginable aim and infinite non-essentialness — the entire light was like some cosmic obsession; perhaps God is mad and this is his mash of consciousness.

How can you make loneliness lonelier? Here there's no day and no night but the two together, as if different pages of the calendar lay scattered about. Somebody realizes after death that the whole sky is terrible deceit: the stars are rusty, the sky a tattered veil, and God is mad. But nevertheless eternity exists, moreover, infinity and madness are inseparable concepts. Life on earth is meaningful and logical only because it's finite. Lea had always been afraid of circus clowns: on this otherworldly landscape she transformed a clown's portrait into the sun, stars, sea. Here the shadows too have shadows, and those have shadows as well; the sea is nothing other than liquid glass, and liquid glass is shadow pressed to matter under the immense pressure of loneliness. Here loneliness does not culminate in singularity but in the countless multiplicity of the adversary. Everything wants to scare — singularity means an infinite number of horror-monads. The sun's green fluff-rays, the light's aimless luminosity which roams space unhindered and falls back invariably into its source, the waves' susurrus, the shadows' molten but strictly consequential raising-to-power: they all want to scare — as though the sum total of natural phenomena could be suffered only if ten, twenty, thirty thousand people watched them, divided them up into small parts, neutralized their accumulated fate-poison and madness, that pours on people with excessive force in solitude.

The most tormenting thing in this grand guignol theater (still meant to reconstruct the 'seriousness' of the grownups) was, that the whole universe turned against the lonely Leatrice with an utterly personal tendency, but at the same time also cleared her out of the way with contempt. Because even the remotest pink cloud wants to scare Lea, she almost pours over into that remote cloud, & the central feeling of loneliness will consist in the whole world being full to the brim with her singular body and soul, so that it cannot contract (thus loneliness is the horror-anatomy of our body, constructed from nature's primal elements): the madness consists in our dissipation into a thousand directions, like mercury droplets popping from a thermometer — we can't rest because our thousand arms' ten thousand fingers grope in unknown places in the midst of destiny's mendacious undergrowth.

Lea tries to close her eyes, but in place of her old child's eyes there is only a blue lake, on which mist splays in enormous blind haystacks — pink clouds whose billion rounded little side-forms would be enough to populate a new world with plastic ideas (pink is probably the most dreadful color in this landscape: it emanates irony, death, female charm, innocence & lunatic hypocrisy; this cloud made of gorgeous vapor-clusters could well be the parody of optimism, as it hovers ever higher above the night's flute-voiced lakes, like the bright and shameless nude of some 'Tomorrow' — but what is the point here of tomorrow, of future, of birth? although this pink cloud-tower is the embodiment of the feeling of tomorrow, the hope of tomorrow that swims in vain in eternity's praesens-jungle): in vain the memory of eyelids closing in the old days lives on in her will's impotent tension, like the past-framed shadow of a forget-me-not in a tautened silk scarf — she can't move the cloud's pink galley, the lake's ulcerous afternoon, the mist's moldy cotton stacks.

So the hostile lake, the hostile cloud, the hostile mist are her own body parts: it's herself she should fear and if she looks at her own hands she screams like the guignol figure whose hand was cut off by a machine and the doctor sew another man's hand in its place. This is the plenitude of loneliness. Is this then the grownups' world?

simile: a landscape on a German postcard, and a corresponding simile: the Berlin performance and stage setting of Kabale und Liebe

Once for Christmas she received German postcards illustrating the seasons on enormous landscapes: idyllic works of naïve painters replete with academic sentimentalism and precious salon-folklore, and yet it was on these pictures that Lea first felt the congestion of loneliness, the syllogistic hair band of infinity and madness, the eternal holler of death sounding from our own bodies like from an intricate but common musical instrument. On the picture depicting summer the wheatfield bulged a bit, as though it tried to give a measure of the roundedness of the globe itself; behind it another strip of land in darker brown, on which a cloud cast its shadow; to the right yet other fields in the most varied hues of yellow and brown, bowing into the gentle lap of perspective, as if vision were a magical breeze that bends objects into one sole drooping wave like mimosas: there was nothing refined about the images, space's cone thrusting into infinity was not torn into rugged distance-stairs or affected simultaneity: that's precisely the reason why it had such an overwhelming impact on Lea. Behind one strip of land there was the next one, behind that another, and so forth, as far as color could be diluted, as though the whole thing were the color advertisement to an idyllic Bavarian Gaea. The clouds too were listed in similar catalogue fashion one behind the other: in front of an enormous white foam-rose, followed by smaller balls with greying sides, and in the end only parallel dark strips.

The whole thing was close to the semblance of a map, like a mountain panorama: it was on the point where everything still retains its earthly reality, but one movement is enough to shift them into the map's abstraction. The illusion of infinity is never given by the horizon's inert dimness-blaze but on the contrary, by those all too visible hills, lakes, mountain-barricades and completed villages that succeed one another under our eyes — it is the scaled multiplicity of precision and not dimness that best suggests infinity.

Next to the lake, the sharp outlines of a sloping meadow, followed by a wood's black toothbrush, the grey-blue blot of a clearing, then the slanting houses of the village, its towers with their slanting shadows, the slanting streets (all uniform in their slanting: if the airplane turns over in the air, the whole world morphs into one slanting style with mathematical rigor), whose one side is tilted facades stretched to dry, and the other side, rooftops, bird nests, slate, frustum, shadow-mosaic, dry redness, two V-shaped book-tablets set on their edge; behind them, the river, which is nothing else but the scintillating and unexpected plagiarism of clouds and sky — like a 'foreign hand' in the uniform text of codices; next to it, a thin row of trees that looks like ten hairs blown upward, for otherwise they wouldn't manage to stand upright — their crowns are the floating and stuck dandelion (or milkweed?) fluff — but the landscape doesn't end here: the variegated coulisses of mountains follow, like in a scene of *Kabale und Liebe*[234] that she has seen in Berlin: on the left there was a giant rococo glass door ("rococo, it seems, was every bit as colossal as Egyptian architecture," she thought), the whole thing made of glass with gold-rimmed grey-white boughs here and there, as though barely-boughs on which the glistening material of glass is built (like soapy water that immediately stretches to a plane if it finds two wires for support) — behind this giant glass door there was another, a bit more yellowish and rendered more massive, but at the same time also more ethereal from the confusion of mirrorings, then a third and a fourth one, so when an actor approached he didn't crash abruptly before the audience but blossomed onto the stage gradually, along the visible pathway of space, of glimmering distance: one after the other he opened the glass doors, which jerked to & fro like revolving screens; the successive glass sheets built up a greyish-yellowish anatomy of space, crisscrossed by checks and powder-brush, as though the director tried to confer plasticity to spatial depth by X-rays; the doors' wooden parts were merely grey splinters that here and there managed to preserve their geometric purity (in one corner five or six identical ellipses were lined up behind one another, each one shifted one millimeter to the left, but under them the rectangles got raveled into that half-confusion which always results when we heap precise geometric shapes into whimsical disarray), so that we could read all the more clearly the infinity of the rococo corridor.

Had the corridor been built not of such clear-cut line-Versailles but from synthesizing shades, it wouldn't have been so limitless — here the source of pleasure was, that the fifth diminished door was still perfectly visible, like a village lying many kilometers from a mountaintop. In symphonies we can often detect a game where from a tragically distorted, passionately thrown-in theme at once a graceful melody is born — the violins almost gild with their buzz the shapeless torso that crashed in their midst like a meteor, and in those moments such manly-ambiguous phrasings of joy are born, which unite the chic of innocence and the grotesque of fatalism. The door series too behaved alike: the clear theme of the first large glass wall was worked into a serene, zigzagging lacework by the small perspective-epigones lined up behind; space was abuzz from the enmeshed lines, from the shrinking forms that nevertheless became ever more clear in their complexity.

On other stages such turns-of-phrase from old plays, like "I see my son approaching," would have made no sense, as no vistas opened beyond the stage in any direction — but here when the actor uttered the sentence above,[235] the audience could see the boy at an almost infinite distance, for the moment only as a cell that needs to perforate the layers of silently closing doors to develop into a full human; every single door stressed, singly and anew, his arrival, and in his person connected space's mystical duality:

the insulated geometrical steps, like transparent white underwater flowers that the water's two-sided and perfectly balanced pressure renders vertical; a petal or thread is swung from its place only by a fin stroke of the odd fleeing fish (the approaching actor sometimes vigorously swung a door, but thanks to the excellent springs it swung only a little in and out) — and melodic continuity, the incessant malgré-tout confluence above the isolated doors, that emanates from the corridor; when the actor finally pushed the last door out of his way, the one who stepped onstage was almost the personification of space, behind whom the line of doors still quivered with golden nervousness, to project his solitary figure far back into living space with the echo of perspective.

In the chaotic landscape that Lea would scare herself with and in which she tried to anticipate, with soon-tiring speed, the grownups' sickly lives, there was more of the exact theater coulisse and analytic listing than fog, black flame, or whale-bodied night; it was always rococo and never Blake (apart from the fact that Blake's naïve-Freudian staffage too is populated with neoclassical, gentle Greek figures, of which Halbert once spoke with quiet acrimony).

Of course this forcing of horror couldn't come close to the grownups' jaded world-weariness: it related to their low-spirited self-importance as the preliminary sketches of certain Biedermeier artists relates to the finished picture — the sketch is full of bloodstains, shredded lines, the shadows are ginormous flames, the movements swell with dramatic pathos, so one might easily take them for a first attempt at tragedy — but in the finished painting the bloody stain becomes a silky-furred lapdog, the shredded line, a pert little snub nose, and the whole tragedy, a plaster on a pimple.

The husband of one of her friends went mad with not knowing how to secure his money from any imaginable bankruptcy (without being stingy by character); at the same time he also had a mania of correctness, so he would detail to every living soul what a conscientious debtor he was. The net result being, that at a certain point a novel taxation was levied on him, where the exact amount to be paid was not yet established, so it was left at the debtors' discretion to decide the amount of the rates, in proportion to the suspected sum. Our man ended up paying huge sums blindly in order to be 'correct,' lest something should go wrong at the tax department. Leatrice, too, resembled this madman when she imagined the grownups' straightforward jadedness to be such dark ecstasy and prepared for it with oversize (overly correct) takings over.

Fifth Non-Prae *diagonal: the diary of the scholar-teacher of a noble family's children*

truth and moment
two plans: De Incongruentia Criteriorum;
 De Vacuis Perspectivis [236]
absolute emotion-life
intellect, emotion, objectivity
comparison to the lover: Diana-statue *under water*
the problem of reality in absolute only-emotion life
the dichotomy of body and sensuousness
the love letter, a melody fragment
the lover: will, therefore evil
annihilating objectivity
an evening walk, death
the theme project of The Honeymoon; *the lover is will, therefore evil*
the above illustrated by shopping for a bag: example of will
imagined happiness: the woman doesn't want him
the epistemology of happiness
sipping tea alone in the dark: philistinism and mysticism
ethical qualms
example of a short story for contrasting pleasure and moral

Sancta **Immediata**
the ethics of action
dressing up the terminally ill cardinal before the evening sermon
by car to the church, rain, crowd
pro domo: why is it that in this work a cardinal is found so
    often in the company of sin?
    — childishness
    — the reduction of the whole world to some abstract ethi-
        cal absolutes, temptation as foundational experience
the cardinal's counterpart: the little proselyte

(...What if? What if? Should I go to the blacksmith's for arms, to time the horses' run in the woods, to go, kill and conquer, or to pray that the patient in St. Andrew's hospital, in the room facing the garden, should die soon and I take his place, if apoplexy smites me sideways like a dropped knife a fancy cake's cream flourish? Will I be a hero or a patient? Sometimes I insert my body into the sunset, among the rigging lofts of pink question marks, to pry on the stirrings of my finger, the first red bruise of fever, like the sneaky opening of an evening flower, and when I feel all love and truth slowly go numb in my head, like ball-leather punctured with a needle, then I blame it on being the alien thorn of action in my veins that strives to pierce them like a murderer.

Because there are two death-paths, one is sickness, the other is action, one is neurasthenia, the other, heroism. Or is it? Is it? In any case I'm lost and I couldn't care much about who my successor will be. A short while ago I still lived in the healthy twilight of love and truth, now I'm up to my neck in their wilting clarity.

How curious: word spread that I'm a great scholar, the man of books, many saw me in the midst of the spread-open palm leaves of folios [I don't like the books which, when opened, fall flatly to the left and right, each page adhering perfectly to the next: my friends are those that open in relief, each page a swelling semicircle, each repelling *the next, each offering itself with a peculiar gesture, truth's gracefully upstart collars], so princes, counts, and bishops started inviting me to teach the children in their families. They believed I was the man of books, which was correct, but also woefully wrong. They never saw the moments when my fingers touched in the most ignoble way truth's ermine pudenda, for those happened in impossible times, early in the morning or late at night, and rolled out in deserted places where nobody would tread who is interested in science for the sake of knowledge.*

But these moments, smudgy and schlimazel-pudic inspirations would have been worth nothing, indeed perhaps they would not have been at all, if I hadn't squatted for the whole day on the grammar bedsheets of books, like a faint-hearted monkey in a thick bush. Whom did I betray with whom? Did I betray the stoical philosopher whom I read in the morning, when I nearly fainted from pleasure in the late afternoon on seeing, in late November, behind the faintly visible net of hoarfrost, blossoming in all its freshness, a flower that usually withers in early October? Or was I untrue to the midnight drop of water that I spied on from the fountain, as it fell on the lake and didn't merge into it but journeyed through its water like a transparent ringstone, a separate air-jewel [tritons' diamond: oxygen], slowly knocked against the shore [half tripping up, half soaked in], adhered to it with one half like the spongy tentacle of an octopus, and then disappeared, leaving behind the chemical formula and living statue of nothingness — was this 'pictorial insanity' a breaking of books? Shalt thou not desire meaningless beauty?

Before starting to teach these, now stiflingly burning [there are few who have watched to the end as fresh flowers burn in daylight with transparent flames], now glassy-luminous, children [perhaps cooled-out herbal teas served in flat wide cups], I was hardly preoccupied by the relation of my books to my forbidden moments [I call them forbidden because I felt that during study I enjoyed truth legally, luxuriating in 'the true' — but water-jotas and belated flowers were my taking advantage of the truth-instinct, my barren loves with unwholesome themes], but now that princes and bishops pay me exclusively for the hours spent in the library, the great dilemma of 'truth' comes to my mind. The book is solely meant to lead us into a completely unknown atmosphere, a lyrical floundering made up of pleasure and despair, where its every word lives on and its every truth shines more than ever, more blazingly than truth, and yet this very swooning acceptance of the book, this opium-faith is already an anti-bookish, truth-defeating, whimsical and flippant heresy. 'Truths' must be 'placed' exactly, in relation to our consciousness, because if they get too close to us, they are lost: they become so clear, so necessary, they pour into the spine of our lives as substitute spinal chord, as to become life, energy, and that is destruction, dance, mendacity. All evidence reaches the point of absolute chaos when it becomes too evident.

There's a crude fiction about geniuses, where the dichotomy above between 'book' and 'moment' [to put it briefly] is as a rule reduced to the uninteresting dichotomy of learnt truth and individually created truth, although, as we can see, nothing could be further [I'm not boasting, I'm copying an announcement: nunc invitamus celeberrimum genium urbis nostrae[237] *— now when I'm standing in front of the two dark gates of heroism or sickness, ingeniousness is for me a forgotten confirmation name, dying-out handicraft], it all comes down to the dichotomy of evident and hyper-evident truth. I did not abjure or supplant the learnt truths, but on the contrary, I have horribly accepted them. Now when I teach them I can't believe in them so completely — but this feeling has of course nothing to do with doubt.*

But am I really teaching them? In the afternoon I sat with a blond little boy in a corner by the praying desk among pillows, everything was violet, and I watched his face as his unknown intellect radiated toward me with quiet certitude, while I was sending toward him the books' content. Did this blue-eyed head and the Greek axioms meet? By the time my book-truths reached him, that head, that whole soul had long left its place and swayed, big rustling violet, by the buoy of my two eyes. Did I teach? For the first time in my life I was learning with genuine humility, when I heard the boy's thin voice and saw his barely-yet-feelings stirring, like the pages of some illicit reading funnel-shaped from hiding under the desk. The boy's face and book-foreign life appeared to resemble my 'moments,' when I was likewise filled with the atmosphere of 'precise secret,' but it was essentially other. In the latter anti-truth, rampant irrationality was still reason's reverie, the nihil flashing forth from hyper-evidence was nevertheless dry positivism — but the secret emanating from the child was devoid of this joy and pedantry.

Is truth necessary? Not for this child: his whole life is a snail-shell, combative virginity against knowledge and truth, whereas I, every time I am overmuch filled with one truth, end up dropping it. Truth is perhaps an entirely primitive means of transmission from alpha-nothing to omega-nothing, or rather, not a means of transmission but simply something 'other' than universal secret, so that the secret may somehow be noticed. We both felt the hypocrisy of learning: when our heads bowed over the common reading we felt that for us the book became meaningless. The sweaty shapelessness and flowery impertinence of my moments meant health: I was not consumed by problems; the questions were no agony blots.

I was made an athlete by secret and nonsense, and truth pushes me into the most flabby neurasthenia. Because if we don't busy ourselves with truth in order to be able to, in the odd moment of hyper-faithfulness, drive a knitting needle into our nipple straight to the heart, but in order to pass them on, then truth will take on perverse forms: not sinful but sickly ones. Truth never stays put in our souls but keeps morphing, whether we want it or not. And this metamorphosis is accompanied by another truth-awareness, more formal than the theme-riddled first one, and that second is accompanied by a third, a fourth one, and so on.

Of course theme and form are merely approximate words here, the thing itself is made of much more cunning fabric. Will I get to write my planned work: De Incongruentia Criteriorum? There I wanted to expose that, whenever the place of a truth is taken by another, then *in fact our overall concept of the truth has to change, in such cases we speak about fully rational modulations: it's not 3 taking the place of 2, or b taking the place of a, but some non-number taking the place of number, some non-letter taking the place of letter, and when some yet newer thing takes the place of the non-letter or non-number, the whole constellation will change again. When I look at the book and its truths during teaching I feel that they are true as far as truth is concerned, but that in existence it's about something wholly other than one thing being true or not true. Here I use a blurred criterion in judging truth, for it stands completely outside the circle of true and not true, and yet it is nevertheless a kind of truth-excitement. All we have is such layers of excitement, every excitement is a whole system in itself, universal perspective, which are of course linguistically or conceptually inexpressible. De Vacuis Perspectivis: this could be the follow-up to the first treatise.*

Eliminating truth doesn't mean the introduction of irrationality, but the installing of a far broader and different concept of truth [of course this is a paradox affair], which [due to linguistic and crude thought-technical reasons] is empty, more formal than formalism itself, and is moreover the taking to excess of the philosophical idea of 'form.' I have perhaps never been so much prey to my drives as today, when I am writing with such scrupulousness about truth. I took up the pen to reinforce myself in emotion, to accept as a style of life the intellect-less, giant-blind vegetation into which I have sunk, and lo, I'm already mechanically rubbing myself up against thought. Even though it's this white-livered hither-and-thithering that I should tolerate least of all — I must drink up unsweetened the black soporific of non-knowing. What will become of me if I don't think? A patient or a hero? Because the edge and number of my love depends solely on that.

What does the only-emotion life mean to the one who has bathed for so long in the light green thermae of truth? First and foremost, that nothing in the world wants my life, there is nothing interested in the least in my life being happy, or in my life being at all. Before I started teaching, every single dark & untanned leaf, every single fishing boat floundering in the bay meant a thought, it illustrated something, or there was something to illustrate it immediately, so it would neatly integrate into some panorama of expediency. Now I learned for the first time to look deep into the eyes of such a leaf as it hangs, inert, in the middle of the night, like the clapper of a wadded bell, and doesn't resemble any kind of thought, doesn't induce in me any kind of ratiocination, I don't want to use it for some describable synthesis; it stands alone, with the walnut-odored asceticism of indifference and hostility, letting it transpire that we don't need each other in the least.

Philosophy, and all kinds of intellectual work, tends to idyllicize everything the moment it touches them: for now, when I describe my perfect lack of erudition during leaf-gazing, I'm idyllicizing by naivizing-into-a-problem. Idyllicize, naivize: let bad prose's gauche rhyme clatter like a Lent rattle in this anguished abandonment, into which I was hurled by only-emotional life. We have plucked you, solitary leaf, of all teleology, as one cleans the sugar from the diabetic patients' food, and now we are left on our own.

Can an emotion that is a genuine emotion be suffered by human beings? I have no time for thinking now, only for teaching and feeling: there's no darker double-decker intrigue in the world than solid artificial truths and virgin emotions. What use to an old coquette if by miracle she reverts to her virginity: she's left with all her wrinkles, all her memories are dense as the orange-lacquered dahlia balls, she just happens to be a virgin, untouched in the purely medical sense.

This is lyricism for me: the blindness of my emotions is an anatomical accident, not a psychic necessity. A thought always has a direction, but a feeling never, so the one who can rely only on feelings loses his place in the world. The black leaf on the tree: its darkness wraps itself around me like a serpent-shaped ring on a yellow column, I have no idea why. Does it have any cause against me, or was it I who was looking for a tighter belt around my waist? Its smell is heavy like a die sinking into the wax, and I'm feeling, distraught, the unasked-for badge of its smell on my soul's pusillanimous walls. Should I suffer it?

or resist it? but if I don't know what it is? When it rustles in the wind I don't know if its mask slipped in flight, or if a stolen kiss' coral trickled down by mistake through the keyhole of the night?

I may well be an old snob who equates emotion & ignorance. Of course I keep an eye on my style and from what I see, it clearly shows the mix of desperate baroque and eerie lucidity so characteristic of dreams. It seems that metaphor remains the most obstinate handle on life's immured door: on touching it we can feel the unknown's reptile-cold and the homely form of easy-to-manage truth. Once I dreamt something similar: I leaned out from a low railing and felt with my fingers the territory lying beyond — it had a human form, the familiar outlines of faces, eye-sockets, ears, mouth openings, but the whole thing was wide, almost infinite, like a landscape, from the facial features yet another nose, yet another mouth-roll followed logically, so the whole seemed even more face-like, and when under a hazy grey light I finally spotted the whole, all I could see was an undulating hill-and-valley territory, sand cones and oval puddles, nothing resembled in the least a portrait or the fragments of a portrait. This was the didactic theater of metaphor: metaphor, too, unites in this manner the cowardice of truth and the gladiola arrogance of nothingness.

This is merely falsifying it, of course: in pure emotion there is only nothingness — how can I put it? I get up in the morning, look out of my window on the trees and know that today I won't mind them, for I will be teaching botany to one of the boys. And then this new temptation starts from them — because I can be in no relation whatsoever with them, they penetrate me deeper than on earlier occasions when I painted them or made verses of them, when they were comparisons in some ladder-dry metaphysics or firestone-ideas in a mannered-blasé natural history. Now these trees finally keep their original faces, in particular one of those midnight black leaves that is fat like an Anacreontic worm and shiny like a prayer-book's leather: I look, look, look at it and nothing comes to my mind, it doesn't inspire me to anything.

This is what I call feeling: the barren, cynical-times-cynical objectivity of things. Do they keep their faces? By the fact that every intellectual image trickles off them, like ink-stained sins under baptism, in fact they keep changing: I first look at the green veins as on things of mathematical or geometrical interest, later the green and the vein become merely meaningless perceptions, I don't know that this is a color, much less that it's a special color, I only let it impress upon me. There can be no difference between nominalism and realism: if the name 'green' is shed from green, the green must change — for two months now I've been looking on its comma-face 'uncultivatedly,' forgetting everything — forgetting that there are such things as perceptions, forms, plants in the world at all: I think that vastly altered the leaf's image. This objectivity, this emotional solitude, this is utter change: the three things, with very likely ill-suited names, always go together, are in fact one.

So feeling and thinking mean two opposite directions on the same level: thinking always adds something to the leaf, amasses words on words — while the feeling always forgets something of the leaf, subtracts word from word. 'Objective cognition': self-contradicting turn-of-phrase, because objectivity lies in the direction of feeling [equals: forgetting], while cognition lies in that of autonomous language. Man is of course infinitely forsaken among such funereal leaves which are objective to the point of emptiness: black aspirates of an alien intention. But I accept this purgatory, for no one can think in truly thought-shaped thoughts who has not intuited, with what glass face the world walks behind the cheap draperies of thought.

It's important to feel the two dichotomies: the one, of which I spoke first, is the dichotomy of book and moment, the struggle of intellectual truth and truth felt to be too true [this was in my 'erudite' period]; the other: truth positivated-to-death for the purpose of teaching [which is no longer truth but merely a schema tailored to the brain] and feeling, by which I mean the infinite senselessness of the things of the world, their being-madly-objects. Schema and hyper-object: now, how can we fit in, between these two 'uncultivated' poles, the ship of love? [For after all I'm writing a love poem.]

Now as I'm standing at the apex of the chance-villa of heroism & sickness, you too, my love, ceased to be the threadball of clever relations. So far you have been like a Diana statue submerged under water — your color all March-green, clearly visible, the downward perspective easing your musical score-crowning forms. But for months now you seem to be slowly emerging from the water, and those parts of your body that passed into the air's silver prose-caustic glow with a light blue as if lit from within with a blue bulb, but your glass-body is so thick that the light looks more color turned to kiss than electricity. Because of the thickness of the glass the blue lighting means three layers: deep inside your chest [this is the place of the lamp in your inner hollow] a dull-white incandescence, followed by the glass' barely-blue Swedish-eye, and finally, on the glass' edges, for instance on your breasts' Koh-i-noor bud, a sharp, glaring blue; white, barely-blue, ultra-blue, this is perhaps an important distinction in the dermatology of 'objectivity.' It's beautiful to watch when an otherwise empty nude strips more, taking off not clothes now but intellectual perspectives; of course this kind of nakedness doesn't really deserve the name nude.

Under water the pudicity-stalk of your knee and shoulderblades were clearly visible, but you were surrounded by the waves' [however transparent] optical ornaments: your brassiere was visible distance, your belt, a dancing color designed of natural signs cancelling accidentals, your mantle a weight sinking in cubic foot. In the differences between water and air the most exciting thing is, that both are transparent, empty, abstract and nixemeral, and yet the water is a thousandfold more positive than its more diluted counterpart. When I had 'thought' of you, my love, you were already lying in the full rhetorical armor of secret on our hidden nuptial beds, but now that I forcefully lost the mere possibility of thought, you are ultimately unknown: not that I don't know your character, but I no longer understand the fact of knowing, of cognition, I can't recognize cognition. Your new nude: flirtatious epistemological lapsus.

You were standing motionless under the water and yet, because of the downward perspective, you seemed to be faintly drifting in a molto cantabile direction: not due to the waves' infinitely little movement, for they were pulsating in disorder, thus there was no question of the cantability of the direction, but simply due to the fact of perspective — with you the water played no other part than to render vision, looking-at-you, a separate material. And vision is an eternal wave that drifts from the eye toward its object. When you surfaced from the pond's vision-silks, this ended: in the air [although here you indeed moved incessantly] you appeared to stand motionless, vision didn't crystallize. For this is true objectivity, when you are sight-ee without looking & seeing, blue virgin in the air.

I'm blind down to the last moment: my imagination, eyes, the distances between us are blind — only when I clash onto you on the last micron-bridgelet do you become visible all of a sudden, and without any vision-preliminaries. Under the water you were more material than now, in the air, although now every detail of your surface can be seen better, glass, stone, marble in their fidelity — and yet all this is in vain, for it is now that you became a spectral formula. If an actor standing in a dark corner of the stage is suddenly lit with a strong light, he will not be any more human, his face any more flesh- and skin-like but rather, more airy, akin to a phantasmagoria in the operating theater. Your legs are still underwater, locked between dark green concubine rails: I still have epistemological memories of you that I would now like to use, not as though I overestimated the fact of knowledge in the moment of loss, but because I'm infinitely weak and feverish and need the envied images of health.

Around you night sets like the irreversible, one-directional movement of the physicist, and you are bluer than ever: pond, trees, sky, railing and stars are all black, but you glisten in your quadratic-equation nakedness above the water. The content of the word 'outside' is never fomented into its meaning with such gnoseological mordancy as in the case of a statue above the water: here it's felt to the fullest that being-outside is not a topographic definition but a theological value signal. My dear love, you are outside everything — perhaps you don't even know this technique of seduction that you now exercise on me: to be annihilated by your reality's reality. I see you from one day to the next, I wipe the deaf monogram of your kiss into my handkerchief, lest my disciples notice on my face the lipstick's misspellings, but all this is only 'some thing' for me: from the rational point of view, next to nothing, and from another point of view (incongruentia criteriorum!), everything. Utter clarity and utter incomprehensibility, these too are love exercises. 'Some thing': the image of this excessively puritanical and exciting trait of yours is found there in the slowly rising statue — as it rises from the water minute by minute one can't notice at all that it takes up some space in the pond which is now emptied, and where water can now intrude: the moment your arm rose above the water it seemed that water was already in the arm's place when the arm was still down under water; that is, the arm couldn't be reality if water didn't register its presence. This is the most precise diagnosis of objectivity: hard stone arm [excess-object] and in its place mute water, there forever, without the mark of the arm [never-object].

You too stand before me now: more body than the body and yet, you have no place, life, something. Because in the air we don't feel the statue's 'place': it had a place only in the pond, or at least that's the only place where it could have a place, but we see that water is there, silent, all-filling water. Does physics fail here — statue and water were there at the same time? Outside the water the statue has ab ovo no place, there it only 'is': in my old life, my dear love, you had a 'place' [this is thought], now your only feature is 'is' [this is feeling]. Of course, the 'place' is clothes, the 'is' is nakedness. What a beauteous and tormenting world, in which it turns out that hyper-object & emotionalism are the same: the trees almost eat themselves into darkness' Böcklin-blankets,[238] sky, shells, garden paths all glide with 'mit Verschiebung'[239] key signature, by quint-steps, into marble-composed silence, and you alone shine with unknown light that is not a spark and not a filtered ray, it doesn't spread one millimeter beyond itself, although it incandesces — a Hartmannesque new disguise, my love.[240]

So one half of the couple became ultimately unapproachable because of complete openness: the above-water nakedness added to underwater nakedness as the second flat accidental to a note that already has a flat marking. My dear ♭ ♭ friend — how is your lover, where am I? You have already evaded from all humanity, but where can I find myself?

Myself: by this I mean of course not the totality of my life, its artistic living-out or any such folly, but some very modest minimum, the point with the help of which I can stand among the other people. By this sharp estrangement into reality's transfiguration, of woman and black leaf, I of course completely liquefied, an altar boy serving on the threshold of sickness & action. The whole reality inspires me to action; action is the only pathway that smuggles our souls to things, bypassing thought. The source of the great action can be only this rabid realism: the blue fairy-statue above the water is surrounded by a high-tension repelling zone — if I try to approach, the invisible force repels me, so I run around it, groping the air: this eternal beating against the invisible force, against objectivity's negative-charged virginity sphere, the eternal trials & hypothesis-grimaces around the untouched blue Diana — this is action. The source of will is the thought, the source of action is not the will but the very impossibility of the will, the desperate wriggling of the soul among realities lapsed into reality-excess.

I was left alone with my body, with my inner organism: is it not sickness that I see you, my love, only as a blue statue, and myself as a mere compilation of blood circulation, vein rigging, and inner gills? Bodily body-awareness is the greatest enemy of sensuousness: when you press your eager kisses on my face, like a four-leaf shamrock into an album, I give an all too bodily reaction with blood pressure maps, breathing legatos, the panting sluices of heart chambers, therefore there is no carnal pleasure at all in my reaction. Sensuous body-awareness is never body-awareness, the theme of the pleasure-nerves is an abstract, out-of-body tune accompanied by the 'body's' artificial pseudo-concept with cheap chords.

So I'm alone with my anatomy [this, as I said, is already a sickness] and I'm alone with the rambunctious springs of meaningless motion [this is the introductory stage of heroism]. Everybody around me is a humanist, and I'm too much of a coward to dare draw openly any de-humanist conclusions from my experience: among my memories I'm looking for those in which I can see myself thinking and see my love for you, my turquoise-scaled concubine.

You have probably no inkling of what a huge change happened in me from the moment I started to have time only for teaching. You don't know that for the first time you became reality and I want to escape you. The only lock that ties us more or less together is that I see gestures mirrored in your eyes, & in your words about me to others, my thinking past, when my body used to be a fiction, humanism's arbitrary imprint, and therefore always ready to accommodate pleasure. One of the main secrets of your body is that it seems to brim with passion, while I felt in it only the doggedness of a dry will. You live a disorderly life, you eat irregularly, sleep at impossible hours, you are fashionable and slovenly, like a fourth-rate actress, and yet beneath all of that one can find a single housewifely will to order.

'Don't take this as criticism, consider that in love criticism and adoration coalesce so much and they are crude only if expressed. You live with your will, and this will wants me: my body, my life, which is here now as it used to be in the old days. Your sensuousness is nil, your wanting my body is merely the dry positivism of will. Your Sapphic ecstasy is the joy of bankers when at the end of the day the balance is square.

Sometimes I pry on you by your window: your unkempt hair flows freely on your shoulder, as if in the first moment it were already flowing in the second, in another key, and the chief joy were comparison with the first; on your knees my effigy, on your face absent-mindedly daubed, glaring make-up, in your eyes some kind of prickly, well-nigh malicious

*curiosity toward my image, as though you saw it for the first time —
and now you cover it with kisses, jump up and sing like a madwoman
and yet I know that this is not passion. Passionate love doesn't need
the other so much: your every kiss is like a foolish colored-beauteous
banner, but stuck at the end of an infinitely long pole — I feel the pole's
hardness. But this alone is beautiful.*

*Could it be that you sucked out my health? Luxurious women
never wear out the male body, but male-wanting women all the more
so. My health, like a pilfered flower, is on you. Go and laugh, laugh
aloud, for who on earth has heard about such a scrawny lover who
demands his strength back from the woman? Twice amusing: first, for
being 'worn out' by love-making in the first place, and then, for going
so far as to ask back those puny energies. And I speak of standing before the kalendas of heroism... Of course I find nothing comical in the
fact that love wears me out, but my friends don't know about this, it's
in their names I invited you to have a laugh. I carry this fatigue like a
mauve robe that shows to the world that I have passed the hard trial of
kennership. I have few other impressions beside fatigue & drowsiness.*

*My spine feels like a defect thermometer into which they forgot
to pour mercury: an empty tube that shows nothing. After one of our
walks I'd like to sleep for days and after a lovemaking, to withdraw
to a sanatorium. The cripple and schnook, too, is entitled to share his
experience once in a while. But there was a time when I was not a
cripple, and I'm looking for that time in you. My sucked-out strength
floats in your enclosed garden like a stolen swan: with the most primitive materiality I feel that it is on you, perhaps in the greenhouse safe
of abortions. My strength was never equal to my self — how much this
is the case I realize only now as I look at the swan. You have hidden it
well: the pond is surrounded by tall, warm grass, like combs softened
by heat; behind them, very large water plants, iris-covers and flying
bullas, which hide the swan's glaring feathers with shocked pudicity.*

*The exhausted can resort only to metaphors: this is his psychic
orthopedics. His muscles are all askew or lame in a zigzagging line,*

there is no object in reality or in memory that he could grasp, thus he needs special handles [empiricism-inserts] that conform to the inner graph of degeneracy, and for this purpose such a fictitious, yet life-giving swan is perfect. Such triads have to be immortalized: for me you are no more than abstract will and foreign excess-reality, and I as stolen and lost strength am present as your swan-shaped tenant.

My unmanly whimper over my lost strength can easily look like the torpid follow-up to the snivel over lost virginity, although I believe it's not. In my early childhood I knew first bodily comfort and not carnal pleasure as the utmost bodily bliss. My parents and relatives always enjoyed and made me enjoy slippers, soft armchairs, long afternoon naps, warm teas [not in porcelain but in glass, so that the dark yellow warmth remained visible throughout] and fireplaces, and I can't forget that. Perhaps in the following I'll touch on something similar, so to say the demonics of philistinism, but it's only a reflex movement and not a genuine thought.

You were far from comfortable, my love: you made me walk in woods steaming with rain, you tore out for yourself the quiet hours of my life, like the color illustrations you liked from a book, and then threw the book back with the ugly tongues of tearing. Your clothes weren't comfortable either. If I looked for my comb it was enough to put my hand in my pocket with a next-to-no-movement, but when I was looking for the yellow trophy of your shoulder, first I had to pull the whole blouse from right to left, then carefully unbutton the skirt somewhere below, unfasten the belt, fold aside the collar with great care to not stretch it, and after all these annoying maneuvers a small bit of your shoulder appeared in a crippled fashion, for you barely managed to stick it into the mingy crater of snap fasteners: on old Madonnas one can see such laughable little breast-orbs flashing out of dressed-to-excess waists, seen through a buttonhole like a figure that peers out from a barometer.

Pleasure and comfort signify two opposite poles; I don't know people but I wouldn't be surprised to discover that by a law of nature *the great debauchers don't love comfort, whereas the great far nientes avoid pleasure. Some time back in my thinking period I might have written a fugato from themes such as 'pleasure is self-torture,' but today I find all expression vanity. I remember our first being together in the spring wood: I would have liked to lie down on the meadow, look up at the sky, fidget a bit with the grass above my eyes, but you flourished your thin black clothes like a stoical lesson. It's not that I didn't want you, on the contrary, you were verily squeezed in the taut nutcracker between will and spring — but I felt that pleasure was not a bodily good but an alien, funereal bliss. Just as bitter and sour stand at an equal distance from sweet, so self-torture and pleasure stand at equal distance from bodily good.*

Everybody was glad that I went for an outing in the gorgeous weather and all were sad when I returned home: my eyes were sunken like a thin cork into a flaring-necked bottle, my skin was leaden like the flesh of an apple if we don't wipe the knife while cutting it up — my every muscle ached and after lunch I dreamed of railway catastrophes and car accidents.

Once I slept through the whole afternoon and when I woke up I thought that I was either dead or had indigestion, and a letter from you lay on the cover — the most beautiful love letter I can imagine. It was such an absurd cantilena of joy like those scores running in extremely high octaves, where the staff remains empty for several beats, while every note is written above the fourth ledger line: this letter and your whole soul were entirely empty and the joy resounded somewhere outside both letter and soul, on a humanless ponticello.[241]

Where is happiness, or, more in general: what is? Like a steamed stamp, from my eyelids the morning landscape folded back slowly, the time-anchors tying it to today having long broken off: starched celestial light with ferns' freckled fans, a few egg-yolk flowers and trill-screw birds. In contrast there was the untimely dream's blanket-brown world, my mouth's salty stomach taste; sleep unifies the body: it takes the mouth and stomach to be one opening, complete with esophagus, so when you spoke of kisses, I looked toward my stomach. The letter preserved my old decenteredness, you spoke of my mouth, but it ceased to be long ago. I had no fingers either, only one big rheumatism from my nails to my shoulder blades: how curious is this swift parody of sensuousness immediately after the kiss — the body changes from the first nap like the most glaringly colorful blouse into black sorrow-gauze in the workshops of express funerary painters. And between this bright morning and my simplified chemicalized body stood your black figure, the slender mast of will, the obstinate literalist of love, its cold anagram. Letter-joy? Will? Body? Dream? Where shall I go? In your light blue letter paper I saw that I was the cause of your joy, so I tried to record it. I forgot everything and lived solely from the letter and for the letter.

I felt that joy was the most mendacious portrait anyone could make of me, but it was a welcome reparation for my lost comfort. Then I learnt the method I am now employing with that poor amateur swan: to relish in your joy my treacherous portrait. Once after we parted on your doorstep I spied on you through the window. I was tired and cross with you for luring me out into the bad weather, away from my books, which I can only get to for a few semi-demi-minutes in months. You threw your coat on the divan and sat down to the piano. You hammered the keys wildly, with all the childish grace and all-too-serious defiance of shrewish improvisation, and sometimes mused like one who is looking for a theme, played it softly, carefully, so that I couldn't hear it through the window, you jotted it down on the speedily prolonged staves of a score that happened to lie about, then returned to playing in chiming and broken chords. I knew it was me, that I was the cause of your joy. I faced these unveiled chords and inaudible recorded theme as a stranger who happened to be me, or rather, with whom I was mistaken. Narcissus never knew this better love: to hear scales and sweet melodies in which to recognize himself as a conquering stranger.

Isn't this the only possible form of love for me: to perceive the joy I induce in another as a strange person or object [swan?], and to worship it? So I had lots of melodies in my hand: my new self. I had no strength [opus amoris unum],[242] because it metamorphosed into concrete music living outside me. The feeling was not serene in the least, but ghostly: in vain I sat down by my green stove at home, in vain I relished too-silent silence, as though drinking tea with one sugar cube too many — in my ears my own existence resonated in precisely definable major or minor, playable anytime, anywhere. Had I heard these aria-torsos played on the piano elsewhere, I might have fainted in panic. I was very curious to see your jotted-down idea of a theme, so I sent a girl to you, a childhood acquaintance, because you made no mention of it to me.

I waited for the shred of paper at home, trembling with fear. The girl didn't bring me any pages but whistled the melody with her pubertal, unripe plum-color mouth. How can I blossom when I'm as good as dead? The theme was so beautiful that I decided to disappear for good from your sight, lest you might notice that your music-flower has no roots in me. It was like one sole electric candle left burning on one of the hundred-branch chandeliers of a vast castle. I ardently wished back the months when I was not yet teaching 'true' things to high-born boys, when I still had strength to waste on you. In the last period I rarely visited you and preferred to send my old acquaintances to you, knowing that you would talk about me, about the living and not the present-day me, and in the evenings I untie their tongues. I called my past strength that you kept, a flower, swan, electric candle — I heard it as green-footed chromaticism. And it was good as it was: because in my fantasy the nostalgic image of my youth kept with you became ever more exotic. And it is the most strident now when I leave you: my body is nearly dead; the strength sucked out from me is nearly a paradise of Eve.

Somebody said that the age of allegory was coming again — let me be a paper-thin stair on its ascending way, so I plunge into the nihilistic diptych — you: blue statue towering-from-water in objectivity's suicidal furore — I: in the shape of my lost pubertal strength, of a tropical garden alien from me and blossoming in you. Love. But I believe I am much more in you than this lost strength. I remember, shivering *and cowardly, our last evening walk together. Our steps were slow and clumsy from the soapy magnet of the unpredictable night mud, we took the flowerbeds for paths, sometimes we rose all of a sudden, like the mermaids of the Rhine in the opera,*[243] *when we stumbled upon huge heaps of autumn leaves. You told me that you wanted nothing else in the world but me. You narrowed your eyes to a slit, shook your head here and there, muttered apologies, halted, pulled off your large bootglove, fidgeted with one of my buttons, saying 'I don't know … I don't even want God.'*

Our long dialogue played out in pitch darkness, so I always added imagined face mimicry to your words — from blown-up leftover leaves, from the boughs' melancholy 'matelassé,'[244] *as they wove themselves into the fog, in general from the details of the garden, so that the autumn's large shadows served your tiniest asides: when you uttered, shy and stifled, that for you God has no meaning, all of a sudden the light of a garden candelabra fell on you and I could see your real face mimicry. One eye looked as if glued together, visibly trembling as it tried to open, and your mouth twitched to the side like when you are served untasty food in a restaurant and inspect it with a sneer, impatiently fidgeting with the now redundant fork, yet in spite of all the puny hypochondria and womanly prosaicness of your face I could detect infinite sorrow being crumpled in you, like a shred of paper absent-mindedly kneaded into a ball in our pocket. This face mimicry was altogether different from the one I lent you.*

After that we again entered the dark and you continued your declaration, in which you spoke only about how I was God for you, and you were unable to live without me. If I should go, you will die. You uttered the word death in the dark, so I could again supplement it with the garden's wet ancillae: to our left was a wide pond with a small artificial island in the far center with a five-columned toy shrine and dim pendant lamp. My clothes were wet from the mist and my palate sour from the thick steam of the fallen leaves. Either I, or death. When you said that for you I was God, I wanted to flee from you with such primal force that for a moment I believed there were years and countries between us. If you can say that without me you'll die, it means you must have been dead for a long time.

And I? I'm a thousand times more dead than you, being undefinably distant to everything. Moreover [the strange chemistry of your stubborn woman-alternative]: I felt not you but only myself to be dead. Either I or death: but even in the midst of my greatest devotion there lurked some foreignness, so for a long time already I can't have meant other than death to you. You now take me to be God, that is, the livingmost opposite of death, even though I can only mean death for you. Is this then love? To keep forever stumbling into the boorish concepts of God and death? White light shone from the small island with a disproportionate and maladroit ruggedness. Death and I were alternatives, so the two were separated in your head as two arriving guests are separated by the wings of a hotel's revolving door, and yet I felt myself to be one with death and was seized by a strong death-fear. You continued my apotheosis with such stubbornness as though you were playing a wild fingering exercise with runs up and down, in counterpoint and canon — while all I heard was the word death, forgetting alternatives, and the fact that you spoke of your, your, your death.

Perhaps this is the only possible female function: to rain on us the deity's November mantle and immediately afterward to flick into the air death's stage fan. If I stay by the woman, I'll save her life, feeling all the while that I am carrying the complete cause for another person's death; it's enough if I make a small move and somebody will die that instant. Does it make sense then for you to speak about your death? For it is a greater death-fullness to be a permanent, lurking death-cause, than a real dead. It is a secondary matter, which of us can lay claim to more 'true' death: in any case there is with us, between or on us, some kind of deafening rabidity. Was this what I imagined? Was this what I wanted when all my childish desire was that a woman should return my love? That she should render me at the same time God and a cause of death? Is it easy to suffer the dizzying arc of my life, the shore of which was philistine comfort, & its first pillar in the unknown waters: my own death-bearing?

There was hardly any talk of woman or love-making: in the beginning cushions, teas, stoves, and tales in the armchair on my grandfather's lap, and after a few years, the awareness that I could kill a woman, that I'm poison. But I should be consoled: I am also God. You are far more courageous than I, you dared place from the first the blue flowers of kisses and the green lance-leaves of lovemaking into the murderous vases of death and God. Contrarily, I wanted to lure love into the childhood nursery-realm of comfort: to draw a forget-me-not flourish on my bed from your eyes, to heap velvet squirrels and droning teddy bears on your shoulders, to play with toy soldiers cross-legged on the floor, but you wouldn't hear about it and performed instead the 'reductio ad mortem' at the second step.

For most boys love turns into asceticism because they contract some disease from ethereal Lanvin nymphs, are tormented by indifferent women, dread brain tumors if their desire shreds sparks alone, get impoverished because of green hats: to me it became asceticism because I was wanted much, humbly, & yet selfishly. Probably this too is a very common form of asceticism, but because I'm only a child, I haven't yet encountered it elsewhere. Summa summarum: I'm awfully proud of having ended up so fast in the atmosphere of death. I can imagine this too under the title Honeymoon: to spend with you the first days of our marriage in a gorgeous villa in a lovely park [the Geneva La Grange?]. All flowers, sun, rattling shutters and rare fountains, and you speak to me of how I'm everything for you, your life, death, god, food & father, with such dark precision & nihilistic determination that for me flowers, suns, and fountains were instantly annihilated.

Perhaps you are mad. You are certainly mad. And I have to learn the most macabresque forms of happiness. Outwardly you are not hysterical: you don't embrace me with knotted muscles and don't kiss me with a biting mouth — it's in your thinking that darkness resides. It's not to say I didn't worship you just as darkly, but I'm far too much of a coward to dare admit it. And the park of La Grange fills with the melancholia of the courage originating in you. Slowly you go mad indeed, but neither you nor I notice it — I almost have the impression that you become more lucid by the hour. Or is it I who am slowly going mad?

If two people see only each other, they have no instruments of measurement for sanity — you are already saying completely unhealthy things and I still take them to be positive womanly truths, because [benevolent little boy that I am] I want to get used to the fact that love is no illustration to Alice in Wonderland but death's paraphrase composed for two instruments: I'm training. I would never have expected such difference between two states of yours — when you are infinitely happy from me, and when you want me very much. I relished your joy and naïvely had no inkling that it already includes this womanly death-thought. For the word death was dreadful not because it brought to mind real death, your corpse or mine, but because I felt death in your hands to be stolen metaphysics, foreign goods: death is no more womanly than weapons. When men speak about death, the warm and steamy boiling water-smell of transience emanates from them like the most natural exhalations, a flower-shaped breath in the cold air above the lips: with you it was a brand-new object bought only an hour before.

I remember mentioning in passing a round, red handbag I saw in the center in the morning: that afternoon we should have met by one of the Roman fountains outside the city, but I waited for you in vain. In the evening we had to meet again at a dinner given by a bishop, where a couple and an old gentleman were also invited. There too we waited for you in vain, so we started dinner. We sat in the midst of a vast, cold marble hall with no windows, no chandelier, no rugs, only three fat but nearly transparent candles on the table.

In the midst of the dinner the door opened, we couldn't see yet which, this baroque ice chamber was so cold, but we could hear the gauche drums of a woman's shoes. In the next moment I glimpsed the huge red handbag and one moment later, you. You came rushing through the vast hall, straight like an arrow, so you missed the table's direction — you needed to take a turn at the last moment [after an infinitely held high aria note, the lapse back into breathing] to find your way to us. You preferred to let me loaf around by the old fountain [how many times I could decipher: CAEL. AQUAR. FONT. BRUGI. II.],[245] you would rather offend the company, but you hunted down the handbag that very day. Later that night after dinner, when I reproached you, you hardly paid any attention and said in passing that you love me the way you want to, even if you hurt me, even if I should hate you for it: but ever since you found out that I liked it, that bag disturbed your mind and you had to have it through thick and thin. You were sweaty and tired, but the bag hung from your hands with the jeering of a ruddy scalawag. First and foremost it was alien, there was still a shop air about it and nothing yet of you. Nothing of you? Did the stubbornness of will, the well-nigh love-destroying defiance of your all too 'individual' love not originate in you?

Foreign object and naked will: this is what I learned from your shopping, and that's what I saw again in the utterance of the word death. On death, too, the environment of the shop could be felt, and nothing of you was added to it yet — it was a crude, new, and boastful weapon. This you felt too and were even ashamed of it a little. Which doesn't mean of course that you weren't sincere in saying that you would die if I cease to be. Perhaps I'm mistaken and death was an altogether inner bud of yours, the hidden door handle of your nakedness, and only because of its embarrassing linguistic expression, did it make such an impression of plagiarism on me.

The bitter theme of **Honeymoon** didn't leave me alone: the grey castle on which reliefs are so flat, the small tilted slats of the shutters so vertical and so tightly packed, that the whole looks like a stretched canvas without doors or windows, and where even the stair flights curving on the two sides from the portico are of the same color [railings included] with the wall, so they seem to be the shadow of the thinning plane-tree opposite. Curiously we don't yet perceive it as a blind wall but a silvery self-mixed surface, as though rococo had morphed into a transparent Japanese quince running all over the wall. Fresco painters would sometimes paint with treacherous skill columns that withdraw into space with the help of meticulously distributed pseudo-shadows: this La Grange villa appeared to be such a painting — if something is rounded in reality, but looks only like a drawing, it's exactly like something that is a drawing in reality but looks perfectly three-dimensional.

The strangest were the wall-grey slats: not one millimeter more inward or outward than the wall [I don't know if that corresponds to reality]. In this way they too became flat, but not so much as to prevent the edges to be seen: they were blinder than a blind window, but more serene than genuine windows — of genuine windows we know they are windows inserted separately into the wall, but these were the eyes of the wall itself, with all their shutness, the wall's organic pupils, not windows but the blossoming freedom of the façade. This is the coulisse against which I imagined you, my love.

That's how I lived in thought your most beautiful and most frightening love state: joy, and wanting-me. There I no longer resembled myself: I was a blond 18-year-old boy who is too early for breakfast after his wedding night, to have an occasion to talk with the servant who is sorting out the cups & jugs: he wants to see a human being instead of the ghost of a woman's will. After breakfast he hides again somewhere behind the grey-white shutters to write a long letter to his ma, in which he relates that his wife said she would 'die without him,' and from this moment he starts feeling his own body dead. Of course his wife is not demonic in the theatrical sense, but on the contrary, infinitely humble and good. She is maybe 30 years old. The story would consist mostly of dialogues which reveal her well-nigh Byzantine faith, that it's only her will that is too sharp, like a metallic E string among soft leaves. But on a quiet, yellow afternoon the boy finds in her the earlier woman as well: when in love-making one feels not the legal or transcendental ring of one person enclosing another, but the atmosphere-imitation of surrounding nature.

Love is bearable only if the actants don't want only & exclusively one another, but on the contrary: if by excluding themselves, they want the whole world. The two worlds of will & joy relate to one another like the mountain-climbing path of love to its path rolling down a slope: on this yellow early autumn afternoon your beauty too appeared anew. Because your beauty is also not your human property but only an infinite little emptiness in the midst of the landscape's richness. Face and will are one thing, thus the face is a hard and foreign exponent on a number in whose power no one is interested in the least. We merged into the willows' long hanging leaves that floated in the afternoon's Tokaji gold like velvety serpent tongues in the prince's transparent handkerchief.

All of a sudden love started rolling: what happened with you? I too forgot about death, and you didn't mention God, future, and happiness any more either. We ceased to be a theme for one another and it seems this was the beginning of happiness. I went down to the park alone, I found the light and warmth so particular; in the morning it was warm but then the whole world is filled with warmth — now suddenly I felt heat separately, floating in the air so insulated as a newly arrived ship in a deserted harbor. Perhaps the surprised Io may have felt the warmth of Zeus' invisible body among the green shrubs: a muscle-shaped warmth inside otherwise warm air.

Afternoon sunshine too behaved in a similar fashion: in the morning one could still feel that the ray and that number resembling a big plaited bread that marked today on the calendar, were identical — but now light peeled off from the sun: they sometimes spread on a dark green tabletop gilded codex pages that have to be pinned down on the two sides by the hands of the bespectacled king reading from them — if he absent-mindedly lapses into gesticulating to explain a phrase, the golden papyrus immediately coils up into a scroll, in stark contrast to the table's rigidly stretched green: similarly, the sunshine coiled up into a separate red-blond scroll, while 'today' [represented by the green table of the mowed lawn] was left in its original expanse.

I saw the contraction of time in general: as if it were stretched on the whole garden with very feeble tacks that fall off, and now the 'today' made of time will end earlier than the 'quotidianum' made of the garden. To put it bluntly [but in love it's sweet to put it so]: the La Grange, the pond were still one single line, but time, gilded transience, was a semicircle swaying hither and thither above it, a cup without a flat saucer that can thus roll to and fro. When I realized that in this way 'today' split into two and one half was swinging on the other, that sunshine and warm air vacillate in it like golf balls around the holes, I immediately felt [such a thing can only happen in autumn] that the vacuum between the line & the semicircle pendulating on it are the atmosphere in which your will goes numb, your personality melts down and you become merely beautiful, as time and the trees too are only beauty without purpose, humanity, the foolish-oversize rudder of your destiny.

How good it was to feel, within one day, the day's yesterday-face: to watch the villa's front and in the same instant to grope its garden façade like a relief made of air. Will, your womanly will & death-composition, cannot bear these benumbing autumnal games of time and landscape: now I was sure that we would be happy. Will wants a fixed territory: when you looked out of the window [as I said, it was the wall opening, not a window — on cardboard boxes often no line can be seen between box and lid, so we only discover where it opens after managing to pull off the lid] with your hazel eye that had a valence of green, you immediately felt how hastening time bends back into yesterday within the territory of today, like a semicircular screen on which the same velvety willow tree is painted, next to which they sat it up in the park. Will flees from the present into the future, from being-here into geographical being-there; but the Geneva autumn outwitted this girlishly rough-and-tumble sport, you didn't know if it was yesterday or today, if you felt the breeze of the future or of the past on your eyes [you felt the wind not in your lashes but with your eyeballs], you only felt time's muddy perfume in general, and your will immediately lost its way like a lizard in an unfamiliar bush.

That's how I waited for you.

It seems that there is a friendly and an unfriendly dehumanization: the former is the present one, when the soft paradoxes of landscape and time take the place of your personality, and the latter one is, when you are a hyper-object, excessively real reality, or sheer will, abstract self-possessiveness. Are you annoyed by the raw statistics of inhumanity: landscape, excessive-reality, will? Not long ago I said that if one is very tired, he will fall back on metaphors — such statistics are merely types of metaphor. It's curious that nature is at its most harmonious, or we might say at its simplest, when a paradox lurks in it: is hermaphroditism a simpler human form than clear-cut one-sexedness? From the point of view of female will this yellow and lukewarm afternoon was indeterminate, but from that of nature it was very calm and restful. Does the ancient statue of a hermaphrodite with its back to the viewer elicit a feeling of disquiet or, on the contrary, of almost-exaggerated harmony? In a thousand cases it's a cause of confusion and unpleasant intellectual dizziness if we can't establish the identity of an object — but not with this human figure: the calm stream of hypotheses flows from boyish into girlish, from feminine into pubertal, without being disturbed by uncertainty, what is more, in time it is overcome by a pleasant carelessness, the quiet half-paralysis of the concepts of 'love' and 'human', a mirroring-opalescent compromise between perversion and 'sex-classicism': we don't know if what is revealed in the statue of the hermaphrodite is the deepest ethical sense of love, cleansed of the gauche problems of 'sexual life', or if we are facing a novel pleasure trick offered by an elegant Parisian cocaine salon.

When I looked around in the gilded autumn afternoon, I saw such a time-Hermes and time-Aphrodite merge into a single figure, without feeling the least disquiet over the ambiguity: what is more, the lurking paradox lent the afternoon a philistine plasticity. We sat by a fountain into the late evening hours: optimistic illustration to the dark dialogues of Honeymoon. Because, just as the sole form of will is naked human speech, the sentence wired around the air like a thorny bough [if I listen to female speech with closed eyes it seems a foreign language — does the word resemble the human body?] — so the only form of joy is the image. Haven't we felt it through and through, how much the image is a thing lying outside every conceivable relation, direction, and meaning? The world is chock-full of the dense implications of relation and meaning, how is it then possible that so much infinity fits between them as can be found in one small landscape [painted or real]? What makes a picture infinite, when its finitude is so obvious?

What is here? A fountain, a wide mowed expanse, willow, thuja, a grey villa, uncertain light: that's all. Perhaps the fact that it contains 10 to 20 components but I name none of them, only take cognizance of them through my senses, and in the great namelessness the numbers 10 and 20 disappear. There is a huge difference between intellectual, nominalist, and merely sensual cognizance: 'fountain' and 'thuja' can mean only two things, but sensuous cognizance knows no such things as 'two' — there it's already a multitude. Not because it also keenly senses the thousand 'nuances' but because it sees them in exaggerated simultaneity: for the intellect something like 'two things at the same time' will remain forever sensational, instead of seeing 'two' things now, it keeps jumping with infinite speed from the one to the other, from 'fountain' to 'thuja,' to decompose simultaneity into the microscopic beat-lets of pre and post: with images this perpetual movement is one of the important sources of infinity.

Regardless, nameless phenomenon is always infinite, or more exactly: absolute. I watch the fountain's small basin: water color, bronze reflection, tree shadows. Here and there mud knots, in other places flowers and floating bubbles. All this I see within an instant: but the soul decomposes them, distributes times, a long one to the water-color, less for the bronze, the longest to the tree shadows. The basin hovers between two hidden caryatids: one is the name opening in me ['basin'], the other, time hovering above it — flora polychronica.[246] We know of even the most banal detail of an image that de natura it can have no name: the rose drawn with the most general features is not a rose anymore but *pencil, paper, the most extreme accident of memory. And that triggers a sense of infinity: to know that what I touch will be extremely chancy and individual. As compared to the concept of 'rose,' the rose is such an alien curiosity that it's nothing short of a miracle that we should call it a rose — but for the senses it's familiar from the beginnings, coeval with the senses themselves.*

The senses are something very paradoxical: they would notice even the most impossible shade on an object, but are almost identical with the object: between the color of eye-ball and roses, the smell of nose-nerve and rose the collaboration is so extremely scrimpy that the rose [echo of German idealism?] is not a separate object anymore, but a rational formula afloat in the process of smelling — there is smelling alone, there is seeing alone. How can this duality cohabit in the soul: hyper-particularity [every rose is exotic] and the complete annihilation of every object in the permanence of perception [every rose is the sense of smell alone]? For every image is sensational in the two ways above, and both are infinities or infinity illusions [which in the case of the concept of infinity is the same thing]. When we were happy, we were happy because of this image.

That's how I imagined it but it's not so. We never came to know shared joy in this landscape form. For you I am either a personal God or death. And besides, our love culminated in late autumn or winter, when we could never substitute one another with landscapes but had to choke in the unbearable pluses of humanity. Because our humanity is much, unbearably much if there is nothing to avert our attention from it. To me you are a dreadful mirror and so I am to you, even if you are often overjoyed about me at the piano and drop themes like sprinkled water on the margin of the score. When I used to have thoughts about you I could still divert the murderous voltage of your electric nudity to more tranquil paths — I had a glass to see darkly, a transparent dulling curtain, you had a shadow, I had a glass sheet through which to see you, you had a hollow imprint in the sea sand if I pressed you deep into its damp bed, you had an alcohol-imbued body glove;

now you are only you in winter bareness, with one sole violet flower on your shoulder — your joy for me. I must flee from you. My organism offers sickness or heroism — what can it mean in a more practical form? Sickness: philistinism; heroism: some church career.

I can't think, I have no strength for reading, so the little time I spend at home between my teaching hours I can only spend in complete indolence. Indolence is a great novelty for me, with huge physical suffering and mysterious joys attached. I know comfort only negatively: if you lure me out into unwalkable snowed-in parks I feel sharply that the warm room is worth much more. But when I'm in the warm room I don't find it comfortable at all. Today too I sat at home the whole day. It was dark inside, on my window a half-thick curtain, through which a streetlamp shone with mauve-ish, theatrical light: I felt like sleeping inside a huge flower that blooms among mist-foliage at an unknown attitude. To be completely without thoughts and yet to feel myself completely as self: this duality made me shiver.

I was surrounded by warm blankets and cushions, with a bottle of wine, apples and cakes at hand. I felt that solitude squeezes out of me the merest possibility of thought like the last trapped drop from a crumpled-up tube. Perhaps I'm feverish. Or a mystic. For the mystic the word 'psychology' has no meaning: if we can talk about psychology, we can't talk about psyche, because the soul starts at the point where all memory, thought, and desire, all the contents of consciousness fall from it. I seemed to have got into this state. Philistinism? Lethal illness? Or San Juan de la Cruz's 'noche del sentido'? [247] *How I'd like to be a human-like human being [you, my love, used to call or rather, greet me with 'is my own chub still chub-like?'], although it seems that 'human' is the most indefinite concept and fact on earth: and if it's so indefinite, how come the obsession with some definite and official human being is so strong?*

As I sipped my tea, at first I thought I liked it more than ever, but soon realized that I was wrong. In order for something to satisfy our so-called animal instincts, the first and necessary condition is that there must be thoughts in our soul, or at least one which is, however, particularly rational: all pleasure becomes pleasure only from an intellectual perspective, in the absence of this perspective there is no pleasure. In the dark room there was not a single thought in my head, so the nerve-friction performed by the sweetish lukewarm tea on my tongue's percept-velvet hung in the air, joyless. If there is one single thought in my soul, pleasure can crop up and rock me into the lie as if there was nothing in my consciousness but pleasure; on the other hand if there are no thoughts at all in my soul, the sensual stimuli are blocked, so to speak, outside my soul and push me into the illusion that the thoughts hovering in the outside world are pleasure-ideas. I couldn't relate the tea to anything, there was no memory and no desire in my paralyzed soul, that is, there was no 'protector' of the nerve-pulsation, it was left outside, it objectified.

And so it was with the warmth of the blanket, the muscles' melting relaxedness, with my eyes' reassuringly narrow and cushioned field of vision: all my sensuousnesses were outside of me, for the slender dock-slide that lets thought into the soul was no longer there. Does then the clean autonomy of the senses equal the annihilation of the senses? My dear love — will it be my senses that weave a thick hedge of leaves to separate me from you forever? I slowly drew my index finger along the warm teacup — I was surrounded by such warmth as if I were by a Ceylon oasis, to one side the sun's burning shield and to the other, the dark blue and cold sword of shadow; that warmth was landscape, battle plan and temple, from which I couldn't escape. Is it possible that the greedy ascetics and tireless spiritual exercisers have not yet realized this? That instead of repressing the senses for the sake of their psychic life, they should repress the psychic life rather and let the senses pulsate freely: by the latter method they will achieve blindness and pleasurelessness far sooner. I'm perfectly sensuous and you are perfectly reality: that's why we die, that's why we turn into ghosts, lovelost. — Philistinism? I started shivering in my new prison.

The window was very indeterminate, like an unknown woman's face that we manage to first observe while she is combing: the room's inner shadows, the crossing of curtains, the circular light of the lamp opposite, which pressed my eyeballs as the empty cap of a lemon peel presses the squeezer's glass cone — I didn't know where the room ends and where the street begins. This is the true Venus grotto[248] *and perhaps the true Manresa:*[249] *my eyes which always brushed against your body like a barren comb lining the snow on a mountain slope, my eyes left my soul and body and surrounded me like a dark green leaf curtain — this way perhaps your beautiful face was forever hidden from me by fugitive and traitorous 'vision'; my hands always in search of your shoulder like a usurer who counts the same column of coins for the hundredth time because a penny is missing, my hands floated away from me like a boat whose anchoring rope dissolved in the water, and now it moved over to be a white bud on 'vision's' light green leaf curtain; my tongue that touched you so often like a sharp pencil, to place the enlivening white dot in the middle of the painted eyeball, my tongue and taste have also deserted me and, like a midnight sun, washed into brownish luminosity the green vision-leaves and white touch-lotuses.*

When I call [call? see?] my senses, which fled from me in allegory's ten a penny machinery, green leaves and virginal lotuses, I'm not trying to embellish them but only to estrange them: I lived so much inside myself and inside my thoughts that for me green leaves and icy lotuses are the marvelous, humorous, and murderous implements of the Inquisition. Perhaps my philistinism was only one step away from a holy life, but that one step was ginormous: I entirely lacked a will to holiness. [By now I can say: in my life holiness and a clerical career were two entirely unrelated territories & possibilities.]

The world was lacking in me, but it was not me who wanted it to be absent: my sensuousness withdrew like fever from quinine, but not because I wanted it to; I was as close to God as one page to the next in the closed book, although I was not seeking Him. The nightly blooming, hostile hedge of my senses was much too wide and thick for me to believe that I could still somehow get across to you. But this is all hot air, self-contradictory nonsense: if I had no senses I could not desire you. Twofold objectivity — first in the shape of the Diana statue as you surface from the water ['I have no thoughts'], secondly behind my living-apart sensuousness-hedge that filtered you thoroughly because of my philistinism ['I have no body'].

But isn't all this mere stylization & lying? Did I not feel in myself at that time too a great and palpable love for you, like a glove we can feel in a pocket when we check if it's there? If the present moment has a shade of 'melancholy farewell,' that's no touch of a Manresa but only of love. This is a question of conscience for which pedantry is needed: which is the greater cult of women [if it's possible at all to separate love for a moment from the human being] — the desire in me plus the woman, or the sensuousness outside me plus woman, where I 'simply see' the latter sum?

But this is the rub: is then what goes on in me really just 'simple vision'? In me the will to love and desire is nil, but you live somewhere in the outer world, and to me you are not otherwise more you than the you glimpsed through the hedge that separates me from you; but because this hedge and you are always together, because that hedge is after all the self of my self, even though it broke away from me: doesn't there exist somewhere in the world a greater love for you through me, even though subjectively without me, than existed before, subjectively with me? Or is this not a naïve bamboozlement by a trivial metaphor, when I take seriously a sensuousness that exists without me and which separates us like a hedge? And if this hedge is reality, then is there any point in raising questions of conscience & speaking of moral: for in that case there is no human individuality, then I'm no different from plants, or I have no boundaries. My brave Catholic dilemma: your head and my joy roll to and fro, their boundaries are metaphor & moral.

To speak in scriptural terms: when you appeared you were already condemned — it took either metaphor and moral, or pleasure and moral, to gnaw you to pieces. Now when I know nothing anymore but *merely wriggle between teaching and inane tea-drinking, I want pleasure and moral finally to confront each other independently of me, as in an old school drama, scanned, intrigued, doodling heroids, scattering red gossip about death and nature into vacuous rhymes. Shall I forever whisper to them and will they remain half-actors: one half of them left god knows where, the other half stuck into me, half-bed of conscience?*

This awful silence that surrounds me cannot bear halves, it demands whole figures. For conscience is conscience precisely because it knows only half-moral and half-pleasure. But why do I then want to see whole moral and whole pleasure for the sake of moral? If one of the two should be completely whole for once, then the other would exist no longer, there could be no struggle, no conscience. Perhaps I don't even want whole figures [wholly divine God, wholly satanic woman], only the half-work of conscience on a very intensive scale. But does it befit a philistine stripped to night, to content himself with intensity? I probably want the confrontation between pleasure & moral because I need to simplify every complicated thing for my disciples. But even though it may be only a pedagogical necessity, it must happen.

How pedagogical this struggle is can be seen in the fact that I have already written a small fable about it. An old man is gravely ill and prepares for his last confession. He had been in love once in his life, but it happened after his marriage and he struggled to forget that woman with long penitence. His wife had long been dead, but he didn't care about the other woman. When he is waiting for the priest [O, didacticism!], the object of his love walks by under his window, young and beautiful as she was 50 years earlier. The old man despairs: he feels no desire for her, he is unable to write in his imagination any abstract 'yes' next to her beauty, but finds that her beauty is already desire itself: enough if one looks at her to feel that his desire had long been inside her and now meets by accident his desire that fled unconsciously to the girl. It's a secondary matter that all this is only fastidiousness and baseless pettifoggery: the essence of moral is that it should lapse into irrationality [this is praise of course]. If the girl is as beautiful as ever, then he cancelled her from his memory in vain: his desire continued to exist, beauty was desire itself rendered plastic. But her reality couldn't be cancelled from the face of the earth, not even with murder, so his desire too will remain. The old man sees his death in his black-robed, white-collared doctor, so he wants to ask him to defeat the girl. The 80-year-old Methuselah is fed up with psychology & with conscience's lyrical nerve-shades — he wants reality. Instead of desire & moral, it is the girl's living body & the old man's living body that face each other for combat. The confessioner arrives. The old man rises from his bed and calmly announces that he doesn't wish to confess, for he realized that the real things didn't happen in his soul, indeed nothing ever happens there, but all the same he asks the priest to stay, to sit down in an armchair and wait until he returns. Because he wants to go personally to the doctor [who is death] to ask him to defeat the girl. Girl & death [if you will, girl and God] should deal with the maddening comedy of temptation between themselves, the old man can't bear it any longer, he will only watch it with the confessioner. He drags the doctor to his castle; the doctor sees that he has gone mad. In the meantime the old man's servants are ferreting around for the girl. The dying man is overcome by infinite tranquility: there are no conscience problems; ethics is a fight of the outer world just as much as that between cat & sparrow, or daisy and hailstorm.

  I didn't know how to end my little fable — should I make a farce of it and detail how the moribund watches the love entanglement of the girl and the doctor, the objective peace of moral and pleasure? Or should I describe how he promises to make the doctor the heir to his astronomic wealth if he defeats the woman [this signals that by reflex he nevertheless feels ethics to be his inner, psychic issue, for his will stands on the part of God]: the resourceful doctor kills the woman with an injection under the old man's eyes? All this is parody or pedagogy [the same thing when it comes to very big truths], and I can't hide it that I was indeed preoccupied by the relation of woman and God there, in the dark room, without thoughts, with a cup of cooling tea.

Why is it so difficult to defeat woman for God? God is infinite, but He is also at an infinite distance from us [infinite even in the Eucharist: the fact of transubstantiation is an infinitely non-anthropomorphic fact]; woman is finite, but she is infinitely close to us, Sancta Immediata. And it is her very closeness that is extraordinary — an object can be without meaning or lacking value, but closeness, the fact of immediate availability is the most valuable metaphysics. It is in fact the protagonist in every love, the positivity in the woman's face is that something is 'quite close' — and that is a worthy rival of God. [One needn't immediately strike down the thing with the Romanesque sigil of 'blasphemy' — this is merely to say that for the average human being the 'close nothing' is a worthy counterpart of the 'distant everything,' it is thus natural that objectively the scales aren't balanced.]

Strangely it's now, when you have become ultimately unavailable for me, that the idea of closeness preoccupies me and I feel for the first time profoundly unsettled by moral. Is it possible that moral rests like a footprint after every woman? It's quite possible, but it will still rest moral. [Adages? Five o'clock?] The 'it's here' absorbs everything: face, character, hair-dye, and of course moral too. Presence is redeeming and destructive at the same time — it acquaints us with the fact of existence, it shows us the most certain signs referring to the validity of ontology, but it immediately devours the things it announced.

Woman is not the existing thing itself, she is only the sure sign of existence and she immediately withers from this attributive, signaling function. This simple etiquette is somehow experienced by everyone, analphabetically, or with sensitive theology: kiss is a scintillating guarantee-bud, the undeniable deposit of the palpable present, and yet from it a pale and air-colored flower grows; love can at most be life but it can never be complete reality. Reality stretches over woman's face as over life-possibility, the way silvery-thin powder covers plums: we grab the plum greedily to taste 'it's here,' but wherever we touch the powder disappears and only life is left.

The preservation or loss of women's physical virginity is irrelevant from the perspective of love, but the wearing off of metaphysical virginity means all the more: the slide from redeeming 'it's here' to the trite level of 'living woman.' Why do we visit for the hundredth time a woman we have long tired of? Because we want to enjoy the experience of 'it's here,' an experience independent of the woman's living individuality — the fact that something that mechanically comes to our mind is really present in the outside world. Thus when I try to confront God and woman I need to feature not woman's sensuous beauty but, on the contrary, her most abstract feature [is it a feature in point of fact?], immediate presence: praesens-inflections from human conjunction. I used to say of your hair that it undulates humbly, because I felt in it the kind of childish modesty with which it curls back into the very midst of the present, its gentle bow in front of time's most tyrannical actor, the 'present.' Present has its graph and the beauty of your hair, face, of your entire figure, was precisely that it was the purest image of the present tense, it was only time, the definition of immediacy. [In the name Immediata 'here' and 'now' are entangled.]

To set up this abstraction as God's rival is also blasphemy, but at least it's more 'erudite' than a featuring of beauty. Or it's not really a blasphemy, for in woman too we see what we always want in God and in everything — something entirely other from what we happen to be, and close to us at that. — So the sin only means the most puritanical 'deed-puritanism' [puritanical because the deed is independent of all human matters — actus purus]: when I see the woman's hair, is the 'immediate being-there' the main source of my normal enjoyment, namely, a feeling concerning such a fact that is entirely divine and moral, but it so happens that attached to it, as infinitely thin addendum, is the 'real hair' to which I hardly have access because of the thick layer of 'immediate presence' covering it — if by great effort and some artificial and unnatural means I manage to somehow get at the only-hair hair and enjoy it, I commit a sin.

It's strange that I think the above and yet by temperament I am as far removed as it gets from all comfortable pan-ethicism. According to 'deed-puritanism,' sin is purely and simply impossible for a human being: when the murderer kills, with the delirium of vengeance or greed in his soul, he also feels something 100 percent god-related in his soul, but attached to this 'holy' feeling like a foreign, inorganic addendum is the action, the 'puritanical deed' of murder, which appears as action only for non-murderers, for the murderer doesn't see it as such, being entirely filled with the impetus [and premeditated action is no exception!], in his consciousness there is no place for 'action,' the action is only the automatic shadow, meaningless side-noise of feeling which, as feeling, can only be 'holy.' The world that follows from the above would be rather too much of a caricature: everything human, or more exactly, intra-human, psychic thing would be ab ovo virtue — & every extra-psychic thing, thus all action, all objects, the whole material universe, ab ovo sin.

Will the fact that I used to enjoy in your hair, my dear love, more the fact of its being close than the fact of its being hair, inspire me to such histrionic heresies? Would then virtue and sin be two superfluous words, whose meanings coincide precisely with subjective & objective: do they mean two circles that touch at one point only, but beyond that the one arcs to the right and the other to the left? To arc to the right from the murdered body is the killer's emotional world: the very last point in the killer's soul is a still entirely 'holy' feeling, for instance, that 'there must be justice at any cost,' or [if he killed for money] 'happiness is the principle of life' [here feeling needs to be supplanted by idea-shaped slogans as the above] — and the next point is already this fact that lies wholly outside the psyche: 'a man was killed' — there is no bridge, no transition whatsoever between feeling and action.

What is then the meaning of temptation? The devil shows us the woman, so that she would elicit in us such feelings that can be 'legitimately' felt only in relation to God. If it is true, then there can be no talk of sin — if Satan, so to speak, disguises women with god-faces, *then we turn to women and pleasure in our quest for God. Sin is imaginable only in so far as we find a transition between action & feeling — here in this silence I saw none. Other imaginings also accompanied the variations above — on the one hand, I felt woman's body itself to be the material of sin, on the other hand I believed that we shouldn't shamelessly want woman because God ordered it so — that is, here l'art pour l'art command, forbidding for the sake of forbidding opposed sin-material woman. Whoever is interested in moral will as a rule go through these atmospheres of extreme like some childhood disease: now believing that sin is an objective plant in the world, and now that sin exists [if it can be spoken about at all with the word 'exists'] only when we break some commandment: the commandment is entirely arbitrary, so God, for instance, could have allowed free love but forbidden the wearing of yellow shoes, let's say, on Monday mornings. Divine arbitrariness or worldly material?*

These were the first, hasty fruits of philistinism. Sensuousness left me but moral started troubling me: moral is nothing more than groping about in a dark world. Around me it was dark, both in reality and as simile, so I lost the ground under my feet and didn't know where I was. I was looking for some stable ground for my empty soul, and this search without seeing is but moralizing — I don't see trees, plants, and sky, I only intuit abstract territories of world: I can't look for a flowery meadow but merely opt for the action of 'going onward' — here, there, nearby, far away, to the right, to the left, these occupy the place of the landscape. But here and there, nearby and far away mean moral territories for the soul. I squandered away the last atom of your humanity.

When I said earlier that for me, an atmosphere of mysticism & the aspiration to an ecclesiastic career had always meant two totally independent worlds I didn't want to imply that I look on an ecclesiastic calling with irony. For me, mysticism and moral were forms of selfishness; I sank into the questions of my own life, I couldn't separate the glance-episodes of my own life from moral, seeing the two as ultimately identical. And the ecclesiastical career meant simply: participation in public ceremonies, reciting truths in rhetorical form to large masses. When I thought of the clergy I was always interested in truth hired as an actor in a theater, and the masses as masses — not once did I come to my mind in the role of the confessioner; whenever something psychological was concerned, that automatically excluded all other people and left me entirely alone.

Besides theatrically treated Catholic logic and the social factor I need to mention a third factor as well — the peculiar face or figure, which was also identical with an ecclesiastic career. I taught the relatives of bishops, I knew a great many priests, so the church career soon became synonymous with the particular portrait. Demonically precise logic, declaiming to the masses, picturesque profile: this was the clergy. Mystical solitude equals such moral punctiliousness that can never be solved — if moral is identical with my organism, it means that it is purposeless, for a human organism is not 'solvable,' it 'complicatedly is' and is annihilated afterwards. While an ecclesiastic career is precisely the practice of 'solutions' that are independent from the human being, the cultivation of definitions and ready-made things — it gently rocks one into the illusion [and of course the word 'rock' doesn't resemble the work of illusion which chases and stifles rather] that the human being, too, has the shape of definition, and if it fails to elicit this deception in us, at least it expresses with positive drama our longing for a definition-shaped life, which could take the place of hypochondria. Church: truth — human being: moral?

For me the ideal image of the clergyman used to be the uncle of one of my disciples, a gravely ill cardinal. This cardinal had the fame of being very holy and a superb orator. Nowadays he spent his days mostly in bed, but at night he would get up, feel fresh, pace up and down in his rooms and talk incomprehensibly to himself. Sometimes he would also speak loudly, on such occasions he would hasten to the church on foot or by car, and start preaching. Word spread immediately and in seconds the church would fill up. Haughty princes & lazy countesses would throw a mantle over their nightshirts, jump into their cars and sprint to hear the cardinal's prophetic speeches. The cardinal didn't use any obscure words, didn't threaten, wasn't poetic. If anything, he was characterized by a certain syllogistic bareness, logical impudicity — the snowy lucidity of ideas almost resembled the nighttime & sticking-out, bed-colored flesh of half-asleep women: perhaps one couldn't deliver a speech of any other color at midnight to such effect.

At that time I lived in the cardinal's house and was still awake when he suddenly tore a window open [a racket fell from it like unexpected silver coins from an envelope] and called out to his driver. The next moment he burst into my room without knocking in his long snow-white nightshirt, with a deathly pallor on his face, with the purple cap on his head & dragging on the floor his long cardinal's cassock. He hurled it to me & stretched his arms like one waiting to be dressed. I have never exchanged more than three words with him; I don't think he even recognized me. I didn't understand much of church vestments, for some time I had stopped serving as altar boy, but I started dressing him. I felt like being submerged under water or between flames, and while I threw around and above me the cracking, blood-colored silk veils, I couldn't ward off the fear that I would end up clothing myself in martyrdom's moiré husk. My arm and the cardinal's glacé fist swayed and floundered among the enormous silk sheets, as the last planks of a shipwrecked vessel — nobody knows what their fate will be. Sometimes I clumsily pushed aside the nightshirt's white string with the big soft tassel, so it flicked in the air like a whip: the cardinal was not only not annoyed but he seemed to enjoy the spectacle. Sweat was running down my spine.

It was the most beautiful landscape I have ever seen: the purple took on the most different hues from light pink to glaring light blue — sometimes the sky looks like this after rain: it showers the whole afternoon, you'd think it's late evening as everything is so dark, but suddenly the rain stops, the clouds are torn apart and it turns out it's still early afternoon, the sun is shining, the sky is green, only at the edges of the unexpected light do violet & claret clouds bulge like special letter papers, 'cerise de princesse' or 'violetta royale.' My body almost transubstantiated from the tempest of strange silks, I felt that my flesh can belong to no one but God: old dodos sometimes leave by will, amid whistles and expletives, their weighty millions to budding bar sirens — now I felt to be some such creature, wanting to leave my body to the sky and only to the sky under the purple. I went wild with strange odors: incense and dull wardrobe perfume from the purple, scented soap from the cardinal's hands, medicine and bed vapors from his whole body — I wanted to kiss them all. I knew that now I was no decadent aesthete: colors and smells were great powers that incited me to the most unpoetic self-abnegation. There was nothing beautiful here, but everything was mercilessly powerful.

A servant came in and took over the task of dressing or rather, of second baptism. For a few minutes we held together the incandescent train, I felt its slowly lost weight, heard on my shoulder its hasty fall as it moved toward the servant, as if through a freshly opened sluice. The servant whispered a woman's name in my ear, I knew she was the cardinal's relative who probably wanted to hear the night sermon and I had to immediately wake her up. I had to go down to the garden — the real landscape felt unusual after the smothering clouds of church vestments. I couldn't see the Moon but it was quite light outside, yellowish and oblique serenity.

The woman's separate little villa stood in the back of the garden. I've often been there; I used to teach her son. I arrived late, for there was light in the garage and I could hear the driver trying to get the car out. All the same I went upstairs. I heard cries from her bedroom; it turned out all the servants were out. I knocked and said my name; she called me in. In the middle of the room a crumpled bed. The word 'middle' is both adequate and inadequate here in so far as in the very middle of the room was not the bed but a circular green lawn pierced through with a strange something that was a globe-shaped, transparent clock, dim lamp, rouged flower and wig-shape fountain in one. This lawn-circle was surrounded in an O shape by the bed. She was *already awake but I didn't know how advanced in the dressing — if she had a nightshirt, pajamas, or upper clothes on. She commanded me laughingly to pass her some clothes, whatever I liked. I took out one dress from the cupboard, too embarrassed of course to even look at what I liked. My nose was still filled with the odor of incense and my body with the desire for purity and right after I was invited to wash in female clothes: I'll go on teaching children with the help of crude examples until those catch on into reality and come to pass. Neither the woman nor the clothes meant true temptation. Some parts of the body rejoiced now and then at the sight, like the dumbmost songbirds in a forest sunk in deep night sleep, but in the place of their chirrup no white hole opens in the night's benumbed blue. Perhaps I was in a state that I imagined to be impossible: I found women's things beautiful, below desire and above æsthetics, as if women were neither biology nor æsthetics but a separate world, like the Moon for instance, with the sole difference that she's a good few kilometers closer. She drove me to the church in her car — for the first time I sat next to a woman to whom I gave the clothes under the top layer. Nudes and undergarments were old acquaintances, but that penultimate whatever kind of item of clothing disturbed my mind. I felt the relation of the man who dresses a woman with that, to be just as peculiar and independent as marriage, extra-conjugal affair, or bachelorship [for that too is a kind of relation]. It was thickly raining, the church stood on the upper end of a slope, so all the cars were roaring but sliding backwards. I would have liked to be as popular as the cardinal: by 'as' I meant precisely 'as,' including the rain, the hilltop church, the night, the downward-sliding cars that harshed sideways against one another. I relished the fact that the crowd was not pouring uniformly into the church but slipping here and there in their cars, the sounds of horns too crisscrossed, and almost nobody managed to get onward. Was this really haste, or the immobile gasoline pantomime of showing interest? The cars' splashboards were all directed toward the church gate, but because they all faced the entrance, they didn't have a place in front to either turn or drive on.*

Those sitting in the cars were not upset; they calmly leaned back and sometimes absent-mindedly looked out the window. This is the very meaning of popularity and success, I thought, these cars almost at a standstill that continued to roar. I watched the acute angles they formed with each other, the looks thrown to one another: they were complete strangers but one great community, almost a blood relationship was foisted on them, in so far as all wanted to hear the cardinal. The concept of the cardinal almost rendered the faces alike, they even tried it out in the rear mirror. I was not attracted by applause and the crowd, only by the soaking cars that didn't manage to move forward in the absence of a traffic guard. In my head there was only the cardinal, next to me the woman in her 'n - 1' clothes, which for me was a little bit like a column of numbers torn out of some bookkeeping registrar — for me it means nothing but I know that for some it may spell out blithe profit, mortifying loss, or the evidence of embezzlement. If I had any penchant to develop a mania for temptation, this was the best occasion — now of all moments, when in my feelings I had nothing to do with this woman, only the abstract figures of holiness and pleasure were found in this school textbook-like juxtaposition. If life performs these tricks, then it's highly likely that we can expect fantasy to practice them all the time.

There are many people who, on seeing 'the holiest' and 'the lowliest' permanently conjoined, inevitably draw the conclusion or diagnosis that it must be desecration, blasphemy, critique. Even though often such dark anecdotes as 'cardinal' and 'coquette' have a completely different source. With me they have two causes, for instance: the one is childishness, the other is the incessant ethical high-strungness, the permanent experience of temptation. For the child there is no essential difference between an illustrated book, the Moon, and a plate of stirabout; all three are blots of color — blots of color a, b, c, almost abstract formulae. I always look around in the world with such child's eyes, thus I don't much care that the one is a human being and the other, an idea, the one a flower and the other, moral, but take every thing that presents itself to be a decorative figure, some kind of drawing template or arithmetic sign that are perfectly consubstantial, it is only their shape that differs.

For the eternal registrars and dictionary watchdogs of 'meaning' something like 'murderer pope' or 'adulterous parson' immediately spells out anti-clerical satire — but not at all for me as child: for me 'murder' means, for instance, night, blood, screams, a trampled flower, the sum of which could also be signaled with x — 'clergy' means light, paradox, universality, solitude and miracle, the sum of which could be signaled with y, for it is such an abstract, human-less something, so 'murderer pope' becomes an arithmetic operation, simple multiplication: xy. This is the child's point of view. The other point of view could be called, by a rancorous 15th-century man of letters, the point of view of 'monopomology' [one-appledness], which consists of the fact that the human soul is completely emptied and one sole thing is left in it, temptation or divine commandment — the world is empty, paradise withers, one sole apple of the tree of knowledge is left as the staffage of naked Adam, accompanied by the remembrance of God's command.

The absolutely ethical human being sees only extremes: in blue eyes, the non plus ultra of immodesty, and in one single prayer, God itself, whose forever changing but always authorized portrait is the pope. If the place of blue eyes is taken by unowned women's clothes, this circumstance makes no change in the soul: what lives on there will be some perpetual image of the absolute of sin [for instance, Gomorrah or murder] — and if a charitable deed takes the place of that of prayer, that fact will not affect in the least the eternal and active symbol of absolute virtue or absolute theological truth [for instance, the figure of a pope]. This is nothing else but the stylized realism of temptation: the permanent consciousness of the combat of sin and virtue, lacking in any small actualities. 'Murderer pope': with me this is the desperate intermingling of sin and moral, the line where the outermost boundaries of sin and moral touch, the geometrical location of temptation in the geography of the soul. My soul is nothing else but eternal calling to virtue, & the world around is nothing else but eternal possibility of sin.

My soul and the world do not exist in separate places and times: my soul is replete with the world, and the world is replete with my soul. But there are obstinate and ineradicable symbols of virtuous soul & world full of sin-possibilities in my fantasy, for instance 'papacy and murder' — the 'anima mundificata' becomes the 'murderer pope,' and the 'mundus animisatus' becomes the 'murderer elected pope.'

Lately my ideal of the ecclesiastical life has been not the kind of the cardinal who preaches at night. In the morning I met on the docks an ugly man with pince-nez who sat on the bench on which I usually rest between two disciples. We watched the workers as they unloaded wares, their slow fidgeting with the veils. The man with the pince-nez started speaking, slowly and with self-importance, like one who discloses great secrets. He spoke of the poor sailors and haulers who have no consolation, although it's right at hand, but they don't turn to it. He held a long pause of effect like a hack orator before repeating: 'it's there, it's there.' At first I didn't understand what he was trying to say, but soon it turned out he meant religion. He took out a huge batch of papers & flyleaves from his tawdry overcoat. He pushed his pince-nez to his forehead & before saying a word he licked his thumb voluptuously several times to leaf through them. He related that he is distributing them among the dock workers. He doesn't speak or explain; he works in secret. He didn't say a word about God or salvation to the first seaman he got to know, only in the last minute did he toss to him one of those illustrated periodicals of the defense of faith, saying he should take a look and might find something worthwhile there, for he didn't have time to look. The worker accepted the leaflet and he, the missionary, watched with relish as the ship sailed out, knowing that in however modest form, the Lord is already present there. He always works like this.

I asked bitingly if he wanted to convert me too in secret, just because he would be a little late. He came quite close to me, like a woman. He had barely any eyes and no eyebrows at all, even his pince-nez was impossibly small, with thin bone frame. His moustache was burnt in places and there his skin was pink like on first scars. His nose was enormous but didn't even resemble the shape of the human nose. His whole physique was repulsive. Should I lie that I was a very holy man to get rid of him? Or tell him my fantastic sins, so that he faints into the sea in panic?

While thinking about such pranks I realized that I had been speaking for some time already: I listened to hear what. To my greatest surprise I had been sincere for several minutes already. And it's true that sincerities told to complete strangers seem to the teller patent lies far rather than truth. If I had lied, there would have been nothing amusing in it, for a completely unknown person is so irreal that the lie addressed to him perfectly befits his improbable figure, fuses into it, so I wouldn't have the impression of cheating but of adapting, with scrupulous precision, to his irreality and copying it by the means of my own thoughts: and such a parallel always begets an atmosphere of truth.

I told him all my weaknesses and he listened greedily. He then went into explanations, which obviously bored me, but I took a fancy to his self-important and secretive manner. It's interesting how for some people the truth is like the plan of a secret conspiracy or opium smuggling. My acquaintance was well-versed in dogmatics and there was nothing of the bad exoticism in his moral principles, it was only his manners that reminded one of the masked thieves of adventure films. He suited the docks' irresponsible world perfectly, he evidently felt at ease here. He told me laughing [only when he grinned could one think that after all there might be something like eyes behind the pince-nez, for around those parts the skin contracted a bit] that the police checked his papers several times and his briefcase & clothes were searched in the customs office, as they took him for a thief or smuggler.

He explained which of the anchored ships were situated on higher or lower levels of salvation. One of the barges was full of glaring green watermelon pyramids, its captain was an atheist drunkard, but the cook did everything in his power to shepherd the crew onto the right path. When they pulled up its bone-dry, almost brittle veil, I felt as though some Hollywood Antichrist had plastered his yellow poster on a market ship.

You see, you see? — he asked, hissing and grabbing my arm. The ships were all in shadow, but the topmost sails were time and again set aflame by the lighter of some passportless luminosity. The whole harbor morphed into a moral landscape ruled over by a dark intrigue-monger, my neighbor. He invited me to his apartment and gave me his telephone number, stressing that it was secret and he very rarely gives it to anyone. He also said that we could also meet on a fishing boat: its owner, an atheist old fogey, was hospitalized, and now the nephew of my neighbor was going to be the 'captain' [he used that word]: a blond young boy who takes communion every day. The boy's career was advancing very slowly and with difficulties, but he can resolve everything. He showed me the boat: a long, completely flat, almost raft-like dinghy full of soot and nets that looked like female stockings.

I tasted a new form of truth: civilian bucketshop mysticism, which I found eminently suitable to the nature of truth. The secret telephone number was almost a philosophical discovery for me, the most truthful effigy of truth. Truth is mysterious and practical, hostile and redeeming, self-serving and sportsmanlike: all this was perfectly illustrated by my neighbor's speech, clothes, thinking. I intuited the necessity of God in this puny, underhand theologizing more than in grand altar mysticism. Salvation is like a bacillus colony that was placed on the seamen here in the harbor, my acquaintance was doctor and a spreader of disease, experimenter and gloating Iago in one person. I have never felt religion to be such an absolutely personal matter as now: it was one form of satanic gossip. Iago and Satan are mere metaphors, attributes of manner, for the cause was the most ideal imaginable.

When we took leave he promised to telephone me and it seems he's as good as his promise, because the phone is ringing on the rug next to my sofa. Or is it you, my distant love? How strange is the thin ring in this shapeless dark room, slightly hoarse from the rug: like the piercing of an injection needle in a long paralyzed body — I don't feel anything, only see its place. Why don't I feel like lifting the receiver? Does the human voice have any meaning and any use in my loneliness?

(Could I answer anything? The voice can be only word somewhere, and I, only darkness — what's the use of dancing at two weddings?

I quietly took off the receiver, so the device would stop buzzing, then disconnected the impatient line. I felt that I became true, with medieval pathos, to something or someone who can hardly exist in the world...)

XII.

*Leatrice's uncle (Peter) visits a female acquaintance.
He waits for the ferryman in a tavern*

She had few acquaintances and even those few seemed strange, dark-faced and foreign, as if the grownups were all ab ovo damned. When she heard the sacristan's story, her naïve pessimism had long worn off but sometimes it was awakened with full force. Peter missed the small propeller that would have taken him across the river, as the bridge was in repair. In the late afternoon dusk the new pillars glowed whitely in the midst of the wooden scaffolding: the whole seemed less a bridge in the making and more a glistening ruin. The river was green from the emerald hue of the giant snow-stars, here and there green tunnels opened in the sky, their points of gravity signaled by the stars: they quivered like the throat of chirping sparrows. It was a theatrical lighting: darkness to one side, drab light to the other (where the searchlight pipe-halo fell); the fragments of day & night lay in disarray above the bridge, like the paintings of the Flemish and Italian schools in a museum corridor that is being rearranged.

This is probably the only possible stage setting of damnation, a luminosity falling strictly above the bridge, like a wall going on forever. Because above the two banks darkness loomed: the thickness of the light was precisely the small river's width — it looked like incandescent green rain whose every single drop-thread has solidified. But the clouds were moving on, opening from black buds into grey flowers, forming islets, ships & metaphysical diligences, enriching the sky's depth. High up luminosity thickened, no threads were visible & even the river's surface was barely touched by a few golden threads, for they started breaking up at the trees' altitude, some longer, others shorter. Night light must surely be the most exact equivalent of predestination, Leatrice thought.

Peter sat on a bench by the river, waiting for the ferryman to take him across. It was very cold; he had a strong cough. By that cough the sacristan, who was sitting in a bar, noticed Peter. He called him in. You should have seen his pallor, he later ts-tss-d. Leatrice felt again, as an airplane feels the sudden take-off, the duality that was her most important childhood memory: the prose of sickness & the stage pomp of sin or of moral matters in general. Poor Peter was a great hypochondriac who immediately held a handkerchief to his nose if there was a bit of breeze, and if he drank fresh wine he felt the cork taste in his mouth for weeks — how cold he must have been on that bench. Inside the tavern it was quiet & jovial; he alone carried an absurd love in his soul. Love? He clearly felt that it was not that. Why didn't he go home? Behind the counter he could see the courtyard — the ferryman, a peasant, was the bartender's brother and was just helping to stuff a very large barrel into the cellar door.

The small, muddy courtyard was flooded with transparent green light & the large snowflakes' pill-luminosity, as if inside a hollow of the shabby little house someone had rammed a celestial cork made of shell-glass. The ferryman sometimes stopped and sometimes made brisk animal movements in which he seemed to have four legs; it was snowing evenly, with a serene indifference toward every other rhythm. The whole bar was slowly rising like an elevator, leaving the snow-dots far below. Sometimes the sky looks as though its lower edge adhered to the earth like a drowsy eyelid, but now there was a gap between horizon and sky — if one walked to the edge of the earth, he could see the sky beyond a deep ravine, on the other shore as it were, like an angel-glacier made of one giant mirror.

To tease the sacristan, the peasants were talking about the church in construction: why a church and not a hospital? They calculated how many plates of vegetable stew could be offered to the world's poor if God were pawned. Peter intervened hoarsely. He got so heated in his defense of faith that all of a sudden he felt a longing for the monastic life, a dark tavern-pesterer who builds marble churches on mountain slopes when people are starving, for no other reason than for making his church-apology all the more difficult to formulate and defend.

Behind the counter the bartender's daughter appeared. Peter looked at her, distraught, with the new church's flaming image on his face & the imagined monk's habit on his arm. The girl asked him with a smile if he was waiting for somebody. For the ferryman, he answered on impulse, although this fact hardly featured in his mind anymore. There were only two possibilities: either to elope to Paris with this barmaid, or to live like a hermit among the frost-breathing fir woods. The barmaid disappeared. He saw the ferryman letting off the barrel slowly (the imagined next movement was slow to leave his arms); it seems she called him to hasten and take Peter across the river. Her speech could be heard like the ringing of a small propeller in the snow-flavored green air, then the ferryman's slow, doubting and lazy answer (with some peasants that's the liturgical form of yes-ing), like the first jolts of a ship's steam engine on the silent water. The girl started laughing and in the next moment she appeared again behind the counter: her leftover smile was like half-wiped grape juice on a harvest thief's face. Your man is coming, she said. Then she turned to a cheese-colored railwayman who stared at Peter with vacuous and incomprehensible eyes, but when the girl continued pouring her words into him, those eyes filled up and overflowed in the form of a laugh at Peter's expense, like a jug that is dully empty but the moment the beer tap is opened it foams over with intelligence. Peter felt humiliated. Love? Love?

about the difference between dream and reality in parenthesis

(Juxtaposed: Leatrice's self-lacerating, fantastic landscape and Peter's tavern surroundings — the most schematic dream next to the most schematic short story-realism. Everybody talks about the dichotomy between dream & reality without knowing its significance; the more cultivated would mention the reality of dreams & the fictitiousness of practical daily life, but this can't be counted as a majority. In the struggle between dream and reality the essential thing is that we split in childhood — there is no telling what the two worlds are that pull us to them, but they are strong enough to make children homeless in two directions at once.

The world of fairy tales doesn't mean the world of happiness, for our most ancestral fears and feelings of disgust do not derive from reality, but from fairy-tale figures. At first sight fairy tales and reality don't even seem to belong to two different sorts: to us the magic crow cawing in the deserted garden is just as dreadful and strange as a father's papers in his suitcase or a mother's cosmetics. For the child both are not, they exist exactly not [in Halbert's clown language, 'hyper-exactitudes of Nonentities'] — she felt herself to be at the geometrical point where two non-existences intersect.

Now, when we need to relate one of Leatrice's amorous scheme-aches, it's inevitable to remember the two irrealities. When her mother once forgot in her room a huge bunch of chrysanthemums that she bought for the dinner table for the unknown guests' visit, Leatrice felt a physical queasiness from not knowing where to place the yellow petal-worms: she could sense something fairy-like in the snaking lies of their weight but also knew that all this was addressed to those strangers, that they were the impotent tools of some adult habit. For a moment she was sorry for them, for they perforce had to leave behind the miracle's quintet-world written for two blackbirds and three skylarks and enter the dreary porch of 'habit,' but immediately afterward she felt that miracle was nothing and habit was likewise nothing. These two abstractions she kept all her life, long after she ceased musing over dichotomies, but she could always feel that to every thing belonged two follies of opposite directions, or two impossibilities.)

about a beautiful woman's beauty

He started coughing convulsively. Is death near? There was a headline about the flu epidemic in his neighbor's paper. And he had caught a cold, there was no doubt about that. He quickly ordered rum and put away two glasses. Was it worth dying for a woman whom he doesn't love, who doesn't love him, who is not beautiful? Against the rum's sun-woven brown background rose his slender cathedral: white like the swinging necks of two giraffes trying to get at the clouds' foliage with their giant, mystical nostrils, to get their fill of transcendental nutriment. Even this barmaid laughed at him: a beautiful woman, but the beautiful woman laughs at him.

The beautiful woman lies outside the circle of love. The beautiful woman doesn't let herself be caressed, you can't weave dreams with her in which slippers & the forbidden fruit peacefully coexist. The beautiful woman is cold and empty like a Calvinist church: beauty is something ascetic, it surrounds women like a thin puritanical armor. Even in his childhood he preferred those helmets that were made up of many clusters and moved like the beetles' thorax glued together of rings — but neither in images nor in the theater could he suffer the smooth, light one-hemisphere iron shakos with at most a heavy curtain-like chain mail fringe hanging on their sides. And so was beauty, a feature outside love, which makes all approach impossible.

Peter felt that love always supplements something, as if a man's life were passed with restoration work and nothing else: his feelings are the material with which he completes the hiatuses in the woman's body and soul — filling in cracks, repairing broken-off noses into snub ones. He had a first-rate eye to spot if a woman was completely filled with beauty's love-denying plenitude, or (even if there was no crack on the surface and no figure was missing from the eyes' niches) if there was a hollow somewhere inside the woman — if she gave a resonant boom when tapped. The beautiful woman always moves in such a way that she is perfectly covered: even in her tumbles or when she makes a nest on the swing (physically) she never uncovers her interior, the psychic landscape in whose murky valleys one could pull up the hostile tent of love. The woman with whom one can fall in love, or more exactly, with whom one can do the work of love, is absent-minded & so leaves a door or window of her life open, and that openness shines like a castle courtyard under the moonshine.

Love is always directed at some body part of the woman which she doesn't know, which is never touched by vanity's independent act, or even if it does (for instance, make-up the lips, or powder the shoulder), it touches them as a cliché (mouth, shoulders), and what the man will like in them is the incalculable chance (for example, the sudden wiping off of makeup, the smudging in strips of powder under the jacket). So love becomes the most regular 'unfair' battle, because it charges in such places and continues the onslaught in such spaces of which the woman has no inkling.

One would in vain look for a better illustration of dancing at two weddings: when the woman sees that the man fancies her, she will spend more & more time before the mirror, elaborating on what doesn't feature at all among her instruments of seduction; while the man would develop to ever more preposterous extremes, and growing ever more alien and distant from the woman herself, the body or psyche-moment silted on the first impressions.

The mirror-mania & the indeterminate moment-stylizing mania countervail: however 'individually' a woman may use make-up, the concept at work in her will be nevertheless as run-of-the-mill that it ultimately falls short of the very possibility of beauty — and the man's impression-stump is so momentary, peculiar, and unavailable to reason that it's beyond all beauty. But he will be unable to steal such an impression of 'officially' beautiful woman: on vast green meadows one may come across an excitingly red small flower, unknown to the meadow (which believes itself to be thoroughly green) — but on factory-made green silk you can't find by accident a bit of red embroidery or external monogram. Beauty belongs to the latter category.

Modern fashion locked women away from Peter and he didn't understand where the forever bemoaned-caricatured immorality of 'our days' may be. The taut, smooth little caps with a small candle-wick on top, pressed onto the left cheek, the hair plastered to the right cheek and down to the neck, like tarmac, the trimmed eyebrow squeezed into the skin, the shadowless, anonymous lipstick, the tight clothes, those clinical sheaths of inventoried muscles; the hard movements, which seem to be permanently launching into the scissors at the uneven bars. All this was so homogeneous that it needed doing something with — to get here and there, drive around, play tennis, dance. But that is not love — he said to himself, not with contempt but with grouching nostalgia. The *Vogue* and the *Jardin des Modes* were in fact the fruit of Reformation theology: women left behind the movements of inner life, those psychic dances that even a lame stylite could perform, switching instead to outward action, to work — instead of capacious gestures bridging in semicircular arches, to small, typewriting-like action-knocking.

There was a time when the non plus ultra of virtue manifested in a single luxury idea, in the aristocratism of self-mortification, later the small useful deeds, petit-bourgeois charity, mercantile thrift and similar moral warrants became the apex of virtue. O, beautiful template moral: what could the daydreaming, hypochondriac Peter do with that? He looked with loathing at the barmaid, on whom the smile left over from the laugh still glittered here and there, just as there are always a few unwiped body parts left on people who have long got home from the swimming pool.

the sacristan's character

The sacristan was half-heartedly defending his principles before the others. In fact he didn't have much connection with his church, being mostly the household servant of its old priest. In the mornings he inspected the horses in the stall: that was his morning devotion. He mucked about with the hay, brushes, listened to the horses' breathing in the warm dimness. Then he proceeded to scold the driver's wife, because her husband was not home yet, although he was supposed to polish the carriage early in the morning, for a high-born guest was arriving who had to be picked up from the train station in the carriage. This unknown guest, on whose behalf he had precise tasks (to remove the old cigar boxes from the guestroom's nightstand, to air the room, hang up fresh towels next to the washstand, etc.), represented mystery at large, the underhand authority that commands the poor, ignorant believers with cold knowledge and disguise.

For the sacristan believed that the whole religion and God were one great intrigue against people, but in his belief there was no shade of revolt, malice, or anticlerical impetus — what is more, in holding the heavens to be such a cunning strategist against himself, he felt a profound respect for religion, the way highwaymen will look with almost pious affect at the gentleman who with unsuspected bravado points a revolver to their chest.

When his relatives, young lovers, and cataract-ridden old women fell for the lyricism and schmaltz in religion, he shrugged with an air of superiority, feeling that truth stands by the side of dark-hot bureaucracy and dry automatism, as he saw in his master. When he attended to his master he always felt that he was lurking around a volcano that might break out any time — not in the form of dramatic pathos but of a small note.

He loved order not because it was truly order but on the contrary: the order that he squeezed out of the 'pisco' (that's how he called the priest, probably from 'episcopus') was so unlike what he himself imagined to be order that this shameless sedition cooled his blood: the 'pisco' would always find order there where his mind detected something tilted, uncertain, & chaotic. In fact he couldn't approve of such consistent turning of things on their head, such cold-blooded & patronizing provoking of lucidity as could also be heard in the 'pisco's' sermons (that is, the sermons he delivered in the church of Z*** where only gentlemen went; the ones he said at home, where Leatrice too lived, the sacristan would not attend, because they were addressed only to merchants and peasants), but this was his revenge on dimwit boys and garrulous girls who would enthuse only for things as simple as two times two.

The sacristan had long carried this silent dualism in himself: deep inside, lucidity, and on the surface of his soul, jeering respect for the paradoxes of the 'pisco.' He got used to the air in the 'pisco's' house where everything was topsy-turvy & when he went home to his family he felt almost sick at the naïve entourage and straightforward prayers. He turned up his nose at the simplest religious deeds and kept repeating that "God is a completely different kettle of fish," and when they asked in reproachful tone, what kettle, all he could see was the shady room of the 'pisco,' the abbey's bastion seen from the window like the chimney of an anchoring steamer in God's China-yellow sea — the 'pisco's' eyeglasses completely hid the priest's eyes, putting two wry aureoles in their place — the empty guestroom, where the fresh towels await the eternal stranger like frozen banners. There's no way one could tell this to the women, they could never understand it. In time he got more and more infatuated with the 'pisco's' personality, the furniture of the small palace (articuli fidei), with the result that he almost instigated the peasants to irreligiosity.

He particularly relished tormenting the candle-lighting peasant girls. If he saw a pale young monk in the morning explaining something to the 'pisco' who merely smiled condescendence and said in an uninflected voice, "— but it will never make sense to melt down our rights with naïve and feminine exaggeration in the fiery souls of romantic Gypsies —," then he lived for weeks on this sentence that he couldn't comprehend, and if he happened to see a peasant girl at her prayers he dropped a satanic jibe to her companion: "these girls believe that if they melt down their rights on their Gypsy hearts, everything will be right as rain" — and looked up with mysterious enjoyment as though he could see the revel's end among the treetops.

Once in the church of Z*** the 'pisco' spoke of the mysterium naturale, of the Aeropagite's hyperphotos gnophos,[250] and of the concept of God in the human and divine mind: mystery and comprehensibility turned in his speech like the wheels of a watermill gliding now below, now above the water — as though God's mystery were not a shapeless twilight and incense-stale shiver but God's simplest trait or daily habit. 'Mysteriousness' is a thing of the exact shape and weight of comprehensibility, but closed. This was a great surprise for the sacristan who had so far felt the thing to be a bird of prey: now from the priest's hand gestures (their brisk energy reminded him of the way he would order recalcitrant dogs to him: the dog didn't obey, but one could see in the 'pisco's' stretched arm, from his fingers hanging down for a minute, that he had confidence in the strength of his order-word, even if his fingers drooped to an absent-minded treuga) he saw that the secret was:

a domestic animal, that the contents of the night were infinitely complex, but it had one point (at the hips perhaps?) where a human arm could enclose its perimeter as though it were an infinite, death-blue sheaf that flares out upwards and downwards (to infinity) but one can squeeze it in the middle with one light, almost phlegmatic grip.

He would never forget the 'pisco's' hand gesture — he seemed to be explaining not an idea but a physical trick from his ambo (so that the sleeve of his vestment slid back up to his elbow) — his white hand could be seen from afar as he made a loop from his thumb and index. He kept mentioning a mask whose features may be humanly simple, but behind it undulates the profile-less face of eternity — perhaps trying to make comprehensible, with repeated images, the two sides of mystery, the finite one turned toward man, and the infinite one turned toward itself: the Janus figure hopped in the air before the ambo like a marionette. The sacristan's head swirled, the word 'mask' had delivered the coup-de-grace: not only was mystery simple but it turned out to be a comedian. Because that's what the mask meant for him. He went home like a drunk or a lonely virgin who was inadvertently slap-kissed by a rambunctious lad.

It was late at night but he went in the church to look at the few Solomonic columns and giant windows lit up by these novel words. Is infinity of the same size then as finitude but with different contents? He groped for a candle in the sacristy. He felt he owned the church, the 'pisco,' the congregation, God, and everything. The poison swelled in his veins. So far he had been the slave of mystery who, even though he didn't recognize the truth of mystery, bowed to its skill with which it got people in its grasp — but now he became the handler of mystery: for we have one side of the Janus-head, the mask; God adapts to man — wasn't that what the sermon said?

view from the sacristy window

The sacristy hovered right above the water like a separate nest glued to the rock face; he went to the window to see in the scarce light which key opens the screeching glass door to the church nave. The sky lit the place like a stage in front of which the last tulle curtain had been drawn; the stars were much closer than the sky itself and floated freely in the air — everything shone in the last act's splendor. In the distance the monastery bastion trickled from the sky like from a blue stalactite cave; a cloud, pondering its own colors in two minds, one red and one grey, let itself vertically down above the tower to lengthen it by 10 meters. Another bright white cloud (also very far from the sky's lonely glimmer) was reflected in the river like a slender bridge stretching beneath the transparent riverbed that continued underneath the city: this way the sacristy swam twice higher than in reality; in the water the sky's evasive blue was ennobled into concreteness, its raw material was fine-polished, without losing anything of its airiness.

The two dark riverbanks with their roof-leaves and tower-branches looked on the river, their soul, with awe. The river stood motionless, like one sole blue tile in the forest: even those small frills, little black wave-beginnings, were unstirring, halting in the same place like the small bulges on crocodile leather. The air-bridge hung in a deep semicircle like those Chinese bridges woven of a few toothpicks & threads (are they authentic? La Chine m'inquiète [251] — as the French heiress put it) that crawl like millipedes across eternity's mirror-fleshed fruit. (Halbert often spoke to Leatrice about his dreams when he could imagine Cambridge only as the headquarters of 'pan-pontism,' and about how he had a permanent vision of bridges when he went to university: on the professors' faces, in the small dime-a-dozen cups of March crocuses, in his own steps, how it stretched through the Renaissance sticking to house fronts as the odd drifting snowflake sticks to the childhood fantasies' silvery, extraordinarily tall & slender bridge made of one sole gossamer arch, which is reflected in infinite depth in the blue waters: the distance between the two bridges is enormous, as if it were the greatest [and mute!] amplitude of the vibration of one white string tautened above the water.)

This whole cult of bridges and bridge-shadows came from Halbert's father who was a vicar at Exeter: it was he who always talked about inexistent, splendid bridges in which he seemed to recognize some moral symbol. The bridge is practical but also playful like a fairy swing; the bridge is a road, but some such minimum of road that it appears Platonic or heavenly irony rather than a carrier of truly human purpose; it is so much only-road & only-direction that this absolute purposefulness almost obliterates the existence of purpose in the world; the bridge is always reflected, so we tread it only with our foot soles, while our soul strays along the reflection's U-shaped underwater diver-corridor; the bridge always stands between two banks, it's a resonant nothing-landscape between yes and no, where we can feel ourselves truly free. The bridge's reflection mirrors not only image but also space; water is incapable of projection, for instance to project a straight line from an elliptic arch — instead it copies the whole space, not leaving out a teaspoonful's worth of the vacuum that gapes under the arch. And this is its greatest enjoyment: visible nothing in water's shiny Versailles, which becomes visible by being in reverse. Is this cheap ethics? Would a vacuous action or barren life, if stretched across the Holy Ghost's celestial basin, become at once rich and scintillating space?

The sacristan had four keys: the 'sword' key whose handle resembled the hilt-guard of a cavalry sabre — it was completely blackened, but its stem shone as though the two didn't belong together; the 'collared' key: under its grip there was an iron ornament resembling the starched pillory-collars of Dutch portraits; the 'squinting' one: this was badly fused, so a second key-stump jutted out around its pivot, as in double vision; and one last, nameless, blazonless, plebeian key that opened the candle cases. The 'squinting' one opened the door to the church and the sacristan found it in the window light: the light almost pulled it from his hand like an acid liquid from the dusk. He scuffled back to the dark door like a miser to his buried treasure. Candle in hand, he entered; the windows receded further from the bumptious little glow. Next to the door stood an old column, a remnant of the earlier church; the sacristan would have liked to pat its neck like of a horse.

It was at the entrance to this church that Leatrice listened to the sacristan's story about Peter. For Peter had his moments of confession-mania; he would never have dared speak about his life to someone more intelligent than him but with the sacristan he felt at ease. The fact that he drastically simplified his 'problems,' which the sacristan obviously noticed and took offence, seemed to cause no disturbance. Therefore the sacristan treated Peter with superiority; in the grip of whimsical humility, Peter suffered this gladly. In fact women were too much to handle for him and whenever he prepared for a rendezvous he toyed with the idea of physically mutilating himself, so he would never again have anything to do with them. Besides, he considered it a sin too, and perhaps the only reason why he couldn't get rid of his instinct was that he kept conjuring to himself the theological concept of sin far too stylishly.

the relation between action and conscience

Overall, however, it was a far greater fallacy that for him virtue was not really possible. Action & conscience were two entirely separate worlds, not connected in any way. Action equaled destruction —

without harboring the least shade of anarchic penchants he knew & had repeatedly experienced that if he did anything, if he managed to escape the grey fog-crater of passivity, that immediately turned into destruction. Why? If we are silent for a moment, one moment is enough for the air, dust specks, light rays to be soothed into a stable position, for a million microscopic phenomena to get into a 'settled' state. If we move then, the smallest change of place upsets, disperses, and destroys those physical & chemical Lilliputians. Affectation? Peter felt keenly that the world was completely filled and so every movement can be but collision, every action distorts the graphs of the world.

Distort? What if it really beautifies? In the present case he could find beautiful only that which was given: wherever he stepped in the world, that territory would undoubtedly split like an ice sheet under a ship's prow, and those two seemed inferior to the pre-movement oneness. It would have been difficult for him to draw a boundary between metaphor, logic, and reality, as concerns moral things: absolute action would have been nothing but the splitting of the world into two equal halves. But there is no absolute action, an action that could traverse, like perpetual, even movement, the world's perfectly stuffed but eminently splittable body. Absolute action would be complete breaking free from the world: all the world's relation-lines would be cut in half in one place, thus willed-to-the-end will would live in their midst, independently, no longer qualifying as will.

All these functions expanded in Peter's mind because he was utterly helpless — he felt like a fakir on whose shoulders birds nest and around whose foot soles gorgeous flowers bloom, wrapping his feet up in their tight roots like in a sandal. How then could he move? Inside him, perfect silence and outside, dense flowers: he felt that if he were to act, it would be not the turning into deed of one part of his soul but that his whole soul, a whole territory of passivity would collapse, so to speak, on the world. For the indolent action is not a particular movement aiming at the realization of a particular idea but simply the turning inside out, the dropping into the world of the entire soul's indolence-ballast: the inner chemical composition of indolence will not change in the least, it is merely shifted to another place, from the soul into the outer world. He always felt of his face that it was incapable of mimicry: so was his soul — it didn't know waves, only the pathos-less possibility of complete flooding. Physically and logically it was equally clear that any movement without destruction is impossible, but Peter felt that psychology too corroborated this fact.

One needs energy for action, and the impotent person can imagine and experience energy in one form alone: at the highest degree. And that can be only destructive. No action is more action than war. Action has to be distinguished from function: function consists in the fact that energy makes a compromise with other energies and together they reach some result, but in that result 'action' plays only a small part, the rest consists of the things given in the world before the beginning of 'action'; on the other hand, action can't tolerate any given thing, it wills only itself, and that of course leads to the logical outcome that everything should be destroyed and it alone remain (we have alluded to something similar above). And war is precisely that: to make disappear everything that it finds on its path, until it sees glowing before it the redeeming blankness of nothing.

He had once seen a peasant flog his wife to death: he enjoyed the spectacle with all the nostalgia of the helpless. Sadism? He didn't look into it but nevertheless felt that his entire soul left his body and started out in the world. What could he do with muscles strained to extreme? Hit, that's all. There are no more kinds of energy: just as we can read in the gospels that he who calls his neighbor a 'fool' is already damned, so in the soul, if everything arises (or more exactly: the entire soul turns outward into body instead of into soul), it reaches such a high tension that it is incompatible with any phenomena of the given world and can only harm them. So Peter's psychology knew no 'creation' (at most as a function), but only two extremes: utter passivity (which he sometimes simply called soul) or destruction.

The logical consequence was that he worshipped authority, not revolution. At the center of revolutions was an idea, if nothing else, the idea of destruction, which made virgin destruction, by definition program-less, radically impossible — wars too are made great not by their purpose but by their purposelessness which blossoms as they unfold. If I indeed want to destroy something, I have already made of the inexorable destructive nature of pure action a mere practical 'demolishing,' dry stonemason's work, which has nothing to do with the empty absolute of 'action.' Peter passionately loathed all the sieges of the Bastille, but he adored the tsar's ceremonial entries and the ovation, he whipped himself to such frenzied worship that everything perished from his soul, his body paralyzed, he had no memories or intentions left, no appetite and no woman, only the lost energy of movement. This carried in itself a greater potential of destruction than destruction derived from the idea of destruction.

Action is like a poetic creation, it's a matter of exceptional inspiration, and it immediately elevates the soul to a height where it can't see the world as of any value but only as its enemy. For weeks he was haunted by the peasant's bloody whip as it lashed with conspicuous slowness into the woman's body, as if it had been not a string but a thin fencing rapier. Such destructive dynamism of action is not related to any form of sentimentalism: it is not some enhanced feeling or lyrical absurdity. When he hailed the tsar he didn't love the tsar and no overall respect for Orthodox power raged in him, it was only his soul moving, and that has only one kinetics for all time. 'His soul moving': this should be understood purely literally, even mechanically, not as a comparison.

How many times he had made up his mind that he would be good, would not commit adultery, and on such occasions his soul indeed filled with moral inspiration, at such times he was not capable of anything else but to scurry hither and thither in the woods or on the streets, & to beat Satan with an imaginary whip, to whack and whack him until his arms ached. On such occasions (goodness! goodness!) he loathed white flowers, because he saw in them the smile of a syrupy mask that covers the sins committed with women; he loathed mothers nursing their children in the gates of the outskirts, because he saw in their stern self-sacrifice only the turning of love into puffed-up red-tape; he would have liked to smash all Madonna effigies; he loathed virtue itself, loathed his own good intentions, for even in their infinite power he felt the mediated power of Satan disguised into woman. That is, if virtue rose to the power of action, it turned into only-action, opposed to all virtue and wanting nothing but nihil.

And there was the other world, of conscience. This was the very opposite of action because it did not annihilate the world but if possible, enriched, tripled, even quadrupled it. The 'thinking about good' will distinguish one hundred sin-shades in one single imagined virtue-splinter, and in these sin-shades, further distinct virtues, and so on to infinity. This is of course the simplest template of vexation, there are countless other methods of multiplication at hand. In this way such a rich world is created between the 'I' and the real outer world that soon the 'I' goes deaf to any reality, and all elements of its content will refer only to another element, never to reality. If a thought is present in the soul, it can tolerate only another thought next to itself, and nothing else. And if an action is present, it tolerates neither soul nor reality beside itself. Conscience is one of the spare rooms of fantasy, with all the balanced richness of pros and cons; action is fantasy-less and chic-less nakedness.

In the small riverside bar only these two representatives of religion were present: the sacristan with his haughty insider allure, whose content could be nothing but the shape of the 'pisco's' hand and the incomprehensibility of the administration of church matters; and Peter, who indulged in naïve logicizing of sin and in the trans-imaginings of abstract tragedies. While sitting in the boat (one riverbank was suddenly bleached, the other was dark like black mud) he felt, with his handkerchief held to his mouth, that he was sitting on the boat of sin steered by a dark predestination-mannequin. His vanity was dealt a blow by the fact that he could never have conquered the barmaid; he would have liked to return with the boat and seduce her, take what it takes. "Women must feel on me that I don't take them for amusement but only the arithmetic reprises of the original sin." The boat slowly wedged into the water and Peter felt that the boatman was sizing him up with contempt. Who would cross the river in such weather? Fools. His dread of disease spread before him the landscape of sin in all its picturesqueness, this ethics-less, hypochondriac mural. The gull-like grey birds were whirling close to the water and the heretic angel was taking him to the headquarters of sin with black punctuality.

With tearful face he looked up at the sky: in the yellow wall of light and beyond the layer of the dissipating clouds moving at different speed behind one another, a small blue patch glowed, looking like something that is not color but speech which his ears alone can't hear. What if God had given him a beautiful woman in his youth? One like that light blue patch smiling down from above the evening's yellow cascades and leaden-blue veils? Is that a sin? He thought of the fate of those beautiful women he never dared acquaint; blue eyes lit up the evening's flu damp with white self-assurance, blue eyes that shine when it doesn't harm men's health, in the most comfortable and most natural places & times. He had always met women at impossible times, in absurd places.

two kinds of shadow

Snow was falling faintly; grey ice sheets floated next to the boat like bits of soaked paper. The luminous shore fell under a grey draught; it was unsettling to see the rushing shadow — one of the houses was still yellow, the next one already grey, together with the pavement and street in front; he would have liked to squeeze some self-mortifying or self-reassuring theory for himself out of the shadow's nature; darkness floated in the air, leaving the houses untouched, even the colors were left intact, so darkening was more a logical imagining inside our brain than the actual soaking-up of shadow into the houses' colorful optical bodies. These two kinds of shadow are clearly distinguishable: the one, meaning no more than a black shadow on a red wall, without darkening the red, or without the red and black forming a deeper shade — and the other, which is no more an external shadow anymore, but the almost inner transfiguration of the red surface. There is no such thing in the world as optical shadow, because the first of the above is merely a logical shadow, while the latter is a psychological one. It's strange that in paintings they mix the walls fallen under the first kind of shadow with different pigments, although in reality the color stays the same and the greyness cast on it is only a logical surplus.

Perhaps sin, too, is only such an insulated shadow on his soul, and the painter who nevertheless prepares the soul and sin of mixed pigments (the old color and shadow) is an exaggerating and bad moralist. In his childhood he often looked at the dark red, overshadowed walls of originally red houses in color pictures: if he looked at them from up close, he could see only one color, the dark red — but if he looked from farther away, he could already distinguish the original red and, separately from it, the blue shadow-air.

He found the struggle of sin and virtue so much a decorative masquerade only (sometimes as a cadence inscribed into Milton) that it seemed only natural to think it was all a dispute, intellectual tournament lying outside his soul, where he is the chained-down eternal spectator.

Peter's hypochondria, virtue, connoisseurship of women

The ferryman said he would pull to the shore further downstream because he didn't want to meet his son-in-law, with whom he had a nasty fallout. Peter was appalled at his ease in announcing this, without as much as asking if he may or apologizing. The forbidden tree of Paradise shot dense foliage: its blue leaves soaked up the sky's little turquoise gazes and all the grotesqueness of real women. He would have liked to bury himself into the foliage of one tree, whose scent, color, weight, and chaos united in itself the contrasting pull of the possible and impossible woman. The ferryman's bluntness forced him into new octaves of fate, as if he had misplaced his life, and his rude music teacher now pushed his hand upward. At the same time the blue was getting lighter, gold-shaded meadow beyond the clouds' eel outlines, when the riverbank started darkening among the clouds' metallic udders. His soul undulated languidly on the waters of the primeval forest, among the effervescent powder of blue sunlight — Paradise is obviously a jungle and solution, the realm of purity and fight.

The more unknown, the more impossible a woman is, the closer she stands to us, the more we feel her presence, her breath, for she was born of us. In dream there is a fair share of drastic empiricism: we walk among positivities, on secure ground, where no surprises can occur. When Peter gazed at the blue patch high above (which started distancing itself, turning into earth), he was overwhelmed by love for the dream: a resigned inebriation ran through his head and he felt that reality could never be so foliage-shaped: leaves above, below, beneath, everywhere.

It's one thing to love the dream for its dream nature and quite another to love it for its reality nature. Peter was far too pessimistic to believe in the primacy of dreams or anything of the kind, but he did believe that the dream images performed such an erosion on his body that he plastically carried within himself the figure of beautiful women. Women opened like fireworks under his skin, like between the slender walls of a castle; desire was so consistent that in his body, by the means of some clumsy transubstantiation (to put it blasphemously) their figures were born and bore fruit. Desires didn't stop but, upon reaching a fulcrum, they suddenly took on new shapes, independently from the outer world, and started another plastic dance.

But this wore him out and made him sick: on returning home from one of those destiny-trainings he would lie down and sleep for long, ask for fine foods, lots of tea, and lots of pampering; his eyes kept dropping tears of self-pity and sudden babyhood. His infinite exhaustion, cough, and racing heart were the best evidence that he was, after all, good — otherwise he wouldn't be so floored with nervousness. At such times he put on his warm leather slippers, sat by the window in his soft armchair, read to Leatrice from some book of fairy tales, and was moved to crying over a sparrow's death. He was overcome by a peculiar serenity, which he interpreted as moral change — for him mortal exhaustion was a great victory. But undeniably from the darkness of the run after women and the ensuing childish, saccharine convalescence, some positivity too remained in his soul: a concrete minus acquaintance with the woman for whom he crisscrossed the whole countryside, humbled himself, fell ill, and yet never received as much as a glance, because most of the time he never met her.

Puzzlingly, Peter knew women exceedingly well. One would think that whoever dances at night with dark angels in the aspful garden of Paradise, to dissolve his crises into virtue with Ovomaltine in the morning,[252] will at most be capable of Salvation Army frescoes and the colorful statistics of primer psycho-machias, but in no case of connoisseurship of women. (Leatrice suffered much from Touqué who never tired of proclaiming that the one who has great psychic struggles, forty horse-power dilemmas, and chessboard black-and-white crises, is surely working on the death of the soul, not its 'complicating.' A hatred of contrast imprinted a sickly grimace on Touqué's face: the 'problems' dull the soul, impoverish it, render it a homogeneous sponge. Solely on passivity's near-dead mirror can true richness emerge. The psychic 'problem' is vital in nature, therefore it cannot yield any finesse.) And yet, Peter knew women very well — he belonged among those exceptional people whose eyes were sharpened by desire, and who could turn those infernal caricatures and ideas refined into a deafeningly pure sound, which were born of his many deceptions and minimal pleasures, into practical experiences. He held only caricatures and ideals to be reality, in his eyes experience was only convention, the affected play-acting of socialites; the so-called experiences traversed Peter's life like a film reel between his fingers after seeing it in the cinema. With him, experience was not spontaneous but rather, a technical conceit to cover up his struggles.

His knowledge of women moved on three planes: the first was desire-knowledge, when the sin's most highly stylized, picturesque-intellectual symbols got mixed with the most real exteriority — fragments of the woman glimpsed; the second was the acquaintance left after 'convalescence': he held this to be the most precious — although this knowledge was not precise and analytic (as compared to the woman's portrait), yet it gave an all the more punctual image of the woman's attractiveness & of everything else she radiated; and finally, the third was an artificially concocted experience, when he tossed the whole knot of memories into the photographic developer of 'practicality' and read the clarifying outlines. Experience showed ever different shades, depending on who the person was to whom he first told it — these pseudo-experiences inherited the godfathers' profile, not that of their progenitor. So the experiential memory image of a particular woman was in fact an exact copy of the various lay or genuine confessors, into which he pasted an original detail of the woman here and there like an archaic body jewel, which couldn't be organically connected to the new portrait. In fashion magazines they write under the pictures of this or that model, 'posé par Mlle N.N.': at some of these experience-constructing operations Peter felt that the one who happened to talk with him about the respective woman, sees the woman and his own perception 'posé par.'

He also spoke about his sins with priests, and one could expect that there would be no difference between the original temptation drama and its polished experience shape, because the given 'godfather' was akin to the progenitor, but it was not so. The battle of sin and virtue looked just as much a formality in his presentation delivered to the priest, as if he had related it to a lumpen fellow. He compared this 'theologicum clericisatum' (being of Jewish extraction, for a while Peter entertained the idea of inventing a neo-neo-Latin tongue) to the refined operation cultivated by an amateur lady painter (the amateurs always set to themselves more 'difficult' problems than the real artist, because they want the difficulty before the actual theme, while the artists discover ever newer difficulties in essentially simple themes) when she painted a bunch of red carnations against a red background, and a green constellation of mugs against a background of identical green.

Sixth Non-Prae diagonal: Chinese marriage, Christian love

> fish and river
> the river at night
> the fisherman and his daughter
> the fisherman's daughter plots to kill the Chinese princess, but the princess changes into the double of the fisherman's daughter; she has the fisherman's daughter tortured
> the bridegroom, a prince comes on a ship
> the old inquisitor and his adoptive son
> landscape under the volcano
> the love of the fisherman's daughter and the adoptive son
> the Chinese wife tortures her husband but he doesn't harm her, regarding his wife as a force of nature
> 'human being' and irreality in love
> logic and church plan
> suicide and hymn to 'nameless forces of nature'

(…To fish here! How can one call this fishing? The water where he looked for fish was not abrupt enough to be a genuine waterfall, but it was no river either, jumping in zigzags on whimsical steps sometimes three degrees into the depth, then four degrees upward, full of rocks, unexpected dams, petrified shrubs and snake-throated whirlpools. The waves dashing against the stones and against the lance-hard, almost lava-like leaves made a deafening noise, inside which a polyphony could be distinguished: most strangely, under the great holler's thunder-domes the small waves' quivering flutes could be heard clearly, and from the riverbed the swaying of the small bastard twigs trickling among the grasses on the banks, as if the greatest noise were not a sound but only a porcelain canon tunnel, under which the most timid sound-flowers can freely open their F♯-C♯-D♯ petals.

To fish here? The waves were tall and narrow like a crosier in the hand of an invisible bishop, with a large white tuft on top, the steaming furs of water-extermination: but that happened only on their topmost parts, otherwise the whole stream was uniformly and shadelessly blue, a rarity that defied physics in such a battered-to-death, rushing river.

And this was not the only whim of nature: from the bottom and sometimes from the top of the rocks flowers bloomed at the end of hair-thin stems, their stems and paper leaves swayed and bowed amidst the water's noise-torpedoes like the midnight clock hand under the lovers' dawn-smothering breath, but never broke; however much the white spume-palms slammed their gentle crown, they rose from the water like trans-virginated flour flying upward through a sieve. The collision of water and stone was so strong that the white spume and blue water were often torn apart like the head and the wig at a beheading: the one flies to the right, the other rolls to the left: the white spume almost flew over the cliffs, almost but never touching their edge like a very low-flying gull, and the adjacent fragment of blue water suddenly calmed down, halted at the feet of the rocks with mirror-smooth surface, without a trace of the clash. It was an immense pleasure to watch this: in the narrow valley the noise wedges into rock face and trees like lightning, the many sounds can't fit in and get curled up like a long lance that they try to ram horizontally between two very narrow walls; the white spumes fly about in the sound-frozen, sound-cold air like angora cats scattered with a shovel — and yet at the feet of the rocks the water is tranquil, almost incandescing with silence, like people's eyeballs under the closed eyelid when waiting for pleasure — with no strength left in the muscles and knowing that pleasure will now be born independently of them. On these quiet rock belts the water is one lip darker than elsewhere: virginity's scattered rings glowing afar — if a monkey looks down from the top of a tree, he will see only white gauze scrolls, from under which dark blue silence-intarsios glow.

To fish here! Where can the fish be? In this water they are wonderful as thin flowers. They exist, but can spend at most a quarter of their lives in the water: big gold-pink, light green fish & glassy-spined sour cherry-red jest-pikes catapulted into the air every minute by the current that hurls them among the rattling leaves of trees that bow to the water — they sizzle among their thick crowns as though tossed into a pan with burning fat; from the branches they drop back into the water, with gills spread outward like donkey ears, underway gathering in a few more slaps from the jutting stones. Freed spumes fly about, & among them, together or sidewise, fly the colorful fish; sometimes only in the last second does the gold-soft tsing-tsang carplet eclose from the spume-cocoon, like a blade jumping forth with delay from the sticky sheath. Here fishing is a bizarre mix of arrow-shooting, butterfly-chase, pole vaulting, and angling — sometimes just tags or nest-robbery.

It's curious how different the colors of fish are from the color of water, water weeds, trees, & rocks — one would expect more mimicry from them. Are both kinds colors — the water's silky, oxygen-trimmed blue and the fish's burning, knotty, inward-sucked and inward-condensed sour cherry skin? Water and fish relate to one another like pleasure and bliss: the one, blue, means the harmonious general state of colorfulness, the other, the sour cherry, color's life-transmission, its sexual tumbles. The two kinds of color are so different to make one believe that only one can belong to so-called 'nature.' The one who lives here [and somebody does live here] will realize before long that everything, first and foremost the human being and his jungle surroundings, is part of one common process, there is no difference between one of his complicated psychic experiences and the trees' nursery-rhyme rain-trickling operations — on the other hand [after filling his lungs with this lesson, like grapes with embryonic wine] he will find that fish and flower, water and air, first cat and second cat are so explosively different that nature can't be regarded as anything but the flea market of the leftovers of some sixty different worlds. In the sour cherry-color fish's color there is some unbreakable limit that doesn't disclose its secret and doesn't filter into itself the features of the landscape, especially of the water: it stands in the sharpest contrast to its most immediate environment and life-giver. And so do the other two kinds, the green rusting into gold, and the light green.

'Is it that we harbor some hazy prejudice about the colors of 'nature' being necessarily blurry, dull, roundabout, could this be the reason why we don't feel fish to be 'natural' enough? Do we link liquid and blueness in the case of water more than we link the fish's oval and the color spectrum? If their redness were at least a bit diluted in water, and around the fishes' body too [whence this obstinate desire?] a reddish stain might be left on the water, the way the rocks' foot is surrounded by an absolutely tranquil dark blue bracelet: we can see such a faint square on coffee where we dropped in the sugar cube. But it seems that there can be no talk of that. Let's say that this landscape is found in Japan or China and that the one hunting the fish is a Christian seaman who was left behind in the wilderness from a ship transporting missionaries.

'Perhaps he can fish better at night than during the day: then the Moon is sovereign and the fish glow. It's not the Moon's silver to fall on the treetops, the fruits' inside [there where a worm dug a tiny tunnel from the peel to the core], but the night sky's blood-dark, bitter, and splendid indigo: it's not the sky that reflects the moon but the sky flaming with its long enamel fountains in the Moon's fireless courtyard. In this blue the fish scintillate wildly like lampions.

'It's then that fishing begins: he climbs into a tree [just as one needs galoshes for protecting against the mud, he would like to have blue-protecting shoes in the stifling blueness] and lets down his octopus tentacle-like metallic net, so that some gauche-sighted fish would jump into it; or he jumps from rock to rock, cracking his angle in the air like a whip, then throws everything aside and lies on his belly in the shallow water and feels the captured creature under his chest as if his heart had almost spilt out. In the violet Moon-darkness the waves' wings have a peculiar resonance and the fishes' colors glisten strangely. The noise is now not directed at the air and the colors are not directed to the eyes: it takes only one great monotony in the world [here, the night's great Danaid terrorism] for the function of the senses to be swapped, confused, rendered utterly useless. The sound doesn't sound but is: man either perceives the world but doesn't suspect he is — or he doesn't perceive nature at all [this was during the night] but his whole body and being is the quivering recording device of it, of existence: so this is the best time for fishing. Above the river the remnants of a bridge could also be seen, but the seaman used the boughs mostly: from them he hung down to the water as a sleeping anchor.

The seaman's daughter used to take the fish to the princess. The princess lived close to the waterfall in her castle made of ladders and giant plants: all its walls and floors were made of very large leaves and ossified foliage, not plucked & engineered together but growing on the spot. The only way to tell the castle from the primeval forest were the thin wooden planks between the scented bastions of flowers & fruits, ladder-like planks on which green toads would walk when kept in a jar, or on which creepers run. The 'castle' made of jungle fern-fans and thin sticks was like the place of a stupendous rhetorical sentence in a learned mandarin's book — but only its place, where only the punctuation signs can be seen, the odd accent, exclamation mark, question mark, or the worrying dash [is there such a thing in Chinese?].

The fisherman's daughter would have loved to roam this neither-flower-nor-house palace — foliage caressed her body like rain, while her arms and feet kept bumping into sticks. The fisherman and his daughter were drunk all the time: he had nothing on him but a blue and white-striped wide jersey, black trousers, and his brandy bottle. The girl was elegant as a Parisian princess, but she also carried a brandy bottle on her all the time. Elegant? She would walk in evening gowns early at dawn, diligently untangling their long trains from the brambles' hooks; she slung the sack of fish on her shoulder & enjoyed the scales' ice on her low-cut, bare back.

The Chinese princess lived a hermit's life so to say, had only two servants but an awful lot of money. Once when she was very sick the fisherman's daughter made up her mind that she would get her money, take what it takes. She fawned, roasted the fish herself, burning her fingers five times as she was so stoned she could hardly see. But to her infinite chagrin, the princess started recovering. She decided that if convalescence took one week longer she would kill the princess. She planned everything carefully with her father, what poison to put in what fish so that the princess would surely die.

The convalescent princess' greatest joy was to put on European clothes. She first tried them out when the European girl was too hot from the sun, alcohol, and the fish-roasting pans, so she shed her clothes on the princess' seat. The fat was sizzling in the pan, almost playing handball with the fish, and the girl got completely immersed in the joys of the game: she squatted to spin the fish, she tiptoed to lift the fish high above the pan with a fork like some triumphal flower whose bud, petal, and fruit is merely fuzzy steam — then took the fish by the head and tail and swung it above the fire, so the flames ran along its sides like violin bows. During this time the princess dressed before the mirror. The act drove her completely wild: the next day she had her skin all bleached with flour and paint, daubed red stains on it, while on the third day she attempted to emulate the European girl's body with the help of all kinds of gels and ointments. One of the servants copied the image of the fisherman's daughter in life size, & while she was sitting for him, the other servant visited the house of her father [it was the cabin of a ramshackle ship] and stole all the girl's clothes.

While she was concocting the poison with her father at home, the healing princess metamorphosed completely into the European girl: now for her to kill the princess would have meant simply suicide. When she nevertheless made up her mind to poison the princess, the two servants captured her and tied her to a bed in the princess's bedroom — her naked body wriggled on the leaves like a glued, sticky-legged worm.

In the princess three simultaneous feelings were awakened: the feelings of personality, of love, and of torture. In her new disguise she feels herself to be 'somebody,' as opposed to her previous self, which lacked walls just like her castle; above all, she loves the woman, something that in her bears not the slightest connection to benefiting the

European girl or eliciting pleasant feelings in her; in torturing the girl she is not driven by the desire to cause and see pain, but movement, vibrating gestures, of which she herself is incapable — no matter how exact a sculptural copy she had become of the European girl, her body and soul are nevertheless rigid, she has no 'psychology,' so she can only find psychic life, psychic mimicry in somebody else — for her, the alien body wriggling under torture equals her own artificial 'psychic life.' At the same time, the feeling of 'caritas' starts dawning in the princess' life as well, for when she sees with what fantastic tear-fountains the European girl pities herself and begs for mercy, then the sight of such a gigantic 'love' [the girl's self-pity] moves her greatly, but of course without a shade of mercy alighting in her soul.

The European girl is driven half mad by pain — while the two servants torture her with all kinds of needles, vicious beetles, the princess walks in front of the mirror in such a way that the girl can only see her reflection. Her own body is green, thin, & bloody, her face covered in wrinkles and dusty tear-mud: she doesn't recognize herself and is startled when she glimpses herself in the mirror. But the princess became her perfect mirror image, so it causes her unsayable suffering to watch the princess arrange her hair with her right hand in the mirror while instead of this gesture she is trying to reach her shoulder with her teeth to scratch the place of a burning beetle-sting. She sees at once the double of her own body blossom into beauty day by day, so that she adores herself in the princess' mirror-image with inebriated narcissism — and is forced to feel in her own perishing muscles ever newer forms of suffering & excruciating agony. She could hardly have got greater punishment for her intention to kill.

The princess supplements the natural course of development of the European girl's physique with cosmetic Stilentwicklung[253] — she puffs up her face, forces her feet into diverse shapes by binding it, lengthens her fingers, squeezes her forehead; the chained girl can ponder if, had she not been tortured nearly to death, her own fingers would have lengthened to quite the extent to which the princess lengthened hers out of sheer boredom. The Chinese woman writes a diary about her 'psychic evolution': in it, the European girl's sufferings are detailed. "This morning I felt that there are two simultaneous dawns in the world, which are bleached by the absence of time caused by their deferral — two silk-grey seas that are both inside me: one of them is the first melting of the future [for yesterday is always an icicle and 'today' is always the lukewarm shape of yesterday turned into water], the other is the white shadow of joy — I have never felt time and happiness so separately-together, like a pushy flower trapped in another flower": for in that morning they threw on the European girl some kind of congealing, silvery liquid that made her whole body shiver so violently that it almost rang like a bell. Psyche Regained. The school and pedagogical methods are consummate — the Chinese woman's 'personality': a mask, her soul: another body's suffering.

In his last will the dying old prince Ming-Hsi ordered his son to immediately embark on a ship, sail upstream on the great river, and marry without delay the princess who lives in a castle of leaves. The young Ming-Hsi had never seen the woman, nor did he care about the whole affair but embarked calmly. The vessel was pitch-black, for it was the same that took his father's corpse to the cemetery — the marriage was no feast of joy and no suffering, the marriage was really nothing, so it could easily be linked to the burial. Ming-Hsi paced up and down in the bow — either standing close to the prow like a sharp-taut string that cuts into two the morning's yellow and the evening's red winds, or walking among the front rowers, cooling down his soul to verses with the infinitely long oars' psychic ruled paper.

Time showed its nakedness freely on the river: there was no pudicity in the hours, the relations between present, past, & future were colorful incests on the water's lazily bubbling stage. Ming-Hsi engaged in voluptuous play with the luxuriating time that caressed the ship like a Circe; he felt that this was his genuine nuptials. Dawn came to meet them, lemon-yellow on the river, only for them, unable to veer to the left or right because of the tall trees on the riverbanks, & the hair-thin oars boldly changed the strings of the non-hedging present. On the mutely winding water, every 'now' was real and true 'now'; earlier, there used to be a pudic drifting apart, gap between every 'now'-word & 'now'-time, but here they stepped immediately into the epicenters of time.

Close by the volcano's rust-brown tent there lived a European youth. His mother had come to China with the missionaries and died soon afterward, so he was brought up by a priest. The priest had been a great inquisitor somewhere in Europe, but he tired of writing and reciting the refutations of errors, sentencing heretics, and wanted rather to convert pagans to the truth. But he didn't succeed: his whole soul was so much set on dogmatic debates, charges, and logical cunning that he proved utterly incapable of conveying the Catholic truths to the Chinese with pathetic simplicity and morning enthusiasm, and this fact saddened him immensely. His sole hope remained an orphan boy whose mother died with the aura of holiness. One night the youth spots the tortured European girl in the Chinese princess's castle. The girl is asleep, her back and head tilt forward like a balance's overburdened scale, on her light green skin there are faded bloodstains like blotted-up ink. The youth falls in love with her, runs to her and covers her in kisses. When the old inquisitor learns about this, he too stealthily visits the castle at night and looks on the martyr-looking girl with profound devoutness and pudicity. When the inquisitor addresses her, the girl lies that the princess tortures her because of her Christian faith.

The old inquisitor is overjoyed that after so many rationalist heretics he has finally met a burning flower of the Catholic love of the divinity: for the first time in his life he sees overflowing, bold, all-distorting emotion. He wants to speak with the Chinese princess, but she can't be seen, she has been hiding for the past days. The half-crazed inquisitor worships the pseudo-martyr almost as a saint, while the orphaned boy learns the ways of love from her. The priest is explaining to the boy the magnificence of self-denial on the very woman from whom he is learning pleasure day by day. During the day they pray with and to her together, and during the nights he is alone with her to kiss.

The priest in a tattered black robe, the boy in tattered white clothes, the priest's hair is white, that of the boy, golden-red — this parroty setting is essential. At last the inquisitor forgets the routine of refined logical debates: the suffering 'martyr' fills his soul with youthful enthusiasm, so he goes out to the Chinese villages on the slopes of the volcano and preaches to the villagers about the suffering woman. Everything he tells them, to be sure, is wild heresy from the strictly Catholic point of view, so maniacal and lopsided is his discourse. He paints romantic word-altars about the fake martyr, and on the volcano's perpetually rusty-leaves and autumn-faced walls the silvery-green nude blossoms like flowers with the scarlet alphabet of blood: now huge Chinese masses worship the suffering damsel. The inquisitor is completely bonkers. The orphan European boy had so far not seen any kind of woman, so he doesn't know that blood-flow and budding fever are not essential features of the female body — for him suffering and beauty are one and the same thing and he praises wailing like others would a chic movement or a fashionable new hat accessory.

On a silent, flowery night Ming-Hsi sends an envoy to his bride, the princess, to announce that in two days' time he would arrive and marry her. The envoy rows his slim boat alone upstream on the river T'ang which winds around the volcano. Here everything, river, trees, & sky are uniformly reddish-brown and rust-colored. This rusty air appears dim during the day like a mist that hides ingles, but during the night it glows like a church candle.

The envoy finds that there is no more mysterious thing than to feel that the whole world is illuminated by one sole twinkling, brown-flamed candle with an ever-present brown light, without this candle being either enormous or possessing heavenly power. The alternation of sun and moon meant nothing on the slopes of the enormous mountain: whether from the depth of the river, from the forest clearings, or from the spring ceiling of air only its indifferent, ironed wrinkles could be seen. Where did that luminosity come from? If he looked at a basalt column or lava trough, they were all matte like a naked foot sole, but *if he didn't look at one fragment but instead gazed at the dim redness in general, he felt that the stones were quietly radiating, that from the curtain-shaped rocks some kind of stale purple was rising like scent. Where the mountain was in fact no one could tell — its red walls hovered among the trees & water like the far-jutting veils of invisible ships among the rooftops in the harbors and canals: he felt it to be not one mountain but literally a sea of red stones, whose waves dispersed among waterfalls and shrubs, like a startled flock's brick-red-wooled sheep; or unexpected banners hanging from the sky which were so icicle-like and transparent, so infinitely tall and shroud-like as to seem no longer a mountain but an air-screen molded of air which the friction of the sunset had colored a little.*

The scattered rocks, hovering curtains, and candle-color night were peculiar enough, but the envoy, for whom 'nature' was after all no theater setting but a more ceremonial gesture of his own body, marveled even more at the curious silver statues which rose here and there among the volcano's hundreds of red cones in the forest, and reflected like burning bridges in the river T'ang. In one place there were 10 such female idols on the riverbank, dipping into the transparent green water like sundial-hand shaped roots. Here the vegetation was so dense that the bumptious color of the Midas-candle could not make its way among the leaves; the branches shot so densely like the left fingers among the right in clasped hands. The water was green like an apothecary's pseudo-hope condensed to deathly poison, while the statues were white like snow resting still in God's basket; we feel the snow on the highest mountain peaks to be not fallen but on the contrary, yet unused material that the January winds would disperse only later on the face of the earth.

The boat suddenly stuck in something: at that moment he saw that under the water swayed not only the conspiratorial drills of reflections but sunken there, too, were such foreign-bodied female statues — love reefs? Water rushed whistling into his boat as though a blooming bough had grown within seconds from the planks — it seems the boat was holed by one of the underwater statues. He jumped to the riverbank while the boat sank on the statue's shoulder like a grinning Gorgon mantle. He went on foot.

This is how he arrived at the princess's castle. He sees with a shock that the bride's clothes and face are not Chinese but that she looks conspicuously like the white statues he had seen in the forest. He announces that Ming-Hsi would marry her in two days' time. The princess prepares happily for the wedding but hides the European girl in an underground den. The wedding takes place, Ming-Hsi doesn't much care whether the bride is Chinese or European; to him she is like a new landscape. In the meantime the orphan boy manages to meet the tortured girl in the underground hideout and frees her. They elope far away in the forest, because the boy knows that if the inquisitor had the merest suspicion that his love is free he would take her by force to the villages under the volcano to have her worshipped like a deity by the Chinese.

For the first time he sees the girl without suffering: he is disappointed at first [he grew very fond of the freely flowing blood's redness] but later this grows into mysterious joy. The forest nuptial has only two themes: itself, and the plans to murder the Chinese princess. The princess is now the erstwhile European girl's mirror image, but the latter has changed so much under torture that if she should murder the princess, Ming-Hsi would obviously notice the change when she takes the place of the murdered woman. The European girl's sole problem now is, how she could resemble her former figure which the Chinese woman preserves as a faithful imprint — the seal is untouched but the die has changed. But the Christian boy is in love with the girl changed by suffering.

The seaman's daughter knows that Ming-Hsi has a fabulous fortune, so she starts molding her body in the shape of the Chinese woman, that is, of herself; what a struggle it is to catch up with herself. The boy despairs, and the girl doesn't want to lose his frenzied worship. She is deeply vexed — she sees herself in two copies, one a shiny Parisian *mondaine with plans of murder, and the other a gothic Saint Sebastian who wants self-serving love. The boy is on the point of handing her over to the inquisitor who would punish her by rendering her a deity.*

The Chinese princess lavishes all imaginable kindnesses on her husband who celebrates his wife in hymns, not as a human being but as a new season in the order of nature. The seaman's daughter reverts to her old drunk and hysterical ways and treats her two roles as an actress: at night, to please her lover, she daubs her body green, paints on it large wounds with red chalk, but in the daytime she disappears to rehearse her pre-capture, mundane gestures, spying on the Chinese woman to learn European face mimicry.

The boy is faced with yet another difficulty: new missionaries arrive from Spain, who would very likely lock up his adoptive father in a madhouse or drag him, Spain's most logical Catholic, before a court for spreading heresies. He would like to save the inquisitor from that fate, something that would be possible only if the new missionaries indeed found the drunken seaman's even more drunkard daughter a miraculous saint. He spends one night in ardent prayer and self-mortification, asking God to make her a saint, so his beloved adoptive father is not disgraced in Spain.

But on this night it is the boy himself who tastes the black-peeled, honey-juiced orange of asceticism: he wants the woman's sainthood so much that he almost becomes one. At the same time the European girl manages to kill the princess and steps in her place. At first Ming-Hsi doesn't notice any difference, as his wife is as gentle, obliging, and humble as before. The orphan boy is worried out of his mind for the inquisitor and spends the second night in penitence; then the murderer girl visits him, drunk, rouged-powdered into a martyr clown. But now the boy has his own suffering, his own genuine blood, his own unpainted pallor: he turns away in disgust from the caricature. After this night she is neither his love nor his saint.

The seaman's daughter longs for the Christian boy and torments her husband. But the husband doesn't suffer at all: moreover, he sees in his wife's frenzied tantrums nature's tragic splendor, its divine forces, and continues writing hymns as beautiful about her as he first wrote about her kindness. No emotions bind him to his wife — for him the emotion excludes the possibility of the 'other person.' By now everything his wife cares about is to find the Christian boy. One night she comes upon him: she is wearing neither the Parisian evening gown nor the drag of martyrdom and she begs his love.

The boy falls headlong into love again. He keeps asking her to leave Ming-Hsi and live entirely with him, but she wants the money. So she ends up tormenting both her husband and lover, but while the former writes ever more beautiful hymns about her hysteria, the second is more and more embittered. He no longer wants to save the inquisitor; what is more, he wants him to perish, for he held the one who is sucking his blood to be a miraculous saint. Why does he in fact suffer from this woman? By no means because she doesn't want to leave Ming-Hsi, not because she 'loves money more than she loves him.' He feels that even if she does not want to leave Ming, it doesn't mean that she values something more than him.

The woman doesn't 'want' the money, but money is simply her spine, blood, her organs, so she can't expel her from herself: the first psychic layer that is bound up with her will is filled with her 'infinite' love for the Christian boy. Because love's 'infinity' doesn't mean that it is more powerful than anything else, and has greater value than any other vital value. So if he, the boy, is so clever to realize all this, why do they suffer all the same? Why do they torment each other? The chase for causes starts, but he doesn't find there anything. Boredom? Routine? Sadism? These are only just effects, not causes. She brings him the Chinese hymns written by her husband to her meanness, domestic intrigues, and nervous fits. There is one in which he sings, in the tenor of nature worship, how she flogs him in the bed one morning.

Love is the crisis of personality; it is simply the most consequent realization of the fact of the 'human being.' When either the girl or the boy look deep inside themselves, what could they see? They feel *themselves to be axioms, that is, something absolutely true and positive, but they have to pay for this absolute with being unable to know the contents, boundaries, and purpose of their personality — 'self-evident, impossible-to-motivate fundamental truth' is a double-edged weapon [and their 'self' falls indisputably into that category], because it means the most truthful form of truth but, precisely for this reason, it also means that Nirvana climate zone characterized by the fact that there the questions of truth and untruth cannot as much as be raised, because there the problem of truth is radically meaningless: absolute light is not a question of optics anymore; in the fact of 'absolute truth' the 'absolute' utterly annihilates and absorbs the 'truth' nature. In love the personality of both sides is such an ambiguous postulate: when they flounder among the whirling hallucinations of desire they are concerned in their most lyrical point but its meaning and purpose remains obscure for them. Did they get to know something, or did they become indifferent toward everything that is knowledge?*

Personality is the castle that protects against everything non-personal, so thick are its walls, but in this castle there is no single plan or lamp, only eternal darkness and groping about. What then is the partner? Even if we would gladly die for him or her, he or she remains a plaything, a naïve and childish ornament hung on the utmost fringe of our personality. The lover who sees in his or her beloved a value or simply, reality is a pathological specimen. This sentence has of course nothing to do with cynicism, especially because here love is treated not as affect but as the formal relation of the logical elements of 'self' and 'other,' the operations with those two abstractions.

Is there any point in logicizing a particular lyrical process? Definitely, because neither lyricism nor logic, nor abstraction or biology are things that exist but only methodological devices, of which now the one, now the other, serves our sense of reality better. Thus in love the following fundamental situation burns in glaring colors: I am before and above all a positivity, but my content, shape, place is unknown [personality is by nature 'impossible to situate']; my partner's shape, place, content is entirely clear, but the sense of 'positivity' is conspicuously absent, for it can only be felt from inside: it's curious that everything is in reverse from what we would expect — we feel lifeless objects to be more positive than people, although we are better able to imagine the life of people than those of things; it's precisely knowledge, knowledge about them that turns them into decorative puppets.

The boy and girl torment each other because in their relation confined to the forest, mutual dependence is enhanced, while at the same time the sense of one another's irreality is also enhanced. In hermitage, the inner life always becomes more capacious [this doesn't mean an enrichment and variety in ideas or sentiments], therefore the hermit will always feel ever lonelier and will start looking for a neighbor — but when the neighbor is found, that doesn't bring any real joy, for the hermit's own inner life had become so wide as to be incapable of reaching out to the new companion through it; so the hermit will fall back into himself, trying to find there palpable, plastic forms akin to those experienced in the companion's eyes, mouth, legs. But it is all in vain, of course.

The old inquisitor had started working on a treatise on logic long ago, when still in Spain, and now he keeps repeating to the boy [whom he meets now and then] that he should take it over and finish it. The boy doesn't understand much of it but knuckles down to the task and amid his love torments he writes the meaningless word on a page: Logic. For weeks nothing else is put to paper beside that lonely word. At one point he makes a doodle of a church: one single laid glass rectangle, including the walls and roof — there are no columns and no division of space whatsoever; can one imagine a neutral lighting where glass is rendered invisible, one with the air? In the midst of the 'solid air' ceiling a black ribbon starts like a runner, shifted and tacked to the ceiling's right side [made of some massive but light material], collides against the rectangular wall delimiting the church, runs along it [again, only on the wall's right side], and doesn't reach down to the ground but bends and hovers midair like a legless table. On the chapel wall's transparent left side a row of extraordinarily tall candelabra starts in a serpentine line, it intersects with the black altar table, but midway in this altar table the candelabra row stops [about 30 reed-thin candelabra]: every single white candelabra is a sheet bent in a sharp V shape whose point is directed toward the nave. The church is ready: invisibility, black ribbon [ceiling, wall, and altar in one] is the image of the massive but blind nature of the 'I' [axiom] — the candle-procession intersecting with the altar only by accident, with its dense precision carnival is the emblem of the precise exterior but inner emptiness of the 'other person' [décor raison]. Or, to weave this schematization further: perhaps the boy was 'truth' and the girl, 'logic' [or the other way round].

The tale, if it is to be regular, bifurcates for a moment at the end: on the one hand it turns into logic and on the other hand, into narrative humbug. Interestingly, the most kitschy stories are those that are the most rational: a narrative that attempts to turn St. Thomas' philosophy or Hilbert's mathematics the most faithfully into plotline[254] *would be more preposterous and more vulgarly common [at least according to a certain conventional æsthetic] than the tritest pulp. Thus the tale's final splitting into two is only an appearance: logic & kitsch are identical [of course already at the tale's beginning the philosophical or mathematical idea can be ab ovo only kitsch, but at the tale's end this kitschiness usually reaches its culmination point].*

Let one more thing briefly pass here: the Christian boy can't bear the woman's hysteria, but he can not bear his own hysteria any better, so he commits suicide. He throws himself into the river which is hammered to bits, into the likeness of almost human fingers in a deep ravine, among the rocks. His head is fished out by the drunk seaman — he had lately abandoned fishing but on that day decided to try again. His first catch that day was that bloody European head. The most beautiful thing would be to embalm it, or at least make a death mask of it, to engrave one of Ming-Hsi's hymns on its pedestal, in which he extols his wife's intrigues like the beauty of serpents dancing among the spring bushes…)

XIII.

the influence of Peter's sin-snobbery on Leatrice; sin and elegance

Leatrice, too, took over this sin-snobbery from her uncle (of course in the present case snobbery doesn't mean the lack of sincerity), but in an altered form: she tried to attain a certain 'racial elegance' through sin and, after achieving this bodily elegance, the annihilation of the concept of sin as such. She felt painfully that there was no highborn ancestor to light up her skin with his blood in 'feudal-cosmetic' colors, while her opinion of aristocracy was resumed to the slogan 'decadence.' She would have liked to supplement the pedigree of her body with sin — in her concept of aristocracy she almost obsessively equaled time and sin.

When she gazed at the face of one of the ladies waiting in the skylit hall she didn't know whether in the complexion's strange material, at once dry like strawflower and transparent like a pink gladiolus leaf, she should look for the stigmata of the centuries or merely for the sins of yesterday. This interchangeability of sin and past led her to feel, after a night of debauchery, when green hollows & black rings circled her eyes, that she managed to push the genealogy of her body one century back into the past. At about that time her cult of actresses started, whom she held to be just such ancestor-supplementing figures. So she fashioned for herself a feigned pseudo-aristocracy concocted partly from Blake and partly from actresses, in which sports-like roughness & splendid madness met.

to the scheme of sin and elegance: Leatrice's acquaintance with Zwinskaya. Zwinskaya's character: morphine and peasant

This she learned from an actress whose forte was the very human recipe above (that is, sport and hysteria). The actress had once been a simple peasant girl with a snub nose and raw skin (like the edge of china where it's chipped), with a caterwauling, grating voice. When she whispered she was always hoarse. Whenever some 'salon corner' scene followed, that dry, almost rattling under breath was conspicuous; one could hear that if she descended to those regions where soft-voicedness rests deep inside one's body like a lake, independent of the voice, there she would be incapable of uttering a single sound; when we hear actors we often have the impression that speech and soft-voicedness are two things made of entirely different materials and not that the latter is merely a shade of the former; there are some who can let words down into silence's deep well like an anchor, and others who can only get as far as the lake's surface (we can almost hear them unreel the whole anchor chain and the moment when it suddenly stops midair). Her actress, too, let down her voice, but after a certain point only the deaf distance could be seen that separates the voice's end from the unreachable mirror of silence.

In those days there was a fad for naturalist plays, so the crumpled everyday clothes penetrated Zwinskaya's body and when she appeared on the street or in restaurants in her full elegance, in her demeanor there was always some Zolaesque or Hauptmann-derived Schlamperei.[255] Her peasant origins and the plays' naturalism nearly converged, but nevertheless remained distinguishable in that paradox form where onstage she consciously stylized her peasant nature, while in her day-to-day salon life she harnessed the literary vulgarity of naturalist dramas for her poses. She was mean and even rude to her subalterns; on occasion she would kick her dresser, and she threatened the driver who stood humbly, waiting for a supplement to the skimpy tip, with shrieks of calling the police if he didn't clear out at once.

It was all the more remarkable that neither her peasant origins nor the naturalist theater's innumerable and openly propagandistic roles of misery made her any bit more democratic — what is more, the stage proletarian postures further enhanced her elegance — she felt there so much only the pose, role, and curiosity that her hauteur was worked up into inebriated ecstasy. She played her wildest and most beautiful roles in high-street textile shops: from the shop's darkness she took the fabrics outside to the street (carrying the rolls in her arms): she crumpled, pawed them in the sunlight (her hands were manicured to death: their shiny, artificial whiteness, the podgy, completely jointless fingers and the nails varnished red, in sharp contrast to the fingers, didn't suit at all her flabby figure and her rough chambermaid face) as she would in the play an actress' head who played a heartbroken prostitute who swallows poison & whose corpse is discovered by Zwinskaya on a battered divan.

She lived in a white villa close to Peter's love, on the other side of the river: in fact her house was made up of five verandahs — all whitewash, cold blue, bright linen tabletops, big shepherd dog, white furniture and a wealth of field flowers. She liked to say in interviews that she loves nature: even from the newspapers' plain letters one could hear her cracking voice which changed flowers into dreary Noras, the white furniture, the garden's fresh, sprinkled, and squeaking little paths into muddy and pimpled small town mews. "I've learnt everything from nature," she would state in her occasional written articles, & by nature Leatrice understood what in her childhood she had understood by 'life': some kind of stifling grownup sickness.

She also heard rumors that Zwinskaya was a morphine addict ("I've learnt everything from nature") & the lover of the very young (at most twenty-years-old) son of a Black Sea port's dock owner. Leatrice knew that boy: a pathetic, awkward, sickly youth, a 'real gentleman' according to Zwinskaya, who wore ridiculous clothes and fell asleep from half a glass of wine. Although emotionally she had nothing to do with him, Zwinskaya was religiously faithful to him and defended him to the point of self-sacrifice whenever he was mocked. There was some glaring amorality even in her faithfulness — she was so ostentatious in her belonging to him that her pedantry breathed shamelessness.

She would sometimes lock herself up in her villa and live for morphine among the whitewashed walls where one would like to have breakfast all the time. At such times she wouldn't even receive the boy, who loafed around the house with unwashed-looking, oily skin; his small two-wheel trap was parked nearby. At such times he placed all his hopes in the afternoon dress rehearsal (for Zwinskaya was as punctual as the ideal coolie and would never be one minute late), which meant she would receive him soon; he questioned the maid, with whom they read the role-books, marveling at the unbridgeable distance between the play's simple, almost doltish sentences ("don't go" — "what use is my faithfulness to you after that" — "if I loved you, I would probably ruin everything forever," etc.) & Zwinskaya's incomprehensible multiplicity. And yet, how easily she can insert her thousand crystal sheets into the role's sheath that offered, so to speak, one single opening. It resembled the stylites' self-denial and perhaps even undressing. When Leatrice heard the role's first words, which were not accompanied by a thousand small fragments of movements as in life, a thousand interrupted splinters of words and sentences that would have wrapped them up in their thick fabric: what sounded in the stage's emptiness was indeed one sole 'sentence' (at the opening of the curtains cold air splashed in her face), in the puritanical mounting of one sole movement: she had the impression that Zwinskaya threw off the thick fabric of 'speech' from her body to hang one shiny 'sentence' stone between her breasts, about whose perversity the fashion reporter of *Sex Select* could digress at length.

In his nervousness the boy ate up the breakfast served on a huge tray, which the actress did not order to her room — how strange that the foods and cutlery that almost constitute our body don't even attempt to adapt to us: even now the breakfast was pulling a 'mens sana' face, while its master was stuffing the night into her veins with injection needles, as if performing a blood transfusion from night's green veins.

The boy knew well the hours after solitude: the actress was pacing up and down in her rooms in a long bathrobe (not pajamas) with blinking, tearful eyes, smudgy face, unkempt, forever resolving some practicality, as if all her peasant thrift were condensed in these minutes — she avoided anything æsthetical with a fishwife's grumpiness, and would talk with her lover like a court judge. All the while imitating the gestures of pie-eyed men with spectacular clumsiness, slapping her thighs like operetta primadonnas in hussar roles with tricot legs and double swords; her movements were traversed by small landowners, hunter and puncher figures. When she dressed she was already in character, disturbing the boy with this alien atmosphere.

Critics always wrote about Zwinskaya's 'individuality' as about something clear-cut, but the boy could see at close quarters what uncertain territories she ventured into; in her eyes, the incommunicably confused dreams that drove her to infinitely distant shores, where the word individuality loses all sense — then at once she takes flight from the dream's immense tension like from a catapult, into her role's other foreignness, forever impossible to anticipate; life is nothing else but the cross-mirroring of this southern and northern foreignness. (Of course he had the most clichéd concepts of life, dream, *&* role, seeing even their contrasts as merely conceptual and not real.)

Otherwise the twenty-year-old son of a merchant lived Zwinskaya's morphine dreams much more profoundly than she herself: he continuously perceived the dream's absurd landscapes around her (are there such?), just as we feel behind a king his country's shiny cities & gliding mountains; she knew this, and even from her gestures one could feel that the power with which she seduces people doesn't lie within her physical contours but somewhere around her in the air (rococo women always sit down after taking a good look around to find a space with a radius of over one meter to accommodate their enormous crinolines: Zwinskaya too felt, like an engineer, the location of the force she emanated, and first looked around in the room to check if her suggestion-crinoline could fit in). She sat in the corner of a divan like an off-handed horse-owner who follows his token animal galloping for the grand prix with only a few casual, absent-minded glances — her self hovered in the air at about two meters' distance from her, that's why her movements were so absent-minded & imbalanced, alluding only drowsily to her distant point of gravity.

Zwinskaya relished the fact that the boy got so easily dizzy in her body's magnetic field, while she couldn't impact him nearly so strongly in the immediate proximity to her body. She drew him into some kind of 'cut-and-dry' rational morphinism; without taking one milligram of the poison, he was continually trying to imagine what Zwinskaya feels and sees during and after her dreams. From her he caught this 'decadent' vision of life like a flu: trying to reproduce with his physique, with his eyes' tearful blinking, with his uncertain walk, his lover's almost wholesome intoxications — while Zwinskaya threw herself into rehearsal work (one word permanently on her lips was 'work'), the boy withered from imaginary poison. Naturally his parents couldn't believe that he was as sober as the most fanatical prohibitionist — he couldn't take wine, and feared morphine like death.

The actress took morphine as a Gypsy woman lights her pipe or rather, as a superstitious peasant woman drinks the concoction of her medicine woman which will surely cure and rejuvenate her. One would have expected her to carry the poison on herself, tied up in a colored stocking. By no means was she looking for the mystery in intoxication, but momentary well-being, a homely sense of comfort; the only reason she didn't find those in tobacco or wine was the fact that her body was too hard and dream-proof to yield to lesser pressure. Zwinskaya often said that she "wouldn't fall for her visions": for her they meant only a small tipsiness — small holes driven into her knotty sobriety. But now and again the authority she achieved by morphine among her colleagues turned her head and she ended up playing the role of the 'decadent' woman.

She also had her raving seasons which everybody tagged 'tattered nerves' or 'approaching end,' although these were perfectly normal tantrums fueled not by dream visions but by petty selfishness. Leatrice didn't see all that and took the sobriety (which culminated in the undiminishable, hoarse voice) & those hysterical inflections and exoticisms of manner to be opposites. When once Zwinskaya wrestled with her lover's father in the docks (he took her to the sea & showed her the ships one by one; she took a bath in the oily water among the cargo ships — that's how his father saw her for the first time), she was only following the example of her sister who allegedly killed a bear single-handedly with a knife. The actress was so refreshed by the fight that every muscle of hers rang out her motto, "I've learnt everything from nature." She distributed her clothes as a trophy to three dock workers who watched the spectacle and on hearing that one of them had a wife, she clawed back everything she gave the other two and heaped them on the husband — then jumped into her car and drove off.

Leatrice met her when the actress ordered two vases from her: at that time she had already made a name for herself in industrial design and collaborated with a ceramics studio, also taking on commissions for vases, tiles, ornamental faïences, fountain basins for halls. To her greatest surprise the actress came late at night after a performance, accompanied by an unknown man. At that time the father sent the docks boy abroad to start his own business. The man who accompanied Zwinskaya was a white-hot specimen of the lackey with ceremonial passion and melancholy pedantry. When she stepped into the antechamber and found it very hot, he let out some booming sound from his body (probably in the midst of the boom was merely a simple, servile-to-the-point-of-swoon 'oh' somewhere around his mouth) and while this sorrowful booming undulated around him, he mechanically reached under her coat to help her out of it. Leatrice hadn't really seen any truly elegant men before but she instinctively suspected that one of the characteristic features of elegance must be the peculiar mixture of pathos & mechanism emanating from the man's booming obligingness and yet cold movements. As if the feeling immediately found its crystallized shape like with a fencing figure: in the duelist the most irregular waves of ire thrash out, & those fiery foams are strained in every moment into this or that mathematical pose, rigid puppet equation.

When she heard the man's first apologetic 'oh' she believed that love's most authentic flute version was murmuring under the green lamplight, and she waited for it to splash into the imitating trumpets' tin jugs, in the form of a million resonant pearls, but none of that happened; instead, he hurled himself forward with one lunge when he jumped to the woman and froze in the movement. The thought that up to that day she had misunderstood the nature of passion and the essence of feelings made Leatrice dizzy: what if all truly grand psychic things were really made of technique, observing certain forms, the gymnastics-like practicing of conventions?

The spinning top always gives fairy-like sounds; with its small tunes (let bud from it by the wind like air mail-spring) it fills the room and the garden, and when at last it falls to the side, it leaves behind a strange, sharp line on the floor or on the thin sand under the verandah; a serpentine, mysterious geometrical figure, perhaps the unexpected meaning of the scattered tunes. Leatrice thought of her past little 'emotional life' & found that she had gone through it in a shabby dressing gown: something kindled her desire, sadness or joy, and she continued that emotion in its raw state, as it were, although you must probably learn beforehand, some techniques need to be used on emotions and, more importantly, you shouldn't behave in parallel with the emotion's obvious direction.

Zwinskaya and the officer

The man with Zwinskaya was an officer who knew that his role was merely one of official accompaniment, but the politeness forms to be used with the actress can be enhanced the way she enhanced her natural complexion with make-up. So, if we take the fur coat of a landowner's daughter by brushing her shoulder with our wrist for a second, then with Zwinskaya we have to do it by whipping our mouth past her shoulder blade, and when she feels that sudden warmth and twists her head back, the planned kiss (which is the equivalent of the lengthy impetus-flourishes in the air before adding our signature to paper) we will smother into one edge of the coat: this little tyranny, of crumpling the other's coat by the collar and compressing all our beastliness into that tiny fur-trampling, like a deathly venom into a tiny wafer — this is the (strictly official & not lyrical) surplus that is the actress' due: if we don't perform it (at least that was the captain's conviction) we commit a gross impoliteness and breach of style. The more wildly beautiful a woman, the wilder the forms of politeness (not of love!): there are brilliant beauties we must make our lovers within five minutes from the first meeting (or at the very least recite such desires in telegraphic style), because their niveau demands an appropriate degree of manner and politeness and nothing less.

love and etiquette

Leatrice obviously felt this pedantry in the man's act of taking off Zwinskaya's coat. In a moment she imagined their whole life, which must be the exact reverse of hers: with Leatrice, the unassuming etiquette she was capable of always shone on top of her feelings — above the black and gold waves of caritas swam those few scraggy petals of manner; in contrast, with Zwinskaya & her officer the formalisms of manner grew, crescendoed, incandesced to the point where the true love-kiss looked a social pleasantry. On what dry logic her life had been based, Lea thought: with syllogistic barrenness she extracted one gesture from her feelings: nothing. For the world is covered in the delicate wiring of convention, and if we link our own individuality to them, the wires start incandescing, burn, and we can enjoy their beautifying light: the human being as such doesn't incandesce (Lea concluded hastily), it's merely the network of formalities that at first merely casts regular geometrical shapes on people's faces (much later it became a fashion with photographers to take every portrait with the striped shadows of a grid), but later developed into curlicue tendrils: yet however whimsical their winding and however whitely they burned, they remained convention all the same.

What a landscape: how much more logical in its irrationality than her own system of 'manner based on feeling' — the snakes of red and white wires swarmed in the night, as if they couldn't bear their own heat; but the chaotic rings still display their original regularity (refrain: is there a more exciting sight than a crumpled-up geometric shape that gets crumpled precisely because in it the awareness of regularity was so strong as to split regularity apart, although even in its most excessive flower-like movements it is incapable of freeing itself from the original outlines of the rule):

while among the wires' red and white groves women and boys stood, cold and matte, covered in the tendrils' sizzling daylight.

Perhaps it is the order of things (as Leatrice said to herself) that if a man and a woman meet, they should suddenly light the wiring of a ready-made 'love story,' prepared well in advance, that had so far stretched between them, grey and lackluster: not to build it from their emotions day by day as a bridge whose two halves advancing from the opposite banks meet halfway, but to relish together the burning formalities. How grotesque it is to grow wheat on two acres, build a wee mill, put a dachshund to draw the millwheel, & at the end to bake the wee loaf in a dwarf oven — when you can buy it ready everywhere in town. Such homemade bread was her sentimental life, too. "She saws herself the love she happens to need" — she heard the scathing comment about herself from a woman who wears prêt-a-porter bought from salons. But where is the salon? Where can she see, in their morning brilliance, the redeeming 'ready-mades' that humiliate her homespun?

love and metaphoricizing biology

How comic it was to remember one of her uncle's doodles in which man and woman were two flowers that undergo preposterous metamorphoses: they stand on the two banks of a milk-blue river — the one is white and flat-petaled, the other (logical contrast short of vision) is black & made of small flower-funnels. The black flower multiplies its clusters to be able to bridge the river, but after the tenth cluster, pulled down by its own weight, it falls into the water which is crystal-clear from the depth of sin & only rusts black from the sunrays; then the white flower grows like a parasite on the black clusters hanging into the water; the black flower continues growing underwater and shoots roots into the riverbed: with this new pivot found, it suddenly fires new stems upward that riddle the water like bullets & radiate toward the clouds like glass arrows, from which they form petals in military discipline; at this point the white flower falls into the water, there it multiplies into a giant dam, so that the glass stems are left without water and snap into two with a shriek; the clouds disperse, water breaks through the dam, etc. etc. — the whole facetious symbolism appropriately depicted the comedy of love's rope-pulling: a long series of patching-up, plastering, restoration, bad forking, misjudged supplementing, imbalance and moral parasitism; a hysterical function gymnastics into which the dullest variables are thrown. Both sides wear the so-called psychic shades and without any design heap on & against each other the bricks and cells, always adapting only to the immediately preceding one. Hence their simplicity and purity.

the 'grownup' meaning of 'simplicity'

Never before had Leatrice felt such a dizzying meaning in the word 'simplicity' (later, when in the theater a young conductor spoke about the simplicity of Beethoven's last works — in which Leatrice had seen the embodiment of complexity — she felt a similar frisson, the alcoholic effect of sudden value change): so far she had heard life as the sequence of independent, so-called pure themes and motifs with naïve melodies (like a 'light' opera), and by that she meant simplicity and purity — but now she discovered that simplicity consists of two or three notes sounding (their relation is mathematically simple, but the whole is not 'melodic' in the everyday sense of the word); these are varied throughout with misty stumbling.

In this, too, she saw the difference in taste between children and grown-ups: in the raw 'purity' of marches you can hear only noise, in the blurry boredom of 'monotonous' quartets you can only feel purity. Of course the main beauty of this purity was (at the point where Lea started enjoying it) that it never quite shed the childhood taste of 'blurriness.' Because the simplicity of the grown-ups has nothing to do with a geometrical or a certain ornamental simplicity; the grownups' 'purity' is worlds away from clarity, hygiene, or bareness. Purity and simplicity immediately bring to our mind the conceptual content of the word, the definition of its meaning, but in our inspired moments we are suddenly compelled to use the word 'simplicity' for something obscure and blurry, as it were, to elevate its conceptual peasantness to the peerage; we realize that in using the word 'simplicity' we have so far stood under the arithmetic terror of 'one,' but now we shake it off because we have discovered its true meaning. This latter 'simplicity' as content had been floating on the bottom of the word all through (even when we meant by it only something linearly simple), because otherwise we wouldn't reach for this very word when what is concerned is not naïve-linear and few-component simplicity but apparent complexity.

But what if the whole thing is sophistry, and this second simplicity is not simplicity at all? — Leatrice thought with scrupulous honesty. She could see and touch the previous simplicity, it could always be reduced to an exterior graphic scheme (whether speaking of music or ethics) — but she felt this second ('grownupish') simplicity to be an atmosphere born inside her, an alleviation of weight, a greater possible assimilation to infinity. To put it arrogantly: simplicity is not the point or straight line but boundless space, whose positive point of gravity and cohesion force is, however, consciousness. So the limited 'one' fell from simplicity & its place was taken by undulating infinity balanced with consciousness (... *Simplex* nihilum significat in simplicitate, quæ conjunctio æterna Conscientiæ ac Infinitatis est).[256] Or, even more bluntly: in the grown-ups' sense of simplicity the greatest analyzable complexity is matched by the greatest unanalyzable dynamic balance.

the concept of 'simplicity' and the trees and leaves of the gardens of W***

She first started formulating this jagged thesis when she walked alone in the gardens of W*** on sunny mornings and observed the trees' branches, crowns, the hundred forms of leaves; the horse chestnuts' palm-leaves all hung their fingers slightly toward the ground and rose above one another like umbrellas or Chinese conic hats — Leatrice particularly liked the fact that they didn't strive toward the sun but rather, bent back toward the lawn; that's why she liked best those trees that were very tall, but their leaves akin to infinite grass blades poured back smoothly toward the region of the roots (every branch a giant skye-terrier) like a silky waterfall: one can't tell if the tree is rising upward or pouring down from a height, or if it eventually hovers on neutral space-stairs between earth and sky. There were abrupt gaps in the body of the foliage: as though they pressed the originally five-pointed stars into a large pyramid mass which, desiccated in a very short time in the sun, starts cracking; black burrows, inorganic hollows split into the formerly continuous mass of horse chestnut leaves, which lack the mellow tonalities of shadow and its affectation indulging in transitions.

In natural history books, trees had two characteristic features: the trunk, signaled with a sole vertical stroke, and five-branched geometric graphics that stood for the leaves. Leatrice observed the vegetative inebriation of regularity on the tree with strange disquiet: how the regular five- or seven-pointed stars turned into swaying fans, veil and zigzag — without the melting apart of the original geometric atom. One could imagine a horse chestnut tree (perhaps Leatrice would have created one like that) in which the five-point star's shape starts metamorphosing from within, and so the 'five' will prevail only in the barely deducible inner structure of the individual leaves, like a hidden dynamic backbone: in reality, however, the exact opposite occurred, for the individual fives perfectly preserved their geometric purity, but they were heaped on one another in vast quantities and along a winding network of branches. Leatrice knew that it's always Dame Nature who is interrogated on her greater or lesser intelligence, so she remarked that perhaps some kind of (otherwise evident) lesson is enclosed in this duality — the tree is entirely algebraic & crystalline but, taken as a whole, it is nevertheless a quixotic wave, romantic form-gossip.

As though the world were created in such a way that regularities, structures, can exist only in the form of tiny seeds, which are then amassed in the most whimsical disorder in the various corners of the world. They are small light bulbs with their own definite shape, size, organism and number, but the light they give in the midst of the foliage is only an indefinable spot, the shiny zone of probability of shadows and lights that condenses, spreads, etc.

While she was brooding over these gentle observations, the word 'simplicity' kept stirring inside her. How come — she asked with childlike purity — that I feel in one and the same moment the air of nature's absolute simplicity, when I can't exactly identify one of its cunning structural tricks? With her eyes she experimented further on the leaves: on the foliage's lower end, on the long, hanging branches the leaves thinned (like the few separately engraved lonely star-eyes next to the Milky Way's star-flour: like drawing a blown-up blood cell next to a colored stain that depicts the redness of blood), they seemed hardly to belong to the branch's knotted black veins, but to hover over them like a quivering butterfly: she also found it strange that the leaves 'grown into' their branches were by far not in such organic and close connection with them as the former ones that seemed to hover next to the branches, independently from them as it were.

The sun shone through the leaves; all she saw at that moment were so-called 'delicate' lines without the least geometric regularity, and yet they were undoubtedly 'geometrics.' When she enthused her eyes almost into a microscope, she saw only greenish blobs, tiny blur-knots — as if that certain structure, geometric order, could exist in matter only in one perspectival point: if we look at trees from afar (and this looking is not only optical but also of thinking 'sub specie') we see nothing but absolute contingency, clouding whim, and when we look at them from very close up, we again find only pulsating blobs, hesitant nuclei; so Leatrice looked at the leaves' quintal number system with naïve awe, for she felt that both under and above them is chaos, and the structure that is visible barely just is, in one lucky moment only, and so at any moment it can vanish forever from her eyes.

This order can exist only on one tiny point of an infinite scale, there is a blur before and a blur after it — with almost every object one could single out the number at which it appears 'order,' as against the scale's other numbers. Or else, the human 'order-eye' is sensitive to that alone, it cannot perceive the order situated beneath or beyond it — the way we see certain rays not as color but feel them to be heat, so we experience certain order-vibrations not as geometric compositions but, let's say, as the atmosphere of beauty, of chaos.

æsthetics and the stylistics of nature

Two things are certain: pro primo, no æsthetics had ever been made based on the exteriorities of nature, although everything is found there, if anything is; the way we say of a painting that such and such a feature is typically 'Raffaellesco,' so it occurs to us with a flower or leaf that such and such a feature is typically 'natural': thus we need to punctiliously assemble the stylistic features of nature, its authentic mannerisms, what its characteristic devices are, et cetera; and pro secundo, every thing in nature elicits in us the 'grown-upish' inebriation of simplicity: the more colors & shapes are amassed, the more the internal dynamic equilibrium is felt, unity culminating in one single point. Painterly impressionism leads to philosophical dynamism: it will always see the ultimate positivities, the last pivot of order in terms of forces.

Such a compensation plays out in the experience of 'simplicity' as well: the complicated phenomenon suddenly burdens the eye with an absurd weight, but in the next moment the whole thing turns into feather-weight, for our consciousness switches the whole play over into dynamics, and so a thousand leaves become merely immaterial color-fans behind the ethereal strings of a single power-resultant. (At that time four concepts swung in disarray in Leatrice: nature; simplicity; dynamic unity; order visible from a single perspectival vantage point. The last two are of course essentially different possibilities of order: the first is entirely common and means that there can be no chaos in the world that the eye would not somehow perceive as order [subjective reflex-order] — while the second means that, on the contrary, chaos has one single pose where it seems order, or rather, it doesn't merely seem but in those cases is indeed order.)

Otherwise, if we try to write an æsthetics based on the forms of nature, it is very important that we should not by any means look for 'Ur-forms,' fundamental schemes of the nature of principles. The way we speak of Romanesque, Gothic, Baroque styles, so we need to speak about nature's nature-style — not as the terroristic Prius of everything but as a variant of equal rank with artistic styles, accident. The reason why it's more important than the Gothic or Plateresque style is not that it's more ancient & more general ("...There Israel in bondage to his Generalizing Gods...") but simply, that it's the only artistic style created not by us but by somebody else: a foreign (or downright 'outlandish') style that seems to be born from intentions so different as to be eventually instructive to us.

Thus nature (for instance, the horse chestnut tree rustling in front of us) is no barren Proton but something individual and hazardous in the extreme, just like a peculiar person, so we have to approach it not with a philosophical mask but with the gourmandize of a Saint-Simon; mountains, flowers, seas are such features of nature as, let's say, military bluntness, moroseness, aversion to books, and constancy was of King Louis XIII ("...The pale limbs of his Eternal Individuality...").

In place of what the Germans designate with the name 'Ur' in the features of nature we have to supply what the French call 'tic.' In figures assembled from back-throat r-s, torn gestures, small household manias, there is a lot more of the 'Ur' (if we stick to it) than in the symmetry mascots. (For more on this see Touqué's little article where he discusses the encounter of the principles of extreme impressionism, and of neo-scholasticism: *Manet and Przywara*.)[257]

Zwinskaya's hat; woman as landscape

Zwinskaya let down her coat only halfway: she crumpled it down on her shoulder blades but not further. She wore a red dress made of some cheap material, which (by having the half unbuttoned coat crumpled around her back and breasts) was very tight and revealed somewhat plump forms. Lea was surprised by this simple fabric. She wore a velvet hat with a vast rim, whose inordinately undulating-drooping ledge didn't seem to obey any master line, but if one looked better, a small, smooth turning-up could be spotted above one shoulder, which unexpectedly summed up the other valleys & serpentine lines, rendering them naïve.

One is captivated by the ruling motif of such a small detail: it soaks up not only the hat's black foams but also the face, the whole body, every movement & thought, as though it were the central character trait. Lea remembered the old-fashioned illustrations in children's books, where thin schoolgirls wore straw hats with very wide rims that were slightly turned up in front, and this openness was the main content of their psychic serenity; even her dolls had such hats, and if the rim was not turned up a bit in the shop, the first thing Lea did was to turn it up herself; she loved to see how, with a few millimeters' curling up, the doll's whole psychic life metamorphosed. She would have liked to kiss the actress for that childish turning up of the hat's rim, which hovered like sunshine above the tree crowns' thick velvet.

She felt she was not standing before an individual woman but contemplating a landscape filled with woman-like entities: the hasty leaves of blond trees sizzle on night's black shoulder as though it were a wind-beaten fleet crammed into the narrow beak of one harbor; above it a flat cloud reminiscent of a sluggish kite, on the edge of which (like the prince's crown in the corner of a monogram) the sun's burning fingerprint shines. Before the narrow harbor a large red island rises like the raw material of destiny — that matte, fat, mushroomy puffed-up redness, of which the female body's veins are made, like the strings on a white violin. The two eyes swayed above the landscape like white-green fans' refreshing wings which swish forth from behind the mountains' green and morose towers into the warm heart of the night. Because the female dawn is not the belated fruit of hours but already paces on night's blue steps like a mute pirate: a worn-out mirror, a truer soul of darkness than the dark itself, a vagrant root.

*female beauty as the Manichean model of good and evil;
about mystical and analytical expression on the side*

Lea felt that a certain kind of female beauty, like Zwinskaya's for instance, is not an æsthetic feature but an embodiment of the human being's most ancient moral struggles, therefore such female beauty is more beautiful than beauty. One can feel this kind of beauty in the works of mystical poets, where it is usually & with comfortable brevity called 'demonic,' independently of the dancer-type labeled a demon. Because this demonism cannot be found at all on the faces of modern coquettes but much rather, on plain peasant and petit-bourgeois faces. It is in these very women that the most blind hysteria & the most exalted ethos live in full animal recklessness — in one common pot, in one sole & identical flower; unio hypostatica: Hysteréthos.

It's as if they signified the beginning of nature in the form in which the court genealogist of Leatrice's aristocracy, Blake once illustrated it: half woman, half specter; quivering through and through with crystalline purity (as if night's leaves were silvery on the verso and if one quietly blew into the black-noon's silence, suddenly that silver verso that fills the velvety dome would come into view; on lips and face the redness of poison blooms like dawn's first innocent pink; virtue and sin, virginity and black pregnancy are one and the same thing in this woman; a monster who is graceful whether she walks in heaven or earth; a beauty that is wired together with the delta of long-polished satanic desires.

In this rigorously analytical portrait there are no colors & no forms, its dreary moralism lacks metaphor altogether: this picture of Zwinskaya à la Blake-Leatrice is first & foremost a moral philosophical graph. Innocence and sin, revenge and caritas, truth & lie, original sin and eternal salvation, sensuousness and holy life:

in the abstract blending of such themes female beauty is born like a mirroring or haunting side product. When one shouts out ludicrous bombast like, "virtue's pale flower funneled sin's thick odor into the objective heavens," the intended effect is not picturesqueness but analysis (or rather, the precision that is as valuable as analysis proper); for analyzing one of those feelings that condition our lives, and which as yet have no practical or concrete content: she didn't think of the de rigueur blends of love & hate, of 'paradoxical' feelings (panis pauperum!) but of alien, pure, & first of all simple feelings which can only be approximately 'analyzed' in the above manner.

These two features: forever thirsty pan-moralism, and 'pure' feeling devoid of all real relation ('pure' not in the sense of virtuous but in the sense of contentless) led Leatrice's perception of Zwinskaya. Thus beauty meant some kind of identity of good and evil, or more exactly, the point of view from which good & evil overlap like in a polarizing device.

The human being is a bifurcating well: on one side it pours over into comb-shaped white pipes & as the thin water-needles slowly fill those glass reeds, they emit precise whistling sounds; meanwhile on the other side water moves in the form of thick blue clouds, steam-flowers in parallel or in counterpoint, like a dream plant whose roots are permanently dancing like an accelerated jellyfish: its petals are blue like dogma-faced impossibility. If we stop one ear we will hear only the sharp ring of the water-strings, the capillaries' 'positive' laboratory scales (analysis?) — if we stop our other ear, we will of course hear only the melodies of the other branch of the well: the great tide of impossibility that embraces our body with its wide rings, dropping at night its velvety wave-grapes into the basket of 'analysis,' so that in the morning there lies among the shiny birdcage's Islamic grids a transparent, pale bunch of water-grapes, mysteriously caught in the sieve (mysticism?).

And this a-logical harvest of absurdity is nevertheless a more conscientious form of precision than analysis. Perhaps — she added cowardly. When she looked at Zwinskaya's enormous hat, her simple red dress, she was looking simultaneously at the water in the well's two branches: the Gothic 'permed wave' and the azure sun eclipse of non-entity. In this vision she encountered anew the same sensation (which Touqué had mockingly dubbed nihilfuddle) that she felt after her first morphine injection, or after yesterday's champagne: she was chasing something into the depth of annihilation only to render it more plastic.

the detective novel as the perfect image of the moralizing beauty-concept discussed above. Example: the violet glove; Halbert's detective novel: The Blessed Practical

So for Leatrice one form of beauty had its origins in moralizing (*Beiträge zur manicheistischen Ästhetik*) [258] — the other was the peculiar meaning of beautiful women featuring in crime fiction. In both, beauty is first and foremost not the cleat of sexual scaffolding (however sexual that appeal may be), or if it is, then sexuality means not the relation between man and woman but only two abstract poles, the world's nethermost structure of pressure, the classical mechanics of moral that every mysticism presupposes as a rule. Sometimes it is God and man, or body and soul, yes and no, virtue and sin, day and night; that's precisely why women understood in this way have such a dreamlike force of attraction (charme théogénétique?), because they come to mean everything — all the seasons, the sum total of sins & political parties.

The detective novels' female figures are closely related to the former: for on the bottom of the crime novel we can smell the same Blake-style moralizing (naturally also nurtured by Puritanical petit-bourgeois thirst for justice). (Halbert's first psychoanalytic study was written precisely on the Puritans under the title: *The Bird of Paradise: From Milton to Wallace*. It traced the lay middle-class sense of justice back to erotic experiences [with illustrations], grouping the whole bourgeois outlook around the pleasures of 'squaring' & 'tweaking'; in crime novels he explored not the game of sin and justice but that of dream and bureaucracy, in which the tradition of the Milton-'complex' lives on, etc.)

For example, she had once read a detective novel with the title, *The Velvet Glove*. Already the title expressed that alluring duality: the elegance & femininity of the female hand, and the darkness of a (by no means sexual) crime. Throughout, the novel danced along this 'charm plus murder' pair of oppositions: in the first chapter the glove is spotted in a hotel room — it's dawn, a strong yellow light pours into the room redolent of the past — one sees that something had happened there (how much a crime story enhances the pastness of even the historical past): somebody is still pedaling; although the real pianist had long flown away, the sound is still reverberating among the curtains. And now the violet glove appears next to the washstand on the towel hook: all of a sudden the room sinks into the atmosphere of a dark diagnosis, like the profile of a gentle-faced patient on whose knee a tiny pimple was found that foretells a lethal disease: the twin themes of woman and crime flutter through the hotel — from one female portrait we jump to a revolver, from a couple of lovers to a morphine cloth.

In a showroom the first drop of blood appears on the splashboard of a barely used concours d'élégance award-winning car that had been so far mostly kept in the depot; on the owner of the most exclusive fashion salon the signs of slow poisoning are detected (in the meantime a big fashion show takes place: a new zebra-suit, a new gramophone hit, a new symptom of poisoning); a long needle is found missing from the cosmetic institute (mirrors, surgical instruments, arithmetic whiteness; two lovely women whose artificial beauty is almost sinlike — blood drops on the tiles); on the Longchamp race the count's young bride goes missing: a moment before she was still radiating on the lawn like an ornate glass cork on the green flacon flatter than a gramophone record; the beauty of nature too is drawn into crime's circle of light: solitary gladiolas turn into corpus delicti, the most gorgeous alpine landscapes into the escapee's murderous path, the Arosa ski resort is suddenly striped with the rail tracks & switches of the mysterious murder.

In the end, as a culmination point it turns out that two almost identical-looking women featured in the story, some 'Phlara Sisters' from a cabaret, & so beauty itself is doubled, the readers can materially palpate this metaphorical doubling in their fantasy: if we look at our face in a concave metallic sheet, after a quarter circle's distortion our portrait is split into two, getting separate arched portraits above and beneath — this heroine too splits into two in the mirror of her beauty and crime, one single reflection couldn't carry all her tension. And this whole narrative lacework is in fact nothing else but the exhaustive analysis of the concept of the 'velvet glove.'

(In his above-mentioned essay, Halbert has discussed at length the common root of horror & idyll, those writers in whose texts the spilt blood, disfigured face, or the yawning metronome of conscience are only decorative units in a poetic demonstration, minus-sign forms of poppy petals, squeezed fruits, or of the wheatfields' monotonous gold crises — at the end of the day crime and beauty, mystery and evidence are one & the same.

The preciosity of the crime novel was especially interesting from this perspective: in fact the events are transpositions into narrative of 17th-century 'conceits'; certain puns about blood become actual events, grotesque rhymes give birth to grotesque people or things: glass keys, projected lovers, violet nail varnish, a serum which, if taken by the young mother in the fourth month of pregnancy, turns the fetus' heart into an unknown gemstone that can be taken out only when the child had reached its fifth year, but the mother goes mad from it in the eighth month of gestation, etc.

There is one single color scale, but we are conditioned to perceive the strong and deep lower colors as crime, sickness, and horror, & the colors upward on the scale as fairytale landscapes: underneath, red bloodstains on the killer's hand, above, small red flowers on a thick white-branched shrub: there can be no talk about qualitative difference. So through the precious crime novel Halbert accused the Puritans of erasing the essential opposition between God & Satan, smuggling in its place the mere difference in intensity, as if the vibration number of heavens were 579 and that of hell, 786.)

Halbert had also written a kind of detective novel with the title *The Blessed Practical*: in this the detectives (the chief representatives of 'practical reason,' together with an assembly of agents & salesmen) are unable to solve the riddle of a crime, and at this point a theoretical physicist, an Indo-German linguist, and a botanist join forces to uncover the mystery with their own methods: one, with the help of Eigenwert, the other by seeing the analogy of common roots in a small, inorganic-looking coterie, and the third, inspired by the main principles of his overarching critique of Linné; together they deduce the errors of excessively logical reasoning. Each of them had started out by applying in jest the concepts & abstract methods of their field of study to this actual fact of practical life, like a 'naïve' professional comparison (one-sided, pedantic, school textbook-like!), and in the end these very comparisons uncover reality. The whole thing is topped by a half-mad musician's deed: he is the one who captures the murderer along the lines signaled by the other three.

the reciprocal influence of naturalist dramatic roles and chic on Zwinskaya's manner; her movements, play of muscles

Leatrice felt simultaneously (in the evening antechamber lighting) Zwinskaya's mystical & criminological beauty: there was a distant ring of bells and if the Moon had suddenly asked the city, which of its ears rang, the city couldn't have answered. The actress pulled her coat tightly around herself under her breasts; perhaps the penitent Magdalene squeezed her body so when she had to cover it in her hair during the heyday of the Eton crop. Zwinskaya's body was a blend of squeezing-tight and free falling. On her, tightness didn't look piquant but rather, homely growing out of clothes.

In the actress' plumpness the only surplus on thinness was of the degree that would invite the following exchange to play out thirty times a day: "Z plump? I'd not call her that by far." — "Yes she is, look at her when she sits down and crosses her legs." — "Dear God, even a greyhound will look fat in certain positions. Anyway I've never noticed it when she sits but rather, when she props herself up or leans out, like in yesterday's play, with her back turned to the audience."

Her movements, the rich modulation of her 'hidden' thinness, was accompanied by the deep piano chord of this small, mobile plumpness (like the balancing weight on the one-arm scale): if the basketless crescendo of the breasts arched with too strong an impetus into the next hip figuration, then a faint muscle chord chimed in with velvety darkness, to underscore the transition. Sometimes her breasts hovered in the morning breeze, in the caoutchouc coat's pneu odor, like pegged handkerchiefs hung out to dry — but if she turned one centimeter to the left, a form appeared that was one shade plumper: in such moments her voice, too, deepened (because she was conscious of that line) and she threw a glance on her blouse as the heroines of naturalist plays on the hospital note announcing the death of their illegitimate child (the beastliness of pain lends actresses some typically 19th-century misery-elegance and fate-chic, as they give a generous tip to the nurse bringing the news & tell her in a shrill voice: "Thank you, dear. Now go, dear.").

With this naturalist pathos Zwinskaya accompanied her body's vagrant plus-plumpness (the eternal bubble of the leveling device glides up and down in this way in the slender glass tube): wherever it appeared, her eyes immediately threw on it a 'coup de décadence,' like the most jaded of her dressers. This gave Lea much food for thought: how she managed to use the naturalist play-acting style as the backbone of her mundanity; through what capillaries and filters did the sickly socialism go over into the egotistic order of hotel movements? Naturalist dramas, in which suffering was as a rule represented by the conventions of fever, hysteria, & paralysis (the contrast between reality and dream was replaced by that between misery and nightmare: most of the naturalists did write so-called 'dream plays,' which were nevertheless not much different from those about drunken cabmen but rather their simple sequels, so they did nothing to widen the writer's 'world'), enriched first & foremost the impassive & neutral gestures of her life: Zwinskaya used especially the prestige of fever, the artificial insulating tricks of dark hysteria, for rendering her manner more aristocratic.

When she pointed at a beautiful hat, she immediately adopted the style of obsessive or sleepwalking women (Hannele ou la mondanité?): 'this, this,' she boomed mulishly, as if a cello & first violin sounded at the same time in her soul — one embraced the object in a melancholy gesture (so does the prole embrace a delicate artificial flower: the whole encounter is in fact the propaganda-coitus of two social classes), sprinkling its whole individuality on it, as air pressure sprinkles mercury in the form of rain through a cork sheet; but the first violin sharpened its soul into a woodpecker beak, which (while rain fell) rattled the object: 'this, this, this.' Thus in her stylized gestures she preserved theater's socialist propaganda even at tea in the Ritz.

In her gestures she used only a part of herself, like those candelabra chandeliers from whose 24 light bulbs now six, now 12 are lit: similarly, the flower of the Victoria Regia always blooms on the edge of a giant leaf, as if avoiding its own central point, the essence of its own character, always showing of itself only segments fashioned for a lay audience, tangents arguably even more important than the essence. When she started into a sentence, her body stirred under her momentary will as a string under the bow or a twig from the bird that drops on it (one could see in the forest another miniature twig's image in front of the twig, as in a musical score we see before regular notes the microscopic natural sign); nothing could penetrate that whole body, only parts of the body — the rest was merely a resonance box. And yet this economy was neither blasé nor nonchalant (gothic oaks stir only their small secretary-twigs in the fiercest storms, as if that reaction were a simple formality that a subaltern could carry out), but bespoke some lazy village nit-picking: she kept placing her movements next to one another as a little girl the goods bought from the fair.

When she sat down and the pressed creases seen at the bending of oven pipes ran through her, their tiny lines bringing anew into play the theme of 'plumpness,' while her other body parts hovered freely like wind-blown silk paper that only tautens in the immediate proximity of the seal-wax dripping on it — sometimes the outlines of heavy ships are smudged into light runs by the approaching small dolphin-motorboats or wave contours in search of geometrical likeness. By the fact that around the seat the folds could be heard almost in pizzicato, while the hat surrounded her with its rings of Saturn, to Lea it seemed that Zwinskaya's soul, gaze, head were only bright reflexes that can be obtained by placing her legs in a tight press.

Thus the actress' tight skirt didn't mean coquetry — much rather, some peasant bravado with the motto, "go ahead, you foolish thigh, if you tug at the leash so hard." Zwinskaya handled her desires like dogs or other capricious pets. She let them run loose not with a charitable sense of bowing to some higher power, but rather, that she was letting loose a raving mad creature or silly dog: across the lawn, rolling in the grass, and when the dog romped its fill, she patted it: 'you fool, you fool.' Her tight skirt, too, was such a 'fool dog,' not her coquetry but the legs' childish insistence to go their own way. Why should she curb their joy? What was the heroism in this, Leatrice couldn't have said, but she felt that Zwinskaya's love is doubtlessly 'geharnischte Venus.'[259]

the difference between girls' and women's vanity

The concept of 'woman' started crystallizing in Leatrice's mind first while she was looking at those thigh-creases: always meaning by woman the manly treatment of girlhood, as though the hunting attitude toward virginity immediately turned one into a woman. Thus Lea's concept of the feminine derived from rather contrasting directions — meaning partly a sickness (the 'women's affliction' of Peter's love), partly the peasant lads' healthy carelessness with which they let the berserk animal run amok until it tires with no more than an expressionless oath.

To 'woman-hood' also belonged the fact that the actress' dress wasn't made of some delicate or ornate material but, as we said before, of simple red fabric, as if puritanism too were an important component of being-woman. The woolen fabric wasn't feminine and thus it gave a peculiar taste to the feminine forms: wool had always signified manhood for Lea, not because she always saw it on men but because in its manufacturing she sniffed some kind of matte masculinity. There lurked on the actress' thigh (above the creases' blister-rayé) this indeterminate masculinity and alien-substantiality. For the first time perhaps she noticed that in comparison to the female face's reflex-like lightness, the female thigh is disproportionately massive, and she didn't yet know the contours of 'style Nature XIV' sufficiently to realize that these asymmetries are the most characteristic features of life's technique. She suddenly imagined the female body seen by non-human eyes: above, a knotty little button on a short stem, followed by a broad bulk that continues in two pipe-like offshoots — it's a comic pretense to speak here of 'golden ratio.' Perhaps the 'womanly' quality consisted in noticing that inarticulate block-likeness within the so-called 'feminine forms.'

With girls the soul tightens the body as alum does the shaved face, or a button sewn too high the whole coat: but in the time of womanhood a giant ball lets drop from the soul's roulette a thigh, a hip, a breast, according to the unexpected intensities of centrifugal force. How comic it is that these accidental forms (flattened ellipses, hollowed rubber balls, pneumatic pliers, etc.) are treated as absolutes by the ladies' tailors: 'the hips' — this they pronounce the way a mathematician pronounces 'rotor'; 'leg-shape' — as though saying, 'the melting point of natrium': although they are only the hazardous forms of lead in the water bowl at New Year's Eve. In jest we would sometimes pretend to be amnesiac or blind, whose eyesight is restored by surgery (the latter being the evergreen & inglorious habitués of psychology books): so Lea looked now at the actress' legs, which nearly burst the skirt, and she saw them for the first time as accidental forms. The girl's body rid of the gathering force of 'the human': is this then woman?

So the female body progresses on the same road of constitutional evolution as the complex empires: first the many joint states are subjected to the mother country; later they achieve more & more autonomy, and slowly the suzerainty of the mother country fades. Zwinskaya's legs were on the level of the Statute of Westminster. When girls pull on their stockings, manicure their hands, or bathe their dogs, they regard each body part as the indispensable, but not very authoritative member of a players' company, which has no erotic autonomy whatsoever — together they compose the ensemble of 'prettiness': here & there one of them gets decorated with an order, some légion d'honneur in the form of perfume or a shoe, but that never lends them actual legal privileges. As good schools put every pupil to recite in every class, so there too every body part is permanently put to work, because they mean the tiny developments, variations of the fixation of the 'pretty girl.'

Everything is a pretty, but abstract Ur-mist (on a studio stage of course: perhaps the whole wee scented chaos amounts to no more than one & a half cubic meters), in which only the lines of the tracks play a part, together with one or two more solid, hesitant balls (like a distracted knot in the midst of the tree's infinite year-strips); the incipient autonomy of the breasts is captured by the legal formula warranting the absolute sovereignty of the 'pretty girl' (in young girls' lives this juridical system barely differs from the Kant-Laplace theory), just as the hips, the spine-valley, the shoulder-blades' bone-cape, the ankles' hourglass-like thinning are merely the folkloric play on this or that body department, which have no legal binding power, however colorful, striking, even essential they may otherwise be. The thighs' Monroe Doctrine is the product of later ages. That doctrine isn't born of conceit or energy: rather, of a certain bureaucratic melancholy. The earlier buoyant joint dance can no longer be continued: the separate body parts have crystallized into individuality, like notes falling out of a chord. The leg can no longer be appeased with a casual order of merit — a whole committee is necessary that investigates its local problems and tries to find solutions for them.

Zwinskaya sorted her stockings with dry eyes, as though reading a bulky dissertation on minority rights or selecting diabetic sweets for a patient. The leg became an institution that one had to permanently monitor like a stranger. Once she played the role of a half-mad girl who goes down the small town's high street at night, muttering mystical commentaries on each house: she blesses the house where her father had betrayed her mother, puts a malediction on the house where she had spent the only happy hour of her life, she thinks at length whether to bless the baker's house or to set it on fire, then in tears she places a glossary on the vicarage's plaited bread-rococo: so did Zwinskaya walk among her own body parts (this, too, is a case of that fruitful plagiarism that the 'grande dame' committed against the prole dame) — she thou-d her legs, addressed her hips with the French 'vous,' and caressed her arms every day with a yellowish-brown cream like one rubbing Lourdes water into a paralytic sister's arm.

She treated her body as if it were only consigned to her: her gestures clearly showed it. Among her movements there was a shepherding, flock-ushering gesture: she always needed to gather all her body parts into one group like waves, difficult-to-symmetrize flowers, or dog breeds. From here derived that characteristically womanly richness of space around her that girls lack utterly; every single body part of hers was surrounded by a selfish aura, an individual atmosphere and air pressure. When she moved, she called to mind the movement of a flock of sheep: the vibration across one another of unity and falling-apart. When in speech she aimed a glance at her legs, she was in fact sending a reassuring telephone call into the rigorist capital of a faraway ally. For Lea this was very grown-upish, as she saw the little girlish-trivial meaning of 'beauty' extinguished in it.

Zwinskaya's vanity entirely lacked the quest for æsthetics. When she put on lipstick she wasn't trying to embellish herself, but adapting to the mouth's inner laws: it was puritanism, not luxury: she was only replacing the weather-beaten barn roof with a new one. Women are trying to exhaust the dry conceptual content of the legs, not to force beauty into them — this was Lea's swift grown-up-imagining. A cathedral may look like the plenitude of harmony from afar, but from 10 centimeters? And women look at their legs from 10 centimeters — this is their 'womanly' trait: they are scrupulous butchers. (Here the word 'butcher' bears no medieval criticism and no touch of the ascetics' usual uncouthness.) Women bleach their skin: there is nothing else before them but a whey-bluish, half-slippery slab ('leg'?) without any touch of harmony or purpose, and they are lacquering it with the help of tubes, small flasks of medicine, brushes, chamois dumplings. By 'cosmetic' and 'prettify' Lea always understood in her childhood such things and acts whose every millimeter and momentary fragment makes it obvious that it's all about æsthetics: but here everything played out differently.

People presuppose that the female leg is beautiful, without it being actually & from its roots beautiful. Zwinskaya's body here again pendulated with a lilt to the bright tracks of convention: as though the whole female magic were only an adopted, arbitrary value (as her mathematics schoolbook would put it) in an empty function. Perhaps men are the independent variables who throw such value into the dependent variable's humble rubber cup which corresponds to the altitude they (the men) want to swing up to, under the influence of the dependent variable they created: as she looked at the officer standing behind the actress she could see how with his manners the man foists female beauty on Zwinskaya, so that he would have something to adore.

Otherwise the officer's rigid obligingness stood in sharp contrast to the actress' tired movements: one was the tree-trunk to which the martyr to be arrowed was tied, and the other the wounded, bleeding body untied from the tree, which now & then bends back, propped up by the tree's fossilized column. Zwinskaya pressed her crossed legs even harder, so that her upper body, neck, head looked even more like vapor let off by the knees' press and the legs' pliers — when snakes lie entangled under a bush, moving their small poudrier-heads on top of the conical spool and now and then stick out their black spark-needle tongues, one has the impression that it was the screw press' immense pressure which set off the hovering little alternating current-bud of heads and tongues (the blue-mute electric power of huge wires, the dancing little ampère-pollen).

Thus the beauty of the female body is like crystals among stones: scattered among big, clunky rock-creases and irregular crevices here & there a mirroring flower-cup shines, more geometrico, only to continue in colorless stone knots again — the one is mere amorphous mass, the next one is already a transient, dancing, ungraspable rule. Leatrice felt the reality of this 'distribution' in her moods: when she thought of herself as 'woman' she always felt to be at the same time a charwoman & a celestial rebus: her hands, legs, waist were great ancient ruins, passive Cyclops meat, but it was precisely this ballast, this pessimistic 'cargo' that made possible the slender veil's delicate, trembling movement (the sea is the clock face, the mast the minute hand, & the stars are the tiny, burning lines of the scale?).

one of Peter's novelistic themes set against mundanity: the vision of moral fastidiousness (Scarpellino)

Probably Peter didn't suspect that female beauty is something so uneven, with as many hiatuses as the inside of Emmenthaler cheese, for otherwise he wouldn't have hooked so many fancy dilemmas on it. Love shouldn't be allowed to coarsen into homogeneous desire, for it cannot get close to the true beauty of women.

Like caustic soda, Lea's scrutinizing eyes started corroding personal unity from Zwinskaya's body —

Peter's tragedy was perhaps of conceiving every woman overmuch as 'one person.' You can hang all kinds of stories on 'one person,' but to this white hand that runs up night's black wall like an anemic coral, to scare away the grey-blooded veil-fish like an electric creeper: to this no love problem can be attached; can this leg stuffed in red fabric, which reminds one of the heavenly sponge with which the resurrected bodies are washed into eternity at the Last Judgment: can this transcendental cosmetic device have any meaningful role in a series of events? Poor Peter became a true martyr of the unifying fiction of 'human being.' For love needs to be made of the sub-human (senseless figurations of matter) and the extra-human (the hypotheses & arbitrariness of convention). She compared the actress' legs to Peter's novelistic themes: it was impossible to find any connection. One such theme of 'human being':

> The young Scarpellino destroys his life with an early marriage: for him ever since his wedding all other female beauty is identified with sin — blue landscapes where he would like to live with a young girl mean the color of sin (because woman always also means a landscape, so do landscapes get diabolized). Scarpellino is barely 20 and his future stands before him in the shape of one huge adultery. Because he knows with fatal precision that he would need another woman, but also that marriage is a sanctum. Even the cathedrals turn into symbols of his sin to come: he imagines each one with a different woman. How infinitely strange it must be when a woman's beauty & virtue are not mutually exclusive. Scarpellino wanted to build a gigantic cathedral & so married X*** because she had a prodigious fortune. (The cathedral would be so

fantastic that you would need private wealth to fund it.) In the meantime the fortune disappeared & Scarpellino couldn't build the cathedral. Now for him there is only sin: for trees, seas, ships, all feature in his mind as sceneries he would enjoy with a woman, that he would paint for a woman, that he would build the magnificent churches for a woman. Somehow he manages to build one: its every column, every leaf on its capitals, the aisles' ground plan, the façade's nearly transparent wall-sheets and wind-ruffled scales, all proclaim 'female innocence' (Peter imagined the virtues of women to have altered shapes like their legs), but Scarpellino knows all the same that this church is the symbol of sin, having been inspired by an unknown beautiful woman, so the first mass is going to be held in the stone hypothesis of an adultery.

How does the entire nature change under the influence of guilt-feeling? How should he examine, in the laboratory of scruples, a daisy's colors and shape, with the radiation of damnation all around? At about this time does St. Ignatius found the Jesuit order; he too would like to become a friar by all means. But it could only happen if his wife died. Thus he has to wish for his wife to die in order to carry out his own ascetic program of holiness.

The dual game starts: either adultery or holy monkhood at the price of the wife's death. He has yet to meet the woman with whom to betray his wife, but he's waiting for her every minute as for inexorable fate. Sometimes he has fits of asceticism: on such occasions he would like to have solitude, independence, but the family's idyllic concept and its reality stand in his way, interfering in the disarrayed monologue of saintliness. Suddenly his wife dies. He feels it is God's finger — not in the sense of God willing him to become a Jesuit but on the contrary:

of God showing that Scarpellino's secret thoughts about his wife's death have indeed killed her. He feels he is a murderer: he killed his wife because he wanted to be a saint living in solitude.

He retrospectively realizes how his secret planned adultery & his secret planned desire for sanctity have wilted his wife day by day. He wants to repent for wanting to repent too much in her lifetime. Paradoxical double sainthood? He wants to be a saint, so God would pardon him for having wanted so blindly to be a saint.

To these two kinds of variations on sainthood a third one is added: the automatic, non-willed, impersonal sainthood — this is ensured by his monotonous grief. He wants to repent his sins of thought committed against his wife by praying for her day & night & having masses said for her non-stop: but so he ties himself to the family again, it is not free saintliness but last-ditch, past-gazing, past-repairing sainthood: sorrow's restorative saintliness in place of free, creative saintliness. If he doesn't pray for his wife he is a common criminal; if he prays for her he is a chained man, the slave of the family. His saintliness cannot be complete, but his adultery can: so he starts looking for the redeeming sin. Although his wife is already dead, he knows it is a sin nevertheless: it's he who killed her for another woman.

In the meantime Scarpellino becomes a magistrate and the woman charged with murdering his wife is brought before him. All evidence points toward her indeed being the murderer of his wife. If he pardons her, he will offend his wife in the otherworld; if he sentences her, he will deliver to the scaffold someone who opened the way to his sainthood. For what if he is a saint indeed? He feels all three forms of his sainthood to be dilettantism, but perhaps the third, the automatic one, might hold some value: perhaps he alone sees it as grey automatism, although what penetrates him & makes him insensitive is in fact the blinding & paralyzing ray of sainthood — true exaltedness is found not in dithyrambs but in deaf swooning. Perhaps he is a saint after all. He pries on the opinion of his fellow priests and clerical superiors: they all consider him a man of extraordinary virtue. Shall he then sentence the woman, the enabler of his sainthood? Shall he set his wife's murderer free?

Then the last chapter in his life starts: 'Dialogues in Prison or, The Ultimate Optics.' He watches the murderous woman as God's positive herald: her every word and gesture is a divine revelation; she is the rope that hangs down into worldly hands from the heavenly rigging loft. He falls in love with the woman, the cause of his sainthood. He loves her both with sinful worldly love as woman, and as the divine trigger of asceticism — the ultimate optics is the last dilemma of sin and virtue, love and saintliness. They hold their nuptials in the prison: the first real love encounter in Scarpellino's life (he is already 45!). Afterwards he is tormented by visions: his wife is stalking him. In the morning he signs the death sentence. Description of the ceremonial procession to the scaffold. The judges, the woman, the audience, the trees, the sea, the thoughts of the first cathedral. In the middle stands Scarpellino: half dead as if he were the one led to execution. On the scaffold the woman kills him: a great tempest starts, stars fall — the crowd is convinced that the Antichrist or the great whore of Babylon appeared. They scatter in panic. In the last description of the tempest Peter expressed all the confusion that the idea of woman (not one particular woman, for he had never known such) meant.

Leatrice and the 'anti-tragic'

Lea wouldn't resign herself by any means to taking over that tragic conception of love, with the wide-reaching allegories of impotence for social life: she was conscientiously looking for a counter-poison to everything tragic, although her own nature also showed a bend toward the lighter paths of tragedy. It was a girlfriend who acquainted her with the 'neo-Ghibelline' snobbery, fashionable at a time with the Germans: for her this became the æsthetic recipe of the Anti-tragic, which the only theoretically pleasure-seeking, but in fact heavy-handed Leatrice grabbed with superstitious & entirely foreseeable greed.

The German-flexible concept of 'demonism' encompassed all the tragic twilight, fateful redness that characterized Peter's impossible love torsos, but at the same time also the victory, the optimism unfolding from the yellow trumpets of negativities, the ethos hovering like a magnesium-Moon above basins of low-caliber lies.

Peter was driven to despair by the thought that for him, sin and beauty had always been opposites; but this Ghibelline stage setting æstheticized sin, made the greyest laicity incandesce mystically (as against the clerical), yielded some cherry-lipped classicism to the crumpled layers of chaos. Among pale Romanesque arches and grey mosaics red-haired, red-skinned, and blue-eyed figures walked; the heads of lanky, white Teutonic boys were crowned with the charms of the Orient; a strange mix arose of anemic bourgeois jasmines & incongruent Hindu birds.

It was around this time that Leatrice's desperate new 'ethics' started developing, the forced weapon of the chase after the Anti-tragic. Peter had often composed gaudy mythologies, but their very gaudiness showed how cowardly they were, childish compensations, wie's im Buch steht.²⁶⁰ These made a great impression on Leatrice, but it was the Ghibelline ethics and æsthetics that really satisfied her for the first time, because mythology was no maypole refuge there but an actual belief. Its basis was the above-mentioned duality: the simplicity of the early Romanesque, mixed with something antique-oriental, perhaps with the stone moment when Greek and Persian or Greek and Indian art were the most ideally one. Hence the ethical suggestiveness of this modern Ghibelline style: Greek purity burns through Romanesque puritanism, and the dull redness of the Orient radiates through the former; asceticism & ornamentation have the same roots. (It's a secondary matter for our purposes here that historically genuine Romanesque taste is no more 'puritanical' than the Greek one is 'pure.') At that time Leatrice had not yet read Leville-Touqué's *Comis Teutonicus*,²⁶¹ where he parodied the Germans' Mediterranean nostalgias & the concept of 'demonism': he ridiculed Stefan George's ideal of the Jüngling together with the fashion for Friedrich II.²⁶²

Leatrice's body and Romanesque (eros and Ghibellinism)

This Ghibellinism is interesting in Leatrice's life story in so far as it changed into a practical manner: gestures, words, intonation, clothes. Her own body came to mean early German Romanesque taste: the word 'Romanesque' gave a brand-new mood to her body, bleaching it, making it thinner in certain places and thicker in others, for is there a more ambiguous thing in the world — she thought — than a Romanesque row of arches, let's say a scale of semicircular arches crowning a cloister? The Renaissance semicircles are worlds away from this inner disquiet and outer harmony (it also goes the other way round, they're just words) that the Romanesque semicircles carry. Mass runs into floating curves, only for the line's momentum to continue again in a block of matter: the pure ethereality of arching and the deepening ballast of matter don't play with each other in such equipoise on the semicircular Renaissance gates or courtyard-frames: there the weight of matter & the arch's geometrical 'pneuma' merge in some kind of median, an engineering and not psychological equilibrium.

Of course for Leatrice this duality was a question not of art history but of fashion & bathrooms: a more exact cosmetics. If she perceived her body as a Romanesque building, the arches were always born anew from her movements, like small geysers that run their 180° course & return to the earth: large surfaces of flesh were left inarticulate and the arching only accidentally flashed through them. Renaissance movement & poise is the exact opposite: harmony traverses the body through & through, proportion overruns the veins and blood like a parasite; by automatism, harmony turns into empty hygiene.

Plastered to massive castle walls, or in the middle of church-brows, the Romanesque semicircular arch blooms like a rare aloe, crowned by all kinds of rich and mostly inorganic serrations: when the half-circle of St. Woolos is surrounded first by small [263] triangles and then by striped zebra cones, those irregular wreaths are not the organic and thematic continuation of the semicircle (in that, Renaissance architecture follows the barrenness of the sonata form) but naïve celebrations of the semicircle shape: to celebrate the emperor's brow, they don't place on it moldings that organically adapt to the imperial brow's form (in this respect Renaissance architecture is reminiscent of the gypsum models of dental technicians) but a flower wreath that only loosely follows the shape of the head: these wave-lines, stone X-s, cubes, and checked snakes that surround the arch also stand for such arch-celebration, peasant arch-hedonism, as opposed to the Renaissance arches' impotent logic. Here the first arch stands before our eyes in the pubertal nakedness of utility, of raw necessity: much as its ornaments are autonomous, added (and thus subtractable) embellishments, the basic form is purely-utilitarian, only-practical gesture.

To bathe in a cold lake on cold mornings: the water, sky, the trees' leaf-fog are all grey-blue, only here and there does a long silvery strip show: the Sun looks like the Moon and trembles on the water as a dropped ball when it performs the last jumps of elasticity before stopping. Leatrice felt like a divorced woman in whom the old nuptials' central heating and the icy ventilator of the new girlhood (some kind of legal, theoretical virginity?) work at the same time. Romanesque triggered in her a landscape and a role: the first anti-tragic symptoms directed against the memory of Peter.

She didn't feel in Romanesque simplicity, for example, the willed & formulated Calvinist simplicity and intellectual moral — on the contrary: Romanesque simplicity could be at times gaudy and crowded, not coinciding with the 'meaning' of simplicity: what was simple was the perception that willed those forms — akin to God's simplicity perhaps. In Calvinist churches she always felt that something had been taken away, something is missing — but the 'simplicity' of Romanesque churches meant something positive, from which nothing is missing: like the face of a daydreaming figure next to a fainted one, like a bud next to a plucked flower.

Romanesque kiss? What is the truth of this affectation? Angels' steel wings collide in the hot Tyrrhenian blue (the water burns the ships' bottom so much that they hover a few centimeters above the surface, like the drop of water lifted by its steam above the hot iron sheet): their white limbs meet in a frosty embrace, their hair, clothes, and everything is glaring white, as if they had been amalgamated in the Moon's round basin: the debate not of angel and devil but of angel and angel, the image of battle lurking in the self-identity of virtue. In the end they meet in one kiss:

in one sole red worm-gear, like the Easter candelabra — in the middle of the Moon blooms one red flower which fills the night's blankness with its scent. These are all mere hypotheses of course. Field flowers too belong here, those trademarks of early Catholic simplicity: what would flowers look like if they had been invented by Puritans? The daisy's life is every bit as sensuous as the most tropical flower, it hosts ruthlessness, frivolity, and sin to the same extent, and yet it is pure & simple; it looks like a girl, although it's a divorcé. How come the only stylistic kin of robust castle walls is a tiny daisy? It would look more likely for flowers to be siblings of Gothic or Baroque: how can they then live in chiming eadem canon with Romanesque?

the relation of the two worlds of over-the-top self-consciousness and over-the-top caritas in Leatrice's life

What are in fact the two worlds that have entirely overpowered Leatrice's soul? One is consciousness, the other is caritas. Are these two not the most European of all things? The one means the ultimate drowning-into-flowers of psychology (some are in the habit of calling, in short-sightedness or a comfortable penchant for metaphor, infinitely condensed flower mass a fruit), the other the most lip-colored mania of Western moral: soul & agape-eros are the truly European products of the technique of manufacturing humans. Psychology and caritas are somewhat allegorically charged, ponderous words, and Leatrice had just enough feminine chic and barbarian scientific bend to load this two-chamber brassiere of our culture not with her live and sensate breasts (as with larger-than-the-net fish) but with two experimental Ersatzes: for her, 'psychology' consisted in the morphine-induced disturbances of consciousness, and 'caritas' of sometimes willed but mostly willy-nilly loves. Europe and the little girls became more & more conscious, the 'self' got in behind the soul and 'trans-vital ego' behind the 'self'; behind that new station of consciousness, the 'analogical infra-subject,' and so forth. Leatrice had little inclination for such philosophizing, but underwent all the same their de rigueur European enhancements of consciousness.

The gift of this process is, that in time her life became so self-conscious that no more contents of consciousness featured in it, only empty frames of consciousness, and her psychic life was reduced to arithmetic operations with those numbered consciousness-frames (mostly combination and permutation). She could best observe the progress to consciousness contours rid of all content in her dreams and in half-sleep: for a while she dreamt of themes that were sharply isolated from her real daytime life, while later she started dreaming about herself dreaming — at that point there was no clear-cut delineation between awake-consciousness and dream-consciousness: she didn't know if she was indeed monitoring herself, or dreaming about the fairy-tale shamelessness also called 'self-observation.'

When she compared the two kinds of self-observation she obviously needed a third kind of consciousness, which she could no more locate. The tension was so high that she felt she woke up. She looked at her watch: this operation brought two oddities. First, the phosphorus-imbued numbers glowed with a sharp green light, although the chandelier light was on in her room and the phosphorescent numbers only glow in the dark. The situation was thus irreal, it seems she was not awake after all. The other oddity was that the clock distinctly and unmistakably showed 27, an impossibility. So it was certain that she was sleeping and only dreaming that she wakes up. But she kept on experimenting: that night she wanted to go to a concert of Haydn's Quinten Quartet. The concert was scheduled at eight. Haydn existed in reality, didn't he? He did write a Quinten Quartet. Eight o'clock was a sensible hour:

how can all that prosaic reality co-exist with the numbers phosphorescing in the light & with 27 o'clock? She tried to laugh out loud at herself and in a certain sense managed to, because a loud laughter came from the room — it was not she laughing and neither some banal ghost, it was no impersonal laughter either, for her self was actively involved in it; only her mouth was 'deaf,' her will and ear were fresh and strong. But the fact that she found some things real and others irreal was no guarantee that behind the real effect were indeed real things — it could as well be that only the two kinds of 'senses' were left in her consciousness, neither of which was objectively relevant. Later she lost her way in the line of 'dreamt wakefulness,' 'dream imagined while awake,' etc., but felt that each one of them represented a different type of consciousness which intersect like colorless grey circles in the neutral, slightly pain-imbued air: there is nothing else but the circle. Could this be the fabled 'psyche,' the fulcrum of individual inner life?

And when she woke up after such consciousness-crossings (with new surprises of course, as it turned out that there was no concert, & somebody from the neighbors said, "I haven't laughed in months," etc.), she immediately came face to face with the fact of love or love-making: she had no idea if she was alive or dead, if she was awake or if she was merely time's fishless gill, where and who she was — & her mouth was already blackened by the strange kisses' umbrella which covered everything again, like the snapping trap the barely moving mouse's leg; she wanted to ask a question, but before she could utter a single word, the kiss' Christian calmative silenced her again. What exactly localized love may be like, the love that is addressed to a definite woman in a definite time, she didn't really know: she was touched by kisses and arms when she didn't feel that she had a body or self, but only blind-anonymous circles of consciousness undulating behind her lips.

And if she felt herself to be not a human being but the hundred permutated rings of empty self-observation, neither could she perceive the man as a living individual, but merely as kiss' impersonal European mechanism in which there was and could be no difference between sensuousness & neo-Platonism, diluted-doctrinaire neighborly love and tragic interdependence: it was the most universal 'agape' function that one could metaphysically imagine. Love of human beings without human beings? Leatrice saw the image alone: intersecting circles & on the side, again sectioning them, one red stain — it's indistinguishable whether it's a mouth or a flower, blood or traffic light. She tried in vain to force some human content under the kisses' meaningless dactyloscopy. Slowly all her understanding of character disappeared, she saw the mouth alone. This had the consequence, in part, that for her the experiential quality of agape or eros ceased altogether, in that relation she could feel, know, or plan nothing — on the other hand, she saw the fact of 'caritas' in its undreamable objective reality, material graspability, which in itself excluded the possibility of undergoing its experience.

People usually say, rather gauchely, that they 'came to know love' when they are truly in love or when they have been recently in love — and that is meaningless, because one can only know love at a time of utter love-impotence, when it is no experience at all but mechanical to the highest degree, and when the very last splinter is long extinct in memory, that could have referred to the erstwhile experience-like loves. With her 'humanist' self replaced by consciousness contours, Leatrice was the world's best kiss-insulator — if that Venus letter catapulted from a red typewriter landed on her lips, she couldn't refer it to her self, for there was no her 'self': she merely left it on her thousand-possibility mouth, like a chance fish fallen into a chance net, which nobody wants to eat. Cynicism is a ridiculously artificial and intellectualist technique of murdering experience — the contentless, Leatrice-style consciousness belts mean an organic & natural device for indifference, one that nevertheless makes the very thing it is fatefully indifferent toward, incandesce into the most attractive, seductive, most logical form. In place of love's 'I' and 'you,' versions of vacuum and insulated kisses: the latest-fad disguises of psychology & caritas.

dream and church plan

Later thus Leatrice didn't dream about anything else but the most marginal categories of dream, time, space, reality, yes & no. This was connected to the fact that she watched with increased attention her nightly wakings-up, including those that were indeed wakings-up, as verified the next day. They were of roughly three types: one was the waking up that signaled getting enough wholesome sleep, the second was the typical insomniac waking up, and lastly, the temporary waking up, which she felt would last for a very short time. She religiously kept track of them because they happily lacked consciousness' carnivalesque pranks, but they wove like ornament into her 'only-consciousness' dreams.

Waking after a slept-through night was like a lying log that is suddenly cut into two in the middle, the cut-off left half is the already-slept sleep, the right-hand half the eventually to-continue sleep; in the first moment she thought she would sleep on. But she soon realized that the log to the right only looked like a log for a moment, it immediately shot leaves, bloomed, bore fruits, the log disappeared from it, small garish-blue birds chirped among its branches, each one of them the trace of dawn's teaspoon (convex? concave?) on the freshly bleached sky: after the section of the log, it's already the rootless flora of daylight.

The insomniac, nervous nighttime waking up is utterly different: there a huge, obtuse-angle wedge was driven into the lying log, the cut-out lump was thrown away beyond reach, & the two parts of the log were pulled apart by one millimeter where the wedge's obtuse angle had been: the dream cannot be continued for two reasons — one stolen bit is missing, & there's a hair's-breadth gap where the already-slept and the yet-to-sleep dream touched.

The schema of the log cut in half can be applied to the temporary waking up too, at such times the cutting-off happens in the following cunning way: somebody presses the blade perpendicularly to the lying log, but the moment it starts cutting the wood, it is tilted & drawn lengthwise at the middle to the right-hand end of the log, there it's turned & again drawn lengthwise to the left end, continuing this undulating move until the log is cut into two: in this way it is expressed that the dream reaches, protrudes with all its length into the dream to come after awakening, & that this dream to come is already inexorably woven into the past dream in the shape of huge advance-veins — let's imagine two interconnected spur wheels where the wheels themselves are one centimeter in diameter, their spurs are 10 meters long, & on each wheel there are 10,000 spurs.

When she was still dreaming (for 16 hours a day most of the time), the greatest reality (in the everyday sense of the word) was the series of gestures she performed half-unconsciously, which she yet sensed all the more keenly. These reflex movements are extremely important next to the empty consciousness-vitiosi, so this or that movement of hers was accomplished architecture, a completed church, bedroom, or triple-basin fountain. One morning she woke up to the collision of her two hands and knees: she didn't see and feel anything else (not seeing her knees under the duvet) than two glaring white balls for which cowardly & greedy hands reach out — there was the apocalyptic altar-wall, all ready.

The wall is pitch-black, made either of the kind of glass that carries blackness as ground glass does blankness, or of excessively lacquered funereal plaque. In front of it stands the altar, made of a similar black material, the simplest rectangular slab with a black cross, with candelabra consisting of a single pencil shaft, with flat stairs: the whole can be barely distinguished from the chapel wall. Two large, shiny white billiard balls stick out of this wall, a third one is glued to the right side of the altar stairs, between two steps. There's a white drawing on the wall (in the color and style of woodcuts), or a sketchy barely-relief, asymmetrically crossing the altar and its steps: two figures trying to catch the three balls — the scene symbolizes the end of the world, when all stars fall into nothingness.

A figure lying on his back is trying to save the ball on the altar steps from perishing: his legs are still on the vertical wall, his knees already on the altar slab, his waist and arms on the altar steps. There's a sharp contrast between the balls' plasticity & the figures' porous sketchiness. The church's 'pessimism' is mitigated by the two side-walls and the chairs: in the church's interior in front of the two transparent and luminous lateral glass walls, there is a zigzagging folding screen made of light grey, almost white net-fabric, several rectangular sheets of the left part are smaller than those on the right and have fewer folds. In front of the altar there are no seats for a while, only more toward the back do the fish-shaped, glistening little steel armchairs start, in whimsical groupings. Net and fish: Saint Peter's net & the fish caught in it.

The gesture is architecture & the gesture is moral. The movement can be exploited for ethics in two ways (for now let ethics mean a pure science of action, with no concepts of value attached): I either investigate the space in which the gesture played out, or the relations of muscles and play of strength inside the gesture. Every gesture disturbs the homogeneity of space and gives different thickening and rarefying graphs: Greco's paintings are precisely such ethical 'space-graphs.' But if I investigate the inside of the muscles, I will come upon the rules of dance, of ritual dance, where 'value' will again not feature. On these two neutral poles of space-ethics & dance-ethics did Leatrice live, but this fact didn't immediately bring with it the disappearance of struggles of conscience.

Touqué and waves

It was Touqué who once contrasted synthetic frivolity to short-sighted essence-micrology, and this contrast resembled in some respects Lea's duel between the tragic and the anti-tragic. There Touqué described a summer bathing: the waves came mutely ashore, for the waves' essence is swelling, rising, which happens soundlessly, and only annihilation, picturesque impotence, brings all kinds of armored sighs; just as the wave has no contour at its fulcrum (muteness coupled with contour would yield cacophony) but only the shapeless hovering of volume can be seen: the passage from valley to crest doesn't happen along a scale, degree by degree, but by encompassing depth and height in one moment and mirroring them, there is depth & height everywhere, there is a whole wave everywhere, and yet the whole wave is a perpetual torso, a direction only and not a statue — as if the four players of a quartet did nothing else but play the same rising scales with increasing intervals and ellipses, thus while the first violin plays sixteen notes (that is the whole wave from valley to crest), the cello would play only two, the eighth and the last (that is, separately a half-valley, and separately the crest of the comb), the viola four, et cetera: such mathematical arrangement could illustrate the rhythm of the waves' rising, their hesitant & yet fateful-precise swelling in its simultaneity, in which a rising line and a shapeless volume (first violin and the cello resonating like a megaphone) merge.

When Touqué was in the valley, he saw a surface changing in every moment, which nevertheless retained the preceding episodes, the way pedaling makes the keys struck before reverberate, thus past and future formed a swinging amalgam where they continuously substituted each other for maintaining balance — a balance that had no time-skin, however. He saw the water around the girls swimming toward him now in the shape of dark green, blind disks, now of transparent light blue mist: the bodies were now concentrated like the ceramic vase on the potter's wheel, almost falling in love with their own axis, their flesh becoming merely the flapping shawl of their weight-line — and now dissolved like a lump of sugar in hot tea. The 'crest' of waves always already means their decadence — originally they are supposed to be rounded.

Touqué watched the small dimples covering the waves' green rubber domes: these relate to the weight's serpentine transience as the violinists' nervous brow-creasing and blinking relates to the celestial lacquer of the sounds pouring forth around their necks: the water too bites its lips while trying to launch huge masses of material to the shore in one regular arch. When a weight-patch reaches too high, an obliging whirlpool-pipe immediately appears at the bottom and sucks up the superfluous weight in a moment, only to disperse it at the whirlpool's end in complicated 8s; the whole is like a vast geometric palace whose every floor, staircase, balcony, and pillar keeps changing all the time, but Neptune as hotel owner must keep the place in walkable, inhabitable, and symmetric order.

Vision and sensory effect are in playful relation: the wave's fast running-ripening fruit is still far away, but it already makes the leg twitch; and yet when we really see the wave under ourselves we feel that the plenitude of momentum has far surpassed us: energy & form run toward the shore in incalculable counterpoint; they vaguely resemble pendulums swinging counter, which only rarely meet.

The human body is generally unused to feeling pressures of different strength within its surface: on the leg, a wild push, on the hips, a gentle caress, dull stability around the head. When in water, we naively hold on to the fixture of some kind of academic wave-scheme (which at first the eyes appear to confirm), to sinus-lines, shell-inductions, & other such spiral harmonies: the disarray of layers of pressure is evidently at odds with such preconceptions — if one's body could easily divide (like wooden planks piled on one another & exposed to the waves), the legs would be thrown to 10 meters' distance, the hips to three, and only the head would remain in place. These distances would have to be brought together in one average and united with the school textbook-like wave-ballet, for us to obtain a more positive wave-formula. Great weight and weight-free space alternate so unexpectedly & irregularly in water that in-between small pauses appear, like between an infinitely long, hanging honey-thread and the swollen honey-drop falling from its end.

chaos and order

It is as though nature always tended toward the greatest possible chaos, and at the moment when disharmony almost sets the world upside down, with a hair-thin regulator at once it tilts the whole thing back: when one balances a vertical stick on a fingertip he will often have to perform the most grotesque jumps, squats, and bows to prevent it from falling off (children will climb up on the table or sofa) — the entire nature gives the impression of busying itself with similar chores: the stick is tilted ever so slightly, only one millimeter (could the fact that the Equator is not perfectly perpendicular on the Earth's orb also play a role from a bucket-shop metaphysical perspective?), but it can be kept in place only if the one carrying it scurries up hill and down dale in the direction of the tilt, to be ahead of the upper tip and so to be able to push it back into full verticality: in this way perhaps the stick will never fall over, but the one balancing it will not get a moment's rest, and so in undulating waters, in the trees' branches and the scent of flowers precision and tumble, purpose & caprice will be together forever. This pace is the tempo of the anti-tragic set against the feigned order of tragedy.

(The human being à la Peter, with his simple-minded mechanical thinking, imagines life as the gradual & homogeneous running out of a spring — Touqué too imagined him as a spring, but one whose spirals now thin, now thicken, now are magnetic and now insulated, now are dense and now so wide as to look almost like vertical threads: common in the two springs is only the compression force loaded in them, and even this force is fragmented into the most diverse segments, in complete disregard for proportion.)

bathing woman comes ashore

Touqué spotted a woman who was trying to come ashore from the waves: already around her chest the salons' light muscle-movements showed, but her knees were still entangled in the water's azure lassoes. The blue blades sawed off preposterous torsos, cutting her body in half now at her waist, now (with unexpected & not at all actual pole-vault) up at her neck, and now tossing her whole body out of the water (like a sizeable chocolate bar from the slot machine) like some unheard-of novelty, so that one would think that if water gets shallower than the ground, it will continue uncovering ever newer body parts of her for meters on end.

In water people get used to taking waves for their own body parts (they gesticulate with faraway water stains); when they come ashore, their gestures unexpectedly tighten, become ridiculously short, as if a whole lot of their essential limbs had been amputated in a moment. Automobiles are tailored like speed's abstract shape, but people cannot mold themselves to the waves and are generally very ridiculous & parvenu when in water: that red swimsuit will hang on, with myopic Harpagonade, to its own shapes and will refuse to smudge its form (as a splashboard would into the wind) among the glass arches of water: the human body has an unstylishly stubborn cohesion.

The girl's swimsuit consisted only of straps, a one-centimeter patch of fabric was held in place by 10 kinds of straps on the shoulders, hips, & armpits (to a yacht's handkerchief-size veil belong 50 kinds of ropes, wires, & buckles): in front, in threefold X-s, on the back in parallel lines — how could those be connected? As a child he used to play with wallets made of two cardboard sheets held together by two rubber bands, one in X-es and the other in the form of equality marks, and if you stuck a banknote under the X-bands, after opening the two cardboard sheets in the opposite direction the money was miraculously found under the two parallel bands — this woman too was such a banknote, as Touqué watched her from the front & back.

reason and unknown in nature

A beautiful woman like that probably has the character of a 'signal': annunciation and commentary, solution and problem at the same time. This duality is the most thrilling thing in nature and women: they show in the most definite form the face of some decisive argument, ultimate evidence (a flower's scent, the silence of a lake, a female calf in a high-heel shoe), but all the same, we are left empty-handed; it's all a matter of questions, an indefinite start toward a solution we can barely hope for.

This is to say that when we look into the glaringly blue eyes of a blond girl, we are in fact standing at the tail end of an extraordinarily long line of argumentation performed by nature, whose every step is expressed in a language completely unknown to us, and yet we feel the truth and definition value of the end result, just as a blind man will feel from a floating whiff of scent that there is some very great positivity behind, one that only shows its illusion face to him. The female eyes are the 'understandable' scent of an incomprehensible & hidden syllogism — we know only that it's the definition of something, and that this definition was preceded by a long premise-slope.

When writers describe those blue eyes, they in fact define a definition but do not deduce the definition's meaning: they merely prepare its syntactic scheme. When in a basic description I call blue 'blue,' I perform an operation similar to the following: 'the table is a piece of furniture with four or more legs & a horizontal top' — a given definition; now comes the writer or painter who will illustrate the rhythmic image of this string of words (not ideas!): a short strip, then a zigzagging longer one, and lastly a shorter one, which is much clearer & sharper than the first. But this procedure can by and large be ushered in the category of falsifying. If I see blue eyes it's painfully evident that here color, form, erotic suggestiveness are all merely the scent and relative reflection of something else, of something intellectually concrete.

Nature is full of graphemes and we hardly ever think of deciphering them — as though we had dealt with Egyptian writing by trying to attach all kinds of names to the characters, signifying the signs with arbitrary new signs, instead of looking for the meaning of the individual lines and drawings: for instance, by calling the grapheme made up of three parallel lines (whose meaning would be, let's say, 'proteract') 'silver wedding,' or — and this is literature! — signaling it with three small semicircles, we considered the whole question of the hieroglyphs solved once & for all. When we describe blue eyes as 'blue,' we content ourselves with placing a parallel, comprehensible language next to the incomprehensible one — in the former, comprehensibility supplants truth, names supplant meaning (see 'anti-logos logic').

It's ridiculous to try to unthread by the means of psychology the ready-made definitions of nature (in them the 'ready-made' quality is very strong; with their gilded sheen they resemble gold coins — 'hard cash' — much rather than the theoretical value of bonds): to derive the psychic analogies of roundedness from rounded shoulder-blades, et cetera; it's as though we dubbed the pages of a math manual where only short equations of a few symbols are found, 'puritanical mathematics,' while those pages where a wealth of symbols feature with an excess of indexes, 'tautological mathematics,' instead of studying their arithmetic meaning. If we want to bring the image of 'flower' closer to a blind man and render its meaning more concrete, we have no other means at hand but to intensify the scent to a fortissimo and to intoxicate and smother him with the scent: the scent will be so strong as to almost reach the degree of plasticity of meaning, the image, although even then it is at an infinite distance from the image.

And art is nothing else but such frenzied intensifying of the scent: to intensify the definition-character of nature's incomprehensible definitions to such degree, to exaggerate it to such extent that they should appear to reach the limit of meaning, although they remain infinitely removed from it throughout. A threefold period: the first one is invisible, as it is constituted by nature's overlong intellectual syllogisms. The second (let's say, 'blue eyes'): the ultimate conclusion, about which we only know that it is a conclusion. The third: the æsthetic degree when we describe, paint, musicize the blue eyes, but by doing so we don't reconstruct the unknown first stage, we merely place the second stage under a microscope and photograph its image magnified a thousand times. (The two things in parallel are important: to always look for some logos in every phenomenon of nature, be it with the help of Catholic theology, naïve heretical rationalism, German automaton-Platonism, or mathematical analogies, but invariably stressing 'reason' — and at the same time to bring to light the ineluctable irrationality of all logos, the absolute panorama of unreason.)

the sienna swimsuit

Thus Touqué came out of the water in possession of two maxims after spotting the woman: in nature, order and chicane go around like alternating current; the forms of nature accommodate burning reason-possibility and absolute unknowability at the same time. A blind wave splashed behind his heels, looking with all its strength for some resistance, but by that time Touqué was already running in the sand, anticipating in every muscle an all-fours landing, so the wave ran into empty space with an ungainly sprain, like a taxi that realizes with a rasping brake that it took the wrong turn. The blue eyes meant a lot: he saw an incandescent light-blue street where the tree-crowns and the house-walls were the same, and not even according to the 'house during the day — tree during the night' system, but all the time the thin slabs were made of smoke, of blue mist (molded smoke? pressed mist?) and they drew their sap from the racket of gaudy horns; around the pavement ran sharp and cold sparks, as if existence underwent here its first friction against a foreign body in its timeless run.

The sienna swimsuit glowed for long among the blue tree-crowns, continually neutralizing, as it were, the glaring bronze of its wearer's hair — the hair's ringlets repeated infinitely across the blue walls (glaucous mirrors), as though fate were a monotonous photo-mixer that screws in the permed hair among gas-shaped glass walls like a drill: in contrast, the swimsuit's dull redness was a dry patch of color splaying with scholastic 'ante rem' boredom. With a trimming, everything would have been different on it, but without such frame the swimsuit abruptly disappeared. The hair became ever more linear and in the end it wedged into the sky's blue like the peach kernel's bumps into the fruit's flesh: behind the golden creases of undulation deep ink-turquoise scars stretched on the ethereal skin. As the swimsuit sprawls more and more (space? plane? contourless planes are always redolent of space), Touqué feels that the true anatomy of women is hiding to this day in the side-themes of old wives' tales.

'I' and perception in love

There is a bassoon-colored desire heard ceaselessly in us: woman is felt to be made of different materials than those found in the handbooks' descriptive passages grounded in palpation. Just as our emotions long for us to feel something that is neither joy nor sorrow nor irony nor sentimental 'dupedness' but 'formal' emotion, akin to the emotions triggered by music: the pure formal criteria of emotion are brought to such fateful incandescence that these radiating frames make all emotional content entirely impossible.

What then is love? An exotic image, in which incommensurate materials meet, foreign and mutually exclusive traits are playfully amalgamated: this is woman. From his own viewpoint: life is nothing else but an entirely transparent and yet unbreakable glass wall that stops us from identifying with our dreams & logic. The 'I' is separated from dream not by some deep ravine but by a transparent but eternal glass wall. Everything is found beyond the glass wall, this side of it is only a little button on which the world-all is fastened from the other side, but the little button is bigger than the buttonhole through which a tiny chain ties the button to the rest of everything. The 'I' is nothing else but the force — impediment or resistance — that makes it impossible for Touqué to be that woman.

Individuality is a simple negativity: in desire's riverbed an immense mechanism and flora pours over into the woman (one would believe it to be all of Touqué, without anything missing), but it is caught up on the last colorless little button. This colorless little positivity, this button is called Leville-Touqué. (The choir intones the tune of 'A non est B'!)

So do then Touqué and the Naiad in the sienna swimsuit confront each other: Touqué = 'the woman in the sienna swimsuit plus a small black dot' (but that small black dot transforms the woman into a preposterous figure). And so does the entire society consist of such two-component molecules: on the one hand, of the great dream-pastiche of 'othernesses,' and on the other hand, of the abstract force of resistance of 'individualities,' which have no content whatsoever, only force. We can also signal the make-up of the human being mathematically and thus the sum total of mankind, if we mark with n the totality of being ('pan-alterity') and the 'I'-s with numbers: $n + (-1)$, $n + (-2)$, etc. The gist is that by n we should understand infinite bizarrerie (and by no means 'objective reality,' the 'concrete outside world'!), and under the numbers absolute colorlessness, active abstraction. Individuality is missing from the whole, but that lack alters the face of the earth with positive force — a subtraction is added to it.

This rhythm is an essential trait of the whole fundamentally simple play: the simultaneous blooming of two mathematical signs. Point and phantasmagoria, a force and a content: every human being is knocked together of two such opposites, two extremes — in their images there is no force & in their forces there is no image. Hence Touqué's sentence-portrait, and only sincere signature is: 'Every inch in me is filled with the woman in the sienna swimsuit, in me there's not an atom's space left for anything else, and yet I can't write under this all-filling content that "it's I," but I need to learn that the content & I myself are two distinct things.' The image of the woman in the sienna swimsuit is traversed by the black rays of the other element, the 'I am not, after all,' the way a shiny landscape is traversed by a cloud or, if you will, a purely burning planet (the woman) is traversed by a distant shadow ('I am not the woman ...'), and thus the signature is revealed to be just a sun eclipse.

Three sounds heard one after the other, pure, concrete, and simple, in whose material there is no ambiguity and yet they are able to uncover two planes in one cross-section (joy and sorrow, irony and faith, despair and salvation). Touqué felt that certain images, certain visionary kitsch, were similarly able to gather into a single chord (what different kinds of things the fingers can clasp at the same time!) the tormenting duality that features between self-identity & otherness; to harmonize the small point of 'I am not her' with the infinite being-image of 'woman in the sienna swimsuit.'

He wanted to invent a certain type of image which could serve as a common sheath for the upper two. In embracing the woman we want to render ourselves more precise; the kiss is a stroke added to our own contours, the coitus a new marble block added to our own statue. One is always swinging between I and the other — what is the form in which this swinging can feature as self-evident? One needs to get rid of the analytic instinct: if we hear the three above-mentioned sounds one after the other, the analytic instinct will see in them, let's say, the synthesis, the fusion of joy & despair — although that's definitely not at stake. At stake is a third, one-component mood that cannot be decomposed into its elements as one would decompose light with a prism.

against analyzing the soul

Psychic life is unanalyzable: it's not about synthesis but (to quote a psychologist) 'a two, three, or multidimensional monothesis'; there is no such thing as a complicated feeling. Feelings develop just like technology: a contemporary feeling of 'joy,' let's say, relates to the joy expressed in Beethoven's *9th Symphony* like a modern luxury automobile to the diligence; feelings are progressively cleansed of their rational components, of the mud of consistency, to reach their pure forms. In their transitional stage (of course most stages are transitional) the emotions look naturally mixed; when the first naïve, almost entirely rational (ice or stone-age) emotion, for example, 'joy,' starts transforming and refining, we have the impression that it grows more complicated, fills with contrasts, revels in paradoxes & dilemmas (in middling French novels: amer plaisir, joie cruelle, ironie pathétique, désespoir bleu, mélange du sérieux et du frivole, de la dignité et de la gaminerie, du féminin et du brutal, de l'ecclésiastique et du gaillard, etc., etc.), simply because we always approach the task with intellectualist percepts.[264]

Once Touqué suggested to a novelist friend (or himself: O Sun, who sufferst eclipse from thine own self-essence) that instead of using ad nauseam those stone-age, clunky 'mélange de *x* et de *y*' schemes, he might dub them with new names or letters, so that the technique of emotion might move on and not be doomed to forever call the airplane a 'mélange curieux de carrosse et d'oiseau.'[265] The essence of the soul lies in its tremendous simplicity, not in confusion. The current primary-school 'ambivalence' of joy and suffering would be better signaled with a capital *K*, Greek *γ*, or something of the kind.

the 'second precision' and an example of it:
a mystical story of Tyato and biologized dogma

Touqué's first such 'ambivalent' feeling arose when he saw the flowers of a still-life painter in Montparnasse: sunflowers that at a first glance imitated in every detail the magnifying-glass picture, but on a more attentive look one could see that they merely imitated the 'microscopic style,' not genuine small details, and for that reason the paintings made a dreamlike impression, of opium-balderdash, while they also retained the relief of the first 'scientific' impression. This was one 'mélange de' about the painter: 'de la science et du rêve'?

The other was the following: when walking home on the rather dark Raspail, those sunflowers glowed around him like gas lamps on the street, like giant Auer-floras that do not light up the night but only reflect their gilded threads in darkness' vertical pools, primavera negra, homespun Elysium. And in the morning he read the following sentence from the newspaper's white Gobi desert: 'cette fleur de P... est une critique de notre temps.'[266] Touqué recalled his inebriation of the previous night, in which blackness and gold merged with Worth fever, and on the spur of the moment baptized that careless state 'critique du temps'[267] — and felt a great sense of pleasure. This was the second 'mélange de...' (needless to say, these pubertal-age artistic surprises run together with the love-surprises' muscle-scale).

To represent emotion in intellect-free purity is a more intellectualist task than translating emotion into intellect and tying it to the tugging-apart threads of rational percepts (cf. Touqué's little sketch: *Mallarmé ou la 'Deuxième Précision*).[268] When Touqué watched the blue-eyed girl in the sienna swimsuit as she stripped off the sea and dropped the landed spumes on the sand like mirror-chemises, he had a similar impression written in 'second precision.' (This artificially chaotizing style, that chaotizes for the sake of precision, has in fact two types: of the one we have already provided a sample above, when the forms of the girl in the sienna swimsuit are further replicated in geometric inebriation; of the second a template follows below, when of the girl's forms and of the exaggerated impressions mythology-likenesses are born [landscape myths]. Both the geometrical and the landscape-mythologizing, experimental disturbance are in fact unclean 'disturbances' in so far as both still stand under the ægis of the fixation of logical composition, worlds apart, for instance, from the Mallarmé of Touqué's choice, where the 'irratio pro ratione' is much more virginal and accomplished.)

A grey sea heaves in sight (the perspective, not the color, is often found in Capri advertisements), like grey champagne in a tube-shaped champagne glass filled from below between two vertical rock faces; on top the Sun's sienna orb falls abruptly, like from a grey bunch of buds whose every drooping leaf is an autumn ocean; this matte Sun turns inside out like a cyclamen, its red shadow is still 'straight,' but the real globe of fire is negative and only hangs on its shadow, like a ball about to break out upwards — the whole scene reminds one of the stunt films where skiers fall over first, then fly, and in the end return to the jumping ramp. Grey and sienna, the sacred colors of sunset: not purple & blue, but grey, barely-greenish, barely-golden pigeon-grey water, which rises up like a ground glass slab towering above the Sun, which appears like a flower with far too large petals or a butterfly with far too large wings in a speeding glass case, shattered on the existence ladder of a thousand-pater-noster skyline. Horizontal flames run along the grey water, as though the Sun were a large poppy petal blown in three directions by the wind, they sometimes get stuck in the sea's blind jelly & wriggle, like a live ruby caught on flypaper.

Deep inside a well on the shore a giant black flower grows in a blue cylinder; its petals and flower-cup are like an open parachute that rises from the depths into the height, like a gasometer's circular walls rising on the outskirts. Bell chimes are heard from high up, each one different — one is steely and tightens the soul to a narrow blade, with which one could pierce the sleeping god's silver heart which throbs in its green glass body in the forest (it radiates faint green light on black mosses, tarred leaves: green bice pulverized to melody), and somebody can already hear how their lives tightened to a small dagger could shatter the glass god, whose legs have already lost the shape of bones and muscles & absently aggregate into rectangular crystals. To kill the god before it turns completely into an icosahedron — is there a more actual juridical or theological idea than that? But in the next moment another bell-chime falls on the sky, loosening Tyato into a current, so that its waves catch the god's body, as if the shoulders were a pristine Ararat on which the glass statue founders; it has to be carried on the surface with the utmost care, because the glass heart is not tightly fastened in its glass case, so at the smallest concussion it would break the body (thus, in contrast to fountain pens, "it can't be carried in every position").

Tyato is waiting and praying for the swelling black flower to reach the well's rim, because then beauty would fill the world and wrap the velvety-petaled Sun the way a black lampshade covers the light wounds of grating light bulbs (comparison?). On the acid grey horizon the Sun is pining for beauty's black lampshade to dress its wounds; the poppy-trinity rattles palely like a water wheel's blades. But cardinal Mordano can only live if the black flower never reaches the well's rim and never wraps in its black glove the Sun's three waving fingers, which are raised for perjury from the ocean's budding swamp. Mordano had always been aware of what a fanatic æstheticist Tyato is, who doesn't care a continental about truth.

Mordano is lying in his canopy bed, pale, and decides to stop the flower's rise from the well, because he needs to become pope to save the world from Lutheranism. Under his window candles burn, of the height of a tower, so the cardinal's villa looks like a prison covered in a netting of white wax grids — at the foot of every candle a cardinal prays, prostrate (they haven't yet heard of Tyato's black flower). At the end of the candles the flames lengthened by three angelic fingers dance like inarticulate screams during the morning organ rehearsal in the church. The cardinal is sifted through the net of prayers like flour, but he is also caught wriggling in it like a giant green-scaled carp in the golden net. Tyato is his secretary, confessor, diplomat, factotum, who throws the cardinal's nightly confessions into the well to water the flower's roots.

Mordano sends his mother to kill the flower: that depraved woman gallops on a white horse, sails on a white ship, debauches on the deck and in the woods, becomes Tyato's lover, and in the end Tyato throws her body into the well. French cardinals elect a new pope: Mordano is desperate. Blue French landscape: light blue to the point of whiteness, full of thin white monks; from heaven comes a continuous chiming: 'cela s'arrangera, cela s'arrangera.'[269] The glass leaves of Avignon Castle shoot from the earth: the walls rise from the grass, the towers descend from the sky, & the new pope walks laughing among the walls and towers which do not touch (encycling with a blue tongue), like a butterfly between the lips of a carnivorous plant. The pope is surrounded by runaway angels that have fled heaven but would not go to hell: they stole the god's silver heart and threw the glass body, punctured and clattering, on Italy, the moment when the black flower (like frothing-over milk) pours its venom-grace over the rim.

Mordano is cured and sets off to sea with a new conclave: huge tempests throw the ship about toward unknown tropical empires, but even in dying the cardinals only live for their work. They elect Mordano their pope. Truth has prevailed: on top of gigantic black waves, like a hairpin stuck into an Utamaro bun, truth's ship scintillates — but what is it worth? The cardinals die off one after the other — every agony is a red cyclone on the sea's black trunk; the waves are gigantic growth rings and the priests' death is a red creeper on the branches. The waves' crest is sometimes horizontally sectioned by the light blue Avignon, with the pseudo-pope's court (so does a snowy-beaked flock of gulls dash against black columns): we can see such ice grisailles on Francesco Francia's paintings.[270] Around the ship dolphins devour the agony-roses, the undigested death of cardinals Celano, Valdemero, Ruspoliti, Gelarazzo & Ugolatti glare in their light green georgette stomachs like the evening flower on a dinner jacket's ledgers.

The theme of deserted truth and lie transplanted to Provence revolves behind the woman in the sienna swimsuit like the tide in the wake of the Moon. The pope's ship sinks; the silk-barbed sea turns into one sloping wave on which the ship glides to the bottom like a broken ski: the wave that St. Peter's magnet pulled toward the sun like a black wreath has risen so high that the whole ocean is hovering at an altitude of about 20 meters above its bed, in which not a drop of water is left for at least two minutes; the wealth of corals, shells, and bloodless water plants looks like Pompeii — the white-muddy static drama of a cosmic anemia: the fish's gills turn outward like umbrellas in the wind, and surround their glassy foreheads like pink diabolo haircuts; their bodies are like blunted knives; the shells are plates and fancy saucers piled up high for the washing up; oysters look like uneaten oysters.

But in the next moment the wave that leashed too high collapses on its bed again, like a bell clapper whose home is God's Golgotha-red coat; the fish's gills turn back and the bois-de-rose ear-haircuts are replaced with linoleum telephone receivers — that is how they wait under Australia for truth, for the pope. O, corals: la vraie morale se moque de la morale.[271] The pope tries to preserve his human character and the anthropomorphic shapes of truth — he continues writing encyclicals from under the water, which he entrusts to the dolphins, but they devour the papal circulars as they earlier did with the cardinals' red deaths: the encyclicals bloom, impossible animals grow out from the dolphins' stomachs, absurd flowers, reeds, bullets, creams and vacuum-filled bassoons: is this what happens to truth if it ends up among non-humans?

The pope's body too is progressively changed; the tiara is made not of three crowns but of 3333 water rings and molded bubbles, which rise from the ocean bed's silvery-green twilight until they reach the upper waves' black barrels; moreover, they rise above the surface (on modern posters they sometimes draw a string of pearls across a white and a black plane: in the one they draw the pearls like crotchets, on the other chess-horizon like whole semibreves).

La vraie morale se moque de la morale. Truth, too, is in fact a sickly amorphia, irregular fever which, if put in the appropriate 'truth-transmitter,' will proliferate, chintzify so fantastically as the most exotic and hazardous water plant. Two milieus: the black waves, on whose edge the Sun's gold sits like the thin gold trimming on God's incognito soutane that gives away the wearer's rank in the end — and the April carnival of the corals, beam-mists, light-blisters, electric sponges and opalescent silt: tragedy and pristine insania — these are the two autonomous forms of truth for the pope.

Above Avignon, too, hover the proliferating circles of the tiara, as if the counter-pope were only a worm, around whom Saturn multiplied itself a thousandfold. The pope-hoops rise revolving from the sea: everybody in Avignon is dizzy, they hang gigantic black curtains in front of the castle's windows, which look on the walls like the tongue of a behemoth smothered animal — one incessantly hears the sound 'oa,' which escapes in the moments of choking when the tongue is thrown out.

And a miracle also happens: they spot the Virgin Mary above as celestial gardener. The people believe that the miracle legalizes the pope, although the miracle touched there by accident like an apple dropped from the basket (this is its theology). The miracle dashed against southern France like the arrow obliquely burring into St. Sebastian's flank (this is its physics) — it diagonally intersects the perpetuum mobile tiaras & diagonally intersects the walls of Avignon Castle, as if trying to hang the tiaras on one cane (children used to play this game in parks: throwing high in the air a bunch of rings, trying to catch them with a stick in their fall — their arms were loaded with the caught rings, but many dropped on the heads of slumbering elderly gents or German governesses: 'Willi gib' Acht!'),[272] at the same time sketching an improved geometric ground plan to Avignon Castle — to cause truth & lie to tremble in one flash, and then to leave both to their own means, like a composer who in exalted indifference lets two themes splash against one another, as though choosing between them were impossible.

---

*the example of the 'second precision' continued;
the image changes: greyness first, then a red flower on a salon table.
Comparison with the red flower*

At that point the play suddenly comes to a halt and a single lacquered greyness fills Touqué's visual field. The grey photograph color of 'smart' magazines drops out of the comedy like the essence or intermezzo (French literary historians would call such inserts 'siècle'), like lemon seeds in the glass press: with a solitary splashboard on the bottom, of which one could make the same kinds of charts as of a heartbeat. For the moment let this suffice: photograph grey (this is present-day 'luminosity': is it light? twilight? We are talking about clear, high-contrast images and we invariably mean greyness. Where is day and where is night in them? Where is Avignon and the sea bottom? 'La vraie morale' and 'la morale'?) and the trembling of a darker strip. To the left, in elliptic blank patches, a house's edge rises slowly: whitish knots in the grey lacquer, the shape of bones on X-ray images, whose most thrilling fact is that no connection is visible — sketchy pearls in the direction of the threading, but without any thread. A filtered & distilled rain runs across empty space, as if it were gliding like a quarter-millimeter eternal lacquer down a small, mauve-yellow gelatin slope; here and there it creases on the image's margins — as water curves slightly upwards on a glass' walls because of the cohesion of matter, so does the rain's colorless tissue condense a bit, divide into fibers on the horizon's edge, and create disturbances of the shape of small fluff-buds.

It is 11 o'clock in the morning, neutrality runs slowly through time's flat veins (in the old days they rendered them rounded, now entirely flat like certain pencils or cigarettes that fit practically into their cases): the two clock hands are two injection needles that let their abstract points drop, one after the other, into the grey reptile body of time, injecting it with more neutrality and coldness. The clock's small ticking are bubbles left behind in the emptied syringe: five or six small blisters proliferating backward, stopping, bursting, leaving only their ground plan on the syringe wall; the 11 o'clock too makes a tiny inoculation wound germinate into the twilight, but no other exterior change can be seen. A loud, strong honking is heard (sometimes in films a face runs so close to the camera that the pupil fills the screen), not even the shape but only the heart of the honking from very close up (in this manner certain Chinese gods devour only the cyclone's core & throw its horn-shaped, conical flesh back into the water, on the ships): it was first heard conically, but in the end it left only a velvety-polished, thin cylinder in the soul.

In the middle of a salon (which is as grey as the one in which Lea once waited, and which he, Peter, had already tried to symbolically harness against the last specimen of the caste of tragedy), in the midst of the silver tea set there was a small bunch of blood-red field flowers: one would expect that among sugar tongs, rum flasks with a roller-bearing-like cork, Mephisto-eared tissues and toast racks the small red flowers would look embarrassed, but this was far from being the case: even though many acquire mundanity through experience, there are always country lads, students of mathematics perhaps or music who, when they get into high society's strictly classical-frivolous salons, turn out to be the greatest charmeurs & bon-vivants without ever having practiced that art. Just like music or painting, or any other art, this mundanity is not based on experience but on itself — and it dazzles in the first suitable company. As a rule it even surprises those very people & they watch with passive inebriation how automatically the presence of a beautiful woman triggers in them the compliments, gestures, and wordplay ('enfin en face') which send their sparks in the direction of both wit and inanity.[273]

This kind of elegance is undoubtedly of a melodic nature: it doesn't stumble from case to case (as it does, for instance, with most officers, whose elegance is bluntly sachlich; they always add a word, grin, or offering gesture to something that presents itself: everything is mere unconnected splinters, and for that reason can never be 'politesse,' that is, mirror-like polishing; even in women they see horses and machine gun pieces to be assembled in five seconds — ambidexterity, quick adaptation), but flows forth from the man in one continuous line, being in fact the passive poetry of the man's whole existence, which reaches with its whip-end the woman opposite like an artesian fountain when the wind blows its water-drops in a given direction; but it is not first & foremost for the woman. And this trait women love & readily recognize.

Such men can often behave impolitely (politeness and mundanity mostly go different ways), because their elegance is not strictly parallel to the woman's life; rather, it surrounds the latter like a vague lamp which sometimes lights up her face (although it's perhaps her shoe-lace that got untied) and sometimes leaves it in shadow, or even throws its long beam on a distant point & so rather impolitely sections the woman's small partying exigencies; its purpose is merely to unsettle the woman's essence with irregular waves: even when she is looking for the sugar on the table, he keeps gawking at a lonely Eve & takes no notice of the escalating sugar crisis in the cooling tea.

Its whole technique is grounded in letting this Eve-fixation develop to the threshold of breaking up the company, & in the last moment (like a race-car driver in the hairpin-needle curve after 5 km of straight road) reduces her to the real-life, clothed woman who in the present moment can only be satisfied with half a sugar cube; the half-second emaciating of the whole biblical Golden Age down to the soirée, then its abrupt untying again toward the authentic Eve is one of the most pleasant rhythms & the basic tempo of mundanity.

The man of this tempo always enters female company as though entering a brothel, but a thousand small veto signs keep warning him that he has to behave differently here than in the establishments mentioned above; the real man of society is he who thinks 200 times per second that he is now in society and not in the Maison Tellier, and so keeps running into impediments: he would like to embrace but offers sugar instead, would like to kiss but speaks about Mauriac, in short, he performs indefinitely the swinging 'from Eve to the present woman.'

The charme starts from the thousand collisions: in the champagne-pouring of some, technical mastery betrays the fact that it's all about the vacuous brilliance of a dead gesture; we see that the other bloke nearly bumps into the champagne glass, of which he had no inkling before, believing as he did that people by nature quench their thirst by drinking water from a mountain brook in the cup of their own two hands. This explains that whenever an outsider gets into truly refined society, they leave not with the impression of having seen the fresco of tact, delicacy, hypocrisy and gentleness, but on the contrary: of stumbling among naked savages, bloody beasts, and perverse demons. In vain they would recall the elegant dresses, stylish perfumes, and ethereal foods — the central smell remains blood and the most primitive compliment ('with you I might even go'), the sadistic challenge of death.

Tilia Parvifolia's salon: the squat furniture

That small red flower also behaved like a non-empiricistically educated mundane figure. Countess Tilia Parvifolia slowly pushed[274] the sugarbox to the side to untangle her foot from the lace hook in which it got caught, all the while speaking about her son: what a curious role the boy, the whole family & household had in Tilia's life. The small tea-table stood by the fireplace: the fireplace was squat, barely reaching to one's hips, the table, too, looked rather like a footstool (her car too was very low, & she always drummed on its top when she stood next to it, waiting for some friend who tarried more in a boutique than she had), and when she threw a casual glance at them, she looked like one sponsoring orphan children in the feverish pose of caritas.

Because all her furniture, interior decoration, and car were so squat, one always felt like a slender geyser or giraffe-bodied stylite, and this greatly influenced the progression of their logic and feelings. There are caves where some poisonous gas stretches immediately above the ground like a blanket, so people are warned not to bow down: even if the biggest stone from their diamond ring should fall, they must not reach for it, for they might drop dead. In Tilia's rooms too one felt that 'homeliness' was situated half a meter from the floor like some poisonous gas, and above it up to the ceiling, the thin, hygienic, and bare world of people. Thus between sitting and standing up there were very big, so to say religion-historical pendulations: to sit approximately equaled Buddhism, whereas standing amounted to a heresy that appeared after Wyclif but long before Luther in northeastern Sweden, among the resettled half-peasantry on the land strip between Falsö and Ingerbalg.

In geography Touqué learned a lot about the vegetation belts of mountains at different altitudes. Within 200m above sea level the mountains' etiquette prescribes palm-trees, cactuses, Rubeids, Canozoida, Felizoida, just as another etiquette prescribes low-heel saddle shoes, nickel-button tweed, and pheasant applique between 10 and 12 in the morning. Tilia's home raised the grooming problem, what kind of moral mimicry-belts people should put on around their legs, hips, or head to suit the layers of atmospheric pressure suggested by the squat furniture, in order to be homely in that room. When a new guest entered, their legs moved among the horizon blocks congealed to mud as though wading in shallow seawater, pushing aside the low spumes with their feet. Perhaps there was a time when all this was not so squat: the fireplace may have been of the height of man, for example, and only later did it sink to the floor, like the slowly separating substances in the sterilizing tube, which are just an idea heavier than water. And just like these silting substances, which, although they reach the tube's bottom, are not permanently stabilized but keep being pushed hither and thither by the inner waves, so everything was indefinite in Tilia's room, not only the buffet table on pneumatic wheels, but also the fireplace. It made Touqué's head swirl.

the armchair; Tilia and her son

When he sat down in the armchair & his knees knocked against his jaw, he felt that some obscene gesture had burst from his body, as it sometimes happens when dreaming before our mother; instead of precious, ethereal hovering-sitting he found himself in a slippery, almost mucous hole. For the first time it occurred to him, there in Tilia's sponge armchair, that comfort is something dark, almost fateful and diabolic. He thought of the original sin. In the armchairs he had tried so far he experienced various comfort-tricks: the armrest of one imitated the form of the human underarm, as though it were a piece of elegant cutlery for those who prefer underarms for breakfast ("scrumptious! Where did you find this spoon? It's excellent for taking things"); another's back was hollowed out in such a way that if mankind went extinct, from this negative the shape of the human shoulder-blades, spine, and basin could be exactly reconstructed; but these armchairs in fact all went back to the schemata of orthopedics & were simple at heart.

In contrast, Tilia's armchair didn't display any anatomical pantomime grimace, but was an incalculable mass: cloud, sand dune, fallen leaves and knotty stirabout in one. When Touqué sat in it he felt no resistance at all, no exciting form-echo for his back or lower arm, but the utter end of friction, the fairy-tale compliance of matter. His arms and legs kept sinking and undulating, but the wished-for resistance didn't come. Is this then comfort, if one takes it to its logical end? The other armchairs all meet one halfway — the spine would fly on, the arm would sink toward lower-lying territories, but matter doesn't let them. In Tilia's armchair, however, the armchair doesn't meet one halfway; it lets the body walk down the whole stretch of the road to complete annihilation. Touqué had so far only felt such softness in bed under the duvet, that's why the thought first occurred to him that by the simple-looking movement of sitting down in the armchair-proton, he became eo ipso naked to Tilia and the other guests.

He landed beyond redemption in the nether regions of the original sin, and this he could clearly read from the nature of the upholstery: golden boughs on a black background, white apples on the golden boughs & among them, scaly birds, whose ad hoc anatomy always resulted from the amount of superfluous to-fill-in black background left by two boughs and a white apple. Why does nobody take the logic of textile painters seriously? Great methodological revolutions play out on divan upholsteries, but they are met with deaf ears. He saw this upholstery from too close up and he could experience that things do not end on their surface and need to be conceived of rather as the color stains signaling the varying depths of water on the ocean maps (permed spongecakes, pre-fission cells): this upholstery, too, immediately filled his brain with birds of paradise (the paradisiac thing about them is precisely that it is from space they turn into birds, a much more edenic symptom than 'in principio erit avis'[275] — it seemed to him that he had no acquaintances all his life but the birds of paradise:

there is an unquenchable 'becousining' family instinct which projects on things seen for the first time an improvised, artificial Ur-relation, in which the oldness of times, the past's odorless gas, is supplanted by the ongoing ornamentation of the surface, space-slice standing for time-dent.

Tilia was still talking about her son — how she adores him, how she loathes him, how puritanically she wants to bring him up, how she spoils him. Of all that Touqué felt only that it was told in the nether regions: before the fireplace opening. Of course the fireplace can be compared to a great many things, but for the time two will do: it resembled the elongated openings cut into the entrance door, through which letters are thrown in (they graft the noble substance of the news onto the house's ignoble trunk, so that next year it would bear noble fruits, nicht wahr?), and it resembled the sleeping alcoves in opium bars. Now no warmth came from it, but much rigid disquiet (o, kaminal ananké!),[276] brick-odor, cement, stone powder, phenol.

One essential variety of the suffering in the next world will be that the torture cabins will be only half built & they will spread an eternal reek of quicklime. Can Tilia who so 'adores her home' and drips liquid armchairs about the place from Lar-ok tubes, relish in such stone-cold holes, cellars protruding into salons? Why does she tolerate this wound in her home? Why is it not poulticed, powdered with yellow cement powder to scar faster? Surely she cannot patronize such vulgar harmonies like 'heavenly armchair and infernal fireplace,' can she?

It was thanks to the cooperation of armchair & fireplace that while Tilia spoke about her son, Touqué felt that this woman is praising her lover (this is the armchair's mathematical 'operator' effect), who is, however, and without this detail changing in the least the nature of things, a corpse laid out to view (this is the fireplace), and Tilia is doing her best to pass on the man to her lady friend (at present Touqué felt like a heavily made-up confidante).

Seen from a certain angle, Tilia's motherly love related to the love of mothers known by Touqué as the jellyfish-armchair to the regular armchairs. On the one hand, it was much more dry, formal, & abstract, on the other hand it strongly approximated a Phædra bluff.

— But I had to take him flowers; it's natural that the mother should give the child flowers, isn't it? — she asked Touqué as though speaking of the unknown rule of some unknown science and asking the authoritative expert in that science, Touqué, for confirmation. But at the same time her eyes burned and she clasped the small chair's hand rest (for Tilia wasn't sitting on an armchair) so that she wouldn't swoon in her enthusiasm: in her voice Francesca kisses were rationed in milligrams and sent toward an invisible Paolo.

— He was so alone, poor darling — in this lachrymose, pampering & Duse-stamped [277] sentence Touqué again heard Tilia's duality: the moment she uttered 'poor' he saw a foreign landscape, the bloodless region of moral indifference, where a nameless little boy lies who perhaps doesn't even exist, or is at most a cinema actor who would play the role of the sick little boy for a thousand dollars, and Tilia is now distractedly enthusing about his acting in the theater buffet — "how sweetly my little darling played, it's astonishing how intelligent they can be at this age" — but when in the next moment he didn't hear the word 'poor' anymore and could only experiment on its echoes, he saw a gigantic red bunch of dahlias, which a goof porter threw in the wrong window of the train which is already pulling out (instead of the secret lover's sleeping car), while Tilia is watching his return at the third-class waiting room window, interrogating him on the face the belatedly-crowned and hurriedly-dispatched Paolo pulled.

He thought of what would sound nicer: Leville-Touqué or Leville-Oenone? [278] What will the fate of caritas be, if it is bypassed from two sides: by the way of social etiquette ("I must send my son such & such flowers on such & such occasion"), & by the way of perverse exaggeration ("my God if you could have seen his mouth, I can't even tell…")?

Baroness Ajuga observed that her son too was treated in[279] that clinic but she was not satisfied with anything, for the sole reason she took him there was that she knew that at the time the head physician there was R*** (not the one who became a full professor at the university now, Ajuga's R had been a full professor for five years at least — no, no, at least 10), & when her son was admitted, R*** himself came to receive him, you know how awfully nice this is of him, for they always send some junior nobody or a resident with the papers, & imagine, my son hadn't been there for three days when I learned that R*** was transferred to another clinic, they say the clinic's professor wanted to get rid of him by all means, but my husband knew that professor and didn't let me take my son to the other clinic, for you can imagine that was my first thought, but I gave in, and whatever happened afterward and however kind the personnel was, for one assesses a clinic in the way we assess a better-class hotel, don't you think so? — I'm telling you, with whatever delicacies they spoiled him, I couldn't be objective, you know in what an impossible situation you get when you can't be objective. "For there is nothing else, really nothing else — she said in a sniveling voice, turning toward Touqué — but objectivity, it's our last resort!"

She puckeringly sucked up one corner of her mouth, shaking her head in small denials, all the while looking into the void as though giving it a second thought and trying to find a possible refutation to 'nothing else,' something that had hitherto escaped her attention, but no, no, however hard she may look, she finds no counter-argument.

Potentilla was sitting a bit further off in a sunny patch, leafing through a fashion magazine.[280]

— À propos clinic — she said with a softly rustling smile, as though speaking through a mouth organ improvised of silk paper on a comb — look, I just saw here a sanatorium interior, it looks like a modern girl's room, with blue flowers, blue mural, light chairs, it's smashing, have you seen it?

— I can't stand those fancy hospitals. A hospital should be a hospital & basta, what's the use of those futurist-flowery boutiques in an operating theater?

— O dear — Potentilla said with tired, softly refuting intonation — it's really not about that (that 'really' was her longest-held word), but the wards, corridors, shared rooms — why shouldn't there be flowers on the walls?

— Where's that hospital? — Ajuga asked and pointed toward the magazine as if trying to flick the ashes of an inexistent cigarette by pulling the old-fashioned trigger of the index finger.

— Whe-ere? — Potentilla asked in singsong innocence and leafed back.

— Never mind, it's not important.

— But it's there, I remember, I'll find it in a second, Dusereel or Nusereel, I forget.

— I tell you, that will be the photographer's name, I've often seen that name. What is that magazine, the *Chic-Chic*?

— Are you sure? No, look, you are wrong, it's not the photographer.

— Silly me, to mix up things like that.

morning shadows

The sun shone on Potentilla through the window pane: the window was green and showed every dot, scratch, or defect of manufacture, and they caught on to Potentilla as a disease: her face, dress, the pictures of the *Chic-Chic* filled with black and green pimples. It was still raining and Tilia's salon looked so ethereal that one feared it would melt. Simple French windows were lined up next to one another with thin planks; they looked extraordinarily thin because the outside light and the rain's soft brush-threads (they use such brushes for combing the fluff of newborns) fell obliquely on the panes and almost insulated the salon.

A moment ago light still fell perpendicularly in the room and the shadow of the distant fountain fell exactly in the middle of the wall opposite the French windows — on the smooth white wall the distant fountain looked like the first movement of a primordial animal, or a blazon whose surrounding feathers came to life: yet with all its trial-and-error nature it still managed to thread the room on the slender axis of a cardinal direction. But now the fountain's shadow shifted to a corner, broken, closer to the ceiling than to the floor, and at the same time much blacker and denser than before. And with it the other shadows too ran into the corner — as if everything wanted to flee from the salon, which the sun had tilted and would turn completely on its side in the next moment. It was dizzying.

But in fact here lies the greatest pleasure of a sharp quartz-lit morning spent inside a room: on the one hand, it's all wholesome light, the secure glance of fresh cleaning, the defiant flexibility of unused-up forces — & on the other hand, the shadow's astronomical perversity, sophistic chess-schemata, the sickly allures of celestial geography forcefully undermined the rise of the former's bonds.

Arguably the morning's most authentic theological spectacle was Potentilla sitting by the window: the external light (linked to the rain's vectors which were 5° more tilted, like tracks in train stations merging at the switches after a 5° divergence) was almost parallel with the cross-section of her profile, casting thus a black, well-nigh mauve shadow into a very distant corner — shedding even under way, of course, small galley proof-like preparatory shadows that could have been the acacia leaf's 'you love me, you don't love me' positions; in addition, it also copied a realistic but elliptic portrait on the windowpane itself in the original colors and with the original proportions. This portrait on the window-pane was like a stamp placed on a sealed apartment: it showed that light didn't penetrate the room but was merely parallel with it lengthwise, like barriers at a level crossing: the windows didn't let in the light but showed a side view of the light.

This constellation of light rendered Tilia's motherhood more comprehensible to Touqué: there, in those feelings too everything was burning light, deafening magnesium, but for the same reason the shadows tripped over into a buffoon coordinate: only madness is capable of approximately representing the joy that spiritual health causes in people. In front of Touqué countess Tilia Parvifolia's maternal correctness and horrible health appeared like a slender iceberg that lets off its hard, mirroring sheen in arctic light.

So far he had naïvely imagined every mother he spoke with or heard about as in 'eternal labor'; when they uttered the words 'my son,' he felt that the woman's body was giving birth to the child anew, for the first time (the way certain philosophers argue that God is creating the world again and again in every moment), and so he never managed to imagine the mother's body as free and independent, but only as a gorgeous Heliogabalus statue on the museum corridor that is fastened to its sign with twenty-five ropes to secure it against theft. Tilia was the first mother on whom he didn't see these continuities of the body directed toward the son. Perhaps that was because of her extraordinary thinness: she was like a paper scroll rolled on itself to the thinness of a cane, so tight that it doesn't have as much hole as a straw, so there's no place for imagining a uterus that could swing hither and thither like a balloon. Her 'my son' has a rigorously rational ring to it, the tight muscles and close-fitting clothes seal off the mother from any biological splaying toward her son.

'My son, my son' — the words rang in Touqué's ears, prepared in the morning sunlight, which, following from light's etymological quirks, struck not in the direction of the root of 'my son' but only pulled its surface aside, like a rubber strudel: the word's content couldn't be placed back in the mother, just as one doesn't manage to replace an already opened map, a supplement to the lexicon's entry on South Africa, by folding it to fit the lexicon's size. Not to mention the soap bubble that one would like to stuff back into the straw. This maternity, in which a revue girl connected to an abstract thought (the theoretical definition of motherhood?) was much more mystical for Touqué than the other one that he experienced at home in his own mother, who lacked such plaited extremes. There where the relation of mother and son was not so rational as with Tilia (because Tilia probably didn't even give birth to her son from her body, but caught the idea of 'motherhood' from some American *Family Magazine*, or eventually a 'gospel commissioned for the day, written after Matthew'), it was not possible to perform maternal feelings as pathetically as with her.

Only a role can truly exhilarate us, reality doesn't have that effect, similarly to the flowers of Lycohydnum edulorium, which grow a huge ovary with heavy, gall bladder-like seeds, but the flowers grown of these seeds, which one would take for the essence of the Lycohydnum (the ripe ovary is like a gigantic embryo from which the mother's wilted body hangs like a degenerate vestigial petal) turn out insignificant small weeds; yet if we grow the new Lycohydnum not from the seed-substance but from the hair-like side-branches, we'll get gigantic petals & triple leaves. Maternitas inflata.

the relation of speech and the female body

Tilia wore a red leotard dress surrounded by rarefied but widespread cigarette smoke; when Touqué leaned toward her, the smell of perfume and cigarettes came at the same time — the perfume obviously suggesting to Touqué the portrait of a strange woman, the only truly important one, of whom Tilia would be merely the impresario. Tilia talked passionately; the role of rationalism consisted in removing the small bits of tobacco from her lips by stopping in the middle of even the most sentimental word, pulling her mouth open sideways as if trying to make a needle-thin peg of both her lips, and pecking at the tobacco thread nervously and crudely with her nails, as if her fingers could command a spectacularly lower degree of precision than her mouth. Meanwhile, one hand got caught in her pearls and she didn't have the patience to gently disentangle it but, like a silly sparrow, tugged this way and that among the stretched threads.

Next to her there was a black vase with waxflower: it was absolutely black but also absolutely transparent, and in fact it should have continued Tilia's role, because for a few seconds (in such cases novelists usually put 'a few minutes,' which is highly unlikely, being an extremely & impossibly long time) Touqué saw it as the nature of motherhood. Tilia was impatiently waiting for the bishop who lived on the upper floor to return from the morning mass, as she wanted to ask some favor for her son, a priest. The young priest had stuck his head in the salon earlier, but Tilia sent him up to wait for the bishop. When she told this Touqué was already immersed in the deepest night, as if the whole world were a giant telephone receiver: he is lying on the membrane and has to decipher some love message from his body's trembling; above his eyes hovers Tilia's face, who is anxiously looking for the message and fawning with light blue kiss-rings — if Touqué touches the message with his body, he will receive a real kiss, but decipherment is entirely hopeless.

Tilia spoke on, twisting her pearls around the syntax as Henry III did with his beard, interspersing the syllables with her shoes, supplanting characters with her clothes, so that Touqué created for himself an impossible new language and linguistics, in whose vocabulary such items occurred: "But he's been there before" — this sentence equals: 'before' means time's large and empty, silky & transparent shell, from which the only pearl was stolen & in its place Tilia's ruddy stockings were put, like a St. Nicholas gift in the shape of a slip of the tongue, and which rise inside the shell like octopus breath, escaping beyond the shell to the sea surface — in it, the sentence's furthest category wave ('time') & an incongruent, inorganic fragment of an object were together.

The meaning was enormous, like an opalizing lake, but words related to it like so many patent worms that are on the lookout for the virgin fish of meaning in their capacity as bait — otherwise the entire oscillating basin, with all its fish, is a function of this small patented earthworm: it was thanks to Tilia's words that Touqué really started relishing the legal rapport between language and meaning.

The apparently simple fact of language was the dope with whose help one could pour over, expand, change density, crease into the most diverse shapes, or cease altogether. Thus the new linguistics resembled geography best, as it slipped in a Tilia map next to the sentence "but he's been there before": her head was pale like the northern reaches of Greenland, the legs too featured in some indifferent color, but the hips were marked with an emphatic brown strip that deepened toward the breasts. The arms were colorless but the tip of the fingers was again burning brown, to the same extent as the breasts, signaling that circumstances of the same intensity prevail there.

Every word engages another body part, every sound shifts the phonetic point of gravity: these create much richer variations than sentiments; if we compare psychological maps to these colorful sketches à la Touqué we can clearly see the difference. Every word asks for a special anatomy, under the influence of our own voice we dissolve into millions of portraits — it would be far more amusing to keep leafing through these maps than to listen to and read the words themselves. The sentences formed a thin thread (Tilia let them out of herself like a spider), around which she could weave her body, so that now the thread became a geometrical axis in the midst of her red leotard dress, and now she eluded it, diverting from it, twisting herself around it, crossing it, etc.

Sentences are always the same: each one of them is a colorless straight line. But the body that is connected to this thread runs around it in broad, colorful strips: however much the colorful strips depart from the pencil line, they evidently depend on it even in their wildest asymptotic defiance. In the meteorological atlases the black contours of Europe are unchanged but the red, purple, and orange strips signaling wind and rain are situated above them in varying undulations: Tilia's body resembled these climatic zones, and her sentences the black contours of Europe.

What a revolution it was for Touqué when at school he saw for the first time a map on which the anthropoid political borders didn't feature at all, only the geological formations: there where European metropolises are located, only grey cataracts showed, barely noticeably, but Greenland, the ocean, Scotland and Finland were one continuous carmine formation, as if the Earth's most sublime flower purpose were flaming there forever. It was not so much its redness that was inspiring but the fact that it linked disparate, utterly foreign territories and thus brought water and dry land to a common denominator: the ocean and Scotland glared out from the map in the same shade of red.

But the color too meant a lot: as though the regular sources of the green, yellow, black had overcome political boundaries, setting alight blossoming patches in place of the puny human demarcation lines; these patches had no stable boundaries, or very rarely — they either poured or fractured. Needless to say, all this romantic flux or fracturing was thrilling only because underneath lurked the pencil drawing of Europe's contours. Tilia's Proteism too would have been tedious if it hadn't been for the mathematical function of her words' grey Morse dots.

Language, human speech, is the most comfortable tool of dehumanization: one of Halbert's favorite writers did nothing else but project the language-induced shiftings of the body, external and internal anatomical reflex mimicry back onto the tissue of language: treating the map of climatic zones as a political map.

Tilia's essence: the alien vase

Just as one can construct the *Idylls of Anti-Psyche*, so one can compose the *Atlas of Anti-Psyche* as well. Touqué wanted to escape the pathologically-concretized human being of psychology by two routes: one was the naïve medieval, fable-bound anatomical Sachlichkeit, in brief: *Adam Nudus*, the other was the complete annihilation of the human being, the psyche-less emotions, character-less humanity, where the accent falls on the barely visible reflex movements or the objects surrounding people.

In the principle of the 'individual' mankind had invented an arbitrary and enforced, artificial boundary for itself, which lacks any concrete foundations — for example, by drawing a sharp contour around Tilia which would bigotedly entrench her body & being from the black vase, although Touqué could positively see that in the present moment Tilia Parvifolia's raison d'être consisted of that black vase: her motherhood, the portrait of her son, the quarter-hour delay of her relative the bishop, were all synthesized in the shape of one vase resultant.

Analysis (voilà encore la bête noire!) proceeds in the opposite direction from life when it tries to find the 'ancient center' with its mosaic art: for in us there is no ancient center at all, only without us, in the infinite distance of time (or space?), which draws us to it like a magnet, and our psychic complicatedness will only look complicated if we're prepared to forget that the millions of waves and creases are the result of one sole external pulling force — synthetic creasing, from which the magnitude, shape, distance, stave can be deduced: and this deduced image of force will always be simple, homogeneous. The naïve borders of the 'individual' will melt, and Tilia's portrait will be at the very least 'Tilia's body plus the vase': not in the way in which it appears on small-town or 21st century photographers' work, where the vase is a simple ornament, but as real, anatomical connection between woman and vase (needless to say, this connection has been there since primordial times, it's only the verisimilar portrait that's a new invention) — and this is of course the anatomy of 'anti-anatomy.'

Some specimens of Melaurea sinaculata grow huge flowers, others huge fruits, while some of the third type, an exalted mass of leaves: if one looks at a flowery specimen he feels that something is missing from the portrait, because the fruity specimen 20 or 40 meters away too belongs to it, being itself only a torso (however much it looks an 'individual' at a first glance), and it needs the distant foliage-growing exemplar — thus a genuine Melaurea personality is located in a very wide perimeter.

Individuality is like a ball placed on a slope: it rolls from step to step, from rocks into the water, from a field into a muddy well, always growing newer and newer milieus, as though every rolling substance were an avalanche that spools around itself utterly alien milieus; it is always looking for the simplest ways for itself, always following the earth's gravitational pull, and thus it balances all the landscape-masks and time-poultices it hangs on itself underway with the otherworldly simplicity of one force.

this is the foundation of 'anti-tragic' thinking, that is, of the greatest conceivable opposite to Peter's thought (cf. pp. 1020–1024)

The most efficient counter-poison to the tragic is frivolous morphologism: Peter used to think in characters — he calculated women, the sum total and the proportion of his loves in characters (like in some cheap currency): of women he believed, perhaps in Leibnizian pudicity, that 'they have no windows,' although in fact they are almost entirely windows (intentiones omnifenestrales), that is, they continue in the confusion of impossible landscapes and atmospheres, and their blood circulates primarily in these continuations, which, being already devoid of character, are perfectly able to bear the absurdities of love. Peter was like an ingenious art historian who wants to study the southeastern façade of Villa Rospigliosi and in a hot summer season finds the solution of assaulting the paralytic porter left behind by the family vacationing in the Engadin with heated declarations of love, supplemented with his æsthetic analyses & his drawings of the façade — only to despair afterward for not succeeding to resolve the façade's artistic 'radiation of problems.'

This is the tragedy-logic, which Leatrice too felt acutely, & which Touqué tried to appease with local calmatives. Leatrice could hear and see that for Peter what the women said and did was still important (O, teach him how he should forget to think of that porter, that porter!), so he created all kinds of spurious connections between the thoughts and exterior of women, instead of proceeding onward along the direction, leading far away from the woman's interior, soul, and deeds, of a pleasant bend of the neck (sotto voce), or a cantabile shoe heel, looking for the true theme of those character-less suggestions; instead, he returned to the 'meaning' of the woman's words and brooded over her thoughts; and while the body was a huge window, metaphysical train depot, instead of the foreign panorama Peter insisted on fidgeting in the room's darkest & narrowest corners; armed with his oversize luggage, he went out to the train station only to perch in the facilities, with the defect electricity, of the third-class waiting room (Cabinet de 'caractère' pour Messieurs: occupé).[281] (Touqué hummed to Leatrice: 'Ich will nicht diese halbgefüllten Masken, lieber die Puppe'[282] — either 'Puppe' anatomy or wide-perimeter Melaurea anatomy: countess Tilia as either Tilia puppet or as transparent black vase: these two concepts alone enable love, there is no third.)

Tilia speaks

The main characteristic of love is that it is incapable of eliciting independent feelings: there is no 'feeling of love,' but at most other species of feelings assembled of excerpts in a fan shape, plagiarized around a sexual germ; the way the monk crab makes a hideout of a foreign shell and protects itself with foreign armor, so the poor little vulnerable and transient fruit of love wraps itself in the thick & comforting wadding of alien feelings. Many men fail to notice this parasitical nature of love & believe the stolen shell to belong to the monk crab.

One of Touqué's experiences of love was countess Tilia's chattering: by far not in the sense that he fancied Tilia and lived with her some great love adventure in a nutshell, but because the æsthetic pleasure caused by Tilia's acting got linked in his mind with a blurred female portrait from yesterday — she was sitting across from him in a small confiserie in a purple-red coat with a black collar and in a black cap, and told an unknown boy: "I'm not joking, I'm telling you if you talk like this I'll be most embarrassed" — and with her face she mockingly imitated the pudic heroines of hundred-year-old comedies: she was doubly embarrassed, in part sincerely and in part in her fear that her parody was not chic enough. Touqué recalled that girl's face, insignificant to the point of being virginal, when listening to Tilia's chat about her son, and that maternal snob-pathos brought yesterday's nobody-sketch (entirely unexpectedly) to a point of red-hot incandescence.

"I've always told him not to study so hard and not to exhaust himself, because once I've read that the king too fainted several times from too much studying and I shudder to even think of seeing my son fainted, I've seen him once and it was dreadful, I kept it secret from my husband because he too had been of a frail constitution, and whenever my son looked a bit off color, had a headache or didn't eat up his lunch he immediately had remorses of conscience that from him my son inherited poor health, and the like." — Tilia spoke of the frail constitution of her son and husband as if it were the most individual trait of those two people, that cannot possibly occur with anybody else, least of all with Tilia herself: one could see that the countess handled suffering like a favorite food, incomprehensible passion ("Oh dear, with men you can never tell," etc.) or quixotic artwork which they pass on from father to son at majoring in her husband's family.

It was the theme of sickness that elated her, not her husband's sickness, & the luminous but not at all warming declaiming suited the pastel colors of yesterday's little portrait like a glove. Touqué was overcome by an infinite sense of comfort, because he didn't need to formulate his love (nowadays you need to formulate not only the expression of feeling but even the feeling itself), Tilia spoke of her son with gestures that entirely satisfied Touqué. He simply placed himself inside Tilia & didn't need to think, "oh my, this sounds like a declaration of love," but could root, without the least bit of naïve analogy-mongering, for the boy who studied an awful lot, never gave a fig about lucrative connections, & whom they now want to get in with the bishop cum jure successionis.

At once Tilia seemed to start chasing the little face from yesterday, wanting to trample it, she reprimanded it for everything, smashed her riding gloves in her face ("Since then Z*** has long become a bishop, although he's dull as a door. At a meeting they held at some point, synod or whatever they call it, there are too many names I can't remember, there it turned out, you won't believe it, that he didn't even know the rite of baptism by heart, he blathered something about the oil that should have been about the salt, I'm too stupid for these matters because I've always stuck to the saying, Roma locuta causa finita,[283] but he, God pardon me, he might be expected to bother to look up those things, especially for somebody who became a bishop at such a ridiculously young age, for let's be honest, what else does he have to do, I can see well on my uncle..."): but why did she persecute that poor little figure who is certainly baptized and washed clean of our original sin, something she's so happy about that she keeps committing smaller sins on a daily basis, but even if she committed great ones, none could be as great as the original sin, although in that gluey movement with which she pulled the spoon out from between her lips squeezed to dishwashing sponges there seemed to lurk some childish nostalgia for the original sin.

But her sister is certainly more important than her, because she has to have a sister, the shadow of the older sibling is always left on the face and nothing can wash it off (except from certain materials perhaps): whenever Touqué met a woman he immediately constructed a sister, & only with the help of that assistant figure (a kind of mathematical dummy who remembers the equation in a flash and primly discloses the value of the unknown) was he able to have social intercourse within human parameters with the given woman. Tilia was an exceptionally strong developer of sisters — the hatred with which she agitated against Z*** became a ready-made portrait of a sister — the little confiserie girl was transparent like a small jug of baptismal water, but the sister was an authentic replica of original sin. Tilia's son and the girl from yesterday, it seems, were really only there to create an inexistent sister.

theme for a short story (a fastidious bishop and the girl who fled to the woods)

That sister would pine for men as only men are able to pine for women: she lived alone, retreated to the woods with a white stag, there she studied from morn to night, she was death-pale but still stuck to her cosmetics because she was a hermit in body only, not in soul. Sometimes she received her younger sister in the woods. The sister disappeared all of a sudden: only the smudgy ice cream cup was left on the table, and the tip's ghostly Charon money, which a fat apprentice harvested from the marble planking with a combing gesture — the new guest is already there, and even if he sits there for three hours and a half he will still count as the new guest.

A bishop had a hunting castle in the woods, the distraught family hurried there to inquire and investigate if he had seen the younger daughter. The elder sister comes out of the woods and settles for good in the city, because she managed to dip her suffering into herself, even if not quite to nip it: there are bodily pains that don't stop from an injection but only congeal somehow in our body — so far we have felt them inside like a burning ball or object of another shape, & after the injection we will feel not the ball's heat but only its weight and especially its surface, like some pain-negative. The sister too felt it appropriate (in this negative state) to come out of the woods, but her younger sister remained there: in the suffering-set so alien to her, a birdlike white week-ender.

Touqué thanked Tilia Parvifolia in thought for enriching him with this image of a trinity: in a great, wood-shaped vegetable pain (piacevole) an inane small joy, or independently of that, some rigid, colorless, and lousy beauty-conducting pain. His love usually turned on this key, and always carried that triad-theme — it was enough if an amiable female profile, a better-ranking painting or a more recent automobile model appeared somewhere.

("Yesterday a friend was with my son, I don't really know if he's a friend, he's much younger, I can't stand him, he has awful manners, I think he's in his fourth or fifth year, I never know these years with priests at their university, my son has explained it to me five times at least but I still don't get it, great use it would be to me anyway, in short, I hate it that he always makes friends with these impossible little figures, not as if I didn't know that everybody has to be young once in life, but he's always hanging around with these boys instead of ever visiting my uncle, you can imagine how unpleasant it is for me to ask for his patronage, and my son never went to see him, and still he always asks about him, what my son is working on, he's such a darling, and he told me to send him up, fat chance of that as you can imagine, once he even said that my son imagines that the whole Catholic church is only there to put the stamp 'nihil obstat' & 'imprimatur' on his philosophical dissertations.")

The bishop vacationing in his hunting castle was easy to accuse of having seduced the young girl: he was a robust man with a high color and thin blond hair, with barely a touch of eyebrows, who always returned from the woods covered in colorful pheasant bodies like a circus clown. And yet he had nothing to do with this woman, and in fact he never had anything to do with any sin, he only walked in their proximity: his face was sometimes pale with desire and his eyes sooty from temptation, his hands trembled with the imagined harvest, but he never got as far as sinning. And the next day his face was serene with satisfaction, his eyes polished with silence, his hands worked quietly, as though absent-mindedly repeating the beats of a well-known melody on a secret keyboard: everybody believed that he had satisfied his desires during the night, but it was the other way round: he defeated them, that's what refreshed him. There was a long strip that led to sin, it was followed by a one-millimeter gap (this is a kind of moral linear color spectrum, with the sole, slender black line of the absence of sin), & after that the long strip continued again, with the full external and internal paraphernalia of the retrospective relish in sin. What affectation it would have been to think that sin was absent from the glistening & public strip.

When the bishop found out that some suspect him, he was seized by a frenzy of conscience: he felt that his innocence and chastity was no real chastity — the temptation-strips were so long (weeks, months) and the moments of innocence, of active, willed innocence were so brief (when the woman finally appeared and he turned around and ran away) that now he wanted to repent and took on himself the charges: he sent all his servants in the woods to find the disappeared girl, bring her to his hunting lodge, so that when they come to search his house they should find her there and believe that he had abducted her for love.

When Touqué listened to Tilia he relished in and cared only about this duality: the red skull of the bishop in the woods, penetrated by sickly fastidiousness like by a capillary drill: the relation, atmospheric proportion of these two, was in fact a variation of the first, in which in a large brown sorrow-wood the blond little sister careered (we will signal her trajectory on the map with a gold-yellow line, in places with hypothetical dots).

Love indulges in formal things, not content: in Touqué's feelings too the dark brown, ethereal but thick forest signifying sorrow, and the skull's large crab-upholstery had exactly the same value and meaning — on the other hand, the yellow trajectory of the fugitive girl (Avicellus Rosalyndus)[284] & fastidiousness's similarly yellow drill. The wood was melancholy, the bishop's head, robust health; the girl was serenity, while scrupulousness was a disease. But all that was secondary to the fact that both sorrow and health formed an extended and patch-like thing, in comparison with which both the girl & scruples were a linear, trembling element: it seems that truth expresses the formal elements of certain truths and 'raison facts,' while thought expresses the content elements of the same truths.

For Touqué all this could mean one thing alone: to defend the bishop. This was the third symmetry: to the rigid figure of the 'negatively' suffering girl who returned to the city from the woods corresponded Touqué's cold defense attorney-like, casuistic furor. With the one it was about apathy, with the other, about dialectical drunkenness, that is, of dichotomies of content, but nevertheless formally the two had a common graph. Therefore the birth of feeling is nothing else but the birth of such a formalist graph or scaffolding, which will automatically grow around itself all kinds of logical, epic, or painterly contents of the most quixotic contrasts.

The fugitive girl became Hereticus' concubine: it was from his bed that the bishop's servants kidnapped her. Touqué defends him, knowing that the girl is not in the bishop's castle. In the meantime she is brought there. The bishop prohibits defense. Hereticus himself appears, accusing the bishop and generalizing; the bishop comes to his senses, realizes what folly it was to adopt such a mendacious form of repentance, for he ends up compromising his Church. He loathes Hereticus, but the latter finds the girl in the bishop's castle, and unexpectedly she starts into a long oration about how superior a Catholic lover is to a heretical one. Touqué himself is now convinced of the bishop's guilt. The bishop escapes together with the girl and, after making her his lover that very day, he writes his memoirs where he exposes how everybody who condemns him base their accusations on an erroneous calendar: at the time of his great condemnation he was still a virgin, and sin only began after the day of accusations and of the sentence ended.

The essential thing being of course, whether his sentence was just. Years later he is rehabilitated: his third successor somehow unearths that his predecessor had had the girl kidnapped only in a perverted self-laceration of conscience, but he has no inkling about the fact that the girl indeed became his lover on the day of the elopement or rather, of disappearance, because the girl's family, in their attempt to stop the scandal, spread the rumor that their daughter is dead. The fugitive bishop learns about his ceremonial rehabilitation: is that really due him? For up to that day the girl had indeed not been his lover, but she had been his lover ever since. The whole ethical affair becomes a problem of chronology, the play of hours, an alibi jest. (The 'bishop' here is not a genuine Catholic dignitary but an abstract English chess figure.)

XIV.

THE MEDITATIONS OF HALBERT'S FATHER, AN ANGLICAN VICAR OF EXETER

Exeter, 1933
on absolute individualism

It is perhaps this precise degree of physical pain that suits me best: were I in greater pain, I would perhaps turn into a Catholic, yielding to the hot allure of martyrdom; & if I were to feel less pain, I would be at most a philosopher, poet, or pundit on public health. This Anglican pain, this illogical, half-baked illness of compromises is precisely what I need. In point of fact you can't really call Anglican rheumatism & Catholic exactitude of pain by the same name.

When I sit by the window watching, my limbs in the clutch of cramps, the statue in the niche of the corner terrace, which I had restored, the youthful portrait of John Frazer Williamson, while pain chains me more & more to my armchair (with suffering I get accustomed to grotesque postures: the more it prods me to jump up and scurry along the stone pipes of the cathedral's brow, like some woodpecker-lunatic, the more impossible I find it to move, so I must look like those comic snapshots where the hurdle-jumping horse and the tumbling jockey are seen eternally fixed), I feel the temptations he had felt during his illness, to spill over from Calvinist suffering into Catholic martyrdom like one modulating between tonalities. He was young and one should forgive him for being unable to preserve the puritanism of his disease, for liturgizing his fever and trying to ease it with the thought of some 'universal suffering' of the world, but I will insist on keeping my own ailment an individual torso, in the same way in which I and my ancestors used to interpret the Bible individually.

Is the liberalism of pain the authority-based 'imprimatur,' or rather, 'indoleatur' instead of pain?[285] Perhaps it is; never mind. Sometimes it would help to light a candle and canonize my torment in at least three rooms already in my lifetime. But I cannot make my spasms bring me closer to God; there is some insulation in all my muscle-aches, from which no true lyrical theodicea will spring. Nobody knows genuine individualism better than I and perhaps a few more people in this small town; whatever I say or do, it's clear as daylight that I can have nothing to do with that matter.

For how do we stand with that fabled Reformation 'individuality' and the universal human being modeled by 'authority'? All my life I have grown more and more individual, singular, but what did this mean? I have always harked to the quarter-notes of marginal nerves as well, relentlessly bringing to the surface the most disguised intrigues of my organism, with the result that a hundred thousand conflicting emotions, mutually exclusive ideas, ran through me — so on the apex of the cult of personality I felt myself to be a hundred thousand different persons: that is, I turned into the most regular garden of universality, having exhausted all possibilities. I was at once 'every man' (because our face may be one for practical purposes, but if we scrutinize every single wrinkle with the liberalism of neurasthenia and with the free-for-all method of illness, we will discover that on our face we wear the face of every human being, the way the nymphet of the hair-dye advertisement sluices all imaginable colors around her brow with her saccharine comb) and completely alienated from myself: sticking to the rules of individuality-gardening, it was precisely 'myself' that I failed to be.

My colleagues consider me a nihilist or lily-livered impressionist, when I am a 'universal human being' with more rigid bigotry than all the Catholic and classical ideals put together. There are three degrees: the first is the theoretical command and principle of 'individuality'; its continuation is hysterical actorship, the setting free of all the secret shades of the human organism; its culmination is the classical 'general human being,' the mechanical integration of all the neuron-roles, from which one alone is missing — the experiencing one. A gigantic zero and a gigantic sum total, this is the result. But the I, the I? That is not.

In my youth I read many historical novellas whose authors relished with decadent psychological gusto the extent to which history's great heroes were divorced from the historical mask that posterity imagined to be their truthful effigies. In these writings the youth of discovery lead to much naïveté; what I feel now is something much drier & much more devoid of tragedy.

suffering, distance from God

For me tragedy, too, is something Catholic: the more indifferent I become toward religious & logical 'questions,' the more jealously I guard the pristine purity of my Anglicanism; it is only natural. I'm no hero of any tragedy and can never become one: I lack the necessary bauble, the psychic undulation, the suffering inflicted by suffering. Which is not to say of course that I suffer cheerfully, that I bear the blows lightly, not at all. On the contrary: I suffer so much that I shrink from adjectives, from all æsthetic, moral or eschatology, like a rococo snail or female mimosa.

For this is individualism, this is fair solitude. To run out to the woods and cry with the trees, to sail out to sea and quarrel with dactylic tempests: that is social snobbery, protectionism-searching, romantic schoolboy eminence. Melodic solitudes, Catholic motif-technique. I am a single deaf-and-mute organ pipe-point: there is no skeptical distance between my primordial self (O unctuous joke!) and my role, for I do not doubt my priesthood and do not doubt God — I believe in everything. Perhaps this is Calvin-style salvation: indifference. The indifference that is a greater bliss than the visio beatifica. I must be the most redeemed redeemed, for I'm not interested in anything. One might organize a new 'one-ness of saints' from the grey record-holders of indifference, from its virtuosi. Doubt and faith, denial and affirmation, are jejune juvenile antitheses that today have no meaning whatsoever.

But to be blasé (is that the word?) has a new pathos, and I'm writing these pages because I want to compete with several authoritative English poets; not with their cheap pocket editions but their most ornate forms, printed on parchment & illustrated with color woodcuts. Doubt and faith: these are necessary until one finds one's own life and soul; and they are opposites only as long as one remains in constant relation with others, depending upon others and making others depend upon him. But when radical solitude starts, the instinct of connecting and weaving relations dies off like a surgically removed appendix, & then it turns out that the fact of 'contradiction' only exists in a social framework, never in the soul. And not by any chance because of 'finding true riches inside oneself': no, my innermost soul is no panorama, it's no lyrical, let alone transcendental, bellevue. Richness, the play of emotions, the logical vacillations of changes of mind: these are still the fiction of the companion-seeking period.

The soul is better than social life not because it is richer, more colorful, or more true. For none of those would it be worth choosing the solitude of the soul. I could say, with a paradox-tic left behind from my childhood, that the soul's greatest virtue is its capacity to liberate us from the thought of the soul: a fact from an ideology. But this is merely a sketch or game and utterly unimportant:

it doesn't befit a respectable elderly gent like me to disguise things with definitions, to smuggle facts with the fake passport of precision into the histrionic (Catholic?) world of raison.

What would I say if all of a sudden the Archbishop of Canterbury or the Dean of Saint Paul's entered my room and asked, "Answer me this, you lurking intrigue-monger, and declare openly, what is your relation to God?" — I would no doubt answer, nil; that the most valuable achievement of my life is the annihilation of the concept and fact of 'relation': I see trees and buses clearly because I never climb them, because I'm not allowed to eat fruits, because I'm cold in their shadow, because from their flowers a white dust drizzles on my black overcoat that can't be properly cleaned in hours, because buses have high stairs, rattle badly, and I can never find their schedule in my drawer when I would most need it. But that's precisely why I see them clearly.

It would be an anthropomorphic fatuity to label the above 'objectivity': I remember very well when I myself was objective — it must have been about 22–23 years ago, it was very hot & the Sellwyn dried up — it was something entirely different; I was objective toward one thing because I was biased in favor of another (if I'm not mistaken, I was in love, with terrifying blindness, with the mythological lexicon definition of 'truth,' & I was objective for its sake), but now it's about something completely different, now I'm not looking for truth, because the world is not 'true' or 'false' (these being much rather social categories), the world is outside them. (But it's certainly not my ambition to turn into a philosopher.)

Shall I tell the archbishop that things are merely parallel with me, that God is only parallel with me, but we never approach one another: we both rush, God as well as I, like a galaxy in space, perhaps we are filled with temperament and even with finalist obsessions, it's only toward one another that we don't grow tentacles, relation-channels, and the like? Rigid simultaneism, they might write in a London paper.

about the concept of 'complexity'

Londoners are very superficial: they are far too sensitive to notice or learn anything. Are they too healthy? They keep noticing finesses, although reality doesn't want such finesse, I believe. Complexity? Oh charme de ma jeunesse dorée...![286] Perhaps people imagined the notion of the 'complex' too homogeneously: they considered a thousand-component system complex, and if they heard 'excessive complexity,' they imagined a hundred-thousand-component system, if they thought about infinite complexity, they imagined an infinite-component system: mathematically multiplying in the self-same direction.

However, perhaps the more complicated thing doesn't relate to the less complicated like a thousand-wheel wonder-clockwork to a two-wheel alarm clock. Why should we always stick to numbers? Sensitivity irritates me if it's mathematical. Complicated = many: what an obsession! Whenever Londoners are nervous they start counting. Does the finesse, the complexity of matter, reside by definition in its composition? And that of the soul, in the plurality of layers? In my soul there is probably not a single layer: the whole thing is one point, & yet I feel it to be so fine, complicated, & (O, Malvolio!) modern as an 18th-century beau felt his vest to be, as he was parading on the Bath promenade.

What if complexity has two ways: one mathematical, multiplying, mechanical mirror anatomy, & another, where the 'more complex' relates to the less complex as two different spatial poses of the same simple geometric shape: the principle-décor is shifted here and there without the simple form coming to contain more and more elements — only its situation will be different in a 'philosophical' space. ("He was a rotten scholastic, heretic & elegant": such an obituary the parish ought to write for me.)

I can imagine two kinds of Gothic (from the window I can see the cathedral's encouraging-patronizing, old man's smile): with the one (and I hate this), they perforate a smooth wall, so it would have ten columns, then in the next century they perforate it more, so it has 100 columns, and so forth, until in the end the whole cathedral looks like a gossamer-thin fishnet stocking on a female leg (in my congregation I have sternly prohibited this stupid coquetry). The other Gothic (this is mine!) consists, let's say, in placing that smooth wall on its head, instead of rarefying it into a comb; in the next century from the mountaintop I will tuck this same smooth wall under water, tilted, and later yet I will place it in a cloud's lap, and so forth: 'complexity' will consist only in the new position of the one-component thing, in the new perspective of principles. School textbook sensitivity knows nothing about this second kind of complexity.

When they took this caricature concept, 'complex emotion,' for reality, they naturally believed that analysis (textile-educated Gothicizing) was the most suitable technique for representing the soul. For me analysis can mean nothing, it's at most some kind of space geometry or dimension tennis: my joy of yesterday moves in a different direction from that of today, that's why the new art finds the flower's essence not in the petals' cells and in the styles' imbecile pollen, but in the flower's place. There is only one flower in the world, only its coordinates differ: that too is the case with botanical space theory or psychology.

But after all, what did an emotion look like with me, which people as a rule mechanically dub 'complex'? It always consisted of two elements: the one was some abstract movement, contentless inner direction-dynamics, and the other always the object, outward reality, where I happened to be. Among my amorous delights and doubts I felt a million 'shades,' knowing well that the word 'shade' is nonsensical, and then I realized that complexity consisted in the accidental relation of my soul's pure only-movement and the outside world's objects harrowed into it. If during an emotion the outside world suddenly disappeared, we couldn't feel anything else but what we feel on a ship if the deck starts sinking under us: an empty direction-nausea. Space-in-movement plus magnolia leaf, space-in-movement plus wind-shaped snowstorm-breast, space-in-movement plus tautened thesis of thinking: this is in the place of 'complexity.'

Oh, goût amer de la distinction,[287] I could say with the Picard poet to be born in the next century. We are the truly nervous, the country folks, the people from small towns, not the Londoners: it seems that to my old age I've become such a snob as to boast with my snobbishness, like a football club with its champion players. Every epoch needs a union slogan, some kind of 'me also' poem: about Arcadia or neurasthenia. Perhaps it's a very shop-soiled fad, but things arrive with some delay to the country and last of all to a parish priest.

7 o'clock bells, subjectivism

The clock strikes seven: first, the cathedral's sound, then my clock. As if the fog had collided into the Gothic walls, giving that booming sound: a scene from some unpublished Wagnerian 'Zeitdrama,' in which time's ship knocks its foggy prow against the shore. Do the sound waves disturb the fog? The longer the bells sound, the faster the dissipating patches of fog drift upward, baring the rose-window's black glass. My time, my rose, I think under my two-second inspiration: how black, empty, and cold is this church window, which they call rose. There is perhaps a Gothic Pandora box: liberated time flees, booming, on this black-mossy, round opening. (Let's hurry with better analogies, for soon it will be over: only five big & two small strikes left.) How confusing this time signal: the rigid façade is all excitement, together with the fog, the birds, the rose's vulgar wound, the street lamps' small pink lights, these small time-calmatives with which they try to benumb time's great waves. As if 'seven o'clock' were not a date but an event that branches out in space, like the arrival of a ship: its prow is already fixed, its stern is still swinging on the water, the bridge has already been let down, the passengers have yet to set foot on it, the huge engines are halted but smoke is still pouring out, all the space-defining prepositions and suffixes have become effective, but everything is fleeing, hesitating, being nowhere. There is fog-seven-o'clock, bird-seven-o'clock, window-seven-o'clock, and perhaps even clock-seven-o'clock: this booming vespera maneuver is at once a frozen anchor and a rowboat gone astray. Why does time's chiming ripeness resemble so much the ravages of fire?

However ridiculous it sounds, I started fearing: did some catastrophe happen? Because the bells went on for too long, something must be wrong with the mechanism, and now the same thing is going on, as on the stage when the hero has already replaced his flute in his pocket but somebody in the orchestra is still playing out in his name. Shall I send my houseboy to see? James! No, no, perhaps it turns out to be some childish prank. There's not a soul on the street, and yet I could swear that revolution broke out. The unemployed smash my Biedermeier furniture. Let them. There was a time when I would have been ashamed of such self-obvious associations as 'chiming' and 'riot': today I clasp fatuity as a blind-born pope clasps Peter's key in Luther's antechamber. He clasps it so hard that he can no longer feel if it's one or two keys. I don't know if I open or close something with it: I merely keep smothering these banalities, with the smell of phosphorus sticking to my hand and the iron heated to a fever.

This empiricism and homegrown positivism is far from comfortable: my fingers are in the clutch of dark spasms and the key turns red-hot. When I read the analyses (analyses?) of Locke and

Hume in our limited school manuals I see not lucid bookkeepers of perception but kangaroos shrunk into the panic of cowardice. Facts, facts! My facts, my realities: can these words have as much as an approximate meaning for me nowadays? I wouldn't like it if the portrait I'm painting here of myself turned out too melodramatic: I'm neither autumnally resigned nor a dyed-haired gigolo in chase of bygone youth.

What is fact and what is non-fact? What is objective and what is subjective? (I'm not asking melancholically.) Can my present radical solitude be called subjectivity? When a tremendous anger overcomes me, as it does a pregnant woman when the daisy's petals are not white in the way she had imagined during breakfast before her constitutional walk, I don't feel (as I did in my 'objective' period full of self-pitying affectation) 'oh, on what nonsensical rages I'm wasting my energy instead of putting my pathos into worthy causes' — but on the contrary, I feel that I have never been more objective, fertile, saintly, & true than now, when I'm wasting myself on so-called pure balderdash. I feel that every inanity, every sensuous lilting, means for me some undefinable universal concreteness: the wearing-off of my slippers' lining, the unsalted soup, the dusty leaf all make me turn over & over the most important questions of life.

Which are these? I have no idea, and neither do I search for them. Is it subjectivism if I adore myself? And why should I affect in these notes: I do adore myself. Shall I cite Germanic Schul-paradoxes in my defense, that with me the 'I' is something much more universal than 'objectivity' with others? It's pointless to engage in correspondence with my former professor in Heidelberg: he is forever hammering out definitions on the basis of nonexistent criteria. Facts! Facts! Where is their boundary? This is not to argue that facts go over into mysticism & the other way round: that way we would be merely applying a legal trick, affirming that 'every thing is its own mix' and that everything that exists is a dual citizen.

The bell is chiming, chiming still: is it a fact or a theory, an object or a fever? Can it mean anything that a seaman goes bonkers trying to decide if to go closer to Scylla or to Charybdis, when in fact he has to sail between Alaska and Kamchatka? Fact and illusion, error and reality, hysteria & lucidity are mere grammatical opposites, & most moody-brooding spirits of yesteryear have worn themselves to tatters, kicking against the artificial pricks of grammar. Relativism as worldview: the acquiescence of the only-grammatically-living human being in eternal word-captivity. The form of interest that wants to distinguish between reality and illusion will simply fall from people.

My favorite company is those who are slightly older than me, but only when they eat. Is there a more profound relationship with reality, truth, God, & ourselves (these four concept-children are approximately the four 'enfants gâtés' of our spirit, as a poem title in my French textbook had it)[288] than the one we reach by eating? People like to say that all those old fogeys care about is filling their paunch.

True sense of concreteness is every bit as rare in the world as true vision. People have some abstract ideas, arbitrary concepts about reality, possibility, experience, & then they try to adapt to these concepts in the most whimsical way. They take a pebble in hand and affirm that this is a more experiential experience than when they only looked at it. They weigh it, break it into pieces, melt it, and cast a dubious light on it with the arithmetic square of distance: now they feel experience to be even more experiential than when they only held the pebble in hand. If I don't take this to be reality, then I consider something else to be reality, and what can possibly guarantee that my reality is not arbitrary? (I'm sure in seminars and in political meetings they still call this a logical question or polite counter-argument.)

O, it's not the soul, or the nobility of our sentiments, and not even revelation that I feel to be reality. I feel that the world is in a great reality-sphere, without it being assembled from given truths or fact-mosaics. Some German visiting professor held a lecture in Cambridge, if I remember well, about various theories of matter: I read one sentence from it in a paper: 'Die Masse im einzelnen Raumpunkt ist Null.'[289] With charming patriarchal dilettantism I said to myself that it's going to be the same with truths and facts: if I take out Lincoln Cathedral, the digestive system, or the Planck constant of the totality of the world, on their own they will not represent or mean any fact or truth, but from the perspective of truth will be simply nil. Truth and reality are continuous: one great process that has no atom-like points. It is evident that when I utter 'ist Null,' I'm not saying that the facts mean something spiritual. Not that I'm ashamed of placing something spiritual before a material thing, but here it's not about that. It happens extremely rarely that I cobble metaphors out of a German thesis for home use, and it's due more to my son's influence than to my own penchants.

O, the booming of the bells! What does it remind of? Of some beautiful image, I know. Yes: there was a painter, unfortunately I forget his name, although I always write with great pleasure the names of those I used to love, because they are few (probably because I started my career as agape's heavyweight professional: it seems that people don't want to be loved too much), he always painted ships in the making, half-ready or in repair; in the middle of the painting there was a gigantic black body like a funereal carp that hangs from a nail: half its body is vertical (this was the prow), the other half is lying on the ground, slightly twisted (this is the ship's bulk). The latter, the longitudinal slab with one of its points rising high, was surrounded by scaffolds: small planking networks, toothpick-towers, the ladders' space-budding creepers.

The bell-chime or the cathedral are like this half-built ship in the docks: a gigantic yet slender bulk (this is the most beautiful thing about ship advertisements: each represents enormous weight and blade-like slenderness; it is one of those rare domains where the rendering of tons is conjoined with grace), and next to it, the millimeter-netting of lines, behind which the ship appears, black like a statistics stain on the chart paper; beneath it, the sea's isolated small waves (they look like the unembossed white glue-strips next to postage stamps), meek, homely harbor waves. These ships are awful with their elegance, cargo, death-profile and optimism. They are like the bell chimes: the houses stand still, and yet some movement goes through them — not everything needs to 'move' for the world to fill up with movement. By magic the bells smuggled the absolute of movement into the mute, frozen town, but nothing stirs. Perhaps this is the most beautiful thing about it; perhaps that's why I feel that for a few minutes I've been witnessing one of the most immoral disproportionatenesses of the world. Reproach and encouragement: let me be incestuous if I haven't been so far, but all the same it also lets me know that I've been predestined for damnation.

Every bell is at its root a moral insanity. Which is the more horrific part of catastrophe: the outburst, or the regular continuation, the wound, or the quiet blood-flow, the first sound-attack, or the air's apoplectic fidgeting? I feel, as a doctor with the patient, that the sound-ailment is at a new 'station,' in the state of inexorability, when there is no longer any bell and church, sound and time, only floating deafness-islands above the houses, like the dark smudges of coal on the illustrative cross-section of a silent colliery. This is a basically 'quiet' station: water streams through the broken dam not with a howl but a resilient swish. What is it going to end in? Why do I lend myself to the childish game of feeling the bell-chimes to be a personal moral crisis?

moral

Perhaps because every bell makes a tragedy out of rheumatism, and pours my personal ailment into the mold of an empty pain template? Yielding it a bit of æsthetics, which I enjoy? Perhaps ethics at large is no more than the æsthetic qualification of small domestic glitches, shapeless action-stems? Ethics: when my former professor uttered this word in Cambridge, I always felt some broad stylization: a stylization of I don't know what, but a bigger shape of something smaller, the ceremonial larva of something that is utterly trivial and transient. I had colleagues who called themselves immoralists, but they merely held other things to be ethical than my professor, and were no less slaves of this Sunday allegory than he.

Moral, moral: by this I meant some kind of subjective lightning, the incalculable metabolism of my most personal tissues, badly botched dreams or dreams snowed-in with mathematical functions, the self on the self-th power, that is: while others invariably saw in ethics universal rules to which personal will is subordinated, I understood ethics to be precisely what is the most indeterminate, strange, meaningless, secretive in the individual organism. During my first moral meditations I felt that for a start the arbitrary relationship between action and moral needs to be torn apart: why should ethics necessarily be a concept of dramaturgy, or a sports rule of the will? At that time ethics meant for me something like this: if a kind of psychic intensity that is entirely meaningless gives the impression of being absolute value, we are faced with an ethical matter.

Utter lostness and utter value-theoretical stirredness at the same time: this is what moral then meant to me. Much too erotic? Too lyrical? Indeed. When we gazed overmuch into each other's eyes with a girl, I learned to define moral as follows: a gaze, the tying of perception's green rope to the harbor's swaying iron pole, has nothing else but the shady-lagoonish owing up to the fact that being human is entirely incomprehensible, that every word of ours is trying to thread thin needles with the thick fur mittens of secret, and yet, this is the greatest inebriation and the most dissertating logic one can imagine.

Love is the best humanist training because it lights the human being into an axiological spark where the abscess of nothingness happens to bloom. Just as water and blood poured out of Christ's side in heraldic-colored ribbons, so the following two brooks pour out of the nuptial bed: nothing and value, exile & burning home. But they are individual nothing & individual value: only complete observation of eyelashes, intonation, embrace-stumbles can get us close to it. Of course in this way every great emotion, every new swelling of the soul's veil, whether driven by the North wind or sickly Passat, immediately turned into ethics, and my whole theory of ethics was no more than an artificial apology for sentimentalism. Was it comfortable? The question hardly occurred to me.

politics and morphinism

All my affinities pushed me toward violence, but I still couldn't identify ethos with suffering. Later I had to pay the price of my passivity, and the repressed action surfaced. At that point I was seized by a manic desire for action, I wanted absolute action-like action at all cost, but not for the sake of moral. My resolution to become a priest goes back to those times. By action I meant exclusively the leading of people by rhetoric: I wanted to play a comedy before them, to surprise them, to instigate, stir them with the help of the most conceptually complete demagogy.

I had two 'ethical' postures: one was the nightly swim in female eyes, hypochondriac roaming among the willow-tents of gazes — and the other was preaching, the ceaseless confusing of people without any purpose or content of value. Love lyricism & oratory of faith: at first sight this was its duality, but in fact it was politics & morphine. Because with the help of drugs I could intensify my individual life to the highest degree, for out of every association a wave-shaped deity was created, so that I could better see how empty and at the same time how powerful it was. Morphine is the great aperitif of humility: it uncovers such richness of the chambers of the self that we cannot possibly put on it the clunky seal of ownership: this richness rules over us, terrorizes us, & we devoutly close our eyes before it. And only-action is politics. True politics occurs very rarely, good & useful politics occurs all the time. I am a true politician, although I have never gone into politics, however ardently I would have liked to: I didn't believe in ideals, had no practical plans, didn't care about humanity, history, future, I only felt an elementary urge to carry out a grandiose buffoonery, dimeshow hypocrisy, & gossip-trumpeting in public. True politics: people don't conform to principles, 'accomplish ideals,' but imitate the gestures, gaze, hair color, mouth-twitch, & shoelace of one impractical harlequin. Prank, paradox, bluff? In old times they used to say things like, 'history is only a comedy,' but they sincerely regretted that state of facts. And now, let's admit it, comedy and serious reality, philanthropy & vacuous mass-shaking, are not opposites but eventually identical.

Politics and morphinism are only seemingly a dichotomy: the reason why one shouldn't give 'ideals' to the fabled people is that ethics is always already contained in the gesture, hair color, shoelace, just as ethics as chemical component is already there in the lovers' gaze at each other. More chemistry and less theory of will in moral! It doesn't matter if the above is a badly warmed-up baby

Machiavellianism or an empty play on words: this too was only a part, one small part of my inner ethical nature. I've never been and am not a buffoon, a conman, because I'm full to the brim with scruples, ethical worries, the Gospels' great neurasthenia-registers. Program: to betray my wife and devour with well-nigh Catholic devotion the living matter of moral in the lover's smile; then to preach (not against and not in favor of carnal pleasure but only for the sake of the word): here moral is nil; & finally, to perch all night on church benches, frightened like the worm dropped from the cut pear on the knife-blade, with half-sorrows, prayer-sheets, trembling from eternal damnation. A lousy moral full-pension, to live on such a diet three times a day.

Perhaps I have to say after all, what is the difference between a metropolitan snob-cocainist and a morphinist parish priest from the deep countryside. When I hear this bell-chime I see the broad draperies of 'ethos,' some bogus-flamed pseudo-Greek morphology where action is like a Greek statue, one can see the whole even in its fragments: O, how it sometimes pays off to have been to secondary school! The whole! The bell, too, preaches this obsession of the 'whole.' I feel myself to be a fragment, although there is no kinship of any kind between me and the Impressionists. (In these diary lines barren routine visibly accumulates in rescuing myself from any imaginable category or dichotomy-trap; after all, every old fogey with his mania.)

moral and problem

Varietas non delectat:[290] I would still somehow like to relate my life, not in line with the wide-berthed prose of the 'whole,' but with a more naïve gathering instinct. If there was one thing that attracted me in my life, it was the so-called 'ethical problems,' but only in their barely-observable, pre-rational nakedness, devoid of all melody. Because once it becomes a thought-through problem, every trouble turns into æsthetic; sadism is a consistent, therefore absurd ethics. The 'problem' is, by nature: melodic, Cambridge-educated, beautiful. This cannot be counterbalanced with any spurious papier-mâché misery. I alone can counterbalance it in my silence, solitude, reclusiveness.

In these lines I would like to recount my silence, those silence experiments conducted with inept methodology, which I carried out for twenty years in the shadow of the cathedral. I would like to show those prudent, scrupulous, loving gestures of mine with which I tried to grasp an ailment or suffering of mine already in the state before it became a 'problem,' before it became a formulated 'issue,' before it was inserted into the gilded-black scale of ethics; when it was still a biological doodle, an alien-nameless, pure cell.

What is the use of busying oneself with such vacuous preciosities for 20 years? That's all I was good for, at work in me was one sole giant energy or, to give it its more refined name: sterile nervousness and nothing else. My associations were meager, my will nonexistent. What I am doing here is no pessimistic settling of accounts. My life has been unsayably barren, but this doesn't depress me: on the contrary, it gives me almost rancorous pleasure that I'm a stubborn goof, because they can drop me into the coffin with triumphant sulking, flowery defiance. I aim no lower: to display this dark, unexpected, bitter, & yet nourishing bringing to fruition that fills me these days. In a fashion magazine I've seen chemise 'fantaisie'; I say to myself: goût 'experience.' What is this? Altersstil?[291] More exactly? This bell-chiming lures me to formulate my life in Hardy's style, but that would be too easy, and what is more, beautiful.

childhood fairy-tales and 'grownup' materialism

Who spoilt my life? The nanny. The ethicists and the immoralists join forces in hijacking & withdrawing those fairy-tales that nannies tell. (I never had a nanny, but in 'nanny' I have a generic noun that could be just as well a delta or lambda sign.) Thus my study of the law was ineradicably the constitution of Arcadia, and my theology, a couple of gourmand-miracles with bearing on me: I have held on to these early pedagogical gains all my life. I'm fanatically selfish and decayed-into-I. But this graceful, slender, feminine, and stealthy English letter I, which is my arithmetic representative in chemical sentences, was an expensive key that opened every beautiful door which objectivated the various shop-window secrets of the spring, sometimes managing to intone meaning behind love's empty cacophonies, & spreading before me the great cadaster of chastity, God, self-abnegation.

Somebody set up a scheme, with a glib orthodoxy characteristic of epileptics: sin is the precondition of becoming-righteous, moreover: sin is already full of the premium-alba of righteousness. Either way it's a dead end: by saying that sin and virtue exist separately — or by saying that sin and virtue con-flue in an indistinguishable mass. There are other formations, we need to shift ethics to other domains of phenomena: relativizing is no uprooting, relativizing is no innovation. Perhaps it's all about movements, colors, not sin and virtue. Something other: limes-other. Something which, if we think it, already bursts into air, meaning no longer 'other' but nonsense. I love myself infinitely for the sake of the world; it was my dream-radicalism that showed the face of the world. Experience: two things at once. Every profile, plant, animal, concept becomes more blunt, precise, more bungled-definite

(O vulnera circumscripta, pedanteria mortis):[292] but on the other hand, every profile, plant, animal, concept is surrounded by more mist, mystery, twilight, and irrationality. It's particularly easy for Englishmen to be whacky plant collectors & melancholy pantheists at the same time. Snow and mist at the same time.

his wife's castle park

I first saw the castle park of my wife's family in the winter, there was a thick mist and the branches were covered in snow. Strangely enough, the branches were located under very broad snow strips: I expected exact nature to give me the branches exactly in the middle of those wide snow strips and not underneath, with such gauche asymmetry: the whole thing looked like the illustration of a cheap pocket edition, where the printing frame got shifted a bit: all the trees, mountains, houses, grass stumps were pushed at least one centimeter lower on the world's page than planned. That was also the first time when I saw that mist was not an infinite expanse but porous, tattered here and there, of varying thickness.

Only this bit now about my two unforgettable friends (snow, mist): the one was all edges, icicles, stars, lamina; the other was all movements, flowing-apart, indeterminacy. Hiems Janus:[293] experience, too, sets a face before me like a rough crystallogram, a rule, but at the same time as a hesitant trying-on of face powder, impersonal climate lampion. What pleasure, what bliss it was to walk in this winter landscape for the first time, coughing from the spreading doses of uncertainty, preserving on my gloves' black leather the snowflake stars like ladybirds from heaven, discovering with a sniff of naïve nature-historical laurels, that these are not closed stars at all but five-point compass roses, Andrew-crosses and it's-not spirals: not small territories delimited by spiraling lines but branches that dehisce and flash out into the air. Branch, branch: how strange all those innumerable branches on the trees, the trunk barely amounts to something: all those branches are means, and the means have made the purpose disappear. Trees shouldn't be like this, there should be more trunk & less branches; the branch for the branch's sake: an abuse. Hindu gods have so many arms that from among the arms' thorns the seed, the god proper, cannot be picked.

In my childhood I experienced everything that exists to ceaselessly fill and sharply delineate itself: only in this way was it massive enough to qualify for the order of Great Existence. And here everything was the other way round: lots of empty space among the branches; instead of enclosing itself, the tree's whole shape seemed to tend to scatter itself, and because of that it couldn't appear to me as truly existing. At that time I thought I could correct this fact by being, once I grew up, at the same time a Casanova (mist) & the Archbishop of Canterbury (snow). That's when the scintillating thesis of suffering began.

toward the most perfect pain-formula; logic and dream

That was the time when I started working on a great deduction which, instead of wearing out the play-chromaticism of a great disillusionment-novel, was meant to resemble the foundation of an arithmetical thesis. After the canonical series of small theses, supplementing & hypotheses akin to modern cactus stands, this Christmas I finally felt that the formula was almost ready. I have always been intrigued by the formula, the sinful formula of my sufferings (here 'sinful' is a cretinous word, but I often imagine myself on the pulpit and there such an adjective may even look pretty — a sign left behind me in the air like the electric ads of shops left on above the pulled-down blinds on Sundays).

Gentle reader X, you know all too well that with me this 'formula' can only be metaphorical, not genuinely mathematical, so you despise it. And you of course unveil my greatest sorrow, my great jealousy: alas, there is no science on me. But perhaps you are not entirely right, my lord reader X, because even though in reality I cannot churn out an arithmetic formula, my experience may nevertheless be characteristically non-literary, non-psychological. I agree, it's a burdensome fellow who has no science but only some scientific inspiration. I would make a lousy scientist, so in my humiliation I dupe myself that I might yet pass off for a beautiful life. Sometimes I'm satisfied with such Woolworth wares, while at other times I turn up my nose even at God Himself. Science? Life? Brrr: again, two dictionary words. Ever since I started taking opium & morphine, I've felt both in my blood (is it a bad place?). Perhaps I have long felt them in my brain, because their blend is served up to us in a great many books like some hors d'œuvre identity: but I didn't like it in that form. It is probably not what I feel and see in my dreams nowadays. The sole virtue of all dreams: not the chaos of images but on the contrary, the complete transformation of our logic, weaving of thoughts, deductions, moral opinions — in general, of our technique of thinking, all the while faithfully preserving the peculiar flavor of raison, logic's ancient nature, even intensifying them.

In dreams the good and useful part is the abstract bits. How many things that we believe to be completely other are still reason. Our logic in opium: delicate net in the wind. The net is made up of exact squares, but the wind presses into it an alien movement. Astonishing wave-shapes, palm variations, diminished-third string nests, space-planes and other vital curves emerge without the net dissolving and without the squares disappearing in the act. Let's imagine a simple syllogism & throw it into dream's creative Föhn: while its logical cohesion will not halt for a moment, it will take on the most fantastic wave faces: we would have no other task but to express again in a rational form these transitional dance movements (which are infinite of course). What seemingly absurd variants could one add to any simple statement. Nobody has as yet meticulously reported their morphine logic; they always talk about images that are not valuable in themselves.

---
defending himself against the accusation of 'materialism' and venality; asceticism and private property

---

When on a Christmas evening I was looking at my wife's castle (at that time I barely knew her), it was the nanny working in me again: it was she who pressed my head to the fence's planks like hair between the curling tongs; it was she who asked for the girl's hand in marriage, it was she who wanted the gardens to be mine, or rather, her own. She was a Parca and a tyrant; every confession has to start with her effigy. In children's tales there is no difference between matter and spirit; there the coveting of gold, of treasure, of the thousand-windowed palace is not materialism. I'm not trying to say that it's something spiritual, although it falls quite close to it. Because in every fanatical desire, ab ovo for being desire, there is more spirituality than materiality: to yearn very much can only be something spiritual. This is especially valid for childhood: there the 'biggest diamond' is so much surrounded by the spirit of rarity, impossibility, distance, wondrousness, as to be rendered entirely spiritual.

Why do I go to such lengths to articulate this? I do it against a charge that I have to refute. My wife's relatives consider me a materialist, money-grabbing, sensuous, and slothful: I would readily owe up to this charge, moreover, I would even consider it much too benevolent, if my accusers could only know what money means to me. I use this quaint affected sentence, 'what money means to me' instead of the mercantile-blunt 'what I spend money on,' because if I used the latter phrase I would falsify things. I need a great many luxury objects and private properties, but I only touch them, I never penetrate them: I play with the abstract atmosphere of the sense of property, not with property itself.

I cannot really 'immerse myself' in physical gain, in women's undigested lucrum carnis:[294] even if for years I submerged into the distant carmine of the senses, there was always something trying to throw me to the surface like a corpse or life-belt. (I am not trying to suggest that beneath my love or money-sexual sins some exploding innocence would have radiated throughout, far from it; I'm not saying that 'deep inside' I was situated at a great remove from my precious properties, but merely that in the articles of comfort I did not relish the comfort they were created for: in women not the love, in slippers not the soft walk, in gardens not the fresh air, in flowers not the scent. Every single one of my adored properties were infinitely flexible: if I wanted to penetrate it with my hands, the property didn't let me but got smeared left and right around and next to my hands, like a half-inflated rubber animal. I was the sensualist and connoisseur of the property's theoretical surface, like a blind man who knows everything by touch. Infinite poverty together with richness: to not enjoy anything but to palpate the notion of 'enjoying something' in all its imaginable logical shiftings.)

'Gain of material for denial of material': perhaps this is long familiar to many. I saw my wife's castle & gardens & came to love them before my wife: this is obvious. They are right: I wanted the park, not the woman. So the nanny, my childhood dictated. When I wanted the park, for me the park was a fairyland, the solution to all the childhood sufferings, and what is the most important and the reason I wanted it the most: the park meant the absolution of my childhood sins. One should sweep aside everything, so that only two entities are left on the stage of these *Meditations*:

the nanny *&* the park. What was I, compared to them? The insignificant train of their silent work, its side-product or laboratory rabbit.

In childhood one wants the greatest pleasure and the holy of holies: so my eyes have always fused together the priesthood and idiotic secret sins. Later the place of idiotic sins was taken by the park, the castle, the cars, the populous parties: but these too were identical with my salvation. Matter-worship? He who did not fall in love with matter in his childhood fairy-tale dreams and does not try to expiate the sins of his childhood with them, is indeed a worshipper of matter, if he worships matter with the greed and intensity I'm capable of. But before every luxury object there stand two natural signs, like embossing on genuine silver spoons: my childhood, and spiritual purity. The park meant the recurring or belated child's dream and at the same time, the scintillating guarantee of virtue: if from now on I persist in sinning (for I will, I must), but with the park belonging to me, then from the park's wide, fairy-tale perspective the sin will not look a sin. Matter purifies, matter sanctifies: to hang around with a filthy prostitute — sin; to do the same with an elegant lover in a fairy-tale park — not sin. Ego sum sacerdos![295]

And still, how could this identity of the thirst for money and the thirst for virtue develop in me with such unusual intensity? Money meant elegance; elegance meant a wild-Cubist home and eternal journey east and west. For me both the Cubist home and travelling meant disquiet, space-vertigo, time-vertigo, fears and universal strippedness. By instinct I'm drawn to old-fashioned country houses where I feel no inclination to get out. The new style and flying to great distances are only shapes of my aborted creative penchants, themes: if I realized them, I would feel that I have worn myself out but I haven't ever really wanted them. I dreamt about funnel-rooms made of crushed glass and for a long time didn't notice that I merely wanted to bring them into being, not to live in them. If in real life I got into such cup-shaped salons I felt what I feel in my dreams when I'm not able to open my eyes, and instead of the sharp contours of printed text I'm surrounded by uncertain smudges. These modern rooms were all village rooms in a twilight tenor: dream-shaped asceticism, rancorous space-inquisition. It's understandable that the facts of virtue & richness ended up in such close vicinity in my fantasy.

I have often heard say that the rich are after the non-plus-ultra of refinery. For me that certain 'refinery' was the illustrated book of death: in place of clothes, formulae and ripped-out Notizblock pages; in place of words, animal barks and sports movements; in place of beds, snowed-in indoors golf courses where two embraced people are probably in the same kind of relation as two strange golf balls in the wind. 'Bounty' in elegance was not human but logical or arithmetical bounty, that is, pure death-text: the infinitely wide bed rendered infinite not the comfort of my limbs but the number of square centimeters; the greater the 'comfort,' the less the human being: absolute luxury equals absolute suicide. So it is for me, who am a bred-in-the-bone and eternal non-elegant. The bread is like the milk, the flower is like the fine-ground algae, the kiss, like the domino's dotless face, the chair like the balance, the cup like the fan: doesn't the elegant environment become the faithful copy of my dream when at the exam, in the text that I have to read out, in place of the a's my eyes can only distinguish a grey ring, and in place of the k's, only a scratched zigzag? Money as sum never featured in my brain; for me, money meant this human-annihilating elegance. My experience of travel was also such a dehumanizing free improvisation: if I wanted a drink, in the elegant home I had to cut my tongue with blade-harmonica fans — abroad, if I wanted as much as going on living, I had to learn myself anew as if learning the alphabet of a Congolese tribe.

Is this materialism? Can a poor soul who yearns for money be a materialist at all? If in old times or other people imagined great masses of riches as the multi-ton gold cargo of bank safes, then I imagine that gold as an invisibly thin, infinitely long thread that stretches through outer space up to the feet of the angels: infinite money makes possible infinite spirituality, 100% abstraction. Let's look at two gardens: one is the real-life park, the gardens of my wife's family, which meant another form of wealth next to the hypermodern home and travel. That real garden was the realization of the good dream, where the sense of home expands to velvet-capped rocks, night-gloved silence-palm: every leaf is home, every home is warm moral.

But there is another garden that comes to mind mechanically every time I think of money: light blue sky that is so thin, the moon has bleached its god-varnish and angel-watermark so much that it looks almost like white powder (this is what comes to my mind first, not flowers, trees, walks, or loves on the benches), some kind of sugar of yesterday in the raised meaning of 'barely'; gigantic fern-shadows reach into the sky, like medical filters of temptation, so that something of heaven would get caught in them; there is nothing more. Behold, the two illustrated schemata of materialism: idyll-material and inhuman space-material — the child's naïve dream pan-ethics, and the grownup neurasthenic's absolute self-laceration.

My accusers are so doltish that I feel constrained to explain: I know that in point of fact matter will never purify me, but for me it creates enough atmosphere of purification to almost amount to real purification. I need ethics, however sinful and unethical I may otherwise be; I need ethical atmosphere, smell, milieu. Everybody gets their ethics as best they can: I acquired mine through the park, so I had to put all my strength into acquiring the park.

> *whatever he touches becomes an ethical question.*
> *The theme of Juanus Ethicus*

Indeed, whatever I touch immediately becomes, Midas-fashion, an ethical matter. Some priests are priests because of their virtues; I am one because everything is bent into moral in my hands: thoughts, fruits, times close like a mimosa, letting only their moral content get to me through their virgin lock. This is the case with money, and of course with women too.

I'd like to write some theme like Juanus Ethicus: this Don Juan tries his luck with every woman, but then the whole affair is only the hook of moral problems in the jaw of a wriggling male fish — woman, pleasure, play, soon everything goes extinct in the affair, to leave behind only moral scruples, maimed half-confessions, weak-kneed ethical theories and Calvinist lyricism. In vain he runs from one woman to the next to learn true frivolity: he never manages to. He looks mundane, while being in fact the victim of morality.

I would describe the dark typology of his amorous adventures: the first phase is when he likes the woman because behind her there is some wonderful room or landscape. The second phase is the affair proper, consisting mainly of bodily fiascos: after silent lakes, beds rattling in vain, and finally the third phase when in the wake of infinitely positive landscapes and superfluous bodily gymnastics, only moral meaning or meaninglessness are left, the constraint-wine of unwanted grapes. I can almost hear the murmur of the Sils lake on a bitter afternoon, oblivious of women, pressing loneliness even more into monologue in Juan's soul; I see the hotel room with running water, three meals a day, kindly ring twice for the chambermaid *&* once for the hotel-boy; and finally, the great scruple-basin of memory, where the various sin-models try out their greedy petals in the night, so that nothing else can ever take their place. All this is never about love, not for one second: for Juan, the Sils waters' blue kiss-gills are foreign and scary movements; the hotel room has the shape of a bill, and among its furniture tuned to 'pour le service, monsieur' the stripping female body appears even more estranged; it's only the movement of female will, but not the image of muscles melted into love — this environment belongs so much to the woman, in such a hotel room woman prevails to such extent as anthropological specialism, that there can be no talk about love; and finally the memory, the great moral-stock market speculation of time, where only stray hypotheses resist in the rarefied air. How many loves of mine did carry out the threefold woman-denial of nature, hotel-operating theater and brooding memory!

And in the wake of women the pushy alcohol of morality ferments together with the row of bungled misfortunes. Women are sick, jealous, aging; while Juan is racking his brains over the mathematical balancing of faithfulness and unfaithfulness, while he wants to return to his dumbest lover out of stubborn honesty, the women want to torture and kill him and one another. The whole short story could end with Juan watching at night through a keyhole how two of his lovers of old murder each other in jealousy: he had been unhappy with both, both had merely passed on his soul by one station in the relay race of guilt-feeling, and now they are exterminating each other, in the vein of English blood dramas: Juan's last repenting prayer and the two women's realized vengeance run into the tunnel of the same minute.

All my life I've been looking for frivolity with the sweat of my brow, not finding it anywhere, I always came upon hindrances & hooks: isn't this enough for priesthood? I see red hair and I hear the ticking of the clock: some woman does something meanly evil, biting, or murdering somewhere; and I'm mutely trembling from damnation and cannot reject that red-haired woman whom I have perhaps not even touched. Materialism, materialism.

the park's solitary gate

I'll tell you how beautiful the park was; I'll describe it in detail, for this is the arithmetic codex of my morality. If somebody proved that this landscape and castle description can by no means be called morality, it would strip me of everything: I have no other moral. Voilà: this whole love started with a wrought iron gate. A solitary, isolated, meaningless wrought iron gate. The huge park gate had two characteristics: one was that, with all its huge size, it consisted in only a few iron splinters, so a thin person could easily squeeze through between two bars; and the other was (that's what I hinted at in the word 'meaningless') that it didn't appear to continue in a fence to the left and right, neither did any path appear to start inward, toward the distant and invisible castle.

Instead of a fence, shrubs, trees, parasites, and creepers of different sizes started to the left & right; small, thick dumpling-bushes alternated with soft fan-shrubbery that swayed in the wind; the small ball-bushes were black with the metallic, pathos-less green leaves — they were sharp and thorny like the tin acanthuses on grave-lamps; while the fan-shrubs were grey with oblong, octopus-like unfurling leaves and blue-stained brush-flowers. Among them big, broad trees rose, wild like the trees on Tristan's island, but something in their manner indicated that they were somebody's private property.

In those days I could hardly imagine that somebody can be the real owner of things that they cannot permanently take in their hands, which are bigger than their owner: to put it precisely, in the foliage revealing huge ruptures (I'm synthesizing the summer and winter vista here) I admired not the fact that, in spite of everything, property's golden-grey hoarfrost trembles on them (is it light? some kind of dew?) but that people should claim that all this belongs to somebody — what I considered almost impossible. I have still not got used to the mythical correspondence between proprietor and property, and for me the legal stipulations to ownership, leaving by will and inheritance mean the most perverse excitement and the most vertiginous diversion; with what incandescent self-servingness is the independence of an oak tree, a wheatfield, a granite stair or white-mossy flock of sheep expressed, and yet these can and should be placed within the concept of 'property': how theoretical is the idea of 'property' when placed next to the objects of property, and how little they adapt to the proprietor!

I expected that the thin iron net, cloud-sieve or 'property'-spider that I called above a meaningless gate, would resemble the owner, I expected that the oak trees' gestures would be exact copies of the movements of the people living inside (at that time I didn't know that only women lived in the castle). For a long time I tried to establish that unconfirmable shade that distinguishes the landscape beyond the gate from the surrounding one. Both inside and outside there were white-barked & black-crowned trees with gluey, salami-color flowers and soft, elastic cones; squat shrubs, beaten tracks, & car wheel traces hammered of wrought shadow, which almost rose above the ground, were then smoothed back into the ground again, like those plants with the flowers stuck in the earth for wintering out.

Beyond the gate was the realm of pain, this was the difference. The few iron planks rising with impossible slenderness above the shrubs (so then property is thin, zigzagging, sharp and minuet-like: property is necessarily some kind of rococo symptom face to face with ownerless nature — I concluded from the gate's style) made me taste the blind sweetness of predestination, the concrete nature and certainty of foreignness, beauty, otherness, and impossibility. Impossibility: a positive object. Beauty: absolutely another's. The essence of the essence: never-to-exist island. The first equation ('impossibility: is') made me almost rejoice with its empirical transparence: so far I couldn't believe that impossibility is inserted into the world, into geography every bit as much as the milk jugs or the old women's wooden sheds are inserted into the next village.

The landscape beyond the gate resonated like a string orchestra, while the parts this side kept mum like Shakespeare's text in my father's library. I've preserved to this day this childhood correspondence between impossibility and music, fate and cantability, that's why I love Mozart so much (for otherwise I'm tone-deaf), because I see in him so well this Biedermeier gate, engraved on the gold-tormented evening sky behind; the trees are buried in the deaf ponds of miracles, the birds fall back into their nests like morsels between the vacuum-cleaner's lips; the waters turn cold and fragile in an instant, the flowers' faces start glaring like the faces of the agonizing or of London revue girls at the curtain call: and hovering above this sunset auto-da-fé with its featherlike tranquility is the iron gate, like a small blazon or monogram in the visiting card's corner, which fell from Noah's Ark and is floating now, Ararat-less, in the froths of the Flood. (What about true rhetoric? I might get there yet.)

I have also instinctively sensed that the shady thing I felt would be 'life' for good, unchangeably, and so the Raffaellesque Sposalizio with eternal negativity came to pass. Why should I not have been proud of it? By feeling once, more profoundly than ever, that the park, the gate, the paths, the castle were not mine and I could never have anything to do with them, a glaring kinship was born between me and the park; what is more, I nearly took possession of it: this great, wondrous property was mine so little that the infinite sensing of this fact gave me the indubitable right to somehow feel it mine, as inwardly belonging to me, to imagine it as my property. The maximum of possession started with the maximum of giving up. Did I lose it or did I find it? — I mused then, on my way back home.

once again about private property; æsthetics

This, too, is ad acta 'materialism': I was looking for properties, feeling that ownership is paradoxical, in fact impossible, the hurling of butterfly-nets toward fiery heavenly fish; property is always alien, it's always somebody else's, & the more I squeeze it, the more I feel that its legal backbone and moral lips are receding from me. For me every object was the bitter-astringent chypre-paste of melancholia, I smeared them on myself like the balm of distance. In vain I acquired them, the childhood memory remained sovereign: the flowers were not mine, it was just the 'un-ownable' flower that happened to be next to me. Shalt thou not covet what is thy neighbor's? I always covet it, but merely because the moment what is my neighbor's becomes mine, I can truly glimpse in the mirror of 'property' the eternally-young, forever-provocative face of the eternal 'what is thy neighbor's.'

Beauty & the property of others became synonymous: when in the pitch dark I glimpsed the white stones of a garden gathering into large ice blocks the night's clumsily hidden Moon-atoms, that bluish-impertinent path gave me the utmost fairytale pleasure, because it was foreignness incarnate, somebody else's property. Blueness, coldness, direction, surprise, Moon, grooming: they all meant property, they had no independent natural or psychological value. When I wanted them, it was their foreignness, legal otherness that I wanted to embrace: if somehow they had become truly mine they would have been worth nothing, I wouldn't have felt the moon, garden night, coldness under the naked feet anymore, because I had no organs of sense, only a legal hallucinating faculty.

I have already said that I want to compete with the de luxe edition poets. As far as sensitivity goes (probably the least important in the whole bag), I certainly could. When I watched the gate's grid I realized that one of the characteristic features of the poet, of the genuine poet, is that he feels the most actively beauty's remoteness from us: the philistine, the petit-bourgeois as a rule owns beauty: he palpates it in his postcards, food, wife, & cinema. The poet at most wills it, intimates it, sets up hypotheses, has by and large only superstitions about it, but no exact knowledge. In certain manuals or 'Geistes'-books the whole of art history makes [296] the impression of a company or Ltd. that mass-produces concrete beauties, the way the textile industries produce fabrics. Although the opposite is true (evidence? my childhood garden nostalgia which my relatives still to this day cite as the main argument for my bleak materialism): the whole of art history means one great negativity, the spectacle of beauty's impossibility, of its concrete absence.

But what do I care about all this vacuous æstheticizing? My sentimentalism will probably not turn Doric if I dry it into theories but rather, by highlighting its greatness as my personal experience. For me beauty has always been a personal problem: a mix of comfort, London woman, fairytale, God, and Exeter. If you will: everything was æsthetics and nothing was æsthetics. Æsthetic experience? Von unten?[297] Is there such a thing? Is there anything other than that? How limited was all æsthetics when it divided 'beautiful' things from the rest as though dividing asses from horses. Just as everybody feels the Bible individually, so we do with beauty, too. (And why should an Anglican priest not speak in a Luther centenary manner?) Just as the music of the spheres is no supplement, added accompaniment to the harmony of the star orbits, but that proportionability is already a musical focus, so beauty was no separate circuit of experience in me or circuit of objects in the world, but the very rhythm of existence. Pan-æstheticism? Balderdash. Balderdash, because by 'everything' we mean a 2000-volume inventory of the world, and under 'æsthetics,' some kind of fancy sweets from heaven. Is something beautiful because it exists?

Are these vitalist dogmas? Naïve philistinism? Am I being rude? I've always loathed arguments. Let the Catholics argue, they have everything that's needed for the job, theses, uniforms, imprimatur.

Truth is a process that lasts as long as the human being lives. Before death I am not yet truth but no error either. Beauty? Perhaps beauty is nothing else but the potential of one individual & unrepeatable life to be truth when it is completed. Death is the movement when beauty turns into truth: and at the same time, pointless, useless, empty. Beauty is negative truth, truth is negative life, life is negative god…

To make telegraphic statements about the relation of beauty & truth: for me this is a form of swearing, of fatigue. That's why I don't apply myself to the medieval teachings about universals, because to my ears they sound rude: the entirely universal concepts are in fact naked bedsprings, the impertinent pleasure mechanisms of automatism, which make whatever is attached to them reverberate at infinite speed until the point of stasis, be they clocks, love, or philosophy. Between special and universal concepts there is only such a mechanical difference, of tempo: the one works fast and the other slowly.

And there is something provocative in infinite speed, something blasphemous and oath-like. Probably some law of thermodynamics applies to logic as well: in time all meanings will dull down to some neutral level, with the ineluctable sleep-sickness of intellectual entropy, and universal concepts (beauty! truth! acrobat oh! …) are the ones that run at the highest speed toward their own center of meaninglessness. Every special concept is an artificial byway, so that meaning doesn't plunge with a gravitational greed toward its own nil-core.

'universals': non est

Meaning is unimportant, what matters is that on that Christmas Eve I returned home crowned with the wreath of negativities: behind me, snow and summer night, dawn-grey water-velvet and sunset gladiola-pauses, all matter, all true climate, to-be-argumented scent & hour; on my head that certain wreath, the wreath of beauty, life & truth, on which every flower bloomed on another's stem, and every stem grew out of another's root, and so on to infinity: they were positive flower faces, it was only their beginning & continuation, their contours & essence which were running into foreignness.

Everything is, that alone is certain, but everything is only by being something other than it is. Flowers are not masks (beauty, life, truth) but bridges, corridors; the hiatuses between pearls in a great row of pearls that is perhaps twisted around God's neck (Calvin pardon me!). And yet, if I remember well, everything that logic and æsthetic ever speak about are pearls. Poor patronized metaphors, scolded-to-death products of Victorian luxury, what if grandpa pushed you to new authority in the intellectual field?

So on that Christmas evening of my puberty I had one correspondence in my hands (O dualismus pastoralis), the beauty of nature and the negativity of concretenesses, what is more: the beauty of nature stems from the fact that certain thoughts are hesitant: what makes lousy logic can nevertheless serve as a gorgeous oak-tree. Non est: this was my birth-song. It lacked all doubt, despair, blasé acquiescence: I was ruddy, hungry, and my tears moved me to colorful satisfaction. When I look back on those times 50 years ago I have to observe that the 'non est' was not the de rigueur transient and all the more necessary childhood whim, but a genuine life program. And still today I can't say anything else: non est.

Perhaps I will end up in a whimper (perhaps that's what I've been doing all the while), I don't know, but for the time I'd rather go without. And yet I have to mention that all in all mine is not a bad performance, to feel no trace of happiness, no trace of joy in a lifetime: c'est classique.

When I started writing these *Meditations* I also had one goal in mind: to analyze absolute (that is, the one lying far beyond the simple sense of sadness) unhappiness. True joy? Absolute happiness? Is there anyone who has ever felt that? Very many, and we shouldn't turn our noses at everything that starts with 'absolute.' People often tell themselves and each other that 'in fact I have never truly lived,' or, 'there was not one happy moment in my life' (at least half of all the music-hall songs are variations on this sentence), but on such occasions they always imagine events of the kind that lacked the pointed flutes of joy that they had imagined and sought but never experienced, and precisely because of this procedure they never realize how unhappy they are in fact.

When I utter 'non est,' I am not thinking of a happy life story passed up or an unhappy life story lived through, but look on my bare soul without narrative and without object, one single point, the colorless apex of consciousness, its abstract needle-point, for whose sake the whole 'life story' plays out, and which it should shift somewhere, to the left or right. If I relate 'non est' to that point of consciousness (north-pole revolving in one place above narrative's galloping Equator), then I can indeed see the darkness, the lack, the omission, the moronic hullaballoo: not narrative but one sole datum expressed in numbers. I'm not trying to say that what I feel is arid and devoid of feelings. Only something much more positive than I could find if I looked on my life-story.

If one thinks of one's life-story, what is drawn as a conclusion in the most rational and syllogistic way is a logical pain; but if one scrutinizes consciousness' bare point-nude from within, then they will select pain biologically, and it will flood them like new blood.

And blood is always melodic, even in the dimeshow variety theater. Most people are modest by nature, they content themselves with logical pain and do not try to switch it over to something essentially different, the lifelike. (Beautiful tree: pain-shaped tree; perhaps reality is nothing else but truth seen from the perspective of pain, etc., etc., merry Christmas to you, to your mother, to your father etc., etc.).

pain, dream, architecture. Project for a bedroom

When I started taking opium (alcoholism is vile and I persecute it mercilessly in my parish) I had no surprises: I didn't see new visions but recognized old ones, the ones that pain and universal 'non est' made me sketch about the world so far. This too is a version of the above-mentioned 'dualismus pastoralis' (was there an 'o' heading it above?): pain as a wave of emotion and the object world as hallucinating Xerxes pomp, always walk hand in hand. This is what makes visions so experientially drastic, and this is how they serve lucidity. Morphine comedies and modern architecture: for me, two pain styles. I hold a snow-white female silk blouse in my hands: it doesn't bend, being so light that it almost falls, the whole thing is much rather like mercury rolling apart than compact texture: there is no greater pleasure than to sink our hands into such rain-shaped material — one doesn't know if it's heavy & it's heaviness that causes it to collapse on itself so greedily, or if it is light and that's why it is not felt to be real but only a hostage breath entrapped in a cool environment. Half elastic leotard, half dogma-petalled silk: rubber & mirror at the same time. It is (they are) of an unattainable woman. I cover it in the fabric of pain and compare it to the narrow point of my consciousness: that's how my rigorous practical geometry is born, but also, the snake-fugues of morphine dreams.

For example, the pain-form of the shirt is this: a bedroom with sloping floor, undulating like a snowstorm on a hillside. The sloping floor is covered in a long-fleeced white rug (velvet, Smyrna or polar bear: unimportant): an arching ski track. There where the slope reaches the lowest point at the room's end is the place of the bed: there is no bed, only very flat pillows on the Smyrna snow. Above them, a large light blue metal lacework semi-dome: flowers & leaves that barely touch. And nothing else; one wall is glass, the others made of polished black wood — this is the ethical bedroom of the ethical Juan. Pain absolutizes: the shirt-white is turned into one sole Engadin-Sezession and the shirt's blue lace hem, into one linear planet. Every 'absolute' is the geometrical blazon of pain at some unattainable reality; in my Exeter abode 'reductio ad absurdum' is pronounced inductio ad dolorem.[298]

There is something prolonged, gluey, monotonous, & polished in pain, like the mirror of tropical black waters buried in a forest. If the snow-white, blue-trimmed silk shirt is thrown into such a mirror, we will get the above bedroom design with the utmost ease — with its cream-golf course stretching into infinity and its great blue grid-scars. That is, the setting up of absolutes is no logical operation but the most common optical illusion of sentimentalism: our new architecture is not 'rational' (thickhead engineering) but fatally only-lyrical. Under the influence of opium the shapes of the shirt morph not into absolute forms but into movement, eternal change of places: the lace's blue becomes movement, blue-movement, as if the colors' hidden drama-spool were suddenly dissolved and, instead of becoming space wedge, turns into endlessly spiraling time-corkscrew. This, too, is pain's musical impotence-score: the trace of helplessness' propellers on time's impatient waters. That's how my betrothal with materialism began.

musical plans

At that time it had not yet fully dawned on me that I am quite monumentally tone-deaf, so I fooled around composing some dark pastoral around my token 'non est': it began with a star motif, with cold, screeching, sharp violin tremolos which were then taken over and broadened by the violas, cellos, and double-basses, so that the one nervous and drizzling star of Bethlehem is transformed into a star-storm, August night shower of falling stars. After the two kindred motifs of 'lone star' and 'shower of stars' had time to develop, suddenly two blunt, desperate chords sound one after the other, the motif of 'crucifixion': the first on softer bassoons (is this the cross's horizontal tree?), the second on the ripped throats of trumpets (the vertical one?).

After this, the strings' ostinato 'star-shower' is heard once more, for the whole thing to collapse, with almost jazz-like glissando (the word 'jazz' is a gift that the sixteen-year-old boy receives from his fifty years older self) into the night-motif of 'unredeemed world' like burning coals into water. Under the cellos' homogeneous texture uncertainty stirs: on the oboes the Edenic idyll glints here and there, the broken melody of pagan love, then after asymmetrical pauses, the grotesque sounds of sin, grunting, and imbecility: 'the world is happy and imbecile,' this is the meaning of the whole passage.

The motif of the night starts rarefying without being torn up: into the pauses a few of the advance-tones of the 'Mary' motif insert themselves. In part the 'Mary' motif contains vulgarly hard serenity and in part, fateful exhaustion. The next part is a trialogue of three motifs: in the depth the motif of 'crucifixion' continues rumbling and murmuring (winds), and above that hesitant and fiery scaffolding the Eden-idyll and 'Eve' motif quarrels with

'Mary.' Absolute frivolity, absolute purity: both are alien, abstract, glistening, triumphant & inhuman; under them, the ineluctable Golgotha.

Two culmination points follow: the rampant 'cross' motif collapses on top of the screaming Eve-motif, like a felled forest — of the whole chaos only the folk song-like part of the Mary motif is left, very quietly, and under it the string-tremolo of the 'lone star' stretches gradually. These two themes prepare the Nativity. Which is nothing else but the 'crucifixion' motif transformed into a march; a desperate triumph. The whole is completed by a 'landscape-descriptive' passage: the Park. (Obviously this was not music but rhetoric: it was not the 'Mary' motif wrestling with the 'Eve' motif, but I was mixing my Eve & Mary portraits, developed for preaching purposes, purely logically and independently of music, and giving the account of this operation in the style of lousy concert broadcasts. My ears had long been tone deaf, & my soul had not yet been converted to the priesthood.)

landscape fragment and private property

But what do I care about these inanities of 40–50 years ago? I have preserved two images of the castle: one is the solitary hair-thread gate, which didn't as much as suggest the huge fortress it led to, and the other was a fragment of a wall by a small brook, the foot of one of its towers, whose upper part already disappeared in the tree-crowns. How curious that we have no ready-made words for such eternal unities that might represent both these images and the uncertainties that they mean throughout a lifetime.

I said earlier, 'fragment of a wall,' 'foot of a tower,' & 'by that small brook,' although essential in the landscape fragment was precisely the fact that none of its architectural element was definite.

I had no inkling of the castle's ground plan, I merely felt that this bit of a tower must be asymmetrically placed on the building, somehow sticking out of the whole like a flower grown sideways in the pot. As a result for me the castle became a living being, much more alive than the deaf & mute brook or the forever trembling leaves. As though I had unmasked the castle, I watched this ironing iron-like stone grave among the bluish moss & Moon-tinfoiled branches. Inside there was perhaps a big lunch going on, while I caressed them: I put my palm on the wet, mud-slimy green stones, as Catholics touch their rosaries to Saint Anthony's grave in Padua.

There's property for you: grown into water, moss, acacia trees, free for all to touch. It's like a root or a crystal, it's not cropped or touched up 'private.' There's property: first, a solitary grid gate & nothing more; and now a bit of rock with lizard and frog intarsia in the knot of one-meter-tall leaf mineshafts. I couldn't imagine anything more vertiginous (and to this day I can't) than to enjoy here at the same time the glaring Sezession of free solitude and the foreign and cold discipline of private property.

What can property's magnetic sphere be like, how far does it extend with biological vitality, and where does its theoretical legality originate from? At home every object of property was all the time tended to, repaired, the flowers were watered, their numbers known exactly. How can the furniture, the trees, paths and stones feel, knowing that their personal portrait never features in the owner's mind or hands, but only in general, like things falling this side of a certain border? As I watched the stones with the blooming water & rock flowers, it seemed to me that I could discern this indeterminacy and duality in them: the faces of the leaves trembling to shadow-powder were like the faces of wives who thoroughly enjoy married life but never have children. They didn't belong to the forest, but neither did they belong to the owner, and in this dubious juridical opal-field I felt at home. This moment definitely betrothed me with sorrow, & I have been faithful to it ever since. With highborn people I think there was (perhaps still is) a fashion of repressing pain: I have no talent for such clowning, I like boasting with my pain: the only material of my Sunday sermons is the list of my afflictions. The posturing, the boasting with my torment is just as healthy an amusement for me as eating. But so far I haven't got to truly wild self-exhibition, finish-line tastelessness.

against certain kinds of paradoxes

Of course the exaggerated cult of buffoonery in the form practiced by Anglo-Catholics and their fellow converts is not to my taste: buffoon-logic, buffoon-ethics, hygienic sophistry. There is in it a kind of naïve exhibitionism: "Look at me and rack your brains on how Francis' bloody stigmata can suit a floury clown face, and the ascetics' whip, Worthington pale ale. We are saints and look, look, how we laugh out all the while." They are trying to mechanically outdo the depraved; automatons produce such theses as, "the pleasures of marriage are more perverse than those of changing your lover on a daily basis," "Don Juan was philistine, & St. Theresa, an empirical socialite," "God is an eternal sophism, Anatole France is a rigid dogmatist," "Puritans are decorative, baroque Jesuits are simplicity incarnate," "there were the epigones first & long after them came their models," et cetera — these are all the Catholics' shticks: they are true, but their mechanism is too facile, they suit me perfectly, I could even churn them out big style (and with genuine faith, not in jest!), therefore they are suspect through & through in my eyes.

Paradox is probably the only intellectual reality and the clichés above are useful steps, but only steps, which, although they proceed punctually toward the goal, can never reach it. People always walk in the right direction, but what use are directions to us? A direction is ab ovo infinite; a correct 'way' is ab ovo eternal. Truth, the mother-paradox (I'm not meaning this in German, for it would become merely a run-of-the-mill Galton photograph[299] about the series of our psychic fiascos) has to be taken by surprise from the back, by some byway, without allowing the malicious detective instinct of uncovering to get the upper hand on us.

silence

But all that interests me now is this silence around the castle's hidden cornerstone, where the 'materialism' I've been charged with came to be codified inside me. I've been often intrigued by the melodic structure of silence and I would have liked to take apart its entangled motifs, to sound them one by one (do such stupid finesses only ever occur to the tone-deaf?), without interferences, but at the present moment the ethical nature of silence attracts me more. This was already present in me in those days, and now of course all the more: to look for the moral prism through which silence branches out and is broken down into separate ethical elements.

Everybody who has dipped a finger into it at least once knows that silence is an ethical tension, a moral battery. But it seems that without the dandyism of metaphor we cannot proceed, so: is silence a moral fugue with infinite voices? is it mere vacuity? These are my redeeming axioms (to express myself in neo-Catholic fashion): demagogic sound *&* fury, Paul's sounding brass or tinkling cymbal — these are my staple foundations. Have I built anything on them? Hardly. With me thought is like blood circulation: has my blood reached somewhere in its eternal return, does it have a direction? But it means everything. Thought gives life like blood;

it's a biological tool and nothing more. It surrounds me like rustling foliage surrounding a tree-trunk, or bell chimes surrounding a church tower. It's the continuation of my portrait, a layer at least one meter thick, within which I am still very much myself, outside of which I fade out, and then the other person begins. My thoughts are nothing more than the zip fastener on the water that stretches behind a propeller. Neither useful nor empty speculation. Morphine taught me by far the most in this respect: will I ever be able to speak of it?

*the relation of truth and language,
the dilemma of identification or fiction*

Vision cannot be translated: all mankind should be morphinists, but before all the world's members lifted the opium pipe to their lips, an injection should be invented to keep the social instinct alive even during the haze, and so the sleeping could invent some kind of language to convey the morale of their dreams. But that would no longer be interesting: the foundation of all wisdom is, that language is inadequate to a thought we feel. What is truth? — Pilate asked, laughing: they should invite an old Anglican vicar from Exeter who might chat out something to him, provided the Archbishop of Canterbury is fast asleep, his ears stopped with cottonwool. (Is Lambeth draughty?)

Truth is the natural side product of the laughable fact that humanity invented the wrong language for itself, or rather, that every language is wrong as such. So truth is a linguistic question; one sub-branch of linguistics, semantics is concerned with it. To mean something? To misname something? To be identical with something? Can there be some difference between an arithmetic sign & the so-called concrete word? It is such questions that research 'truth.' Truth is a calculus of deferral that expresses language's lagging behind a given phenomenon. A 'great truth' is one that is able to express, in its delayed state & from the elements of delay, the feelings that we imagine to go together with being-on-time: to assemble from the components of a train station, like a mosaic, the face of the distant landscape, the one where the missed train was headed. Let's imagine that the world invents opium language: it will not bring relief. Truth exists so far as fallacious, hiatus-filled language exists. One can imagine an automatically and continuously 'enriched' language made up of an infinite number of words: there where it is spoken they don't know the concept of 'truth,' its problem, its nostalgic images of desire.

There are two things we can do with a phenomenon: we either name it alpha, or we ourselves turn into that phenomenon. We either say a bluff, a factitious arithmetic grunt like 'vetchling,' or join ranks with the vetchling & become it with an Ovidian curtsy. We are galloping big style into the thicket of scholasticism (for even old fogey Protestant priests deserve their funny Christmas present once in a while, don't they?): art does nothing else than attempt to smuggle reality into the relationship between name and object, or rather, to create some relation in that lack of relation, elementary not-belonging-together, which stretches between alpha and phenomenon, the word 'vetchling' and the vetchling. The fallacious index of names should be fallacious to the utmost: this is the artist's best interest.

The world is a model: let's suppose it's a Greek statue head. This is what students (artists) need to imitate and express. (Here I'm not going into the relationship between these two concepts. In the above-mentioned infinite-word language there would be separate signs, for instance, for all the transitional shades and dilemma scales of 'imitation' and 'expression,' so the relationship of the two words wouldn't constitute a problem.) The Greek head is made of white marble. Student number one gets a marble block, on which the model's features are already carved out, all that's left is a few finishing touches. Student number two has only grey marble with features barely signaled. Student number 12 has a box of white oil paint, a treatise on Greek satyr dramas, and Rembrandt's pocket watch. Number 3874 (that's me! Oh charming happiness of Adamus Chrysostomos Paradisopaccer!)[300] has a meteorological time-chart, the model's faithful copy made of stable gas, & a historical hypothesis about the Jews having erased the 11th commandment from the Bible. What a horrendous work I need to do to imitate with these tools the Greek marble statue set before me as model!

But while I crumple, take apart, mix my three absurdly anti-sculptural tools (that is, words), what an infinite number of 'truths' I will discover: proportion relations, the relations between the tools, and those between the tools and the model. Student number one will never discover anything. An arbitrary (senseless) measurement, an unknown phenomenon, and the relation between the two: these three elements are the 'dramatis personæ' of thinking. The relation may be true, but this is always made possible by the applying of a hazardously adopted, meaningless sign ('vetchling'). To put it melodramatically (it will yet serve for a sermon core): on one side, an algebra of whim, on the other side, blind 'Ahumanum,' & between the two, a temporary relation-bridge; temporary, because it lives from the sign, and the sign was created on a whim.

It is silence that interests me now. This silence has featured in a relatively recent opium vision too, & I haven't been able ever since to subtract that preposterous stylization, solution, essence-impudicity from the memory. But remembrance itself already functions according to the laws of opium: that is, it is the source of the laws of editing. True composition? Kaleidoscope accidents heated by the obsession of logical causality (only the obsession stands a chance of being validated, not logic by a long shot): to dream, to sleep, to get drunk, in order to find 'logic' as fever-evidence, a necessity as powerful as sexuality. Logic is the shadow of time on the fruit of yesteryear, and opium is compressed time that piles up in irregular waves in our heads, 20 years in two seconds. To devour time: to fall into logomania.

theme for a short story: the vision of fastidiousness (Avido)

In my youth I wrote an anti-Catholic, anticlerical satire, which I first experienced, when it was very far away from any parody, and then made into a satire, and finally it was placed into an opium constellation where it underwent very real idealization. Opium: parodies turn mechanically into apologies due to the infinity of visuality. Every lie — for example, that 2 × 2 = 5 — is harried into image madness, & will eventually become an arch-truth to worship: pictura non potest esse non veritas.[301]

Parody-thesis goes like this: a married young man is in love with his wife's friend of old, but vows that he will never as much as utter her name or invite her into their house. For that friend lives in a distant, inaccessible castle where one can at most lurk around among waters, towers, bridges & moats. Once he dreams that if he should break his vow, Lauro Avido, the pope's secretary, would die immediately. The young man withers entirely (comme il faut)[302] from his repressed love. At one point he finds out that the friend had a fallout with her family and fled to the woods, where she lives in a solitary hut. He cannot resist the temptation and runs to her. He embraces the girl, who immediately rejects him and sends him back to his wife.

The young man doesn't quite know if he has broken his vow or not: he allowed himself that embrace almost like a prize for having so literally kept his promise up to that point. He has a sinister premonition about Lauro Avido. He goes to Rome. There the following pass: a young theologian has returned from his travels deep inside China with the news that he has found Paradise and Eve lives there in eternal youth. This young theologian is one of the pope's most rigorous rationalists, not one of your loony types: the whole court, pope, cardinals, bishops, abbots sail out in secret toward China. The only soul left in the Vatican is Lauro Avido, the pope's plenipotentiary procurator, almost a pope himself. The empty Vatican: dark green ponds, golden-yellow columns, library, light green night (did the whole story originate in the word 'ponds'?).

Avido falls ill: the enhanced beauty of the deserted Vatican gardens is parallel to his worsening bouts of sickness. Does he fall ill from beauty? From loneliness? Analyses. In the meantime a heretic traveling preacher incites people to abjure papacy. Avido is dying: he raves, terror-stricken — throwing codices about, boozing, destroying, dancing, setting things on fire.

The young man in love arrives in Rome at the same time as Luther. Avido is just jumping into one of the garden ponds: Saint Peter a suicide? There is not a soul left in the chancelleries, there are no cardinals or priests in all Rome: is all Christendom duped? People lose their faith, within one year there is not a single Catholic left in the world. The young man knows that if he had not embraced the girlfriend's knees in the forest hut, religion could have flourished. He had exterminated Christianity with one caress (in fact it didn't even amount to an embrace). People have to be converted again: for decades he walks the streets of Europe, repenting and converting, without success. At some point he gets into a forest: it was here that it featured as my dream-setting (that is, everything) the blue water, bloom-heap, and bud-Schlamastik surrounding the castle's corner.

From the tree's shape, the flowers' color, & the grass' softness the young man concludes that in fact he himself is the pope; for if there is one sole Catholic in the world, then it is self-evident that only he can be the pope. His argument — not that he needs one — is the forest's visual system of emphases, from which his papacy logically derives. In a state of inebriated bliss he runs to the Vatican. Ex cathedra he legislates his most preposterous desires to dogmas. The pope decreed so, thus he must believe it: and believe he does, who is a codifier of dogmas and pious believer in one person.

Meanwhile, the wife's friend had peregrinated to China and met the pope (the real one) & his court; they had found Paradise there and debauched themselves, but there depravity was no sin of course. She steals the tiara & the keys and sails back to Rome. He meets the young man in love, who has just proclaimed to himself (to 'the whole of Christendom'), surrounded by a thousand candles, her worship. The girl kills him with one stab: adulterer. The dead pseudo-pope's wife appears; the girl wants to desecrate the corpse, but the wife, her erstwhile friend, stops her. In response, she has the wife jailed, who continues doting on her husband even now, and although his one caress has exterminated all Christianity, she doesn't consider that caress a sin. The girl feels that she has saved virtue; like a drunken harpy, she squats in the middle of St. Peter's, caressing the tiara & the keys with her long, bony fingers until the moment when their rightful wearer should return. The triumph of virtue: the pseudo-pope husband and the faithful wife (faithful to a sinner!) are damned.

problems and possibilities of editing;
novel structure and ground plan of a villa

I wanted to write about silence and I feel that the previous pages are full of ruckus and mishmash. And yet, silence is the greater unit into which I would like to assimilate my entire life — that silence around the castle's cornerstone. It too was full of dots, lines, colors, different materials and unaligned small movements, but it was mute, not as the opposite of loudness but as an unknown third state. Was it musical? ethical? These are impotent anthropoid questions, to which memory doesn't react. But I would like to imitate the duality I encountered there: how could a million insulated, linearly autonomous leaves become foliage-silence? How could, in spite of everything, the water's soft-rigid spacemirror, the air's million dust-specks, the trees' roughness, fuse into a landscape dream? What was the cause of harmony? How could the catastrophe of my percepts, diverging in a thousand directions, merge into one unified whole?

The word 'merge' is totally inadequate, for silence didn't suck out the buds' individual forms and smells into some kind of common and neutral tedium-mass. My life is unified like that silent forest landscape, and yet when I jot it down for myself it becomes dispersed like any page of a newspaper, on which politics, prose tidbits, murder, weather and the stock market of grain are printed in five different kinds of fonts. Should I kill off my associations, as some London magazines advise? I could never do that: I cannot erase, and neither can I select. Is nature, too, often a classicist? Perhaps; in any case there are still far too many things in it and nevertheless it manages to be harmonious. Did I turn so soft in the head at 60 to take literature for nature? I have experienced that such zany mixing up of concepts can at times be the prologue to bringing essentials to life, that's why I stick, with optimistic mulishness, to finding unity & structure by some 'novel way' (o dear!).

Selection, geometric proportions of chapters: these would be naïve elusions of my crowdedness of today; the tropical jungle cannot be 'harmonized' by trimming it after the fashion of démodé foreign gardens, for in that way we wouldn't harmonize the tropics but eliminate the jungle to the degree where it becomes a scanty European forest, and then gather that scanty European forest into a composition. Of these three moves the second is a hoodwink. Structuring doesn't necessarily mean asceticism, discipline with an ethical content; composition is, after all, not something linear, it is not transparence and not mathematics. Neither was my life, although it is one and 'composed.'

Am I biologizing away æsthetic principles? Are these the sole alternatives then — linearity, or biology? Mathematics or life? Alternatives never say anything, in them it's always about the same thing, never about two. Mathematics and life: here I either take the 'part' of mathematics, looking at things from its perspective, so life is a mere empty biological negative of 'mathematics,' a mechanical counter-image or barren verso; or I situate myself on the side of 'life,' and then it is mathematics that becomes life's artificial pendant, its counterpart that will appear a counterpart only in a decorative sense. Thus there is no reality in alternatives, only some half-reality supplemented with ornamental shadows, toy-contrasts, in which we can never find the rich, alien flavor of true 'otherness,' only a diluted, fainter version of the original thesis. The fact that I don't like mathematical composition doesn't mean that I would necessarily lapse into its polar opposite, biologism; the true answer to thesis is not antithesis but rather, some more elementary and illogical 'otherness.'

There are moments when I feel that composition alone exists in the world, nothing else, but if I check that fact (as I am now checking these *Meditations*) I am disappointed. It is as if a compositional line radiated from space, which influences the objects thrown into space like an electromagnetic field: space as such 'magnetizes' objects ab ovo into structure. A real landscape is always composed; the editing activity is inherent in the nature of all space. Time, however, is its polar opposite: an active decomposing force. (Music always stretches through time in a space cocoon, space mask, like in a diving suit to which life-giving space arrives via a tube across time.)

One form of the lookout for composition, for instance, is that while I write these lines I imagine some building around myself, some kind of physical space that could then exhale the great suggestiveness of order; it doesn't manage to order things, like some Pentecostal Holy Ghost-tongue gone off, which never settles in the apostles' souls but is left forever hovering above their heads, with such light and heat that Christianity withers underneath already in the bud, its history being nothing more than the strange parallel of dead apostles & pointless truth-magnetism.

Now, for instance, I want to desiccate the scattered events of my life with the following lapis lazuli of order: let us imagine a long, open hedge, about 40 m in length, of the kind seen in the Belvedere gardens in Vienna. Now let us place a glass snake on it in serpentine line, crisscrossing the hedge, a huge angular glass pipe, the way a snake coils around some rod on coats-of-arms in a diligent S line. There where the hedge and glass tube intersect, there is not a real shrub but the live shrub's faithful metal copy made of dense, glistening, hard green steel leaves. The glass pipe's U letters on both sides of the hedge are the individual rooms, whose doors are small, short tunnels in the artificial, wild-green hedge-wall. In my imagination I'm sitting in the midst of such a glass U, before me there is the sharp rectangle of the metal shrub, behind me the U's vertiginous curve, to the right, the thousand crammed leaves of the real shrub mass. All my chaotic percepts are thoroughly anesthetized: they are every bit as disorderly as before, but they are mute, paralyzed, ineffective when placed next to the strange, impassive, more spatial space. (Architecture is the digitalis of space.)

'Literature should not imitate nature': O, learned principle! But literature too is nature, and we need to research its natural laws, only from there can we get correct literary principles (are they necessary at all?). We need to examine the composition not of the artwork but of the creator: the relations and waves of the first associations of ideas, there's the secret of composition. Do I hear the finicky warning: 'psychologism'? I would call it rather *esse*-ism, the expression of existence. It's a very broad concept but an altogether narrow fact. To put, retroactively, unifying inserts among the preceding pages: is it a bungled piece of work if we should need pills for that? And yet it is so: it's precisely these 'sickly' violations that lead to the creation or intimation of true composition.

It's not that I am cultivating problems instead of solutions, but I don't sense any difference between the two latter concepts: if we shift the rationalist lighting a mere one centimeter to the side, the questions immediately lose their question shape and turn into facts; problems and answers differ from one another only syntactically. I remember a dialogue, or love of mine (for every dialogue worth the name, of even a few words exchanged with a woman, is already a complete love story) that played out on the seaside: what confusion there was in my soul, in our words and personalities, and yet, the flatness of the sea, the sky & the shore foisted unity on them.

landscape around the wife's castle

I could also consider (instead of the project for a villa above) attaching to every page of these *Meditations* the image of the castle's cornerstone with the porous leaf-canopy above (the leaves are so pressingly dense to render the otherwise perfectly normal phenomenon, of small gaps here & there in the foliage, conspicuous and unexpected): the sea of light green, whitish dots as they rise above the dark blue water and stop exactly 1 millimeter above the surface; not one branch, trunk, or crag is visible, so one cannot imagine why this one-million-piece leaf mosaic stops above the water when it could just as well pour into it like green powder;

in the blue mirror its shadow is an ink sponge that hangs from the real shrub by a hair and can break from it at any moment: then the whole shadow would sink to the bottom, unfishable. The shrub is one gold-dented wig and the water, one black mirror: no ray gets through shrub & foliage into the water. I saw both at the same time; the water had no inkling how close it was to turning into a Danæ.

The sun heated up my back, the water in front put a blue poultice on my face. One wave-valley was transparent like ether in which the pause-sign of a distant radio station sounds, and a wave-crest was dark and impenetrable like basalt, with the difference that one could feel it could become transparent any moment; and were it to turn indeed transparent, it would be not partly so, in rash-like patches, but all of a sudden the whole wave would change into nude transparency; its energy dies down, but its content becomes clear on the whole line.

I felt like being on the sea floor, so deep that even the water touches only in shreds, there is not enough water in the whole world to reach so deep down: the castle's cornerstone is in fact a sunken ship or forgotten anchor among the pearl-budding and grass-haired seaweed. Sometimes a red flower floated down on the brook: not in the water really but above it, because on top of the mirror cohesion was so strong as to expel from the water everything but a meremost minimum of the petals, leaves, and stems fallen on it. If only I could send, refrain-like among the previous pages of my *Meditations* and regularly, such a transient fallen flower or the entire small casket-landscape, or the seaside where I spoke with a film actress who was shooting there (the only extraordinarily beautiful woman I ever spoke with).

*theme for a short story about the beautiful woman,
the psychology of temptation, and the Garden of Faithfulness*

There was a legend somewhere about this 'one and only' (I seem to be evading, by three by-ways, the analysis of the psyche: landscape, architecture, & theme-textile): a man lives separated from his wife without being divorced by law, let alone in church. He is morally fastidious, so he remains faithful to her even in absence: with a dark, hard, sickly faithfulness, across which temptation stretches like a violet wire across the white sea floor. Faithfulness has its own liturgical rituals: lonely snacks in an elegant hotel lounge or at home; lonely springboard diving and swimming lessons in elegant, crowded spas — contrived, unnatural being-alone. His faraway wife, with whom he had spent unhappy years, once wrote him to 'be free,' but precisely for that reason he cannot betray her.

On a lonely evening a gorgeous film actress appears at his home: Susan Fleming? What is the difference between the previous beautiful women and Susan? The previous ones had all belonged to the category of 'human,' but the new woman doesn't; and not by all accounts for being 'supernatural' or a 'souly sort.' On the bodies and dress of the previous hotel-and-strand women there has always been at least one area that recalled the forms of sin, from where the devil typology could have been derived. From Susan's body all sin-hypotheses fall off; hers is a form of beauty that cannot be connected to sin. Newspapers would write things like, 'mechanized beauty' and 'abstract ground plan for showgirl,' 'technically derived impersonal beauty-scheme,' 'naïve philistine dimeshow doll-ideal,' 'apostate puritans' liberated temptation-formula,' 'Anglo-Saxon sex-constant made of cosmetic and medical hygiene-ideal,' etc. For me all that sounds balderdash: I have always understood by 'human being' some potential for sin & tragedy; even fashion, hairdo, lingerie, & interior design proclaimed their doloristic 'character' obsession. Susan lacks this utterly: of course she too cries, suffers, wails & dies like her fin-de-siècle predecessors, but it doesn't show in the least in her image, exterior composition: she stands at a remove not so much from 'being-human' as from the latest 'human-fashion.'

Susan is not external to ethics, as it is impossible: she merely radiates a different ethics than, let's say, a Courbet nude. Courbet and the showgirl: what a nice comparative moral sermon I could deliver on this theme if I were younger & had time. Which is the more moral? How they circle one another, like a propeller's two ends, moral consciousness and moral deed, and how they meet, baby-schmaltz and damnation, fatalism and prancing dandyism. In my young years I used to have Courbet-tailored, sinful desires, now they all have a showgirl shape: what kind of ethical change is subsumed? Have I become more sinful or more innocent? How amusing depravity's theory of forms, the history of erotic sin-taste must be.

The hero of my legend has fought the 19th century blueprint of temptation rather than temptation itself; his lonely years were dominated by a Courbet vision. To him Susan comes as a surprise: she is not tropical, motley, ornate, plump, nude & belly-dancing as the catechistic de rigueur temptation of St. Anthony, but pure, simple, of minimal elements and altogether rather puritanical than grandiose. 'Being human'? Could he have taken that Courbet croquis for 'human' and this real one, Susan, not? How could he be so wrong?

He looks back on the earlier women he rejected: they have all been inhuman temptation masks. (Thesis: "The influence of the idea of temptation on women's external appearance.") So far it was he who wanted women, hence his guilt-feeling — but he wasn't prepared for this Susan, this he didn't want, on the contrary.

It's Susan who wants him. Not with 'desire,' not with 'life,' empty words borrowed from the romanticism of sin-ology and biology, but with a desire style that falls far outside all love territories.

Absolute sexual indifference is the darkest sexual inebriation: it doesn't mean that the 'naïve damsel' is happier than the Freudian courtesan (in this binary opposition it's probably the latter who is happier) but that, just as we like almond-flavored butter more than almonds themselves, we love alien forms of life made of love's material more than love itself. Let's not simplify this hastily to saying that metamorphosed love is better than love's unadulterated raw material: this is not about metamorphosis. There are two separate worlds: the solitary psychic focus of love desire, and the non-love actions and conversations with the woman. The previous hotel and Lido-girls immediately mixed with love's fire, they were relatives of desire, between desire and woman there was a logically incestuous relationship. But between Susan and the old desire there was no relation whatsoever.

He fell in love with Susan immediately because the elastic balm of desire didn't stick to the body but ricocheted into the man's soul, and there it tautened and narrowed into one white point of light; from the woman's body an almost cold wind swished forth, blowing desire back into one point, scraping it together in the man's body. The ancient shtick of 'embrace' floundered: Susan and him were immediately far beyond 'love' and already talking about the stock exchange & African music. The man could resist 'love' but he couldn't resist woman: now he betrayed his wife.

Description of an afternoon tea under the yellow lampshade ('twilight' + actress with 10 lovers). During snack they hear a ruckus, he goes out on the street to see what happened. There was a murder, the watchman was killed by his wife's lover for going back to his estranged wife: fidelity's victim? He watches the street scandal, mortified, the agonizing man, the wailing woman. He cannot go back to Susan: something has intruded into his first-ever unfaithfulness the moment it happened. He runs to the 'Garden of Faithfulness.' Here the potatoes are fragrant but roses are rancid dreck, the corn drops golden seeds on flea-picking, rheumatic Danæs, but the sun gives off no warmth: everything is the other way round, topsy-turvy, in incalculable Nacheinander: this is virtue's madness, or rather, madness as the essence of virtue (no criticism intended).

I used to have a childhood mania: I daydreamed about discovering unknown works of composers from the past, which are indubitably authentic but written in an utterly unknown, 'modern' style; and then I set to compose these imaginary opuses. So did I 'discover' a Credo by Schütz, composed in Venice on Italian commission, which the master compiled from the variety hits of Levantine merchants spending some time in Venice; what was expressed in this Credo was not doubt, far less some pagan irony or anti-Catholic cynicism, but simply the fact that dogmas are strange, alien, sublimely grotesque & tumble-shaped. These Oriental, now sauntering, slowly-blued, now suddenly-luminous melodies in disarray sounded above a constant theme on the winds, more and more entangled with their irregular pause-ribbons, inorganic crescendos and fade-outs.

The legend's 'Garden of Faithfulness' resembled this imaginary Credo. Sometimes night lasts for five weeks, Moon & Sun appear on the sky next to one another, and sometimes the world goes dark for only five minutes, & only a part of the world. The rivers stop suddenly, as though they knocked into the dam of the air; the stars fall like the snow brushed off a blue overcoat, and pink birds sit in the sky in their place: ecce ultima fidelitas. (Moral triola: Courbet-temptation; Susan-reality; lunatic beatification.)

The murdered watchman dies in repentance, with God's name on his lips. After waiting in vain for the hero of my legend to return, Susan Fleming too goes out on the street; to her greatest surprise she sees that the angels have not yet carried off the watchman's soul, so she grabs it herself and carries it, together with the corpse, to a forest. The watchman wakes up, believing himself to be already in the otherworld and Susan, to be an angel. He adores her with ardent love, which he believes to be the heavenly beatitude of his purified soul. The 'Garden of Faithfulness' suddenly splits into two (in Switzerland at night the lakes and sky look perfectly identical, the mountains are merely black belts; empty lake and pouring sky appear on top of one another as the chalice above the head of the officiating priest, if he drinks the last drop too vertically), and Susan sails away with the watchman between the two shores.

My hero rests in the 'Garden.' No sooner does Susan's yacht sail out (its veil is a powdered showgirl shoulder-blade), his long abandoned wife appears. He runs to her but she turns from him in disgust: faithfulness made a cripple, a nebbish, a schlub of her husband. She holds up a mirror to him, then strikes him dead with an ash plant (the pink-blue stem of the Garden's faithfulness-plant). Her disgust is unspeakable.

The boat is flying with Susan: in? In thick white fog, traversed through and through by sunlight: grey substance, one can't see one centimeter ahead, but full of light and golden luminosity all the same. I've always been drawn to this duality: blindness and transparency. I've once seen something similar in a lake: the water was light green, almost leaf-blond, one would have expected even the fish, the Morse-signals at 100 meters' depth (long, even slides with a propeller-stir at the end) to show upwards, although the very opposite was the case — that brilliant, silk-souled water formed such a thick blanket that one could perhaps have a better chance to see its bottom in a black caustic bucket. (My volatile caustic mints happen to be black.) The water is so luminous that its vertiginous luminosity is already dimness: as though it was the thinnest net that one couldn't see through.

the lake's transparency and non-transparency; two kinds of landscape: infinite transparency and finite localization. Their connection to love

Could Susan have a more beautiful environment than this? Among my memories I used to particularize, to the point of frenzy, that bright mist & glistening-blind lake; in imagination I divide them into infinite transparency layers & proceed to examine those — each one is transparent, but on the last point there is something that hinders seeing through them. That mist and that lake are situated between a looking-glass and a window, you can't see through them, but neither do they reflect me; behind them there is some amalgam that insulates the phenomenon of 'transparency,' reflecting back or letting through neither me nor the things lying beyond it, and yet one cannot see through them. They always lure us deeper and deeper, because the ray pulls us through the mist toward the mist's non-existent kernel like a magnet; the lake's green ring-glints, too, pull us downwards; I feel I would need to bow only one centimeter lower to glimpse the resonant flora of the lake bottom (the flower of the depths is the musical score of the surface), and when I bow down and see no more than a closed light-openness, I again believe that now really one centimeter is all it takes to glimpse the foaming scores. And so on to infinity: from transparency, always only the multiplied, arrow-like & velvety-flying 'trans,' never once the palpable 'parency.'

Interestingly, with me next to this landscape type (for this too is a landscape, perhaps the loveliest: the even and infinite light-fog and the light-green lake, in which gilded sun-colored blindness hovers like a nervus vagus) usually its polar opposite also occurs (in my dream? in reality?). With the above-mentioned landscape everything dilates, everything widens to water or mist, while with its opposite everything contracts: the firmament (which so closely resembles the first type of landscape mentioned above) becomes one blue apple, the sea becomes one black bush, a mountain range becomes one black piano key, or rather, they do not become but already are.

This regularity puzzled me & I looked for its cause: why do I feel at ease in these pole caricatures instead of the so-called normal landscapes? Long before I first heard about all kinds of sexual symbolism from my son, in moral self-mortification I imagined I could so enhance my penchant for these two opposite landscapes, that it was my own subjective feelings of pleasure that found expression in the bright mist, in the luminous lake, so flooded by light & yet in which nothing could be seen; while in those contracting images where a dispersing reality becomes a minute concreteness-over-the-top (the sea becoming a shrub, etc.) — in these images the objective, bodily contours of real life, living women persist.

Because these are two different worlds: the subjective upper-C tickling of pleasure, and the objective, material form of certain women; hence two landscapes should go with them — for landscape is indispensable, landscape is the essential, life-most life. ('Life-most life': from such nil-words some charm-remainders somehow, sometimes awaken.) The two landscapes are made of materials of a different order: they relate to each other not like two flowers but like a flower to a mineral. The amorphous landscape, let's call it 'pleasure landscape,' is in fact a new mush, a desire oriented toward the creation of new material: textile-engineering inspiration. On the other hand, what we enjoy in the contracted landscape is substitution (in place of the sea, a shrub), the grating incongruence of the relation: logical inspiration. Textile and logic belong to different orders. To experience the most human and the most dramatic things in landscapes, where the human being doesn't even feature as a stage prop? old fogeys' recompensation? I live on two landscape types, as I have said before, although those too keep changing, kaleidoscopically. O, that kaleidoscope, perhaps that is everything. Am I keeping mum on it? Should I keep mum on it?

> *object before the human being. Its cause; an example: a Stuttgart film about the gloves, titled* Adam and Eve

My son has told me about a film he saw in Stuttgart, whose fundamental idea was taken over from a patient with a brain tumor. If I'm not wrong, its title was *Adam and Eve*, and the whole language consisted in rendering all the passion, humor, fiascos, and tragic openness of a night of love with the furniture of an adjacent room and the woman's clothes scattered about. For that certain patient always spoke of a pair of white gloves, drawing, dreaming, explaining it. Madmen are always in tune with the times and obey strict stylistic rules, something that is only natural, for they got into the workshop of fancifying-in-place from a fixed world of data. And still, you cannot avoid being touched by the manias' faithfulness to actual problems: within an epoch, the collaboration of mad and lucid is almost idyllic.

But all this is secondary: the truly intriguing matter is, why are so many spirits satisfied by objects better than by people? What can I discover in them that guarantees their superiority? That pair of white gloves and my landscapes are no different; landscape and object together possess something potentially more interesting than a character sketch. Can it be that they express character better? For however much one might see in these objects a liberation from anthropomorphism, they will not liberate us from it — on the contrary.

When we enjoy so-called alien movements, autonomous forms independent of man, what causes the utmost joy is invariably the fact that the unknown thing is the expression of a hitherto unknown element inherent in us. We know our own surroundings and then we discover a fantastic ice paradise on the Moon, where the ice-beds are rooted in the air & the blue glacier-curtains float like the clouds hung out to dry, et cetera: when our eyes absorb this impossible landscape, like some dented sheath the fitting screw, we will inventory it not as 'novelty' but rather, as a more precise graph of our well-known, prosaic surroundings, its more precise map, higher magnifying, the essence that out of absent-mindedness or ungiftedness we have never noticed before. And the more fatuous the Sezessions, the more foreign the foreignnesses that we come to know, the more positive the old surroundings will become in the process: every footprint of the step ahead will be shifted behind the point of departure. So is the object more human than the human being.

Sometimes when we believe ourselves driven by the desire to know our fellow humans better, in fact we merely want to get goose-bumps over their revealed, strange traits of character, wanting to taste the social acid of foreignness: the most ostentatious exorbitance is always inventoried like a more precise definition of the homely, and yet foreignness does have a boundary beyond which it will no longer fall back elastically into the known. At such points I want not to know but to repel the other person: during love-making I try to concentrate solely on the woman's perfume, so much so that she is rendered entirely unknown and her very existence is rendered a logical impossibility.

Is there any difference between absolute familiarity and demonic impossibility when a person is enormously important to us? Is the body of a woman we kissed not an eternal swinging between our own copy and a hostile object-god (handkerchief, handbag, sum displayed on a taximeter, etc.)? Do I want to get a fright, or to get used to? I couldn't tell if instead of a kiss I gawk at a manchette, on top of which a garter made of coral thread was thrown: have I unveiled my lover's 'intimacy,' or am I voluptuously forcing myself into feeling a sense of horror, error, deliberate vertigo, engineered amnesia? This is the point where 'Sachlichkeit' connects to psychology: the drab object is a more refined analysis than the logical threading of ideas.

The clothes taken off without the woman have always attracted men: since they could crumple and sniff her clothes, woman was symbolically in their power, like a captive criminal, while at the same time being transformed into the carrier of utter unassimilability, foreign-purposedness, ghostly, funereal lie, somebody one is in superstitious awe of and nothing else: 'character' cannot feel this alternating current on its narrower and more primitive territory. Love parasites the merging of impediment and purpose.

And another thing: the form of life-structure that best suits our ancient instinct is the fuga canonica, but instead of cultivating it, destiny proffers us disconnected, incoherent suites. Objects are better suited for fabricating canonical fugues than people or character sketches. The Stuttgart *Adam & Eve* made this fact forcefully evident: the pair of gloves lay about in a dark room, one on a hand rest, the other on the chair: the two related to each other as the dripping-diminishing stalactite and the ascending stalagmite sheaves. At once they incandesced, became linear and brightened up, light flew apart and the fingers' five forms hovered in it only as quivering sardine spines; later these sardine spines thickened to red strips and the gloves' incandescing whiteness thinned to small waves; it was now the line flaring into a body, and now the body running to a line, now chance flowing into essence, and now essence filtering into puny electric discharges.

Every impression worth mentioning (which indeed deserves that holy name) demands such a glove-fugue, and never the hand after the glove. The glove again, after the glove, this is 'sachlich' sexual instinct. But life brings the hands nevertheless, that's why we need to stick to the object, at the price of however forced methods (film-fugues, etc.). The 'real' hand is not the hand of the human being but the glove processed in the manner of a fugue: substantia equale fuga canonica accidentis.[303]

---
analysis of the stairs

Women always appear to me at the end of some suddenly lit graphic fuse; in the world I glimpse such hopscotchness or architectural scale of spaces and colors that will necessarily have at their end, I know, a woman. My greatest loves are in fact architectural riddles: they started with vast stair fantasies, column-chromatics, or hyperbole-faced double lakes.

One of life's greatest secrets & delights is stairs: once I dreamt of an infinite stair-world where the stairs were located more or less like different-content sheaths adapted to the mounds and earthen waves of a vast hillside landscape (Anacapri exultat glaucos);[304] wide, thick packets of paper tissues, half-open fans, vacillating harmonicas, toppled-over dominos, corkscrews & grit wrinkles.

This was love's ecstasy: all undulations and yet nevertheless regular degrees, geometrical angles. I loitered on the stairs, head swirling, every minute changing in my foot soles the actual and fitting sense of space, like Mercury changing the wing gaiters on his ankles; on the flat, membrane-like stairs that were in fact more the distracted wrinkles of a slope, green moonlight fell, cutting up the handrail's odd & even balusters into check colors; above the thick stair-ends a narrow, concentrated sun burned and washed away the shadows even from the crevices, like a flying razor removing the sky's black beard: this is how the female body's anatomy started, and I had felt a great urge to send this in to some paper's tidbit story-cobbling school which illuminated (practically at that!) such questions as, 'How to build a character?'

I only feel truly well on stairs, only there can I imagine human action, because all my deeds, all my narrative traits that play out in time are the imitation of some lurking female form. In fact a complicated flight of stairs is already heightened drama; if a hesitant page alights on it, he is betrothed to destiny from the first step. When I wanted to imitate Shakespeare in my youth, all I could think about were pantomimes with a great many stairs, on which the heroes and heroines roam about at will.

Quite evidently, stairs are the keyboard of space; but sometimes for a lordly baptism we should humbly dip our souls into the staid waters of the handiest metaphor. The female body is the best form of space in an extremely complicated, dissonant chord, but the stairs prepare that dissonance, allowing us to enjoy the weight, flavor, degree of resistance of spaces one by one. If stairs had nothing but such pedagogical rationale and preparatory tutorial character I would most certainly not like them: but there is something to them that provides a swift answer to an old psychic question. Or more exactly, the stairs are such an energetic sensory revelation that they immediately create a question, create the illusion that we have long asked and demanded it (which is untrue), and we enjoy this hallucinated demand-past even more than we enjoy the answer's meander-trumpets. O flowery night of wild solution's rush: the world is chock-full of answers, solutions, ready-made forms, and around these, like an optical play, colorful rings on a lens' rim, questions arise, not parasites of certainty but rather, its onward-demonstrating second flowerings.

The stairs are firstly a keyboard, but secondly a propeller: they emit sounds and propel in space. Woman is firstly and lastly space: to trigger the pleasure of all pleasures is a space geometrical shape. Stairs are the most primitive 'building,' but they lead the deepest among space's complex tissues, to the important experience of movement and octaves. Every single grade is in fact a horizon, a metaphysical meridian, calculated for me starting from the erotic

Greenwich-point of one female body, which prompts me to discover that the most whimsical zigzag, if reproduced, immediately becomes a rule and constraint. One sole spatial echo (or rather, 'space-reverberation') immediately creates a rule: this is the great utility and sanctity of stairs; I draw a winding line, repeat it 1 cm to the side & above, and lo, the dogma, the spatial law, the rule is born.

Stair-dogma unites the most frivolous method of production with the holiest effect. If we pour soft matter from a tube, molten tar from a barrel, it will congeal in the shape of a gradient hill: each stair brings to mind the invisible tube, and the energies, flagging from one stair to the next, of the individual pouring-out layers. The stairs always lead upward, elevate, but they do so almost despite themselves, because every single sheet of their body expresses the plane, longs for the plane, and flees toward the lyrical sea-level Eldorado: their monomania is the inane plateau, and nevertheless their profession is some kind of elevator. They suffer greatly from this fact. When broken off from the earth's muddy branches, crystals are as a rule shapeless like a glass wart; but if they are shattered, cut to bits, then all the torsos will be regular geometric bodies, mirror-sinuses, light paradigms. So I feel about these stairs; my desire is unnoticed space, combed out of my soul like a sticky bud from one's hair; but if I break (i.e., ripen into torsos) this filtered space (desire), what I get is the stairs' crystallized, cross-section forms: each stair is the cross-section of a longing.

By their nature stairs are a half-thing, like one of the two breakup surfaces of a statue: one always wants to have the precisely fitting, broken-off half. But instead of that other piece it is us, people, longing spirits who walk up and down the stairs, enjoying the non-fitting of the surface of our soul and the stairs' breaking surface. We cannot adjust to the fact that the stairs were made solely and exclusively for our feet, or rather, for our foot soles: when we dream of vast stair-seas, terrace-alluvia, it is not easy to come round to the conclusion that originally all this architectural crystal-jungle served no other purpose but that our foot soles, these comical little territories, could walk a slope more comfortably.

Whatever is needed for the foot sole we will imagine as footprint-shaped, like the forms of the bicycle and sewing machine pedals, or the forms of the foot-sheaths of old stirrups or barber's stools, so we would also feel moved to imagine the stairs like this: as leaves stand out sideways from the twigs, so would the cutout foot-shapes stand out from the branches, into which the human foot could fit. But these vast planes are a massive surprise for the foot soles.

Characteristically, a separate, emphatic form of vertigo is the stair-vertigo, and since I sometimes think that all nervousness and frenzy originates in someone feeling too vividly a truth they are incapable to express (logical discovery forced to silence), the stair-vertigo is in fact nothing else but the intimation of identity relay à la Russell [305] when referred to space: no kind of space can refer to itself, just as identity is not identical to itself, because the things that are in a relation of identity to themselves belong to a type one degree lower than identity: this is the stairs' spatial function ad maiorem Russelli gloriam. That fabled 'quidditas' always escapes next door; one (if he never walked on stairs) would believe that what belongs to a thing most closely is the 'idem eadem idem,' [306] that the closest to something stands itself; but the stairs teach us that the 'idem' is already next door, that the 'idem' itself is already 'alter'; the terza rima occurs to me, standing in the middle of a three-verse stanza like the stanza's gravitational point and essence, or kernel — but when I want to grasp that center and kernel, when I try to feel and palpate it as essence and kernel, I need to read the first and third verses of the next stanza, that is, the frame of another, foreign stanza, its most peripheral, thin surface. It's an old hat that desire is never directed at the woman but at an image of desire, behind which we can never place the actual woman but only another image of desire; desire is directed at desire, & so one desire in fact subsumes a whole, infinite chain of desires: every desire-pistil is the petal of another desire, and not even at the end of the chain (there is no end to it in fact) does the actual woman stand. If we have still somehow got to the actual woman, it's not by the path of desire. One of the most wondrous things, even with stairs, is that on them we still get to the first floor or a hilltop church gate; there is so much infinity in the step, so much impractical pleonasm, that it looks well-nigh self-serving.

Stairs are self-reflexive verbs: first I utter 'I,' then 'wash myself,' here already two I-s feature; then, that 'I know I am washing I,' here a third I is added, and we could continue this to infinity, so 'I' will come to mean as much as an infinite number of subject-zigzags one behind the other; the creation of a sole concept of 'I' immediately stirs into infinite tautology, at infinite speed on infinite waves. The exciting fact that every rational unit immediately multiplies a billionfold the moment we utter or think it — I first felt it in all its flamboyant histrionics on the stairs: viola pomposa tautologiae.[307]

finite and infinite; the relation between medieval allegory and 'sachlich' emblem

'Eternity in the instant,' 'infinity in the torso': I have always found these type of sterile games sickening, they are so much salon postulates. The psychic experience of infinity is precisely expressible, and beyond doubt it becomes conscious before the deduced and secondary percept of 'finitude'; for me the stairs were, among other things, the laboratory where I could grasp these experiences from up close, the most selectively. I realized that 'finitude' and the finite things are only global concepts cobbled together for convenience, pegs with which we can lift infinity at one point. The word infinity, in its theological sense, has never lain close to my heart, and it was certainly not my ambition to defend it for religious purposes, or to render it natural. But I have experienced it myself that man would rather go on echoing in eternal repetition, mirroring, multiplying, overproducing, so it's always by violence that we make a unique thing instead; the artist is the reproducer and the printer is the creator of unique objects.

If I understand the finite as an extract of the infinite, its characteristic focus, it's a completely different kettle of fish than going about with the lyrical swindle of 'the whole firmament in a drop of water.' Some are drawn to feel, so to say, the scent of infinity in a finite object (out of sheer modesty I don't dare think of a Greek statue, because that way I should convert to Catholicism, to confess it as sinning against the sixth commandment, don't Geistesgeschichte),[308] as though it were a mosaic-scale or pastiche made of the splinters broken off from God's body; but I see in it an organic part of infinity itself, one visible, real fragment of it. Yet here the 'infinite' means not religious plenitude, open perfection, not spirituality and truth, but some new thing (hundredth-sameth throat of self-reselving bird), which could be only expressed precisely, without the awareness of the opposition of finite and infinite, without being the lyrical mean of the two. First I mentioned 'extract,' then 'organic part,' and I set both in opposition to 'mosaic': don't extract and organic part stand in howling contradiction? No.

Let me add two things to this: first a historical nota bene, to say that excerpt and characteristic focus are two techniques of symbolization, the former used to be general in earlier times, the latter is general now. For instance the allegory of Nature used to be made (in older times) by daubing together in the one place trees, water, birds, fish, clouds (a kind of ontological 'beef in brief'); and now it is made by photographing, magnified 20 times, a fragment of salamander skin which completely fills the frameless image, so we have no inkling on what part of the reptile's body it occurs, or what it is at all: and it is precisely that, the more-mask-than-mask (a blond girl's potato-nose blackface falls closer to her than the salamander's fragment of skin, scientifically color-objective and magnified beyond recognition, stands to the salamander itself!) that we feel today to be 'characteristic,' 'characteristic focus'; it is only the unrecognizable that we can touch, as a Thomas in reverse: if the wound is a red bracelet, bijou de Herz, bijou de Boivin, only then can we bemoan it as a true sickness.

But now let us place these two styles of symbolism into the logical developer bath of dream: this is the second thing. (To 'dream & logic': the thought, the conscious thought stands in no howling opposition to the unconscious thought, we have arbitrarily designed consciousness as a criterion of value, with an entirely reckless optimism; the wakeful consciousness may be every bit as much a biological whim as that of dream, I feel no precipice between the two worlds, at most a continuity. Consciousness is a deformation style and so is dream; perhaps the one is Renaissance and the other, Gothic, this is all the difference between them, so dream is not more valuable for me than consciousness, merely a useful experimental milieu, just as the fantastic onward-developer of many morphine-induced thoughts is lucid consciousness.)

Before the dream mingling of encyclopaedic gathering-allegory and the salamander fragment let us take one more look at the salamander. It is the very proximate symbol and organic fragment of the same thing (that is, Nature): is this indeed what neue Sachlichkeit means? It is all appearance, and the exact opposite is true: with a symbol quite obviously only the relation between symbol and symbolized thing is interesting, and not the emblem's isolated theme; but in our case the salamander's skin in its isolated image nature is far more remote from Nature than the other, old-fashioned allegory on which trees, clouds, fish featured in a gathering tableau.

The scientific photograph of the salamander's skin can be set in relation to Nature only in the wake of an abstract ratiocination; moreover, like every too empirical fragment, it is itself abstract & so cannot be regarded at all as an organic part of Nature. For after all, the human being boasts with his dreams & for garnering praise he will risk quite a few didactic distinctions. How does the dream see the salamander and the allegorical inventory together? Perhaps as follows. When I'm playing bridge I often pry into the impression a clubs 9 makes on me: 9 independent little leaflets, neither shamrock nor number, and still, it means to me at the same time the unified notion of '9' and the few or many flowers of a falling-apart shrub, not a number but, to speak in the language of perfume, 'quelques fleurs.'

The way a blossoming shrub and a number are evidenced at once on such a card, so in my dreams the catalogue of trees, birds, lizards, and fish, and the black-and-white vortex of the salamander fragment also fuse, on a territory beyond the rough-hewn meadows of logic and image. I know that when one expects meaning and receives a comparison, he pulls a face like on the evening of a long-awaited concert, when he spots the announcement above the ticket office, 'due to the artist's death today's performance is cancelled,' but the whole symbolism issue is my own, personal nervousness far rather than genuine 'issue.'

explaining the catechism in the church

I am really bored, no less than my imagined reader, of these ruminations which are due solely to the fact that I used to explain the Catechism to small children every Sunday in the church, getting second thoughts after each explanation, that I may have told something too playfully or philosophically, or, as the case may be, too mendacious-subjectively and so forth, so in the evenings I would formulate all kinds of cunning excuses to an imaginary controller; sometimes for the sake of a slip of the tongue (symbol-mongering is hardly more than that) I would improvise whole theorems, instead of admitting the plain error of speech. I always remember those impossible Sundays with a shudder, 'l'après-midi d'un faune anglican,'[309] when I was alone with naïve little mouseys and the dim church's disproportionate secrets; in the church's upper regions pink and mauve lights floated in from the windows — the window's color patterns were simple & regular, every color occurred strictly in its place, sharply and exactly, but in the light those blazon fields oozed everywhere, as though they were emblems of the fact that behind every heraldic image some colorful fever is flexing its intrigues; whatever figure was painted on the glass, lions, pentagons, bears with briefcases, or blood-checked ostrich feathers, they could have only one colored strip for oblique projection in God's Calvin-faced hangar; they were indeed horizontally so prolonged that only a line could be seen of them; after all, that is the true, comme il faut Protestant optics.

The big rose glowed whitely, in fiery cream; the whole inner façade was so bleak as though it had been an external wall, & so it turned all homeliness inside the nave upside down. I was so afraid and felt so unsayably a stranger that I could barely concentrate on the children. When I uttered the simplest words I had the impression that I was luring them to sin, and when I was silent I believed I told them an extreme lie; in no way could I balance the children and the upper church's aristocratic phantasmagoria spectrum; all the lordly blazons went through and through me with their falling lights and tagged me with fornicating, heretic rain, as a glinting sigil: my soul was soaked in the essence of strange families.

O, thou Gotha chromatic fantasy, what was I to do with the children, the catechism, and on the whole, how was I to become innocent? I felt pressed down among the most authentic stage props of original sin in the décor-cellar of a dark 'institutio christiana'; I felt that Christianity's dawn acid was wasted on my forehead, because the light of the ripe blazons prancing on the church window performed a guignol-flavored counter-baptism on me, the better to throw me into damnation. The lower church was dark like a random act of some Romantic opera, but I could see no fear at all on the children's faces. One door opened on the lawn outside with a couple of trees, but this offered no consolation; the tree was like a human lung made of cotton candy, with silvery bronchia and dusty sponges.

At that moment all kind of dark anecdotes came to my mind: women and blood, inheritance and doubt, but these lagged far behind the idyllic wave of guilt-feeling. For the most curious thing in all this horror was, that it unfurled infinite pastoral instincts from me, like an acrobat unfurling infinite rolls from a small top hat; all around me death's great schemes lit their semaphores while I continued living among childish kisses, wigs, virginals and Austrian rondeaus. Are blood and childish purity, Gomorrah *&* Greuze[310] so proximate? Or was it simply because there were children before me? No, it cannot be, for children used to be conspicuously in my way whenever I wanted to be 'childish,' and if there is something children don't understand, it is the 'childish' behavior of grownups.

the atmosphere of damnation and idyll

In the meantime I went on with my pantomime and within seconds lived the painted family blazons: death and miming are always closely connected, in my childhood I couldn't tell the carnival masks in images from the ex-libris skulls. For me sin is a theater season, a natural temporal phenomenon that comes to the fore in certain months or certain parts of the day, like rain or wind in geography manuals; now I felt that sin's poppy à-tout was flying in a wide arc toward the fearful table of my soul. In such moments any kind of indifferent, but especially beautiful object turns into a sin: Satanus Midas. The cathedral's walls, the windows' resonant cells, the little boys' innocent faces, the landscape's ambiguous form-secretiveness, our bodies' Maqama-like anatomy: all this turns into sin. Either everything is sin or nothing is, this is my feeling, and of course this has nothing to do with my conviction. I can enjoy these hysterical divertimenti solely because they are isolated & never get as far as my office, where a dog-eared, tilted yellow slab hangs from a pin: no entry for strangers.

It is also regular to the point of burlesque that the most innocent joys, those with 'nihil obstat' vignettes,[311] should elicit the most active guilt-feeling during such sin-atmospheres: a slender poplar with blue sky for backdrop (God sees it as silver, because he looks on it like a suspicious lady checking a fabric vertically in the shop door in the streetlight); under the tree a vague shepherd & a flute de-rusted to incandescence; in the air a well-nigh pious aria.

This Johann Sebastian Theokritos scheme is perhaps a more penetrating analysis of original sin than Saint John's braggadocio-Babylon. One must take refuge in some brutal ready-made joy for psychic purity, because lakes, meadows, chapels and central-heated small town hotel lounges are chock-full of damnation's rum contagion. But I can't possibly talk to the children of anything like this, for that indeed would be sin, genuine sin, not mere decorative, lyrical indulgence. I'm looking for the simplest words but realize with horror that they have absorbed the now-actual odor of 'evil' more eagerly than that of complexity: baptism, God, goodness, promise, love, humility, so many infected words that make my voice tremble. These words have a certain and precise meaning, and in times of such sin-seasons the tiniest sense of security, including the logical one, is immediately enhanced into a perverse sense of carnal pleasure, so that every utterance brings with it the excitement of such an unnatural sin. Every certainty means an elemental bodily pleasure, schmaltz (which is more than the sexual desecration of a corpse), and because on such occasions the sense of pleasure is continuous, by this quaint ethical byway I realize how many certain things there are in the world.

Gomorrah and Greuze? To be sure, every Cysarz-parrot[312] can churn out such opposites ad lib, with blunt and lily-livered dictionary technique; sometimes I myself show an extraordinary penchant for such prole industry, that's why I shudder from it, and if in my psychic life such oppositions nevertheless pop up that resemble this confectionery Hegelianism, I go to great pains to justify myself, proving to myself that they are not logical or concept-catalogue derivatives, but the concrete outcomes of naïve, maladroit childhood memories; everybody knows how to think, but few possess the art of being sparingly dummkopf.

*to the above, a childhood memory:
description of a castle's interior (low ceiling room and coat-of-arms; history; portraits and gnome; the position of the chairs; mossy pond; tapestries, nudes; enfilade and love; Tudor roofbeams)*

When I felt the romantic identity of dark sin atmosphere and petit-bourgeois idyll in the church, inside me there were the memories of my childhood visits to castles, my first encounters with elegance. Small wonder that the beginning of my marriage was also the water-edge cornerstone of an unknown castle and the solitary grid gate of its gardens, for my oldest memory is the inside of a castle that my father showed me, when all my barely-life still consisted of dreaming, fear from illness, and allowed and not allowed, so that for me to this day perception and memory mean a stranger's home.

The first thing I noticed was the low ceiling; inside I was shivering with the excitement of strangeness, unhomeliness, but the too low ceiling gave the impression of nest-like enclosure, the joy of warming up under the blanket; but no sooner did I start dreaming myself into the life of the 'strange lords' (in those times the word 'man' — o, philanthropy — still meant the unknown, the snake-cold, moving nothingness), imagining how they eat in bed, drink under thick covers, walk about in ambulant, but completely closed beds in the garden — than my father gestured with his walking stick toward the door, where I saw a blazon: feathers, swords, stags, from which ladders grew out, instruments, the likes of which were to be found only at the dentist; here and there a chess figure, but the ones I half-identified were cut into two and painted in two colors like the clowns' trousers; the grownups were looking on all that with pious reverence, while I saw in it the hopscotchness of frenzy, fever, of fatal destruction, thinking in sudden revelation that what makes grownups grownup is the fact that they can 'bear' meaninglessness and chaos, while the child is only able to live in logic, order, and the shameful walking-school of the principle of identity, with small reason-gills (I use grownup language because my impressions from now and then are completely identical, and in the 60-year-old's experience the words mean only a ludicrously small added value to the childhood experience) — how is it possible that, on the one hand, they sank the ceiling into a duvet (at home it meant something like a Protestant icon: 'in the heights, my Lord'), and on the other hand, that they had such a murderous and ghostly image carved on the wall, which one can only relate to the thermometer's red numbers and lurking mercury column — a mercury you can never see, neither under the lamp nor at the window, not in mother's and not in father's hand, but heaven forbid that it gets into the skivvy's hands: fever is every number, 37, 38, 39, 40, 41, they can be seen so clearly, and the fever is the invisible mercury, the parents' whispering patience game:

what is the use of reminding people of all that? Could it be that the 'strange lords' are sick non-stop? I was almost ashamed for not feeling indisposed for the moment.

My father remarked that people never lived in this room, that it is only an old inheritance, but long disused, perhaps for as long as two hundred years. Is that possible? That everything is more beautiful than at home, there is more of everything than at home, and yet they don't use it? Then why is it home-shaped? Perhaps not even the blazon-feverish sickness is high enough for the 'strange lords' and the only thing to satisfy their richness and desire for life is non-existence. They don't live in it: we could never bear to do such a thing. I was choking with repressed sobbing, for in this moment I felt with material certainty that I am forever banished from highbornness, because not even with the most whimsical child optimism could I imagine ever building a house and not being in it — of being present everywhere, but invisibly: if I do, buy, own something, I will surely be there too, my parents too were there, we cannot not be there for two hundred years; the mere fact of existence and self-consciousness proved that I was a plebeian nobody.

While I was mulling over how I could somehow eventually manage to not-be, my father dragged me to another room, where King James I had once slept and declared war on someone from the bed while having coffee. What is history, after all? For me for the time being it was no more than the draught at home, which in an instant can cool out the rooms we heated with such hard work: it can't be nice to live in a place where something awfully big happens (I felt history to be not time but a distant milieu in the present), or rather, where something happens at all, for at home and in the circles of all our relatives nothing ever happens; for me King James's yawning declaration of war and a bus accident at the Exeter level crossing were similarly 'history.' The unsolvable tasks multiplied: I had to be nothing for 22 years, and I also had to happen, for without history there is no beautiful room. I will not happen.

Comfort was completely suppressed & flooded by the vast amount of objects of comfort: foot cushions, fireplace banister, bookstands, newspaper openers, buffet trolleys, ubiquitous cigarette boxes and ashcans, like the haunting election urns of narcosis; all that seemed rather like a hostile network, a wire fence impeding my view. It was not that in my imagination the instruments of comfort caused me physical discomfort, but that their infinite number gave the impression of some arithmetic glitch, deduction bloomer, being in pursuit no longer of the human body but of the self-serving logical world of its own arithmetic relations. The way a speed higher than the speed of light can only mean stasis, the being already-there & already-elsewhere before having started even, so this cosmic and self-overtaking, self-driven, absolute speed of comfort was also in vain, one could feel in it the meaninglessness of 'overtaking,' as if a participant at the September 1 car race rushed past the finish line on August 25th; one could not enjoy this comfort, because the frosty vacuum of logical overtaking was felt in every armchair like an electric repulsive force. In such places one could intuit the kinship between Gomorrah perversion and the lukewarm family-puddle à la Greuze: all comfort and still, infinite distance, armchair and reckless, boundless logic.

On the walls portrait after portrait hung, further emphasizing the elevated being-nothing of the 'strange lords' (face to face with my rough existence), instead of making it more verisimilar. I and my family were made of matter, our existence hung on our desires like a rain-soaked overcoat, but I never felt that we had a face, that our butcher's-shop ballast could invite an effigy: whereas these people had no bodies, they didn't even exist, but they had all the more portraits. The associations of concrete and absurd go back to that.

When I walked into a wainscoted room, I could again enjoy the shrinking, the idyllic toy-likeness, because the wooden squares reminded me of the caskets and boxes at home, of a more interior, lining-like interior, in contradistinction to the home walls that were like the coats one could also wear inside out, with only two outsides and an unknown inside. There were inscriptions here and there, which I didn't understand of course; I badgered my father over one, if I remember well it was *loyal yet free*. I didn't understand the concept of loyalty, far less the slight paradox; the one thing that rested with me was the airless defiance of 'yet' as abstract grammatical gesture, accompanied by 'meanings,' that is, darkness to the left and right. That insulated 'yet' was my first attempt at the psychology of will: I, too, wanted to be of some kind, & yet otherwise; for me, to will to this day means the grammatical staging of a paradox, a fair share of my ethics flared up for the first time around that 'yet' (slight psychoanalytic joys?).

I saw a room with very little furniture, one or two small tables & a few chairs, but the chairs were set in such places that no one could ever sit on them: for instance, one was immediately next to the door, to the right, far from the room's center, far from any table — who would sit on that? For me it was a herculean work to tear up the vulgar association between chair & sitting down, & to look at the chair as at a decorative flower that we only sniff and say compliments about, for instance, who could have expected to find one blooming so late in the autumn. Isn't it natural (O, psycho-psycho-psy...) that the abstract (or rather, all too biological) ground plan of such an impression should remain on the ethical and every other plane: idyllic object of public use linked with never, ornament, self-refutation?

If I looked down from one of the room's windows I could see a huge still water right under us, a green, weedy, swamp-smelling and unclean water, on which a few mysteriously beautiful flowers floated, out of place, as if they had been dropped on the water with someone crying for them, but because no one came to fish them, in the end they were left behind. As if it didn't suffice that the 'strange lords' exist on nothing, they have faces and history, but to cap it all, nobility also includes this sewer-panorama of dirt, this uncleaned, miasmatic stagnation? One drinks water, watches it in the form of a fountain or river, but I have never seen such a big morass, such slimy, snail-greased and weed-plastered green puddle, with those exciting, entirely unknown flowers. Is dirt capable of apotheosis? Moreover, is dirt mandatory for apotheosis?

Above the water, which related to the afternoon's time span as the poured-out contents of an ashtray relate to the sloping dreams of a man drowsing off next to it, there was a stone bridge leading into the castle, if it could be called a bridge at all: its arch was so flat that even there where it curved the highest above the water the untrammeled and Ur-eared water plants got entangled in it and glued to it in the wind. This infinitely flat arch only enhanced the time-urn's reflection-foliaged boredom, apart from the vertiginous change of the meaning of the word 'bridge.' King James I is continuously happening, and this here is standing in such a way that, if I should die, my consciousness could never stand in such an impossibly staid manner. Nothing should be the way it is: a part of the walls were run over with pitch-dark creepers, with the windows showing among the green cascades like scorn-tonsures bitten out of a satyr-hedge. At home the green creeper was friendly and modest, but here it covered everything, like an incurable skin disease.

I met again the arithmetic error of multitude on the tapestry corridors, where the human figures covered the walls like saltpeter, hanging down between my shoulders like drying clothes in Venice: people, people, & people everywhere. The pictures were themed and let the wall be seen here & there, but the tapestries reached everywhere, and instead of doors Prometheus' light-green nude could be seen; cupboard, table, chairs, bookshelves were all filled with, or supplanted by such faded-green planimetric company, as if there were no objects, walls, windows at all in the world, only people and people, scenes and scenes.

For me it was a big thing to intuit as possibility that the world consists entirely of people, that even ceilings are knocked together from innumerable Ganymedeses, and the most abstract architectural angles are in fact the mold-silvery muscle ornament of female hips. The way the infinitely numerous instruments of comfort stood in no relation to comfort, so this all-encompassing plane-blossoming of human bodies washed out the meaning of humans as living beings or as otherworldly secrets: they became pure playthings, like my collection of glass balls that could always be supplemented from the shop; the whole thing was nothing but satanic ornament.

Two-hundred-years-old nothing-man, strange only-portrait, and million-shaped kaleidoscope-human: I wonder what the owner would have thought of my dogmas of elegance? As for those few women I speak with, aren't they forced to endure being talked to as either tapestry-lovers, portrait-Venuses, or the ones who, for two 200 years, have been the non-tasters of their own eros-chalices?

One can't forget the tapestries: the human figures as rain, as air, the people I'd like to hold on to but cannot, because everything, earth, sky, window, vase, is people: because of the tapestries' mathematical frenzy, the idea of 'humanity' has all too much filled with the duality of sin and idyll. With me sexual perversion is no more than the body's adjustment to the tapestry-rooms' hundred-percent loading exclusively with people: it is not the relish in the body of one neighbor, but the pouring forth of bliss into the world made up of only-people, of an infinite number of people.

I don't want to delight in the light green embroidery-ephebi or in the living ones, but the fact that I keep bumping into them makes the impression that I'm fantastically at home, in my mother's lap or in my tiny child's crib, drinking warm milk, but if they lift me in this crib-and-milk-drinking pose from the tapestry-room's sketch of people, it suddenly transpires that I'm living in the scabrous pose of some sexual Sezession. With me perversion is no pleasure or chasing of pleasure, but simply the passive awareness of a mass of human beings hoarded with the tapestry method.

Of course this could not last long, for my father drew my attention to the grand & lordly fact that from one room you could see into five or six other rooms, or rather, not so much into other rooms as into the house's structure: one window opened on a narrow courtyard with close-set, vis-à-vis windows (it's rather unsettling when a window serves the only purpose that another window opposite should fit into it: lovers can see each other's eyes in this way, if they press their faces closely together, as it were, without sight, placing eye on blind-open eye), with a gaunt fountain in the middle, on whose water the afternoon sunlight crept in loose whorls like a scraggly vine; from a door you could see into the staircase where the stairs rose not evenly but at irregular distances and with the most diverse degrees of abruptness: where a high story was situated, there were no stairs at all, while there where the plane remained on the same level, a small stair-mold rose abruptly, only to descend again on the other side; at another window I could see anew from the outside the same room inside which I had been a moment ago, so that with the 'strange lords' the outside is still inside, in another room; departure from home still happens at home.

First the tapestry-people pressed me into the homogeneous thicket of numeric, infinite corporeality, while now I am roaming the vacuums of eternal space-openness, as if I were not a valuable and closed human-text but merely a template-printed invitation to a ball or advertisement, delivered by the post in open envelopes. Does Pieter de Hooch then work against,[313] or for sexual perversion? The question could be best probed in its didactic duality where (since there was a large entrance hall) the wall was covered in tapestries, but inside the hall balconies jutted forth from the wall: I was swimming at the same time in space-nihil and in the shower of bodies.

Did these two motifs not alternate in all my erotic memories: one sensuality, directed no more at the woman but simply, at the consciousness of corporeality built up as infinite geometric list — womanless, humanless, pleasureless; the other sensuality, likewise not directed at the woman but consisting in the experience of 'pure localization,' the abstract joy of 'there is something somewhere': the way I saw from one room not a positive other room, but only the shadows of the meaningless, so to say exactly-imbecile stair-flashlights, structure's vacillating space-switches, so in the female body, too, I relished not the muscles' good-for-nothing anatomy but the uncertain embrace-gaps, body figments in the dark, similar to a dilettante pickpocket's gestures.

Curiously, even the castles' names stood for these two poles: the place I visited was called some kind of *abbey*, whereas the family's other possession, some *place*; neither was a true home but either concretely other than what it was, a Catholic monastery, or an abstract and passepartout, empty noun, simply: place. My kisses, my kisses: the pulling-apart V-s or bumpers of abbeys and places — either non-women (for instance, mirrors), or only-spaces.

The last room I remember was in a separate little house with rough-hewn rectangles from which huge, tarred black beam-X-s stuck out, signaling the most primitive method of architecture: from such beams Noah once built his Ark. Here lighting consisted in lots of candles set in big leaden-spurred, weaponry-faced candelabra. Allegedly a hunting abode; for me a kind of spiritual exercise room. I could never warm up to candles or to flayed walls: in vain I received what they said was a gourmet buffet breakfast, all the food stuck to my palate like wallpaper, and my gullet worked like a propeller above the water. And all that was a 'home,' the place of idylls and well-being, among bier candles. When I tried to express my trembling desertedness in the church, I had to plagiarize back my childhood & say that the church was as ghostly as absolute 'home.'

―――
*to this, a further example of idyll: a banker and his wife
(the wife in the car at night in front of the bank; telephone call; metaphysics of grids; the connections of money and rococo; woman, value, and purchase; money clinic; the porter's wife and death)
— the end of the two themes attached to 'damnation and idyll'*
―――

When after the catechism class I tried to account to myself exactly about what happened to me there in the cathedral, I jotted down more or less this: a bank director wanted to go on a journey with his wife immediately after their wedding, but trains were stopped because of the severe snowstorms. He loathes all hotels, so there is no alternative but to spend the night in the bank, in the director's room. The big car stops in front of the bank at half past midnight. The bank looks like a Venetian luxury villa; although left and right from the entrance there are numbers of starting capital & 'cambio valute' on marble plaques,[314] the windows are covered by chessboards, angels, clavicembalos and masks, looking like a rococo creeper.

The car is unlit; with her glowingly pale face, the wife sits in the green depth of the car's 00:30 A.M. depth like a larva inside a carnivorous plant's leaf-stomach; curiously, the big luxury car happens to be a *Phag*. The husband realizes he doesn't have the keys, he fidgets in panic; in the end he rings. He sees that the porter's cabin is lit but there is no one inside; moreover, the glass door is evidently locked, because the door handle is switched to the right.

All the while the car burrs quietly; it gives off a sound between cello and drum covered in funereal fabric, the snow around it is painted violet.

The woman is half asleep: she sees the car's window frames as slender black columns and the enormous blanket on her knees, once the coronation mantle of polar bears, as a green fountain foaming into the night among slender arches, and she is the ex-matriculated nymph condemned to forced labor who, naked, must blow this green geyser from her mouth into the snowy air; the water is so cold that the snowflakes don't melt on it but stay compact like on fir trees; the whole car is a gorgeous black villa built opposite the bank, and she is a guest who mistook herself for the watchman due to the simple fact that she's the house's mistress. But if she is three persons and still blowing the artesian fountain from one mouth, then the Nympheum will surely punish her, and secondly, they will sentence her husband for polygamy, thus she needs to warn him: to rap on the window, or to step out, virginal torch in hand, on the car's balcony.

She wakes up to this. Her husband tells her that he needs to check the porter's cabin at the back entrance because there is no one in the front cabin, although the lamp is on. She thinks it incredibly beastly to hold a wedding on a day when there is no one in the front porter's cabin, although it is lit, and she doesn't know if it were not better, however much it would shock her family, to have a mass officiated for her husband like for the poor porter who is not, although he is lit.

The husband has switched off the car's big flashlights, so she is left in the dark and observes that darkness, too, comes from some kind of reflectors, in her face, and at this discovery she hides her legs with the blanket, because dark falls precisely on them, so in front of an owl she is ashamed of her negative staredness-at. On the whole, darkness contours her body with overmuch precision for herself; suddenly it has no other theme. It insults her that her husband starts stripping her already outside on the street, and the more she wraps herself up in the blanket, the more naked she feels because of the friction; otherwise the whole blanket-wrenching seems like trying to smuggle milk-cream back into the tiny opening of a crumpled tube, in serpentine thread, that it might look brand-new: why does her husband not do that?

In the meantime her husband had gone around the bank; by the wall, in a small marble trough, there is a bit of green lawn with huge mauve flowers which looks like the secret taps of night spraying the walls with 'flood-night'; a heavy, unexpected scent rises from them, probably delayed seven and a half hours because of the snowstorm. He lifts his wrist to his eyes, not for checking his wristwatch but for checking his shirt, specially made of a fabric that always absorbs the dominant color of its environment and gives a variation of it: indeed it looks a pleasant greyish-mauve.

He finds in his pocket the key to the back door, enters and telephones the backdoor porter, wasting a lot of time as he didn't know the big telephone set with the 27 banana plugs, sockets, all shapes of wires and cords. He makes eight erroneous calls and feels he is provoking God when he rings into those silent nighttime business assembly rooms: although he receives no answer he feels that those numbed and spectral company representatives, head accountants, directors and board representatives had heard and recorded his blasphemous abuse, to avenge it with no delay in the netherworld; at each wire-switch, at each lighting up of the red lamps' microscopic hell he repeats in weeping voice and apologetically the useless daytime names of the people working in those rooms. He feels ashamed in that nothingness as a cripple in the dance school.

In the end the porter's voice answers, to whom the coin falls after half an hour, that the director wants to spend his lordship's wedding night in his office: for half an hour, when he didn't get the director's meaning, his voice darted toward him, but when he finally came to understand him, he told the rest of what he needed to say in this already-emitted voice so that he continuously sucked it back through the wire; the fidgeting husband understands solely from this change of the voice's direction that the porter got his meaning.

In the meantime the wife sees the car horn's flexible nickel tube as a snake that could only be paradisiac, and she would have liked to ask the traffic warden to call her lady friend and tell her that it was not Eve who seduced Adam but the other way round, and *The Hibbert Journal* must fuse with *Vanity Fair*,[315] for otherwise it would founder in moral insolvency. While this goes on, the porter receives the task to serve a cold dinner and make the bed; the director had often slept at the bank when he waited for telephone messages about other banks' late-night assembly meetings. The next moment all the electric candles of the hall are switched on, before the husband gets back to his wife who is already asleep in the car.

The woman believes that she had got among a late Baroque stage's layers of décor where there are so many horizons pressed behind one another as there are paper napkins in a napkin holder; whatever is one step behind is painted vertically, so distance is not a horizontal momentum but a shower of verticality, as if the most practical way to build a ballroom's glistening mirror-floor were by pressing one million blades vertically to one another. This floor construction seems the world's most absurd technique, although sometimes it can be considerably economical; with three vertical planes one can suggest a far greater distance within one sole centimeter than with a horizontal plane across one hundred meters. Strangely, this technique should be at once precious and expressionistic; it's as naïve as a wig and as poisonous as morphine.

One can make a selection of distance and gather cross sections: and this bank entrance hall held together those vertical space samples (a salesman's fabric collection) as the various-hued cards on the occasion of a space-slam. If distance's gentle, horizontal continuity is suddenly cooled down in the extreme, then one gets these crystallized spades, diamonds model sheets, et cetera, and the young wife would have loved to start a card game with all the Baroque spaces, as if those were various patience-prefigurations of the new fashions of space (Anschaulichkeit der nichteuklidischen Geometrie?).[316]

She had already felt at the convent school that in the meek Biedermeier gestures there is something of the cripples' movements: the curtsies, révérence-s, humility-lunges didn't remind her of idyll in the least, but rather, of Cimabue's sacred rachitis.[317] When she entered this rococo hall she felt this in an enhanced form — the entire space & its analytic perspective reminded her of distortedly sketched limbs, orthopedic whims seen on pedicure advertisements, wild foreshortenings.

Otherwise the 'distance' seems to be such a shtick institute: a mixture of opium, Inigo stage,[318] and anatomical lottery. One behind the other, different copper lacework stretched toward the tabernacle of credit: each full of girlish metal embroidery; in themselves they were magnified shirtsleeve trimmings, but compared to one another, in the demonic matrix of Nacheinander there were only three brutal space-findings full of positive data, as if space were crammed with the inner wounds and bacteria of proportions and dimensions. Upwards: the porous mask of Rameau's soul: a mesmerizing and tormenting space surgery.

When she needed to cross these hanging horizon-filters that within seconds sieve one's broad-drab space-percepts into precision space-mimosas, it occurred to her that in the war many soldiers' lives were saved by the notebook pages that stopped the bullets: she, too, felt that she couldn't go further than three such copper nets, they condensed so many kilometers in themselves. She felt that this walk was one of the finest cosmetic treatments:

one needs time to walk distances, but here she felt infinite distances within seconds. Of course she felt these seconds to be years, without those years aging her body in the least.

A woman can hardly have a more intelligent experience than feeling time's waves (her greatest enemies) to be a cosmetic radiation. She intuited that time was the true material of beauty, its radiating source, but in life woman is doomed in tragicomic fashion to fight with the utmost Darwinian rigor against time. She nearly fainted at this thought, so her husband had to hold her. What use to proceed onwards in space, in the democratic directions of horizontality? It was as if so far she had only watched the spirals, marble patterns and gilding painted on the books' edge, and now for the first time she realized that to these colored page-edges long text-sheets belong, three of which would take her much further than one thousand of the colored edges: for the first time she read the text of perspective. Horizontal and vertical are siblings in theory, but in reality of course not; are a book's text-page and page-edge of equal value? The page edge can be tranquilly taken for nil, and the horizontal distance is made up of such nils: after all, absolute silence too can be recorded on a gramophone. Her previous sense of space had been only such a 'half-tone' needle, which ran along the blind grooves of horizontality.

If we want to safe keep it in the neglected depot of our percepts, we need to comb space every so often in the direction opposite hair growth, because only then can we feel its million vertical leaves. Even as a child she had loved to assemble the grownups' pack of cards from tree leaves, to regulate the value of a chestnut against an acacia and lilac leaf; now as she lay half fainted in her husband's arms, cards and plants merged before her eyes and the only thing she knew was that her beauty has dehisced.

What a laughable wedding present is space, she thought, and perhaps it's even used for immoral purposes. She felt her body turn into mercury, shrinking more and more among the vertical degrees of the big space-thermometer: a space is the more intensive, the denser its vertical coulisses; already at the third bank door her mercury-nude had contracted to the minimum. She realized that whenever they ironed plissé or gouvré[319] on her school uniform skirt, it could be only a compromise: had they done the harmonica-folding radically, there would have been no skirt, but only a single line that one couldn't possibly put on. This bank-vestibule was exactly such an uncompromising skirt: in it distance was ironed into such a harmonica that it narrowed more or less to the 'width' of one thin glass pane: 'portable' light year?

But what curious and beautifying 'base' delight it is, to be among dense vertical curtains that cross our bodies, like the parallel strings of the egg-slicer. So did the young wife's body get sliced like homogeneous light on a thousand black evening waves: thousands and thousands of 'fadings' censured her flesh — what was the point? The mouth existed separately, the navel separately, the shoe-heel separately: the parallel sheets cut her into pieces, as though the thermometer's individual degrees penetrated into the mercury column's body and sliced it up. But all the same, the parallelism, the orphic monotony of planes illustrated the perverse garden of order: the celestial pathology of the rule. The parallel blades yielded autonomy to every single body part, or the stumps of body parts, which then blossomed independently toward unknown formations, berserk and dehumanized (ça vous plaît?)[320] — but in the meantime a thousand parallel planes glowed above them with geometrical furore, as absolute (that is, drunk) order.

Because of this duality the bank's entrance hall had a cosmetic effect on the young wife and thus, she felt, also an erotic one. If in good bourgeois fashion they wanted to take a wedding photograph of her, the following would be seen on it: on one side a wealth of sharp, parallel lines (like the wireless' tuning filaments) — on the other side, the scattered bits of the body cut up by this many-edged space-plough: fragments of lip-, hand-, hair- and wrist-meters. I emphasize on behalf of the little wife that this is not a frivolous ordering spree, being a metaphor only in so far as we ourselves have been metaphors before being nonconformist preachers or bankers' spouses.

How far this is a positive date from the life of the young finance wife I can demonstrate with a historical example from the realm of botany: long ago an Arab gardener from Spain made an experiment with a creeper, of leading its long tendril through parallel walls (on each there was a small keyhole-like opening), & in each resulting cassette he used a different kind of soil, irrigation method and treatment, managing to get different kinds of flowers between the different walls, with different colors and shades of perfume.

The wife, too, was like this plant among the bank's grid-walls and curtain-doors. And this is evidently the picture of amorous disposition, metrum epithalamii: [321] from the same stem the body develops the illusions of utter dissolution, anarchic plots (some kind of Gomorrah) and dogmatic standardizing, scholastic or pettifog order (some kind of Greuze). (Both also remind of the structure of death.)

It's important that the bank was built not in modern but in rococo style: that's what suits money the best, as the wife's feminine-homemaking instinct immediately realized. On the banknotes' greenish-pink paper rococo lines run in infinite density in various graceful distributions; tight lassoes, pudic and mathematical interferences, rings and parables, where cosmetics and theoretical physics freely alternate. Money-paper has always attracted her with its old-fashioned drawings, of the kind she had first seen on her great-grandmother's ball invitation: ever since that time, each banknote has reminded her of 18th-century carnivals and Weber-Aufforderungen,[322] together with those primeval forests and monsters that are part of a Puck dowry far rather than of the genuine jungle. Is there anything more beautiful than a ballet about

Prometheus, a dance movement called 'pas d'Hercule,' a small variety opera about the fall of the Titans and a new face powder that the Exeter apothecary baptized 'Minos' Shower'; what rambunctious instinct prodded those musicians and apothecaries to visit the world of monsters, giants, and multi-ton gross-pay heroes of all worlds, when they used to create precious wee chamber pantomimes and perfumes?

Just as in those days such partly tragic, partly athletic psyche-pillars used to be surrounded by mademoiselle embroideries and cuckoo meteorological signals, so now the brutal nakedness of money, of gross business sums are again caressed by rococo flourishes and color-changing calligraphy: what a mushy continuity, she thought. The watermarks that her husband would sometimes check by holding the banknotes up to the window almost invariably represented some mythological face with a transparency that recalled a grease stain: a Medusa or Mercury head, the spectacular bon vivant of thieving. Above, the script is printed with the most regular visiting-card sweetness, the thin lines fade into downright ethereal piano, while the thick fortes are as deafening as an abruptly amplified, automatic mechanical whistle.

'Fast transition' is a strange concept, but with this provocative-pristine calligraphy it's quite understandable; thick & thin lines alternate densely, and the whole is one big transition. There is some deliberate flirtation in this, as though it represented the musical stock exchange-mimosa nature of the value of money; one thousand dollars: how many obsequies, curtsies, how many palings and things tolerated (behind the paper, the Dalcroze sheets[323] of the gold-standard), how many jumps & swan's deaths are in it. And beneath the writing's rond-serpentines the ghostly, but gentle Medusa head (like a banished little baroness behind the lettering glued to the café window — ƎᖵAƆ — so does the watermark hide behind the inscription of the nominal value); Perseus didn't need to look Medusa in the eye, but he spied through a mirror her lethal face mimicry: likewise, the handlers of money get the Gorgon only via such discreet reflexes, through the faint, televisionary attempt of the watermark.[324] And among all these, the green guilloché, like a forest of sling stitches fading into gentle pink.[325]

Calligraphy! Green forest! Mythology! These three things are indeed worthy of eliciting our love for money. Sometimes on banknotes we even encounter statesmen in wigs or Rubensian cavalry battles, but these attracted her less. For her the concept of 'value' consisted of the three above-mentioned decorative elements, and when she entered this rococo bank hall she felt that her dreams have been but snub-nosed little empiria with the capacity to thrust toward reality.

Sometimes 'value' was brutally in her hands in the shape of shameless and exhibitionist cash, at other times only as some kind of credit, trust, or deposit and other symbolic and spiritualist matters that flared around her with the Vestals' pink peplums. She felt the whole scale of value, and each shade of value irritated her skin differently, depending upon how close or far it was from blunt cash. If she bought something with a bill of exchange that lost validity in two weeks, she would buy different kinds of goods than with a bill of exchange valid for two more months; these value-avatar moments determined her brain, fleeing from mimicry to mimicry, with different radiation.

To the bills of exchange correspond violet shawls, fishnet stockings, modest evening gowns (the whole dress is one ribbon that stamps an X on her back and a Y on her chest, or the other way round: the material's modesty creates a much more modest atmosphere than the body's modesty) and 'Bouche d'Iseult' perfumes; while to cash (to mention only such vulgar extremes, although only the in-between ones would be truly exciting) swimming trunks, calf tattoos, muscle-electrifying, massage, and usually expenditure touching directly on the body.

Sometimes she simply forgot her wallet home, & so received a two-hour credit: this again created a peculiar atmosphere around her body & the purchased objects, which only seasoned plein-air painters can render adequately, for the particularity of the grades of credit is expressed in the color of the air. She had always identified credit with virtue: there was some kind of homely trust about it (as far as her shopping goes), purity, sacred hygiene — perhaps it's really the Vestals' invention. The Vestals always stoked some fire, & its imagined pink, its coals carried around in sieves & onanized forth from fruit stems suited well the faint moral portrait of credit.

For her modesty always consisted in such a gentle, economic, and transparent image, as she had been pathologically visual in her girlhood (she heard of a girlfriend becoming pathologically auditory since her wedding), that's why she felt that her allegedly most immodest dresses were in fact the most modest. She had a violet evening gown that was but a crêpe-de-chine Auftakt,[326] as if one watched a nude with a dim lorgnette; she felt that the soul-like delicate material, which was light as a breeze and violet as newborn pudicity, and transparent like truth-saying itself, was the most perfect expression of virtue. The Vestals used to bring water from the Egeria spring themselves, and underway they were not allowed to touch their jug to the ground: this glistening, almost flying water preoccupied her almost for weeks, and when she saw it again in lamé and rhinestone, she placed on her body only a scarf that hung from her neck to her toes in the front and behind — this minimum-element simplicity, brook-faced modesty was her virtue. But at the bottom of all these pure visions worked the various inspirations, atmospheres and intuitions of 'value'; she was fully aware that everything she had on, and even inside, was connected to 'value': axiologia effeminata, pastorale commerciale.

To reach the director's office they had to cross one large marble hall, in the middle of which, like an airplane taking off abruptly, there twisted the stairs (because the stairs were in the open, one didn't feel like leaving the hall: when one was on the top stair, one still saw the hall and its floor — only the very last step hurled one unexpectedly, like the suddenly-swinging hook of a crane, onto the next floor).

This second-floor room barely preserved anything of the rococo & on the whole resembled a clinic rather. The counters were low and wide, like operating tables, with wide, frameless frosted glass windows, like the geometric glaciers of the various exchange rates — one behind the other, with undulating, angular, or serrated edges. The ink holders, pencils hanging by springs, adding up and multiplying devices, mechanical file organizers, telephone centers, and metal rulers, were like the medical appliances necessary for some complicated surgery; even lighting resembled liquid spirits, in which the utensils swim on a sadistic degree of sterility. Here and there a white coat hung on the hanger; from a small washstand hung, like old military banners in Gothic churches, starched-ironed towels. The floor was of cold marble, and the air smelt of menthol.

Perhaps money is a great disease for whose treatment there are various methods, slow and exciting therapies. There's always silence in the banks, because somewhere a monumental patient is lying on the operating table: the bill blocks are doctor's prescriptions, the columns and exchange machines are collective thermometers, the tension- and pressure-meters of cash registers, with an objective scale. Objectivity always impressed her, just like ties: typical male wear & yet gaudy like artificial flowers.

This great currency-clinic seemed to her the atrium of objectivity, with all its disinfecting externals and deadline-décor. As a dutiful woman, in objectivity she liked especially the ornamental side: 'O, men are so terribly vain, aren't they?' What is this jumbo drawer-garage if not the house of men's childish posturing, the tricky games of objectivity? Her love for her husband multiplied tenfold, because she could see from these multi-story glass walls and six-propeller ventilators that her husband was a poetic, childish, rhapsodic, and unserious spirit.

While they crossed the polished & multi-edged refrigerating room of value, the porter's wife was arranging the pillows and bedsheets in half sleep, scattering lots of notepads & bills from the desk, so the young wife could have been a Danae with the wealth of notes and invoices still flying about in the room when they arrived. The porter's wife didn't get it that the young couple wanted to spend their first night together there — she imagined someone must have felt sick, the director or his sister, & needed to lie down at once.

She was fully familiar with the external signs of death: car stopped at night before the bank, telephone calls, switched-on lamps, making the bed, renewed telephone calls, and in the morning, when light leaves the objects in one's eyes like the lost ring or swimming cap on the black bottom of the swimming pool after draining the water, in the morning there is only death, which hardly has anything to do with the nighttime hurly-burly; if there were no night there would be no death either. What's the use of all that hubbub, when in the morning everything will be still anyway?

In the head of the porter's wife the connection between finances and stroke suffered during inspection was forceful as the one between cognac and delirium tremens. The stroke was a thing and activity every bit as serious as a board meeting that goes on into the small hours, and in fact she felt no difference between the two: work is work. For her death was such an execution procedure that foists glory on one & validates honesty almost with sums: a black appointment. By so integrating death into the normal functioning of bureaucracy, her excitement was not at all painful while making the bed. She came to only when her husband started laying the table with the buffet provisions: green, yellow, red sandwiches, the trembling trumps of life and appetite ...

ontology and masquerade

This is how far my jottings about the church frisson go, & I was perhaps guided by the age-of-Mozart 'magic tragedy' atmosphere that has haunted me my entire life: although in reality all my moral crises consisted of barren and altogether banal hypochondrias, the moment I tried to find their kernel they somehow transformed into madrigals — from sin's atonal stump, into such a rococo bank. In me all these are women's attributes: Gothic conscience and rococo poeticized out of money. These marginalia wanted to be first & foremost about women, and I cannot approach them with either Exeter twilights or journalistic ariosi. More 'jagged' experience: should I then prescribe this to myself? Isn't it just drunk empiricism when I strain to render reality thousand-masked, with all kinds of association postures?

Allow me an entirely prosaic consideration: if I go on to process all the world's existing material into masks, in the end I will have only reality's positive sludge in my hands. And if I keep changing the masks forever, there will be no difference between the material and form of reality on the one hand, and the material and form of the masks on the other hand. If, instead of a blue bell-flower, I show the beak of a red buruburu bird as mask, in the name of a naïve-comfortable empiricist objectivity, some buzzing objection might be raised; but if I use every single flower as raw material for manufacturing an infinite bird mask, and then every bird-mask for manufacturing flowers, then all difference between mask and original will be nil, ontology and masquerade will be de facto identical, even in the chemical & arithmetic sense.

But in order for the lie to rise in rank and be on par with the absolutes of reality, you need an infinite number of lies, a transcendental combinatory, which, when applied to the issue of the artistic structure of these *Meditations*, implies that I should write forever, that I am not allowed to ever end, precisely for the sake of empiricist honesty (or, if you will: 'laconicity' in the theological sense!). 'Infinity minus one' number of lies (the rococo bank is such a lie) still allows for distinguishing ontology from fiction: only an infinite number of masks will become identical to reality, but then immediately — to infinite reality. The only classicism of these *Meditations* can be, of painstakingly refraining from all beginning-shaped beginnings and all ending-shaped endings: because it works with masks, it must be eternal and directionless. (Doesn't physics, too, try to defeat Cartesian mathematicism with all too mathematical means: the more it tries to set the real thing in place of the mathematical mechanics, the more it is chased into baroque algebra. Affectation is the fruit of fanatical empiricism.)

―――
the irreality of female beauty
―――

What kinds of women did I know, what did I do with them, what did they do with me? In this moment (and probably only in this moment) I see the following three stages: the acquaintanceship of ugly girls; one masked woman at a ball, whom I don't know to this day; and finally, an imaginary landscape. This is a strict scale of values: ugliness, anonymity, and magic landscape. The beautiful woman has preoccupied me all my life, but only as problem, as the poppy-shaped diagnosis of the sexual tinkerings of my solitudes. Today I found a mask in my drawer, that's why I'm writing about the mask. I could have found out who it was, but I didn't want to.

Before I spoke with this masked woman I had no inkling that it is possible to feel such a profound, indeed wild, love for somebody without a face. I almost wrote that I felt 'compassion,' because while I was courting her, and especially after, some deep &

unearthly grief undulated inside me; I felt the facelessness to be an apotheotic surgical-clinical illness, which makes the woman's mindframe much sharper and clearer, but still an illness nevertheless, just as the angels' incorporeality is an even stronger form of the same illness. Now I felt that the body's shape had lost all its humanity, because the face didn't draw an I in front of the individual muscles' bumptious zeros; and now I felt that the hips, legs, and the dress' frills are just as much portraits, portrait features as the real face.

I have tormented myself my entire life over the questions and facts of beauty and ugliness: now a woman appeared with whom this didn't occur; for me it was a far greater salvation than a true beauty's appearance could have offered. Beauty is always a problem; it's always a separate personality next to the woman's actual personality, and I am confused by this dualism; just as we feel one ball to be two balls if we rotate it by throwing our middle finger before the index, my soul grabs women too like such a scissors turned inside out, forming a vexing duplicate. Beauty blocks something, it makes something impossible: it is pressed into the middle of our soul with such determination that it can't be dislocated. Women know this well and every act of vanity demonstrates how they cultivate a strange person, the figure of beauty. A beautiful woman always sets this figure of beauty in the center of the dialogue: the woman stands behind it and the man before, they are in three. Beauty is her essence, and yet we feel it to be some kind of alien armor, as if beauty could by no means be an actual person, just as the absolutely 'intelligible,' too, can be only immaterial. There is something impossibly immediate in beauty, something theologically clear, & man cannot approach and grasp this personally.

In evidence there is a lot of self-annihilating, self-effacing purity, so beauty nihilizes the female person. It is a mathematical form in which symbolization is carried out radically, and at the same time the whole chain is also axiomatic, it naturally lacks sense — I remember coming across something like this. I feel the same with beauty: it includes a whole network of truths, but it has no human or other meaning — the most divine logic excludes sense, the most consistent beauty topples beyond the human act of 'seduction' and is non-æsthetic.

One feels the anatomy of the beautiful woman to be homogeneous: there is nothing behind the surface, only the same surface beauty — the woman is either thin as a paper sheet, or her lungs, heart, soul too are likewise a continuous portrait. If so, then she lacks real dimensions, and up and down make no sense with her: one of the foundations of love is laid precisely in a bourgeois-Euclidean space. I cannot approach her or distance myself from her, go round her or cast a shadow on her: she is always consistently present, and omnipresence always means being away.

Hence perfect beauty is always something ascetic: it's like an infinite eel, one can grab it continuously, but it will always glide out of our hands. Beauty is motley validity, which exists uniformly everywhere (for us God doesn't differ from the dead), that is, it fills our soul; hence our sense that no space of movement can be created around it where eros could move.

In certain psychologies the cognition of the object consists in the soul becoming, so to say, identical with the object: the soul immediately takes on the form of beauty, and so, in the inebriation of impression, our own soul becomes the beauty of the admired woman: the one who comes to know is only a fateful actor, who is compelled to take on forever, willy-nilly, the role of the things of cognition. So does the lover wriggle in the stifling role of beauty: the woman's beauty becomes his prison, immures him, and he literally undergoes the fate of the drunk who keeps revolving around the advertising column and palpating it in the middle of an empty square while muttering, — 'good God, I'm walled in.' And so we live like a fly accidentally caught inside a massive soap bubble: the glossy prison-globe bears the surrounding world in all the colors of the rainbow, in unearthly forms and vertiginous perfection, moreover, the fly sees there the yellow fruits and glinting candies too, it is their very beauty that surrounds it like a mirror peel, barring it from reaching the real fruits & candies — it is separated from the beautiful things by beauty's murderous coulisse. Lame-winged fly; wretched country parson...

In fact there is nothing human in beauty, that's why we always look for another person behind the beautiful woman's beauty, like the children who don't yet understand the perspective of photographs and keep fingering the pictures' verso, to feel if the plastic details visible in the image and receding into the background do not bulge backwards. We are like a mistaken animal with dual instinct, whose eyes react only to a certain plant's fruits, but its appetite, its shady self-preserving instinct, can only be appeased with the plant's root. In this way the beautiful woman is divided into strange items: into one concrete miracle, beauty's untouchable positivity, which, however, fills our soul to the point of paralysis, and so it keeps occupied all perspective terrains; on the other hand, into an imaginary human being, hypothetical person, whom our instinct feels with the utmost certainty, but whom beauty's Chinese Wall forever bars from our touch.

Sometimes I tagged beauty as 'vindictive perception,' because I had the impression that instead of approaching the woman's whole reality, like an entrance hall the interior rooms, it suddenly becomes independent, splits off from the woman's body, comes to me, but doesn't take me back to the entrance: I don't know if such madness exists, but in any case the beautiful woman chased me into this; like a thin nude-envelope, exterior beauty splits off from her, alights in my soul, but then it stops there and doesn't return to her together with my soul, that I could know her: midair it becomes an independent, vindictive perception. With tormenting certainty I intuit that this beauty-peel that split off from the woman used to be above something personal and human, but I cannot come to know that, I hold only an empty dress in my hands, which wants to lure me to believe that it is a real person.

Such an independent perception hanging midair is a ghostly affair: its true uncanniness is not its twilit nature but its poignant luminosity, directed at something I cannot know, I cannot know where it belongs. Thus beauty runs on a parabolic course, it means an eternal interruption — it starts from the woman, reaches me, but it never returns to the woman. (Somehow I am the man of these parabolic, vengeful perceptions in every respect.) When I try to court her, I need to address this perception-puppet moving along the parabolic course, so I am forced to stylize myself as well out of all eros-willing humanity, and to acclimatize myself to beauty.

It is an old habit of mine that, depending upon the object I happen to be looking at, I feel I have the face of that object: when looking at the gramophone box, a mustachioed dragoon brigadier, when looking at the yellow lampshade, a female Bach, when looking at my own reflection in the mirror, a live candle snuffer, etc. Beauty as an exact, object-like thing also elicits from me some kind of imaginary personality, with which I have nothing human to do and with which I have no juridical relation, merely a formal compulsive movement depending upon the given beauty's suggestion. Therefore my love which gains support in beauty is infinitely irreal, ghostly, and merely-ornamental.

The sole gist here is: female beauty never triggers one of my characters unknown to myself, it doesn't provoke a character role that is foreign to me (it would be so trivial to be hardly worth recording), but it changes me into a graphic system so to say, independent of character: from all kinds of intellectual inner contents and physical gestures, my whole psyche constitutes a supplementary image to the woman's beauty. I was made to see this process in all its puritanical nature by the drugs' simple explanatory images, scriptura illiterati.

One minimum of this love situation is also revealed by a dream unbenobled by morphine: one night I looked for a long time at the nude of Andromeda on a relief, and when I dozed off, I myself became Andromeda, without losing any bit of my real bodily or clothing personality: cassock buttons, white stocks collar, my blue veins worming with greying hairs were built, by the power of some transfiguration architecture, into Andromeda. That is how our dream love began, a particularly exciting form of canonic monologue; by resembling the woman, the burning otherness and sharp bodily distance of Andromeda split from me, from my own soul and physiological inside, with unexpected petals. I could feel Andromeda's figure inside myself, for I changed into Andromeda, & I could touch her forms inside my body; in that moment I felt what the stranger, what the other is, what surprise is.

If we could feel for once during the day the inner weight relations, personal muscle elasticity of a stranger's body (not merely the other's exterior image), only then could we start intuiting something about the 'other.' To feel the 'other' is always identical to the feeling of 'infinity'; something strange cannot be imagined as dimensioned: alteritas aeternitas. To feel in ourselves Andromeda's sole shadow: to feel God's plenitude: Ens habitat alterum.[327] So I changed into a clown's mask during my courtship; my whole anatomy resembled the Futurist pictures: I produced colors, weights, sounds, when I knocked into beauty's floating perception layer. However human beauty was, it represented a human face — by being so independent, I could only become worthy of it, akin to it with such irreal Proteanism, with dehumanized shticks.

the masked woman; still,
the most ancient human inclination is goodness

It was all different when I stood face to face with the masked woman: then the emphasis fell on the 'human being.' I can easily imagine that if this diary ends up in the hands of some reader (I imagine my son like that too), the respective reader will be much vexed by my distinction between beauty and the human: for those graphic deeds of mimicry, pronounced irreal, which I have performed in front of beauty, are no less human than my other actions; dehumanization too is anthropomorphic. To this the answer can be the following: the concept of the human that we feel behind the words anthropomorphism, humanity, or humanism, is a theoretical, logically derived concept of the human: it is a real concept and not a human being. Whereas the other thing we call dehumanization, and which is the meaningless, object-like heap of colors, weights, meanings and moral-tumors, which can never for a moment resemble a concrete human being or human life, this 'futurist' bluff is in fact the expression of the human being's most primal biological layer, the most scientific expressionist style of the center of human life.

The man of 'humanity': a concept; the man of dehumanization: a life-principle that is alien to life, perhaps even contrary to life. Woman's undisguised beauty terrorizes us into a dehumanizing pose (that is: into the possibly most human one), but the masked woman unveiled to me the traditional features of 'character.'

If I address my words to a beautiful woman, they leave my lips like a rivulet, which the sunshine immediately absorbs and annihilates into steam — I am like a mute who is moving his mouth in vain. When I spoke to the masked one, the face didn't immediately drink up my words, but I saw them in front of me in the cool isolation of responsibility. This was the only occasion in my life when I came to intimate what a superb role speech too can play in love. Because here everything was speech, and the words took upon themselves the role of beauty: here too there was a third one between us (let me resort once again to this still-usable symbol), but it was speech, with rich bodily articulation. Speech was the big tree on which both she & I were only swinging parasites; words were sizable and our bodies insignificant.

The heads never match the body: the simple proportions of a nude with the mosaic-like 'Kleinkunst' of the female face [328] above has always seemed to me a stylistic error, like a Gothic window-mask glued to a Romanesque façade. These wee art historical touchinesses are of course utterly unimportant, but now they proved to be useful because I have never before seen bodies so calmly. The headless body, too, is individual, but it's a more moderate and discreet form of individuality than the face, which is incapable of connecting to another face; people look each other in the eye because that's the one thing that somehow best resembles another's. I was overcome by an almost philanthropic devoutness at the thought that all mankind would always go about in masks and would feel a universal fraternity. I couldn't understand at all the curiosity that looks for the face behind the mask: why should I remove that visual muffler, to go deaf again from the cacophony of over-the-top individuality? This muffled individuality resembled the surrounding hills in the afternoon: one was oval, the other a bit flattened, the third one very gently serrated, the fourth undulating — in masks this would be all the difference between women.

One could think that I'm a very superficial observer if one mask is enough for me to muffle the outlines of a woman's individuality. When I speak about the muffling of individuality, it doesn't mean that I wouldn't notice differences and shades: on the contrary. The 'individuality' evidenced in the face is particular to such an exotic degree that two such infinite particularities cannot be set in a relation of difference anymore, just as there's not much point and use in speaking about differences between a cat trinket and a Phoenician astronomical hypothesis. But the difference between oval and undulating landscapes is all the more enticing: the more generally similar two landscapes or two female nudes are, the more we observe the differences, shades — that is, it's precisely the refined observer who turns away from the faces to pore over the bodies. The foundations of fraternity (so the philanthropist went on in me) are these very small differences, whose only role is the better to emphasize kinship.

It's much healthier if the speech partners unwittingly make up some kind of blurred portrait on the basis of the sentences uttered than if nature threw before us its senseless ready-made. Because such a portrait will emerge anyway, but adapting exactly to the style of the body and grammar: all syntax is always a nude, and not the expression of the head; in grammatical rules and grammatical harmonies the body's simpler but more instinctive waves persist, not the face's over-evolved contours.

The dress was a bit strange, because although its tailoring followed the body's shapes, still, the clothes always refer to the face, it is the face's contents that the clothes try to imitate with their rationalist balm. The skirt was taut on the legs, like a candle-flame-shaped candle snuffer, but even so, it didn't refer to the legs but alluded to an unknown face instead: as if not only the dress but the whole human anatomy slid into a routine of 'face'-centeredness in our brains; I felt that at the legs, hips, and shoulder blades it was almost impossible to get rid of the portrait's no longer actual dissection constant. Although in them there was, tense, a new, obsession-less autonomy, like scholasticism lurking in the texts of certain 18th-century relativist philosophers: their sentences may still bear the limpid meaning of doubt, but in the more real body of the words and concepts the great tensions of absolute swell — what a sterling game, to express with the absolute's realist vocabulary the heresy directed against the absolute: what a sterling game to assemble the face-less woman's new anatomy from the figments of the 'face' obsession.

Perhaps I was faced with the trivial biological phenomenon that, if I cut off a lizard's tail, it will grow a new one, or if I tear off a semorancus' four legs, it will develop a veritable net in their place, with which (with its cripple organ, that is) to catch even more small fish than it could have with its four healthy tentacle-legs. This woman also concealed, annihilated her head with a black silk lorgnette, and in its place her clothes grew into a face: O, sweet aequi-finality. Ever since that evening, whenever I see gorgeous evening gowns in shop windows, I never imagine nudes under them but see them as faces; for me the Bond Street seamstresses mean the National Portrait Gallery.

From the music & champagne I gradually lost my conversation partner's dimensions and the directions of her body, standing before her like before a large snail, which has no head at all, or the whole animal is impossibly only-head, a kind of Pliocene thermophore; or they have several half-heads where some highly precise, face-like detail is found — the dumbest animals are replete with such too-precise portrait fragments: under the octopus' eyes Torquemada's wrinkles tremble from the sickly satisfaction in truth.

Once I watched a woman through a keyhole, whose head I could also not see: homeliness radiated from her clothes, a kindness and goodness directed at me. And then as well as now some kind of Inquisition horror story occurred to me, because the best match for the body's outlines are the outlines of sin, as if the spirit of goodness could be best expressed with the sketches of sin. The image of sin can better resemble the essence of goodness than the image of goodness itself: with schoolboy-like snugness one sees the 'essentials' as lazy croquis, and those always resemble the sketches of sin. People of course take the 'sketches' of sin for sin itself, and often feel guilt, although they are merely trying to express their elementary goodness and thirst for goodness with narrative, painterly, or merely action contours.

In relation to the female body (especially if there are clothes on it) I clearly feel that from the body, the golden anxiety of innocence suddenly drills into me, crumpling up all my percepts, like a zigzagging heavenly magnet the gold smoke that one minute before was hovering, mirror-smooth; one would believe this is what sin's topsy-turviness looks like, although they are the decadent figurations of innocence. As concerns innocence and the graphic outcomes of virtue: they are all full of fin-de-siècle bizarreries (the Garden of Faithfulness!). Sin is only a Nice must-mask on the face of goodness delighting in its own plenitude: the expressionistic style of virtue. (For a dull person sin is the only artistic means of expression: they cannot write, play music, or paint, but they can commit crimes — this is their style, their æsthetic.)

I have always watched with ruminating doubt the people who think they can discern the bugaboo of sin on the bottom of all virtue; I would do it the other way round: instead of lurking sadism, I would talk about lurking saintliness, and I feel a great gusto for a reverse moral-Freudianism, which could analyze the base dynamics of goodness out of everything. In place of the original sin, we would have original virtue; eating the apple would be only a decorative, embellishing expression, merely-external, histrionic staging of primeval goodness — for Satan too was an angel, 'man kann nicht unbestraft unter Jesus wandeln,'[329] perhaps his sin is also nothing else than the expression of a half-baked goodness; virtue molds into form, or shudders into form before ripening, because its holy dynamics is always in excess: this premature reflex-form, constraint-decorum, is sin: 'ars,' the impatience of virtue.

Above the body, the face is the ungainly seal of finitude, like some official stamp on a Persian rug's edge, signaling that it's reserved, it's pawned. But without a face, the body is the vast landscape-sofa of infinity, regulated by the unequal ebb and flow of innocence and sin. The moment the head disappears, innocence alights. (This is not what certain sexual lyricists froth at the mouth about, that there is 'some inherent goodness in the body,' or that nature equals virtue. For me body and virtue, naturalness and innocence, are sharply distinct things: for me the body evokes, creates, triggers virtue, but is by no means identical to it.)

If the numbers on a clock face were once to put on masks, like this conversation partner of mine (not even my dance partner, because I can't dance), then the clock-hands would continue moving, time would open, so to say, like a boundless sea: only the slow rhythm of passage would stand before us, without any concretizing number. This fact alone would bring to mind some 'goodness' — with the numbers masked, time is ethicized on the spot, at least this is my mood, which now in my old age is as much a dogma as it used to be in my puberty. Although time becomes infinite this way, still we feel that the entire time-complex has become humbler, more modest and melancholy, closer to us, to our Kleinmensch needs — is unpunctuality philistine? Is this the illusion of virtue? Let's admit that we have always been the troubadours of the clock hands & not of the Zifferblatt.[330] By this I don't mean that women's bodies are more sympathetic than their heads, which now features as the unknown of an equation, or more precisely, like the zero in an equation reduced to zero.

Is there anything more exciting than an equation, on one side of which there is a whole charivari of values in the most bizarre relations imaginable, with the characteristic modulations of life, & this whole equals a 'zero,' or else, the whole family of values can only be matured rationally if we keep in mind the zero glowing beyond the equality sign; how richly can one express zero, and what new feelings one can attain by zero. Royal Exchange: at first glance an infinitely long math formula, which equals zero, does not seem doomed to death at all (tiny kitsch humanization:

Euler libera nos!):[331] what if the whole of nature is reduced to zero, only we don't realize it? If I beheld with a simultaneous gaze the trees' branches, the birds' song, the mountains' ground plan and periods of arctic light, performing all latent operations and grouping them according to plus or minus signs, subscripts and superscripts: I would get zero. Royal Exchange: zero gets such a fancy tautology, the whole world, like one side of an equation; and the world gets a constant inspiration, possibility to generate value, solution, meaning and reality from the fact of being reduced to zero. But it's unwise to start gossip right away with 'what if the whole world'; every eros-cobbler to his eros-trade, to the masked woman. Here, reduction to zero means reduction to a black mask; the equation's other side is the lonely body. It was enough to cover the face & everything else opened: the night landscape becomes visible to us if the headlights of the car approaching from the opposite direction are switched off.

Personality, rigorously localized 'character,' illuminates nothing: it's merely the selfish points of the headlights' carbon. One cannot get rid of a face, continue it into life, into nature, the face is a state within the state, nature within nature; this exponent-portrait alone is such a complex system, that only the (always rhetorically apostrophized) belated grandchildren can be expected to find the time for the concrete raising to power.

Before the girl's mask I felt like a bank robber before the closed eyelids of the banker sedated with chloroform — to him that closedness is almost visually identical to the openness of the forced-open safe; if that pair of eyes is closed, then suddenly all the villa's other secrets are thrown open. Chairs, rugs, doors, cupboards and vases all transubstantiate into infinite openness the moment the banker falls asleep; the thief's soul becomes vastly selective toward the 'gospels' of every single little enamel casket: he hears everything, he sees everything before him, everything presents itself to him in the best possible form — that pair of closed eyes sends life-giving electricity into the smallest objects, which start resonating with the strict harmonies of a classical orchestra. The 'out-wearability of everything' is a worthy counterpart to the 'Wohltemperiertes Klavier': it's one of those structures lined with absurd dependents, which are known only to the greatest artists' desires.

When in this way everything of the woman became evident to me, I took her by the hand and pulled her after me on a balcony. 'Now now, I don't think we should smooch,' she said, and those frosty words put an end to everything, paralyzing me. I had wanted to see the landscape, the moon, the mountains. Of course I went out on the balcony alone, after my love period that had ended, and started musing about the 'ideal' masked partners who are not spiteful. A moment before, when desire was still at work in me, I went over all kinds of bloody scenes in thought: now when I loathed my partner to the point of annihilating myself, no revenge cliché occurred to me, so dead I felt from those words.

Because the small feelings, small sorrows, small angers are like a vase's 40, 90, or 120° curve, that's why they are visible and audible; but the most tremendous feelings mean a complete psychic turnabout, the complete circumnavigation of the globe, returning to the point of departure, the vase's 360-degree curving away from itself, and that's why they remain invisible: the great feeling is no longer a psychological fact but rather, the curious mixture of time and logic, a clock that is a whole day ahead of time — everybody believes that its number-face is punctual, although lurking behind it is the corpse of a hastening, triumphant, and nonexistent day. Old rococo operas came to my mind, where masked figures or a group of masked characters appear; music plays, dance goes on gingerly, only those mysterious intruders do not mix in with the fête's lilt. What kind of strange sympathy did pull those souls of old to the dance and mask: as if there were more real terror behind Donna Elvira's mask than in the murderous illustrations of medieval danses macabres.[332]

Even then I felt an inclination, as always in my puberty, to simplify love to a grouchy, testy symbol: for instance, to an old beggar torturing an overlong harmonica, desire's mewing garland, & above him, a half-veiled Venus statue of the outskirts, whose drapery is lifted for a moment if one throws a few copper coins into a slot (since then the mock-harmonica has become desire's great cocaine-graph, whose expandings & sinkings are well known to me; 1. *Analecta Morphino-Mathematica*, tom. III. Vol. 8. fascic. 17 a.); I recalled that belittling formula, but now I find it vulgar & too petty.

hatred of the woman

The loathing of love somehow spread to the whole soirée company and could have found satisfaction only in a peculiar form of permutation; one woman related to another, one mock-candle to another man, one buffet waiter to the other garde-nanny, and all of them to one another, separately and in groups: loathing was enclosed in one abstract formula expressing all these imaginable relations, rather than one single old-fashioned and macabresque movie poster. My hatred was unstoppable, that's why it became so ethereal and why any parody or satire could only have impoverished it; for if once hatred indeed finds the place in a woman's being that deserves hatred, it hits a moving target, which buzzes over into another object, there it is linked into another person, then God, then tax regulation, and so on to infinity; disgust's thin, dancing wire runs across the whole world. All that has nothing to do with any 'hatred of the world': although disgust circulates through the entire world like through an excellent conductor, alternating, I still loathe the woman and not the world; but the woman's essence is a dancing atom, it whirls almost whistlingly.

Whoever grabs something fixed grabs something unessential; all the ancient ens-es are transient and forever careering. That's why satires are so laughably impotent: they cling to their theme, and so clang empty. The one who reached his goal deludes himself: if he reached it, it couldn't have been a goal. The intelligent point keeps jumping; it runs away, but all the same, I can possess its course.

All these ruminations probably originated from the fact that my hatred was an empty glass, and around me lots of unknown people swayed on the freshened springs of the dance (my old lyric-etiquette: inside me, active nothing, around me, passive anything), but I felt in each moment that in the next moment my brain would dull forever, and instead of healthy-English, patriotic inductions I obeyed only the Neuron's lazy program: I deduced on a whim. There was a quivering, bright synthesis in my hatred: it was like a ringing summa shower, Mozart stigmata, which never reaches the ground.

The real, great destructions, the undoings corroding the ontological tissues are always so melodic and playful as this ball, with its replayed old dances. Perhaps on such occasions it becomes clinically evident that people do not know the incalculable 'largesse' of true naiveté (my wife always utters this word like the name of some Tropic of Capricorn insect), and woe the one who even for one second believes the music. Gigolos do not cultivate credulity: what a pity. Credulity is the only true, entertaining way; the one who always kicks against the suggestiveness of externals will end up living in his objection's homogeneous water-shade, like a big, intellectual white corpuscle in the virginal vase made in honor of cowardice. Those incredulous ones are far too virginal for any virtue to aggregate in their brains. They would hold it as incest if their brain merged with a flower the way the flower (rather explicitly!) seems to demand it; and yet only this eternal incest, the nauseating liaisons of superstitious perceptions could ever teach us anything. Ontologia est incestus, there's no changing that, but girls will hardly take notice. And I bemoan this fact now, aged sixty, as if I were still fifteen.

The relation of death and idyll was always regular on those 'champêtre-s,'[333] balls, May Days of my young years: with a girl I reached an infinitely beautiful stage, and at that point I noticed that she was not with me, only her cheap copy, & the whole thing had been nothing but a monologue. In fact nobody ever interrupted me: from the glass lampshade of my monologue-body, behind which my relic-like random-brain went on ticking, the adventurous little flies bounced back as if struck. Thus I had all the disposition to elevate the stylite 'cogito' into my life's positivity, but the thing backfired: every inch of me belonged to the one who was outside the lampshade.

theme for a short story on the eternal relationship between death and idyll (interchangeability of kiss and murder)

The above regularity could also be framed as follows: in Venice there lives a gorgeous woman who is involved with two men. One of them is a Catholic priest who is in love with her, the other is a Protestant diplomat-agent from Geneva, who must kill her. She is a regular mix (not psychologically but from the perspective of bodily stylistics, of artistic representation) of the duality of the touristic Venice: doge history & Lido, Byzantine St. Mark-bone and New York maillot. (Her teeth, especially one of the incisors, sticks out a bit, so if one kisses her on the mouth, that bone cuts his mouth like the jutting-out mosaic stones of San Marco cutting into the foot sole, especially if one is in tennis shoes. She wears a brick-color shirt, black Chinese cloister pajamas made of heavy evening-gown silk, and a huge-rimmed straw hat imitating a wrapped-around, thousand-fingered palm branch made of metallic greenish parchment.)

The story's time setting is obviously blurry: there where woman and fashion are in the center, the action cannot be set in one single period, for the so-called feminine psyche is so whimsically ahistorical with its poses of primeval animals, remainder-ideals of historical ages, nonchalant time-flicks or hysterical thirst for tradition, with its anatomy that simultaneously represents different geological eras (how can a physician not conversant with the Cretacean bog-snails and the quack nutriment of Babylonian hermaphrodites treat them at all?). And to complicate things even further, they also crisscross to and fro between nature and time. When she puts on the green palm-hat, this obsession-blazon of Palm Sunday in a slightly loose shape, who can tell if she is sticking to a certain date, or indeed submerging into pantheistic indifference.

The entire life of the cardinal (let him be a cardinal, for a cardinal expresses the absolute with poppy-abstract simplicity: the absolute of moral, of dogma) is a continuous torment, temptation-confectionery, for he is trying to defeat his love. The two of them keep loafing about the woman's quarters, one with the intention to murder, the other, to kiss. The critical night comes in the end (Calvin, Edgar Wallace?):[334] distraught, the cardinal murders the woman, he gives her poison and disappears. After him, the Geneva agent enters, finds her in a half-swoon, now he could easily kill her. Instead, he takes advantage of her and wants to flee, but he is captured at the gate, for in the meantime the Venice police got whiff of the planned murder. They find the woman dead upstairs. The Protestant man doesn't deny anything; his whole life had been one continued plotting to murder, and only in the last moment did he kiss; he is the murderer, he cannot remember any love, with logical clarity he feels the kiss to be murder.

In the meantime the cardinal wants to confess but his confessor has sailed out somewhere, he follows him on a boat, catches up with him at sea and confesses immediately. He confesses his love: his whole life had been one incessant plan to kiss and he only murdered in the last moment: his is an amorous sin, he cannot remember murder, with logical clarity he feels murder to be kiss.

The story concludes with an open heap of metaphors, with the identity of love & murder evidenced everywhere with the help of the woman's dream-anatomy: the angels pick the covering scales of San Marco's white domes like artichoke leaves: hors d'oeuvre petals of the large white cone, each one a flat little apothecary parcel with medicine or poison inside, yellowish-green snow blown everywhere on the square, so powerfully fertilizing that the girls by the tables of Florian or Quadri, like express Danaes, immediately go into labor, & the café owners send up huge umbrellas into the air, which press like bras on a circus pseudo-Hindu god's five hundred breasts, to cover up the fact that from each of those breasts blood flows instead of the commissioned perfume, but the pigeons find this immensely chic and dip their wings into the blood-Worth, causing a Lido Quaker minister to convert to Catholicism on the spot, because he had heard of such a miracle, etc.

microscopic threads of faithfulness; fear from damnation

I have always remained faithful to everybody: 'oh royaume précaire de ma fidélité.'[335] And even now I hang on the lines I have once seen around the ankle of a girl who was traveling on the same bus with me, like Poncelet's ticklish hyperbolae:[336] I have never known her & will never know her, it all happened 20 years ago, but I preserve them in the Exeter vicarage office, like medieval chapter houses or chanceries storing last wills with red seals (ankle? seal?). That other faithfulness, which ties a husband to his wife and the lover to his beloved, I have never known: I can only produce faithfulness in the relations of impersonality. I am thus surrounded, and tied down by the fine but dense network of faithfulnesses (like violin strings on their keys), and I have never broken a single one: I have known two or three of the big ones, but those I have torn apart in two days, or perhaps they never even got to the point of solidifying into a cord.

This faithfulness does not mean forgiveness: the countless tiny threads of faithfulness that tie me to a million important trifles, compelling me to this world like comb-shaped mist, all contain the duality of love and its exact hatred-foil; for the likes of me, love without hatred is like a line without length. Every tiny episode splinter gets its validating small nausea-pigment, like the trachoma-infected eyes getting their eye-drops at the polyclinic, lined up, one after the other, regularly.

I had other types of faithfulness too, for instance, now and again to my wife, but these were ascetic selfishnesses, laboratory experiments, loneliness' wounded-from-birth, bitter hypotheses — who would ever call A's relation to A in the relation of identity, faithfulness? My wife considers me faithful in the last decade, and I rarely go into definitions at the table. My small, meaningless faithfulnesses will all be annihilated with my death; or else, they will surround my Anglican spiritus, like an airy birdcage made of hoarfrost, through which my soul will, however, never manage to ooze onto God's vast highlands, or if it does, whatever of it oozes through the sieve of gimcrack-faithfulness, will hardly make it worthy of salvation. Lethal sicknesses are small bacilli only: the small faithfulnesses are the greatest heresy.

Lately the thought that I would be damned has been tormenting me. In vain I keep repeating to myself that from the infinite line of small sins no big sin ever aggregates, I cannot tell in truth if my sins are small. The old mathematical dilemma: what result does virtue raised to the power of sin give — and what is the power of sin raised to virtue? What has my whole virtue been? The upper-class technique of disillusionment; the ceremonial stylizing of pain. A tad too little to be called virtue. I have been merely sad for 60 years, & this I took to be goodness: why does sickness not save me, O, my Lord Jesus Christ, why do you not count death as the greatest virtue? When I kissed bad women, wasn't it a virtue that I didn't like the taste of those kisses? And when good women did not want to kiss me, although I would have loved to — wasn't that great blindness on my lips virtue? And the eternal chain of fiascos, why does it not turn into virtue from the touch of your divine finger? Why doesn't, why can't the unsuccessful sin become: virtue? For then, my Lord, I could be a saint — 'capitaliste de la grâce,'[337] as a Lyon Catholic friend of mine has put it.

Sometimes I'm overcome by anxiety in the evening (how I'm attracted to belletristic set phrases: I'm tormented the whole day, least of all in the evening, but still I write, 'when in the evening I'm overcome by...') that hunts down my virtues: I'm not trying to cure myself with the radiation of sorrow, but trying to pit against my sin-cells small discovered virtue-cells: if virtue outnumbered sin by one cell, then I could be saved without sorrow, automatically, on statistical principles as it were. I shudder from sorrow, because I don't feel my sins to be defined enough; that's why I cultivate instead this bacteriological bookkeeping. Perhaps I shudder from sorrow because my guilt-feeling is so universal; sorrow is something planimetric, narrow, and lean, while my whole sin-soul (and not my 'sinful' soul) spreads in vertiginous stereoscopy: you can't eradicate an enhancedly spatial phenomenon with plane-like instruments. Euclid's virtue and Riemann's sin:[338] these can be translated into one another's language without a rift — can then perhaps the strained dimension of my sorrow also be converted into the bloated multi-spatiality of my sins? I feel myself to be the most snobbish flower of predestination's model garden.

utopia of absolute sorrow; hysteria and Satan

The heroism of fastidiousness? Humbug. Sorrow & sin are made of such vastly different material & are so different in form that I cannot relate them ('ta vague littérature':[339] when I lie dying I will sorrow as hard as I can, for that's all God wants, not the permed psychology); sorrow is a too tight Fénelon wig that the scornful[340] wind had hung on the wide-reaching plane tree of my sins: I can't fit into it. For sorrow to be worth anything, it should be able to grow into the tissue of my sins: by merely surrounding them like some inorganic and retroactive veto packaging, it cannot annihilate them. Sorrow should adapt to the chemical material of sin, to melt and mix into it (so at the moment when theory-sorrow really becomes biological sorrow, at that moment it could no longer be told apart from sin).

I can't even use the word guilt-feeling, for my sins usually appear to me like independent actions or objects. Because 'my sins' have been those family crises, hollers, ravings, and womanly self-lacerations that sometimes appeared in my Exeter den like natural disasters, Persephone's sudden fall into the pomegranate's dark shadow (meliboia! polyboia! arrètos!).[341] Hysteria I have always regarded (like a chaste little teacher of Greek) to be Persephone's unexpected kathodos,[342] and that sudden darkening, artificial, and empty shipwreck was the body of my sin, my sin itself.

Sometimes I was a few minutes late for dinner, at which my wife threw a terrible tantrum, she fell into fits, out of the blue she started biting and kicking like a perverse ship that finds its satisfaction not between the waves' blue thighs but on pencil-sharp rocks that crush it. The sadistic ship and the image of Persephone moving to hell appeared joined to me ('...on your lips rusty kiss-Morast,[343] your brow an arched gnome landscape') in my wife's raving.

When I saw that disproportionate fire and fury, the thought of 'sin' occurred to me: what if this is sin, hysteria, this posture-epilepsy & senseless wriggling, stylized primitive? Sin is inside my house and I am the cause of it, I thought. But at times like that I felt the need for exorcism rather than repentance; I felt that I had been a careless master who left the garden gate open, and so the devil got in. Devil and sin featured separately in my life; the only devil I have known was external to me. The devil doesn't haunt, sin is not something psychological, the devil *is here*, for instance in my wife's raving, or not here. This was one of my moral moods.

And I hedged in other matters too. The last time I arrived home late because I found it beautiful that the sundown is not also a landscape-down, and with what brooding laxness the town acknowledges the strictly private affair of the water, hill, and sun; I could almost see the angle of interest that links the earth to the sundown; Exeter became a peg-thin angle, so dis-identified with the green code of the firmament. When I got home my wife burst out. Mugs and plates were lined up cleanly and coldly on the table; from the shape of the plates and spoons one could of course guess the dishes to be served, as if to lie before me were the different stages of time, the anticipated splinters of not-yet-existing endingness. My wife's face, clothes, essence did not suit at all the blind thermometer of the laid table; I have always felt how mismatched are cutlery and the living persons' style. I was still chock-full of the setting sun's bohemian parallaxes and found these phials, pegs, the cosmeticized operating service of anticipated 'lunch time' even more alien than usual. My wife fell into a fit; the paleness of frenzy, then the green fog emerging under the eyes closely resembled the morphology of sundown, for every late afternoon is one such shrieking drama, only so far away from us that we cannot hear it, all we can see is the green powder stains death places there (something drawn again from the epoch of pubertal metaphors, but when I remember my wife's hysteria I too am depraved), and the pallor in the rivers' aphasiac mirror. The earth is far too small to be able to completely appropriate the sundown's theocratic diagonals: the female body is far too modest a building to reproduce the devil's whole scale.

If the neighbor's drowsy bees could see my wife's funereal gymnastics (all hysteria is labor: the devil fecundates my wife, and now brings to life its invisible but ginormous child, my objective 'sin' — 'liaisons dangereuses')[344] from afar: they wouldn't hear the holler, wouldn't see the wild gestures, ripped stockings, bitten pillows, but only a fall and shrinking of a big, heavy shadow (tuned green and white), the way I saw the sun: daydreaming basso continuo in a home orchestra. When people use the word 'destiny,' they see a comparable image and hear a black-saccharine buzz; my wife's zigzagging quirk was the thousandfold magnifying of the word 'destiny.' So far I had been only walking on the yacht's deck, on the delicate lacquer of metaphysical imaginings (in fact I'm loath to illustrate a purely spiritual thing with a purely material one, but…), but now I was close to the engine house, the blurry center of pistons, dampers, valves and tandem-engines. How little the movements of the engine house resemble the yacht's movements, even if they are almost identical. How little the sundown's green continuo resembles my wife's moral epilepsy, although the two are identical — the sun is on the edge, hysteria in the very middle.

My wife is then a mechanism, the mechanism of sin. This mechanism shouldn't be visible, just as we shouldn't see the mechanism of pocket watches either, and still, a few clockmakers do lay bare the device, partly to boast and partly for decorative purposes; it seems that God is of the opinion that such a cross-section, ethical spring-galimatias would suit a Calvinist minister's room sterlingly.

At once I felt that my wife had unveiled all my furtive desires; she was probably raging only for my being five or ten minutes late, but I, with namby-pamby loyalty, imagined into that anger all my planned sins that I myself was hardly conscious of. I was stranded between two ethical realms: I have already mentioned one of them — those tiny threads that tied me to the ankle-bones of unknown women, or the ambiguous stigmas of weird inflorescences — a kind of sin-chinoiserie. The other realm: my wife's grand hysterias, lyrical epileptic fits, of which I was the immediate cause, but never with some positive, great, so to say 'normal' sin, only with words that she misunderstood, or small grooming errors. Deep inside I was carrying the rumbling hypothesis of an adultery, but they had no inkling of that fact, or if yes, they didn't much care; the reason for the raving was being five minutes late, a political or literary opinion pronounced with a tad too much nonchalance, or, as case may be, my father's youthful adventures.

prayer in the church

To partly explain why no true guilt feeling could develop in me are these two ethical realms (tertium non datur here either):[345] barely-sins and pseudo-sins; a million moral sporules and a few great symptoms of women's afflictions; a wee belletristic game-monadology and a few pathological chimes of the clock. I didn't know where my true, empirical sin was, but in any case my wife's ravings indicated that I am in a dark kind of relation with sin, & some heresy from the first centuries A.D. would no doubt primely suit the sin-atmospheric type I represent.

To get at once to the gist of the process: it all started with stubborn Persephone associations & ended with light-Cubist church restorations. I have already alluded to and used Persephone and a ship comparison; now is the time to throw in the church business. This I will digress on, for it's not about three random little pictures but about three essential phases, none of which can be left out, and far less can another one be added ('for decorative purposes').

There are no undulating transitions between Persephone and my church-building projects, and no cadence bridges to insert either.

I usually answered my wife's hysteric fits with counter-hysteria, with bites, kicks, the boxing of my own head. After, I ran into the cathedral: as if running to a distant balance with my newborn babe, whom I want to drop on the scales with frantic excitement. I wanted at once to carry rage's sickly antiphonies before God: to simply, passively lay them before Him, for Him to illuminate, to radiate on me some kind of diagnosis based on such howling symptoms of moral life.

I have never been the praying, but merely a 'churchy' kind; whether I had some joy or sin, I always wanted to present them to God, like a warehouse dummy the clothes hung on it, without adding any kind of commentary in thought, meditation, or prayer; I simply sat in a bench or knelt before the altar for ten minutes, a quarter of an hour, intuiting that God was not taking a snapshot of my soul but an old-fashioned daguerreotype picture which necessitates at least one quarter of an hour of exposition time. Prayers were supplanted by such barren model-séances: let God make my current portrait, for I couldn't have lived without being so inventoried & booked-up from heaven, but nothing more followed from my inner impulse. I felt my body to be a complete prayer; I loved the anatomical knots of my existence more than a Catholic does the devotional pepper grains of the rosary.

If singing is double prayer, then body-statuary is triple singing for sure: by the fact that I have undergone something, a prayer-action passed — for what else could I say to God? My body is a component of His body, my mouth is sealed by His mouth glued to mine (that is, any psychology is out of the question, for I am a sealed letter to myself) — in this desiccated erosion-embrace it makes little sense to speak, for God sees me so thoroughly, His eye is so analytical, that with the words of prayer I couldn't possibly goad my falling-apart atoms into synthesis; perhaps from the crossings of a ten-voiced sorrow something might develop, by drawing together all the fields of responsibility (splayed in different zones in my body beneath God's murderous summer) — but I am much too tired for such toil.

description of a church; metaphor and Cubism, church plan

I don't know exactly myself, what kinds of self-architecture problems I wanted to solve with my frequent but passive reporting myself to God: to set unity in place of the dispersal of life, or on the contrary, some coelesta-entanglement in place of the unity of the vital action, another confusion in the wake of a tedious confusion? When I entered the closed church after my wife's and my own hysterical fits, my first thought was that I would entrust this whole scene to God like a role, who would know how to play it best: that I would hand over the sin to God, who could defeat it instead of me. There was undoubtedly some lurking repentance in this impotent role-change; I would have liked to watch the withering of my sin at the touch of God's body. All I could see in the dark were columns and grids, the kinds of successive grid walls that were the protagonists of the bank nuptials; the columns and capitals were red like pineapples or palm trunks assembled from burning coal scales in a forest where flowers are trunks, foliage is trunk, fruits are trunk; these immaterially incandescing & yet positive bridge abutments were connected by the blue steel cables of the slender lance grids.

 I didn't feel under a roof among walls but rather, in the midst of a giant netting or sieve that was lowered from the sky into Exeter's red cellars to fish me out — in old times Ganymedes was clawed into heavens by a bird, but Christian heights still employ the old threads of the net with slow patience. Or perhaps it is the other way round & it's not God who fishes me with those blue grills but man who had built the cathedral as a monumental radio receiver, to trap God?

In sundown's red interference the hesitant gills of God's spirit move to and fro: could they get caught in the church's metallic traps? And I, a little 60-year-old hunchback priest of the great snare, am peeping to see what the hunt will yield? I see nothing but grids that go on forever; if God rushes through them in the shape of wind, his spirit will be combed, which had been sad in freedom but is now happy at being caught by man's net. One grate is wide, the other is low, one is dense, the other is twisted, one is set lengthwise, the other across, so they await God, and God is rushing into captivity, looking not for palms and shiny roads but for these handcuffs prepared for him by man, which arch above the vertical sound boxes of the sunset like the parallel thicket of strings.

A nice Exeter intrigue against God, grand slovenly backstreet docks: here & there a collared candelabra sticks out, like the logs from the lagoon's water that serve for tying the boats to; scattered on the floor, ringed matting, like spare halos left behind in the wardrobe (looking for blasphemy today, Lord, aren't you?); the black-and-white tiles running out in every direction in the hyperbolizing diluting liquid of distance, as if a chessboard was flattened into a 179° rhombus; lying about in the choir stalls, deserted prayer books, autumnal devotion-leaves fallen from the trees of heaven and not swept up; the statues are green from the decay of loneliness, among the blind amperes of silence: sitting in their narrow sheaths like green peas about to fall from their pods; the fan-tracery ceiling funnels are the angels' uncomfortable nests: a cack-handed beekeeper makes such bungled hives, which look like ornamental vases, into which angels need to be packed so that their wide double wings hang out like petals on the vases' brims, with no place for their feet; because of the gallimaufry of the background the lamps seem to be hovering far away from their suspending chains, and in the air they are like bladder-defects in glass, or knots in wood; and the windows are the flaming circles through which over-trained horses are made to jump, to test their discipline.

And in this catalogue of comparisons there was my sinful, or perceivedly sinful soul, like an unwise sundial needle, & started what I earlier called light-Cubism.

I saw the church metaphorically, and I wanted to realize the following metaphors in stone — so did I get to Cubism or at least to something that resembled Cubism. Three cathedral stages: the real, the metaphorically seen, and finally, the Cubistic. Curiously it was precisely the completely dissipating metaphorical, dreamlike perception that provoked in me the Cubist desire to build. And this desire to build was my sin & repentance in one. I shrank the choir's surface to a minimum, and you could not walk in the middle because it sank conically to a low point. The big armchairs were lined up close to one another in circle, like teeth in the hollows of a human jawbone, or the numbers in a roulette wheel; as one can build a piano with quarter tones, so here was such a quarter-tone keyboard, where the chairs' backs rose up to the cathedral's ceiling like muffled fluting; and the organ almost hung from the air into this tube-choir with its free-standing pipes: Damocles' resounding stalactite chandelier. There was no difference at all between the organ pipes and the rising continuations of the armchair backs: the entire architecture looks like frozen electricity circuits going from floor to ceiling without wires.

Thus the source of hyper-geometry is again (for the umpteenth time) my insurgent metaphorical outlook that loosened everything into natural images and which calumnied 'order'; again it took the over-explicating and popular evidence of morphine to drive this fact home in its full rationality. The true structure of the human being is not the skeleton's primary-school anatomical calculator, but those patches that emerge always elsewhere, in different groupings, or from ſtrong physical decentralizing. The skeleton is a regular but unreal composition; it is neither logical nor æsthetic. Cubiſt geometry doesn't represent essence or syſtems — on the contrary, it is the result of metaphorical chancing-apart (is this a word at all?), a more sincere impressionism. So after each sin period of mine a new church plan was added to my notebook.

---

*one needs to die with all the memories,
not juſt those of the laſt few days; about great unfaithfulnesses
after 'microscopic faithfulness' (see pp. 1198–1200)*

I have often vowed to write of women for myself, not for other people to read it but for carrying them easier into death: I want to die with my entire life, not juſt with the laſt days as moſt people do — when they lie dying they condense their whole life into the laſt hours, and die as if those few hours had been their entire life. Because indeed death does not reach back into the insulated paſt of the healthy decades, it cannot caſt its shadow over those; God had tailored the cloak of death so short that life ſticks out as a Concert Mayol showgirl's nude from under the cynical velvet cape. But I don't want to become such a Concert Mayol figure, hence I need to ſtart melting death into those old periods of my life where it couldn't possibly penetrate, reach back to, in my laſt hours.

What do memory images do after death: the wealth of memory images that death has never touched with its chemiſtry? They hover, unowned, beyond life and this side of death. But if we inoculate in time all our memories with death's serum, they can accompany us into the ſtrict ozone of the predeſtined ſpaces. If I am damned, I want to see around myself the collaborators of my fate, the classified caryatids of Calvin's truth. With them I am like the stamp collector with his stamps; there are some sealed and unsealed ones, to one or other a figment of the envelope or postcard sticks still, another is shown off in a separate little frame, untouched; one is exotic and of little value, another looks like an insignificant receipt-stamp but has immense value; in the album there are great gaps & unglued small bunches ready to be swapped — I think the assessment of women in my life happened differently from what I saw around.

I have talked about the thin but eternal ray-reflecting capacity of microscopic faithfulness, but here I need to say something about the nature of the great unfaithfulnesses too. Because from time to time the adulterous hypotheses came to pass, but in those cases the rift opened not toward a woman but in general, toward the crisscrossing, straying paths of the living women (on an alpine landscape: underneath a motorway, perpendicularly above it a viaduct, still higher the large rail-bow of the railway, which loses track even of itself in the great direction-unfaithfulness of the Albula line):[346] in those cases faithlessness consists not in betraying my wife, but in later betraying the lovers with other lovers, etc., so faithlessness meant not that bridge, not the movement leading out of the family, but the company of 'more women,' that is, the geographical foreign ground where the bridge led — and that is a huge difference.

When I embraced a strange woman, I was still up to my neck in ethics; I was a prey to remorses of conscience, but the strange woman emanated moral mass in such quantities that I took no notice of its charge (sin and virtue are not two opposite numbers but the same number with opposite signs). Thus adultery sat in the moral commandment of 'be faithful' as a live flower in one square of an infinitely abstract system of coordinates: the mathematical place of the live flower was indeed the square of sin, but the abstract location could not in the least influence the flower's life, its absolute goodness, its moral concreteness. The same woman was surrounded by double brackets: the one was the narrow braces, tailored to her body, of her own autonomous goodness, *&* those braces were surrounded by the abstract square brackets of 'adultery' — can a pair of brackets change absolute inner value? But if I betrayed the lover with a second lover, I instantly felt that I was in the positive realm of unfaithfulness: I didn't feel remorse of conscience, I didn't find myself immoral, but I discovered, Columbus-fashion, the psychic concreteness of unfaithfulness, and what is more, I discovered its extra-psychic material existence.

Betraying my wife has rather propelled me into ethics-in-extremis, because it made me discover the difference between moral coordinate and moral mass (I will call it yet somewhere a moral 'Sachlichkeit') — but betraying the lover led into nothingness, because it proved how utterly incapable that moral concreteness was of attracting and keeping me tied to itself. How many times I have gone through this moral trivium: marital faithfulness as abstract parenthesis — the lover's kiss as the moral concreteness of heavenly caritas — the kiss of the second lover as the utter annihilation of morals, of personality.

For me unfaithfulness has one sole meaning: it extinguishes my faith in the human person, becoming thus not simply the opposite of 'faithfulness' but that of reality. The perfume of the lover (the first one) is lay grace chemically changed in a small phial; I believe in it, it will save me. But exactly when I am deep in faith and devotion, an upstart sidewalk minute-hand woman arrives out of nowhere, and I immediately pursue her, and the perfume loses all its power. The second woman causes no pleasure, I don't even like her, it's only that she is walking, and my legs walk, carry me with her, independently of me; the whole thing is the purest, most abstract kinetic mimicry. This has always happened: being moved to the utmost religious degree on an object, landscape, time-color belonging to a strange woman, and immediately afterward the abstract, almost unself-conscious fall for the 'first second' woman.

How I'd like to be faithful to the perfume but I cannot, the simple movement after the second (or third, if we start counting from the wife) woman pulls me. Because nothing but kinetic neurological disease ties me to the second lover, I don't feel that I have 'betrayed' the first lover but that I have annihilated both of them & myself into the bargain.

Later, when I had an affair with a woman, I sought a second lover literally out of moral self-abnegation and wild asceticism, who would annihilate the moral concreteness received from the first (face powder! shoe-last! armpit razor!) and make me realize that it is all an illusion.

the mutual exclusion of love and the human being; two lovers; their psychology, moral, connection to Juanus Ethicus

How extra-human are the paths of love: the first lover's sin-insulated virtue-Sache[347] consists of an intuition of such profound layers of life from where the human being, personality, social being had long disappeared; and life with the second lover is only a dry rhythmic adjustment and nothing more — so the fact that I can betray anybody at any time, or rather, that all I can do is betray them, derives from the fact that in love the human being as human or the human being as personality never features.

When I hold my first lover in my arms I feel that divine fate had wrapped me around this woman for all time, like the lid of a sardine can on a can opener, then the lover's human portrait is only a thin membrane above the erotic-moral wave of emotion that could be called an absolute dependence-on-the-neighbor or dissolution-into-the-other-person: and the upstart new lover stands in no contrast to this wave of emotion. There is no connection whatsoever between lover & the love running to her: the lover-human has no power because the lover-human plays no essential role; the emotion is paramount, and that remains untouched, irrespective if we have affairs with anyone in the meantime. One only understands this fact when having to do with many women, because first we all set about love as some essential humanity. And it really drives one to despair to discover that there is nothing human in it, that the eyes' goodness-Basedow,[348] the kisses' faithfulness-wax, the hands' sacrifice-daffodils and the embrace's god-pressing are merely toy masks over one sole amorphous emotion vortex, which doesn't know this eye, those kisses & embraces, because it moves in a far more blind and deaf depth: the greatest love is the most impotent, most unfaithful love.

A paradoxical feeling: when we embrace the second lover, we feel two things: first, an infinite sadness that we 'betrayed' the first (& now we think of the first lover as human personality, as only-portrait) — & secondly, how little contradiction there is between embracing the second lover and the love for the first lover (& now we only think of the feeling toward the first lover).

What torments us is that even the greatest love can 'suffer' the second lover — if we could forget the first, if our feelings for the first could be exterminated by the second, we would feel ourselves to be far less unfaithful: but precisely because the feeling for the first lives on unmolested in its plenitude, for that reason we feel ourselves to be unfaithful — so does embracing the second lover play out above the reflecting wave of the emotion for the first lover. The annihilation of human personality doesn't occur in consecutive absences but on the contrary, in the simultaneous, real presence of all the lovers, and the absolute psychic experience of unfaithfulness consists of the equal, eternal presence of many faithfulnesses (the problem of *Juanus Ethicus*): because my soul can bear complete faithfulness to three or four lovers, the lovers' person is probably no more than a ghostly surface but never reality, for otherwise they could not be fitted inside my psyche.

Is love transient? Nonsense. It is truly not transient but eternal: that's what the great unfaithfulnesses have taught me. If all the lovers of old were to completely die on us, it would never occur to us to talk of transience. It is the eternal presences that represent annihilation, with a kind of inverted syllogistic example: Mary lives, Eve lives, Anna lives, therefore I am nothing, therefore they are nothing. We would like to be seduced through thick and thin & in vain we expect women to seduce us: the first lover is far too strong to be obliterated by the second, but the first lover is also far too weak to not allow us to be seduced in one blink of a second.

There is no more consuming sorrow than seeing that even our 'greatest' loves are completely unfettered. Why is it that faithfulness to the person (and not to the emotion) can be willed only, that it never becomes natural? There is not one micro-millimeter of a magnet in the lover's person — why, oh why? Why does the lover allow our betrayal? In the end, unfaithfulness doesn't exist — reality: nostalgia for the faithfulness that is directed also at the person. (The *Juanus Ethicus* will feel the moral bonds in retrospect, I have systematically looked for the annihilating second lover to see the extent of the destruction, the impossibility of love & personality [female portrait]: who of all women would be prepared to believe this asceticism?)

the ugly women

I have written something about the masked one, & now I should say something about the ugly women. How should I knuckle down to the broadest common denominator of my life, which is no longer a universal (for that is always something well-delineated; even the remotest universals are tightly tailored to the body of something, they are exactly universe-shaped things, although the brain could deal with much broader matters) but, to drop a nice botanical name: *polyvalencia theopathologica*. With me everything revolved around the ugly woman: my God, my faith, my moral, my æsthetic. In puberty one can still afford to think of satires, all kinds of graphic distortions, but now in my old age I see ugliness differently: not as parody but as religious principle, materia prima, so to say, from where the meaning of my life derives. Thought has been the content of my life, or rather, it has been my life itself, & thought has been in an essential brotherhood with ugliness, with the physical ugliness of my fellow human beings.

Curiously ever since my childhood I've had the statistical impression that there are many beautiful people in the world and still, all I ever encountered was ugliness. Because I've been so systematically surrounded by the ugly, I'm inclined to see the situation harmonically: I've been born to decay, to moral and æsthetic half-bakedness, but without any externalities and romanticism attached. The ugly people who surround me are in fact no cripples, and when during a concert or after my sermon I say to my wife, have you seen that cripple, she is outraged that although I'm a priest all I see is the 'appearances,' and anyway, that woman was really not ugly ("now you can really not call her ugly").

Somehow it's me who exaggerates ugliness into them, because I see its germs, and I can tolerate only logical images around me: if a woman's chin is one millimeter thicker than ideal, the rational possibility of a triple chin is verily present, even if there is no biological possibility for it; if it occurs to someone to give a syllogistic twist to that chin, it immediately morphs into the rubber-ringed poster of the Michelin pneu.[349] Only unnaturally can the millimeter rest one millimeter; the logical onward-spark hovering in it lives and sizzles on in my head.

the heresy of identity (the bending of 'parallel' lines)

In my childhood I had the following favorite pastime during dull classes: I drew a closed plane figure, let's say a triangle, trapezoid, and then drew a series of parallel lines to it: around the first triangle, a bigger triangle, a bigger one around that, and so on. At that point it occurred that I could understand the sensorial, dynamic experience of parallelism only if I drew those lines not straight but curved: each successive line became more & more curved, so that the third and fourth triangle drawn around the original one ceased to be a triangle, for the three curved lines didn't cross each other anymore: facing the original triangle's three sides three parabola lines emerged, whose rounded points were situated around the middle of the triangle's sides, but at the triangle's points where the intersections should have been, they ran far away from the triangle; that is, I felt the lines to be truly parallel when I copied one closed triangle in a lifelike manner by drawing in place of one closedness three open parabolas running into three directions.

The triangle's biology is to look like a triangle; the triangle's logic is, that out of its three sides three parabolas should emerge, situated around one point in the way the three leaves of a shamrock are situated around the stem; on the three points where intersecting lines should be, there are three infinite opennesses. If I imagine the triangle's sides to be made of the violently straightened thread of a spring, then the three spirals uncoiled from the three points will rebound into three circles; behold, the illustrative logic and congruence of the triangles: three independent circles.

I have unwittingly applied a similar method of rationalism to the women too, trying to find the logical engine of given points in their bodies: which is the infinitely alien and unanticipated female form that still logically follows from the given woman? Certainly by this method it's easy to syllogize several ugly women even from a veritable beauty; if the triangle's essence is, that its three sides should burst into three circles, then the circle too (as an infinitely many-sided polygon) will have the logical essence of bursting into an infinite number of circles — from the beautiful woman the reason for an infinite number of uglinesses can be derived, more than from an already ugly woman.

senses and intellectualism

The fact that I was so sensitive to women's appearance shows best that I was a typically non-sensuous man; like a naïve rationalist I would analyze through and through the bodily figurations, just as the first precondition of wine connoisseurship is, to not be a drunkard. My childish acquaintances would often say of me that I 'notice everything in women' — although that is perhaps not true: if I look back on my life I feel that I've made one million empty & abstract reflections on women, which I then artificially visualized with the help of their most trivial bodily traits: and that is a far cry from noticing. Or does all observation live off the prestige of that humbug?

Observation: frivolous crystallography; our gaze scatters the metallic netting of prejudice and fishes from it all kinds of arithmetic figures for the brain, to make the women's world even more fragmentary and fractured. Because one cannot talk about love, only about loves, about one million erotic 'hapax legomena,'[350] which do not illuminate each other in the least, do not throw new glossaries among the statues of new women, from whose insulated arcs no pedagogy can be bent toward the other. I'm tied to one woman by a series of disconnected love-roots, the most diverse scale of desires that cannot in any way be attuned; hence the characteristically asocial nature of love, and the ease with which it can be pulverized into reason.

There is a threshold of the density of sensorial impressions, beyond which they can only mean intellectualism; there is a tempo of the pulsation of desires where everything lapses into reason. Is there any theory to propound that in time, matter will metamorphose into light, and its tiniest energy cells, into photons? I have felt this Ovidian shedding in my sensorial impressions, ever since I started living for love: a mass of colors and shapes starting toward me from a woman's Phryne radiator,[351] like material complex — & which already reaches me in the form of relations, values, recursion formulæ & paradox equations.

Nota bene: the photon doesn't relate to matter as soul relates to body; this is not to say that my soul, like a kind of counter-mimosa, would suddenly spread out into reason's strutting fan under the influence of bodily stimuli: no, it's to say that each sensory impression achieves such a strong local sensorial impact in my body, that I am unable to gather myself into the model sheath of one sole desire: my arms, wrists, nails, spine suddenly start living an insulated, independent life of their own, which has nothing to do with each other, with the net result that I feel my love anatomy to be a relation set of incompatible (but all too sensuous!) desires — the only synthetic thing I feel is the constrained intersection point of all those desires (and of that, only the projection intersection!) in my impotent consciousness.

Thus absolute sensuousness and absolute mathematics are identical in love: if my body is girdled by thirty erotic zones, I feel not the zones themselves but their abstract relation. Consciousness is utterly orphaned in this process: the thoughts, desires, movements jut out far beyond the horizon of my strength and dance on the outermost limit of my personality, like colored powder on the ego's barely-magnetic ledger; the sea breeze of the unknown woman blows on it, stirs and scatters it, and the magnet barely manages to withhold it. Ratio est forma colloidalis sensus?[352]

Love's lesson is precisely that it yields and defines the liminal values of the senses, of matter; with its sizzling decentralization it leads into the beatific world of the logical estuaries of matter. In our folly we need such a terroristic external lesson-kiss, which could ultimately compromise the nonsensical difference between love's so-called 'materiality' and 'spirituality': kiss partitions matter so much, it disentangles so much the compacted tissue of our nerves, that on the one hand we get more matter, enhanced variations of matter, and on the other hand, their infinite number already gives the impression of an abstract geometrical structure; matter is so plural, its variety so luxurious, that whatever is so infinite cannot be self-serving: it is precisely the infinity of matter (the pathological plenitude of sensuousness) that proves how it cannot be all-important (qui est theomorphus est harpagonus):[353] only those relations are important that emerge among the infinite shades of matter. Baroque in the shape of a jest: metaphysics is the erotic Harmonielehre that tackles the finite number of differences of infinite-component matter.[354]

Very thin women are beautiful because they are such an embodied difference-tone. There is nothing 'spiritual' about the thin woman, on the contrary! But she is sensual in a very different way than the recent past's courtesan conserves. In the old days there was the female animal and the heavenly angel, now we have a clever compromise, the thin body. The thin woman is no substance but a burning limes-flower, matter's hair-thread ontic.

æsthetics; dream as producer of categories; category as producer of beauty

---

The natural history of ugliness still impresses me in my old age, but I cannot touch it anymore, for I feel that I haven't yet got the beauty of beauty into such a form that I could take with me. Today too I dreamt something about a quiet little street in the country in the spring, and during this dream such an atmosphere of beauty flooded me that it makes tinkering with ugliness impossible for the whole day. I have often tackled beauty as a curiosity (blague cosmique?),[355] as a special case of mathematics, which appears under the catalytic effect of certain peculiar values in a neutral environment, but which I have never as yet considered as a narcotic atmosphere that can be felt in my blood, as stifling inebriation. I have the feeling that one could concoct the chemical compound, pharmacological produce, which could physiologically elicit in our nerves the mood of beauty.

One needs to attack æsthetics from two directions at the same time: with such a pharmakon and with a mathematical formula. Perhaps beauty is not even unitary, and the æsthetic experiences are not made up of that physiological vibration of the nerve pulsation & mathematical order at all; both function separately, exert their influence separately, and they cannot be brought together under the crudely simplifying term 'æsthetics.' One of them dwells at the depth of the body & can be felt in dream like an unknown function of an unknown organ; the error of the 19th century materialists was to have been not radically materialist enough and not penetrating to the senses of the senses. They stopped at a few banal, sensory phenomena and didn't attempt to find new senses with unknown new functions.

Now when I'm waking up from a dream I have the hasty impression that beauty comes into being (at least in dream) by way of a hidden organ of sense, the 'sense of categories,' perceiving phenomena: for instance I see a red book cover in such a way that I immediately see with it & feel with it, sensorially, the two great categories of time and space; included in it is the nostalgic free course of spatial distance and some kind of historical disquiet of the temporal situation, the asymmetry of passage: it is from those two sensorial surpluses that the red book cover becomes beautiful; to put it in grammatical forms, I see it time-red and space-red.

Morphine is nothing else but a substance triggering one to categorical vision; there everything becomes only-category, phenomena lose their cohesiveness & become merely the impotent mathematical functions of time and space — and because morphine corrodes & irritates precisely those 'senses of category' which are needed for the autonomous perception of time & space, we have the impression that we live in a chemical coitus with the material of time & space: this is one possibility of beauty.

Or perhaps it is the other way round and there is a primary material of beauty that we immediately perceive in the shape of time and space, on account of an optical illusion or of the make-up of our hidden-most æsthetic organ of sense, so that our experiences of time and space are only the naïve masks and natural constrained hypocrisy of the original, a priori given beauty: a simple perception is so strong and brutal that nature made sure to fragment it into time and space, so that all perception would come to us by the diminishing, intensity-muffling wires of those two categories.

biology and mathematics

Undoubtedly beauty shows a connection, on the one hand, to some well-nigh counter-vitalist, overmuch-biological matter (life's most shameless asymptote), and on the other hand (as I have signaled above), to logical absurdity, rational excess-Sezession, the most virginal basic paradox of the intellect. These are two poles, whose dichotomy, emphatic difference, we stress until we realize their identity — in Deo: is the life-most life, the lowest point of existence, not already identical to God's life-giving thought, idea? When God invented existence and it appeared, in the first moments of the beginnings of time was the most ancient, most primal life not identical to the most absurd rational punch line, moreover: wordplay? For life indeed appears as a strikingly absurd lack of proportion in comparison to the eternal non-life preceding it, and to God: when compared to God, an amoeba is a joke, a farce, wordplay, paradox and sophism; but the same amoeba or protoplasm is the most ancient form of life, its cause and germ; it is also the concrete root of instincts, organs of sense, loves and æsthetics — that is, in Deo the most biological and the most mathematical (arbitrary-paradoxical) branches of æsthetics are identical, they are one.

Here we should turn our attention toward the colors mostly; to the sole worthy theme of æsthetics, where the close unity of maximal vitality and maximal logic is felt the most obviously, and from here we should turn our eyes to the woman, the woman, the woman: *Kritik der reinen Frauen-Chromatik*.[356]

experiment: a peculiarly quaint, pedantic style elicits the absolute experience of beauty in the author of the Meditations

Why is *this* beauty, this precise, isolated, punctual one I am about to describe here, why do I always feel beauty to be a frenzied 'question of detail,' unexpected throw of the dice, why do I feel its essence, its almost murderous definition in the palimpsest of one moment?

Spring is always cold like a bathroom facing North, and violet like the robes of the two lean cardinals who are fervently praying that the old priest they hastily elected pope may live for at least five minutes more, to have time to sign a new declaration of war and a novel dogma scheme; one article of faith pressed into text and declaration of war against the emperor: for this is what spring is, especially the lilacs smelling like soap, from actual politics &

slowly oxidizing dogmas they all swell into the photographically exposed lungs of sour shrubs, as if the angels' breathing & credo-inhaling could only occur on such ornamental lungs.

Lurking in a black angle among the brambles, like the dark co-tangent of life, there is the prae-purrita harmony of the rendezvous;[357] the leaves are sharp like the angels' glassy replicas or like official love's bumpy-green kisses: the agape-blade will draw blood from amor's fatty hypotheses. (Why is *this* beauty for me, why do I feel this to be reason's purple-pointed 'Ille sufficiens' encyclical? Why is it precisely here that I feel the classical & cooling arteries of æsthetics? Why do I feel beauty's peasant pulse beating at such vision-qui-pro-quod? Perhaps the way in which God's most autonomous deed after creation was self-destruction on the cross, so beauty's most self-akin form is the stretching to breaking point of the springs of existence?

Spring is always black, like the first towel of kiss rising from the waves of its lies; a large, fluffy black robe that administers the stolen chrism to illusions. What if the only handcuff-like positivity can be that in which the dependent counter-harmonies of being-out-of-place reach the geyser status of ineluctability; for love may well be the worst of all balances, but its weights, which have grown like reefs into the objective scales of our palms, nevertheless belong to God's alphabet. In the lilacs' twigs the sky's blue blood circulates like alternating angels; my love's forehead is surrounded by a lovely blue garter, like a Capricorn diadem surrounding the globe. The great Tesla rhymes of empiricism resound in my ears like some scholastic notion, like the self-forgetting triumphal chant of a God lurking incognito.

I feel that in the spring the sky is empty; the clouds' great devotion-diaries peddle in the seraphic propaganda of dethronement. God's style is always something sharply anti-divine, not out of some love of paradox, but because the more ancient disposition of rendezvous wills it so. Does this woman want my faith in her entirely without God? To take advantage of God's great happiness game and baptize it into frivolous denial? Does she not realize that the spring is a great hypothesis & God, one time one? Can God understand the world? (Ornamental heresy in me; petty pseudo-Augustinian dandyism. My Sunday pleasure: who can devise more heresies starting with P, in five minutes.)

Spring is a shrub in all its mathematical prole nature; in the plenitude of godlessness it is a greater mystery than God: what is æsthetics if not the inkling of the excessively-divine degree of non-divine things, heretical theogeneia? God's punch line is the luxury of the infra-divine contents; God carries an infra-god in his womb, who is a trans-god in its æsthetically aborted state (Ens matinale?).[358] (Here God simply means some superlative in general.)

Come then, my young lady, to our rendezvous among the lilacs, ad hoc showpiece of an eternal substitution. The blind nil-seal of your place surrounds me like flour-grid snow; now you became a positivity or rather, 'position,' now that the imposture of the imagination humiliated you to me. Why is beauty born in me like this? Why is it that for a sixty-year-old peasant-born Calvinist minister fact becomes a fact in this way? Where is the glitch, where is the miracle in all this? Humbug phosphoresces around me like the Redmount meadow in the winter: the whole world is blue, as if they had made a huge blotting-paper out of God's love, to soak up with its violet capillaries the last remaining Calvinist staffage of the world — what is the bloated authority of the lie? What is the Don Juan-esque allure-secret of truth? What is the great image-depository of our virtue?

I cannot ever feel dizzy, I cannot draw a crooked line, I cannot, woe me, I really cannot: play — now when my hands try to filter the source of beauty, those hands do not tremble, being far too healthy, like prize-winning livestock. It's not I who feel dizzy: it is from the facts that some alien matter irrupts; it is God who sweats godlessness into the lukewarm veils of the spheres. Perhaps I am only a brazen fly fallen into Christ's clotted blood like into a flytrap; perhaps I am a true heretic, or a mediocre short story writer; an angel, or a mask of validity.

For me, my dear rendezvous partner, woman has always been at the same time technique and death; that's why I smuggle you into the lazy tress of 'aisthesis,' that's why I pour in you the sleeping God's splendid isolation blood.[359] What is beauty if not the fact that all essence is merely relation, and you, O, Flora Ambigua of æsthetics, are the expression of all relations? When under the bilabial suction-pump of the kiss, death's black veil appeared, preventing one single morsel of the kiss to fall on life's blind floor (so did the wise women in Rome guard the host before the altar rails, I've seen), & slowly covered our lips in some kind of lipstick called 'cimetière de Céline,'[360] so God too could take it as some secret-prohibited pill: was it not the love-ingredient in love, that of all materials, only the truly-material leads from one person to the other; nova lex geminorum pulchritudo.[361] O, my love, beauty, thou great popularizer of death, in fact perhaps you dilute the non-protons of things into hyperbolic mannerism. When you pour the horizon-pools of great categories under hazardousness, don't you feel that those shiny universe-mirrors, great perspective-trapdoors of vanity, are in fact what is pressed out of the nothing-part, nothing-roots of things; nothing pours out of the world like resin from ill pines — categories are the great Venus-gardens of counter-ontology. Beauty runs around categories like a murderer around the place of the murder.

Death was present in every blooming lilac, syringa mortalis, but not as death, only as the spraying fourth or Bacon fifth of a distant violin; æsthetic expresses some multitude that is unbearable for matter, one half of that multitude — the other half of that multitude is processed in the shape of death. Death is God's glossy therapy-trouvaille against nothingness; the philosophical weeds of nothingness have morphed into death's noble rose; caritas mortis, pulchritudo Dei, impossibilitas materiæ, affirmatio inversa etc.³⁶² If death is God's cosmetics among the material's great popularities, then beauty has a lot to learn from that celestial mundanity; for me, O my dear friend (you hang on this appellation a bit like an ill girl's clothes on the hanger in front of an operating theater), death has always meant raw common death and this beauty-kinship, and when I drank from your mouth your scant-cream sibling-whey, I felt I was fighting death with another death; that I was fleeing inside, not outside: merging into the prison walls, not into the surrounding landscape, and so managing to free myself from the screws. But God has made everything in such a way that only after the most absurd metamorphoses can his things be grasped: beauty performs this complete turning inside out, the *nonsense training of distancing*.

Bitter pudicity on the Exeter waters; in my files the past's ebbed prisms and emptying pipes; time has been an adverse multiplication above your head, petite-amour, the groves were singled out by the angels on defect telescopes, the Sun is raging for new quotas: the more I press the impossible words into things, the more bloodily they labor themselves out from God's stingy womb. How consciously I attach vignette after lousy vignette to the heavens' tidied-up drawers of the heavens; on the lilac bush, this: "death's open pose, kiss-nihil equals beauty-everything, God is a rising mercury column among the world's Celsius ladders" — on my soul, this: "predestination theory as the dehumanized mind's movement in vacuum, and so as one mask of beauty; peasant prolegomena, cocksure crossbuck in the way of all mysticism; physiological sex-mimicry to the glaring-blue heavenly bushes of 'primum mobile'" — and yet another label, let's say of style: 'cœlo-sexualitas coeli,'³⁶³ to make visible the test-tubes of conscious lying.

When I am experimenting I am in a fever; in vain do I know that I'm lying, I believe those lies, what is more, it's precisely faith that makes it possible for their lie-profile to be wholly contoured

& become an essence-portrait; on the other hand, it's the analogical breadth of the lie that makes possible the fermenting acid-love that can already be labeled the basic form of faith. The method immediately adds a lesson to beauty: something is concrete in so far as it is impossible; beauty only lets itself be seen through such 'estilo culto' forms.[364] Raw mysticism works with raw contrasts: yes and no, empty and jam-packed, etc., & rightly so; it's these contrasts that I would like to gloss, expand, rationalize, with all their capillaries: to place in the center of madness another, second madness, whose relation to the first would be so alien as to push one almost automatically into the well-nigh superhuman state of pure reason. Only once would it be possible to go mad again inside madness, that is, to go-further-mad, to go to the length of a whole madness further in madness — perhaps then we could realize something.

beauty

Beauty is the domain where it becomes evident that any object of the world can bear any other object of the world, mirrorium morale. Beauty is so important that I sometimes have to adopt even the sickening occasional articles of two-pence mysticism for blood in order to get closer to it. God cannot be called 'prima veritas,' because truth is a human concept: and beauty emphasizes precisely that God can have nothing to do with any truth whatsoever, only with the happiness of existence. And this is no cowardly eudaimonics:[365] this 'happiness' is the lyrical dimension of simple existence. For there is some measure of quality in all æsthetic phenomena; a system of pluses and minuses, proportions, scales and degrees, which surrounds an unknown, anti-number nude (without defining it, for dimensions never justify).

Beauty is the great, par excellence rational precondition to the reason-less conclusion that presses on the statics of things; by beauty we mean the reason over-swollen with divine happiness. Because this 'felicitas' is the ultimate important thing: all the beautiful things explain the fact that there is a form of life devoid of truth. Devoid of truth, not opposed to truth, not false, not irrational, not something in any way opposed to truth. Any programmatic devaluing of truth is foolish and laughable, but nevertheless it is a fact that soon we will have nothing, or next to nothing to do with truth in general; among the few haughty and orphaned stars of the highest constellation truth can never feature.

I started this whole artificial madness by treating myself to a few local mixed metaphors about the spring, my lady friend, lilac bushes, and raising the question, why I happened to feel the essence of beauty in this utterly peculiar metaphor-cancer, although that's precisely the style I try to avoid most, as a defiant Adam tries to avoid the apple orchard of charabia.[366] In theory I'm attracted by theses like, "French Surrealism is nothing but the consistent imitation of reality," that is, that the intensified factification of fact can only be completely resolved with the icy methods of the denial of facticity, tyrannically causing the fact to virginate back into something only-semantic; in reality though I loathe all mechanical confusion, even though it is through it I know everything I know. (Most autonomists of dream have no inkling about morphine images; and it's no help if they taste morphine.)

I will jot it down for myself as a curiosity, choice meditation tidbit for a priest: in history, substances are always entrusted to apaches, because essence is like the unidealized, gross sexual organ next to its veiled social functions that mean the forms of 'love': somebody who boasts about their essence (that is, their sexual organ instead of love) needs to be exceedingly base; in order for someone to cultivate the most authentic bacilli of beauty on their own style-skin, they need to be 'artistic insanities.'

Such naïve venery of orthodoxy has always been alien to me: instead of the blunt orthodoxy of 'beauty' I've always been drawn to the preaching & pusillanimous neology of 'art.' But in my old age I had better show enough manliness and puritanism to resort to the material of swindlers, if that's the only place where I can find the raw and true values.

*about the styles of the different epochs;
the different epochs' view of themselves*

It's a curious & remarkable thing that every epoch sees in its own style not an ornamental approach to unattainable beauty, but an X-ray image, principle-scaffolding of the very essence of beauty. That's what I feel with 'neue Sachlichkeit,' Surrealism, and a few more of their ilk: I don't find that they produce beautiful things but that, casting aside the tradition of the artwork, they are exploring beauty itself in the self-contradictory form of experimental metaphysics; as though it were not a style that was beginning, but an anti-style; after the amateurish hedgings of art, beauty's concrete physiology.

Interestingly, every style has the shape of 'essence,' that is, they have a central feature that can always be imagined as the paramount trait of 'essence': in Gothic, infinite ascension, in Renaissance, infinite harmony, in Baroque, infinite spirituality, in today's epoch, infinite lifelikeness. Any of these features would be enough on its own as exclusive characteristic of substance. If somebody is in pursuit of verticality, they will not realize that what they do is Gothic, but instead, they will have the impression of drawing the most universal, thus the most a-temporal feature of 'essence'; every style consists in trying to draw the most universal feature of life, but in the process it ends up producing the most ephemeral toy-things, like a man who writes down a long text with closed eyes: during the writing he feels the pure shapes of the letters, but when he opens his eyes he can see the bunkum he put to paper.

But as a rule an epoch never opens its eyes. (Of course it's also possible to imagine the thing the other way round: every epoch plays, & every next epoch hallucinates the essence-searching nature back into its antecedent.) Style is followed by style: they say the style shift can be imagined to infinity, that is, there is no single kind of beauty but a million, which equally possess an equal degree of beauty. In my opinion the fact that we can make infinite variations is the most glaring proof that we are speaking about one unified thing; only that one, unique thing, or, to speak in cant, 'mono-physical' thing is inexhaustible; because the 'one' is closed, something that cannot be penetrated, only circled around, and there is an infinite number of positions on the circle's circumference. Infinity & One are the world's oldest pair of twins.

---

in connection to the number of styles, games about numbers in general; what is true structure? About the swapped letters à la Bernouilli

---

In my childhood I used to imagine numbers like the different degrees of openness of a spiral; '1' was the start of the line, where spiraling is present at an absurd degree in so far as it circles around itself (being lock and key in one person), squeezing completely around itself and closing to one point (its difference from the point is that a point is not something closed, but this starting point exists due to its closedness, its numeric self-stifling pudicity); the 2 is the slightly more open, widening portion of the line; the 3 is even more open, while the ∞ is a spiral widened to a straight line. Therefore the 1 was no longer even a number but only a center of barrenness, the infra-numeric nucleus of closedness. The first member, labeled 1, of the line of numbers is an organic '1' — but here it's about something much more important than the spiral: the inorganic 1, which has nothing to do with the number-1.

The imaginable infinite line of styles revolves around such a non-numeric, ex-arithmetical 'one and only' beauty; this 'infinity' too is only the décor-like integration of the idea of intensifiability — when we imagine the infinite line of numbers (or styles), we keep counting up to a point, after which we imagine the inebriating concept of continuability, nurtured by the pathos of the preceding great counting — from the territory of counting we move over to the alien territory of dynamics & convince ourselves that we are still inside the world of counting, which is patent self-deceit.

Counting and infinity relate to one another like the following two things: a man travels by boat to huge distances; another never leaves his spot, but with the help of a peculiar drug he inoculates his dreams with the experience of travel, of departure (if he had been departing in reality, he could never have possessed the experience of distance with such dreamlike exactitude): the first gent is counting, the second gent is infinity. Thus in infinity we find no trace of numerical multitude: infinity is simply something other than numbers; it doesn't relate to the colors of the spectrum as yet another million imaginable colors, but as one (small!) form.

This little mathematical clarification of the relation of beauty & style came by as accident, it has never been dear to my heart, but all the same, these three counter-number number-like concepts may have some bearing on however little sub-specie-aeternizing history: 1. the '1' outside numbers, that is, shapeless 'seipsum';[367] 2. the pseudo-numbers, for instance those of the styles; a line of numbers with an open end is no longer a line of numbers, the empty space at the end of the line retroactively impacts the numbers (in grammatical terms, 'regressive assimilation'); and finally, 3. infinity's characteristically anti-mathematical, dynamic, or psychological concept, whose content is the pure movement of numbers, but never any kind of number. In fact, there are, or more exactly, there should be devised as many numbers in the world as there are kinds of things to be counted, specific countables; if we denote three things with the number '3' & four, with the number '4,' and following that, I take that 3 & 4 as consubstantial things, as the two members of the same Numerus family: I have committed a great lie, because 3 and 4 have an utterly different inner structure; the fact that in 3 there are 3 units and in 4, 4, would be yet a very naïve reason to regard their anatomies as related; the game starts with '4' having an essentially different anatomy than '3,' it's only that so far no one had given this the least attention.

Thus we either declare that the number is impossible (*Unmöglichkeit der Zahlen*: Jena's slender daffodil),[368] or we need as many types of numbers as there are numbers: 3, 4, 5 make up not a line, the way an antelope, a hamadryad,[369] a carpenter's plane, and a Leibniz portrait don't make up a line either but belong to four different worlds; there will be a separate theory for 2, a separate taxonomy of 3, 4, etc.

Because the human body and a stone too can be divided into parts of the same size and weight, a common divisor can be found, but what an external and artificial cause it would be to declare the human body and a stone to be members of the same family, although they have 3 and 4 as common divisors; the one is just such a meaningless, extraneous, and contrived something on the two alien bodies of numbers. (*Eine bio-organische Auffassung der nicht-homogenen Zahlenkörper*: the dark blue lily of Göttingen.)[370] (The biologizing of numbers is ridiculous, for numbers were purposely made in order to express, or more exactly, represent, a side of life devoid of biology. If they were made with an anti-life purpose, why am I objecting to the fact that they are not treated like lifelike facts? Simply because in my morphine dreams I saw even abstract numbers as lifelike, non-homogeneous logical bodies: even 3, an empty, fictitious, counter-life, rational figure appeared as a living organism to my sensitivity — not in the form [that would have been useless] of seeing behind it 3 apples or 3 jockeys for that matter, but because I saw its very abstract nature [being made up of 3 units] as fantastic, sensing in my nerves, for instance, the uneven, indeterminate, and undulating nature of the 3 enclosed units' intellectual weight.)

Why does the drowning root of beauty live for me precisely in these small mania scales: the spring, violet lilac, the pope elected when he lay dying, the rendezvous, death — why is it that these burlesque protons and spurious plasms, whose premises and even relations are the most whimsical imaginable — why is it that of all things they have for me the nature of passiones entis?[371] Perhaps God is nothing but the moving synthesis of all indeterminacies, the likely origo of the thousand-thread coordinates of uncertainty? Beauty appears to be the formula that expresses universal exchangeability: quaestio curiosa ex doctrina combinationis,[372] to go back again to my favorite theme, the Bernouilli letters.[373] He asked how one could swap an infinite number of letters, to which an infinite number of envelopes belong, in a way that exhausts all possibilities, putting each one of them into a mismatched envelope. And they found a formula for that, which expresses the sum total of cases of swapping.

Beauty relates to the world as this found arithmetic formula to the letters and their envelopes. In Surrealist short stories and paintings I relish this rigor of permutations, the absolute precision of swapping; if someone could present the sum total of the world's phenomena in all the imaginable permutations, or find the formula that expresses that possibility, he would come across something absolutely beautiful, managing to pluck and make resonate the primal spine cord of beauty.

What is true structure? Bernoulli's swapped envelopes are on the true degree of artistic composition; because every unit connects to every other unit without exception, the units get into such transcendentally close relations, such connection-panic that cannot be dissolved by any means. The formula expressing infinite exchangeability causes twofold bliss — first it brings to mind retroactively the chaos preceding the formula, the spasmodic states of exchange, when there is no regularity at all in the disturbance, there are only letters stuck in the mismatched envelopes, which fall apart in isolation; but in the next moment when I throw the formula among the cases like some theological yeast, in an instant I see it all before me as a harmonic world, the proportion-piling picture of rhythm, order, of correspondences.

If I imagine the letters and their envelopes in space and watch the directions of exchange in the air like concrete lines (like the planetary orbs: letter a into envelope b, letter a into envelope c, letter b into envelope a, etc.), then from all these exchange orbs I will get the world's most beautiful and regular space-net. The idea of absolute permutation expresses my life's two basic states in one synthetic formula: the psychic hither-and-thither undulation disarrayed to the point of madness (perhaps the adjective is not appropriate here, for madness is not disarrayed but on the contrary, punctilious and pedantic), and the psyche-denying perfect architecture that is at a remove from the human.

Psychopathology and architecture, dispersing hypochondria and absolutely-geometrical architecture were one and the same thing in the Bernoulli-Euler formula:[374] here the basic type of exchange, error, glitch took center stage and from this the rule, the absurdly-complete order was born. The 'meaningless' hither-and-thither swaying of associations is a frivolous & barren game only until it covers all the imaginable erroneous byways and derailments — after having walked down every byway, we recognize in it the image of the perfect linear system. The logical end point of patho-psychology is, even unwittingly, architecture, just as the rush of a million ephemeral celestial sparks through dark space will trace a million red lines, and when they have all disappeared, we will still see red cones, snake-balconies, and uneraseable stair-spools on our eyelids: reality is not the spark but the orb that rests behind even after the disappearance of the spark.

It's interesting to observe the moment when the rail-comb of the associations gone astray suddenly steps out from the human being into the extra-human architectural space: the pictorial or intellectual content of the associations falls back into the soul's worthless urn like a spark into black water, but their trajectories stand in space, rigid like an objective grid, Bernoulli-Cubism in the outer world. (The Bernoulli letters have shown to me the identity of absolute order and absolute disorder, and thus faithfully symbolized my thoughts about literary style: for me two possibilities of writing and language exist, if once I should want to write something that indeed asks to be written — the one is the medieval Latin tongue, this lies in the dimension of 'order'; the other is an entirely dishabilly, frivolous, topsy-turvy mongrel lingo that nettles every national academy, a pure macaronic. Now when I'm writing this diary, these two penchants are at work in me — Latinity & international cant.)

three editing techniques

I have experienced three major editing techniques: one of them is the pan-permutation editing mentioned above; the other is the 'magnetic' one, when a center of force draws around itself the subordinate elements (in the permutation style there is no subordination!); and finally, the biological cell-style, when the given individual cells are drawn together by life, by organic force, and the place of order here, of order understood in formal terms, is taken by the mystery, 'why is it that cells stand forever in this precise order and not otherwise?'

In the first case the structure runs across an infinite thread (a million orbit combs, orbit ellipses, orbit-spirals on the blue atlas of 'permutational beauty-firmament') — in the second case, the structure thickens into one single point of the magnetic center (that is, one thing is very one-shapedly one) — and finally, the third case, of vital, organic cells is characterized by a structuring that occurs even despite the denial of structure — 'life is that which is absolutely structured even without any structuring device.' (All this is the coming to the fore of the above-mentioned formless non-numeric unity, of pseudo-numbers and of the similarly counter-number concept of infinity in the world of structure: interestingly, the order-features of absolutely artistic structure are not in the least numeric, mathematical features, what is more, they are their three principal enemies. The Bernoulli style is an infinite mass of relations fleeing into space; the magnet-style is the applying of unity; the biological cell-potpourri is the coming to the fore of pseudo-numbers.)

I hold the first editing style, pathologically pure combinatorics, to be of prime importance also because this is what most resembles the mind's exigency for absolutes here on earth; 17th-century concettismo, neue Sachlichkeit, Surrealism (the Euclidean three dimensions of the self-same taste) all work in this compositional manner.[375] In nomine Bernouilli: '... spring is always cold like a bathroom overlooking north, & violet like the robes of the two lean cardinals who are fervently praying that the old priest they hastily elected pope may live for at least five minutes more... slowly oxidizing dogmas... like the dark co-tangent of life, the prae-pourrita harmony of the rendezvous,' etc., etc. — these words perform the grand, frivolous asceticism of swapping, that is, they serve to draw those permutation lines among the world's scattered phenomena, which mean the superlative knotting technique of inter-connectedness; when imagination performs violent erroneous connections, it is then that it ties the wildest twin knots;

in one image there are flowers, horse-hams, vase bases, & profile shells, as they say, 'heaped' on one another, although here a stricter & closer structuring manner is construed than those of the Cids: it's not tying a thread around one set, but the individual, separate connecting of every single element to every other element, like with a variable electric wire; instead of the composition proper, a pan-relation.

---

woman and beauty, Bernoulli permutations and 17th-century Baroque or modern Surrealism; experiment for analyzing beauty: woman at night in the hotel hall

---

In broad outlines, the connection between woman and beauty is by far not as simple as one might imagine; sometimes I feel that at one end of a linear color spectrum stands the permutation, while at the other end the woman (here I always mean a woman dressed according to the latest fashion, because for me the naked body is æsthetically worthless), but I cannot grasp their kinship any better. In a London hotel I've seen an elegant woman arrive from the theater; the lamps in the hall were already switched down, only the porter's small table lamp was glowing, but the central heating worked at full gear as before, gaining peculiar importance in the dusk, as though it had been the nightly vapor of things, the secret but unveiled fever of beauty.

For the things, too, move sufficiently much during the day, so that in the sudden evening silence heat pours out from them — how many times we hide even from ourselves the lurking bodily fever, & when at last we lie down in bed, heat at once floods the undressed body like a suddenly cleansed, wide melodic territory; in the dusk those columns, armchairs, palm trees and writing desks seemed to transform into the warm fictions of their own 'central heating.' In such moments one doesn't dare touch anything, the objects appear so much as the autonomous images of sickness; in order for one to dare sit in an armchair, it would be necessary for another person to sit somewhere around, who could conduct the hallucinating charge of 'objectivity' into his own body, like a kind of patent objectivity rod. One person cannot accept reality, the objects' histrionic fact-corporation for practical purposes, because he is a far too rudimentary transformer to be able to muffle the disproportionate intensity of existence — he is like a small light bulb connected to a 10,000 Volt electric circuit.

As under normal circumstances one doesn't sense what a superhuman energy-terrain the heart is, so he will not notice what energy-romanticism is raging in the simplest objective facts; is there anything more innocent than a small porcelain tile — and yet this night, in the central heating's ontology-fever we intuit the fantastic mass of energy that this small existence develops for a few degrees above the level of non-existence. And like at times when we wake up in the middle of the night from the racing of our heart and cannot imagine the cause of its repeated thumping, when it would be so much easier for it to stop and sink to the lower energy-Celsiuses of non-existence: that night in the hall I couldn't understand why these experiential energy-crystals sustain themselves with such frenzied effort, with the digitalis of forms, when they could all fall back to the great energy-equipoise of non-existence?

The objects stand in the air like an iron ball that is only forced up in the air by the pressure of light rays; how much light is needed to lift up an iron globe with its sheer pressure? Because one has to imagine the same amount of energy for existence too, which happens not naturally but with the wildest arbitrariness. If a man were born who is endowed with hypersensitive organs of sense to perceive force, he would be annihilated by the simple existential energy (which is a far cry from vital energy!) of the smallest splinter of matter situated in however far a district, not to mention this hotel hall.

The woman returning from the theater walked into this ens-feverish dynamo-flower, like a stray butterfly; the objects' artificial existence-throbbing suddenly sank to half from the fact that somebody shared with me her radiating energies, and I thought of Robinson who stood in the dual focus of the circle of existing things, and there was no one to share with him the great 'voltage paré' of existence.[376] Above her forehead there was a twisted, long, see-through feather, which bent over her nape, reaching her right shoulder and in front partly fell to her breast, and partly twisted to her left shoulder; large beads hung from her neck; in places her dress was so taut as to make her flesh a phosphorescent mere-concavity, the surface was pushed back like the blazon's negative on a signet ring — in other places it was flaring and wide like a parachute, which scoops out huge hemispheres from the air's body, to adorn her figure with such atmosphere lampions: crinoline Picard. The ostrich branches divided between her breast & shoulder revolved around her eyes' black fatigue like tethering electron orbs, shifting incessantly to the side with the momentum of petal-like parallelism; as if God's prison too were a pink fireworks-foliage and the smoke-shape falling from that foliage.

$$n = n + q$$

For me this woman was first and foremost an image, in the most exploitative sense of the word; secondly, she was a shapeless, but at the same time awkwardly sharp desire to act. The moment she dropped from the hotel's revolving door, like a glass splinter dropping from a wrecked kaleidoscope, this bifurcating experience was born in me — complete only-image and complete possibility of only-action; I defined the woman from these two distant angles as one can measure the distance of stars from the angle of two distant telescopes. Because these are indeed two distant things and they best illustrate the redeeming, but impossible nature of love. Pragma Gynaikos:[377] first the woman's image appears, or rather, woman as image in its analytic richness, with a multitude of lines, colors, shadows (anatomia vere digna et justa: *umbra*)[378] & (this is the important part) with the well-nigh perpetual further possibilities of lines, colors, shadows; every moment conjures ever newer diatonic developments of graphic elements onto the face, body, clothes.

But perhaps even if these many possibilities emerging in time were not given, and one single, eternal, and fixed drawing stood before us in woman's phenomenon, even so, the drawing, the image carries infinity in its essence; the black needle-tablature of a row of eyelashes, as it arches with the semicircles of small ebonite bridges over vision's slow Huang Ho (one of the greatest wishes of my childhood — in connection to the word 'Cambridge' — was to build a bridge that would consist not of one wide road but of dense, narrow, and parallel one-person arches; five thin bridge-cathodes and bridge-anodes bending like thin pipes above the green veins of the colleges); the combed-back strips of hair and the muffled explosion of wave-glitches at the nape: if we could run a membraned needle through all the small dimples of the hair, we could get the positive melodic findings of woman; the logarithmic charisma of a feather's white pipe and selective foliage; the shoulder-strap's lonely pudicity-Styx, as it burrows alone into the shoulders' Pascal cone[379] (perhaps it is the shoulder-strap that I feel to be the most diaphanous beauty in love, and which constitutes a separate permutation territory on its own, like for instance the permutation style) in order to proclaim the naiveté of clothing (because the clothes didn't grow into us but only hang on us, from top down): all these image-nesses, precisely by being image, are infinite; the image is eternal multiplication — so that next to each woman we should place the arithmetic factorial sign, to warn that we need to multiply with each other all the images, down to the present woman: the facts of 'image' and 'factorial' cannot exist without one another.

The image is always open, spreading in plane, and is mathematically always more than it is; so here we always have $2 = 2 + q$, and $n = n + q$. It is the q that renders the image an image; the image is always a sum that is only identical to itself when there is some surplus added; certain chemical alterations only happen in the presence of an extraneous (unchanged) compound — similarly, certain self-identities in the world can perform the exact adjustment to the precise idem, only if an extraneous material, q is added to them as surplus.

Because the phenomenon of identity plays out on a certain trajectory of identity: with 'A est A' the A sets out from itself, covers a circular, elliptic etc. trajectory, and only after this logical promenade does it get back to itself: the image always means this logical identity-detour. Thus the image is logically a half-state, and mathematically, an infinity status; it is the cross-section or snapshot made in the course of the identity-slip of the A returning into itself (this is its logic); the elements are always higher in number than their sum total (this is its algebra).

For these two reasons everything that is visible is paradoxical, and the organ of sense is nothing but the aide of the brain that can nevertheless squeeze with *one* peg, with some masterstroke (impression?), the limbs of absurdity; the senses manage *&* process all the absurdity-material of the world.

visuality and reason

On the other hand, the plenitude of visuality omits the 'sight,' because it discovers so many new fragmentary visions within one vision that the component-visions risk decomposing the original, unitary image — that is, the more visually I react to an image, for instance to the image of a woman, the more wildly I will be destroying that image: vision and strong visuality are mutually incompatible. This trivial phenomenon I could experience with the hotel woman. She appeared in the entrance and shot a savagely eye-wounding image at me, like the poisonous arrows of imago at a cowardly St. Sebastian; this was the first vision, verisimilar despite all its relativity, the authorized version. But in the next moment the eyelashes turned into geissler-bridges,[380] the gaze into Chinese flood, the hair into logisma-plate, the shoulder-strap into a species-blazon, the belt into an instinct-loupe or auroscope, which all started living an independent life: the murderous parasites of metaphor undermined the life of the image.

The original image, the portrait of the woman returning to her hotel from the theater now consisted only of the insulated relation of those images; visuality consisted merely in the ability to make an image appear as a wealth of other things instead of what it is, and thus always seeing the original image as the sum total of the relations of alien images with no connection to the original; in brief: visuality always abstracts. (Narrative, if it is serious, does the same: the so-called novelistic character [if an I?] is entirely annihilated when it gets into the hands of a veritable, bred-in-the-bone narrativist, for it faces such a mass of details that the character is stripped of its initial character nature — the characterization of one sole novelistic figure is in fact the series of an infinite number of anti-character ideas & images; if the sciences too feel more at ease in the world of the cells instead of the drab exterior of matter, even though the cells don't by far look like the trivial forms of appearance of matter, then why should the narrativist not feel more at ease in these anti-narrative milieus, where they must needs get under the pressure of their talent?)

*another experiment for the analysis of beauty:
project for a consciously over-the-top 17th-century horror drama:*
Night of Innocence

In fact it is all the same if I talk about this female face or for example about a juvenile theme for a play, which I wanted to develop in the 17th century's horror tonality; I didn't think of horror as a moral or neuronal concept but, among other things, as a special branch of the theory of colors, one species of the theory of intensities: at stake in it was the trinity of color, force, and rational purity. A force is given as 'horror,' with me this immediately has the shape of color, because I have the impression that color is nothing but the energy surplus left behind unused from the things' 'thingly-existence,' that is, a force, which (in the case of 'horror') is, let's say, light violet (silver or mercury, combined with lilac flowers: psycho-Patou),[381] & the light violet Faraday-trouvaille is something coolly spiritual or at the very least, air-like, one epidemic-tube of space. In this percept-trinity (force, color, raison) which came to my mind à propos the concept of 'horror,' again my penchant evidenced with the drawing of the hotel woman's portrait comes to the fore — to feel visual & emotional facts as abstract things.

The title of my horror drama is *Night of Innocence*, its theme is more or less this: the protagonist is the Avignon sky with its white stars, lined up as regular destiny-points on the clerical apsis —

the heads of popes & cardinals are covered by such fitful, Técla-system astronomical chequer-fridge [382] (here I must amass image sperms with experimental lopsidedness). This is the night of innocence, the Avignon sky with snow-color castle walls; the whiteness of the papal castle and the stars' whiteness are made of the same material — the viewer would expect that in a few months nothing would remain of the castle, as all the walls will have dissolved for starry purposes.

Innocence is something white, like those stars or the papal castle's wall, but they are surrounded by night's Neptune flora, the dark hectares of negative God-frescœs; that is, innocence is a mathematical function-whiteness, it depends on some darkness that is not sin but rather, virtue's embryonal mash where the sexes (that is, original sin & ecstatic virtue) are not yet distinguishable. Hence one cannot speak about the morning or summer of innocence, because that would be self-contradictory: innocence hypothesizes the night immediately with itself. (For me there is no separate light and separate darkness — both empty concepts — but in their place there is unified naturalness, that is, this 'innocence-night.')

The protagonist of my play is some cardinal; you have to believe that no anti-clerical impetus prodded me when I wrote it. The cardinal has two positive traits: he has a homogeneously red and grotesque Italian profile — both the infinite color (in the homogeneous something heterogeneous is subsumed) and the infinite caricature of the face are bifurcations of the same rational factor, which continued to preoccupy me for decades. So when that cardinal or another commits atrocious things, I have him commit them for the sake of a *Raison-realistische Farbenlogik* (am I English? am I at all?).[383]

The cardinal kills another cardinal in the Avignon castle under the star-sirens, because he wants to get rid of a potential rival at the papal election; he wants to, or can get rid of the corpse only by dressing it in a girl's clothes & taking it across the river in a boat. He will sing serenades to the seated, wigged corpse in drag with guitar accompaniment; spring incognito. In the play everybody is evil, sick, or a caricature, but the play's style renders everyone innocent, happy and full of Adonis-tics.

The cardinal's murderous plan is secretly known to a girl who is in love with him; this girl has a dress made that looks identical to the ones the cardinal had made to dress the corpse, what is more, the girl even gets a mask, so she would better resemble the murdered cardinal. The deceit is successful: the murderous cardinal takes the girl in his boat, imagining her to be the dead cardinal. Serenade on the water.

The body of the murdered cardinal is lying inside the castle with its blond girl's wig, in an elegant mademoiselle dress; the wound wasn't lethal, the cardinal gets up and walks to the mirror: he sees a woman with blond tresses. Great Websterian monologue: the cardinal comes to believe that he is a girl, & goes mad with the thought that he is a girl and cardinal in one. In the meantime the real girl leaves the murderous cardinal and falls in love with the madman who walks in the mirror image of her clothes: she fell in love with the stranger's face, but in time the cardinal comes to resemble the girl exactly, under the influence of madness (innocence! innocence!), so the girl too goes mad with the thought that she is in fact in love with herself and is then perhaps the actual corpse. So she pretends to be dead. And the mad girl-cardinal becomes Hereticus' lover in a northern Italian town, on the banks of one of the trans-Galatea lakes: Lago di Pudore. The murderous cardinal had no idea what happened to the corpse while the living girl and the feminized cardinal-believed-to-be-dead went on their dubious honeymoon; when the murderer heard that people believe the 'murdered' cardinal to have died of natural death, the criminal masks himself to better resemble his victim and has himself buried.

*parenthesis: the lurking homage to Catholicism
of the author of the* Meditations

(I started these marginalia mentioning how I strive to avoid the Catholic forms of suffering, choosing the unadorned, dry, lay formulae instead. Weaving an asinine 17th-century theme that would be so suitable for naïve and shamefully demagogic [because there is also a redeeming demagogy] anti-Catholicism, it's here that I feel my relation with Catholics to be at its strongest, like feeling my temple or artery while picking flowers — how many times I have crawled on my belly among the forest brambles to pluck a hidden flower, trying out one by one my limbs & organs if they would fit into the opening where the small flower stood among rocks, briars, and cage-twigs [its pose betrayed that it had no inkling of the nobility foisted on it by its self-appointed bodyguards]: I fitted my arms, legs, mouth, and nose among the dusty branches, like mismatched keys into an obstinate lock, when all of a sudden I finally felt the little being's natural & unexpected warmth, without being able to see that disproportionate little fever that we can't even sense in a landscape looked at from without — I wanted to pluck it, I squeezed my fingers or tried to grab a leaf with my lips, carefully cushioning the edge of my teeth with my turned-in lips, and then it hit me that what I believed to be the flower found at long last was in fact one throbbing station of my own blood circulation, that I was palpating the velvety beats of my own temple, the blunt minute-hands of my own blood instead of a caught-out leaflet.

And now I feel the same thing about Catholicism: there, an unexpected stumbling-into-anatomy instead of an outsider flower, while here, mushrooming homage instead of comedy. If the only way I can express my lurking homage to the Catholic ecclesiastic order is, to invent inane, scathing burlesques — that means I am walking down the most well-trodden path of all mysticism: to express the superlative degree of love with the superlative degree of blasphemy. But there is no such thing as conventionless mysticism; the two concepts exclude one another.

Perhaps I am driven by some kind of pubertal aristocratism when I put to paper these fresco swearwords: I can truly love, respect, and defend only those whom everybody else considers ridiculous and pointless. I could never respect the saints, because they are howlingly respectable from center to circumference. I always want to defiantly mine whatever I want to respect and adore, from impossible depths: to distort women to hunchback witches and within that state to find beauty's absolute; to have logical principles ruminated to smithereens in a madhouse, and when they are reduced to a rotting intellectual chyle puddle, to chemically extract from them truth's virginal cells; to banish great cardinals to the dross of pulp guignol theater, there to ridicule and impossibilize them until no one would find any value in their lives: and once I can be statistically certain that everybody despises these Roman-red dogma-roses, then and only then is it worth it for me to love them, to suck out their values with holy gourmandizing like a complicated fruit's juice that conceals in a small membrane ball beneath a thousand sickening peels some miraculous sap.

Perhaps some day I will be able to clarify if I have been a Protestant or a Catholic, but for that I would need to write two big books, and neither could be diaries — the metaphysics of neurasthenia, in brief, *Metaneuron*, and the metaphysics of European history, in brief, *Metaeuropa*. When we express values by attacking values, we undergo, willy-nilly, one liminal case of the fight between eternal human hypochondria and eternally alien 'action.')

sensuousness toward relations: the outcome of the second experiment

This drama theme closely resembles in its structure the face of the hotel woman; on that face there was such an infinitely dissenting multitude of visual elements as to render every tiny visible element immediately autonomous (that it sparked a million possibilities of metaphor in fact meant that it broke up into a million concrete kinds of matter; from the center alpha-, beta-, and gamma-biologies started radially outwards), and in place of the original image there emerged the relation-tissue of other images; and this relation-tissue is something abstract & rational. Thus metaphor is a product of decomposition, or rather, one half of the image's way of decomposition; the image reaches the state of abstract rationality through the intermediary stage of metaphor.

In this drama theme metaphors are supplanted by plot-exoticisms, or more exactly, every quirk of plot can be considered a huge metaphor (this way history is the greatest metaphor we can experience empirically), and in the drama the stress falls not on the individual actions but on the relations between them, on their relation map, and that is something abstract and non-emotional. Everyday action fragments hardly yield such sharply perceptible relation graphs, and therefore they are not suitable for the production of abstraction; the wilder the contrasts, narrative paradoxes, colors, horrors and absurdity-balls that feature in the work, the faster the image will reach the stage of reason; the so-called irrational stories (*Night of Innocence*) and the so-called irrational images (*hotel woman*) elicit the raw material of reason and signify 'intellectual' art.

Because here we are talking about looking for the material of raison instead of truths, for the atmosphere of intellectualism instead of intelligence; truth doesn't make reason visible, being made of another material (or having no material at all) — in contrast, the torsions of madness show the raison-space, where truths are alien knots, insulated islands. Thus beauty is a forever busy, unquiet bridge, where true phenomena hurry to the other bank to turn into reason; so are colors, for instance, left-behind truths, and yet-unreached reason. (When I distinguish between truth and reason, I am not implying that the latter is something subjective and relative [it is not mind!]; reason, too, is objective and absolute. The relation between truth and reason is far rather like that between seed and flower; so far truth has stood in the center of human inquiry, although it's merely a seed from which the more absolute, objective flower of reason develops, or can be developed. All these inklings of mine are expressed in mutually contradictory metaphors, for it is difficult to express the new with the old; so, for instance, under 'intellectualism' too I meant something objective and not psychological. The only reason why it's worth jotting down this naïve apology is that it brings to mind another, novel treatment of the theme of beauty.)

Before putting to paper this other possible meaning of beauty, I will place here a few pages of an earlier notebook of mine, because the psychic processes described there are very close to the sense of the style of *Night of Innocence*. The purpose of *Night* had been to allow the smothering accretion of picturesque, psychological absurdities to end not in picturesqueness, mysticism, or simply in bluff, but to create the impression of a rational and abstract work: so that an extreme comedy may run its course to become extreme abstraction. These notebook pages illustrate a similar trajectory from my life: how extraordinary intellectualism turned into an empty movement of the soul, devoid of ideas, how extraordinary ethical sensitivity became utter being-outside-of-ethics. But I feel these ultimate (ultimate?) stations of development to be not derailments, no, and not 'disenchantments,' nor apathy either, but a logical culmination, the most etymological content of intellect and ethics. I wrote these pages when I first came into contact with my congregation.

the clergy: the relation of the author of the Meditations *to sin and God*

Perhaps there are two kinds of clergymen after all: the good priest in the practical sense, and the priest who is very bad in the practical sense, but who is nevertheless a very good priest from some perspective, or a priest in a very priest-like manner. Because to be a good priest and to gnaw away every layer from us, down to the kernel of priesthood — they are two utterly different matters. This I felt immediately when, for the first time in my life, I came face to face with my future congregation. From that moment I loathed their faces, longings, humility and goodness. Of course it was not them whom I found intolerable but the situation that I had to stand in front of them and do something within a short time. It's about God. But they stand at one end of God and I at the other. They feel and do of God what exists from the earliest times of him, while I, what barely is, what is a forever dehiscing actuality, wriggling advance-season, the needlepoint of time or the widest surface of the god-bubble.

It is not worth mixing in clever objections, that God isn't divided into a rigid trunk and an ephemeral flower, a frozen eternity and zigzagging hypotheses. It's about God: they believe in Him, and I am escaping into Him. Idle wordplay? Perhaps. Is it possible at all to do anything else with words but play with them? But it's a fact that I am lost in God, that is, I am lost in the clergy. I am incapable of seeing the matter from outside, God as sculpted relief and my soutane as fabric. To them God's portrait as portrait naturally looks in some direction and points at it; the bitter gondolas of nose, eyes, mouths all mean one direction: for one moment they glance at God's portrait but immediately turn their backs on it, for in the direction of his gaze they are looking for the object of that gaze — they scuffle, claw on that 'direction' as the blind on a thin bridge parapet. I, who am inside, see no direction of course, only prison and darkness: to me the concave eyes & trough-shape lips show no way, they only signal that I am captive in a finite space.

For me it is all the same if I go right or left, it's all the same if I am a moral insanity or a rapacious missionary, I live not from directions but from atmospheres. How can I say something like that when God doesn't will it? Well it's you who say that God doesn't will it — to me one sole positive religious experience was given: to feel God's shadow above all, to the point of the soul's decomposition. Comparison? predestination? Freudianism? It's all the same what rubric I fit in. I am to God not in the relation of faith but in the relation of the desperate and perhaps fleeing blotting-paper and ink; my veins fill with his existence, and my bones are surrounded by those green, selfish snakes, like the sinking brow of Medusa. My faithful speak about moral deeds, they want and like such things, although they have no inkling of the deed so long as they insist on seeing a traffic sign in God's profile: a deed that aligns itself to a direction is no deed, but the rendering-plastic of the direction, its underscoring and barren doubling.

The action can truly play out inside the God-portrait or behind it: in the non-gravitational, neutral, forceless space where there is no temptation and no seduction. That's why I have little sense for sin when I commit them — I feel that in whichever direction I move, God's shadow is on me, the celestial leeches of existence suck my blood all the same even on the most prodigal poles. And this is my only apology for my clerical calling, this pallor that is due to the fact that God left very little blood in my veins. I am barely human; I am like a gnawed-to-death blanket, the leftover of the banquet of a million moths. I am not standing at the altar and on the pulpit because I could lead, teach, or heal. I cannot do any of them; I barely intuit the meaning of those words. I am solely a spectacle: I am the softest material that the angels, metaphysical worms, God can chew. I am an anatomy illustration in the church, like those boards with large numbers, the numbers of the psalms or pages. But under no circumstances a human being — forty years of comparisons have amply convinced me of this. They wanted to kick me out many times, but I left no stone unturned to stay: with hypocrisy, lies, bribery I worked to remain a priest, to rest here.

I feel God's closeness not out of mysticism but out of hypochondria. Here no one has yet been a hypochondriac to this extent, & I have to take advantage of that fact. But can I call it advantage, if I keep kicking up scandals? If I almost purposely compromise the church? But I don't, I can't give a continental about the light, about showing the way — all I am interested in is the fires, eerie patches of light, jack-o'-lanterns. I don't want to hygienically divide God in Exeter, righteously as a good husband divides the felled game; I don't want to design a comfortable central heating from his shapeless fieriness, so that I can charge a higher rent to the theology students.

Because it is imperative to choose: God is either present, or we follow him. I am nothing but the wriggling grammatical tense expressing presence, the important inflorescence of prae-sens, a bad priest, an absolute priest. Am I calling my ilk peremptorily absolute priests? The priest's essence, cockade, and umbilical cord is God. Is it peremptory to call absolute the one in whom the divinity as existence is alive and destroys in the most active way imaginable? I am a laboratory rabbit, on which one sole thing can be researched through a waste of rashes: that God is, is, is. Existence as such has no ethics. Whoever has read into these jottings here and there will know that the reason I hold on so frenetically to ethics-less divine existence is, that I believe overmuch in my congregation, not in my own God-feeling. Yet another duality: I believe in my congregation, yet I follow myself.

his intellectual life, ideas, and the place of ideas

What then is my moral and intellectual life? To keep twisting and turning, disassembling, setting in motion (and here I am not proselytizing against analysis — in disassembling we should notice not the laughable puniness of small details, but the size and sharpness of the analyzing talons, their beastly rapaciousness, and then it immediately ceases to be idle pettifogging) every kiss and thesis to the point where I reach the last imaginable extremity, consequence of that kiss & thesis — to distort and virginate with fanatic instinct, to force through every contrast, so that in the end only a hair's breadth of concreteness rests of it. Every imaginable kiss-gesture, moral and mathematical kiss-commentary is left behind; I have tried out each, and the second time I was unable to return to the first kiss. Here it's not necessarily about real kisses — in thought I have experienced every possible kiss-ness of the kiss, so that soon there was no more possibility left for new meanings.

Today for me a kiss is a million outdated encyclopaedia entries, the thick layer of a million thought-to-death & intuited-to-death meanings in the past and one sole illusory shadow, dancing silk thread in the present — then it's all over. I stand at the very end of the kiss' long way, where only vacuum follows. My congregation are the other way round, for them all the meanings, all the moral & æsthetic contents of the kiss are somehow lined up before them, for them everything is always yet future, in their imagination the world is tightly packed before them. For them God too is a tree-lined alley with 10,000 trees, which they are going to walk down, down to the 20th tree, to the 1000th tree, but never to the end.

But I am at the alley's very last tree, I can no longer see the last one either, for it is behind me, only if I sprain my arm backward can I touch the blond leaf of its last bough, which grows so tenderly on its trunk like a theater ticket's one half on the other where it is dotted for the controller to tear it off: absolutely thinking idea always tends toward the very end of its theme, its culmination point, the way a cork forced underwater tends to surface, so that I almost slip from my themes and lovers, come up before them, take over, defeat them, that is, I lose everything, I am nothing. Can I thus meet my congregation — lead weights on the sea bottom?

My congregation believe that everything is: something. Like the black circle in the middle of the bullseye, so the content of every idea stands in the middle of the idea — they believe. They believe that the deeper you penetrate something, the harder the kernel is that you will find. They want to learn, which means the superstition that the idea tends toward precision, toward a root of meaning. And I want to simply think, which means the fastest possible flight, wild escape from the world of knowledge, of 'something,' of meaning toward nothing. Growing horizon? Of course, but if we want to be sincere, that means growing emptiness. What torment is each sermon, when I have to feel under my shirt the duality in uttering every single word: my congregation want to get into a forest, want to get inside the meaning of an action, its value-grotto, to see that a kiss is this or that, exactly that and not anything else — while my soul wants to get out of the forest, to the last tree, to the horizon's great it's-all-the-same growth, to nothing, where kiss consists of maybe, barely, & everything.

By no means should you see in the latter process the scheme of relativizing. It is indeed perhaps the very opposite, because the nothing into which the kiss kisses itself after the whimsical psycho-pedagogy of mouths, is in fact the synthesis of the value and strength of all kisses, it is not nil but only an invisible force where every objective & painterly feature fades. Kiss, knowledge, moral all ran this course: they lost their somehowness but they retained their resilience and elasticity. I have long forgotten the kiss, the shape of the mouths, their x-lining, breathing, remorses of conscience, stopping-earlier or stopping-later, but something remained of it, some rhythm, force-splinter, eternal dance — it lives on in the striking down of flowers, in the irresolute spending of my ink (this is not psychological but logical Freudianism): the kiss became a wide ring, inside which I keep hopping to and fro, somersaulting, sinning, wading, idealizing. Is there even one of my congregation who would gladly blur the somehowness of things, draw an abstract ring of them, akin to the circle around the discus-throwers' feet, and evaluate the whatevers thought or done inside that circle, instead of the old one-and-only somehowness?

It's curious how the greatest intellect doesn't want itself and walks with empty hands. I consider myself to be so, and I dare confess it and it is no arrogance because under 'intellect' I don't mean excellence, value, or anything of the sort, and by 'the greatest' I don't mean a first prize, competition record-breaking, or success, but rather, perhaps, the sickest, the one who is the most mechanically consistent with himself, the most naively mechanistic. So the category of 'the greatest intellect' ends up being the habit of humility on me. Perhaps the greatest moral too resembles this. It's only when I face my congregation that I see, first to my great shock and panic, then maliciously, as a tabloid sensation, how little my ideas are ideas but only swinging attitude gymnastics, which have meant neither feeling nor reason (that's why they are 'attitudes'), only the soul's eternal disquiet around things. On this ground I was no more than a half-talented would-be painter, for in journalese it's that kind who are forever racked by 'disquiet.' But I was a lot more, for I never wanted to paint or create.

The first reaction when I find myself face to face with my congregation, all of whom have ideas, is, as I said, panic: for there is not one idea in me, how could I ever feel clever? What was this or that train of thought of mine? The place of one nothing and the place of another nothing, and between the two there is a nothing that happens actively? Is that intellect? Nonsense. But now I know that it is no nonsense after all; that is intellect: when instead of 'ideas,' there are only abstract traces of forces in the soul, which dance along decorative orbits, not along the thematic leashes of 'connection' but according to the situational chance energy. Frivolity? Word! For my congregation ideas are moving and crested waves on the sea surface, they are the internal movement of water that cannot be seen, only rarely, on the aquarium walls or on an artificial rock as passing shadows, transient change of color. And why couldn't the same apply to moral?

action; the struggle of moral value and dehumanization

For my congregation action is a well with a regular-shaped bed, or a geometrical fountain; for me that water is a one-millimeter spilt layer on a map, with the same amount of water as the well or the fountain, but spread to invisible thinness, moving hither and thither, changing its boundaries, transparent like air. There is no other way for me than one comparison after the other, it's only that the word 'comparison' is false, because it's always the thing itself that I write down, not its image.

Ergo, in fact there are two kinds of action in my life. One is this infinitely thin action-layer, a membrane on everything, spread out like a Jansenist raincoat from my cradle to the grave:[384] my whole life is in fact one sole action, an immense fabric on which I work day by day. The other action-world is the infinite & varied series of small deeds, perhaps the restless to-and-fro movement of the hand weaving the fabric, which cannot refer to me and cannot be my own actions, because all my moral threads are used up without exception in the fabric of the single life-action; these actions are barely just movements, but not the sport of my moral, what is more, they are indeed the swaying to and fro, in vacuum, of the empty, impersonal body, stripped of moral (but not 'immoral,' in the criminological or sinological sense!).

Grapes & wine? Is the wine the unencompassably broad fluid of the 'one action,' while the grape stalks would be the other actions, in the dust, anywhere, everywhere? In fact I don't know, I could never know the one great action of my life; it is so large that I cannot understand it. And the small ones I barely notice, because they ring hollow. Do I have 'sinful' embraces when I don't know that my life has long been absorbed into a divine action, & these kisses, tragic somersaults, sonnets & forbidden operations are only rattling stalks, rolling-away grape seeds, spit-out peels? My celestial nobility lives in the sky like an eternal ethical flower, and on earth I'm no more than a genteel signet ring, blazon tossed about, which I press into the grass, into stone and art without making any imprint, because nature, love, beauty are all far too hard & cold.

Pointless blazon and meaninglessly distant-great aristocracy: behold my two ethoses. My congregation know the difference between accusation and defense, but I don't: I have a celestial title, which doesn't mean goodness, it might even be the shadow of ab ovo damnation on me, but I can't know. All I know is that if I look at my congregation I see that they lack this eternal estuary-flow into God. Who I am, what I am, I don't know. My deeds, my seductions, my boo-boos and whipped-cream ornamental prayers are all alien and dreamlike — I know that they really exist-into society & can be empirically perceived, but to me it seems unjust. Why did the Lord form me so, that both my ethical forms should remain in fact unknown, illogical, inhuman, existing outside of values? How I'd like to commit an act that could truly be mine, that I could know!

Perhaps this very state of mine is a sincere predestina-experiment: my ethical existence stays with God, unknown, & my body, which is independent of ethics, I can use to anything. I glimpse a woman in a white-serrated, padded swimming trunk, like a healthy index finger in a hypocritical gauze turban, and immediately want 'sin' with her (to borrow the vocabulary of my congregation) — where does this reckless flight toward the 'sinful' liaison come from? Because I feel that the body is nothing, my personality, my whole psychology, my primal sincerity, lyricism & rattling of desire, are all the meaningless leftovers, litter of the celestial nobility, that is forever celestial and has no connection whatsoever with my life: I am so much absorbed into God, that nothing is left here, just as the soap bubble bursts the moment it is sucked back.

The emergence of this duality can be explained not only with such image-theology but also with psychology: in my youth my whole life consisted of the desperate settling of moral prohibitions — I fixed my eyes incessantly on the principle of 'don't.' The first consequence of this was the blurring of the difference between small sins and big sins: from the two commandments of 'don't pretend' and 'don't commit adultery' I only experienced the abstract, objectless concept of 'don't,' which was the same in both. Thus the 'don't' & pretense, adultery, stealing, lies, etc. gradually split off, the 'don't' alone filled my soul, and the concrete sins you were supposed to not do faded from sight next to the abstract mathematical sign of prohibition. If a rubber band is painted & we stretch it too much, the varnish will not dilate all the way with it, but crack, flake off, go to waste. So did the attached deeds flake off from the infinite tension of 'don't': my life consisted of a sea of 'don't,' which ridiculously shrank all the unsecured kisses, gurgling lies. The more wildly one experiences the prohibition-nature of moral prohibitions, the more easily they will slide into moral indifference & frivolity.

When I glimpsed the woman in the white swimming trunk, the 'don't' immediately grew into such a fantastic cloud around her that its prohibiting force could not be used to the setting in motion of one single action or will, it was only possible to get inebriated from it and impotently to fall on the swimming trunk's serpentine belt. If steam is infinitely strong, it will not drive the engine, then the engine's only energy will be its own torque of inertia, its own dumb and pointless weight; it can roll at most. But that rolling cannot possibly be a sin.

When the woman in the white swimming trunk became my lover, it only meant that I became her, because I couldn't be myself anyway, given that my self was already at God, and I dropped only leftovers, morsels from the predestination banquet into the woman's basket of existence, for want of a better place. I always committed what my congregation would call sins in a holiday mood: two bodies are only the playful friction of two leaves in the wind, as compared to the two ethical celestial flowers that have long been blossoming at God. I enjoyed it physically that our love-making is unable to disturb the burning schemes of our two separate, independent morals, just as the sea's heterological exchanges of waves cannot alter the compass' single direction.

Action and moral are alternatives, they exclude one another: from a practical point of view here on earth moral is an acute and poignant nothing — while the action is the million waves of the moral-less human being. Human being and moral too exclude one another. What features under the labels immorality, perversion, etc. with my congregation, only meant carnival, disguise, masquerade, just as nobody would take the thousand directions of the waves to be a sin against the north-south direction. Comedy and sin were for me medically identical: five lovers at the same time are not five offences against God, but five clown-poppies daubed on my cheeks.

To be human means to be empty, to be morally sucked out: if the air is sucked out of the rubber duck it can be thrown about on the tarmac like a rag, like an unowned handkerchief. I duly strove to blackmail my life into such an infinite burlesque, to take advantage of the holidays, of the fact of being only cast-off peel. It seems an old fatalistic routine: 'everything is decided beforehand anyway, do what you want.'

But this is only an appearance. The reason for my moral ambivalence (I'm saying it again with the country upstart's shameful braggadocio) is a modern setting for two: the celestial moral, the predestined ethical stain in heaven — is no article of faith, no lyrical template, but one of the foundational concepts of the new thinking: the absolute, which, precisely by being absolute, means nothing, a positive force, the most elemental component of existence, but it's blind, illogical, empty. And the other, the earthly actions, the thousand whims of comedy are the other foundational concept of the new thinking: relativity, randomness, the meaningless thing, which is nevertheless ontologically powerful, logical and redeeming. Relativity ended up with all the features of the old absolute, but we consider it much more insignificant than in the old days; the absolute ended up with all the old features of relativity, but we believe in it more wildly than ever. On the woman with the white swimsuit even the smallest angle of the sandals is an ontological certainty, infinite concreteness, and yet for me it's no more than burlesque, Aristophanian reprise. And my moral tie to God is eerily invisible, impossible to feel, unthinkable, and yet it is the sole reassuring real reality of my life. How abhorrently difficult it is to speak of 'moral actions' to my congregation, when all I know is either burlesque or magnetic nothingness, there is no third option.

*the dilemma of identity: tautology or otherness;
its significance in the investigation of beauty*

Lately I've set up a hierarchy with three ascents: truth, beauty, reason. (I even used the obscure expression 'true phenomenon,' because seen from the highest intellectual viewpoint of reason, logical and empirical coincided.) I represented the three stages dramatically — in time the logical morphs into beauty, and in its turn, in time beauty morphs into reason. But if I compress this hierarchy widened into time, it thickens into identity, and results in: truth equals beauty, beauty equals reason. Every lucidly and every artificially thinking person shrinks alike from such setting of the ultimate categories into an equation. And still, they end up on the tip of our pen because, while we are thinking about them, in fact we don't see them as categories but on the contrary, as utterly peculiar physiological functions, empirical accidents, thus when we put to paper hollow-ringing sentences like, 'beauty equals truth,' we feel as if saying, 'belladonna leaf equals probability calculus' — for us even the ultimate category is an individual, portrait-like thing. 'Beauty' and 'a beautiful flower' relate to one another not like 'world-space' and 'a seat in the train compartment,' but as a seat in the compartment *&* another seat in another compartment.

What does it mean, that something equals something? Such 'identity' is excitingly double-edged: on the one hand I affirm (for instance, in the equation 'beauty equals reason') that the other thing, with which the first is identical, is in fact not an other thing at all, since it 'equals' the first (for instance, in the equation 'beauty equals reason,' reason is not reason at all but beauty); on the other hand, I affirm that the first thing is not identical to itself after all, but something completely other, for if it were not completely other, it would not be worth setting up an equation at all; it's precisely the notable otherness that gives meaning to the relation of identity (for instance, reason is essentially other than beauty, that is, an equation is always an unveiling, as though it were correcting an optical illusion).

This means that an equation or judgment can be understood in two ways: as tautological, or as productive of otherness — in other words: as barrenly superfluous or programmatically anti-equation. When I say, 'the cat is an animal,' it is either about cat & animal mingling in the same mass of identity, in which 'animal' features of course not as feature but as something of the same rank as cat (I don't feel the difference between judgment and equation), or otherwise: the cat entirely soaks up the animal; in both cases, the observation is pointless & empty (something that is particularly valid for the so-called synthetic judgments), it merely hollows out identity into even more identical identity.

But perhaps with the case of 'the cat is an animal,' the accent falls on 'animal,' and then the equation expresses precisely non-identity: it is 'animal' that soaks up the cat, or rather, it is no longer about the cat, the cat is insubstantial, the only essential thing here is the 'animal,' which is genetically other than cat. The outward form of the equation doesn't signal this alternative between tautology and anti-equation, it is only us who feel it.

So an equation always expresses one thing only, never two (although, having two sides, mathematically or grammatically it seems to express two): either something that is precisely that something, or something that is precisely not that something it seems to be, but something completely other. To generalize: between every idea & every idea-object there is some similar relation, in so far as an idea referring to a theme means either that the given theme is that very theme — or it means that the given theme is something completely other, the given theme is not the given theme after all, but something that is the exact annihilation of that theme. And here my musings connected to the idea of beauty:

I had the impression that the beautiful things' beauty consists precisely in the duality that they suggest at the same time a thing's self-identity that runs back into itself, & the thing's utter having-another-meaning.

In an artistically depicted tree in fact the artistry is, that it depicts the tree as more tree-like than it is, i.e., it emphasizes its self-identity to such extent that it is provoked into essence; on the other hand, that the tree will express some principally non-tree, what is more, anti-tree and never-tree, as if the point was to express with it the most tree-less world possible; beauty differs from equation in the fact that it doesn't take the side of either of the two things expressed in it ('cat' and 'animal'), but keeps both active poles, tautological identity and self-annihilating otherness, in equilibrium.

If we apply this hypothesis of beauty to the female face and female clothes, it's not difficult to imagine the peculiar eros-pendulum set in motion: in one moment love reflects on itself by piercing woman's essence as an injection needle stuck into the most important vein curve — and in the next moment it realizes that its desire had sought something typically non-womanly, or even anti-womanly, and yet this element absolutely devoid of woman is the very essence of its interest in woman. And yet, all this is directed at woman, her bodily appearance; and yet when I saw that woman in the hotel hall, in addition to seeing a vision I also felt desire. In the image there was some self-evident infinity-likeness: in the direction of openness. Because that feeling condensed my whole inside into one single desire-ball — while the image spread out in plane, the desire directed at it resembled space or rather, an ever-shrinking globe.

This metaphor brushes past the essence: because the more desire is preoccupied by possessing the image, the denser it becomes, the more it approximates psychic ball shape, and thus the further it gets from the desired image. That's why the expression, 'desire directed at this or that,' is misleading and erroneous — for the essence of desire is precisely that it cannot direct itself, because the more I intensify its force, the more it thickens into itself; if in the beginning it still had arms, jellyfish-like mother-of-pearl lassœs, then with the intensifying of desire these arms grow back and merge into a central globe.

The scheme of the game (and there is only a scheme!) is this: love's imagistic part spreads planimetrically, to my right and left, but never toward me, because when I face the image, I'm evidently facing the plane, not its edge; and love's desire part becomes forever more intensive, that is, it bends my individuality, which could have had surfaces parallel with the image's plane, increasingly into a sphere form, away from the image, into cohesion's narrow, onanistic infinity shape.

In any case, this is how I might play Romeo and Juliet in a Futurist cabaret: the woman would be a continuously spreading, millimeter-checkered paper sheet — & the man, a mercury drop in the air, which is rounded thinner and thinner. If we feel this duality for long, as I did, then the untidy & unclean concept of love in fact ceases to exist, giving way to two independent and forever alien, but separately crystalline facts: to the independent worlds of image and desire. I have never felt love, but I did have woman-eras, when I was much taken by the æsthetics of woman's exterior (elegant clothes with face); and I had desire-eras, when in the windowless dark of my soul I fed instinct's black chubs (not with women!), like the royal fish at Fontainebleau. The two had nothing to do with each other. Because the image of woman, as visible sensation, is something situated beyond love (gyne meta-eros);[385] desire, on the other hand, is some shapeless existential gymnastics, something situated this side of love (cupiditas Veneris semper prae-venerica).[386]

alienness of woman-image and desire-image

That here we deal with two utterly different things is shown the most palpably by morphine's Ordnungslehre exercises;[387] they show not the faintest kinship between woman-image and desire-image, not even the most minimal formal link can be found between the two — if the two ornamentations featured together in my dreams (something quite frequent, naturally), the two form styles could be distinguished as white & black thread twined into a cord. With similar clarity was the relation of identity, that is, of otherness represented in my dreams, as the gist of equations and one hypothesis to the nature of beauty; I don't know whether with these dream images the sensing of things is not more important than the seeing of these things — if one can distinguish them at all.

Because the essential difference between the 'normal' images of daytime life and the morphine images of dreams is perhaps that the lucid daytime images are indeed images by their nature and because they are images — but the morphine-images seem to be images only by constraint, they seem to be just barely images for want of something better, because they would not want to be images; every one of them is merely relation perfected to sensuousness, logical movement, which brushes past the upper world of images by accident and mirrors it (logos: satin bleu patine très brillant),[388] but it is not at all their purpose. My instinct for images has always been brutally strong, but I've always been aware that in it a decisively anti-image penchant is let loose; because in its two most obvious forms, in dream-relish (aphroneira non-conformista) and in morphine-etudes I have never found a single 'true' image.[389]

In dreams I relished the utter diversity of the components, that is, the way in which every component realizes another perspective, a separate space, disproportionate autonomy, being pushed the furthest away from what is image-like; a woman's face is small, the sentence she addresses to us is an enormous, insulated world of sounds, independent from the woman, not connected in any way to the woman uttering it; the sentence's time-color and place-graph is completely different from the woman's portrait, which is similarly no real portrait but the throbbing-on of a distant house's colors and ornaments, which somehow got entangled in the face's empty logical model, & so by accident the house-colors and house-ornaments (let's say, a Belgian house's red bricks and a gilding-curlicue) became a portrait, the way freely-flowing water suddenly takes on the shape of the rococo iron embellishments of a storm drain's grids with its trickling-branches if it happens to flow that way: one single dream image contains a million perspective splinters, almost perspective dust, colloidal logic, in which first and foremost the abstract preconditions of 'judgment,' the rational adhesive intonation, of intelligible order rule supreme, like a power-netting suddenly magnified to the point of energizing, and among whose rationally distinguished netting-threads lie scattered, like insignificant shreds or secondary coffee grounds, the images.

Every dream is in fact a reason-crystal or, if you like, a 'logo-eder'; the leftovers of images or barely-images make up the crystal's sides, as it were, and the image-wrecks' relations, that is, the dream's essence make up the crystal's edges. Every dream shows a different crystal formation; the forever-differing relation-body of fatefully heterogeneous consciousness layers, and it was always in those proportions that I sought a logic of a novel nature.

These proportions were somewhat spatial: I felt that wakefulness and un-self-consciousness are the starting point and end of the same scale, between which the floors of consciousness are layered, and the dream undulates in an elastic serpentine now in the direction of the lower and now in that of the upper boundary, like an eel between the surface and the seabed: I always felt to be

'logical' a line that whimsically zigzagged in difference-density, &
that line was in fact the symbolic expression of the relation-changes
occurring among the dense differences. *Ratio sit phosphorescentia
liberata relationum semper mutatarum propter hysteria innatam mentis
inter imagines hypocriticæ.*[390]

As I mentioned earlier, with the morphine images I felt even
more strongly that the image expresses only the negativity that
where the image is located there is for the moment no idea-shaped
reason, or rather, that there, only reason's lower, blurry root-
capillaries, chemical pre-portraits and mask-protons feature (I
am systematically using the primeval and mask as synonyms),
only for them to express their gesture into a surface raison in
the next moment or on the next millimeter (with these small
relation-stirrings — 'veritas tremens' — the moment cannot be
distinguished from the millimeter, just as in the case of a musical
theme made up of 5–7 notes we don't know whether the small,
seven-tone unit got glued together in time or in space).

In the case of morphine I imagined (my Lord, I am a priest,
not a doctor) that there would feature such organs of sense that
normally only condition the general disposition; freed from their
ordinary daytime routine that one could call muffled synthesis,
they now engage in autonomous stimulus games. In dream layers
of consciousness and unprocessed raw image-torsos featured;
with morphine, solitary nerves that are only attentive to the interior,
& well-nigh infinitely processed image fragments.

Let's take a fallen leaf: this becomes special in dream (that is,
it becomes reason) by being shifted, let's say in its full daytime ex-
perience-size, above a miniature time-droplet that trickled to the
very edge of consciousness: one time-sonant and one independent
space-sonant together give a dissonant, absolutely false time chord
(this relation of falseness is the dream's logical yeast), but the fallen
yellow leaf doesn't undergo any kind of interior processing; in the
case of morphine (or even of fever and of ordinary daydreaming,

but there not in essential form) a nerve unknown to me runs with enormous sensitivity-energy, like unexpected electricity, into the fallen leaf, and immediately processes it into its own symbol of intensity, so that from the first moment it ceases to be the fallen yellow leaf and becomes some abstract figure — the way that leaf forms an abstract spiral graph if it adheres to the spikes of a wheel and is rolled along the road.

imago habet suam essentiam in non esse imago

Let's set aside for now the medical reality of things, which doesn't interest me much here, and look only at the two worlds of image style, of dream and of drugs; we can see that with one the essence is, the opalizing of relations, while with the other, inner nervous sensitivity dynamized to the point of abstraction: *imago habet suam essentiam in non esse imago*.[391] This can again be linked to æsthetic caprice as a third voice, so that complete reason, the barely-image image and beauty may again be together.

The disproportionateness of nervous sensitivity interested me much as the source of a novel truth-taste, for wild-red is interesting because it exists next to faint red, or because it spreads its redness to an absurd degree, developing into a state beyond color, which relates to the old, trivial redness as the satisfaction of desire relates to the desire that precedes it: the intensifying of desire reaches action, which has even so far been the inspiration-essence and center of desire, its everything, but the action itself as form, as situation, is utterly alien from desire. And in this way, if with some substance somebody is made (gradually) infinitely sensitive to red, at the end of the intensification an alien event will happen, which yet signifies the essence, like an entirely novel kind of satisfaction at the tail end of the kindling of desire; to put it bluntly, the person in question will come to see or experience the 'purpose' of redness, which will no longer be the everyday redness of the color red, but some suddenly manifesting, new phenomenon.

I have experienced that the intensification of sensorial impressions doesn't mean that red appears ever redder, pleasure ever more pleasurable, that is, it's not about intensity being self-directed; on the contrary, intensity means a continuous derailing from the starting point, the intensification of redness (or of the sensitivity to red) shows a regular derailment curve from red, even from colors in general, which we can call infinite (the parable of idem-fugue?), if we should so relish the lack of punctuality.

Ever since childhood I have felt in sensitivity some dramatic disproportionateness, some murderous asymmetry, and I kept comparing it to a balance: when a balance was in equipoise because there was a one-kg weight in both its left & right scales, and then I took off one weight, that is, took off half the total weight, immediately the balance tilted, and with my child's mind I found this very disproportionate: I have only taken half of the total weight, and yet the equipoise was destroyed not by half but completely, the balance got unhooked, the scales' plates turned upside down, the twines got entangled and my parents scolded me. I always expected that, since I took away only half of the weight, some kind of half-order would be installed — this unexpected and brutal destruction of the equilibrium felt almost sickening.

Ever since those times I've been a bad mathematician and pedantic connoisseur of bad numbers. I remember this childhood mathematics-romance every time I think of the enhanced sensitivity of certain nerves: I only tilt them a bit, and immediately vast landscapes of the soul are exposed to me, only a little redness needs to be added to the red and immediately some utterly different 'loguisage intime' appears from it:[392] the sensuous phenomenon (however intensive it may be) is entirely small, yet the rational vision generated in its wake is disproportionately vast.

For our senses realize an extraordinarily, indeed laughably small part of our real capacities, so they can be in harmony with one another; because otherwise, if all their strength were set to work, each would be a new world, a new person; from a mass of impressions and a mass of nerves only a complicated and dispersing society would be left behind one sole person, and it could not be kept together with whatever socialist projections of the co-belonging of whatever truth specimens, since any given truth is 'zoon-a-politikon.'[393]

incandescing self-identity amounts to self-estrangement; to this, the lesson of a glass mural (the two kinds of stars)

Earlier I had compared the feature of enhancing intensity, where the absolute of change and the absolute of selfing the self coincide, to the Janus-style identity of desire & action toward satisfaction, but because in general it is the whatness of beauty that interests me in dream and woman alike, I could have taken an example from the art of our days as well. The other day I had to make a visit to a high-born family for some church-related affair. I was kept waiting in the hall, where my eye was caught by the painting on a glass ceiling: the ground was black glass, and the individual images were made of different shades of grey (the grisaille is made of sheer relation calculus, therefore it is the worthiest form of contemporary art: before the concrete appearance of color the grey value-spectrum signals only the conditions of light, as it were, the colors' unfilled local values, as though a Milky Way of intonation were hovering above, followed only later by the smothering skivvy world of color-syllables, without those grey strip-glasses having anything to do with the abstract 'forms' of classical philosophy, brought to life in a next step by the accidental circulation of colors:

they remind rather of the most aristocratic guests of aquariums, mirror-crabs, & electric spiders, which mean at once pure life, bigoted linearity, absolute glossiness, & floreally faithful love-blindness) — among other things the stars of the sky were represented on it. The stars realized the same drawing in two forms, and in my pedagogies those two stars will correspond by and large to the relation of desire and its satisfaction, red color & color-no-more ultra-redness: here too the two stars realize the same graph with the help of polar otherness.

The ground was black glass, and one of the stars showed the forms of the simple rosetta used in printing: four white lines intersecting in one point. But next to it, the same star was rendered as follows: on the big black ground a small white, more or less circular form was drawn in sfumato, and they left the place of the eight-pointed star empty, so that here the universal black of the whole glass ceiling shone through the small white powder stain.

The first star was made of lines, positive thin lines — the other was no longer of lines, because there where the white sfumato was left out, an empty place resulted, which couldn't be perceived as positive line but only as the wide but negative riverbed, virtual place of the lines. The first star featured on the infinite black ground-sky; for the second star to exist at all, they needed to create a separate little finite, white astronomical sheath of couleur locale — that is, with the first the star itself was concrete and the black space behind it a Kant-masquerade one could treat as negligible quantity ('the space'?), whereas with the second star the star itself was only a black potentiality, absence-calculus, the precision sigil of non-est, & the true reality was that small white powder-space, the positivity was precisely the category-mignon created with separate activity, the space, the background.

I understand the second star as a further particularization of the first star's incandescing, that is, of its particularity, with the result that all its components have turned into their opposite, moreover, the place of the star is taken by the star's space; dehiscing from the bud of accidens like a tropical flower is the flower's impossibility-to-exist. But this only renders the bud more bud-like — not by placing it on the doubtful platform of infinity, but tracing it back to bud-ness — identity, otherness-identity, counter-identity, more identical identity: these are the two stars, this is desire & its satisfaction, this is the psychological adventure of red & red enhanced to absolute with me. Beauty suggests some similar mechanics.

self-doubling

When the concepts of the splitting of the 'I,' schizophrenia, self-doubling come up in conversation, I absent-mindedly think about these stars: with one man two selves seem to feature, although it is precisely the regular polarity and antithesis that justifies the existence of the single 'I,' as though the negative and positive ego-charges were engaged in a peculiar dance of alternatives, not insulation and not electric discharge but some kind of logical esse-optics. I said regular polarity, although people have hitherto not known that truly regular polarity that I've seen on the stars painted on the glass ceiling, that the positive part is depicted as complete absence and the insignificant space is concretized as a little active object, thus the swapping of constellations doesn't happen only within the object, mosaic-wise, but becomes the logical exchange of the whole universe: from space-nothing, space-everything results, and from object-profile, absence-mask.

The same can be imagined in psychology as a form of an exchange of consciousnesses: the way in which the image's infinite black sky becomes a small white powder patch, so for instance in the psyche a very broad moral attitude may become the hallucination of one sole quarter-note, & conversely, in the way the positive white star-branches became a black negative vacuum-graph, so in the psyche from the small red-perception of a red poppy petal a great I-vacuum, new consciousness-frame, infinite ego-angle can emerge — this is psychology's true after-image, the complete and absolute after-image (schizophrenia?), which is nevertheless still the lyrical path of idem-searching, moreover, of idem-finding.

What will the end of my beauty hypothesis be, what sentence will be the last conclusion: raison luxe? Today before dinner I walked again on my way back from the church, and watched the sunset, which is for me the greatest event here at Exeter — it compensates for the absence of women, deities, health, and itself. And then I found out, quite by prophecy, that my fate will be like these sunsets watched a thousand times. At the end of my life I will finally come to know a woman who will not turn my love for her into æsthetics, sin, boredom, experiment, and my own private business, but I will love her only, through her I will finally find that caritas that I lacked all my life: for up to the present I have always hated; through her I will learn that love & God can be related without maudlin vacuity, and when I live the most harmonious moment of purity with her, when finally after 50 years of hatred I will have learnt for the first time the unknown taste of self-sacrifice, and smuggled into my heart for a moment the inebriating psychology of virtue like a ball that was swimming inside a bottle, but when we want to pour liquid from it, the ball slips to the bottle's mouth, blocking it completely — after this heart-virtue movement, damnation comes: perhaps by my killing some of my close ones for some trifle, with the 'hiératique maladresse' of fate-distractedness (as my Lyon priest friend used to say),[394] or simply because my former sinfulness would direct me to damnation after death anyway, like an automatic railroad switch.

about the nature of goodness

Why was I bad, when every moment of my life was filled with the desire for goodness? And my last end too will be the absolute knowledge, moreover, possession of goodness, but the fact that 50 years ago I already married a woman has placed the toxin-sign of evil in front of all my so-called idylls & idyll-thoughts to come.

Because goodness is something fatally outside the soul and outside the self; the moment the soul takes possession of it, it immediately turns into evil — the good deed is like a foreign instrument, a harmful and blind little mechanism one has to handle gingerly, because if we go very close to it, our body will be spoilt and the machine too will break down. On the occasion of my adultery before death (it will be only a passing embrace, like in one of the themes jotted down earlier in these *Meditations*) the sensation of goodness will again be inside me and that will spoil it; it will become the joy-component of my body, although everything there is prepared for damnation's straightforward operation. Could it be that I handle my depravity too boastfully? Perhaps — but perhaps this is what it takes for my congregation to be duly edified (they won't).

Obviously the woman whom I will love then with absolute virtue-happiness will immediately afterward commit some small, low-caliber inanity, just as some species of beetles or bees or whatnot perish immediately after using up their sting; this woman too, once she has shown me her sole flaring-up of caritas, will drop like the currant stem from which we have combed the currants with a special fork.

Goodness always undulated between two factors: it dropped off from an unself-conscious stem, or rigid scaffolding (like that woman to come), insulated itself like a celestial shedding, & then fell into the distorting chambers, into the chintzy comfort of my egotistic soul. But if I know so well that even that last woman will be only a slimy springboard for a daring foreign angel's feet, how can I say that I will love her with all my faith and that she will even radiate into me the violet criteria of self-sacrifice? It's possible only because I have always belonged to the paradisiac wuss species, and when I embrace for the last time her unexpectedly thin waist (crocus-time: Calvin-time) in Cambridge (for it will happen there!), I will forget everything, to record only the virtue-happiness' angelic bellevue.

When I call myself a wuss (my diary is a lordly antechamber where I am the haughty porter who can abuse at will the lily-livered chap waiting to be granted an audience, who is also me), I'm not doing it in self-laceration: I am not so mad as to spend in self-laceration the few days I have to live before damnation's green feast. Under wuss, with all the insulting intent, I am also sending myself some love; one of the greatest torments of damnation is precisely that one doesn't even love oneself, and cannot take refuge from God into the last-ditch dualism of self-love — I will have to send myself a few urgent & postponed billets doux while I'm still up here.

But on the other hand, when the object of my love shrinks to a bare virtue-hanger, the goodness of my wife will blossom all the more; in her, in whom for 50 years I've seen nothing but the symbol of small-mindedness, in her I am going to glimpse positive goodness, not as infinitely-beautiful vision which my soul's concave mirror æstheticizes into her, and not as the soul-skin of an alien 'psyché-maîtresse,' but as rich and limited bunch-courage: field flowers squeezed into a ball. Field flowers? Now this too is only vision-bijou, this too is merely beauty. My wife is indeed something more valuable than beauty, so I will not insult her with such 'field flowers.'

types of virtue; ontologizing ethics and action-ethics

How is it possible that God tolerates the utter perversion, that I can see virtue only in the most frivolous, and in the good I can see only sins? What is the cause of this predestined perspective? (Do Chypre and Ypern resemble one another?) I've always seen that in inebriation drunks are looking for something beyond life, obviously God, for nobody else lives in empty Beyond Street; their eyes were pious, and when they beat their wives, it was heaven's Serenissima Iris taking revenge on earthly blindness. Where was goodness? Not in the drunk and not in his aged wife, who was scanning some new homespun apocrypha to Iris' barbarian; goodness is far too paradoxical a symmetry for the soul to realize it. Goodness means some concrete act, in which the transcending power is so disproportionately big to explode it altogether: it's either complete transcendence to God, and then the earthly concreteness of the good deed is exploded, or I realize the good deed, but leave transcendence out, and then it ceases to be goodness.

Which of the two would God choose? When I don't take the hand of a strange girl, do I have to deny myself the taking of that hand because there is something evil in the hand itself, or because there is something holy in the principle? The principle and the actual deed are not parallel: for God it's all the same whether I take that hand or don't, but on the other hand he wants me not to take it, that is, he is demanding something extremely artificial.

Is virtue indeed artificial or does it belong to the very essence of nature? Is it a luxury or a component? Deciding this question is not as easy as my respectable colleagues imagine. Anyway, one can't talk about virtue in general, but only about different virtues. But since the difference of the different virtues is so paramount, can they all equally represent goodness? When I help the poor

I feel that the specific gravity of my soul is identical to that of the atmosphere of goodness: it swims inside goodness; when I practice sexual self-abnegation, I feel that I am performing a stylized variation on the theme of virtue & not practicing goodness itself, merely a human technique of goodness, which is only the bitter opium of the feeling of virtue and not its further development in the direction of virtue.

Caritas is always transcending, union; asceticism is only personality's self-enclosed modulation toward an unreachable tonality. The material world was created by God, so the trace of his hands is present everywhere: my type of goodness (this doomed-to-damnation one) is forever chasing these dactyloscopia that dropped from infinity and stick to nature, for me goodness is identical to the infinity-scent of the creator, not merely on the basis of decorative analogy but of positive identity; the frivolous spendthrift who squanders his money on dancers is no caricature of goodness and creative charity but its factual realization: in him such a 'dactyloscopy' is at work, a lonely transcendence.

Ontologizing ethics: the trace of God's hand is present in the very act of giving, not in the purposes or the one to whom the gift is given. But then here are the great ascetics who breathe the scent of infinity to a far greater extent than the cretins of champagne. Perhaps, but here I am talking about the petit-bourgeois champions of virtue, about an Exeter company to which I myself belong; I am asking who may be more virtuous below a certain degree. And even aside from these restrictions, the squandering of the frivolous is sometimes more exciting than the charity of saints: in the saint's deed personal will is so strong that the deed itself cannot be peeled off from the soul's bumptious dynamics, the saint's virtue is always psychological and not ontological; but in the squandering of the frivolous the giving itself can prevail more purely, because it is not willed as virtue but rather, performed in posturing, imbecility or utter unselfconsciousness — the soul's lack of virtue as insulating material renders the deed's goodness-content denser & more strident.

Virtue, the real one perhaps doesn't belong either to the world of human will (Christianity) or to the humble-drunken underscoring of biology, to the ritual following of nature and instinct (paganism, Orient), but is found in the gestures devoid of the human being, this or that well-nigh a-psychologically strong wave of emotion: it's some kind of odd bridge between the human psyche and nature, far from both like the rainbow, which ends precisely where it touches the earth.

virtue and damnation

The drunkard's wife is an inventionless, limited animal, but one who has no sins, so even God will save her. This means that the action is important, for which even a laughable minimum of being-human proper is enough. Thus God handles those traces of infinity that he left behind from his own being in matter, like belletristic comedies: he has separated goodness from them. Through goodness we can also feel that, but mere transcendence into infinity is not enough. For me approaching God could only have happened with giving up infinity, concealing God, moreover, with God's terroristic banishing: faithfulness to my wife would have pushed me into petty preciousness. He who reads this diary as an opprobrium to God is wrong, & they are wrong who try to find here (pluralis doloris) some 'critique' of Christian ethics or a testimony of malicious doubt.[395]

I cannot imagine any other ethics than the one that killed me, perhaps because I feel my damnation to be unjust: perhaps that's precisely why I intuit divine syllogism in it. This may of course be mere priestly fancy talk, decadent routine, & belletristic tour d'esprit, but on the bottom of such things there is always some hard knowledge. I am a thousand worked-out and no mere simile heresies, but always feature only as a vase: the sole, orthodox vase of a thousand heresies. Is it unjust? If God is infinitely just, then infinite justice doesn't resemble earthly justice in the least, just as an infinitely broad circle is no circle anymore: as long as it is a circle (in the imagination) it is not yet infinite. Infinite goodness, too, must be something typically amoral.

I don't want to commit blasphemy when I opine that it must be darned hard to be a divine balance, on the scales of which our sins land and from which they take off like butterflies with their motley umbrellas, or hornets with their small ventilator wings; the scales sway from one second to the next, the intersecting sums of pros and cons are distorted into the klutzy columns of irrational truth-numbers — the strongest motivation of my faith in predestination is that I see the same kind of necessity in meaningless damnation as in wars: if truth cannot be clarified with legal disputes, let the 'brainless' weapons come; if the gross instrument of the ethical canon is lost, let the more precise radicalism of impotent judgment take over.

Every evening when I looked back on the day in an exam of conscience it was my subjective feeling that behind me stretched a chessboard of half-sins and half-virtues, which can at best be destroyed but not judged; this was no justice but the impatient crumpling of a botched preliminary sketch: I imagined the same of God and this lyrical infatuation wasn't helped at all by the certainty of salvation. Moral and destruction, ascetic attempts and self-evident damnation were inseparable concepts with me; I felt that every absolute, whether logical or moral, by its nature had to aim at the destruction of human beings — even in the beauties of nature, not only in the programmatic Exeter sunsets but also in the Riviera mornings, I always relished that outsider status, that radical incongruence stretching between my psyche and nature; the beautiful landscapes were the practical pre-figurations of damnation, the popular movements of the perfect things' indolence.

Perhaps my insignificant persecution mania should have been treated by fashionable doctors, who would have put their finger double quick on the motif of all life-giving errors in the registered lexicon of causes, and so that connection, religious percept-suturing, that I have finalized between perfection and going to the dogs, would have been dwarfed to puny henpecked romanticism: but the grand lies of healing & harmony never attracted me, hygiene is not the gods' etiquette.

variation on predestination; thinking in moral absolutes

I chose pain because too many signals pointed toward an ability of mine in that direction, and I sought to keep it clean and dry like a blind crystal, pointless plant, or empty formula; I protected it as best I could from the dimeshow transformers of bows, rhymes, and colors. Everything acquired moral nature because I knew that everything would be sentenced: the burning fleet of poppies among the field's icy waves became ethical persons because they played the classic, long-winded soliloquy of purposelessness. Thus I and the world filled with the robust importance of purposelessness, and my pessimism was devoid of all artistic Schlamperei, all impressionistic decadence masterstrokes, all doubt and pastel colors. It remained like a Protestant church not requisitioned from the Catholics: clean, scrubbed, hopeless.

My moral fastidiousness showed the thousand-shade color spectrum of truth, and after successfully dispersing the original unity of truth and virtue through the psyche's prodigal sieve, I could no longer reassemble those colors & had to look for some new unity. This new unity was damnation (Death Standard, behind

God's dancing currencies?) to which I was doomed; in this black burning glass the squandered colors of fastidiousness were again reassembled and gained meaning.

I still marvel today how it is possible that my mind is satisfied by such senseless destruction, and perhaps my thoughts have nothing to do with predestination but I simply feel that I love my small sins better than I love God, and I expect that I will die without sorrow. I would like to see the world from some absolute perspective; & if I am unable to see virtue's scintillating monism behind the false chromatics of poppies, at least I keep placing behind it the great common denominator of sin. For when I busied myself with my damnation, in fact I never thought of God at all, but judged myself, and the whole affair was nothing more than a false and comfortable suicide.

Why did I end up among the small lots of sin? Perhaps because from the beginning my ideal had been moral absolute, a kind of moral exoticism that only Catholics are capable of, and because I couldn't find it in myself, far less in my fellow human beings, I hated myself, my wife, my congregation, & God. My will was an infinitely tall and slender grey flower, which grew a giant capriceflower in the clouds' pointless height: who has ever seen that flower, who did it spread its scent for, for whom did it scatter the nostalgic statements of its colors? I myself only told stories to myself about this prodigious flower, feeling at most the twitches of its stem like a fishing line when a fish swallows the bait, but I knew nothing closer about it.

I had two great desires: perfectly self-abnegating holiness of life, and perfectly self-satisfying love. But I imagined both in the shape of utterly special moments, in the present moment for instance I see holiness in the comfort of my legs resting crossed, because in this imagined pose my conscience is so calm that I can cross my legs in siesta; I imagine perfect love as a vast meadow from where through a window with half-shut blinds you can see into an empty green room: the external wall is old English brick, inside the room there is angular modern furniture. And these meaningless spectacle-splinters are coupled with logical absolutes: to trace love's internal guidelines, suggestions of power down to the last point; to palpate even the highest-voltage frames of the concept and meaning-zone of asceticism. Struggling in me were not desire & God but desire's logical reductio ad absurdum with the similar reductions of virtue. I could never reach true desire and the living God; even today I am calculating the semantic purport of desire, and poring over the most closure-like conclusion of virtue. In the brain's pathologically perfect soil both develop to perfection hey presto: from the jutting vein of a poppy the figure of a girl is textualized, & from our distractedly touching fingers God's electricity sparks.

remembrance of a 'sinful' kiss

Virtue & love are forever open; the hand kiss is no ending (obviously the complete possession of the woman, too, is only an open beginning: an angle, not a boundary), Our Father is rendered Our Father only by a second one, but that second one only becomes really second if a third one is given; the moral act never becomes a positive fence bending toward us, but an open gate, which always lures us toward a yet non-action act. If I could even for a moment feel a kiss to be closed & repentance to be closed, I could have been a good man, but because I worked with the forcibly drawn conclusions of my acts, I ended up forever wriggling in the shallow waters of fastidiousness.

When I first kissed a girl somewhere in Switzerland, the mountains were blue like the sky, they were only large glass clusters in the azure-rain to measure the increase in degrees of the blue's blueness; here and there a bit of snow shone on their edges, as if miniature tents were lined up on the sky, whose bottom was not visible; under us the lake was green and full of the mountains' anchored shadows which quietly knocked against the thin buoy of silence; the meadow was full of spring flowers, & our mouths were merely one atom of all this luminosity, cold, colorful pudicity, but I kept thinking about what the logical consequence and syllogistic culmination point of that kiss might be; I didn't want the girl to become my lover, I only wanted the memory of that kiss, which flew about in the air like tissue blown off the terrace of a mountain-top hotel, floating among the mountains' blue, the lake's layered green & the sky's vast Torricelli aula; it was so clean, transparent, light, white, and pointless.[396]

In that moment I felt that I wanted to run away from that girl with the insulated memory of the kiss, but in the meantime I was thinking that the love of the kiss' memory can be nothing else but a self-deceiving, hypocritical form of the desire for shameless love-making, and therefore it must be a sin. The thought of the sin made my head swirl: when afterwards I noticed with delight that my hotel room's window-sill had been scrubbed, I thought I could not rejoice in this fact if I didn't carry the memory of the kiss, which was one form of sinful desire; there is no gaze, holding of hands, hand-kiss, mouth-kiss, embrace, lovemaking, perversity — there is only one thing, impudic bodily desire. Of course I didn't feel that desire at all, I merely thought that lovemaking was already logically pre-programmed in the hand-kiss.

The next day the mountains' blue (mountain cliffs & plateaus were only small rings through which ran the sky's unstoppable luminosity, like a blue finger through a white ring) became sin's ritzy ancilla; the lake's green, solidified to silence, turned into sin's mire, and the spring flowers' naïve 'imprimé' fabric meant for me sin's alphabet, its signatures to read. But was fastidiousness indeed no more than shallow water, and my fixation on absolutes, barren nervousness? Didn't I manage to dip my fingers into the ancient material of moral, like one who leans out from a boat to dip his fingers into the lake so much that he ends up drowning? Is damnation perhaps only metaphor for me, and destruction, only a word of braggadocio for moral's true 'material'?

night in the Swiss hotel; he goes for a walk

Around that time I slept very badly and always had sleeping pills on me; inebriated with happiness and guilt-feeling, I ravished my clothes about the room and was only consoled by the thought that my parents were playing cards downstairs in the hall; their quiet amusement subtracted something of the strength of my sin. Then I went over my suitcase for pills and found the thin bottle among my ironed shirts; the shirts looked utterly deserted in the foreign hotel room, like chess figures on a lawn, but the anonymous medicine bottle suited the anonymous hotel all the better; nowhere do health's Latin-faced phials look at home, but they are everywhere in place, as if in general our health were an unhomed, strange abstraction, and only our sufferings and nightshirts were tied to the self and its well-worn environment. I didn't know at that moment if I should link my sin to the individual nightshirts or the impersonal medicine bottle, but I realized that it can by no means be tied to the nightshirts, for it is entirely new and shapeless, like borrowed clothes.

Before taking the medicine I wanted to fetch a glass of water, but the tap was broken, so I had to go out to the corridor for water. I put on my breakfast gown and went out stealthily; in that precise moment the girl from the afternoon went up with the elevator to a higher floor; in my hands the pill, like the symbol casting into foreignness, of the most impersonal, well-nigh extra-human health, on my body the old Exeter nightshirt, which stuffed me back into the narrowest cell of my personality, as if my soul had been forced into my self as a huge filling into a narrow caries; between them, like a pasteurized angel enclosed in a bottle, flew the girl; the liftboy's hand on a button, above which a small red lamp glowed. Only the movement of thick iron ropes followed them, like in a rigging loft after the archangels' number is over, the smell of oil, & sweetish buzz. I stopped to listen for the slamming of the iron door and the door of the elevator: where should I put my sin?

Suddenly the light on the corridor was turned off, so I couldn't find the common water tap. In the dark the afternoon landscape glowed before me with the great rational retouching of insomnia, the blue mountains were soaked up into the sky, like breath on a window-pane, the spring flowers as small buttons and patent buckles of impossibility — then I found the sink and turned on the water, the neutral, empty, principial hotel water, which is really not one shade more than official water. What is health, what is peaceful sleep? — I thought, as I gulped down the ice-cold water with the pill; what meaning can it have among the murderous hypotheses of nature, sin, and hotel?

From the bar came the sound of music; I felt that I alone was a sinner in the whole hotel, I, whose brain is turned into a motley duvet by the field flowers, and not the figures who cut themselves with razor-sharp shirt fronts; it gave me almost childlike pleasure that I can see and find sin even where others only suspect innocence, and armed with this Exeter vainglory I doddered back to my room. My mouth was full of the medicine's crumbling clinical taste, my head of the flowers' simple colors and of the elevator's rushing angel-cage, as the boy keeps pushing the same floor and door-number under the red light; because the elevator circulated non-stop among the floors' porous diaphragms, like blood, I didn't feel my room to be isolated but something permanently afloat in the hotel, that mysteriously crossed the girl's room too, so the electric current of sin went through her as well. I almost fell into an idyll of fate, so I rang for the chambermaid because I wanted to talk with someone; when she asked what I wanted, I told her in a panic to refrigerate my pills because otherwise they would go off.

When she left I bemoaned my damnation for a long time, and now that I would be damned for her kiss anyway, I wanted to make the girl my lover. What is sin? What is virtue? And first and foremost, what is guilt-feeling without sorrow; the matter that I imagined to be matter because health, too, was pressed together in the sour-bitter material of medicine.

I switched off the light; my room suddenly filled with lights and shadows, which were in their place in the first moment, without any movements of finding a place, although they moved across the most complicated surfaces. From behind the thick curtains the windows shone through at once, with the blinding light of the arc lamp in front of the hotel, & of the slightly vague and crumpled veil of the hesitant snow seeds. I would have liked to pray, but didn't know what to choose: gratefulness for the kiss, or pathos against the kiss? For the one nurtured the other, which made it all so exciting. The arc lamp swayed a bit in the wind, my room switched to the left like a swing above the shadows' rigid wall bars. And all at once the kiss was red, as if the lamp had pushed the room exactly in the place of kiss-incandescence.

For the kiss occupied a wide territory and was full of magnetic rays; my room stood above it, hanging on the zebra rigging of lights and shadows, like a tilted veil on a foreign mast — the wind wraps the stray veil like balm on the other mast, & the ship doesn't move forward. I felt that my room was slightly tilted in the same way; on the one hand, it was fixed in possession of the kiss, and on the other hand it was also about some great untidiness, sliding-off and false harmony, like in a domino stone that presses to another with ideal tautness, but its number of black dots doesn't answer at all the dots of its companion. One of the main reasons why the kiss could radiate so ideally was this alternating atmosphere: the boundless certainty of dream, & the unexpected tilting of reality.

The certainty of the kiss continued incessantly; I didn't possess its memory as a flower is possessed between the lexicon's pressing pages, but as a forever deferred goal, infinite sound, which continues across a long series of dividing bar lines, hanging by the eternal bridge arches of the ligature lines: this is the positivism of dreams, where that which is certain forever runs on, is prolonged, spreads, attracts, and rises. I felt in half-sleep as my soul runs after the kiss like smoothly running black water; remembrance consists precisely in trying to lure the image glowing outside the image's frame inside that frame, but we never manage, and so only movement is left for the soul. This movement at once became so fast that I was forced to wake up.

In the room there was profound silence and I watched the furniture as I would watch the stage in the opera where the overture is already over, but the actors are not yet onstage. I decided to go for a walk; I have never gone on such a nighttime walk after interrupted sleep: it caused me peculiar Schadenfreude that the sleeping pill would work on my nerves in vain, I will be roaming outside in the cold, snowy wind. I felt certain limbs fast asleep, like uncoupled carriages in small deserted train stations, while the train rushes onward. The sleeping body part is the 'healthy' one, I thought with a laugh, and this widely awake one, upset by the great acceleration of memory, is the nervous one. Where was the memory now? How did the vague mathematical function of virtue and sin stand? In the night silence I had no instruments of measurement; in vain I tried to apply the numeric systems of nature, soul, dream, memory, none would turn into my decisive measures.

One would imagine that in the silence of the night the soul flies direct to God, but it was the other way round — the daytime confusion was the form of irrigation that bent the soul, with the help of virtuous thoughts, toward God. I quickly dressed and ran down the stairs, where the rug was so soft that you barely felt the angles of the steps; it was like a slope really. Underway I met two women; I couldn't tell if they were richer or poorer than me, as in their lives there was no short sleep between dinner and nighttime lucidity, which can present one with the absolute feeling of recklessness; was I purified by the dream, or did I betroth myself with sin? Now when this short nap urges me to run, am I trotting because I want something else than kiss, or because I can see even in the snow's thick soufflé nothing else but love's white-clad dams?

I felt an extraordinary desire to talk to someone who had not slept yet today, to feel and make them feel that almost moral surplus that my interposed little nap meant; in the hall the eyes were haunted by sleep's malaria season, while my eyes already showed the freshness of dawn, like the editorial of a morning paper, which some screwball publishers allow one to read already in the evening. What for these drowsy American women was still active today and living present, meant for me already past, a closed and withered world before falling asleep: when I picked up a dropped card for an old gent at the bridge table, I secretly enjoyed that he thought, I too lived now and this moment of mine is utterly parallel, what is more, consubstantial with his moment; he has no inkling that I am one or two hours ahead of him, and I pushed the card back from the pool of the future into his past, into what from my angle is the past. Thus for me everything was two hours behind, women, trees, mountains, snowfall. Does this help or hinder moral?

I certainly managed to get rid of something by this time difference, but I didn't know if it was the feeling of responsibility, or merely the unpleasant dam-taste of the feeling of responsibility; of love as thorny theory, or of love as the curbed routine of concrete desire? In general: did I burn with the fever of thinking, or with sensuous insatiability? Sleep divided me from the hotel and from nature, but a little bit also from myself. Was a wakeful part of me watching, with the excitement of discovery, a sleeping part of mine, so making me become a conscious watcher of my dream, or did I get into sleep's central belvedere, from where to listen to dream's triumphant commentaries and look at them, referring to wide-awake daylight consciousness: am I the maximum of consciousness, or dream's blind servant?

The remembrance of the kiss (not as image but as broad territory) meant the crisis of individuality; it partially freed me from all real bonds & lifted me into solitude with no way out, because every small flower was full of steaming mountain fog — and partly tied me to this sole memory, human being, movement, moment and place. Now I felt my self to be nothing, a mere, vast mist-world — and now I felt it to be small data characterizing some stranger, as though I were the specific gravity, boiling point, constitutional foundation date of that girl, or something in that line. Which is reality here and which the dream: the fog, or those small data? the psyche's ascetic flight, or the small philological footnote of the memory?

the basic difficulties of virtue'

Virtue struggles with two great difficulties, I thought when I stepped out of the hotel: one is that with every significant impression the psyche overflows, as it were, the 'normal' boundaries of human character, the new impression gets into one's center, and the psyche flows out and apart in the world, being squeezed out (the impression is the castle and the psyche is merely the surrounding moat); when thus it should take a stance, should will and trigger to action, it had long forgotten the narrow territory of the 'human being' and spreads to foreign territories, like a straying river forced out (by the strength of the impression) of its riverbed.

The other is, that for the psyche no action-models are given; the action is so immaterial, will is so absolutely lacking in the world of surrounding nature, or rather, the psyche gets so much used to nature's images, movements, and manner, that it barely manages to develop the model-less world of morality.

Sometimes a beautiful face or snowed-in fir tree makes an extraordinary impression on us, and this impression consists in the psyche fleeing from us & reaching an unknown, entirely new state that is utterly alien in its every part (if we can speak here of parts), which it doesn't understand, cannot measure, compare, or express. The natural thing would be for that beautiful face or snowed-in fir tree, as image and practical phenomenon, as the well-defined sources of the impression which estranges us from ourselves, to immediately come to our assistance and guide us. But they do nothing of the kind; if it had once made an impression on us, if it had been engraved in us even for a moment, a natural phenomenon (woman or tree) can no longer be of any use to us — the cause and source of the impression is unable to offer however transient a shade for understanding the impression. Therefore we are left hovering between two foreignnesses: between the object's nameless & meaningless data, and the feeling's energetic emptiness. How should we place the 'action' in this estranged world?

Otherwise absolute goodness doesn't mean something unified for us, it is scattered in the small hollows of different moments — the great virtues, the asceticisms and moral trials tautened to the limit of their volume's elasticity and beyond, could not mean the apex of virtue for me, or rather: they meant the apex of virtue, but not its goodness. Just as absolute beauty never appears to us in a single work but is pressed together from one movement of a musical piece, some love memory, political theory, and a few unattainable desires, & is made of the nostalgia that thirsts for a work that could unite those fragments.

Absolute: lots of disconnected fragments, plus desire, ambition directed at the future, which will perhaps supplement these with a new unity. The most important moments of artistic beauty-experience are exactly these transitional time-kisses, in which all kinds of plagiarized fragments are coupled with an unknown, an entirely unknown possibility. Composition, design, means far less the proximity of beauty's absolute than the moment when only a blood-red autumn creeper leaf and the glaring trivialities of a botched-up piano sonata exist, reflecting in the passive mirror of impossibility. Impossibility here is not melancholy but on the contrary, it is concrete like a color, and the absolute is always that fortunate moment of plagiarized banality when things are forgotten behind their shadows. I mention impossibility and possibility as consubstantial words: what a mystical thing an unknown possibility is, and how real a known impossibility.

---

the painted-over clothes of the kissed girl: from beige to green; their analysis. In the meantime, the wife's modified clothes

---

On the girl whom I kissed I loved two things: one was that her dress was from the previous year, painted over green; the other, that her cheeks were badly rouged. Both showed a typically cheap tendency; the dress' green dissolved the memory of the previous Swiss summer, dissolved her body, dissolved me and foisted my words into green gloves; while the misplaced rouge was transparent, like porously traced, thin aquarelle; instead of painting a focus, it looked rather like Flora's March kiss-smudge. The dress used to be beige with dark brown polka dots, which could barely be discerned now under the uniform green paint; but it was precisely their quiet darkness that showed peculiar resilience, as if, independently from the girl's body, these polka dots wanted to preserve the memory of my fingers from yesteryear — while the psyche, the will, the eyes glowed utterly independently from her, the dress showed the plenitude of faithfulness, of unwitting, animal, almost musical faithfulness (she had the dress painted over because of another, strange boy!): its new dark green color looked not as an extraneously added, new layer, but as the inner development and deepening of her inexorable relation with me. And this dress triumphed over the female body: in vain her white skin performed its actual, new season mimicry, the irrepressible dark dots surrounded her with the conservatism of wrinkles.

Before touching her with my fingers I felt that thanks to the painted-over old dress (which became ideally old, in a purified way, precisely because of the painting-over, that is, the denial of the past) my embrace was around her hips; as if the frills, seams, slackenings & side-shifts were my well-trained fish that are now doing their well-rehearsed number around their new mistress' body; their capering caressed her body, but that caress was solely the result of my training. With great anxiety I watched my gesture-disciples who lived in the dress, & whom I haven't seen for a year.

The girl's face has changed far less than her dress, and yet it was with the dress that I conversed first. Rarely can we enjoy so purely the coincidence of old & new, where novelty works for the old & the old produces the novelty. The entire dress appeared to me as if I saw it on the bottom of a lake, behind fir tree-green reflection floors, and it thus distanced the girl's figure into the green skies of the past (air looks blue in the height, while time looks green in the past): perhaps its embrace meant that one threw oneself into the green waves and swam for hours toward the dress' yesteryear beige and dark brown.

Change doesn't usually show on people in the form of such naive dualism: time alters, processes the elements of yesteryear rather than adding a new layer of color over the old in such a way that the old shows through; otherness as a rule is something consubstantial, while in the case of this dress it was two-substantial; there was no development, no metamorphosis, all time-biology was absent; everything related to modern time-gourmandizing as the naive, glued-on time-cubes of medieval miracle plays to the latest time-cells' telescoped fission screw-threads.

Earlier I saw the new color as development and now, as naive-blunt jump: if an impression is strong and precise we can fit anything inside it. The old dress showing through the paint was in any case the past, and the new dark green color was the present, but the two were not connected by the mythological and snobbish umbilical cord of time and of passage: during the game the girl's substance-partie had two, arbitrarily drawn cards.

I could refer the dress to myself only — objectively the dualism meant nothing for the girl's body; it was not her who multiplied from the dual fresco layers, but my body that lay between the two color strata like a living mummy. With all its darkness, the green also radiated spring glee, like an alto-voiced woman singing a laughing arietta, & in this gleefulness everything seemed homely to me, because girls usually don't wear their painted-over dresses on solemn occasions, or if they do, they would drop in passing, 'O, this is a trifle, a painted-over blouse from last year, really a rag.' Last summer, last year's embrace (it was barely a touch) is thus secured and rescued under the new layer of paint; if she hadn't had the dress painted over, its oldness wouldn't have come to my mind and the dress would have been exposed to new events chafing off last year's months from it; but now, even if I am met with only rudeness from her, it will not affect me, because as compared to the dress' transparent dark polka-dots from last year, they are only impotent vapeur-s and humeur-s, as they would put it in old comedies.

This painting-over meant for me a greater proof of faithfulness, of the preservation of my personality (she nearly became the lover of the boy for whom she had it painted over) than any imagined letter in which she would have declared her love for me. For a year I heard nothing from her, but now I found myself in the dress, not so much her fictitious-decisive faithfulness to me as my un-self-conscious faithfulness, of which I could say like Molière's upstart, with no inkling that so far I had spoken in prose: c'est la fidélité![397] If this woman had this dress painted over, then I have been ceaselessly faithful to her all the while, always longing for her; the darkly showing-through, almost bassoon-like, crackling and hooting-through, big polka dots suddenly radiated into me a desire-past, not as though I had lacked desire, but because so far it had always appeared to me as barren, self-mortifying, and pointless: now these two color layers reshaped it into law and melody.

(Since that summer I have often had the occasion to enjoy painted-over clothes, my wife has been wearing such clothes for years. She had a 'puritanical' upbringing; in her grownup years she had no money, so the two circumstances met in touching harmony. When we had guests I tried to hide the fact that she had an old dress on, and employed such adjectives that are mostly used for new clothes — at such times my wife interrupted with a wry little laugh, 'Our dear guests know anyway that we don't have the money for spring apparel, and they can see very well that this is my green dress from last year, I only had the middle of it painted over, and twisted back the belt, and here in the front where the old seam's place showed, I made large cotton stitches that look like ornament. Then they botched the painting in the workshop, one part of the skirt was lighter, but I left it so, sewed on a line of buttons between the two colors, and it's quite becoming.' She even went up to the guests and showed, folded over and buttoned, the parts that betrayed the piece's age. The women praised her handiness & modesty, her behavior as a real priest's wife.

Of course her satisfaction had nothing to do with virtue — first I fought against it, but I resigned myself to it in the end. I watched her as she leafed through the Paris fashion magazines with genuine greed, without any personal desire or sadness mixing into her infatuation; then she started mending her stockings and explained that she sewed up the holes so that they looked more artistic than the most complicated arrows, palm tree-rayons and other stocking inlays. Occasionally she had a few fine dresses, the results of lengthy theories; in theory she knew fashion far better than other women, but less from the perspective of fashion than of the arts, which she learnt from me.

I thought that if I inserted modern clothes among mathematical ideal theory, Parisian post-impressionist painting, and other such general period characteristics, with such bait I could lure her out from her raw and literal-minded 'puritanism,' but the shtick didn't work — she designed such absolutely modern clothes that they were barely wearable, and got immersed overmuch into the world of theory. Moreover, she treated painting-over, retailoring, & cross-stitching too as Sezession experiments, all the while led by the 'simplicity' she inherited from her parents.

The awareness of art historical actuality isolated her even more from elegance, because in the shop windows she saw not separate, wearable clothes but only fashion arguments, which can be all reduced to a few technical & fabric-logical devices, like for example, 'asymmetry,' 'rayé & smooth,' 'discordant materials,' 'rococo variation and Cubism,' etc. — and she could very well apply these principles to painted-over old clothes; she sewed on the neck lace from her mother's old underskirt [this was rococo variation], but tore off all the skirt's old ornaments and ironed out all its creases [this was Cubism]. My desire was not directed toward such mundanity in theory of course, and it suffered greatly.

We had acquaintances who wore much more old-fashioned clothes than her, but their relation to their clothes was more modern; these women went without lengthy deliberation, the knowledge of every imaginable type of textile and the awareness of their value [my wife knew every kind of fabric], just as they never criticized the seamstresses' style; only the hasty unthought of vanity worked in them. In contrast, my wife's vanity was hard, arduous, fastidious, and joyless, almost as much of a disturbing strain of womanly life as the monthly indisposition. To this stealthy vanity was added [a typical feature of puritans] her appreciation of the 'reliable respectable'; if once in a blue moon she bought herself a hat, it would be an outrageously expensive straw one, dull as ditchwater, but if marinated for half an hour in chloride and 'stretched' in coal gas, its threads never curled, not even if rubbed with manganite, which is beyond a shadow of doubt the best evidence of perfection!

I hated her the most when she sat before the mirror; her hands, in which the brush withered, were not led by instinctive vanity, nor by art historical prancing, but by some drowsy bigotry around the concept of the 'real lady,' & half-baked health advice. Perhaps she suffered much when she sat before the mirror, perhaps she felt the torment of banishment — I could see only that every trying on of face powder, hair adjustment, destruction of skirts, was a beginning anew, the utter lack of routine, something I have also noticed in our skivvy, who recalibrated the order of coffee spoons and fruit-preserve bowls every time she laid the table; she never felt that one had to adjust to an immovable order, but decorated and changed cutlery three times a day, as a painter would do with his colors.)

The beauty-possibility of this painted-over dress was, that it meant at the same time the old color's blossoming, like a flower-funnel's ever spreading, widening ledger, which is nothing more than the flaring of an initial, narrow little tube, eventually its turning inside out, and yet it also meant the independent duality, the anti-development beginning-anew, Arcadian inorganic mutation. In other words, it could be enjoyed psychologically and geometrically at the same time. At that time I was reading the *Urteilskraft*,[398] and I still vividly remembered the few moments when I passed from the chapter on 'beauty' to the passage on the 'sublime,' where such words featured as formless, pointless, chaos, et cetera: without feeling the dress' new dark green color to be sublime in the least, I nevertheless related it to its color from last year as this later chapter in Kant to the earlier one; psychological representation likes compiling similarities from flowers & philosophy.

The color of last year, the dull beige, was beautiful in the way Kant would have liked it, it was free beauty and purposeless purposefulness at the same time, it was equally free of gross color-sensuality and of the cheap regularities of Pfeffergartens,[399] it was far removed from all objective cognition, but precisely for this reason it had some peculiar logical flavor (for me Kant's most charming characteristic was also that sometimes he would isolate the experience of beauty so completely from every form of cognition, that in consequence it gets some nervously intellectual coloring, the way a mirror absorbs the objects departing from it more symmetrically toward its center than the objects approaching): I arrived at the consciousness of the beauty of last year's dress by demonstrating to myself with a wealth of arguments, that the experience I am undergoing can be nothing else but the experience of beauty, and if we approach something with rational steps, even if the purpose should be completely irrational, it will rest rational forever, the way we can imagine a pristine, self-serving point on a field of snow, to which long footprint-radiuses arrive, and only around the center does the snow-field rest white and untouched: and yet that untouched center cannot get rid of the black footprints, and we enjoy the footprints' black star far more than the solitary center. That beige corresponded to the Kantian vision: in the middle, the object, which is always surrounded by the ring of beauty.

What the Königsberg booklet calls sublime is perhaps nothing else than a small change of places: in the middle is beauty like a busy well, and only as a weak filter does the object's concept or positive existence surround that dark green well, which is, however, now and then carried away by central beauty, as tennis nets are sometimes carried away by a gust of wind. There is thus no difference between beauty and sublimity; with the first, the object is the subject and its beauty is the predicate — with the second, beauty is the ab ovo existing subject and the object is the small, frost-like predicate, which even the faintest breeze brushes off the top of the overflowing subject. The expression of the latter condition of beauty is the ever-widening flower-cup, on which we always see one dynamic trait, ever-rising intensity, and its object nature, its concrete shape are merely characteristic data and measures to express force; these funnel-cupped flowers only have shape (accidentally) because something interfered with the free development of intensity; object-like shape is nothing more than the sum that expresses the missing dynamic continuation.

I observed the same on the green dress; its cut, its material shape, was like the image of a freely springing water jet when it splashes against a glass pane — what had been a simple water jet running ahead will draw all kinds of wide-corpulent shapes on the pane set across it. The dark green beauty was something peculiarly ever-flowing, so its turning into a dress was solely thanks to such a hindering transparent pane set in its way. But since the green-shaped beauty was an undulating force and the dress' cut was a transparent, but all the stronger dam, beauty kept fretting behind it like a nervous lizard, in whose path a giant wall is raised, and the small animal scurries left and right, up and down, looking for an escape route.

The beige dress was simply the world where my psyche stopped and left room for the new phenomenon: a last-ditch room toward the girl's essence, but it was not I who took that step, it was the dress that took that step to me. With the green, however, it was the green dress that flowed out to me, and I could take one step only toward it. All these flowings, flower-like onward-dehiscence, predicate-meltdowns and Urteil-swings are typically psychology-flavored interpretations of the painting over; the psyche lives from time and force, that's why it favors biology and philosophy. But I did everything to free myself from this routine and interpret the relation between beige and green in a drier manner.

I was surprised at how the green dress, which looked so much an eternal expansion, March-melancholy onward radiation, could nevertheless fit into last year's small beige territory, for 'intensity' is probably only a turn of phrase and in reality it was the dress' expanse that grew bigger. And yet it didn't become any wider, and so the only way the operation can be imagined is that the second green dress is the ably placed orthogonal projection of something much bigger (let's say, of the green-veined ellipsis called 'spring'), the way in which some modest circles plotted inside squares or rhombuses are also the orthogonal diminished projections of distant ellipses.

The beige, last year's dress, in general the women of yesteryear, the times of yesteryear were the narrow frame, tyrannical fate, the rigid mounting of remembrance, and into this fell the infinite green, the spring melancholy, the haughty pubertal girl-present, the whimsical 'pattern' of hic et nunc as small orthogonal projection, in which two large polka dots featured only at 3 cm distance, but two running rays somewhere around the mountains' murderous rice powder and the sky's azure oases showed those two dots at a distance of 3 km. So it could happen that a far larger time pool fitted into the tight beige dress; the swelling present fitted, in pill shape, into a narrow little past-tubelet, like my sleeping pills into the tube that I gave to the chambermaid to put in the refrigerator.

Colors mean different times and different spaces; one could experiment with placing vast amounts of time into someone's consciousness by the means of green, and with the same green to exponentially increase their perception of space. All at once the new dress gave me the impression that I could dispose of much more time than in reality; my parents had planned our stay here for three weeks, but ever since I saw that unstoppable green layer over last year's layer, in its place, I felt that I would be together with this girl for three years, as if one could go not only forward in time but also across & upwards; the beige is its width, the green its length, or the green is already the new, multi-dimension world of love, but in any case time's thread-like dimension-loneliness ceased and it widened into a pool, where one day meant at least three days — swimming forward, across, & down into the depth.

It's curious how such a new layer of color over the old one means not only a simple plane-surplus but the milieu of an abundant well; I couldn't tell myself if it meant time or space, I only felt that it was a life-base, as if a discus thrower, around whose feet a circle is drawn which he must not overstep when taking momentum, once dreamt that the circle is exactly as large as the world's horizon, inside which only the momentum's blissful and empty sweep exists, and the dry excitement of the throwing cannot come to pass, because preparation too is infinite and the act, the throwing, cannot possibly be more than the preparation. Thus according to this green dress the act of love (the throwing of the discus proper) shifted over into infinity, and I felt the moment of preparation for love to be an overlong, prolonged time; the second of glimpsing and first self-ignition was prolonged in the dress' dark tranquility, like the shadow of a match from the generosity of sunset. Because only shadows came to my mind, which grow so fast in the evening, I soon started interpreting this much-hailed gain of space and time (it was as if I had put all my desire to one number and now the roulette's hazardous green gave it back 36 times) in a sorrowful key: all expansion, gain, the flowers' spreading petals (according to psyche), projection of an ellipsis within a small square (according to reason), all that is merely a mechanism of shadows, and so it presupposes the wearing out and ending of something, just as even in my wine-drinking I would mourn, with redundant compassion, the shivering skeleton of the maimed vine stock.

the paradox of 'infinite' temptation

Let's suppose that the momentum for throwing the discus is not yet sin, but the throwing itself is already sin, & so the momentum doesn't aim at the throwing but is only an absent-minded experimental movement that might or might not continue in the throwing of the discus, and then even though this eternal momentum twists toward the throwing, the discus will never be thrown (I surrender entirely to temptation's slope, but it is so infinite that I cannot reach sin in space & time): I was in this moral state the night when I got up after my short nap to go for a nightly walk on the snowed-in paths & decide if I was sinning or not. The green painting-over, reminiscent of unfathomable lakes with its dots coming from deeper yet, rendered the beginning of love infinitely wide and large, and this put me in a rather paradoxical moral situation; if the beginning is infinite, then it never attains the sin, but on the other hand even at the very beginning there are sinful germs, like minute bacteria, and now even they were infinitely magnified, so the apparently comfortable situation, of resting forever at the beginning, cannot offer any consolation.

If the green dress' tropical river-mirror, with its slow flow, boundless riverbed, & lacquer-clotted silence had not magnified the first moment, the moment of seeing the girl again, then at least the innocent adoration, salad-Platonism could have remained great and the sin-part small — but in infinity these proportions were not preserved, for there sin, too, became infinite alongside innocence. Perhaps it was not sin though but only the seeds of temptation, and all in all, an infinite temptation is not yet sin.

The magnifying didn't happen, however, on a geometrical sheet, but on the feverish soil of my most vivid feelings; inside me the seed of temptation lengthened to infinity, and such a thing can't play out in the psyche without triggering sin, just as the revolving of a propeller under a bell jar will not result in forward movement, but the moment it is dropped in water it will dash forward & transform into movement.

Does the infinity of infinite temptation presuppose that one cannot resist it — that it must needs trigger sin? Because my moral balance revolved around this question while I was playing with the hotel's enormous St. Bernard dog on the threshold. To my delight the porter allowed me to take him along on my walk. The infinity of temptation can only mean an infinity of force, so nothing could be simpler than to set against it the infinity of resistance, & in that moment it becomes superfluous to even mention infinity, for the situation is exactly like a finite one, this being a case of direct proportionality. But temptation always resembles nature, while will doesn't; seemingly it's difficult to think of a finite tree, snowed-in pine, or a beautiful female face as infinite, although it's the other way round: we always feel the matters of the psyche to be like coffee spoons and knives of baby cutlery, faced with the objects' immeasurable 'plat de l'éternel.' [400]

the creation of numbers and moral

In fact we have no idea how many moral traits lurk in our everyday visual experience and artistic hallucinations, which modify them; we can't even imagine the state when the eyes saw only objects, felt only instincts in the fingers, and no do-s and don't-s interfered. For these two arbitrary addenda to things completely change the technique of the most straightforward color and sound perceptions, the technique of impressions too: an object and the same object plus some moral addendum relate to one another like a word's etymological spelling & its modern pronunciation; nature is orthography, the psyche is phonetics. As the language keeps altering the words like water the pebbles, so does moral use alter, in part polish, round, and in part fragment, tear up the everyday visions; the eye slowly transforms into a moral mill that grounds the objects' rough grains into the fine flour of do-s and don't-s.

Perhaps a slightly parodic image of this process could also be the way in which I compared the duality of beige and dark green to the Golden Age relation of 'one' and 'two.' When the human being knew no number and moral yet (if such a state doesn't square with historical reality, let's imagine it) & saw a flower, whose cup kept growing, widening, flaring, and even curling back at the edges, for the petals' plate-like splaying inevitably leads to a narrowing, the edges coil backward in the shape of spring-like tresses, under themselves (the earth too is rounded because it expands too intensely and continuously), then that human being will not relate that great quantitative increase numerically to the initial form, the petal-start — for him, all this will be one and the same thing, for he had not yet divided up the magnifying, and for him the expanse will mean a qualitative change within the same quantity, the 'one': where the dark green color-canopy (green sky, green clouds, green stars, green Milky Way of creases, green day and green night etc.) could be imagined above the old beige according to the psyche's tastes (as I mentioned above) as follows: the beige's closed bud opened, its stingy leaf-buckles have fallen apart like sigils snapped into two, and now on the new meadows the eternal flower's green flooded everything in its abundance, being far more than the original wee beige-root, it is in fact a multiple of the beige, so for a refined brain it meant the multiplication of the one-beige, as a great number of petals is, mathematically speaking, always a multiplication of the bud's initial sum — but now we are trying precisely to get rid of that 'refined' brain and enjoy the Pliocene or Miocene arithmetic, which will see merely the atmospheric shades of the selfsame 'one,' and not its multiplying, even in the exponential growth of quantums.

When does 'two' come onstage in this comedy: when does this continuous spreading split into two parts? Anywhere. I couldn't for my life say why (that's why I called the above parenthesis parodic), but it is my obsession that here the strange elements of licet and non-licet got suddenly mixed into the process, interrupting the eternity of expansion, the infinity of the '1' like a current interrupter.[401] In the beginning, before the incipient neurasthenia of licet & non-licet, there was no '2' yet, at most 'an other'; when I related the green to the beige according to the taste of the psyche, I was fantasizing about the 'other,' which is at most a role of the '1,' a role behind which it remains 1; and when I proceeded according to the arbitrariness of reason (or, according to my latest intuition, according to the arbitrariness of moral), then I suddenly split development into 2, and beige and green became separate mathematical figures, the green was no longer a mask of beige but a strange, second thing.

Thus the coming into being of the concept of '2' didn't interest me in the least, if it started with someone spotting a second, separate flower next to a flower — but I was always drawn by the forced presupposition that a single flower-cup widened, expanded, like water pouring out on an absolutely flat floor, & this spread is somewhere, anywhere split into two from some reflex-like spasm of asceticism, probably not evenly, so that this algæ-like '2' is no regular multiple of the '1' but disproportionately small or big as compared to it.

When I stood between the beige and the green, enjoying the ethereal fruitfulness of comparisons, I felt to be among such antediluvian number-algæ, in the arbitrary rift between 1 and 2; 1 and 2 related to modern number-hygiene like primeval flying lizards to the 20th century's regular & respectable little bourgeois insects. Because that ancient '2' which suddenly broke off from the slender stem of '1' in fact represented all the other numbers, the infinite richness of all the imaginable numeric systems & their unprocessed content;

one moment before splitting off it still belonged to the exclusive and private anatomy of '1,' but when the split occurred, when it dropped from the edge of the spreading petals, it pendulated into another extreme, becoming not simple 'other,' a kind of charming pendant-sibling next to the pristine '1,' but all the world's strange things, the accumulation basin of complex otherness — perhaps this split-off part was smaller in quantity than the original '1,' for example, & yet this small '2' become independent had a far richer content and significance than the 1. Hence the overwhelming disproportionateness, the mathematical contradiction that the green dress' dizzying depth meant for my pedantic eyeballs.

problems of the analytic style, its nature of leading outside itself; the part of something and otherness

The color green obviously meant the most contrasting things for me. Not from the beginning though, and indeed it all started (as it does with all imaginable analysis) with me sharply separating this case of painting-over from the ordinary consequences following such paintings over; for example, I stressed to myself that the green didn't emerge from time's continuous stream but was an isolated new time fragment, thrown on top of the former's body; later, when I further investigated the excitement of the new color, I found the exact opposite of that assertion also true: flower comparisons and presuppositions of the emergence of numbers developed the green from beige, gradually and according to biological fashion. One can hardly imagine a greater contrast, and yet I found both to be equally characteristic of the girl's dress; as if it were in the nature of analysis to find everything, even mutually exclusive things, equally pertaining to a thing.

The analytic instinct starts first into fanatical insulation; it singles out and differentiates to extremes a small fragment from the rest of the world's things. To achieve this differentiation, it needs a great amount of small analogies, metaphor-pegs, scheme-sheaths; yet we draw and borrow all these small analogies, metaphor-pegs, and scheme-sheaths, with which we want to surgically remove a small shade from the body of the real, in order to elevate it into the microscopic idol of difference, from the same world from which we attempt to separate the given part (in the present case for example, the green dress): I need to cobble together the fence I am trying to erect between the green dress and the rest of the world from the elements of the rest of the world — thus the fence only differs from the rest of the world by being otherwise grouped and organized.

At this point the fence displays a cancer-like disease, an infinite swelling of the insulation material; because the fence or insulating material differs from the rest of the world only in its order, the analyzing, that is, insulating instinct tries to magnify this upsetting of the order, so that the fence may appear all the taller, thicker, and pricklier. In fact I am not analyzing the internal nature of the painted-over dress, but the wall that separates that dress from the rest of the world, but made up solely from the elements of that 'rest of' the world; and this I need to make of many elements, so it is not easily mistaken for the rest of the world, because in contradistinction to the world, only with many elements can I achieve a juxtaposition in innovative confusion. Thus the analysis refers first and foremost to the hedge and not to the so-called analyzed object, and with the hedge it can no longer be called analysis, only a simple multiplication of elements; there is no singling out of elements but only a mathematical multiplication of those elements (elements referring to the non-whole). That such procedure is oriented more toward truth than conventional old analysis used to be, will perhaps be proved by the emerging style of our days.

When isolating analysis transforms into a mechanical multiplying of elements (if the instinct of analysis is indeed strong; if analysis is not the chosen research method but the most primal movement of constraint of the soul), it will naturally also line up self-contradictory elements. Thus the analysis that started as rabid insulation technique ends up by expressing its theme (for example, the dress painted green) with the whole world, identifying it with all conceivable things, sciences, myths, numbers, human beings, nothings. The analytic instinct will 'individualize' the green dress to the point of spreading it to the whole world, everything will be in that green, red for instance, blue, yellow, the whole color spectrum from which the green was initially to be separated, but the special atmosphere of the green can only be expressed with the help of the red, blue, yellow and the whole spectrum.

Thus the radical style of analysis extinguishes the classic concept of 'the whole & its parts,' and in their place it develops the style of independent parts referring to the non-whole — needless to say, at that point 'element' is no longer an adequate name for it, because of its suggestion of a whole. The thing has to be imagined as starting to decompose a flower to its component parts: this is the start of classical analysis in novels, psychology, and medicine alike.

But that flower can perhaps also be expressed otherwise, or that desire to express and define can be lived in another form as well (and nowadays this new taste is spreading, as far as I can tell from my country parish) — instead of dividing up the flower, like a mystical divisible integer with some arbitrary divisor, I pick a few elements from the world surrounding the flower (arbitrarily, or so it seems), and I usher these elements picked from here and there under the flower's old name. This method (if such a frivolous-looking game or barren sophistry may be called a method at all) is no artificial conceit but the natural consequence of the classic analytic style, its logical meaning. In classical botany there will feature 5 petals, two million cells, 8 leaves, 1 stem, 5 boughs, a root branching into 29, and 13 leaf-stems: all separately, but out of them the whole flower can be assembled (at least in theory). In the new, post-analytic 'element' style (I haven't yet invented a new word to take the place of 'element') stockings, zeta-functions, short story titles, spouses and legal penalties will feature on the analytic pages of botany: from them the original flower cannot be assembled, not even in principle.

Before it got to the short story titles from the branches, to the stockings from the petals, the furore of analysis used to be continuous, consequent, and seamless, but the same way couldn't be covered backwards, these elements couldn't be led back to the flower meaning the original starting point, that is, they could no longer be treated as 'elements.'

Two concepts feature here: insulation, and analysis proper. The slicing-up of the flower is such a blindly-complete practical example that one can no longer feel in it the fact that it is a dividing analysis, in fact theme-dissecting technique is from the very beginning an insulation technique; it is merely an optical illusion that I tear petal after petal from the flower and tear up the psyche to its associations (as if the novelists and psyche-healers of old played a psychological 'you love me, you don't love me' game): in fact even there I am selecting illogical elements from the flower's environment, which are drawn under the name of the flower only by the flower's magnetic force; the relation between the plant's sheer name & the units of the surrounding world unrelated to that plant is a much stronger, well-nigh logical cohesion, than the relation between the whole flower & its real petal, stem, root, etc. parts.

Attempted comprehensive analysis wills many elements, and in time the concept of the element fades, leaving only 'many' in its place; instead of tearing off the petals, it will foist ever newer unrelated petals, even whole flowers, in the end probably even animals.

These many ersatz-petals and inserted addenda-animals burst the frame of the flower and yield a new graph & new plasticity, which doesn't resemble the original flower a bit, and yet they adhere to the flower's name. This new plasticity, the product of interpolated strange elements, will be the new flower-Anschauung,[402] the new classical structure. The process started as the generation of mathematical fractions, developed into an interpolation of integers, and this new, enriched series of numbers suggests new figuration, new lines of composition, some new whole that we will link to the old concept, or rather, to the 'sheer name.'

There is an ambiguous moment in the history of analysis, according to the above, when an 'element' is still half a component, that is, part of the original whole object, but at the same time it is also an independent formation, some other thing independent from the original whole, which belongs to the face of the surrounding world; in part petal, in part white ellipsis, which lives its ultra-white and exclusively geometrical life independently from the flower. Perhaps the next moment it would bend back into the flower's unity like the flowers that close on themselves at night, but perhaps it would develop into the ellipsis illustration of a white tennis dress and a scientific treatise; analysis is caught between post- and trans-analysis.

The analysis that reaches the post-analysis stage thus performs a two-directional reduction: in the direction of the concept it will leave only the name unaffected, the bloodless-emaciated nominalist clown's mask ('green dress' or 'a flower'); and in the plastic direction it creates plasticity, strange, illogical plasticity in excess, triple-foliage and octet-fruits in place of cells, which grew on a different kind of tree (in place of the original image of 'green dress' for example, the image of a red sea fish, in place of the 'one flower,' three Old Persian family names as the non plus ultra of analysis!).

But there is a strong attraction between the empty name and the strange-new plasticity — if that didn't exist, the game would not be worth playing; a red fish interests us far less qua red fish and far more if that red fish, as material reality, means a 'green dress,' adheres to that concept, or became the content of that name at the end of the analysis of the 'green dress.' There is an optimistic morale to this: fear not if analysis should 'particularize' the psyche and the world to death; on the contrary, that way it will create new, great bodies.

the color green and a comparison to it, of a fictitious green plant

Since I saw that painted-over dress in Switzerland, the color green has been for me like the Aphatyrum Minangium II blooming on the sea floor, which has the unique trait of always blooming twice: one of its inflorescences adapts exactly to its surroundings, so if the crack in the rift happens to be oval, its silk thorns too will be arranged in an oval, if in its close vicinity there is a three-branched crack in the rock, then these silk thorns or macaroni tendrils will always develop in three regular mimicry groups; but at the same time, in miniature next to this actual and accidental fashion-form, and as a rule regressed and barely noticeable, another, but constant inflorescence will also be present, which is always unchanged, whatever the splendid adapting inflorescence may look like, with its pink sponge-purée and combed rainbow skeins; somewhere close by, hidden from view one can always find the basic form's moldy, grey rosette. Ever since that moment, with most of the important events that happened around me and related to me, the color green played a part; the events were different as the Aphatyrum's ornate and adapting flowers, but the color green always featured in them, just like the unchangeable regress-essence.

association with the color green: meadow between Cambridge and Ely, where he met a half-idiot girl; landscape and caritas

I came across the most memorable Aphatyrum find in the afternoon when I met a half-idiot girl on a green meadow between Cambridge and Ely, when my wife's mother attempted suicide with some glaringly green poison. On that lovely afternoon my mind was mostly preoccupied by the thought of agape, and I observed sadly that it is and must be completely missing from people, being not human-shaped; the moment it becomes anthropoid it already morphs into something else.

I was giving a speech in some religious society about the great creases of love in Christ's soul, and while I was dramatizing my theme into a more logical form for my own understanding and watching the finished, concrete faces of my audience, I saw love bloating into a lonely, bulky storm cloud among the hostile winds of my metaphors, and this grim love-cumulus couldn't land anywhere, couldn't let out rain, couldn't dissolve into white or golden-blond rain, but remained a big shadow in the air's purposeless emptiness.

All my sermons shared the same mechanics: I wanted to foist my most subjective moods on my congregation, to graft the most human things on the next other, and the more I spoke, the more lyrical I waxed, the faster the theme split off from both me and my congregation's souls; at the sermon's end a strange shadow, a dark, isolated idea-mist hung from the church ceiling, which had nothing to do with anyone, least of all with me.

On that Cambridge afternoon too I left the society's boring assembly room with these feelings, and I felt that love is made up of vast movements, physiological comedies, death, and the soul's impossible meteorology; caritas is not identical to humanitarian goodness, or in general, to any human moral; caritas is purely and simply the functioning of all life, the blossoming of flowers and the contract breaches of Halley-stars in heaven, the carnivalesque squandering of truths and solitude's spherical egoism, all these together are caritas, that is, all life, with the sole difference that caritas is not there for life's but for something else's sake, for anything's sake.

At that point I felt only these two features of caritas to be authentic: vita omni-viva and 'anything.'[403] And this cannot fit into the abbreviated souls of people, for they never live through all livables but only the conspectus of life revised & abridged for humans, and yet caritas begins where 'everything' features, and a quartet cannot be transcribed to one violin; secondly, people don't know the atmosphere of 'any kind of strange purpose,' but only its opposite — they will see the essence of every deed, flower, flavor in the safe deposit of cause and purpose.

Before me was Cambridge, green meadows dotted with flowers scattered in groups, like icing sugar on the fancy cake at home when cook was in a hurry, and instead of icing it evenly, she dumped all the sugar into one corner; here and there a thin green brooklet lying deep, like the low-lying tracks of the ceinture railway around Paris; gentle bridges which, although they didn't droop their arches with such vertical one-sidedness into the dimension of sorrow as weeping willows, nevertheless looked much sadder, because instead of fleeing into the free light-wells of the brooklet, their quivering shadows grew back into the abutment with sudden maudlin, the prodigal son's worthless gesture; instead of taking advantage of the counterfeit passport of shadow provided by the bronze-oblique afternoon sun, and evading themselves, they chose to fuse in a barren spring kiss on the other bank like the Sapphic bowling pins of Magdeburg; on the streets there were a few blond boys in Harris tweeds & black-robed lecturers; in the doors marble plaques that supply remembrance with memorials;

among the pebbles, buds like ill-threaded, shabby beads on crooked wire: one is a small green dot, like carbon dioxide in mineral water, running toward the sky's slowing lights like a sparkling curtain, and some Elizabethan bird chirps the overture to accompany it ('twittering joy-points of poisonous Perchance...') — the other is a white wadding-fluff that seems to have got accidentally entangled in the crags' out-of-tune strings; the green dots grow on crooked twigs, the wadding-buds on regular arches, and the latter soak up the sun like blotting paper, so a peculiar shadow is cast around them, not black but colorless sun-vacuum; from one of the fountains an inebriating water-smell rises, a cold, muddy, deep, and Shakespearean smell, into which inspiration sends its fast-chained buckets.

It was clear to me that this is true caritas, the great tranquility of time & existence surrounding me; towers, poppies, the hourglass' forever-shifting dune strand, where only the shore knows ebb, never the sea; statue-bowling pins napping between the columns, from which the multiple meanings of English history will perhaps rise, like shiny moths, at the Last Judgment; cardinals, heretics, kings & ladies-in-waiting were all mere blind worms pupating in college-cracks after their deaths, & I was waiting, with Christian excitement, for the surprising great butterfly of Albion Protestantism to come on that tremendous day: oh, papillon noir de ma pieuse espérance! [404] If this is true caritas, it will indeed be found in few people, for barely have three or four truly insatiable people been born since the creation; the world is chock-full of satisfied beings, for even the most bloody-minded revolutionaries are satisfied to see a new, second order in place of the old one; caritas will achieve nothing with such meek, prim lads.

I was floundering out of the town, head swirling, bemoaning especially the girls who don't know caritas. At that time there were two or three weeks to my wedding, and I was looking for some thought that could make me forget it. Why didn't I run away from marriage? Because there were moments when my bride too (what an awful word that, I feel in it some Völkisch syrupiness) belonged to the clock face of my life; I was the distraught and precise clock hand, surrounded by numbers like on modern clocks where the numbers are no longer written but only an identical-looking line is engraved everywhere, so you can know the time only from the position: my wife too was such a modern number, with no independent value, only an independent position in my life.

I felt marriage would smother me, but the adoption of smothering too belonged to plenitude; whatever presents itself has to be borne, because the moment a thing appears, even by the most cursory act of noticing that thing became self, and I cannot cut off and throw out slices of my self at will. When I was horrified of my bride, I was thus not horrified of a strange human being but of an ineradicable feature of my soul, of my body's incurable disease; although the girl was an 'adopted' feature of mine, it gave the impression of being born with me, like the sense of touch or original sin.

The true impressionist is not the one who tears the Rouen cathedral's stone laws into light's vibrating doubt-scales, but its very opposite: the one who imagines even the river's transient shadow-currencies to be his life's pivotal contracts made with Satan. Even my most frivolous impressions meant some obligation toward fate, that's why I was unable to even think of escaping from the cul-de-sac tunnel of marriage. This obligation-panic brought along with the tormenting wealth of my impressions could provide an explanation for the emergence of my caritas concept; under caritas I felt the impression-sea that doesn't carry the weight of obligations: vita omni-viva, which is yet made ethereal, free, & blissful by the 'anything,' the some 'other purpose,' whose meaning I don't know. On the other hand, the 'everything,' the insatiable multitude belonged to the essence of love so I could have greater hope for the purpose, the moral thread getting entangled, enmeshed, broken: the wadding-buds on their own could still have meant some obligation for me, for example that I become a founding member of a society for protecting plants, or express my gratitude to God for repeating spring, or buy a bunch of flowers for my wife, etc., but if I placed the green bead-buds next to the wadding-buds, and next to them, the slack G-minor bridges with their slightly dissonant shadows, as they clumsily modulate toward freedom's purer tonalities; and next to the bridges, the colleges' memorial plaques, wells and relics, the clouds and skies of the surrounding landscape: in this way all practical purpose was lost on the way and only the world's active beauty was left for me, in which I could swim freely and where getting sucked in by a vortex meant triumph, spasm an advantage, and death, the purpose.

the infinite love of Christian love

Love is not the nauseating turn of one person to another, but the blood circulation among the world's most distant objects; logical blood circulation corresponds to God's idea of creation, and the blood circulation of love, to God's appetite for realization. My caritas drunkenness consisted in mediating kisses among buds and ticket controllers, memorial plaques and shop windows, prayerbooks and weekend tickets, not resting for one moment, just as blood circulation has no bombastic Sabbath either.

At first sight then my caritas is nothing but vitalist salesman's thrift or too deeply inhaled æsthetic. Vitalism is the world of the surface-most layer, poetry, science. Ontology is a tad deeper, because existence is more than life, but still, it's far from being the ultimate. Deepest of all is the world of caritas; it is concerned not with the flower's life or its existence, but with the psychic movement with which God had once wanted to create the world:

this movement doesn't resemble the flower at all, it's simply the rhythmic passage from nothing into something, which wills not logic, reality, or life, but wills merely something, thus it is a love gesture. Because the world cannot mean reality next to God's reality, it cannot mean truth in relation to God's existence beyond truth (or rather, it can mean only 'truth,' to be understood as a term of abuse, a scathing remark), the world can only mean some 'lyrical' thing in God's life, and this impregnated God-lyricism is what I call love. Where are its boundaries? It is ever-present in souls & objects alike.

People like talking about feelings like joy and sorrow, and about their shades too, but they keep forgetting that the greatest feelings, those decisive for our lives, and which, if once tasted, we seek as a morphinist seeks drugs — these emotions are not joys or sorrows but absolute tensions; they are not artistic inspiration or rabid will to act, but the intuition of the moment when God created the world. You could say that I make use of God here as a rhetorical device, the priest-like avoidance to face my lack of talent for analyzing emotions squarely, although it is not: when I look at a gorgeous flower I am not overjoyed or sorrowing, I don't want to emulate it and turn into a flower, I merely feel that my soul fills with infinite movement & intensity, the way it must have been in the celestial will that willed the world into existence; divine cause does not resemble effect, it is no bud & no beginning, but a rolled energy-ball, from which something comes forth, anyhow, anything.

This feeling could perhaps be called an infinitely passive and infinitely action-ignorant will to act: love, too, wants lethal embrace & canonic tranquility at the same time, when it tautens all our muscles into a bowstring stretched in acute angle. Perhaps the reason why I always felt so lonely among people is that I haven't been living on joy and pain, on joy of life or artistic inspiration, but on these nameless intensities that are inhuman, destructive, & frivolous. How is it that the greatest emotion has no name?

For in comparison joy and sorrow are not even emotions but merely slightly fanciful judgments; instinct and existential mysticism are dilettante ersatzes: you need to study love, which barely has a name. The only way to live caritas is play-acting, the circus pomade of blood and lies: I'm wriggling under the buds' springtime machine-gun kisses, they are chasing me like the angels' green whip-ends, I must run and devour them like a neurasthenic roe deer, even though I'm not hungry, I have no rhymes, and I'm not interested in waking or life.

What is then this primal savagery? Caritas: caring about something. I care about the buds. I care: nothing more. They don't interest me, I don't admire them, but with unsayable and amateurish mania — I care about them. And this is what caritas means: to care about things, independently of the things, to be roused by them until you drop. Bud? What can this small vegetal slip of the tongue mean, this vapid, soggy snafu: beauty? But it is ugly and laughable. A symbol? Who on earth would lap up that hogwash? And yet I see blood, murder, escape, dawn, damnation and the proof sheet of deities all around it. The whole feeling is so unknown that all I can do is to roll the rattling peas of commonplaces above it — it doesn't express anything, but at least in rolling the theme resonates beneath it. My millipede reason recoils from the paradoxical forces of caritas, so shapeless are they; it kicks left and right like an upturned beetle that tries to get to its feet again, but I cannot listen to it: I let myself into love. Am I styling up my trivial hysteria? I am, for sure. But is hysteria a sickness? What if it is theological poetry? Caritas, caritas!

about the so-called 'contradiction' of emotions, example:
he is going to meet a girl in snowy weather

People are chock-full of 'contradictory' emotions — but can they be anything other, if they are emotions? If not contradictory, they are not yet emotions. They always try to force emotions into parallelism with people, landscapes, events, without succeeding of course, & still with some logical obdurateness they insist on calling those permanent failures exceptions. Once when I went to a rendezvous I got lost in the woods, snow flaked off the morning's grey hide like shedding fur: it was not falling vertically but like a spirally unfurling rug, which keeps coiling up even if they smooth it out — the snow came down to the ground in a half circle, then again arched high up above the grass on the wind's trap-spring, it covered anew the downward-sloping line, more outward, and hastened toward the clouds' sleepy pastel croquis.

My eyes were full of sharp snow-splinters, the way a pomegranate's skin is full of red sugar pellets, the air was white, snow piled up on one side of the trees like a supporting plank, there where the wind dashed it against the trunks — but there was none of it on the ground, the roads were black like damp lignite, the small iced puddles brown like half-stirred coffee in milk, the whole mass of snow kept revolving in the air in parallel circles. I was inebriated with delight, I kept licking the snow from my fists as if it were glass buds, and pushed my mouth to the great fabric bolt of the wind as I would push my fingers to the moving parapet of a subway.

I was going to a woman and I relished the fact that this sieve-tearing salt shower ('ab ship,' as the shop assistants put it) erodes all love, desire, memory from me — by the time I get to her (but I hope I never get to her), the woman will become an empty association key to press, a 'noiseless' sign in my life. The snow whistled among the trees' moldy reins like ill-tuned radios, my body fell on the morning's whitewashed nude like rushing water on a slow millwheel's blades hungering for maculata conceptio, but silence was there nevertheless, I felt I could find it at a few meters' distance like some geographical reference point; it stood, rigid among the hours' slowly released barrel hoops, like thin scissors next to a small visiting card which it would cut in two, who knows why, between the first and the family name.

The morning silence: everything. Is it joy? Is it sorrow? No: caritas, the very it. The previous evening when we agreed to meet, silence surrounded the woods like green oil, soft, dissolving, caressing — so does the juice surround the dreamy, hovering pear faces and peach breasts in jars. In the morning silence didn't embalm with its vaseline the burns that existence inflicted on the trees, but jutted out separately, like a nest of prickly wires, leaves and dagger-thorns, inquisitorial threat beneath the snow's great spinning top. Snow filled my soul like a picklock filling the unknown keyhole; I opened, although the guest was a stranger. Every single drizzle-grain was a cynical weight in love's balance; my scales kept plunging so hard as to make the trachomatic fishwife of 'fiat justitia' seasick, and the flame flew out of the other scale like a misdirected roulette ball. The snow rang on, in my ears it became a million bicycle rings and hummingbirds, and when I finally felt my tympanum becoming a bloodied bandage, it poulticed me with grey gases, with smoke hovering around the branches. What is snow: shrieking thorns, or muddy liquid? I felt the moment had arrived to touch the very depth of my emotions, the snow's corrosive acid had burnt away all psychology from me, and through the caritas-world beneath ontology a seductive fragment showed, like a bit of bared bone.

I was in the plenitude of will, without purpose. I thought I was lashing out against the woman, wishing her to be buried under the snow's doorknob-less door, and kept kissing the air, because I felt in it the fugitive scent of eros: here then is at last the much-quoted 'contradiction.' Of course it is a contradiction only in so far as we keep palpating the finished world's cooled-out seal wax, into which one monogram is frozen, and in vain we try to etch a B above the A's gorges — but if we play out the round of the creation when the wax is still hot and its shape inchoate, when every drop wears a flame-bun and the sigil is lying about in an unknown place, then there is no contradiction, then kiss and death, woman and snow, inanity and exchange of rings are simply images and movements without a rigid meaning, everything is merely scena caritatis. When under the snow's big imitation polar bears I glimpsed a drowsy green, sunken pond with no ice or snow on top, I suddenly felt an urge to fish for my lover, to let my string into the hard water's cataractless iris, so that instead of a kiss, a hook's thorny question mark would get between her lips: real kiss would be this, the hook's bloody article between two rouged eros vouchers, as I hurl it with a whizz from the depth of the waters to the coughing lightness of snow-compact air.

there are no 'emotions,' only one basic psychic intensity

Love appears destructive, vacuous adjective baroque or schoolbook sadism because it is a creative act not in the artistic but in the divine sense, it doesn't 'create something' but keeps training, barrenly and forever, the celestial psychology of creation. Love cannot make distinctions, for that is a belated, human industrial product, for love a desecrated corpse or the canonized kiss cable alike are 'things to be cared about,' it doesn't seek anybody's good, neither is it self-seeking, for it is not on the lookout for itself either. Somebody had been vicious for 10 years, repents in tears, then continues to be vicious for another 20 years — the caritas value of that one-minute sorrow is not damaged in the least by the fact that the ensuing action didn't correspond to it.

A great sorrow can never be practical, because a great sorrow means great emotion, ultimate intensity, and a great emotion is no longer sorrow but only emotion, something that lacks an object altogether, the light speed of themelessness. There is another man who lies about in a drunken stupor, in half sleep thinking about his lover's shoulder as it rises & falls under the blanket, like the seal's back in the zoo pond: he is not thinking of the woman either, he doesn't want the shoulder but merely the movements that roll from the shoulders like eternal growth rings, waves, that is, the emotion itself, the untitled lakes of intensity.

Didn't people realize how much alike extra-great repentance and extra great chase-for-lovers are, how ridiculous it would be to distinguish them according to their themes? Both are giant lakes, but on one it was a withered acacia leaf, while on the other, a rolling pebble that traced a hair-breadth of a crease — who gives a fig about these ephemeral causes and even more ephemeral effects? Needless to say, as long as people don't realize that there are no 'emotions' but only one basic, for the moment nameless intensity (here and there psychopathology attached a name or other, but certainly not for the purposes of idealizing!), which is at the same time death, eros, etc. (this ridiculous idiom of dichotomy will not last long), as long as they don't realize this, there can be no talk of poetry — in reality poetry hasn't even existed so far, as there hasn't been conscious emotion.

PRAE II · XIV

description of the half-idiot girl; her caress: absolute caritas, perhaps more absolute than a charitable deed; what is the surplus here?

When I formulated for myself in the clearest terms the impossibility of love for the human psyche, my attention was caught by a bus stop where a woman descended from the steps of the vehicle, extremely slowly — they lifted her off like a corpse, the ticket collector, driver, passengers all together with their arms, on their walking sticks and shoulders — I was almost reminded of the movements of the descent from the cross, which I always gawk at during my sermons in the above-mentioned religious society. For a while her whole body was visible above the people's shoulders, the sun poured down on her flowery dress and snow-white face; she lay on the bridge of helping arms like on a chaise-longue let far back; then she vanished altogether among the standers-by, like a statue dropped in the middle of swarming waves; and then she was seen again standing, shrunken and bereft of her previous sunny luminosity. She adjusted her hat and sought to get a better grip on her walking stick, one she was probably long used to.

I went to get a closer look. One of her legs was lame and shorter than the other. She wore a brown fur coat open in front and not covering her sufficiently in the back, which perhaps rather accentuated her hunch under the broad, drooping collar. Her hair was shiny and pitch-black, with a very large frou-frou reaching down to her eyebrows; its hair started from one point at the top of her skull, broadening to cover her whole forehead. On the sides and in the back it turned back into small curlicues, like the paper with which they wrap the bare flowerpots or branches. Her eyes were dark and so huge that the whites couldn't be seen. Her face was powdered to death. Both lips were extremely thick but without a shade of pouting: two magnified mouth-arcs, not at all distorted, only disproportionately multiplied as compared to the face, and painted poisonous red. She kept her mouth open. You could see that she was mentally impaired. Lots of white imitation pearls hung from her neck.

When the bus drove on and I was left alone close to her, she turned to me and asked for the address of a nearby villa. I happened to know someone living there and knew that the street was in repair and could be reached only with great detour, so with unusual courage I told her that I would see her there. She said nothing, only stroked my clasped hands with her right; extremely slowly, distractedly pulling her fingers and palm, stopping now and then, halting with a twitch, as if every movement were only an involuntary reflex, the body's asinine nervousness; some annoyed little smile accompanied these stirrings, the way pianists shake their head if their pianissimo turned out too loud.

It was in this slow, unending, unexpected caress that I first discovered the plenitude of caritas, of Christian caritas within the human body, enclosed in a human movement; just as in my childhood, when I learned to play the organ, I had always wanted to compose an absolutely unplayable, technically impossible 'difficult' piece for the organ, so that in a coming century a mysterious virtuoso may be found who could perform it and I could relish the success of my composition in the grave (because in the performance of such works from the first moment the creator vanishes next to the mystical virtuosity of the performer, only to ascend above him with all the darker modesty), so now I saw caritas as a technically unsolvable work, yet one which an unknown artist can play with the utmost perfection.

In the previous moment I still saw the essence of love in what is beyond the human, in the complete but purposeless sum total of life being created, and now, when my whole body is crossed by the stifling heat of the caress of unknown rhythm, I suddenly felt the whole of love to be the human being's innermost trait, the one that alone distinguishes the human being from Cambridge's yellow columns, red doors, and deaf-and-bothered buds. I felt that one needs to be a human being for this heat (for that's all it was at the moment, a heat of unknown degree in my body), but the heat is not anthropomorphic; there are feelings for which the human body and soul are the quintessential nurturing ground, but they immediately leave behind the roots' inescapable microscopic terrain, the cause's laughable little boutique, to swell its leaf canopy into the world of autonomous bounty and boundless denial of humans. I found an inebriating petit-bourgeois pleasure in the fact that caritas' limitless fever should issue from my body's insignificant Biedermeier drawer; I felt it to be infinite precisely because my body appeared such a finite, such an infinitely finite small cause conserve.

What was the peculiar surplus in this caress? I felt that the caress is the girl's natural state, it was not her hand stirring but her whole body was identical to it; in my previous statistics of pamperedness, among the data collected at liquidating my pessimistic cuddling-balances, every single caress used to be a separate gesture, the so-called expressive gesture of the emotion of love that just happened to be actual.

Caritas begins where it is not something psychic but the body itself, not metaphorically, not as biological simile, but so to say according to the rigid clinical criteria of theological anatomy. Lately I have read several books where the Ich is distinguished from the Seele;[405] those loving caresses that I had hitherto enjoyed always issued from the Seele, while the Ich, the most central kernel of the human being (needless to say, I use 'central' here for want of a better word), knew nothing of them.

When people (especially women) believe that they love someone or something, that love is always only an assumed trait of theirs, it was not present in them before, but now it is, like a new bacillus in their spleen or the new blue fox around their neck, and they now put it on and don't take it off for the duration of love; for instance during a three-month liaison or lifelong marriage the true love-time is not three months or a whole lifetime, but perhaps the length of only 15–20 hours or 8–9 weeks, because they attach the surplus of love, the emotion-suffix only occasionally to the lonely noun of their self, otherwise they don't even know about it. Lots of photographs could be taken of people who have the reputation of 'amour fou,' psychic photographs from the most different hours of the day, when they don't show the faintest trace of love, just as of all the X-rays made of the sword swallower on only very few will the sword be visible at all, on the others the body has nothing to do with it.

With the fox there are two cases: the woman either puts it on her shoulders or leaves it at home, but she will on no account turn into a fox, with whatever degree of fakirism she may gawk at *Vogue*. So it is with love, too: on certain X-ray images love will alight on the peripheries, while on others not, but when it's positively present, even then it will be merely above the epidermis like a thin ointment that you need to apply before powdering, so the powder doesn't harm the complexion.

What is that impenetrable Ich, on which every love gets caught, every love ceases and only the ego's lonesome humanity lives on: is then the human being's essence the lack of emotions? The Seele's tedious world, its pseudo-loves and pseudo-friendships — or the Ich's insulated defiance, fateful selfishness? What should you teach of these matters, bald-headed vicar? The girl's caressing movement was first of all no 'movement': not the representation of the idea of love, the way dated neumas represent still valid notes in medieval missal scores, but it was love itself, which in the case of this excessively rouged, half-idiot girl penetrated the Ich, too (to fully harness this Germanic-flavored distinction), including the center of her personality, of her humanity, which center in Castor knew nothing of Pollux, and in Pollux nothing of Castor.

absolute love and the psyche; personality is the death of caritas

Earlier I found perfect caritas to be outside the human being, now to be burningly inside the human being, but is the matter really so simple? For true neighborly love is found only where from the soul's motley & elastic peripheries it has conquered the self's immovable essence-point; that essence-point, the personality's frozen stone-root is, however, entirely free from content, it's merely stubborn negativity, as much as 'I am no other,' 'I am not the world' — that is, the innermost individuating-kernel of human individuality is something utterly colorless, empty, and lacking in perspective, therefore if this is what love penetrates and if I call this penetration 'burningly human' love, I am not wholly justified to do so, for beside being the essence of individuality, the Ich is nevertheless barely human, perhaps barely individual either. Yet if caritas is not the adopted trait of the soul that provides its circumference, but rather, the self's eternal nature, then the self's rigid meaning as detailed above ceases altogether, because the 'I' is nothing but the inner psychic remainder, which can never be reached by even the most resonant tones, the brightest colors, or the most pragmatic kiss, just as there are homes with a room where the sun never penetrates, whether coming from southeast or northwest, in early dawn or late afternoon: that one room or the room's one corner will forever be left untouched by warming sunlight.

The human being's internal life is a great circle, into which impressions fall from without, like a lake lined with cypresses on every side, into which the cypress shadows fall like the immaterial level crossing barriers of a Böcklin sundial;[406] some points, or point, or stretches of the lake, will perhaps be forever untouched by shadow (here as far as possible not the astronomical truth but the Böcklin one is meant): this negative place, where the cypress shadow's end point or the last vibration of impression never reaches, this powerless place, 'magma impotentiæ': the 'I' proper, the center of individuality, the ego's passive-throne.

But the loving soul doesn't live off the cypress shadows, that is, it doesn't have the zebra grids of impressions tattooed on its psyche, but it starts with the flood, it overflows its riverbed and with all the excited bubbles, ravenous drops, & light green Venus-sinus of its water it embraces the surrounding trees, it brushes their crowns with rain and is soaked up through their roots into all the imagined and unimaginable, tentative buds: it is not the lame instrument of impressions (as though the psyche were only a container fitted out with a greedy centimeter scale, a kind of impassive impression-meter) but on the contrary: themeless aggressiveness, amorphia impudica.

The simple-minded practitioners of love would often complain that they don't feel the girl's or boy's love for them to be individual enough, they don't feel that their partner's soul is the exact envelope of theirs, the two souls are either too tight or too loose for one another, therefore they are ill at ease in this, as they put it, mendacious tailoring to size. Although, the more they correct and tailor to individuality the occasionalist chanciness of love, the more diligently they are excluding love from it; the undulating, Christ-like frivolity of caritas goes extinct and in its place two wry portrait-jokes are left, a boy clad in a girl's clothes & a girl clad in a boy's clothes, individualism's two badly botched fake signatures. Instead of searching for love, they are fidgeting with the mosaic of individuality, as though there were anything to do with individual psychology.

I went through all the tedium and purple cock-ups of humanized-to-death love; now when this seemingly idiot woman left her hand on mine I knew that the caress was not meant for me, that it was entirely anonymous, like an election poster that is fitted out with a slogan for millions, but it boiled up my timid blood chambers precisely because it enclosed such universality; spring does not start with it being expedited to my name and address, registered and with return postage enclosed, but it is 'publicly announced' in clichéd democratic fashion — yet it makes me happy. And this impersonal, purposeless caritas which can't distinguish one human being from another, grips and satisfies our individualities much more powerfully than the other one, tailored to 'individuality'; for above all we want the very plenitude of love and are well aware of that fact, it's only that we don't know how we could accomplish that; we believe that individualizing is the safest way. In the meantime we forget that the purpose was the whole caritas and not individuality, which had been originally only a temporary and hypothetical trial instrument, and so end up squandering our time on carving one millimeter deeper in our partner's soul the forever out-of-place psychological altar niche of our own individuality. So does the dilettante morphology of eros evolve, although eros can only begin when all morphology crumbles to comedy; for that certain Ich knows no forms, characters, images, or piquancy, narrative or sexual heresy.

The moment love is specialized it becomes self-contradictory; just as a tropical waterfall with a double spume-chin and pearl feather-boa ceases to be a waterfall if it is lead into terraced marble troughs cut into the letters of the Greek alphabet inside an individualist week-end palace. But on the other hand if deep in the forest I stand next to the waterfall's foolish riverbed with my loosened ears and unshuttered eyes, I will nevertheless become the owner of the most personal experience, because our innermost desire is never to forcefully disguise waterfalls into our arteries like émigré blood, or to individualize the spring's thousand-floor Volks-theater into our intimate temple movements: we just want to see, look, at most get lost into them, to get enmeshed in a place left empty by chance between a bud and a bird-throat.

If we want to enjoy the truest love, then we'll have to look for it in women who love not only us but anybody, women who are love's living water in which anybody can bathe. Because that perfect degree of the gross sensuality that prostitutes offer not even the most perverse but not professional woman will ever be able to reach: it is good because it's not meant for us, and yet we can participate in it.

We have to enjoy women like nature: broad, forever continuing, like the unending hand caress of my new acquaintance. I have also realized that there is truer caritas, more monumental manliness in the pietistic whimper, in the apocryphal indolence of the Alumbrados,[407] in general in all the mechanized snivels of lachrymose literature, than in the cheese-advertising Jäger æsthetic[408] or psycho-pedagogical hygiene of the sober orders.

Caritas can never be healthy in the naïve-medical or idyllic sense, for neighborly love is always excess, it is always everything, whereas health is based on the affected pickiness of Cathos and Madelon.[409] But even if caritas is not health, it can by no means be neurasthenia, for neurasthenia knows far less about true love than health does. Neurasthenia is the ongoing development of the self toward an even more self-shaped self, that is, it works in the opposite direction to love; it too is construction, moreover, sensibility also has its Doric style, but it's not capable to prepare the only important caritas architecture.

Love has no mythology and no analogy: with all its nauseating Eve-stylizing, with its satanized apple orchards and its morose 'post triste' Adams,[410] with Jupiter's uninventive and mongrel-empirical metamorphoses, with the million misprints of nymphs and extragalactic pleasure abodes: they all belong in the Seele's everyday little rings and do not start from the Ich's empty but redeeming center. It is pointless to address a definite individuality, for the sentence is immediately caught up in some thorn, just as a silk stocking gets holed in a thousand places if I try to pull it on a rose twig; but it's all the more worth conversing with the 'love' woman who emanates amorphous caritas, the waterfall and the spring can be meaningfully apostrophized, the way the silk stocking is not tattered if I let it in the rushing wind's eternal waves like a stringless kite. Needless to say, such women are not looking purposely for the maximum occasions to love; they are not so-called 'pandemos';[411] for the latter doesn't love everything and everybody, but only a great many 'particulars,' and this fact immediately excludes erotic caritas, if I am allowed to construct a phrase that would equally gall the one thirsting for pornography and the one thirsting for sursum corda.

We sauntered slowly, holding hands, on a green meadow, which was differently green if you bowed your head and peered among the grass leaves than when you looked straight ahead and only brushed the head of the grass with your eyes; the one green was discontinuous, problematic, and alive, as though it were the color's very biological workshop, where in general everything is always essential but at the same time also doubtful & caricaturistic, but the other was hard and homogeneous, squeezed in between the school textbook margins of perspective, like primer handwriting, when a long sentence needs to be fitted into one short line. The grass heads' green hooks got caught in the afternoon sunrays, like little melos-claws made of barrel organ disks, which plucked the chords regularly when rotated. From the uniformly tall grass a few white, blue, red flowers jutted out with prancing significance, like quarter-notes from Hába's enriched scales[412] — although the tonal difference is very small, still, the new keys are just as big and hard as the ones used for striking full and half tones: so too are these empty flowers nothing and yet they double the color keyboard of the Cambridge meadow. The red petals (they seem rather like beetles standing still in the air, just as there are unmoving stars) slowly turned mauve from the evening sky; the sky showed the deathly pallor of gold (gold too is sometimes in ruddy 'high color' and at other times pale, even deathly white, preserving its goldness all through), which fell on my new acquaintance's inexpressive, happy face.

face mimicry, perception, and pan-love

This too belonged to caritas' essence-mimicry: the face was utterly meaningless, but if ever so small a thought-wrinkle ran along it, it was lit up by the infinite smile of happiness and joy, all its imaginable facial movements immediately became caritas' landscape. In people life normally suppresses the love-portrait, the elasticity of skin and muscles immediately ceases, so the moment they are relaxed we find not love's insatiable serenity but some vulgar hodgepodge, the silted leftovers of thought, fatigue, death and individuality.

This girl lacked the bollixing instinct of self-preservation; if anything touched her at all, she loved immediately. For her no other relation was possible but love, or more exactly, she stood in no relation with things at all, that's why she could love them. For we have one true organ of sense and that is of love, all æsthetics (perhaps a small blunder will help the cause) is the unself-conscious catechism of the sole charitable eros. I didn't come to this realization because I am a priestly priest but because, bad priest as I am, I have always sucked up God on lay straws, finicking, and not from public & subventioned Sunday wells. All perception has to be love already, not 'perceptio amorosa' but 'perceptio amor,' that is, the green meadow doesn't trigger the adoration of green but immediately sees something love-like, loveable in the green, and barely any green, only a love-shade; one can physiologically demonstrate that this girl is color-blind and is able to value green in the most green-worthy way because she reacts according to love's pulsation number; her spectrum, her scale, is love, her consciousness is love — she doesn't say 'I love' but in the Augustinian way, 'the love that loves loves, because it loves' — subordination and coordination mean the same, where the Ich is dissolved into eros.

I watched the meadow's tranquil afternoon green with the girl's eyes and I came to intuit (although I was of course incapable of understanding it in its perfection) the redeeming lopsidedness of perception that is meant by mad caritas in the literal sense of the word. The first words she addressed to me were, 'I'll go pick some flowers. Violets I'd like.'

the half-idiot girl's mention of violets, analysis of the violets

She uttered the first sentence with uncertain intonation, but the second already with certainty: as though it were highly doubtful that there are flowers in general, and any kind of definite things in the world, but as if the greatest certainty were that there must be violets. Caritas is as a rule blasé toward all material things, it permanently looks upon the world from doubt's useless and steering wheel-less fishing boat, but if it needs something it gets it with the unexpected liveliness, primitive and defiant creative gesture of the imperative; it sets out to fish without net, hook, harpoon, or bait (this could be felt in the first sentence's immeasurable distractedness, tired of all the world's flowers), it doesn't believe in the existence of any fish, but when it gets in the middle of the lake it suddenly wants a particular fish, perhaps of a kind that is long extinct, and gets it by jumping from the boat, diving underwater, ordering time to move backward, and with vaselined fingers clutches the fleeing winged reptile.

That was the first occasion when I experienced caritas' order-logic, so I was quite dizzied when hearing the girl's first sentence; all cause, all guarantees withered in this logic, she forgot everything, all categories lost their significance, only one little specialty, one final side-result was left, the violet. I have fallen out with most girls, in fact with all, because they would stress the everyday sentence above in the exactly opposite way: stressing the flowers and barely mentioning the violets. In love, in me, in money they would be looking for the most general conditions of love, man, or money, like someone who rents a third-floor hotel room overlooking the Seine only after carefully checking the geological strata around the river's source, to see if they are not prone to earthquakes; girls are maniacs of insurance; when their eyes keep looking for the Greek-style palaces of Assicurazioni Generali, they are in fact practicing one variety of persecution mania.

When I heard the girl's violet-desire, in one second all natural history was turned upside down around me; all flowers went extinct, but the violet absorbed all ghosts, God, and moral prohibitions: when I said that love always wants everything I didn't imagine it as sticking the affected ex libris of property next to every single entry in the Encyclopedia Britannica (how curious that on these ludicrous little signature posters the naïve poultices of ownership always draw death's skull heads, naked women, or oboe d'amore, as if the owner's posture and the symbol's lyrical klutziness were inseparable), but the way in which this idiot girl wanted the violets: the strength, the swish potential of all things is compressed into one single petal, which fills up with the huge reality of dream, losing at the same time all its naïve material significance. Which it only possessed as far as the petal was among the other things.

Was the violet she wanted to pick a flower at all, or simply a fashionable dress of desire that she tried on for a moment; were her nostrils trembling, like leaves in the wind, with real violet-odor, or did she want to flex her muscles & mentioned violets to me out of habit, because one needs to say something — I couldn't tell. First, the broad and secure notion of 'flower' ceased for me, then the mythically one-and-only violet appeared, and finally I felt that she was lying.

But were not these the three stages that I had aspired for since early childhood, and were not these the very things I never managed to find in anyone? I remembered the expression 'broken triad' which accompanied harmonic triads in my childhood scores: all the other girls broke caritas' triad, its logical chord, but here it sounded in its purity: an atmosphere of doubt, commanding over-the-top certainty, and infinite lie. The root and fifth, doubt and lie, differ from one another like black & white, but both belong to the foreign tonality of the natural sciences inspired by love.

Love is the most perfect form of freedom, and the lies of madmen (in spite of all their rigid neurological determination and monotony as compared to themselves) always boldly open the unbroken sigils of reality, its turned-off taps or secret evacuation doors; by believing something to be other than it is, first they choke reality but then they render the supplanting dream a positivity, and with this dream they suggest a new meaning in the old thing they had misrecognized (the alkalic grace of a mismatched comparison).

True love cannot exist without this divine game, which means one of the absolute technical conceits of 'in medias res': it annihilates 'res,' elevates 'media' to the rank of real divinity, so that it obviously stops being 'media,' although that's the very source of its divinity; such a god is like a rootless tree or trunkless foliage, but then, love's garden always soothes with branchless leaves, its source bathes one in dried-out flooding rivers, in brief: it nurtures with the hovering and irrational manna of senseless effects. I have never felt such all-consuming, moreover: sickly desire for violet-picking as now, when first I felt the utter lack of value of all flowers, and then the mendaciousness of violets themselves; between these two stages all the violet's velvety shades, cool scent, canary bird heart and false Lucrece-ness hovered in divine light & infernal mauve. Why?

The 'in medias res' also had an external form, for the girl said violets straightaway, she didn't prepare the ground with other words, with the slowly ascending stair-rings of sentences, from whose perspective scrolls the violet could have emerged in due time, in duly diminished proportions — instead she immediately started speaking about the violet, with dissonant unruliness, that's exactly why it appeared to me, in the bluntest geometrical sense, as huge, therefore a lie. When unknown people begin to talk they always start the conversation with anthropomorphic things, & I got so used to this fact that now when I heard the violet slap-bang, without any humanist garnishing, I unwittingly imagined it as anthropomorphic, forgetting all actual dimensions.

The beginning, the 'one' is far greater than all the numbers put together, and yet it is unity, the foundation of numbers, the very number 1 which, precisely for being so huge, is the most ridiculous specter & optical swindle in the world of numbers. For me this violet was a lie in two senses, as conventional conversation starter and as fateful myth. The violet was a quite complicated world, with mauve book pages, green grids, yellow twisted columns and scented cloud inlays. The convention was the violet's denial, myth an exotic pseudo-violet, which was nevertheless nurtured by the lie, by obsession; without sophistry caritas must needs perish. This wondrous violet, rendered wondrous by its unexpectedness, brought with it a wealth of naïve percepts in a sweep, as if true kinship could be recognized only if the central figure is distorted. So the violet filled up with wordplay-like meanings, to foist even more celestial splendor on the object that a lie helped to deify.

First, this wonder-violet brought to my mind the real, modest, and small violet which the wonder-violet surrounded and chokingly superseded, as the embroidered ducal blazon of a huge bedspread covers the scrawny boy adopted only five minutes earlier: it was both familiar & immensely strange to me. Then from the word violet the root *viol* took over — the thought of murder, injury, death, and vengeance, to lend its place to the word's other meaning, *viola*, viola da gamba, etc. I intuited that with words where the contrasting meaning between dark blue-phial murder and minuetting rococo violin is not so readily at hand (it's curious that while the piano's frame had long left behind its Biedermeier ground plan and we have long been playing Cubistic pianos, the violin had to preserve its essentializingly naïve, anachronistic, f-keyed and cartouche-contoured form), even with those words the arbitrary etymology of caritas plays out in full. A cult of opposites?

Something more important: the lookout for suffering, for pain. The childish contrast-etymologizing, which suddenly came upon the forking of murder and gigue among the violet's blindflamed petals is in fact merely a superstitious form of that cultivated fixation, so indispensable in eros, that every existing thing can be expressed as suffering, or rather, that in all existence there is a trait of suffering, just as in every man there is a backbone or diaphragm. It is the paperweight of suffering that withholds the freedom of lying from utter caricature, so the violet's wondrous love-light that fell on me from the girl's empty mouth in the bus stop, flared equally from the dual foreignness of suffering & of lie.

Because we need to abstract suffering from the humanoid trait of bodily torments & psychic repression, and we have to take it as the lie that we relate to the concrete violet; suffering is an entirely fantastic, but ontological accessory, existential mode-sign, of the violet as the lie, with the sole difference that it works in the opposite direction. Perhaps this concept of suffering is entirely artificial but I felt that nevertheless it was an operator of the caritas procedures, and it was there before the 'true' suffering, the one within the human being, of which I've long been the 'self-made' expert.

absolute love's relation to 'homo' and 'humanum':
body, soul, artificial body, artificial soul

So the essence of love is insatiability, almost the pole-vaulting of desire, but precisely because it is insatiable and pole-vaulting it hurls itself past the goal, flying above the bar or tautened rope; in fact it fails to reach its goal just like abstemiousness, but whereas the latter stops before the object, the former, beyond it; love's wallpaper is patched together of kisses scattered far beyond the mouth. That's exactly why I have avoided of late both neighborly love and eros, knowing that by their essence they are in vain; they live off people, feed off people, people are their purpose, their dependent variables, but it is not people who satisfy them: *omnia circum hominem et nihil humanum in amore.*[413]

Only love can teach us the huge difference between 'homo' & 'humanum,' and in the half-idiot girl this tragic difference was entirely lacking; her meaningless face was at once a portrait and washed-out symbol, insulated character and ever-changing everybody's-mirror. This is precisely what love needs, the alternation of character & indeterminacy, human being and rainbow. They speak a lot about the female body and female psyche separately, and they do well, signaling in the least with whatever gross means that love isn't directed at one thing alone; it is made up of more things, of at least two elements foreign to it; our love is not bodily in the sense of being only interested in the anatomical part of woman, and it is not psychic in the sense of being attracted by the girl's moral qualities.

We are always interested in the body, not because it suggests some kind of body-character, not to say body-soul, which has nothing to do with the real soul, the one taken in the religious sense of the word, but it's the female individual's law-shade, thanks to which our love appears not a whim-chase but a universally valid and relevant law-analysis; and we are always interested in the soul but only in so far as it conjures up an unknown pseudo-body next to the real one, the moral personality draws its own invisible new Andersenian anatomy, which in its turn bears no resemblance to the real, material female physique. So do body and soul come to feature in love, but that body is rather a body-shaped soul (artificial soul) and that soul is rather a soul-shaped body (artificial body); human desire flounders among four great thorns: real body, artificial soul, real soul, artificial body. Hence all love is an infinite-risk patience game — we must shuffle the above-mentioned four cards and, abandoning ourselves to chance, lay them out in such a way that they make up a certain number, 21 or 13, with all kinds of additional stipulations.

As a priest I should not care about the artificial soul, only the real one, although I never could; the true soul of my wife is the richest well of love, benevolence, self-sacrifice, faithfulness and piety, and it never interested me, because it didn't project an attractive character-body on her real body, with attractive caritas-lips, benevolence-shoulders, self-sacrifice hips, and piety-knees; her qualities were stifled by the pseudo-soul or body-soul emanating from her real body, which showed an unamiable, tired, selfish, & indifferent figure. If she did something good to me, if she said a word of real kindness (she often did), I was immediately faced with pure virtue; goodness evaporated from her body with the energy of the central heating's sudden warmth coming through the grid under the windowsill. Goodness immediately left her body, virtue immediately flooded me; in my wife's soul the beginning of virtue was just an immaterial point, sense or sensibility-point, which could not for one moment delay inside her but bounced to me at once and flooded me, inside and out.

I had no possibility of seeing the biology of virtue, the tumultuous material of virtue, because it was indeed great virtue, truly virtuous virtue; in the woman's brain a spark-shaped desire and spark-shaped idea, which, if indeed absolutely virtuous, cannot remain in place but must hurry toward its goal — if even for one moment it rests inside her head after coming to mind, it is no longer absolute virtue, because for example 'to help' means to help at once & with all my capacities, for the missed half second cannot ever be made up for. But when the virtue, which in my wife's soul was an infinitely small but absolutely strong motif-point, jumped to me at the moment of its birth (what is more, almost preceding its birth, the way the truly holily social soul offers the beggar bread and thinks only afterward that it would offer bread), completely flooded my being, so I again couldn't see the 'material' of virtue, because it became one with my whole body.

Perhaps this too is the tragedy of the holiest virtues (if you look at them from a sentimental viewpoint of course), that their nature is absolutely pure and they attain their goal perfectly, and from motive to goal no time passes, the whole thing is infinitely fast. I didn't find any joy in this goodness, which was so absolutely divine and conceptual, so absolute even from the practical point of view; however, it was not absolute from the point of view of my own 'charitable eros.'

the difference between moral act and moral Sache

When the half-idiot girl kept stroking my hand almost continuously underway, it was obvious that the two above-mentioned absolutes were missing; the punctiform motif was missing, which immediately lashes out toward its goal, so fast that even its place of birth is before itself — and likewise missing was the utter goal-fulfillment, goal-flooding, the wild squaring of realization.

Instead of these two absolute terminus points I could see the way between them, virtue's slowed-down orbit, which was without cause or purpose, it just kept proceeding, moving, living, spreading; it was no rushing waterfall but a lake, which perhaps rolls waves that go all its length, but all the same, those can't be called flowing or progress. Yet can one speak of virtue at all where there had never been any goodness-cause and where there will never be any goal of charity? It's not important that we call it virtue; it's a fact that I saw goodness' ethical whatness punctually in this idiotic caress; here the thought of goodness, instead of immediately shooting its arrow toward me (the way goodness burred against me from my wife) was left impotently behind in the girl's body, so to say, flowing all along it, and thus it conjured above her real body uncertain virtue's apotheotic & mendacious virtue-anatomy & shadow-body; if the punctiform virtue, the practical-minded virtue-idea flies out immediately, it will obviously cast no shadow on the body — for that delay, laziness, unreasonable relativity are needed.

The 'Sachlichkeit' of moral theory and Christ's ethics are mutually exclusive: I either enjoy the material of virtue, virtue's 'Sache' part, & then the motif will not be absolute & the goal will not be attained; or I am truly religious, and then I must not stop the virtue-point rushing into its goal, slow down the point of departure and point of arrival, which almost fall into simultaneity. In all domains, 'Sachlichkeit' means this: in painting for instance the sachlich representation of a horse chestnut tree's foliage — that is, its most materialistically material representation — means, that I paint a surface filled with one leaf alone, on which there is no branch, trunk, sky, cloud, flower, bird, but only a five-lobed leaf and on top of it another leaf and another and yet another, with the result that I represented no longer the chestnut tree's foliage, no longer any foliage, but a green 'penta-quint,' a counter-theme, anti-Sache abstract-sensuous thingamajig.

There is thus an essential difference between absolute foliage and Sache-foliage, they are eternally incompatible: I either represent the foliage's absolute sense, that which makes the foliage foliage in my mind, & then I need to draw a whole tree, on which I will be hence unable to depict the foliage's material in all its exclusive materiality; or I depict not the sense of foliage but its material, & then its foliage nature will immediately cease, turn into some new decoration, and this is precisely the divine paradox of 'Sachlichkeit.'

Let us now place general virtue, or one specific virtue in place of the foliage, and we face the same dilemma: either to choose absolute love, which lacks love's infinite-anarchic emotional material; or to look for love's emotional materiality, which lacks that conceptual and practical reason that in fact renders it virtue. To join the two: Christ-like ethic (or absolute ethic) is the one where foliage and trunk, sky and birds are in perfect harmony; Sachlich ethics is the one where only a cutout foliage fragment is visible, without dimensions or sense — it's only leaf, leaf, leaf. My wife was such an 'emplaced,' harmonically blooming tree; the half-idiot girl's caress was a dimensionless, solitary, cutout foliage-Sache.

The Christ-like ethics' interest is directed at the moral human being, while Sachlich ethics takes an interest in independent patches of morality; Christ-like ethics condemns the coquette, but Sachlich ethics is able to find in one gesture, word, or gaze of hers such ethical material (I called it 'patch of morality' above) that can surpass in value or mass of energy the love actions practiced throughout a lifetime by some saint (this is no blasphemy but at most literature). When it depicts foliage, Sachlich painting has long forgotten that there are trees in the world; likewise, when Sachlich ethical theory talks about love, it has long forgotten that there are human beings in the world.

Can it still be called ethics what starts out from utter dehumanization & examines the virtues not as the components of the human

psyche or individual character, but independently, like the alien &
disproportionate crystals grown on the soul? In Sachlich ethics this
disproportion is paramount — it can observe love's vast material,
its butterfly-ulcer, if the human being on whom it has grown is
underdeveloped in all his other virtues, puny, transparent, and
unautonomous. With the virtues of the saints (and this is no critique — here 'saint' means just an abstract didactic extreme), even
if disproportionate, this disproportion was metaphor far rather
than reality, for with them the entire personality, all its movements
were molded to, elevated to the main virtue's infinity, so that only
the whole person was disproportionately big as compared to other
non-holy human beings, but the given virtues were proportionate
& regular among themselves, just as a giant's heart, liver, stomach
are all gigantic and disproportionate when compared to us, but
they show no secession from one another; for the same reason, in
Sachlich ethics it's not the saint who is interesting but the insignificant and sinful human being, on whom some peculiar gesture
or rather, reflex movement has grown out of all proportion, like
some cancer or thousand-flower parasite.

Now we're at it, such 'apologies' are not without precedent,
where the sentimental charity of prostitutes was judged superi-
or to cardinals growling their 'pas de grâce,' but they differ from
Sachlich ethical theory in the fact that they claim to have found
genuine virtues in prostitutes, they recognize one kind of virtue
alone, which they find not in saints but in prostitutes. Sachlich
ethics doesn't mean this Hugolian method; it doesn't value the
prostitute on occasion (it doesn't value the prostitute as such at all)
because she possesses virtues, for instance, giving alms to the poor,
nursing sick colleagues, keeping her mother, etc., but because in a
non-virtuous gesture or reflex movement of hers, not ethical when
seen in itself, it glimpses the material (but only material) of virtues
(never existing in the form of deeds with her) — for instance, in
the way she laughs at the movement of a cat jumping from a floor,

in that laughter perhaps it sees so much material of love that its caritas-mass exceeds that found in the acts of virtuous people. The Hugolian tendency had been to oppose the 'virtuous depraved' to the 'stone-hearted priest' — however, here we do not render the depraved virtuous, but discover in their indifferent-looking small side-gestures, primitive frolics, in the gaze looking for the last station of the run in a stocking, or in a whistled music-hall song, the emotional material of the great virtues that they too lack.

Æsthetes of old used to stress that the raw green color squeezed from the tube does not elicit an æsthetic effect, being only a trivial stimulus; beauty begins where that 'rough' stimulus material is turned into shamrock leaves, acacias, lilac bushes on the canvas. On the contrary, today we don't feel that the paint squirting from the tube is a lower-than-beauty stimulus-skivvy with no æsthetic value in itself, but we enjoy it as material (as Sache) which can bring new artistic surprises before a painter has used it for anything. When in a coquette we are looking for the material of virtue and not for virtues proper, we are doing the same as when we examine & enjoy not the painted foliage but the paint itself. (I'm up to my neck in tautology, but there's no helping it, for thinking moves in me like trains pulled from one track to the other: the rails branch out like sheaves outside the station, beyond the hangar, and if a train stationing on the eastward rails wants to go over to the westward tracks, it can't jump directly but needs to go back, along a redundant and repetitive-looking trajectory, first pulling into the station, and only from there can it start out westward. For one myopic shade I need to repeat the basic idea, only from the axiom-hangar's well-worn starting point can I move on, with refrain momentum.)

On a healthy body or soul the soul's essence is obvious, but its material only becomes visible in sickness & madness; when God created sickness he did nothing else but pass to biological neue Sachlichkeit; when life turns against life, then and only then can it be seen in its reality. (So the Sache is nothing but a concept that makes the distinction between substance and accident redundant; although it's not a mix of the two, it represents both to an equal degree, without naïve dualism.)

*the visible end of love (the opposite of caritas);
analysis of the speech of women from this perspective*

With whatever woman I have spoken so far, & however kind she may have been to me, I have always seen the end of her neighborly love, I've seen that love is situated in her life as the half cocktail left in the glass by yesterday's guest is situated in the morning; it's a gorgeous landscape but its horizon is too close. Therefore it could cause only struggle and sorrow, for whichever thought of hers I touched, whichever body part of hers I invented, I could read from it how much longer her movement directed toward me may last yet, the way they register on used cars, how many thousand km they can still run before breaking down irreparably.

In this respect my sense of observation has grown very acute, so when I saw a woman approaching from 30 meters' distance I already knew from the small tilt of her ankles that today she needs to be home earlier, I could read it from her belt that tonight she needs to change before going out, I felt from her handshake, when her hand chafed against mine, that tomorrow she would leave the town, and from her eyes' landscape-prying, that she can't invite me to her birthday party because it would be too conspicuous.

So I immediately detected the end of every gesture, from the beginning I calculated the gestures' end with such mechanical self-lacerating that I would unwittingly greet the approaching girl with a 'so long.' I calculated my whole love backwards, with Hebraic algebra, so that only the images of leave-taking were left in their plasticity; since eternal being-together was not an option ('eternal' here meaning, 'as long as I feel like being together'), every meeting was only a meticulously prepared parting, thus not even with the best of will can one talk of joy. I read backwards even my free loves imagined in the distant future, and this inevitably showed in my courting techniques. Because I felt the moment of encounter to be already the instant of good-bye, I didn't know the feeling of growing anxiety as the moment of parting draws near; in the moment of the handshake I already knew that something would break away from me, & everything that followed was mere cockatoo variations on the blunt theme of 'sic transit.'

Thus the end, the impossibility of being-together, was immediately given, the conversations only followed it. For instance the woman observed that she had a hard time coming here through the meadows in the thick mud. This was the first variation that formed a meaningful idea from the theme of the end, so that the 'coming here' sounded exactly like 'back,' 'away from here'; the 'I came' sounded like 'I went,' and the whole idea, in which the word 'hard' was the most revealing, because it signaled that her being-here is the chanciest chance, therefore it is not even real but a momentary tricking of fate rather than the will of nature (love needs universal acquiescence: every mother, liquid gas, brother-in-law, stray dog, and Eskimo household god has to uniformly want it that she pays me a visit).

The whole idea brought the woman not to me but distanced her from me; by placing before me the practical phases and accompaniment of approaching me, the way, the mud, the distance, the time, it let me know that her place is somewhere else, not here, not with me, not for me, for a way is far too big a thing for its goal to be, that one given person treads on it toward me; the mud is a mystical hindrance, on which the woman might perhaps at some point topple over toward me, but at other times she would hardly go to the pains of making her way through it.

If a girl should name and formulate her act of 'coming to me,' then all of a sudden the thought of coming-to-me created such a logical luxury space, dilated orbit of movement around her real body, into which the real act of 'running away from me' could be comfortably fitted; in fact this is what the reading-backward of love ultimately meant. I shuddered at every definition of presence that the girl uttered about herself, for the formulation stripped the act of exclusive unambiguity and washed it over into the opposite possibility (I saw being-here only as thought, and in thought 'at me' and 'not at me' are infinitely proximate).

I saw the musical scores of the theme 'end' in their full clarity; in its musical variations we render a characteristic formal relation of the theme with the help of strange sounds, not only with repetition — here too certain tones of the end appeared before me, for instance upon uttering the word 'way.' The way is something frightful: although it branches off from the main road, it happens to lead right in front of my gate, thus forcing the most egotistic graph under the visiting woman's feet, still, when she uttered the graph's name (way!), then I realized in all its naked certainty, that in vain the way winds in front of my house with precise selfishness, there is not one speck of dust in it that would bend the traveler, the walking woman, in my direction; on her lips the word 'way' sounded as though it were a celestial curlicue somewhere among Chinese clouds, coiling like the itinerary of patience riddles ('which way can the cat reach the mouse?' — on the penultimate pages of children's magazines), and it would disappear somewhere in the midst of the stars' green beards; on the one hand, the 'way' is only the uncertain symbol of a kind of logical croquis, distance, vagrancy, on the other hand, it is a blind force of nature, a solitary and self-serving fact that can never have the merest consideration for the personal nitpicking of tiny rendezvous.

Conceptual dilation & natural monumentalizing: there is not one pale conjunction or mystical pronoun that has not undergone these two tortures of estrangement. If she uttered a pampering 'you' (meaning me), she only distanced me further. You? Around female words synthetic and abstract categories spread like the rings around a pebble on an infinitely good wave-conducting pond. You? Lots of people who are not I; the word's outlines are completely melted on her lips, she is forever unable to enjoy or address one concreteness, so even her kiss is always a broad synthesis-kiss. You? It suddenly turned too empirical, my modest little self could no longer recognize itself in it, seeing only some ridiculous, big man-idol, the robust god of women, to pat like a horse's neck.

Scientists and poets have equally bemoaned the contrast between the greatest experiences and words, but they have never yet realized this contrast to its full extent. What is love directed at? At a face, clothes, gesture, life possibility, landscape — always at something utterly new, individual, something we haven't known or even intuited before.

Love is the fusion of the impossibly differentiated shade and of bigoted monumentality, as is all nerve sensibility. The sensitive relish in a tree leaf first and foremost the changes brought on by the afternoon sun, weather, their own breathing — they would not notice ever newer details on the leaf itself (they do of course, but this is not the important part) but observe the slow changes of the environment, of human mood changes independent from the leaf, time embroidered on the clock face, the lights hovering in the air, and now and again into the stream of these changes they would throw the most trivial template of the leaf. And yet they arrive at the perfect understanding of the leaf: climate neuroses utterly independent from it lend the leaf scientific monumentality.

It is the same with a female face or body: we always enjoy on it ever more external things, increasingly independent from the face or body, and feel the most remote subjective nerve-lasso to be her absolute essence, divine ineluctability. All kisses move their erasers on this duality — on the mouth's infinite personality (infinite specialism already means non-existence) and its evident permanence (the mouth appears to be the most primal natural law).

Words have nothing to do with either: dead individuality and school textbook world-axiomaticity lie equally on this side of language or beyond. When among the night shrubbery's redundant repetition signs the female face alights, words shrink into nothingness like the host into water: it commands us straightaway to fail at the conjunction and declension of verbs and nouns. Our whole life is calibrated to the chase of beauty and happiness, and yet we keep talking all the time, although speech works in the opposite direction. Faces are impossible to describe: blond, blue-eyed, vase-necked, cyclamen-lipped — these are not descriptions, just as the passport pictures inspired by the savagery of analysis are not descriptions either. If it truly appears, blondness means precisely that all our previous concepts, hallucinations (to say nothing of words!) have been utterly misleading & irrelevant when it comes to blondness — what we see is strange exoticism, dizzyingly individual liminal case and precisely because it is so impossible it is ineluctable, with all the catechistic vulgarity of the postulate. All I want is that face, nothing more: who on earth would want to converse with flowers or corrosive-virginal blue fountain-pauses?

I'm not looking for walks, reciprocated love, lover, kiss, understanding, moral support or hush-hushing rendezvous, which are all primer wall posters teaching syntactic rules in place of the sole reality of the face. To grammaticalize love apart forever? To forever chase the face's blade-orthodoxy into the ha'penny heresy of speech? The only meaningful speech between man and woman could be woman's beauty, and it is inexpressible, hinging as it does on microscopic shades. The woman goes here, goes there, eats this and that, dances this and that, sleeps here, is operated there — does any of this have the least bit to do with her beauty, that is, with love? All events are alien — that's why I've so often been taken for a dodo. I want to do nothing with the woman; I've glimpsed her, that's all.

Why don't people abandon themselves to the redeeming sense of utter ignorance, why don't they activate systematically their bamboozlement before female beauty? Of course it's only pathological rationalists who would look for the conceptual freezing point with such gusto, but in general people are not very rationalistic. Our theme is a red mouth, the spur, scribbled in red ink, of autumn's tragedy — why should we talk of else? Love has never yet had a language, not even an experimental one — it always went about in reach-me-down grammars, like a little girl from the poorhouse.

Lovers start talking, they build one word upon another, and they slowly push one another apart with this vast word construction. Silence should be forced on lovers with terror if necessary, and I'd like to write a sermon of 'prayer for silence.' And yet, to write down the unwritable (is it worth writing something that can be written?): the mouth's word-pulverizing, the hips' drama-liquefaction, women's love-subtraction. The moment when rabid thirst for reason appears in people, the desire for languagelessness storms out too.

When we like a mouth we need to forget immediately the concept of 'mouth,' its word, for otherwise the first desire for a kiss and even more, the first kiss are already directed at this grammatical form, not at that 'vibrant nothing plus god-monogram' which is the real mouth — if we don't forget the meaning of the mouth, the kiss will be an act, part of a story, which is already a calculus of people that lies outside of love, the shifting to and fro of the social being on the abacus' crooked wires. It's a naïve but all the same useful medicine to call the mouth at once a mauve tent or flicked pearl and learn it by heart, so it stays outside the mind, impossible to translate into logic. The graph of woman, love, eros is not time, space, or the human being, but meaningless passive contemplation.

Caritas is precisely the positive form of meaninglessness, the nothing-depositing of redeeming nothing. I am not bound by any kind of relation to a woman, nor can I be; moral, contract, faithfulness are all statistical and abstract-mechanical things that fall outside of love: the sole reality is that I like her infinitely, and the cause of this liking is the impossible-to-analyze, chancy-individual beauty — can one attach the artificial bridge of faithfulness to an infinitesimal mouth-hieroglyph? I can be neither faithful nor unfaithful to her, beauty is simply impossible to relate. From beauty nothing starts, only from 'character,' but the character is a fictive social habit, stoical or Christian cut of fashion, grammar's brassiere on the soul. What follow-up can there be to a mouth — to be faithful to redness? To marry a shoe-heel? To posit value in a knee bowling-pin? To mourn for the cloud-footsteps of shoes if she should die? But these things are not the matter of life, nor ontological mathematical functions, but even more primeval design vortexes.

Do I want the woman? No. The ultimate hook of will doesn't get caught in the murderous neutrality of hovering beauty. I don't choose, don't invite, and don't repel her: beauty is, & makes me, happy. Once I wanted to write the story of a big divorce case in whose center stands a man who equally wants his wife and mistress, and equally doesn't want them, because will and non-will are completely identical when seen from the world of female beauty, lying outside every sphere of action. Caritas!

The positional nihilism of liking knows one sole concept vis-à-vis the woman: 'you were,' or eventually, 'you are.' I look at a face that I used to love very much; between us there is nothing but existence's gigantic-empty auxiliary verb. Beauty is — everything else is no longer love but liaison. On these pages nothing can rest of love, it had always been nothing on the plane of reason, thus here it will be unknown. What a barbarous age, when psychology and love could be wrung in a relation! Love is a kind of liking-atmosphere, the appendix of other people.

The unfaithful husband is caught in the act with his mistress — he doesn't understand why they are all at daggers with him &

his mistress, for his love bliss is so much not this woman as 'one woman' among people, and not the love-making, the secret rendezvous (he went through love-making and rendezvous the way the guest goes through the courses he is served, out of politeness), but some inexpressible feeling that no one can see — he knows nothing of mistress, meeting place, he had long forgotten them, he doesn't want the woman, doesn't defend, adore, or attack her; in the instant of the great exposure he barely knows who is in the bed with him, and when the vengeful witness storms into the secret hotel room it's not to him but at the woman in the bed he shouts: 'Who is it?' He denies his mistress because during the divorce case she is just 'a woman,' human personality, not beauty or love.

Autumn leaves' red calendar-stigmata, red-letter promises on the sky's Thomist bill of exchange, among them two hazel eyes, two slow gazes, two velvety nests padded with the embezzled feathers of silence — what can this have to do with the following: religion Roman Catholic, mother's name Mary, last seen her husband on February 23rd, first cessation of menses in March? The air is yellow as though the inside of a lemon had been blown up to a season, the kiss gets stuck under my tongue like a leftover seed in the lemonade, tomorrow tilts like a signature faked with the left hand — lots of prodigal impossibilities, and is the mother of these Mary, and is this February 23rd and Roman Catholic? O, loathsome words: 'you,' and 'way,' and 'I had a hard time coming here'!

Speech and action are things outside love; example:
with a woman at dawn (the color blue); other example:
Dialogue with the Undialoguable *(impossibility of love 'life')*

How much speech and action are things lying outside love I could immediately see in the fact that every woman made first of all a huge impression of color on me, or eventually the combination of several colors: the color of clothes, skin, face powder (not to mention the charis-postulates of perfume), and colors are known for their defective declension of 'events' & know nothing of the director's tricks of the genitive. This immediate streaming-into-color was decisive in love: under the girl's throat, a small light blue buckle or button, like the Buddhist cutlery of abstract beauty, with which I have scooped out the stockings' peach-skin, the corset's membraned pistil, the shoulder-straps' carbonized electric discharges from their object positions and spread them into one sole, eternal wave of blueness, next to which the 'human being' lay like a fishbone on the plate.

Blue gaze, blue kisses' Léman shutters over desire's broken[414] window, blue arms' serpentine grids on the horizon's nihilistic balcony: this is how in my childhood I imagined bleeding to death if I happened to stick my finger with a needle, when the last drop from our veins' thread-flasks is soaked up into death's capillaries and nothing is left but a giant red sponge, bloated with blood's martyr-yeast, & next to it, the corpse, like a crooked hairpin fallen out of a bun, of which one would ask, 'where did this fall from, is it yours or mine?'

Bleeding-into-blue was unstoppable — in vain I pressed words like, 'let's meet tomorrow at half past four in front of the Swan Court construction site,' on the shoulders' silver-azure, chess-plebeian riot: time's small hour-hook may catch fish from whose stupid little throats hunger flares up like a lighter's flame, but it can't pull out the blue waves, the shoulders' 'vers la nuit' tide from the upstart fishpond of existence. The wave is not hungry, it has no anatomy, no name or goal, place or time; when I slowly placed my fingers on its blue roes, all positive forms whizzed out of them like a clumsily caught sparrow's propeller-flight.

I shouted names at the women, the way the police press in-relief or concave fingerprint templates on unidentified fished-out corpses (to press a seal on the seal matrix by all means? ancient love fiasco), but they were blown off by the blue Antipassat, like the flame-red false beard of Richard III in the small town theater where they miscalibrated the ventilator tempest in the wings. Slowly all whirring energy differences came to rest (to rest?) in the neutrality of eternal blueness: St. Moritz lake in moonlit night, when Luna slowly descends into the middle of the water, like the weight at the end of the fathometer, the light of a Cubist church; around it the snow's blue ermine, soaking its glacier fingers into silence's tepid water, like the left hand at the manicurist's while the nails of the right are already being pared — who could express the desperate happiness, asthmatic redemption, that the woman bled-into-blue meant? I was forever cut off from her in the love for her; I didn't know what to do with her.

I have once written a prose poem with the title *Dialogue with the Undialoguable*, where I speak of the impossibility of love 'life' with the blue woman in the morning, on the fir-lined lakeside of St. Moritz.

'Tonight you were born into non-existence, the kiss' bladder-stone sperm fecundated you, and the beribboned womb of your mouth brought your blue non-mouth into the world: do you want to have breakfast with it, tea or chocolate, or explain the Bible, or scrape fresh death off it like a stamp, which has not yet got stuck completely on a mistaken envelope, or let it run for good? The catalogue could be complete: during the night your arms embraced me so hard with the hoary zip fastener of your will, that in the morning you have no more arms, only only doubtful fins leading nowhere. We betrothed each other, I fell silent, you became nothing. Do you feel like playing golf, do you feel like lying? Play golf, trick the waiter, so he doesn't get a fright. Shall we get married? Perhaps I'd kill you rather. But if I kill you they'll lock me up in a madhouse — who on earth would stick a knife into a corpse that death had already turned blue? Perhaps I'll stick a long knitting needle into your heart though, to show me the time, dead sundial, touristy quinquina. Speak, speak, my father taught me to be polite, two sugar cubes, no jam, would you like a return ticket to resurrection too? Who do you want to be today? You can also choose who I should be, we are free.'

Such is the politics of all love: to pour blue poison into the morning drink of our betrothed, to accuse her on her deathbed that she wanted to kill us, to commit suicide, so that we could be in heaven before her death and there gnaw our prayers like a tattoo into the hips of her guardian angel, to keep his protégé alive on earth, then betray God to drop back on earth like the small change dropped from the street phone if nobody answers the call, to cheat on her with the bunny squatting in the snow on the St Moritz posters, to force her hand into marriage, to give her a failing grade in spelling. All this is not some precious inventory of opposites but the soul's natural dilettantism in love: it has no attitude of any sort vis-à-vis the woman.

The divorce novel and this *St. Moritz Undialogued* kind of affair have to be written in parallel. Here it's not about love's psychology, not about now loving, now hating the woman (kindergarten animal picture alphabet: A — ambivalence, B — bifurcating, C — complex, phee) but the fact that vis-à-vis the woman all action is meaningless, out of place, impossible, that is, the St. Moritz poem's murder doesn't mean hatred but x meaningless movement without any psychic, emotional coloring, marriage is the other y meaningless act, far beyond all pro & con quarters.

---

*in parenthesis: new thinking technique;
contrast between thought and thinking*

(It seems I cannot escape tautology and so I can't escape apology either. The opinion & technique of the old-style thinking consisted in observing the ideas embedded in consciousness, imagination dimples and relation-buds, 'bringing them to the surface' — whether it was these it brought to the surface, the ones it first noticed, remains an open question — logicizing, inflecting-declining, teaching them the etiquette of truth and grammar. Thinking and writing were like angling: to pull up the unknown fish from the depth of consciousness, and make it into a delicious entrée?

I proceed differently: when I feel the fish's hunger-seal at the end of my angle, I don't pull it out of the water; when I feel the first germ of thought on the slippery threshold of consciousness, I'm not trying to make it more conscious but leave it as unknown germ, incomprehensible movement, but at the same time my entire soul bends above it — I'm not rendering it meaningful but I'll instruct all my meanings to surround it like a sheath; in the parable of the fisherman: I train the sea above to adjust to the unknown fish, of water I make some indeterminate fish-statue above it.

I don't aim at lifting the fish out of water at all, far less at conjugating its gills: I'm merely trying to imitate its barely-intuited shape with water statues. And this is the tautological style's 'complete angling': it doesn't write down complete thoughts but gropes for the forms of obscure barely-thoughts, without knowing their goal, content, only following the uncertain graph of their first movement. It turns out that the fish don't even exist, they are only wave-models, oval blue water brocade: thinking extirpates for good the uncreditable caricature shape of the 'thought.')

love and inescapable lie

It is by no means enough to write it in a phantasmagoric form, that love is something outside the confines of action — the prosaic praxis of the affair needs to be written too. In the morning we don't pour blue poison into the glass of our betrothed, but we don't want to meet her either; we don't accuse her on her deathbed of wanting to kill us, but we filch from her handbag the 50 francs that she wanted to exchange to liras in the morning; we will not commit suicide, but every word of hers sends a shiver through us, like the hailstorms of anathemas, only for us to gnaw her arm into dental print-templates with our kisses in the boathouse: that's when the parallelism of meaningless, murderous speech and raving corporeality is unleashed. It's like a metaphysical rollercoaster: up, up, up on the glass ropes of unrelated conversation, and down, down, down on moss-thick kisses' woman-parodies unrelated to anything. Word and sensuousness resemble so little the love dissolved into one sole blueness that I feel no difference whatsoever between the words said to the woman and words said to another, new woman: I can take unfaithfulness too to be truth-telling, and faithfulness also to be a lie.

I'm tied by three contradictory relations (not contradictory feelings!) even to the same woman: vision dissolved into blueness (this is the gift, the only love that is amorous love, the feeling itself), the self-serving dialogues and the impotent sex-inquisitions — there are three unfaithfulnesses, three betrayals, I cheat on the same woman with herself, and on myself with myself three times, so that even within the circle of faithfulness I immediately experience the most concrete combinatory of absolute unfaithfulness, the sickly growth of the lie. Even if I never for a moment leave her side, I always feel that she is going to catch me in the act of some unfaithfulness.

Three facts: blue leaves above the lake with the night's still-wet fever enamel; 'tomorrow Miss Lishman is going to sit on our sleigh instead of Adreano'; the planting of my pulse, like a tiny sapling, between her two breasts: are they not every bit as strange to each other as a French Madeleine, an Italian Nicoletta, and a Russian Olga? Where love appears at all, the lie will immediately be there too, inescapably, preceding from the beginning all intention to lie or cheat.

Thus man is depraved even in the henpecked respect for one wife, for he has three lives and into none of the three can he place his whole humanity, something will always be left out; blueness, dialogue, kiss will all appear to him as insincerities, hypocrisies. And this is precisely what elicits the feeling of depravity: in no action can he feel completely present. He will not as much as notice if strange women mix in among the three foreign attitudes: the faithful kiss is just as far removed from the faithful speech as a strange woman's kisses from the kisses of the wife. Speech is the most important preparation for unfaithfulness: the worship addressed to the wife is just as mendacious as the speech addressed to a strange woman. Speech as such, in itself, is already unfaithfulness, next to it the difference between wife and mistress is nil. One can be faithful to blueness, but barely to kiss, & not at all to speech.

continuation of the analysis of female speech

I continued observing the speech of women (the schoolbook opposite of which was the half-idiot girl's speech), trying to locate in the words' foreignness-rings with which women enclose themselves, the trait that is nevertheless the most responsible for the fact that they are incapable of convincing us of their meaning. I echoed the words in my ears & saw that the moment the woman spoke they lost the content that they had represented in my head and became instead merely invisible scaffoldings of her mouth's movements, small sound-handgrips on which lips, tongue, teeth, face, eyes settled with unknown movements. In the first moment I thought that the word's meaning dilated or, if you like, froze into only-meaning in her mouth, but later I realized that it simply lost its meaning and its place was taken by her timbre & face mimicry.

I'm scandalously fastidious around the subject, hence I will also need to resort to the Bible of the poor, the image, to illustrate the important thesis that women's words, even when they say their most personal pros, by their nature sound like cons (and this is obviously not about women's 'naughtiness'). When the woman pronounced the word 'way,' it became a transparent white drawing, colorless figure (on it every speck of dust was rendered precisely, but it was completely immaterial), behind which the strange and adored mouth moved in all its vividness of color. Whichever element of the concept or image of 'way' I tried to check, I also found on her lips, listless and empty, with the face's blossoming fabrics undulating behind. I was faced with the word 'way' like a father who encounters his child, whom he hasn't seen in twenty years, in a foreign environment: it's his son, but a stranger.

Every moment I would have liked to shout at the girl when she uttered 'way,' that she should take care, she wasn't holding it right, here it was too loud, there bitten off, here too colorful, there too logical; I couldn't imagine that it could possibly evolve the same percepts in her brain as in mine, for the word sat on her mouth like a top hat on a kangaroo. The most awkward thing was that, once she had uttered 'way,' I no longer possessed it, she took the word away from me; old art collectors feel such pangs of anxiety when the executor handles a crumbling 16th-century pocket watch as though it were a disposable box of matches; they keep reaching out with trembling hands to save the watch from falling.

So did she wrest from me almost all my cherished words in the course of a half-hour conversation; behind all the words, where so far differences of meaning showed like the colors of the spectrum, she placed her own portrait and movement of the lips, so the 'You' meant laughing eyes and clumsily rouged mouth, with a bit of lipstick smudged on the teeth; 'way' meant a long index finger, rattling bracelets & a small oops, with which she caught her slipping handbag. We feel language to be our most personal possession, like our nose and the sum total of our threads of hair, and when a strange woman uses those same words I go through what the detective novel's robber feels, when he glimpses his lookalike at the cash register: the same nose, the same moustache, the same red ears, somebody from an unknown gang had copied his face down to the last particular. I felt that the woman was hanging my face on hers: perhaps my copy is not the best, but all the same, I must flee from here. What is more, I have to destroy my original, authentic face, such a hystericizing authority does the living copy command over the original.

So I ended up like the magician's apprentice: first I scattered words in the woman's direction and when I got them back, they all tasted of strange hocus-pocus fairies' money, dancing elves' syllables that surrounded me hissing, jigging, and threatening. There is no more eerie swishing than to listen to well-known words we like to use, coming from female mouths; their meaning glows white like silver birch leaves against the iron-blue sky before the storm, their light scintillates with foreign sparks, their voice is a harmony-less cross-chiming. The more I listen to them, the more tormenting this leaf-swish and sentence-sirocco becomes; the enhancement of familiarity itself becomes foreignness' resonant grammar.

In conversation I always see the rushing train on its way to the river where there is no bridge anymore; we pile words on one another, come to 'understand' each other as they say, although all I feel is that I'm being looted, my meaningful I-shaped words are divided among others like the clothes of the condemned, with a throw of the dice; every moment I see the strange person's body grow in place of the word's meaning, and I cannot rule over a stranger's body, the train crashes into the river.

a Magnasco reproduction as the illustration of love's 'impossibility'

The best illustration of love's impossibility, of the reading backward of encounters, was a Magnasco reproduction hanging in my childhood bedroom [415] — or perhaps I learned from it to see in every joy an exciting darkness (exciting at least in its raw industrial form). If I remember well, it depicted a nuptial cortege in dark grey, without colors. The cortege crossed a dark forest; the dark sky's throbbing clouds & the shadow-muscular trees' smoky foliage could hardly be told apart, it was as if God had created the clouds before the sky and the dense network of leaves before the trees. There was no day, no night, no storm, and no sun eclipse, only eternal dusk, which meant not the absence of the sun but the sole possible lighting — sometimes in our dreams we move about in such brown-sooty dusk, which is independent of the zodiac's revolving roulette stars. It was not a thick forest and not a clearing either; such uncertain steppes can perhaps be found in the Catholic Purgatory; here and there giant foliage with enormous gaps, in other places the grey penitential fur of rootless cypresses.

In the middle of the cortege the wedded couple sat astride a mule; behind them a small flagpole and a guitar's string-mast, which I had for years taken to be the tilted cross' two stems. White light fell on their bodies, as if they were ghosts dragged to some kind of witch-burning fete on a mock-ass. The cortege was headed by a dark rider, a cardinal or lawyer, notary or master of ceremonies in mourning clothes, I could never tell, with a small pointed goatee, a haughty, dark, and selfish gaze, reaching out his hand in an unfriendly gesture, as though pushing off all people in disgust. Since I saw that picture, every time I talk with a girl or celebrate a wedding in the church I see that death-faced, French-bearded riding notary. He is wearing riding boots and (in my child's interpretation) the cap of a learned dean; love's cicerone is a hunter and doctor, that is, a murderer and examiner, in front of whom the flowers' fairy-tale-like, chiming G-sharp wig turns into crumpled newspaper, & whose merciless cross-examination fails the forest's Albigensian birds one by one.

Behind him, hatless and much more shady, with a similar posture, rode another gent: hair aflutter in the wind, an untrimmed tomcat moustache. Are the lovers lepers or smitten with the pox, that they ward off everybody from the vicinity of the white couple with such haughty disgust? Or is it from the forest's carbonized foliage-silt and the sky's dying-coal clouds (the remains of a great fire), from their falling branches and bitter ash drizzle, that these dark masters of ceremonies are trying to protect the couple? Are they marching to an execution? Or watching with shuddering pity that two people can find happiness only in each other, and these two gesticulating hunter-cardinals are explaining this fact to the painting's invisible audience like professors of medicine explaining a disease to their disciples: gently stroking the patients to calm them down, saying they would be discharged in two days, while putting the label of Latin and Greek words on the articles of their death for the disciples' benefit.

The mule was led by a little boy, but the painting was so centered on the pulling movement that he looked like he was dying: on the paintings of the Italians absolute purposefulness often leads to the maximum breaking of purpose, and so it happened with this boy. His head was turned southward, his hand westward, his legs twisted into a plaited loaf — he looked an epileptic far rather than a drunken teen or henchman of joy. The same was even more true of a romping beagle: its slenderness was a skeleton's grace, its hopping, grabbing movement an impotent wriggling, as though it were fighting the bride's skirt for dear life.

Behind him a running, stumbling, distraught guitarist forever lagging behind; Lucifer descending into hell may have had such a tattered, sorry-looking orchestra of angels for suit. The painting's disheartening sadness was beautifully rounded off by the last figure: an apostle-like man who sat astride his horse like an evening cloud above a fruit tree, and dropped alms in some direction (at least so I saw in the dim image that was further dimmed by the glass sheet covering it). The nuptials go by, only misery is left behind, some invisible beggar, perhaps the forest itself with its misty trees, with the sunset's undulating paint-steam, to which this superb finale-apostle tosses his alms. For the forest beggared to the point of love indeed needs some shower of grace, divine money; if the warlord-cardinal is dead or takes off his ill-buttoned lace collar, if the wedded couple go to the rocks on the first night's hopeless kiss-surgery, and even the guitarist falls asleep, this flaring, alms-throwing arm will continue to glow, and now and again it will shower the rain of forgiveness, redemption, and sanctifying grace on the bleak forest path, entirely covered in snow as old mirrors are covered by violet, yellow and green stains, cobweb cracks.

*two pseudo-expressions; ideal:
absolute gesture (dance?) and absolute mathematicalization*

In fact the two styles of the natural pain derived from love, which I have jotted down for myself, point at the great absence and helplessness of my life: one is tautological analysis directed at the foreignness of female speech — the other is the pathetic imitation of the Magnasco painting. Both mean an impotent half measure, but hitherto I have been unable to cover even those; both set the great task of pain to me, and I was unable to solve these didactic sorrow examples like an eminent pupil.

Analysis is nothing but a primitive and nostalgic technique toward attaining perfect mathematicalization — but the imprint of the Magnasco word is nothing if not a similar, even more primitive device toward achieving complete rituality, the utterly external gesture.

The resolution of pain is possible in two directions: in the direction of pure algebra, or that of the purely liturgical posture. I thirsted for both equally, but they remained torsos in my hands; instead of numbers, some kind of upstart rationalism, and instead of true 'ornament action,' wallpaper clusters.

When I investigated 'analytically' the ring of the words 'You' or 'way,' two meanings were possible: on the one hand, to present my unified mood as the imagined sum total of all kinds of other moods (that is, to represent one color as the mix of different imagined component colors): this is the most sterile analysis, in fact a mere pseudo-analysis: on the other hand, to depict with abstract traits first the independent word 'You,' then the one used by me and in the end, the one used by the woman, to signal myself separately without the word 'You,' and to do the same with her; then to signal the value of the word 'You,' if I feature in it together with the woman, not as two people but as the homogeneous and anatomical domain of the pronoun 'You': and then to carry out the operation of conversation with these signs, since conversation is just as much a basic operation as multiplication or division, one only needs to discover its method. If we succeeded, then 'foreignness' would not be a misshapen psychological abortion emerging from the masks of metaphors, but a thesis like the following: if the quotient of the impersonal pronominal 'You' and the female 'You' is always inferior to the multiplication of man minus 'You' and 'You' raised to the womanth power.

against 'nuance'; for the kaleidoscope

The other method mentioned, when I'm not calculating with objective algebraic signs but try to forcedly imagine my own feelings as composed of many elements, invariably lures me into the public humbug of the so-called shade; like a good teacher of the catechism I repeat last week's lesson to my pupils: feelings have no shades, the feeling is always one and indivisible, those certain ambiguous, polyguous, everything-uous and nothing-uous feelings that the psychological industry has produced over the last decades are just as straightforward and one-element down-to-earth facts as the most certain joy or the most unequivocal suffering; there are no 'complex' feelings, it's only their rational description and the range of comparisons that is complex.

There is diversity, there is simplicity: the first is, for instance, the various meanings of the pronoun 'You' (not its shades of meaning, for there are no shades in the world of numbers), the other is my unitary, homogeneous feeling or mood arising from observing the various values of 'You.' But my, as case may be, literary feelings spoil and hopelessly entangle this wholesome alternative: they forcefully pull the independent differences of value of the word 'You' into the homogeneous lake of the feeling, but at the same time they cut up its sole wave into tiny pseudo-waves, usher them among the arithmetic formulae of objective values, from where only meaninglessness and tastelessness can result. The 'nuance' is always the mix of an erroneous number and an erroneous psychology — perhaps all 'good' literature itself is no better than such half-baked work.

In the alternative the algebraic case is clear: art needs to change completely into mathematics when it addresses the foreignness of female speech. But what should it do with the other half of the alternative, the emotional understanding of foreignness, with the feeling itself? Is there no other method to express it than the arbitrary invention of nuances and decomposition to shades?

How is that shading carried out? Simply by dragging into a heap lots of great generalities: for instance at the description of a special pink we bring up blood-red, snow-white, brick-sienna and cherry-bordeaux, the conspiratorial vermilion and sunset rosehip, powdered mist and Protestant-converted cardinal robe, the martyr's wound and virginity's linear color spectrum — that is, every single delicate shade, detail-detail, and element-element becomes a huge thing, something greater, weightier, and more universal than the object to analyze itself, the pink. Instead of decomposing a special thing (let's substitute pink with any feeling, the template of the 'shading' will be the same) into smaller elements, we would rather build above that small, special thing a huge and misshapen tower out of all kinds of sweeping generalizations. This method is thus entirely worthless; one cannot analyze feelings or colors.

But we can do something else, so that next to the alternative's algebra-part the feeling-part too may receive an adequate method, equal to the algebra branch. This method would not pile above the feeling a group of much more general feelings but throw about elements at random, which relate to no thing in particular; it chaotically casts about all kinds of colors, different feelings, having no inkling what these meaningless pieces might refer to: what they refer to transpires only by accident at the end of the game, just as in a kaleidoscope we don't take one large pattern apart into its components but the other way round, we shake elements at random and from this one sole (but thanks to the mirrors, rigorously constructed) hazard, form results. This kaleidoscope frivolity is the only worthy counterpart of the algebraic method as a form of 'analysis'; in fact it is not 'analysis' but 'whole-ing,' which strives toward the whole from the hazardous mixing of meaningless fragments, that is, it works in the opposite direction than the old novel's analysis of the psyche. It doesn't dissect the psyche but throws in a heap of unconnected objects to the point where from the jest a soul results by accident.

How do I stand with the gesture part of my pain? I would have liked to translate all sadness into act; what is more, this instinct is a much more beastly perfection of precision in the posture-ceremony that responds to pain, than in impotent analysis. When every word from the girl's mouth rattled estranged on the glass walls of my psyche I felt that it was all about such a permanent sadness in my life as the succession of evening & morning are constant — if I thus accompanied these parts of the day with regular prayers, it's paramount that I too accompany the ineluctable miseries of love with some kind of constant ceremony: to carve a seal die with the word 'way' or 'You,' to stamp this on the girl's photograph, to mail it to my own address, to not live at home as long as the letter strays on the itineraries of the post, to write the girl's name on the envelope as sender (like stamp falsifiers) and call myself by her name, to cross out my own name in three different places & write 'You' instead — these were the kinds of festive burlesques I longed for during my sufferings. But I never got to realizing them, at most I got to an unembellished description of Magnasco-style paintings, for I felt the essence of ceremony to be the infinity of action, the eternal spread of the pose; the ceremony in fact tried to supplement the quality of experience planned by analysis with an infinite-volume quantity of action.

dance and politics

For me there are only two kinds of entirely pure gestures: dance & politics. The 'Bewegungskunst' is a loathsome mechanism,[416] its foundations are mere emotional fatuities & old-maid's æstheticism

— but there is a true dance somewhere, which can somehow lead the feeling's stifling homogeneity along the muscles' dispersive waves, which can create a million shifts and independent actions without breaking into pieces the one-and-only feeling. In this way dance accomplishes what psyche-shading literature is forever incapable of: it piles detail upon detail, without those being the component parts of the feeling, and these details are not rational contents but figurations independent of meaning or language. Dance is the delirium of precision: face mimicry, on the other hand, is always infinitely itself, unmistakable & always infinitely irrational. Precision and reason are mutually exclusive.

The closest match to dance, and one barely distinguishable from it, is politics: while in dance it is with one sole body's muscles that, let's say, the pain of love is expressed, in politics in place of muscles social classes & institutions feature, which are driven by the demagogic (here this is a word of praise!) force of rhetoric. I can take politics only as pure movement; as soon as objectives, future, prosperity, etc. are mixed in it, I turn away & withdraw into my cocoon. In the shortest time many people come to realize that there is more practical benefit and celestial morality in frivolous adventurer politics than in dyed-in-the-wool idealism. Anarchy taken to the bitter end can result in civitas Dei anew: one million historical vector lines running hither and thither are a more ancient-military pattern than the scrawny and unfinishable, solitary line of 'useful progress.'

A Platonic Labor party member splashes like this: he takes a jug of water, pours its content into an utterly straight, long pipe, without knowing where that emaciated sewage pipe is going to end. I, the selfish morphinist politician splash like this: I don't pour the water from my jug into any kind of infinitely progressive capillary pipe but agitate it, tilt it over, and make it wave, so from the infinitely contradictory mass of waves an average wave-graph emerges, the orthodox divine kernel of all anarchies.

return to the color green ((ambridge meadow:
the painted-over dress of the girl 'sinfully' kissed in Switzerland):
the Elizabethan lady-in-waiting symbolizing Cambridge

In fact my whole encounter with the idiot girl interested me not as regards the nature of virtues but because it was one of the most beautiful forms (I don't know myself if I should use here form or content, development or meaning, variation or intensity) of the color green (which I had experienced so intensely in Switzerland on the painted-over dress of a former vacationing companion whom I met again). Behind us the white-golden towers of Cambridge, like Gothic catkins growing around the funerary relief of a high-born lady-in-waiting of bygone days; Cambridge has always reminded me of an oval-faced, pale, etched-lipped woman with golden dress (the skirt is a gigantic dark cone, and her hips are a gorgeous pearl-shed territory from where thousands of pearls pour out in every direction); from her hand a Greek inscription hangs, like a snobbish Veronica veil.

These three elements were dominant in this feminine city: a pale (in all sincerity, barely feminine) face, utterly white and deathly rigid; a splendid dress, whose shape may be stern and rigid like the illustrations in astronomy books, but gold & pearl roll out on it almost dissolved; & finally, a quote from the classics in Greek alphabet, which contains the wise sayings of one of the Pythagorean masters. When I looked at one of the fountains I found it enchantingly feminine, but immediately after it appeared pale & rigid like a statue; when I strolled along one of its sun-gilded courtyards I felt that every single chirp of the birds (residents? commuters?) was one rounded-out, finished pearl, which I could thread on the shadows' wild crinoline; I saw the pearl, the sunshine, but I recoiled from the shadow's ghostly cut — under a thousand pearls and galloons lurked the cellar-like darkness of the courtyards; at first the Greek lines studied here meant a yellow horizon-foam above the celestial flatness, but then they were flattened into dry and laughable nature-historical commonplaces.

When I felt it to be feminine, I thought of the darkest features of women, of the reclusiveness behind the lovely face, of the ineliminable foreignness behind the lovely dresses, of the blind pedantry behind the lovely words.

studying and fugitive impressions (truth and moment); green grass

Cambridge like an Elizabethan lady-in-waiting occurs in every second festive school ode or tourist poster — why do I then stick to this image? Because it featured in many of my dreams when I was looking for the whatness of knowledge; there always featured spring birds, dead ladies-in-waiting, gentle Renaissance school orders, black, black, black banners and odorous meadows. All listing is pointless, for the spring buds didn't occur together with the black banners but they presupposed one another in the dream; they didn't mix and didn't fuse, but revolved around one another in the narrow but fast atomic orbit of conditioning; and the face of the dead lady-in-waiting, besides being a concrete, oval whiteness, filled the whole dream scene.

In dream every little episode-dust features with two values: as speck of dust and as the essence of the whole image, its territory and its frame. The banner is but a small twisting black fabric-band and yet the banner is everything. The dream is an arithmetic operation to be carried out permanently, but whose every phase moment is an end result. Knowledge is always of the past, knowledge is always irrelevant, knowledge can only ever be enjoyed in the milieu — this was the primitive epistemology of my dream exercises.

How much Greek I have studied, how many fatuities in foreign languages, how many valuable moments I had when drowsing in the shade of some tree: what is knowledge?

The houses were old, the pictures were old, the ceremonial robes were old — thus knowledge is what we have nothing to do with; the texts spoke about the bold being happy before the cowards, and that in Pericles' times there were five subgroups in a Greek division — thus knowledge is what tells us nothing; but among the lakes, bridges, meadows, and the shadows that were greener than the trees, I felt a tranquil inebriation, dizziness and certainty, the feeling of the unattainable and of riches I possessed but couldn't spend — knowledge is then what we don't know. For me school and studying always meant this; now when I looked back on Cambridge from love's huge human-shaped foliage, I again felt my pubertal soul floating between the useless past and unattainable future, among Greek commonplaces and incomprehensible tree crowns: I will leave the symbolic dead dame to be.

Has my life changed in any way since studying? When I sat with some book under the first leaves and felt for the first time the foreignness of these two types of knowledge — the one that was in my book, written by somebody else in another language, in another time, written for everyone perhaps, except me, and written for all time except this present moment: can such a thing be knowledge for me? Knowledge is only (this is the other) what in this moment solves the meaning of this moment — the sole reality is the stirring of the leaves, the present throbbing of my life, the present accidental mingling of colors. How strange & doltish the 'eternal value' in my book lay in the moment's divine swing. What is written by somebody else cannot be knowledge, it doesn't interest me because it refers to something unknown, while I myself am only a moment: cobbled together, as the Germans might put it, from the 'Dingaugenblick' of leaves,[417] watering cans, afternoon snack rendezvous, missing small change, too strong reading lens.

That's when I made up my mind to tend only to my dreams, for every book is anachronistic as compared to people. What I don't want I can read at the library, and what I want is so uncertain as the wind of unknown direction. So far I have always walked about in the library with the optimism that perhaps once I would come upon books that might explain something that interests me, but now I realized at once that this is forever impossible.

When my friends talked about their favorite readings I smiled wryly and asked timidly if in their books they found exact answers to what they were looking for. They said they did. I felt ashamed and started reading again with frantic dedication, but in vain; I loved a fountain, I read 50 art historical tomes about it, but there was not one syllable about the fountain. Then I realized that I too loved one moment of the fountain, which nobody had seen but I. For this reason precisely any objective discussion was out of the question, so I resorted again to swooning, to dream.

I recoiled from the thought that someone might accuse me of being solely interested in the subjective part of things. When I went out furtively in the evening to watch the last drops of the little fountain in the sunshine, as they glide on the slippery moss down among the basin's rusty sewer grids, was I perhaps trying to satisfy my own quixotic atmosphere-gourmandize? No: I was far rather driven by a mania of objectivity to chase the fountain's moments and I found the theme of the art historical books pure fiction.

There has been yet no absolute objectivity in the world: for this I started into dream's morphine tactics. I was not looking for so-called 'poetic' truths and not beauty either, nor any kind of symbolism, far from it. I was in the paradoxical situation of knowing that I could only possibly find truth within my own self, but it will be truth & independent from me; no one could see the fountain the way I saw it, for I alone was there on April 30th at half past nine in the evening, but if I can ever describe that moment absolutely faithfully, I will have found the objective fountain, the eternal fountain independent of people, of which no trace could be seen of course in the books whose naïve authors had believed that if in their forewords they glued five lampooning adjectives to the word 'lyricism,' slap-bang they have become factual.

It's a frightful feeling to know that my every moment swells with truths, but there is not one book or one line in the whole world that even approximately speaks of my truth; to be stripped of the pleasure of reading, for every single page is a struggle, it speaks such irrelevant side issues with respect to us; to be robbed of the enjoyment of pictures, houses, music, because they all speak about something other than us, when we look at them or listen to them.

For me Cambridge meant this fear; truth, beauty, and goodness exist only in others and in other times, in us there is something completely different, in myself I am always something else than what has hitherto been affirmed of the human being, all knowledge is useless. One glance of mine at a geranium ruins 10,000 botanic treatises and five million poems about flowers; 'truth' starts anew in every moment and in vain that lady-in-waiting rolls the Greek text with her frozen but beringed, dead but varnished-nailed, loving but paralyzed hand for the boys in tweeds.

When I felt again this utter forsakenness while the half-idiot girl caressed me, I realized that individualism went up in smoke because it had never forced itself to reach the point of asceticism; if somebody dare immerse themselves with absolute excess into their individual feelings and individual sights, then they have to bring truth to the surface. But for most people individual means that which doesn't resemble another, although individuality is something far too wild for the naïve criterion of 'non-resemblance' to suffice. I needed dream because with its help the individual accidents linked into a close structure; thanks to the dream everything gets a fateful and absolute coloring, momentary collisions turn into divine liaisons. But all this was not very important in those moments, for Cambridge and with it, my youthful fretting over the triviality of all science and the inexpressibility of all personal experience, were all behind me — in front of me lay only a green sunset love-landscape, perhaps the last in this life.

And grass really became green now, now when a female human being was wading in it, who wanted nothing but neighborly love; I felt that in order to bloom, nature needs human presence even more than the cool, searching fingers of the rain, which reach for the root's hidden knots like an obstetrician for the baby-head tarrying in the womb. The landscape was fairly simple and monotonous: grass upon grass, then grass upon grass again, and above, branches, youthful blooming shrubbery and prudently budding stingy twigs. But all these scrawny greens were transformed by the presence of love: what was the wondrous part in this, when the feeling itself, by its very infinity, was empty, burning nothing, mere incandescing absence among the things of the world — and the things of the world were far too few to create the impression of abundance.

I was filled with immense happiness, but when I looked around I felt like crying from poverty; in my soul there was no content at all and around me no real novelty. Do I have to lie even now, in what is perhaps my life's last chapter, if I want to write it down?

Let's give it a try: the grass was light yellow from the many crisscrossing horizontal sunbeams; it rolled hither and thither like the golden asphalt being rolled out on the ground, fresh-hot, by the wind's large, cold roller cylinders, so that lukewarm green steam rises from the grass to the clouds; then when the sun sinks lower, violet patches appear on the meadow, as if the ray did not withdraw uniformly from the body of the grass, like a slender drawer or wetness from an ink stain, but went missing only from certain points, while continuing to circulate in the other meadow-organs.

Shall I magnify nature or shall I annihilate it: shall I affect it to value, or preach it apart to nothing? Or is it that whichever method I might choose, its opposite would also inevitably & mechanically be realized?

The greatness of every great emotion consists in our feeling that everything is nothing: I always looked for the greatest love and the greatest knowledge, although the two are... The leaves' small veins filled with happiness, so in vain I would have looked in them for the plants' vital sap; love filled the trees' blooms too with thick powder, which would of course never have fertilized them. Neither I nor nature lend anything of ourselves to new love: is it really now that I would have to fall silent? Do I want love at this price? I hesitated for a moment and lured my soul into shivering yessing. Lie would not alleviate this fundamental ignorance and emptiness into which love has pushed me, so let's stay alone, away from boughs & away from myself. I started speaking.

lack of precision and caritas

— Do you often walk around these parts?

— No, not often, only when I need flowers for the table, and only here can I find the kind of violets I need. They are thin, quite narrow in the middle — (here she pulled such a stern and cruel face as though the violets were scraggly from her peculiar poison; it seems that if love observes something it unwittingly adopts the grimace of hatred and precise animosity, because all 'features' or 'characteristics' stand in its way) — and the petals turn outwards on the edges, as though they had been together once and then, bang, they popped apart — (she imitated the popping apart by hitting her blown-up cheeks — first she hated, now she ridiculed the violets).

But her behavior was exciting precisely because, although she ridiculed and despised the violets, still she was here for them; in her steps I felt the slow crumbling away of the goal, and yet that only enhanced the goal's attractiveness.

— Where do you live in fact? — I asked.

— There — she said, suddenly turning from our direction and looking vaguely toward Ely. Then she pulled a small twig to the side, so I could see better where she lived. — You can't see it from here — she observed, but immediately pushed aside another cluster of leaves for me to see at least the direction clearly. The generalness of direction for domicile suited well this girl of uncertain consciousness; I didn't feel like asking where she lived exactly. — That's where the flowers are going — she said, letting the elastic twigs, like a pair of blunt scissors wrapped in green wadding, bounce back above her head.

It's strange to observe the precision expressed by every stress and gesture of the mad, as they are connected with utterly vague things — or the other way round: they express things precisely, with surprisingly analytic details, but accompany everything with smudged, uncertain gestures and out-of-place actions. Is this not what ruins love, that it lacks such division of thought and action, or feeling and thought: as if women forced love's inner time-duality into a common tempo, so that keeping the beat and reading scores would be made easier. But when women simplify love's genre written for two consciousness-hands and two consciousness-measures into a beginner piano lesson, they do nothing worse than I who appoint myself to professional time-decorator, who can spot 'life-giving' duality in about everything, what is more, when elegantly lurking dualism has grown boring, I can transform it into triple or whatever multitude — shouldn't the infinitely many-dimension psychological game be finally brought to an end? In this life I could draw no advantage at all from the duality of body and soul, but the 'precise gesture vs. vague thought' or 'uncertain half-action vs. absolutely precise goal' have always been domains where I had hopes to build something.

Love is like jumping the hurdle, it's full of breathless running and hurdles scattered about (not narratively speaking of course, I don't mean that such is the life of people in love), what is freedom and what is a hurdle is a secondary matter here, the gist is that we have both: sometimes the feeling is quite simply freedom, and the given female body is the hurdle, but it can also be the other way round, that the woman's humanity is absolute openness (for instance, while dancing, in a new dress), and our feeling, our love is the hurdle on which the female body is suddenly caught.

In this moment I saw this scheme prepared in the mad girl: her body flowed apart in some places, like the thin water-sheet of a threaded-apart and woven waterfall, in other places it suddenly aggregated into whirling wells, into thick water candy-cornets. When I moved closer to her I physically enjoyed this uncertain distribution, as if she were a broken balance on which the weights shift this way and that, never falling into equilibrium, but all the same I was aware that she can afford this game because she possesses a much more profound and more positive equilibrium than the superficial kind we can see in the scales of a balance.

On me the mad always made an impression of exaggerated harmony rather than scatter-brainedness — they hesitate because for them normality is nothing more than a mass of tedious phrases, to which they would only resort with utmost disgust and with a vengeful gesture, living as they do in a more positive world. Madness always seemed only an outward cover; it was as though this girl too revolved at the end of a long, perhaps infinitely long twine, like the stone in a sling — her madness is only the ever-present centrifugal force that wants to launch her into the world of absurdities, but she never flies off the twine end, so that in the end my attention is directed back at the decisive & unified gesture of the rotating hand. Normally I never feel the dual game of fugal and petal forces in the life of girls; with them everything goes either forward or backward, every action gathers all its psychic forces into its present (like an old maid who walking into an apothecary with all her 15 pinschers on a common leash), or every idea immediately uniforms the whole person into idea-livery; there is no trace of the internal delays, disturbances in the train timetable, & fateful misprints that rendered this half-idiot woman uneven.

the outcomes of the half-idiot girl's speech; first conclusion: identity of modern architecture, caritas, and the syntax of madness (architectural example)

But what symmetrical unevenness was expressed in her peculiar syntax and polyphonic facial mimicry: from it I understood the furbishing of modern homes, orchestral scores, and Uccello's perspectival ideas. The girl's speech was an ongoing construction: it went from huge curtain-minores to thick candle-maggiores — when she stressed a conjunction with exaggerated and unjustified pathos, forgetting all sentences, winged co-ordinations or left-handed subordinations that followed, I came to understand those infinite silk shrouds that hang in front of dining-room windows and contain the shifted half of one sole pattern of embroidery, a pattern that, being characteristically small like a conjunction, would otherwise only occur in the midst of thousands of other patterns.

When she started stuttering playfully, without putting up any struggle, as though patting, splashing the first syllable's ice-cold and resistant water, I came to understand those monotonous but active repetitions of the objects of which I saw examples on postcards, where a flute-shaped vase is repeated twelve times next to the window, or instead of balancing a candelabra branch that is so tilted that it almost topples over, they draw some 30 more such candelabra branches next to it in a network: as though all these architectural conceits were based on the symbols of the mentally impaired and were thus illustrating the etymology of caritas, the object declensions of true eros.

These dining-rooms and bedrooms had two typical features: pathos shifted to the side, and inebriated stuttering; large stains appeared there where they could have no practical or symbolic role, for instance the dining-room table was made up merely of two crossing gossamer threads, one couldn't see them & tripped over on them, but squeezed between window and ceiling there was a huge black serpent-buckle, the most important thing in the room; or the bed in the bedroom was merely a light blue crease-paradigm undulating on a 2 cm tall podium, which almost melted under the vacuuming cubes of luminosity, but the candelabra lined the wall in such density as electric wires on a long fuse: that black ceiling-buckle and those dizzying light-stripes correspond to the girl's meaningless intonation, overgrown suffixes, senseless interrogating tics, conjunctions gone wild.

But stuttering too was allowed to run its course: if in the dining-room the knotting of the ceiling became more important than the table and in the bedroom, the candle birdcage became more important than the bed itself, then these secondary objects were also repeated to infinity; for instance, the curtain pattern was only one half of the count's coat-of-arms, but that half pattern was repeated 15 times from the ceiling downward, like the leftover ornaments of a 15-winged, degenerate moth; the great geistesgeschichtlich value of stuttering consists in elevating the fragment above the whole by the means of repetition.[418]

This technique is indispensable in love: most women compose the love events into a so-called 'harmonic unity,' because the human instinct for 'the whole' is much more natural, ancient, and childish than the instinct for the fragment, and by this petit bourgeois-childish 'rounding' they trample all lovely fragments to death; with the idiot girl this naïve harmonizing was entirely absent, her acts, gestures, didn't integrate themselves into the pre-established program of a regular, wholesome, proportional, clear, purposeful and balanced rendezvous, but each fragment remained a fragment, with the difference that they acquired either some ridiculously out-of-place stress or they vibrated, delayed, and repeated by stuttering, like the same fragment of text on the printers' rolling cylinders.

It gave me an extraordinary, perhaps exaggeratedly priestly joy to notice the connection between the fantastic Bauhaus designs and love's most ancient needs: if I saw a lamp, on which everything was tilted and left incomplete, which resembled every spider and gave off no light, then I saw love itself, caritas' precise diagnostic portrait, of the caritas that wants only the fragment and never the whole, because the whole is merely something fictitious, it's always design & goal, and the kiss can never engage with such textbook abstractions.

How curious that the women who live in rooms furbished in the taste of caritas-Cubism and mathematical eros functions, never assimilate anything from their surroundings, and if they kiss, they keep regarding that kiss as the second chapter of the encounter, which encounter is in its turn the fourth *a)* phase of the whole acquaintanceship, and that acquaintanceship is the first of the three major hypotheses that is meant to experiment with the idea of marriage, etc., although the upright mirror with drawers on only one side could teach them to cease making of every love action a victim of narrative symmetry and to enjoy it rather with purposeless repetition, as the upright mirror's half wing does — the drawers far surpass man's head, 20 drawer levels line up vertically: *ut psychologia veristica Veneris ac architectura decorativa riemannisata una et eadem sit.*[419]

second conclusion: detailed orchestral score from landscape scores,
the identity of music, caritas, and the syntax of madness

Because the girl's sentences referred uncertainly to the surrounding world (some words got glued to their meaning, moreover, wrapped themselves around their meaning like the twine with which they tie a horse to a pole: the more the capricious colt tries to escape, the more it ties its slave's chain around the pole; the more she tried to comb the fuzzy sentence-pigtails of her words, the more she got stuck and entangled in the first word, but all the while other words dodged their meaning, the way the birds that had somehow strayed into the room fly by the open window when they try to escape — a thousand times they fly against the wall but they miss the huge opening every time), and in this way the whimsical score notation was visible on the objects themselves (a lilac branch, to which meaning adheres tightly, has a completely different role in the landscape than a green toad which meaning only brushes by, like the accidental, peripheral wave of a wind blowing in a different direction): the whole world became like a conductor's score, with different instruments and tempo markings.

I needed no special artifice to assemble the musical score of my milieu redeeming hesitantly in different greens. The two main groups of strings and winds were supplanted by the earthly and celestial worlds. The staff landscape of flutes was signaled with the red clouds; oboes with the mist-shaped, green, yet sharply silver-lined and engraved-edged clouds; the clarinets with the golden-brown firmament itself; the bassoons with the night dusk exhaled by the valleys. If the girl hadn't spoken of them, all the landscape winds would have sounded in unison on one tone, ceaselessly, as though they were one sole instrument.

But the girl interrupted with, for instance, 'I'm getting cold,' and while she said this, with her arm she pointed toward the dark valleys beyond the meadow, but her eyes kept gazing at the sky, so the sunset's narrow gold covered her pupils & eyewhites. With this small sentence and skyward gaze the winds' inane unison ceased — the yellow sky, that is, the clarinet, sounded for the length of a semibreve, while the bassoons gave 8 staccato quavers. This means that the darkness that we imagine as a rule to be a homogeneous and infinite still wave ('... sans manches en satin gaufré blanc, lamé d'argent. On obtient ainsi un ensemble de petit soir extrêmement pratique')[420] was suddenly condensed into 8 shadow points and gave 8 morose grumbling sounds; in reality too there was 8 separate times a cool night under the yellow sunset sky. Eros' grammar finally managed to disjoin nature's impossible parallelism, its doltish tempo-solidarity.

Needless to say, this is not about 'comparison'; that is, it is entirely insignificant if the golden sky or the black water corresponds to the clarinets: the gist is, that the natural phenomena are metrically differently divided, and this I can only express with the help of musical scores. Thus the landscape score (the object-condensing & object-dilation resulting in the wake of love's true syntax) would look like this: the staff's first line — mountains; second line — waters; third — trees; fourth — flowers, etc. I put down on the flowers' line one semibreve, under which, let's say on the line of 'sky,' I enter 32 demisemiquavers; that is, one sole daisy exists throughout, while the vast firmament repeats 32 times during the same timespan.

The game is always interesting in cases where the larger thing (here, the sky) is only a fraction of the smaller (the daisy): it took the half-mad girl to suggest the love possibilities in landscape score writing with her whimsical words. In a landscape score everything can be carried out that is possible in a musical score: for instance, a 'theme' is first sounded by the sky, then the whole is carried over, diminished by the daisy, & the landscape's different components get into close arithmetic relation.

Of course we can represent not only landscape with this musical score-like method but also narrative scenes. If I want to tell the story of the Annunciation, to give one example, then in the score in place of the clarinets, flutes, violas & double basses there will be such things as clouds, angels, prie-dieux, Madonna, light ray, house, etc. Once orchestration is settled, all that remains to be done is the abstract mathematical work: on the line of the 'clouds' I will enter pizzicato crotchets, while in the line of 'prie-dieux,' rushing-undulating hemi-demi-semi-quaver triols will scream; the whole 'poetic' or concrete moment in this abstract technique is, when I decide what kinds of 'instruments' to use (Madonna, prie-dieux, clouds, etc.) — having solved this, all that's left is an abstract rhythmic work. But it's important to devise, with the help of film, a method by which these abstract landscape scores and narrative orchestral scores can be played and imagistically realized: so that a new side-theme compiled from half a Madonna & half a cloud can become visible in a continuously drawn-out, melting, dilating, permutating landscape: *ut psychologia veristica Veneris ac contrapunctica objectorum realiter dissolutorum una et eadem sit.*[421]

Every word of the girl pointed at a different direction, her sentences rolled apart, but those scattered words were like the waves cut in half behind a propeller — the more fragmented they were, the stranger their trajectories in the air, the more they drew attention to a central force. Where something falls apart, there some unitary force must also exist, where something crumbles into one thousand meaningless mosaic pieces, there one suspects one sole frightful energy. What is more, we feel positive 'intention' to be precisely what cuts apart so many connected things in its own unknown interest; not that I had any naïve-pious respect for destruction in general, but it's a fact that I've always felt composing to be a wuss, fidgeting placing here & placing there; where things meet

& stick together I always saw a smaller force, because everything is so primarily individual that whoever can put them together can only do so by forgetting their individuality, and this makes him completely wane-eyed and helpless; he whose every sentence naturally respects so the program of the grammatical *Latest Fashion and Gentleman's Syntax* magazine, does probably not feel the words' eternal pulling-apart force, he does not try to extend his own terror to the words foisted on him, which therefore can mean nothing to him anyway.

When I say such things I'm not a foe of convention but the frivolous middleman of predestination spite-æstheticism; what I want is not individual language (it must be rather loathsome — it probably looks like a daffodil-shaped rhinoceros) but the simple boycott of language, its ridiculing, its respectable parody. The flower bunch is only a sort of pseudo-composition, schoolbook-like unity, primer synthesis — but in the incongruous nettle leaves, wind-scattered red catchfly stamens, in the worn feather boa leaves of toadflax lying about on the roadside or caught in park benches and on my clothes, in those I see the wind's slender spine, the only selfish and determinate line, something that a flower bunch can never bring to mind. Perhaps such a lopsided, dynamic interpretation of composition is just the aging fuddy-duddy's cold and emaciated theoretical comfort for lost life vigor, but I see the young using similar compositional devices too (because structure can only ever be an extraneous technical conceit & never the well-nigh philosophical symbol of starry-eyed metaphysical unity): in the upper corner of their painting a huge button, and in the bottom corner, a bar of lather soap — in this way they can better, i.e., more uniformly express, for instance, the iffy joys of a honeymoon.

*third conclusion: the moral significance of perspective,
the identity of painting, caritas, and the syntax of madness*

That is also why I felt my companion's psyche to be utterly unified behind the scattered & meaningless words: the given meanings (a sort of diminished semantic eunuch) were located inside caritas' destructive stream (love and meaning are mutually exclusive) as the different objects in the pictures of the Italian pioneers of perspective — the new 'order' of perspective effected far wilder distortions on the words than the more naïve school which preceded it. Perspective disperses, therefore objects pushed apart in a hodge-podge will always suggest some unifying force which stands above us all. There are two kinds of distortions, one inner, flower-like, & one outer, accident-like. There are Madonnas (and these were not shaped by the soul of love — 'de perspectiva caritatis'), who under the Holy Ghost's linear shower don't bend toward the celestial lines' grace-optics but get lost in their own movements; it is the caving-in tilt of kneeling which twists their head, it's the palms joined in prayer which stiffen their ankles: the whole body is a Babel of gestures unable to find their place — a mimicry dictionary with only typos inside.

The speech and sentences of most girls show such distortions: the words go stale on the spot, they spread from the bacilli of their own meaning, as if consequence had been the best perishing conductor; even flowers look like nothing else but a single cell's form-onany, all the spread of petals is merely would-be-spread, for they are incessantly formulating the center, and however many color operations and petal multiplications they may perform, still only the flower-self, the blind idem features in all their exponentiations and logarithms alike. In contrast, there are Madonnas, castles, and equestrian battles where the Holy Ghost's stern wires (all these white grace strings can be tuned on a dove handle) distort, what is more, cut down the bodies in one sole direction; these Madonnas are the opposites of flowers, and they alone resemble love's mistailored words.

If meaning is unity, then variations of petals, stamens, colors and star follicles will be produced: every flower is the exact chemical end product of logical 'idem per idem'; but if unity is not meaning but some external force, then it will not allow the given separate forms to lose themselves into the Baroque sepsis of self-identity, but carry them in one streaming direction where they would fall apart and be prolonged beyond recognition, but every single atom of theirs could receive its own tiny direction-nude from that direction. Behind flower sentences love and the girl are always lost; a word's absolutely reasonable dictionary meaning constitutes such a strong electric charge that I can't penetrate among the electric cores of such high-voltage sentences, and love will have to slightly shift meanings from under the words, as if squeezing toothpaste from a tube: squeezing until the toothpaste trickles and the tube too is twisted and crumpled, and when they have so split from their logical anxiety, all that is left is the memory of one pure force.

At first sight one is tempted to believe that where word and meaning are perfectly one, there true simplicity dwells, yet in reality what dwells there is what I would call 'idem-Baroque,' that is, meaning's incessant self-fecundation and self-fertilization as the basic formula of logical incest (that's what the loveless girl's syntax cultivates); on the other hand, at first sight we are tempted to imagine those sentences whose relations of meaning are loose, where the words' contours and the patches of meaning do not overlap but intersect rather, to be complicated, even forced, although it is precisely in such sentences that ease, purity, and simplicity prevail: even in the simplest case, a meaningful relation of identity is a double-fold fabric of meaning, but where not even this relation features, there identity thins out to its half, and even among those elements there are gushes of air rolling hither and thither.

Perspective never allows any given form to swell into pathological tautology: love never touches on the inner meaning of words, it always rolls and brushes only their exterior layers into one common wave: *ut psychologia veristica Veneris ac prospectiva pingendi una et eadem sit.* [422]

with the half-idiot girl by the evening water and enveloping trees

But all the words the girl uttered were insignificant next to her gestures. When the world became grey and pink we reached a quiet water; I couldn't tell if it was a pond or small river — the bank was hidden from view behind the hanging branches of the trunkless trees. I could see at once that this small natural park corner was the exact copy of that castle corner which was the beginning of my love and later of my marriage, and which for the first time united into flaring religious inspiration the basest materialistic desire for property with the fairy-tale freedom of children's books. I knew that my life can hardly have another such important moment, because I could enjoy at the same time the materialist charms and the mad girl's meaningless love. In the first moment I wanted to run away, knowing that the few minutes I would spend here would offer me such plenitude of bitter happiness that it would destroy all my strength after this encounter — 'the marriage of madness and property' — I would no longer be either priest or Anglican, either poet or animal, either husband or murderer, but only phosphorescent inertia, beyond-morphine dream.

The trees enclosed us completely & the evening chirping of the birds sounded not in our direction but away from us, as if every single chirp had been a blasé tennis ball sent crashing across the black foliage netting, which bounces away unenergetically on the matte ground of the exterior world and can never fly back;

the invisible birds performed a strange distancing, propeller dream-cleansing, as though every throat had been a condensed drop of lemon juice which bleaches the daylight color stains, leaving in their place only pale rings, grey breaths. Every chirp devoured the evening and rendered it more ethereal, as if every tune had a separate, individual echo-orbit and resonance-alley — on the water no phonetic graphs, gilded-quivering fever charts of a single star could be seen, but the air filled with the various tremblings of late chirping, from small quivering zigzags to long drawn-out, wide, almost horizontal waves; and yet even more wearying than the sounds were the sudden stoppings in the chirrup, as if some large, invisible silence-fruit or silence-chestnut had dropped on our knees; our clothes, brows, hands were full of the silence-sequels of interrupted whines and chirping, which fell from the heights at unexpected speed. You felt that all the songs flew up to the firmament, bounced back from there, fell silent, died down, then fell on the trees in the form of black springs.

the fusion of private property, caritas, and nature in ultimate happiness

I perceived every leaf as if it belonged to me — here and now I couldn't have denied that the most primordial passion of my life was possession; I felt that it was a profoundly godless desire, not an idea at all but some incurable organic derailment. In this moment I affirmed the leaves' green hooks hanging down to the water with the warm, melting recklessness of dream, as my property; the small color-coughs of the tiny white marsh flowers, the large traps of shades stretching above the shrubs' small kiss-brushes as half-lowered black piano lids; the first star that vibrated its yellow pudenda on the dark green evening sky as the helpless sparks of a broken cigarette lighter: all these I felt to belong to me alone:

I didn't want to share anything with the poor, not even with the homeless God himself.

There is a point in lovemaking from where the embrace becomes forever irreversible, whether its consequence is excommunication, syphilis, or illegitimate twins — similarly, there is a degree of the dreamlike plenitude of ownership from where no return is possible to any legal morality — there is one direction only, to pervert ever tighter the sensuous closeness of property between myself and the flowers, myself and the birds, myself and the experimental star-virginity on the summer sky. What is then the love of property, that I would so happily accept damnation for its sake? Is it the extension of my blood circulation to the surrounding nature or objects?

The hysterical desire for property wasn't directed nearly as strongly at industrial objects as it was to flowers, water, leaves. Not far from me there was a slender Solomon's-seal in bloom, great evening Old Testament anagram of property: on one side the aristocratic leaves crept upward on its stem, all were grouped on one side with their black creases, black scent lungs, leaving the stem's other side free, where at the base of leaves small, pale, whey-rheumy fake flowers hung — all life, and first and foremost proprietorship, then love, somehow resembles this: on one side the huge shadow-fans, predestination's velvet-gloved muses or wire-veined caryatids lined up in solidarity, while on the other side a mangy biological squiggle, all kinds of moldy essence-doodles of life, of reproduction.

There is an incredible lack of proportion and regularity in every flower, therefore in every property-aphrodisiac as well — I thought, as my eyes bounced, like a myopic, lame old bee, from the leaves to the flowers, from the flowers to the leaves on the whirring wings of its desire. The flower inebriates because it continuously rouses us to imagine it magnified a thousandfold, and to have a home, like for instance the great, donkey-eared, funerary leaves growing on one side of the Solomon's-seal: my rabid desire for property is nothing but the desire for perfecting linguistic expression — for if the leaf's color, creases, placement, shape, clustering, twists and foreshortenings, individually and taken together, constitute my property, then these are a home that means a milieu of expression, but I can express myself with it only if every inch of it belongs to me, if I control them. I want to control them not in order to transform them according to my expressive needs, because the feeling of ownership, the moment it is projected into a flower, will anyway alter, transfigure it into my self.

I often mention the word 'I,' as if in the love of property some kind of naïve egoism or infantile philosophizing subjectivity were doing its rambunctious pranks, although what I am trying to express with the word 'I' is precisely something unknown, impersonal, something that is beyond me. For me the human being is either in a relation of ownership with nature or in no relation at all. When in Switzerland I glimpsed on my fellow vacationer the dress painted over in green, with its see-through dark polka dots, I felt it to be a dark green pond or green carp-globe, something of nature, only because I immediately transformed the dress into my property: my every glance at a girl is a virtual theft, so there was probably not one moment in my life when my hands were clean.

Dream was my great education in thieving: one by one I filched the women's handkerchiefs, flowers, hats and dogs and locked them away in my castle. What is the lake's booming dream-chaff worth if I cannot feel that all this is mine: how could the leaves' green be obvious if they are not kept spite-green in the cocoon of my consciousness?

Curiously I have felt these possession-trances, the candors and dulcors of property only hypothetically, for I have never had property. My wife received one of the family's castles for dowry, but as it turned out soon afterwards, it was so heavily mortgaged that it had to be rented out before I had the occasion to see it properly from the inside, and the tenants also used the park. In time one half of that park had to be sold, so my dreams came to nothing; but ever since I have turned all feeling of property into only-dream. I have been affirming much more positively and with more brutal aridity that property alone can make one happy, then when I used to take 'official' steps for obtaining that property. In fact it's something double-sided: in my dreams property is childhood's gorgeous flower, a nursery poppy — in my principles and daytime desires it is one arid thrill, desire to inherit, aborted stock exchange speculation.

What is the significance of nature? — I asked when I surveyed the grey leaves on the waterside, from whose capillary ends the huge and heavy seeds jutted out indomitably, like the flexibly popping-up scissors from the fold of small pocket knives — what is the meaning of these razor corn-ears, ribbon-shrubbery, snoring roots or croaking frogs, these minus-stamened lake water counter-stars: what is their meaning, what? Undoubtedly, that we may feel to be children and perverse at the same time, innocent and ready to commit any crime, sincere & absurdly lying, at once ever-living and beastly dead, at once the most ancient heirs of dreams and the failed little schoolboys of prose, goals and fatal going-astray.

In nature everything has the same meaning: for me, to kiss my companion had the same meaning as drowning her — to listen, under the kiss' melting wine-press, to the air laboriously oozing from my anxious mouth, or to the grunting bubbles surfacing from the water, mingled with the frogs' croaks, which a dying body lets out: in the bubble's little white foam-ring all the chemical 'svelteness' of oxygen merges into the deathly ruffling of the soul fighting to break free; it would have been all the same, to worship God with the wildest forms of self-mortification, paralyzing my whole body and leaving only as much space in my eyes as to see the straying little yellow star, and leaving only as much strength in my mouth to keep uttering non-stop, 'God, God, God' — or to roast my wife alive, garnish her body with poppies & consume it with this mad girl — both things would have had the same effect on me.

Psychoanalysis? Country bumpkin obtuseness? Presbyterian openness? Morphine tenor? Were these contrasts not ludicrous by this evening water: I knew in detail the life of all the weeds, the leafy pondweed, I remembered their numbers in the botanical guidebook, but I also knew that every night they would flutter in my dreams those eros-strong perpetuum mobiles which obscure the faces of my congregation, my wife's soul, the future of my son, or the certainty of one times one before my eyes. What is stronger in me: morphine, or the retired old botanist? What a nonsensical question on that evening and ever after. I have no health or sickness, I have only one great love, from the perspective of which it's all the same if to deliver the data is dream, or an official Cyperaceæ catalogue.[423]

Property was the inebriation of certainty — but the mad girl's unkempt, more and more ruffled sentences (sometimes the rye's protruding seed-hammers wriggle so in every direction) meant the inebriation of uncertainty. The principal trigger of bodily love is the lie; most wedding nights turn out so tedious, moreover, such irritatingly empty conventions, because the partners know one another already, they know each other's name, know the history of the preceding days, know the exactly laid-down program for the future — from this point of view even the so-called bohemian nuptials mean little more than bureaucratic red-tape grinding.

Sensuality needs vacuum, which should never be interwoven with the thick ropes of acquaintance; if a woman is called Margaret but she lies that her name is Mary, the kiss will be twice more galluptious than if to receive it were the real name. I lied that I was unmarried, I had a brother, a bishop in Peru, and that my greatest passion was playing the piano. When she took my hand I could distinctly feel that to receive that touch was the brother of the bishop in Peru, so I saw my hand independently from me, as though amputated by the lie — but all the same, the sensual pleasure shuddering through her like reeds still jumped over into my consciousness: it jumped, it wasn't simply conducted over like electricity. I wanted to see sensuous pleasure like an electric spark discharged through the air, in the absence of a wire, and so the lie became the mirror in which I could indeed see all my feelings objectivated.

We have a sensual and a rational sincerity: the two exclude each other. I either take on the role of the bishop in Peru (because I quickly realized that my companion found it every bit as likely as my being only the bishop's little brother) and place in this portrait all the lifelike traits of my perceptions, like a foreign country's motley joy-map; or I keep my Anglican priest's robes, but then all my joy will be distorted and turn to lie — personal identity kills sensual identity. The relation between sensuousness and personality should be like that of a red sword and a transparent, mismatched sheath: the shape of sword and sheath, red snake and glass cage is similar but they don't suit each other, they are like two wave-quivers that meet only now and then (this too is necessary: the momentary and chance coherence of individuality and sensuousness, for sparkling entropy-glitches to be produced), but their essence is necessarily different. I lied and the girl was idiotic: the difference between the two untruth techniques was visible to the naked eye, for every sentence of mine underwent a twofold reflection: first it was reflected from my consciousness, taken from the hesitant wave-wall of the mad girl's perception-uncertainty — truth became first a lie, then the lie turned into madness. But this logical phase delay was the psychic toilette, which alone could render us somehow akin to flowers and water, because in flowers too all we can see is that one leaf-shape is repeated by the next in the form of a lie (unless this is self-contradiction, but then again, in the flowers' morphology form-lying is the most basic exposition technique), then on the third branch the lie again juts out in a new phase, in madness' special form tempo. People are so ridiculous in woods or among waves, because they don't practice the more cunning linking methods of currents of meaning, although that is the only way in which they could become akin to flowers.

the analysis of lovemaking

We touched our faces to one another — her jawbone was so small that it fitted into my right eye-socket like some warm, concave blind-lorgnette. With my other eye I could see only big yellow flowers and clothes turning black. I felt on her the paradoxical desire that she would like to make love, but not with the movements of lovemaking; as if she were long used to the fact that everything is in the distance, in the conventional vacuum and distance of visions, so she kept lashing out with her hands and tilted her face and waist to me more out of lack of balance. The fact that from her body the conscious movements of arms and legs were directed at the distance or the wild flowers that happened to be next to us, and at me only her waist, back, and a hard-to-move part of her thighs, had a huge significance for me: just as the words assumed a Venus face because meaning was pulled out of them, as a letter from under an insufficiently sticky stamp, so the lovemaking became more blissful than any previous lovemaking because the movements and their purposefulness split off, the purpose of lovemaking crossed the girl's body through and through, this I could see and feel, but the lovemaking's consciousness of purpose grew an independent and unusable purpose mimicry, which trembled in her muscles like the poplars' leaf-quiver along the branches — the true purposeful movement fell only occasionally from among the trembling leaves, like a big, black, startled bird.

It was good to feel that not the whole body but only its heavier parts leaned to me, as if her waist alone were truly body, while the limbs & breasts were only the quivering & fugitive surfs of the will, or consciousness-dolphins surrounding the body's dark vessel. Body and will meet only at one point, on my face where her face touched; there I could feel on my skin the sparking current of will, not continuously but only with intermissions, but this movement now traversed through & through, and now unexpectedly completely filled with will caused an utterly different pleasure from her waist's hesitant towing-in into the thin but elastic harbor of my hips. She half turned her back to me, and to this back belonged as face not her face but the evening landscape, whose multitudinous greens the evening slowly covered in its own velvet.

On my face I felt the warmth of her shoulder-blades smelling of fabric, but before me I saw the reels' swaying candle-snuffers and the tree leaves thinning out skyward — as if someone in the next room were typing at breakneck speed while falling slowly asleep, so that I could hear the typewriter's rattle growing rare: that was the effect that the boughs' bald ends & thinning leaves had on me, here and there one sole long verge with a loose black leaf-sleeve on its end, like a sword plagiarized from a blazon, from whose point a Turkish head hangs.

So the portrait is the entire nature pressed together from sunset and private property, but the body is only a warm black weight surrounded by the small lacework movements of the will, directed elsewhere, but desired toward me.

The main value of all lovemaking is that weight and will, body and body-purposedness separate in it and run on two orbits; in this way sensuality becomes a genuine new creation of the body, and the will that wants to make love, an independent crystalline formula glistening in itself. Lovemaking is a permanent undulation from unconscious anatomy-mysticism toward any meaningless concrete detail of the outside world, and from there back to the muscles' Pelagian nonsense;[424] first I felt that after my kiss she crushes my whole mouth with one unknown movement of her accidentally twitching shoulder: I would have liked to smuggle my whole being into this movement like a metaphysical stowaway, but then all of a sudden the shoulders' volcanic soil ceased under my lips and I found myself in front of a large yellow tulip, which I hadn't seen before & which appeared there unaccountably, for it was the most striking flower in this narrow foliage-séparée whose every nook and cranny I have diligently vacuumed clean with my eyes. I didn't have much time to ponder this, for in the next moment the girl moved again and a whole unknown muscular mass was pressed to my face, which made me feel like a sickness in her body. During lovemaking, because we press our face and our eyes very close to the woman's body, every little movement appears like a huge rumpus, because if she happens to be wearing a dress with a very small check pattern, from up close even one millimeter shift to the side is enough for our eyes to shift from black to a white square, and that is nothing less than catastrophe.

Lovemaking doesn't take us closer to knowing the body but rather distances us from it; because all it can yield are black muscle atmospheres, measureless weight-milieus, or suddenly glimpsed foreign yellow tulips (nothing of a third order), we obviously need to give up all anatomical gain from the start. As a man from the country I immediately thought that this new counter-anatomy is precisely what makes the city and the woods look identical, this is what would cast an identical image of the strange equations of the leaves' shadow-compounds and the metropolitan shop windows.

Above us, horizontal layers of leaves, through which pink vertical flowers glided down; horizontality was absolute, verticality showed only at its incipient stage. The foliage was just like the lovemaking: weights and forms collided and suddenly new shapes were born, as with chemical metamorphoses — from one black leaf & a thin row of needles a reddish-transparent flower surfaced, like naked hydrogen emerging from shiny water, if natrium mixed in among its Neptunian muscles: one moment before it was a blue lake and now, Mariotte's fugitive & virginal muse.[425]

Within the foliage this equation plays out incessantly — two upward-jutting thorns turn into a horizontal shadow-loop, from the union of a shadow-loop and pink petal-wool a vertical sun-ladder forms, on which the sunset can walk up and down, so we would be naïve to imagine that a chestnut tree's leaves are all chestnut leaves, because every little vein grafts the tree, and a new shoot grafts that graft again, and so the tree dissolves into unknown leaves and impossible scents; fruit trees metamorphose into dimension poison and distances, into weather-beaten circles.

the identity of natural forms (leaves) and metropolitan mirror reflections

But did I not experience the same in the city when I last observed a woman standing in front of a shop window and trying to see something behind the huge glass pane, but not succeeding, because the light fell in such an angle that all she could see was herself; I stood one step from her and could easily discern the large pink hat in the shop window, so it was all the more amusing that a whole honeycomb box of reflections blocked the object from my neighbor's gaze; I could see nothing of the reflexes but I could have drawn exactly that rhombus prison from whose walls the curious girl got back only herself, like a slot machine from which you expect cigarettes but only get the coin you threw in, or with those newly fashionable photo frames which are made of mirror, so that the frame is always the squared face of the one looking at it. Those gestures were very important: now she squatted and shaded her left eye with her hand, then tiptoed, pressing her nose to the glass, but she needed to press her palm to the glass in an impossible position, to lure the reflex-armored object into this shadow trap. In vain: she now saw her own glove or hat, now her umbrella mixed with my black clothes (she too was surprised by the priest residue produced accidentally at the end of the chemical equation), and now cut sharply in two, because the smooth glass panes always cut mirror images with razor-sharp angles; they trace lines, roll spirals from shadows, multiply to infinity, and tune a positive scale from emptiness (one would imagine that 'umbrella' is some kind of antique Italian instrument, on which one can play tunes built up of minus luminosity).

More than anything else, they practice these tricks, and so they coincide exactly with the forest's conniving of leaves piled above each other: here above our heads the horse chestnut tree trembling with chemical valence-swarming also performed quaint lines, infinite spirals, and obsessive tautologies. The girl was like a blackbird, sizing up the pink flowers dropping in her palm; blinking, she looked up at the sky, trying to locate the bough from which they fell, but at such moments every flower is in place in the trees and not one is missing, so she felt that the tiny petals in her hand were some immoral profit, stolen coins, and would have liked to stick them back on the low branches, which bowed all the way down to the earth at about four meters from us: the forest surrounded us like a butterfly net.

I would have liked to heartily laugh at those who see a contrast between the forms of nature and those of metropolitan elegance, when foliage and a Cubist glass hotel display the same ground plan. Such toy words as 'vitalist mathematics' are extremely repulsive, but beneath the word's reductive grossness lurked my most important lovemaking conclusion.

> *the relativizing of order and disorder,*
> *the seceding of forms and contents*

Vogue or else the *Acta Mathematica* ought to publish a big album in which, on two facing pages, there would be invariably a mundane illustration and an image from nature, proving their structural identity, while on the bottom of the dual pages, in the center there would be a formula stating the golden rule they shared in common. On one page (*&* these pages would yield the picture book of caritas par excellence!) there would feature for instance a thousand-stair staircase, the infinite zigzag of stair serrations, on which an elegant woman is walking up among glass walls impregnated by sunshine — but on the other side one cornflower petal in color photograph, magnified: from the infinitely 'regular' stairs' algebraic cube-refrains a playful, flower-like light-and-shadow flora would grow, but from the cornflower's incandescent blue whim some non-geometrical linearity would emerge, so that stairs *&* petal create the same effect, it's only that with the stairs the whiff of that certain 'elementare Unordnung' comes from the rule,[426] while with the flower, order is the vapor of disorder.

When I came upon the realization here under the tree canopy, that there's not a hair's breadth of difference between urban and forest morphology, in fact I realized the meaninglessness of the words 'order' and 'disorder'; from order to disorder and another one that goes from the irregular to the rule, but these are just directions which depend on where I happen to be standing. When I looked up at the tree I had the impression that I have sucked it clean of the marrow of objectivity, and one reason why it is so similar to the grass halls' light-domino is the fact that I see it only as a membrane-statue, prepared only-surface, while 'life' itself, the so-called force, instinct, energy, etc. of nature lies about sucked out, independently of its foliage form, like a discarded big black raincoat. I also sucked out the soul, character, emotions of the woman walking up the stairs, like sucking out a hand from a glove, but even after the hand is withdrawn the glove keeps its form; similarly, the woman's character was lying somewhere in the ground floor wardrobe like homogeneous suitcase stuffing. Foliage and glass architecture, life and algebra, woman and leaf looked alike, because they all depicted thin surfaces only, infinitely small air cross-sections, whose content had fallen off and was lying about in a shapeless mass: 'form' (in the schoolbook sense of the word) became truly itself by lacking content and by faithfully preserving the most superficial exteriority of the exterior; whereas 'content' became more self-identical by congesting, knotting together and existing only as blind weight of inertia, straying far away from its form: forms and contents lived a two-homed life.

endnotes

214. A brand of decaffeinated coffee produced by the Bremen company Kaffee HAG (*Kaffee-Handels-Aktiengesellschaft*) founded in 1906, the first to produce and promote decaffeinated coffee.
215. German caricaturist, illustrator, painter, and poet Heinrich Christian Wilhelm Busch (1832–1908), whose *Max und Moritz: Eine Bubengeschichte in sieben Strachen* (*Max and Moritz: A Story of Seven Boyish Pranks*, 1865), written & illustrated by Busch, is a classic of German comic literature, many of whose satirical passages became dicta in colloquial usage.
216. The frequent English-language phrases have been set in both translated volumes in Scala Sans. All further instances of Szentkuthy's use of English will be signified with the same font.
217. Lat., 'Content-Venus,' 'Form-Venus.'
218. Lat., 'the two-eared chalice of the moving.'
219. Presumably a reference to the experimental biplane designed by Ambroise Goupy and Mario Calderara, known as "Goupy 2" (1909, Blériot factories), a successor of Goupy's earlier biplane & tri-plane designs in the first decade of the 20th century. Known for its distinctive & highly unusual design, the "Goupy 2" had an uncovered box-girder fuselage & a biplane tail unit, lending it a skeleton-like appearance.
220. The work of German humanist, mathematician, astronomer, & theologian Nicolaus Cusanus (1401–1464), *De Coniecturis* (*On Conjectures*) advocates for the use of presupposition and conjectures for a better understanding of truth.
221. Zeno was a member of the Eleatic pre-Socratic philosophical school founded by Parmenides in the city of Elea, in Magna Graecia.
222. Andrea Verrocchio's monumental equestrian statue of condottiero Bartolomeo Colleoni (1400–1475), Captain General of Venice, erected by the city in the latter's honor on Campo SS. Giovanni e Paolo ranks among the chief works of Renaissance sculpture.

223. Ger., "New Objectivity," a defining current in modernist German literature, architecture, the visual arts, and film in the 1920s and 1930s. The phrase goes back to a traveling exhibition of German post-Expressionist painting curated by Gustav Friedrich Hartlaub, first shown in 1925 at the Kunsthalle Mannheim, which brought together a miscellaneous array of post-World War I artists. Influenced by Italian metaphysical painting, Neue Sachlichkeit sets in its center the object, and in time further evolves in the direction of Bauhaus constructivism. In literature, Neue Sachlichkeit is characterized by a turn toward the unmediated exterior world, the use of a wide range of cinematic techniques, and a pronounced sense of the visual.

224. Ger., 'sound-object'; 'not-sound-projection'; 'empty sound-dimension.'

225. Ger., 'new human objectivity,' with a play on *Neue Sachlichkeit.*

226. Fr., 'Stay at the edge of the Psyche.'

227. Lat., 'logical agreement or accord in grammar.'

228. Ger., 'slovenliness.'

229. Advertisement in *Arts et métiers graphiques*, issues 37–42 (Hachard et cie., 1933).

230. Utopian anarchic socialist philosopher Charles Fourier (1772–1837) who projected the ideal cities or Phalanstères, the rationalist architecture of utopian communities.

231. Lat., 'missal of snow.'

232. Ger., upbeat, the opening part of a musical motif or phrase in an unstressed previous bar; metrically, the opening part of a musical phrase or piece that consists of less than one bar.

233. Popular German illustrated satirical monthly that appeared, under various titles, from 1889 to 1928, founded by illustrator Lothar Meggendorfer who remained its editor-in-chief until 1905.

234. *Intrigue and Love*, also known as *Luise Miller*, a five-act tragedy by Friedrich Schiller. In the autumn of 1931, while on his honeymoon, Szentkuthy saw a performance of the play in Berlin, directed by the innovative theater-maker Max Reinhardt, having Lili Darvas, the playwright Ferenc Molnár's wife, in one of the main roles. In a marathonic life interview given between January and May 1983, Szentkuthy recalls the scenography, an infinitely receding golden-

white corridor in perspective with a series of glass doors set behind one another. See *Frivolitások és hitvallások* ['Frivolities and Confessions'] (Budapest: Magvető, 1988) 102.

235. Probably a distortion of the repartee of First Minister von Walter, "Mein Sohn soll hereinkommen" ("My son is to come in") in Act I, scene VI, anticipating the appearance of Ferdinand in scene VII. Friedrich Schiller, *Love and Intrigue. A Bourgeois Tragedy*, tr. Flora Kimmich, with an Introduction by Roger Paulin (Open Book Classics, 2019) 27.

236. Lat., 'Of the incongruence of criteria'; 'Of empty perspectives.'

237. Lat., 'hereby we invite our city's most illustrious patron spirit.'

238. Swiss symbolist painter and sculptor Arnold Böcklin (1827–1901), whose works — especially *The Isle of the Dead* and his *Island of Life* — influenced a generation of European Symbolists, post-Romantic composers, and whom many Surrealists regarded as a forerunner.

239. Ger., 'with displacement, deferral.'

240. Influential neo-Kantian German philosopher Nicolai Hartmann (1882–1950), whose 1921 *Grundzüge einer Metaphysik der Erkenntnis* (*Foundation of a Metaphysics of Knowledge*) established him as a major European philosopher, and whose ontology and ethics stipulates value as a foundational concept. Hartmann's ontology differentiates between the general categories of *Seinsmomente* (moments of being), pertaining to *Dasein* (existence) and *Sosein* (essence); *Seinsweisen* (modes of being), pertaining to reality and irreality; and *Seinsmodi* (modalities of being), pertaining to possibility, actuality, & necessity.

241. It., 'small bridge.'

242. Lat., 'love's sole work.'

243. The Rhine maidens guarding over the Rhinegold in the opening scene of Richard Wagner's opera *Das Rheingold* (*The Rhinegold*, 1869), the first of the four operas of *The Ring of the Nibelung*.

244. Fr., textile, usually cotton fabric with a raised design, or embossed, mostly used in upholstery.

245. *CAEL. AQUAR. FONT. BRUGI. II* — Latin abbreviation of AQUARUM FONTIS BRUGI, suggesting an inscription on a plaque, presumably set up by a certain Cælius, marking the source of the river Breg/Brigach.

246. Lat., 'multiple-season, or many-age plant, or flower.'

247. The dark night of the senses, the first purgation of the soul, followed by the necessary purification of the spirit described in the poem *The Dark Night of the Soul* by Spanish mystical baroque poet San Juan de la Cruz (1542–1591).

248. The *Venusberg*, the subterranean abode of the goddess Venus, where the knight and Minnesänger Tannhäuser spends a year according to medieval legend and in Richard Wagner's opera, *Tannhäuser* (1845).

249. The town where a crucial episode of the future St. Ignatius Loyola's conversion to a spiritual life occurred: after a grave injury on the battlefield in 1521 put an untimely end to his military ambitions, the former warrior and gallant courtier immersed himself in spiritual reading, and at the very beginning of a planned pilgrimage to the Holy Land, reaching the town of Manresa in 1522, he gave up his worldly possessions for an ascetic, mendicant life; it was there that his *Spiritual Exercises* were conceived.

250. "Darkness beyond radiance" (in 17th-century poet Henry Vaughan's translation, "dazzling darkness"): a linguistic hyperbole and oxymoron used by the 5th-century Neo-platonist Pseudo-Dionysius Areopagite in his treatise *On Mystical Theology*, to render a quality of infinite-finite darkness, or hyper-luminous darkness, of the divinity.

251. Fr., 'China makes me nervous.'

252. Swiss-made soluble malt extract containing condensed milk powder, vitamins, minerals, and cocoa powder, originally developed for convalescent patients, later widely advertised as a dietary supplement for building strength & immunity. The original Ovomaltine was produced by the Berne company Wander AG from 1904.

253. Ger., 'style development.'

254. German mathematician David Hilbert (1862–1943), one of the founders of mathematical logic, whose contributions to invariant theory, the calculus of variations and algebraic number theory were decisive for the development of early 20th-century mathematics. His mathematical system relies on the Kantian understanding of mathematics as a set of synthetic a priori judgments describing the structure of space, time, and the constructions therein.

255. See note 228.

256. Lat., "*Simple* means nothing in the simplicity which is the eternal connection (or conjugation) of Consciousness and Infinity."
257. German-Polish Jesuit theologian, philosopher Erich Przywara (1889–1972), a pioneer of ecumenical Catholicism, who sought to reconcile Catholicism with modern philosophy, especially phenomenology, but also with Heidegger's ontology. In his 1932 *Analogia Entis*, a likely influence on the young Szentkuthy's work, as evidenced in many passages of *Prae*, he repurposes St. Thomas Aquinas' distinction between essence and existence, as defining of all created reality and its difference from the Creator.
258. Ger., 'Contributions to a Manichean æsthetic.'
259. Ger., 'armored Venus.'
260. Ger., 'by the book.'
261. Lat., 'kind, amiable Teuton,' with a possible play on the Hungarian *komisz* (whose pronunciation is identical to comis), 'vicious.'
262. The German Symbolist poet Stefan George, inspired by Nietzsche, framed the ideal of a new Germany of the aristocratism of the spirit, modeled on ancient Greek imagery and populated by figures of beauty who incorporate the lived reality of divinity, especially in the volume *Der siebente Ring* ("The Seventh Circle"). The medieval historian Ernst Kantorowicz (1895–1963), a member of the George-Kreis, an influential intellectual grouping organized around George, dedicated a book, *Kaiser Friedrich der Zweite* ("Emperor Frederick II," 1927), to the 13th-century king of Italy and Sicily and Holy Roman Emperor of the Hohenstaufen dynasty, one of the proto-Renaissance medieval rulers of an extraordinary culture, stressing the modernity of the monarch's political and cultural vision. The emperor, who resurrected the idea that the Holy Roman Emperor is the successor to the Roman emperors, while also being, like the Byzantine emperors, God's representative or "viceroy" on earth, had numerous conflicts with the papacy, being excommunicated three times and vilified as a heretic and Antichrist; he often features in Szentkuthy's work.
263. Probable reference to the 11th-century Norman archway of St. Woolos Cathedral in Newport, Wales, later incorporated into the expanded nave. The semicircular archway's chevron or 'dog-tooth' orders cut in stone, recognizable in the description, are a typical ornament of

Anglo-Norman architecture, widespread in 11th–12th century parish churches throughout Norman Britain.

264. Fr., 'bitter pleasure, cruel joy, pathic irony, blue despair, mixture of the serious and the frivolous, of dignity and playfulness, of the feminine and the brutal, of the ecclesiastical and the roguish.'

265. Fr., 'curious mix of carriage and bird.'

266. Fr., 'this flower of P ... is a criticism of our time.'

267. Fr., 'criticism of time.'

268. Fr., 'Mallarmé, or the Second Precision.'

269. Fr., 'it will work out, it will work out.'

270. Bolognese painter, goldsmith Francesco Francia (ca. 1447–1517) was close to the Ferrarese school of painting, characterized by the primacy of drawing, being influenced especially by Ercole de' Roberti and Lorenzo Costa, with whom he collaborated in his early years; from 1506 he became court painter of the Gonzaga in Mantova, and his style shows the impact of Perugino and the early Raffaello.

271. Fr., 'true morality mocks morality,' from Pascal's *Pensées*: "La vraie éloquence se moque de l'éloquence. La vraie morale se moque de la morale, c'est-à-dire que la morale du jugement se moque de la morale de l'esprit qui est sans règles ... Se moquer de la philosophie c'est vraiment philosopher." In A.J. Krailsheimer's English translation: "True eloquence makes light of eloquence, true morality makes light of morality; that is to say, the morality of the judgment, which has no rules, makes light of the morality of the intellect ... To make light of philosophy is to be a true philosopher." In Section I, *Thoughts on Mind and Style*: no. 4, *Mathematics, Intuition*, Blaise Pascal, *Pensées*, tr. A.J. Krailsheimer, with an Introduction by T.S. Eliot (New York: Dutton, 1958) 3.

272. Ger., 'Willi, be careful!'

273. Fr., 'finally, face to face.'

274. The name is an 18th-century botanical term for *Tilia cordata Mill*, the European small-leaved lime or linden tree; its use as a female proper name may hark back to Joyce's playful catalogue of the wedding guests at the nuptials of Miss Fir Conifer and John Wyse de Neaulan, all derived from the names of trees, in the 'Cyclops' episode of *Ulysses*.

275. Lat., 'in the beginning were the birds.'

276. Gr. Ἀνάγκη, inevitability, necessity, also the word for fate or destiny in Old Greek, is personified by one of the principal deities in early Greek mythology, the sister and consort of Chronos and (in some sources) mother of the Moirai or Fates, whose attribute is the spindle.
277. Italian actress Eleonora Duse, one of the defining figures of theater at the turn of the 19th and 20th centuries, signature impersonator of Ibsen's female characters, known for her intense psychological absorption in the figure.
278. The Phrygian mountain nymph Oenone, the abandoned first wife of the Trojan prince Paris, features in many literary works, including Ovid's *Heroides*, & Tennyson's famous poem "The Death of Oenone."
279. A botanical name, meaning bugle or bugleweed.
280. Potentilla is the name of the family of cinquefoils, or tormentils.
281. Fr., 'Cabinet of "character" for gentlemen: occupied.'
282. Ger., 'I don't want these half-stuffed masks but rather the doll.'
283. Lat., 'Rome has spoken, the case is closed.'
284. Lat., little bird Rosalynd,' with an allusion to the fugitive heroine of Shakespeare's *As You Like It*, who disguises herself as a young man, Ganymede.
285. Lat., 'to be printed'; 'to be bemoaned.'
286. Fr., 'Oh charm of my golden youth.'
287. Fr., 'Oh, bitter taste of distinction.'
288. Fr., 'spoiled children.' See Victor Hugo, "Les Enfants Gâtés," the most frequently anthologized poem of the late volume *L'Art d'être grand-père* (1877), often seen as Hugo's most saccharine. A celebration of the untrammeled freedom of childhood, the poem can also be read as a political statement in the context of the republican struggles in the France of Napoleon III, advocating against a rigid education system that it parallels to a tyrannical state and ruler.
289. Ger., 'In a given point in space, [an object's] mass is nil.'
290. Lat., 'variety is not the spice of life, variety doesn't delight,' a play upon the adage *varietas delectat*.
291. Ger., 'late style, the style of old age.'
292. Lat., 'O, circumscribed wound, death's pedantry.'

293. Lat., 'Winter-Janus.'
294. Lat., 'the profit, lucre of flesh.'
295. Lat., 'I am a priest.'
296. Ger., 'intellectual history, the history of ideas.' *Geistesgeschichte* was a dominant, trans-disciplinary field and current of cultural history that shaped German thought in the late 19th and early 20th century; it combined the history of religions, cultural history, literary and art history, the history of sciences, and sought to outline worldviews, intellectual frameworks dominating a culture at a given period. Szentkuthy was conversant with the writings of many historians of ideas of the German *Geistesgeschichte* school, among them, of Wilhelm Dilthey and Ernst Robert Curtius.
297. Ger., 'from down upwards.'
298. Lat., 'induction to pain,' to the pattern of *reductio ad absurdum*.
299. English polymath, anthropologist, proto-geneticist, psychologist & propagator of eugenics Sir Francis Galton (1822–1911) devised a technique of composite portraiture — superimposing the photographs of different individuals and creating an average face — as a tool for visualizing different human 'average' or 'central types.' He first applied this method to portraits of convicts and attempted to establish correlations between certain facial features and distinct types of criminality; later he experimented with composite portraiture of mental patients, tuberculotic patients, & members of races regarded as inferior.
300. Pseudo-Latin, 'Golden-Mouthed Paradise-bungler Adam,' playing on the epithet of the Church Father St. John Chrysostom and the mongrelized, mock-Latin version of the German-Hungarian *paccer*, 'bungler, botcher.'
301. Lat., 'painting cannot be not truth.'
302. Fr., 'as it should be.'
303. Lat., 'essence/substance is equal to a fugue composed on the basis of its chance traits.'
304. Lat., 'Anacapri undulates in blue.'
305. English philosopher Bertrand Russell (1872–1970) sought to ground philosophy in rigorously formalist analysis; positioning himself

against philosophical idealism, which stipulates that the object of cognition is inherently in relation with the subject of cognition, Russell attempted to make mathematics and logic into the foundation of philosophy, and thereby work out a methodology for philosophy that could access and formulate the irrefutable truths not subject to the contingencies of cognition and sense experience. In *Principles of Mathematics* (1903) and in the three-volume *Principia Mathematica* (1910–1913) he treats mathematics in its entirety as logic, which can thus be emancipated from the taint of subjectivity; similarly, a philosophical methodology based on mathematical logic could be pitted against metaphysical thought. In the former work he grounded the concept of the number in a mutual correspondence of equivalence: accordingly, if such a relation exists between x and y, then no other term stands in an identical relation with y, while x stands in no identical relation with any other term. In *Principles of Mathematics*, however, he discovered a contradiction at the heart of the system of logic, which became known as Russell's Paradox. The paradox, which Szentkuthy seems to reference repeatedly in *Prae*, is as follows: some classes are members of themselves (e.g., the class of all classes that are countable), while some are not (e.g., the class of all men). The logical problem occurs if we attempt to construct the class of all classes that are not members of themselves. If we ask of this class, "Is it a member of itself?," we are faced with a contradiction: if it is, then it is not, and if it is not, then it is. In order to construct a system of logic that is immune to paradox, in *Principia Mathematica* Russell proposed a complex theory, the ramified theory of types.

306. Lat., 'the same' in masculine, feminine, and neuter.

307. Lat., 'tautology's grandiloquent blossom.'

308. See note 296.

309. Fr., "the afternoon of an Anglican faun," with a reference to Stéphane Mallarmé's poem *L'Après-midi d'un faune* ("The Afternoon of a Faun," 1876), a dream evocation of a faun's reverie and a meditation on the creative impulse, later interpreted musically by Claude Debussy in the symphonic poem *Prélude à l'après-midi d'un faune* (1894).

310. French academic genre and portrait painter Jean-Baptiste Greuze (1725–1805), famous for his saccharine portraits of children and young girls.

311. Lat., 'nothing stands in the way,' the certification of the official censor of the Roman Catholic Church that a book contains nothing opposed to faith and morals.

312. Philologist, critic Herbert Cysarz (1896–1985), a prominent exponent of *Geistesgeschichte*, loosely associated with the Stefan George-Kreis, was a professor of German literature in Prague from 1927, & from 1938 in Munich. He was one of the first critics to recognize Franz Kafka's value and importance for world literature. The young Szentkuthy read his 1924 volume *Deutsche Barockdichtung. Renaissance, Barock, Rokoko* ('German Baroque Poetry. Renaissance, Baroque, Rococo'), which had a strong impact on his literary sensibility; in *Frivolities and Confessions*, the author also recalls attending a reading by Cysarz at a world literature congress organized in Budapest, at which Benedetto Croce also participated (260–261). From the 1920s, Cysarz harnessed his discipline, Germanistik, for the struggle for political rights of the increasingly radicalized German ethnic minority in the Sudetenland, Czechoslovakia; after moving to Germany, in 1940 he joined the NSDAP. However, he was soon denounced as promoting pacifist and Jewish authors, as well as interpretations — of Nietzsche, among others — which couldn't be reconciled with the party line, leading to his marginalization at Munich University. Given his previous involvement with Nazism, after 1945 his academic career came to an end.

313. Pieter de Hooch (1629–1684) was one of the most significant Dutch Golden Age genre painters; the characteristic feature of his paintings is of setting his scenes of domestic life in interiors where several rooms open into one another, allowing the viewer a perspective inside the house.

314. It., 'currency exchange.'

315. A London-based quarterly magazine of theology & philosophy, one of the leading journals in the field, published between 1902 & 1968.

316. Ger., 'perceptibility of non-Euclidean geometry.'

317. Florentine painter and mosaic artist Cimabue, or Cenni di Pepo, active in the second half of the 13th century (ca. 1240–1302), the most important Italian painter of the generation before Giotto, and the first artist of the late 13th-century Italian Proto-Renaissance that saw a break with the Byzantine models.

318. The most important English architect of the early modern period, Inigo Jones (1573–1652) left his imprint on the architecture of London by introducing the forms of the Vitruvian-inspired Italian Renaissance to England; a decisive figure in the history of theatrical stage design and considered to be the first to introduce scenery and moving scenery on the stage, as well as experimenting with the use of stage lighting & curtains, he frequently collaborated with Ben Jonson.
319. Fr., 'crimpled fabric,' as of crêpe; embossed fabric.
320. Fr., 'how do you like it?'
321. Lat., 'verse meter of epithalamium, nuptial ode.'
322. Early Romantic German composer Carl Maria von Weber's popular piano rondo *Aufforderung zum Tanz* (*Invitation to the Dance*, op. 65, 1819), orchestrated by Berlioz in 1841.
323. Swiss composer and pedagogue Émile Jacques-Dalcroze (1865–1950) developed eurhythmics as a method of teaching musical concepts through movement, emphasizing creativity & improvisation. See also note 416.
324. The noun television refers to a theoretical system to transmit moving images over telegraph or telephone wires. The technology was developed in the 1920s & 1930s. Source: Etymonline.com
325. Fr., intricate ornamental pattern of engraving or embossing densely intersecting or overlapping spirals or other geometrical shapes, often used in banknote printing; term for a technique of trimming embroidery derived from Ger. *schlingen*.
326. See note 232.
327. Lat., 'The Existent / Being dwells in the other.'
328. Ger., 'minor art,' the term applied in the late 19th century to the decorative arts.
329. Ger., 'one cannot walk under Jesus with impunity.'
330. Ger., 'clockface.'
331. Lat., 'Euler, set us free!' Swiss mathematician and polymath Leonhard Euler (1707–1783), groundbreaking innovator in mathematics, especially in the domains of complex analysis or infinitesimal calculus, who introduced much modern mathematical terminology, including the notion of mathematical function.

ENDNOTES

332. Don Giovanni's abandoned lover, who repeatedly and unsuccessfully attempts to persuade him to repent for his sins, in Mozart's opera *Don Giovanni*; in the finale of act 2 she arrives, masked, to Don Giovanni's house, beseeching him to repent, only to witness Don Giovanni's death and damnation in an act of supernatural punishment at the hands of the Commendatore he has slain, and whose stone statue calls him to account.

333. Fr., 'pastorals.'

334. One of the most prolific British writers of crime fiction, adventure stories, fantasy novels in the first decades of the 20th century, Edgar Wallace (1875–1932) was also the author of dozens of Hollywood screenplays, among others, of *King Kong* (1933).

335. Fr., 'oh precarious kingdom of my fidelity.'

336. French mathematician & engineer Jean-Victor Poncelet (1788–1867) was a pioneer of projective geometry, author of Poncelet's closure theorem, which stipulates that a polygon, which is inscribed in one conic section that circumscribes another one, must be part of an infinite family of polygons that are all inscribed in and circumscribe the same two conics. This theorem can be proved by using an elliptic or hyperbolic curve.

337. Fr., 'capitalist of salvation, capitalist of grace.'

338. German mathematician Bernhard Riemann (1826–1866) made decisive contributions to differential geometry, analytic number theory, and formulated the integer. Riemannian geometry concerns itself with the differential geometry of surfaces; its extensions enabled the mathematical formulation of the behavior of geodesics on different surfaces, and ultimately, Einstein's theory of relativity.

339. Closing line of Stéphane Mallarmé's poem 'Toute l'âme résumée' (1914): "Le sens trop précis rature / ta vague littérature" — in Henry Michael Weinfield's translation, "Too fixed a sense erases / your art in its faint traces." "The entire soul evoked," in Stéphane Mallarmé, *Collected Poems*, tr., commentary by Henry Michael Weinfield (University of California Press, 2011) 77.

340. French theologian and poet François Fénelon (1651–1715), archbishop of Cambrai and tutor of the royal infants under Louis XIV, implied in the doctrinal debate over Quietism where he held a

moderate position, was the author of one of the most popular books of the 18th century, *Les Aventures de Télémaque* ("The Adventures of Telemachus," 1694).

341. Gr., 'sweet cow'; 'many cows' — the first is the name of a series of mythological figures, including the only Niobid spared by Apollo and Artemis' arrows; the second is also a theonym of Persephone or Artemis. Arrètos (ἄρρητος): 'unspoken, unsaid, not to be spoken, not to be divulged,' used of sacred mysteries.

342. Gr., κάθοδος: 'descent, return.'

343. Ger., 'morass.'

344. Fr., 'dangerous liaisons,' the title of Choderlos de Laclos' famous 1782 epistolary novel, in which the exploitative seduction games of a couple of former lovers belonging to the French aristocracy are reported from several viewpoints in the letters of a group of characters.

345. Lat., 'no third [possibility] is given,' the principle of the excluded middle in logic, which states that for every proposition, either this proposition or its negation is true.

346. River in Switzerland, a tributary of the Hinterrhein, and the name of a district in the canton of Graubünden that it crosses.

347. Ger., 'object, thing.'

348. Basedow, or the Graves-Basedow disease, named after German doctor Karl Adolph von Basedow (1799–1854), is the thyroid gland's autoimmune disease of hyperthyroidism, the most easily recognizable symptom of which is eye bulging.

349. The removable pneumatic tire was patented by Michelin in 1891.

350. Gr., ἅπαξ λεγόμενον ('being said once'): word or expression that occurs only once in a given text, in the corpus of a given author, or in the written documents of a language.

351. Athenian courtesan in the 4th c. BC, allegedly the model of the painter Apelles' *Aphrodite Anadyomene*, as well as of Praxiteles' *Aphrodite of Knidos*. A gilded bronze statue of her, also by Praxiteles, was reputed to have stood near the Delphi oracle. Famously, she was charged with impiety and defended by one of her lovers, the orator Hypereides, who bared her before the judges, using her beauty to move them. The scene became the subject of many literary and art works.

352. Lat., 'Is reason the colloidal form of the senses?'
353. Lat.-Gr., 'he who is theomorphic — i.e., god-shaped — is stingy.' Harpagon (from Lat., *harpago*, 'hook') is the protagonist of Molière's comedy *The Miser, or The School for Lies*, a tyrannical sexagenarian pater familias obsessed with his amassed wealth and going to laughable lengths to save expenses.
354. Ger., 'the science of harmony,' a comprehensive concept of music theory that concerns itself with the intervals and chords in the tonal system, different tonalities. With the appearance of polyphony, its focus shifted to the simultaneous sounding of various voices and to counterpoint.
355. Fr., 'cosmic joke.'
356. Ger., "Critique of Pure Woman-Chromatics," with a play on the title of Immanuel Kant's *Critique of Pure Reason* (*Kritik der reinen Vernunft*).
357. Translingual joke on the French *pourrite*, an erroneous, child's language version of *pourrie* or *pourri* (balls-up, done-in), with an additional play on *harmonia præstabilita*, 'originary, pre-existing harmony,' suggesting 'originally botched-up harmony.'
358. Lat., 'morning being.'
359. Originating in a phrase of Canadian politician George Eulas Foster, the term describes the pervasive 19th-century diplomatic and political practice of Britain, of non-involvement in the conflicts and alliances of European powers, continued until the 1902 Anglo-Japanese Alliance and the 1904 Entente Cordiale with France.
360. Fr., 'Celine's cemetery.'
361. Lat., 'the new law [is] the beauty that stems from twin-like similitude.'
362. Lat., 'love of death, God's beauty, the impossibility of matter, warped, or twisted, argumentation/demonstration.'
363. Lat., 'heaven's heavenly sexuality.'
364. The 'cultivated style' of *Culteranismo* or Góngorismo, the dominant style of Spanish baroque poetry alongside *Conceptismo*. Aimed at an erudite coterie of readers, the ostentatiously ornamental *estilo culto* was characterized by a proliferation of recondite allusions, striking word coinages, complex metaphors, elisions, chiasmus, as well as highly complex syntax.

365. Gr., εὐδαιμονία ('good spirit,' state of happiness, welfare), in classical Greek philosophy the supreme good, the ability for living a good life, the perfection of virtue; in Aristotle's *Nicomachean Ethics* it is the highest good for humans and the most desirable life, associated with pleasure, political activity, and a philosophical life.
366. Fr., 'double Dutch' or 'gibberish.'
367. Lat., 'himself.'
368. Ger., 'impossibility of numbers.'
369. Gr., Ἁμαδρυάδες, a dryad, a species of nymph, bonded to a tree, that lives in the tree either as a spirit or as a live being. The term also designates three species of animals that were considered to have a strong connection to trees — the king cobra (*Hamadryas hannah*, later *Ophiophagus Hannah*), the Hamadryas baboon, native of Asia Minor, as well as the cracker butterfly, a species that camouflages itself among the leaves on which it feeds.
370. Ger., 'a bio-organic understanding, conception of the non-homogeneous body of numbers.'
371. Lat., 'the sufferings of the existents.'
372. Lat., 'curious question about the theory of combinatory.'
373. Swiss mathematician Jakob Bernouilli (1655–1705) wrote the first mathematical treatise devoted entirely to the theory of probability, which also became a foundational work in combinatorics and permutation: *Ars Conjectandi* ('The Art of Conjecture'). *Ars Conjectandi* was published posthumously in 1713 by the author's nephew, Nicolaus Bernouilli (1687–1759), who worked further in the field of the practical and legal applicability of probability. One of the combinatory cruxes addressed by the latter, & independently also solved by Leonhard Euler (1707–1783) is known as the problem of the misaddressed letters: supposing that someone writes n letters & mixes up their envelopes randomly, what is the probability that all the letters are in a wrong envelope — & how many different ways are there for the letters to be in a wrong envelope? The solution to the problem is a sum that gives the number of possible "derangements," that is, the permutations where none of the members of a set are in their original position. The calculated probability approximates to $1/e$ for large numbers. See: Ari Ben-Menahem, *Historical Encyclopedia of*

Natural and Mathematical Sciences, Vol. I: (Berlin-Heidelberg-New York, Springer, 2009) 1048–1049; Eli Maor, *The Story of a Number* (Princeton: Princeton University Press, 1994) 37. Incidentally, Jakob Bernouilli recorded much of the results and theorizing of the future *Ars Conjectandi* in his diary that bore the title *Meditationes*.

374. See notes 331 and 373.
375. Concettismo, or Conceptismo in Spanish, was a current in 16th–17th-century Baroque poetry that influenced the English Metaphysical poets; its most important representative is Francisco de Quevedo Villegas (1580–1645). According to its early theorist, the Jesuit Baltasar Gracián (*Agudeza y arte del ingenio*, 1647), Concettismo celebrates *conceit*, wordplay, poetic inventiveness, and shows a marked metaphysical bend. As opposed to Culteranismo, a contemporaneous tendency in Spanish Baroque poetry, as well as to Góngorism, which celebrated artificial language games and play with language, Conceptismo, sought to condense in a laconic, elegant form a sophisticated and ingenious idea, establishing surprising relations between objects and themes, while foregrounding the near-hermetic difficulty, opacity of the poetic language.
376. Fr., 'ready voltage.'
377. Gr., 'matter of woman.'
378. Lat., 'anatomy truly meet and just [is]: the shadow,' with a play on the words of the opening hymn of Catholic liturgy, 'vere dignum et justum est' ('[The Lord] is truly meet and just').
379. In projective geometry, Pascal's theorem states that if on a conic six arbitrary points are chosen and joined by line segments in any order to form a hexagon, then the hexagon's three pairs of opposite sides meet on a straight line, called the Pascal line.
380. Reference to the Geissler tube, an early form of gas-discharge tube designed to demonstrate the luminous effects of an electric discharge passing through a low-pressure gas between two electrodes. It was invented in 1858 by German physicist Heinrich Geissler (1814–79).
381. Paris fashion house created in 1914, which also produced prêt-à-porter clothes.
382. The Técla laboratory in Paris produced cultured pearls, widely advertised in the 1920s.

383. Fr. and Ger., 'reason-realistic color logic.'
384. Inspired by the religious teachings of Cornelius Otto Jansen (1585–1638), the Roman Catholic reform movement of Jansenism sought to reconcile free will and human agency with St. Augustine's doctrines of predestination and the necessity of divine grace, stressing the inherent corruption of man. In the 17th century the movement spread to France, the Low Countries, and Italy; its most famous adherent was Pascal, who wrote an apology of Jansenist teachings in his *Provincial Letters* (1656–57). On account of its closeness to Calvinist Protestantism's doctrine of predestination, the movement was proclaimed a heresy by Innocent X in 1653 and came under increased attack in France during Louis XIV's reign, leading to its gradual eradication.
385. Gr., 'woman beyond love.'
386. Lat., 'love desire is situated this side of love.'
387. Ger., 'order theory,' classification science, the science of ordering & retrieving information.
388. Fr., 'very shiny patina blue satin.'
389. Lat., 'non-conformist aphroneira.'
390. Lat., "Let reason be the phosphorescence/radiance liberated from the conditions that are forever changing due to the mind's hysteria born among hypocritical imaginings."
391. Lat., 'the essence of the image is in its being not image.'
392. Fr., Szentkuthy's neologism, perhaps 'intimate logicizing.'
393. Gr., 'a-political animal,' from πολιτικὸν ζῷον, 'political animal, social animal' concerned with the affairs of the community (derived from *polis*, city), Aristotle's definition of the distinctly human in *Politics*.
394. Fr., 'hieratic clumsiness.'
395. Lat., 'the plural of pain.'
396. Italian physicist and mathematician Evangelista Torricelli (1608–1647), Galilei's pupil, one of the first scientists to recognize that the atmosphere has weight and exerts a pressure on surfaces; his early investigations into atmospheric pressure led to the invention of the suction pump and the barometer.
397. Monsieur Jourdain, the comic would-be-gentleman protagonist of Molière's *Le Bourgeois Gentilhomme* (*The Bourgeois Gentleman*)

learns in Act 2, Scene 4 with great astonishment from his teacher of philosophy that all his life he has been speaking in prose. The phrase quoted here features, however, in *La Jalousie du Barbouillé*, Act III, Scene VII: "C'est la fidélité que tu m'avais promise? Sans ma feinte, jamais tu n'eusses avoué Le trait que j'ai bien cru que tu m'avois joué. Traître…" "And this is the fidelity you promised me! Had I not deceived you, you would never have acknowledged what I suspected you instantly of having done. Wretch!" *The Dramatic Works of Molière*, tr. by Charles Heron Wall, Vol. I (London: George Bell and Sons, 1876) 124.

398. *Kritik der Urteilskraft*, the *Critique of Judgment* (1790), is Immanuel Kant's third Critique, after the *Critique of Pure Reason* and the *Critique of Practical Reason*, divided into two parts discussing aesthetic and theological judgment; it is in this book that Kant theorizes the concept & sense of beauty.

399. Ger., 'pepper garden.' In the conclusion to the fourth moment of the aesthetic theory of *Critique of Judgment*, concerned with the theory of taste, and before introducing the theory of the sublime, Kant contrasts the inferior aesthetic pleasure offered by stiff regularity with the pleasure offered by that "with which Imagination can play in an unstudied and purposive manner." He gives as example a pepper garden, a compromise between unbound, irregular form-generation and objects which display a regularity of form, only to affirm the supremacy of untrammeled natural beauty, not subject to artificial constraints: "Marsden in his description of Sumatra makes the remark that the free beauties of nature surround the spectator everywhere and thus lose their attraction for him. On the other hand a pepper-garden, where the stakes on which this plant twines itself form parallel rows, had much attractiveness for him, if he met with it in the middle of a forest. And hence he infers that wild beauty, apparently irregular, only pleases as a variation from the regular beauty of which one has seen enough. But he need only have made the experiment of spending one day in a pepper-garden, to have been convinced that, once the Understanding, by the aid of this regularity, has put itself in accord with the order that it always needs, the object will not entertain for long, — nay rather it will impose a burdensome constraint upon the Imagination. On the other hand, nature, which

there is prodigal in its variety even to luxuriance, that is subjected to no constraint of artificial rules, can supply constant food for taste." Kant's *Critique of Judgment*, tr. with notes by J. H. Bernard (London: Macmillan, 1914) 99–100.

400. Fr., 'eternal dish.'
401. Lat., 'it's allowed, it's not allowed.'
402. Ger., 'view, perspective.'
403. Lat., 'all-living life.'
404. Fr., 'O, black butterfly of my pious hope.'
405. Ger., 'I' or 'self'; 'soul.'
406. See note 238.
407. The Alumbrados ('Enlightened') were adherents to a 16th–17th century mystical sect in Spain, persecuted by the Inquisition, who believed that the human soul had already attained a sufficient degree of perfection to allow communication with the Holy Spirit, therefore all participation in the rites of religious life, just as good deeds, were unnecessary for salvation.
408. Ger. 'hunter'; probable reference to the ablist, vitalist ideal body propagated by eugenics.
409. Two would-be précieuses from the country in Molière's one-act satire *Les Précieuses ridicules* (*The Affected Young Ladies*), who come to Paris out of a desire for a life of elegance, and are outwitted and exposed by valets masquerading as masters.
410. Lat., '[is] sad after,' from the saying 'post coitum omne animal triste est,' 'after coitus all animals are sad,' attributed to the Greek physician Galenus.
411. Gr., Πάνδημος, 'common to all the people,' epithet of Aphrodite.
412. Avant-garde Czech composer, teacher, and music theorist Alois Hába (1893–1973) experimented with athematic and microtonal music; in his instrumental and vocal-symphonic compositions he used quartertones & sixth-tones, and constructed keyboard instruments and woodwinds capable of playing quarter-tones.
413. Lat., 'everything is around people & [there is] nothing human in love.'
414. Lake Geneva.

415. Genovese late Baroque painter Alessandro Magnasco (1667–1749), noted for his sketchy, near-impressionistic, nervous brushstrokes, dramatic use of light, and penchant for bizarre themes — frequently, torture scenes, or genre paintings with bandits or Gypsies.

416. Ger., 'the art of movement,' the name designating early 20th-century movements of modern dance, eurhythmics, and emancipatory dance pedagogy, all of which broke with the conventions & strictures of classical ballet.

417. Ger., 'thing-moment, object-moment.'

418. See note 296.

419. Fritz Riemann (1881–1955) was an important German architect in the interwar period, an adept of the Bauhaus principles of functionality and geometric purity. He designed many social housing units and apartment buildings of standard size, especially in Leipzig; among his most important works is his housing project for railway workers in Lindenthal, Leipzig.

420. Fr., 'sleeveless in white embossed silver lamé satin. We thus obtain an extremely practical petite evening set.'

421. Lat., "that the veristic psychology of love and Riemann's ornamental architecture are one & the same." The reference is probably to architect Fritz Riemann, see note 419.

422. Lat., "that the veristic psychology of love and the study of painting is one & the same."

423. Family of grass-like flowering plants known as sedges.

424. A 5th-century heresy that takes its name from the monk Pelagius, which opposed the dogma of original sin, stressing the inherent goodness of human nature & the freedom to choose between good and evil.

425. French physicist Edme Mariotte (1620–1684) discovered, independently from Robert Boyle, the empirical relation regarding the compression and expansion of gases at constant temperature; Mariotte's law (also known as Boyle's law) states that the pressure of a given gas varies inversely with its volume at constant temperature.

426. Ger., 'basic disorder.'

AFTER WORD

Dogmatic Accidentalism.
Miklós Szentkuthy's *Prae* and the Chaocosmic Novel

ERIKA MIHÁLYCSA

Preparing for exile in protest against Hungary's slide into fascism under Horthy, Béla Bartók allegedly recommended one recently published book to his friends: "Keep an eye on this chap."[1] The chap in question was a schoolteacher of English in his 20s writing under the flamboyant pen name Miklós Szentkuthy — meaning, "of the holy well" — whose two-volume doorstopper, *Prae*, was seen sprawling in Bartók's home, weighed down by a few wooden flutes. The image of the folk instruments on top of the daunting novel has a charmingly surreal quality, but there is something to the connection: after music, experimental modernism made a none too timid entry into Hungarian fiction.

The book starts with Leville-Touqué, one of an eccentric group of characters of the author class, summing up the problems of expression, of bringing fashion, cosmetics, mathematics, psychology & philosophy to a common denominator, in a formula he dubs Dogmatic Accidentalism:

> Leville-Touqué wrote an article on the subject of 'Outline of a Starting Point, or New Composition,' for his periodical *Anti-psyche*. In this he had advanced the case of an imaginary novelist, or maybe a philosopher who assumes the role of a novelist purely in order to gather arguments

---

1. Miklós Szentkuthy, *Frivolitások és hitvallások* [*Frivolities and Confessions*] (Budapest: Magvető, 1988) 348.

for his new logic from another field, and he gets that character to observe the point before which there was not yet a logical or artistic inspiration to write a new system or a new novel, but at which point the first germs of inspiration were already present; and with the help of the very first germ and its immediate continuations, he attempts to investigate the nature of the new compositional fashion, the special relationship of analysis and unity, fortuitousness & regularity. After the 'Outline of a Starting Point' he had provisionally summarized his conclusions in a second article entitled 'Toward a New Culture of Wordplay, or Concerning the Rules of Dogmatic Accidentalism.' (*Prae I*, 3)

The theory, occasioned by spotting a hat in a shop window, & one of hundreds of theories that litter the pages of this quixotic novel, is pursued with less than dogmatic zeal, and in fact falls much closer to the leg-pullings in the early novels of Beckett or Flann O'Brien than to Stephen Dedalus' aesthetic ruminations. Yet, even though Dogmatic Accidentalism, trumpeted in a spoof manifesto in a student magazine in orthodox avant-garde fashion, is soon ousted by the next fruit of the group's sparetime literary activities, the novel playfully attempts to put it into practice. Leville-Touqué's coterie of like-minded friends includes an Englishman, Halbert, and an industrial designer and *femme fatale*, Leatrice. The latter's portrait starts, jocose-laboriously, from a postcard and soon morphs into a passage that reads like the literary equivalent of a crossbreed of a Cubo-Futurist study of movement and Surrealist collage, culminating in the candid appraisal, "Her brow was not big and, seen from the front, it was shaped like the white bone handle of a moustache brush — an anonymous oblong oval" (*Prae I*, 69). Nearly 600 pages later, at the second volume's beginning, the aborted description is taken up again; this time Leatrice becomes the image of "everybody" that has to be assembled, with the methodology of a medieval *typologia universalis*, from the chance impression of four women in swimsuits, and further still, from the absolute externals of fashion: shoes, stockings, and shoulder straps. The latter passage, a veritable tour-de-force, runs to hilariously over-the-top analyses, in the course of which the female leg, a geometrical cross between sphere and cone, is described through the analogy of a corkscrew and macaroni. The incipit of the shoe's description well illustrates Szentkuthy's method, of conjunction through an apparently endless chain of striking visual, verbal, & conceptual associations, tongue firmly in cheek:

> The shoe's line is first of all a dramatic glissando: from the culmination point to the tip of the toes one breathless plunge, like the line that stands for a tragedy's synopsis in school manuals, which at the fourth act soars to an apex and from there falls, with an avalanche's dopiness, to the tearful and hygienically too-hollowed sink of the fifth act. Such is ski jumping: a superb arc, melodically polished drawing above snow and fir-trees — constant death-fear &, eventually, too short time by the chronometer. Every female shoe brings these three as its sine-qua-non dowry the moment it alights on the horizon of a bus step: melodic arch, tragic free fall and time's odd jolt, as if two successive seconds piled up in panic, like a pair of too tightly connected rail ends in the heat. It is worth poring over the shoe, for nowhere else can we relish melodic plenitude and deathly derailment at the same time. (*Prae II*, 771–772)

The book ends with the diary-cum-manuscript of Halbert's father, an Anglican minister in Exeter; in its closure, abruptly following an ecstatic epiphany of love where eros and agape merge in love-making with a "half-idiot" girl (a love-making that can't be safely told apart from rape), another hat is spotted in another shop window, and the thesis is re-orchestrated that mathematics & fashion, absolute order and "elementare Unordnung," are facing pages of the same book.

When *Prae* appeared in 1934, its author was barely 26 and known only to a small coterie of literati. Printing the book privately obviously didn't help its visibility much, but as Szentkuthy's further volumes followed in quick succession — the diary-like volume of numbered reflections, *Towards the One and Only Metaphor*, the novel *Chapter on Love*, and from 1938 on, the monumental 10-volume series *St. Orpheus Breviary*, a playful *catalogus rerum* of meditations on history in the disguise of pseudo-historical fiction — it may well have saved Szentkuthy from persecution for blasphemy and obscenity, charges that could have threatened his teaching position and resulted in worse consequences.

Known as Miklós Pfisterer in civilian life, the young bookworm and polymath allegedly acquired his pen name from a train directory, when his eyes fell on a lackluster village outside Budapest, Szentkút. The only son of a high-ranking civil servant, he chose to study English and French at university at a time when both countries and cultures were viewed with hostility in post-World War I Hungary, not lastly by his father, a jingoist nationalist. Yet it was that same father who took the young Szentkuthy on a classic Grand Tour in 1928, and who would indulge his son's passion for books, buying him everything from the classics to botanical atlases and contemporary art books. And even if the son looked on his parents' petit-bourgeois tastes & social snobbery with bemused horror, one can detect a residual guilt feeling at having let down their expectations. As the writer recalls in a series of marathonic late-life interviews, the unsold copies of *Prae* were piled up high in the room where his father lay dying: "My father's last glance, imagine that disappointment... Even on his deathbed, with his last glance he can see, that's all his son ever accomplished."[2]

The quixotic novel was written in 1928 as a young man's response to receiving the shock of Europe seen during his travels with his family and during his one-year scholarship to England in 1931, spent between Bloomsbury and Exeter — and to contemporary modernism spanning everything from German Expressionist theater & fashion photography to Joyce's *Ulysses*, read in 1931. The ghostly bookshelves that can be discerned behind the book would be loaded not only with the works of the usual culprits — Joyce, Proust, Gide, Valéry, T.S. Eliot, Huxley, et cetera — but much reading from his beloved Baroque period, from the Metaphysical poets through Burton's *Anatomy of Melancholy* to Ben Jonson, on whom he would write his dissertation, and whose *A Tale of a Tub* provided him with a template for viewing human affairs in terms of puppetry. Equally importantly, *Prae* playfully digests a potpourri of modern physics, mathematics, and biology, ranging from Schrödinger, Einstein, or the brothers de Broglie to Brown's description of molecular movement, and Bernouilli's mathematical combinatory, all of which underpin the text's self-definitions as organized around the principle of chaos, entropy, and absolute contingency. The latest additions to the book were the "Non-Prae diagonals," partly tongue-in-cheek aesthetic theories & self-commentaries,

---

2. *Frivolitások és hitvallások*, 85. The father's only reaction to the book, which he never touched, was, "You should at least have written something patriotic at the end!"

partly torsos and caricatures of the anecdotal short story form, often spurred by philosophical or theological jokes, whose lurid guignol narratives run to would-be-conclusions that question traditional narrative, providing it with bifurcating or multiple non-endings:

> The tale, if it is to be regular, bifurcates for a moment at the end: on the one hand it turns into logic and on the other hand, into narrative humbug. Interestingly, the most kitschy stories are those that are the most rational: a narrative which attempts to turn St. Thomas' philosophy or Hilbert's mathematics the most faithfully into plotline would be more preposterous and more vulgarly common [at least according to a certain conventional aesthetic] than the tritest pulp. Thus the tale's final splitting into two is only an appearance: logic and kitsch are identical [of course already at the tale's beginning the philosophical or mathematical idea can be ab ovo only kitsch, but as a rule at the tale's end this kitschiness reaches its culmination point]. (*Prae II*, 985)

* * *

It is no sleight of hand to call Szentkuthy a cultural accident in Hungarian literature, an author who would have been as likely a denizen of Dublin, Lisbon, Buenos Aires, Odessa, Istanbul, or Alexandria, as of the Budapest literary stage of the 1930s. With the experimental late modernists of his generation — Beckett, Flann O'Brien, Borges, Carlo Emilio Gadda, Máirtín Ó Cadhain, Ahmet Hamdi Tanpınar, Arno Schmidt, to name but a few — he shares a pervasive sense of secondariness and lateness, of an exhaustion of possibilities, especially of the novel form. A profound skepticism moves him, like the above, to impishly puncture any form of authority, be it cultural, political, religious, scientific, including the authority of authorship, often embodied by the towering modernist masters. *Prae* is exhilaratingly dotted with parodies of philosophical schools, especially Heidegger's existentialism and Husserlian phenomenology. The former's jargon is caricatured in such nonce concepts as *reine Und-heit, absolutes So-tum* ("pure And-ness, absolute So-ness"), to which are added a plethora of fictitious philosophical treatises and spurious scientific books — for instance, the intimidating title by one "L. Brehle," "*Heidegger'sche « Sich-vorweg-im-schon-sein-in » und Neue Sachlichkeit: Nichts als Sache*" (an approximate translation of which would be, "The Heideggerian 'Self-ahead-of-the-already-being-in' and New Objectivity: Nothing as Object"). Mock-manifestœs of latter-day -isms jostle with each other in Leville-Touqué and Halbert's debates, cousins twice removed of Beckett's *Le Concentrisme* and Flann O'Brien's exercises in the genre. By and large, *Prae* could be described as a carnivalesque comedy of ideas, whose motto could be a gloss from its pendant, *Towards the One and Only Metaphor*, "What other attitude can I have but the medical and the parodic?"[3] Like Beckett, Szentkuthy wrote his graduation dissertation in French literature on Gide, & suffered a veritable "Proust trauma," which he sought to overcome by proposing to write a "space-Proust" in *Prae* (*Prae II*, 817); from his 20s he wrote extensively on, and translated, both contemporary and Baroque and Enlightenment English writers, the latter helping him to forge an alternative version of modernism, one suffused with Sternesque jokes, mock-anatomies, and a vision of history seen as a grand-guignol pageant.

Szentkuthy can be situated in a loose network or undercurrent of late modernist meta-fiction and experimental works.

3. *Towards the One and Only Metaphor*, tr. Tim Wilkinson (New York: Contra Mundum, 2013) 242.

His true intellectual space was a Borges-like, boundless library that exceeds national and linguistic boundaries, as well as the boundaries of disciplines, encompassing about everything from music to botany, from mathematical theory to cosmetics. Moreover, he also emphatically blurred the boundary between his autograph writing and his reading: not only is much of his text-world a commentary or gloss written around and across existing and imaginary works,[4] but, like Arno Schmidt, Szentkuthy was unequivocal about considering the margin notes of his multi-thousand-volume library, and that library itself, everything he had ever read, an integral part of his major work, his diary estimated to run to more than 100,000 pages.[5] It is seductive to see this as an extension and self-cannibalizing analogy of Gide's central conceit in *The Counterfeiters*, and a relation of sorts of the student-narrator's diary-cum-manuscript in Flann O'Brien's *At Swim-Two-Birds*.

In a penetrating essay, Colm Tóibín links the conditions of the emergence of Flann O'Brien, Borges, & Pessoa, as writers coming in the wake of High Modernism in semi-peripheral post-colonial, post-imperial metropolises, who grew up with a sense of homelessness in language, in somewhat inchoate cultures that were mimicking dominant cultural poles & positions. The coordinates fit Szentkuthy's fiction as well as his Budapest, uneasily transitioning from a multilingual imperial metropolis to the increasingly mono-lingual capital of a shrunk post-World War I nation state:

4. Two volumes of the *St. Orpheus Breviary* — *Marginalia on Casanova* and the later *Reading Augustine* — are in their entirety commentaries on other texts, inspired by the methodology of Karl Barth's scriptural hermeneutics; a long part of the novel *Chapter on Love* consists of a highly unconventional explication of Empedocles' philosophical fragments.
5. *Frivolitások és hitvallások*, 9.

Their books did not come from the world, their books became the world: in the beginning was the word, but there was often nothing except the word and its hollow echoes, and this gave their playful spirits an edge that was often melancholy, often manic ... Yet out of the emptiness, out of the non-sacramental, at the heart of where they were, [these writers] found words and literary forms, old ones and hybrid ones, fascinating ... The idea for them of what lay between the old and the hybrid, however, was a problem; a great tradition in fiction in which characters had choices and chances and possessions, and destinies to fulfill, was for them a great joke, a locomotive in a siding whose engine was all rust. They began by dismantling the escape routes and then removing all the wheels. For them the notion of character, and even identity, was to be undermined, or driven over. Then they set out to undermine not only choice and chance and destiny, but the idea of time and indeed space — and the idea of form.[6]

Tóibín's hypothesis, that some of the most daring experimental fiction of the 20th century could have emerged only in such spaces and at times of crisis when the political project of the nation failed spectacularly, finds an eerie echo in some of the responses to *Prae*, stressing the book's "homelessness" in Hungarian literature. Antal Szerb, virtually the only reviewer to celebrate the novel as a monument of modernist literature among responses of half-hearted praise or forthright mandarin recoil, incisively linked the novel's singularity to its existence in a vacuum, writing, "Artistic form is not an æsthetic but a primarily social factor.

6. Colm Tóibín, "Flann O'Brien's Lies," *London Review of Books*, Vol. 34, № 1 (2012) 33.

Form is a social consensus, by which the artist may communicate himself to his audience. The writer who discards conventional form to such an extent discards, *eo ipso*, the reader as well, at least such an overwhelming majority of readers that the remaining can hardly be called an audience."[7]

In all probability *Prae* did not come from the outside world, at least not the outside world immediately surrounding its author, but that world is subliminally present in all the novel's heterogeneity, fuzzy contradictions, & bewilderingly anachronistic points of reference. The book's bare bones of anecdotal narrative, as far as they exist, seem rooted not in some well-defined organic social world but in a wildly incongruous assemblage that makes the reader wonder at times if the setting is really contemporaneous or medieval rather. Fashionable socialites live in villas that morph in a single paragraph from Cubist interiors to emblazoned & bemoated fairy-tale castles, and their utmost ambition is, to secure a bishop's mitre to their sons. The image of the automobiles stuck in a midnight traffic jam in front of a church where an eccentric prelate delivers one of his rare sermons, and in general the obsessive Catholicism of the book's imagery is less surprising when seen against the backdrop of Szentkuthy's Budapest. With all its vibrant modernist scene, the city added but a thin veneer of metropolitan modernity to a semi-feudal country that lived by different clocks, and whose preferred mode of self-representation, the operetta, well illustrates the generalized social titulitis and cockamamie cult of the army & clergy.[8]

---

7. Antal Szerb, "Szentkuthy Miklós: *Prae*," *Erdélyi Helikon* (July 1934) 549.
8. See social historian István Bibó's by now classic 1946 pamphlet, "A kelet-európai kisállamok nyomorúsága" ['The Miseries of East European Small States"], an unsparing anatomy of the social psychopathologies characterizing the region, caused by a toxic mix of incomplete modernization, frustrated nationalism, and deeply embedded feudal authoritarian reflexes. *Válogatott tanulmányok*, Vol. II, 1945–1949 (Budapest: Magvető, 1986).

Apart from the similarities of context & background, Szentkuthy shares in common with his European and overseas metafictionist peers an all-pervasive sense of a crisis of authority, which fueled his tendency to amalgamate incongruous source materials and cultural allusions, as well as his refusal to align the text's structuring principles to the image of a single authorial personality. In consequence, the authority of the author is dispersed across the text that grows out of hand as (self)-commentary — a feature also evinced by the numerous inserts in brackets. If Flann O'Brien's *At Swim-Two-Birds* opens with a writer-figure contemplating three possible beginnings (and for that matter, one hundred times as many endings) for a satisfactory and democratic novel, *Prae* opens with one of its author-figures introducing a comically pretentious tripartite scheme for bringing a Cubist-looking hat to some common denominator with philosophy & science. This series of "unconnected starting-points" reined in by an "associative mesmerism of objects"[9] includes a theory of wordplay that functions as a theory of general relativity and contingency, as well as of "the annihilation (or over-realization?) of 'person' or 'romantic hero' in the dehumanizing novel technique" (*Prae I*, 2). This poetics of anti-anthropomorphism is conjoined with a writing of "virtuality" that resists closure & realization precisely because it would foreclose other possibilities for its realization (of which the actual, formless form of *Prae* is one example); as Ferenc Takács writes, "a book which is only a *prae*-paration for an unwritten (unwritable) novel, can maintain, on the level of fictional illusion, the freedom and openness of its potentialities."[10]

9. István Vas, "Miklós Szentkuthy, a True Avant-Gardist" [1969], *Hyperion: On the Future of Æsthetics*, Vol. VIII, № 2 (2013) 52.
10. Ferenc Takács, "A Comedy of Ideas. Miklós Szentkuthy: *Prae*," *World Literature Today*, Vol. 55, № 2 (Spring 1981) 355.

To this day, Szentkuthy's status in the Hungarian literary canon is somewhat marginal and his model of experimental modernism largely unassimilated. The inevitable silence to which he was reduced after the 1948 Stalinist takeover in East Europe provides only a partial explanation; like many of the finest writers of his place and time, he turned to translating as a creative outlet and a way of making a living, eventually rendering into Hungarian such works as Swift's *Gulliver's Travels* (1952) & Joyce's *Ulysses* (1974), and writing fantasist artist biographies in-between, mainly from his beloved 17th & 18th centuries. It is no coincidence that his critical renaissance started in the Paris-based magazine *Magyar Műhely* in 1974, the prime venue of the Hungarian literary emigration and the most important platform of Hungarian neo-avant-garde and experimental writing, with strong connections to French and European literary scenes. It was also through the mediation of the magazine's remit of authors that Szentkuthy was first translated into French, finding, belatedly and anachronistically, his place in the wake of the Nouveau Roman, some of the preoccupations of which he seems to anticipate. By the time when one of the leading Hungarian publishers, Magvető, started a new Szentkuthy series in 1973, a new generation of Hungarian postmodernists — most importantly, Péter Esterházy, Péter Hajnóczy, Péter Nádas, László Krasznahorkai, but one may also add the older poet Dezső Tandori — had brought about a poetic turn, carrying out work on the Hungarian language which could be seen as the equivalent of the work done on English from Joyce's "revolution of the word" to the dismantling of narrative conventions in contemporary Anglo-American fiction, or on French by the experimentation of the Oulipo. Their writing, much inspired by Szentkuthy's Wakean rendering of *Ulysses*, created a secondary frame of reference for Szentkuthy, so one can say that, albeit anachronistically, the "holy well" found his place in a lineage.

Szentkuthy started writing at a time of a *rappel à l'ordre* across Europe, on a literary and critical scene characterized by peculiar and often contradictory æsthetic and ideological leanings. At the time of his West European journeys and one-year scholarship in England, the experimental fervor of the 1920s abated and the dominant voices were of cultural conservatism and often neo-Catholicism — the later T. S. Eliot, Graham Greene, Evelyn Waugh, Robert Graves. He recalls how these voices, of the new "rebellion," engendered in him a derisive and triumphantly blasé attitude, of not striving to differentiate between the "mendaciously sincere" and the "sincerely mendacious."[11] The recollection evinces a disenchanted equidistance from these diverging æsthetic programs, and illustrates the impish irreverence with which Szentkuthy would treat the established voices of cultural *&* artistic authority, including the modernist masters of the earlier generation.

These intellectual and political fracture lines make only an indirect entry into Szentkuthy's writings, in thinly veiled parodies in historical disguise on the pages of the *St. Orpheus Breviary*. In the later work, the gaze at the historical events around him — the nativism and shrill anti-Semitism of the Horthy regime, the years of terror in 1944–45, the Stalinist takeover after 1948, the crushing of the 1956 revolt — remains at once detached and perceptive of the continuous disaster unfolding in history. As he himself put it later in life, he would remain a specialist of looking at all epochs as simultaneous, "sub specie mortis, sub specie aeterni," and, one may add, with the formula of *Prae*, quite often "sub specie whatsit." Together with a Benjamin-like awareness, that next to each monument of culture (and, indeed, underlying it) an act of barbarism is found, such equanimity also evinces a lightness of touch that treats history as a continuous journey through the heart of darkness, where such events as Szentkuthy

---

11. *Frivolitások és hitvallások*, 242.

lived through are at most "pimples, silly flaws."[12] However bewildering this lightness of touch may be, it is also worth keeping in mind that Szentkuthy's favorite philosopher, the one whose insights he used most in his work next to Pascal's dictum, that true philosophizing makes a mockery of philosophy, was Simone Weil. In the closing scene of *Chapter on Love*, a pseudo-historical novel written shortly after *Prae*, the imminent slaughter and destruction of the town, and of the known order, is present in the form of a dissonant chord in the Requiem music, which reinforces polyphony and the polyguous nature of meaning: "Sounds have a thousand meanings, but polyphony has 10,000. The choir swelled, rose, the sharpened lament of the violins soared ever higher on the tide of newer and newer chords: at the end the light-blue sea of harmonies flooded them as the Flood's burying waves did the 'it's useless'-foliaged souls of those who don't deserve life."[13] The closing chord of the 1938 *Black Renaissance*, from a diary of the tutor of the future Queen Elizabeth I, is an affirmation of the impotence of words and established knowledge when faced with the ultimate mystery, being face to face with the other — a strikingly Weilian, even Lévinasian admonishment to a future monarch, and a conclusion that brackets any suspicion of ethical relativism: "… the essence of the heresy known as 'the other' is that it is always just a single portrait in a flash of a single historical second. Something that, in any case, cannot resemble Pharaoh's horses and the tired-scented fruits of cypresses going back millennia — it is a solitary wonder that has no premises, its conclusion unknown."[14]

12. Ibid., 339.
13. *Chapter on Love*, tr. Erika Mihálycsa (New York: Contra Mundum, 2020) 379.
14. *Black Renaissance*, tr. Tim Wilkinson (New York: Contra Mundum, 2018) 279–280.

AFTERWORD

* * *

What kind of novel is *Prae* — indeed, can it be called a novel at all? The writing is more essayistic than anything in Thomas Mann, Musil, or Hermann Broch; the scant vestiges of plot, character, and dialogue are merely pretexts for further discursive forays. If one of the characteristic preoccupations of the modernist novel since Henry James and Ford Madox Ford had been multi-perspectivalism, showing a set of events and figures from divergent points of view, in Szentkuthy's novels the place of these reflector-characters is taken by personae who appear rather like mouthpieces for varieties of theorizing. Devoid of nearly all the usual attributes of fictional characters, of a psychological profile, biography, and recognizable quirks of speech, they are mostly discursive instances in a text structured like a musical variation of sorts. And if in modernist novels the chain of free associations and flickering perceptions are elevated to the prime mover of interior monologues, taking the place of outward accident, causality, and what Joyce called the "goahead plot" propelling narrative onward, in Szentkuthy's writing they are replaced by theories begetting theories, as an unending associative chain of images and theorizings that proceeds by simile, juxtaposition, contingency.

Ever since its first publishing, the ultimately undecidable question remains: what is *Prae* after all — a mere juvenilia, as the title implies, a preparation for writing proper? A loose assembly of commentaries, embedded essays, pseudo-scientific or mock-philosophical treatises, spoofs, aborted short stories and caricatures of the short story form with an attached moral lesson? Or is it the dispersed fragments of traditional narrative form in a state of entropy? The book was almost immediately dubbed a 'monster' by its critics, a verdict certainly helped by its typographic layout: of a length almost twice that of *Ulysses*, the two-volume book came in 14 paragraphless, uninterrupted chapters reminiscent of the *scriptio continua* of medieval manuscripts.[15] The book's thematic concern — insofar as it has any, & insofar as this *any* is distinguishable from everything we know about the world-all — is that forever receding instant of the arrival of 'inspiration,' ungraspable for conceptual thinking; this the book attempts to codify, taxonomize, dissect and circumscribe, write across, around, apart, trying out on it the jargons of (mock)-science and (mock)-philosophy; in more than one sense, a grandiose parody of *À la recherche*.

At first glance, the novel's most radical feature is its ostensible lack of structure — or rather, of its making of negativity into a prime narrative strategy. Allegedly when the young author complained to a lover about not finding the adequate structure to hold the book together, she quipped, "But to be sure, the paper-clips are its structure."[16] Pursuing the images offered in *Prae* as analogies of itself, no conventional novelistic form and no stable composition can ever result, since the novel's form is formlessness itself. A late addition on the difference between *Prae* and *Non-Prae*, which disconcertingly starts on, "Does *Prae* have anything to say about what it wants? No. It does not. It does not even come anywhere close to itself" (*Prae I*, 97), reveals the true encyclopaedic scope and inevitable defeat of the text — of including everything, even what it leaves out, of not being self-identical but merely the trace and effect of its own lacunae. The gesture is at once a jocose reduction ad absurdum of the grand modernist encyclopædic projects, and a bona fide

---

15. Only the second, 1974 edition, edited by Mária Tompa, introduced subtitles and broke the text into smaller units, a layout preferred by the author himself (*Frivolitások és hitvallások*, 345–46).

16. *Frivolitások és hitvallások*, 374.

emulation of the principles of modern quantum physics.[17] The relationship between the text of *Prae* and the "Non-Prae," running behind, beside, & around it in an accompanying stream, is likened to the relationship between a tautened bow string and the arched shaft of the bow: accordingly, the poetics of this newfangled self-generating text will be one of negativity, where the absent presence — the bowstring missing from statues of Eros — determines the sculpted marble bow:

> What exists, which is to say *Prae* itself, is a continual blunder, institutionalized prevarication ('truths'); what is truly exciting, interesting, the one true faith or the actual, by its very nature lies outside any narrative, and that is the inaccessible, the '*Non-Prae*,' which bears the same relation to *Prae* as a tautened bow string does to the arched shaft of the bow. On statues of Eros the figure of Eros is sometimes shown holding a marble bow; this has no bowstring, to be sure, but the bow is nevertheless arched in such a way that the viewer cannot fail to imagine the non-existent string as being there. In the figure of *Prae* there must, therefore, be some sort of positive signal from which the tensile strength of the '*Non-Prae*' that is constantly running in coexistence to *Prae* can be made perceptible, deducible. Principle: to utilize the essential impotence of literature with productive optimism as a useful structural factor: to make the constant

17. See the discussion of the formless form of *Prae* in Gyula Rugási, *Szent Orpheus arcképe* ["The Portrait of St. Orpheus"] (Budapest: JAK — Pesti Szalon, 1992), and in Gyula Rugási, "Leatrice görög arca. Szentkuthy Miklós: *Prae*" ["The Greek Face of Leatrice. M. Szentkuthy: *Prae*"], in Mihály Szegedy-Maszák et al., eds, *A magyar irodalom történetei*, Vol. III ["Histories of Hungarian Literature"] (Budapest: Gondolat, 2007) 310–322.

> ghostly absence and its continuo of otherness a harmonious component, to incorporate the 'Non-Prae' into a work's preserve in much the same way as in the Pantheon there also used to be a positive altar to the 'unknown god.'
> (*Prae I*, 98)

The result is a fragmentary, hybrid text that foregrounds the infinite web in which everything in the multiverse is interwoven, and which shows a constant drive away from anthropomorphism. The awareness of the impossibility of the task and of the impotence of narrative does not generate, however, a writing of melancholia or an æsthetics (and heroics) of "fail better," but rather, a baroque gleefulness and 'productive optimism' of the *sub specie whatsit* perspective.

This constitutive formlessness is jocosely demonstrated at the book's beginning, when Leville-Touqué improvises a preposterous historical yarn involving a nun, a Venetian merchant, a Spanish king, and a pope, intended solely to punish a girl in whom he takes an erotic interest, but whose puritanical tastes in matters of clothing put him off. The parable is duly engulfed in a mise-en-abyme of digressions conductive to a new editing technique, that of *detours*. Simultaneously, another prime strategy is paraded in the work-within-the-novel (and, by extrapolation, in *Prae* itself): of differentiating between theme-writing and novel-writing, where the first would approximate the form of algebraic formulae, closed in themselves and non-narrativizable: "the plot meant nothing, the words which played a part in it, like Venice, duke, Semite, Lutheran, or pope, had no conceptual scope: they just touched on the notions and immediately dropped them, otherwise they could not have become part of the structure: structure excludes 'meaning'" (*Prae I*, 13). A "theme" — that is, pure composition — is, however, no more indebted to mathematics than it is to biology, to organic cell growth and proliferation. The result is a protean text that incorporates everything without retaining anything, and which collapses present, past, & future into simultaneity in a sweep of self-reflexive elaborations. Szentkuthy's meandering, parenthetical sentences even stylistically enact the self-generating nature of these techniques, growing to monstrous lengths as they follow a chain of comparisons that never ends but is merely discontinued:

> A 'theme' and a 'novel' are separate genres, and the two have nothing in common: one cannot discover even the remotest relationship between novelists and thematicists. A theme, which has no novelistic aim, means pure composition, and in my 'elaborations' (which of course are not based on any 'theme') there have occurred 'themes' as compositional plans; those compositions, however, did not signify the structure of the work, the whole work, but 'structural' chapters inserted as interludes, or in other words, if I had written two chapters (without a 'theme') and afterwards some compositional trick or compositional possibility came into my mind, I did not set the two already written scenes into a structural unity but used the 'structure' as, so to speak, a third scene after the already finished two scenes. The so-called artistic structure was not the skeleton, a coherent system of girders, of the novel, but an independent character, as if one of the active roles of Romeo and Juliet were to turn into the plot line of the same tragedy. The composition thereby becomes unending, it proliferates forever, constantly changing shape, incorporating everything, but at any moment it might also lose everything, but this structure elevated into a separate character will float as a cork ornament above the eternal foam of this continuum of elaborations: as if I were suddenly to deprive a white

lily (which previously, with the aid of a cactus & white hatpins, I had been able to express more precisely than with itself) of its contours and thus end up with only an endlessly crumbling and contracting, stray white stream, a white stream onto which I toss the lace-like sample of a now self-reliant contour (painting has been using this technique for fair time). (*Prae I*, 12)

'Theme-writing' has a further vital ingredient: a radically de-anthropomorphizing gaze, which collapses the subjective and objective perspectives ('total impression hedonism' and 'mathematics'). Such playful oscillation and fragmentariness is correlated to philosophical and physical theories of space and time, revolutionary at the time of the writing of *Prae*. It is such space-time concepts that frame the narration and anew force a rethinking of narrative structure itself: accordingly, structure becomes a character in fiction, and fiction is reimagined on the analogy of contemporary experiments in the visual arts.[18]

Contingency, contiguity, chance, and radical provisionality take the place of the outward organizing principle. The novel foregrounds chaos theory — it even uses the adjective *káokozmikus* ('chaocosmic') some years before "in the chaosmos of Alle" was added to the galley proofs of *Finnegans Wake* after 1936[19] — and toys with replacing structure & conventional notions of beauty with absolute chance & entropy. The figure for the latter

18. Rainer J. Hanshe sees in this an early anticipation of William S. Burroughs' cut-up technique, but Simon Hantaï's *pliages* might also be cited. For Hanshe's take, see "To Humanize and Dehumanize: Imitation, True Contrasts, and the Faustian Pact," *Hungarian Literature Online* (16 December 2013).

19. See Dávid Szolláth, "Leletmentés. Válogatott szentkuthyzmusok az *Ulysses* szövegében" ['Archiving the Finds: Selected Szentkuthysms in *Ulysses*], *Alföld* 9 (2010) 73.

AFTERWORD

is found in one of Jacob Bernouilli's cruxes of mathematical permutation, the probability calculus of randomly mixing a set of letters and envelopes in such a way that each letter ends up in the mismatched envelope, the mathematical term for which is, aptly, derangement. This classical mathematical problem occasions an original definition of beauty and a rethinking of structure: "Beauty relates to the world as this found arithmetic formula to the letters and their envelopes," in a Surrealist "rigor of permutations":

> What is true structure? Bernoulli's swapped envelopes are on the true degree of artistic composition; because every unit connects to every other unit without exception, the units get into such transcendentally close relations, such connection-panic that cannot be dissolved by any means. The formula expressing infinite exchangeability causes twofold bliss — first it brings to mind retroactively the chaos preceding the formula, the spasmodic states of exchange, when there is no regularity at all in the disturbance, there are only letters stuck in the mismatched envelopes, which fall apart in isolation; but in the next moment when I throw the formula among the cases like some theological yeast, in an instant I see it all before me as a harmonic world, the proportion-piling picture of rhythm, order, of correspondences.
> (*Prae II*, 1233–1234)

The principle of permutation, of swapping and derangement as the methods of infinite connectivity, is constantly at work in the book's distant & seemingly unconnected parts, coming from the pen or mouth of its various reflectors. In the same vein, Leville-Touqué presents an earnest proposal to replace the traditional methods of analysis with the kaleidoscope method, by which the chance constellation of disparate elements which surround the object of analysis at a given point in time might be taken to define it, by accident: "in a kaleidoscope we don't take one large pattern apart into its components but the other way round, we shake elements at random & from this one sole (but thanks to the mirrors, rigorously constructed) hazard, form results" (*Prae II*, 1366). This device is employed in the novel long before its formulation — among other examples, in assembling Leatrice's portrait, and in most of the mock-essays written to counter received psychological and novelistic discourses of analyzing the psyche.

However, the most striking instantiation of this principle of absolute contingency and universal relatedness is Leville-Touqué's theory of wordplay from the book's beginning, which embraces everything from language to contemporary architecture, and which probably shows most eloquently what Szentkuthy assimilated from his readings of *Ulysses* and *Finnegans Wake*. Winding "the phenomenologist's open helical spool of self-repetition" (*Prae I*, 20) beyond endurance, the demonstration rushes the reader from the moniker Hyppopochondra Stylopotama, which forces the utterly foreign entities of hippopotamus and hypochondriac onto one another "in order to make their shared area a single, true substance" (*Prae I*, 28), to a survey of modern architecture, and eventually results in a full-blown manifesto:

> The whole century is progressing toward wordplay — Leville-Touqué wrote in his essay. Wordplay is an expression of the instinct that we consider relations ordained by chance as being much more eternal realities and much more typical beings than the individual things which are the characters of the relationship. One can imagine a new arrangement of the world whereby trees vanish from an alley of trees and only the smudges of

touching boughs are left; the constitutive elements disappear from chemical compounds, and lines of bonding force are all that remain as sole material reality; the cells of living tissues have all been annihilated to give way to the relation between cells: in the places where hitherto there had been nothing, where only purely intellectual bonds of relation had run, in other words, in practice, an emptiness yawned, that is precisely where realities live nowadays. Every right bank and every left bank fades away, but the world is filled up with an endless multiplicity of solid bridges. If previously one had been interested in rose gardens because of the roses in it, one is now interested in the area between roses; in other words, for us a rose garden will not mean the aggregate of roses but something like a house painter's template, being a single large sheet of linoleum, out of which, however, the roses are cut off: that sheet of templates can be perceived as a separate space of the relationships of the roses, a materialized mass of relationships which is so dense that the roses are negligible abstractions in comparison. (*Prae I*, 30)

* * *

It is unusual for long literary works to be translated years apart by different translators, yet such is the case with Szentkuthy's *Prae*, which comes in two voices to the English reader. The first volume was published in 2014 in Tim Wilkinson's translation — the third of his four translations from Szentkuthy, preceded by *Marginalia on Casanova* and the idiosyncratic book of reflections, *Towards the One and Only Metaphor*, and followed by *Black Renaissance*. Wilkinson was a veteran, virtuoso translator of Hungarian literature, known above all for his magisterial rendering of the works of Imre Kertész; his English Szentkuthy was rightly hailed for its stylistic fireworks & inventive word choices, as well as for the elegance of the sentences — something which, with Szentkuthy, means endless wandering, spurred by additive comparisons and associations begetting theories. I had the occasion to edit Wilkinson's translation of *Black Renaissance*, a task he couldn't undertake on account of the illness that was to claim his life. That close reading involved fine-tuning syntax, with special attention to the timbre of Szentkuthy's voice — a German and Yiddish-infused urban Hungarian dotted with multilingual erudite terms and wordplay, and with an anarchic, elfish grin always in evidence; it inevitably meant immersion into the voice and idiom of the translator, which I tried to respect in all the alterations that revision involves.

With Tim Wilkinson's demise, *Prae* seemed to be doomed to a half-existence in English. I undertook the work of bringing the missing volume to the English reader, having previously translated myself one novel by Szentkuthy, *Chapter on Love*, written shortly after the completion of *Prae*, and in which some of the figures and ruminations of *Prae* are resurrected in a different guise. I am an academic translating into an acquired tongue, with a background in Joyce, Beckett, and translation studies. While I obviously attempted to harmonize the text of the second volume with my predecessor's translation, my timbre will be inescapably different from his. My priorities were to approximate Szentkuthy's distinctive mix of a hyper-erudite, often mock-pedantic lexis, a pervasively self-ironic tone, and a liberal use of urban jargon — ill fitting the norms of stylistic propriety in the Hungarian literature of the 19th and early 20th-century. I attempted to blend an idiom that could fuse, in the same sentence and often in the same compound, the pedantic-quaint with the wacky-demotic. In order to render Szentkuthy's Germanisms and elements of Yiddish-inflected Hungarian, I peppered the (mock)-scholarly passages with Yiddish English and extra foreign terms. Occasionally I resorted to anachronistic usage — a pervasive practice of Szentkuthy the translator and author of pseudo-historical fiction in the *St. Orpheus Breviary*; so does, for instance, "snafu" make a casual appearance in these pages. At the same time, I didn't try to smooth out asperities. Szentkuthy has a strong penchant for word coinage, especially through agglutination and compounds, often of elements taken from incongruous registers or domains of knowledge; and while word-splicing comes natural in Hungarian, his multiple compounds are a distinct stylistic trait that far exceeds standard Hungarian usage. At the risk of favoring an oddity, I sought to recreate these coinages in English. Overall, what guided me was no principle of fidelity to period diction — a preoccupation conspicuously absent from Szentkuthy's practice as both writer and translator — but an attempt to create a hybrid idiom in which high & low, learned and facetious, mingle, and where the guffaw of the anatomist of Spieß-Bürgertum enlivens Art Nouveau decadence and grand-guignol. To compensate the inevitable loss of domestic intertexts, often used for a punchline, I inserted echoes from Anglophone classics & moderns. In some ways, I used an interventionist, recreative translation method on his text, a method that resembles his own.

Szentkuthy shares with Joyce and with his Irish contemporaries Beckett and Flann O'Brien a sense of unrest of spirit and foreignness in the language he was born & educated into. One might say that for him, Hungarian was an acquired tongue: both his parents — his father of German, his mother of Jewish extraction — were first-generation Hungarian speakers; both were by temperament taciturn and uneasy in an imperfectly mastered language. In the extended Pfisterer family, polyglossia was an everyday reality, making language visible as language. In *Frivolities* Szentkuthy remembers his linguistic apprenticeship: "even today I sometimes think that my affair with the 'mother-tongue' is like that of the child whose parents never taught him to walk: out of necessity, and in order that he may pass unnoticed, he learns to do tumbles."[20] This self-diagnosis was corroborated by fellow writer István Vas, who commented on the homelessness of the Szentkuthy idiolect, suffused with the German and Yiddish-inflected 1920s–30s jargon of Budapest, through which he "acquired an intellectual impact and precision which would have been hard to achieve in a spicier, full-blooded Hungarian vernacular," and which he appropriated & recast to such an extent that it doesn't appear obsolete long after the demise of that idiom.[21]

At the end of *Towards the One and Only Metaphor* Szentkuthy describes a veritable epiphany of language. During a brief illness his wife read to him in English, and as he listened to her voice, the words suddenly lost their meaning, becoming erotic entities floating in the air: "I was only able to pay attention to the savor of the words, irrespective of their meaning … it was more a question of my enjoying the meaning of each separate word, its etymology shucked, *insulated*, rich in semantic annual rings (independent of the sentence and the writer's 'thought'): a single sentence length in twenty or thirty cross-sections."[22] This episode of language suddenly turning into an opaque sensory continuum that has to do more with a certain distribution of muscles and flesh folds than with semantics, grammar, and syntax, was preceded by his reading of Joyce's *Work-in-Progress* and of Sir Thomas Browne. It takes no great stretch of the imagination to spot here a moment akin to that experienced by Watt in Beckett's eponymous novel, as he finds himself incapable of linking the word "pot" to the pot of his master Mr. Knott. Yet the

20. *Frivolitások és hitvallások*, 60–61.
21. István Vas, "Miklós Szentkuthy, a True Avant-Gardist" [1969], *Hyperion: On the Future of Æsthetics*, Vol. VIII, № 2 (2013) 53.
22. *Towards the One and Only Metaphor*, 299.

outcome is not ontological angst but a baroque buoyancy in celebrating language's "colossal, elemental filthiness" (305). Tellingly, the ferments of this new "sensitivity to language" are labeled "language-mushrooms," unruly organic outgrowths — deliberately or unwittingly echoing the "moldy fungi" into which abstract words turn in Hugo von Hofmannsthal's 1902 *Lord Chandos Letter*, one of the fundamental texts of modern Sprachskepsis, a condition Szentkuthy was intimately familiar with:

> In recent times there has been no literature for me, only language — every book is inundated, drenched, destroyed as a 'work' by the language in which it is written ... A writerly writer has to feel, before he starts writing, that his instrument is ... materialized inaccuracy, chance reflex crystals (which is what words are, after all), a whole lot of debris out of the utterances of big brains and phobia-lashed primitive humans, the muscle-twitchings and cerebral vegetation of a heterogeneous and contourless shoddy mass (that sort of thing is politely called "word" and "thought"), the impure cultural sludge of practice and sorcery, decorative barking and fallacious sound etiquette: that is language and that is the instrument of literature.[23]

In *Prae*, too, the reader often encounters porings over this constitutional impurity of language. In the *Meditations* of Halbert's father it is the lesson of the Bernouilli letters, of the coincidence of order and absolute disorder, that opens the way for two opposite literary styles and languages that would be eventually merged in *Prae* — "Latinity and international cant": "the one is the medieval Latin tongue, this lies in the dimension of 'order,'

23. *Ibid.*, 298, 304–305.

the other is the entirely dishabilly, frivolous, topsy-turvy mongrel lingo that nettles every national academy, a pure macaronic" (*Prae II*, 1235). Szentkuthy's own coinages & occasional use of macaronic Latin would certainly have nettled his former university professors, let alone the pedants of the academy, but the best example of his mixing of erudite allusions with cant can be seen in his translations. Indeed, it was in his *Ulysses* translation, published in 1974, that his stylistic signature was established — his contrived, multiply allusive Szentkuthyisms. Since he worked at a time when most Joyce scholarship, including Gifford's annotations, was not yet published, he inevitably missed many contextual references, covering these up with interventionist, often multilingual language games; many of these portmanteaux suggest that Szentkuthy may have been packaging the reading experience of the *Wake* into the Hungarian *Ulysses* text. One such characteristic translatorial intrusion occurs in the closing part of the famous "Oxen of the Sun" episode, made up entirely of style parodies that follow the evolution of English literary idioms; in the episode's Coda, the drunken company spills out on the streets in a poly-cacophony of voices, dialects, accents, slangs and pidgins from all around the globe. In one such aside somebody voices his sympathy for the orphans left behind by Patrick Dignam, whose funeral Bloom attends earlier in the day, in a picturesque jumble of Hiberno-English & caricature Black American English: "Ludamassy! Pore piccaninnies! ... Of all de darkies Massa Pat was verra best."[24] This, in Szentkuthy's translation, becomes a flamboyant linguistic conceit:

> Circumdidit in pacet. De nekem most erről ne circumdadogj... Az egész nacionálgaleriben VII Piás vere Dignam volt a legbecsületesebb fickó.[25]

24. James Joyce, *Ulysses*, 14.1555.
25. James Joyce, *Ulysses*, tr. Miklós Szentkuthy (Budapest: Európa, 1974) 531.

AFTERWORD

To begin with, the utterance conflates the formulae *Requiescat in pacem*, and the funereal prayer *Circumdederunt me gemitus mortis*; on the distorted Latin Szentkuthy inscribes the stuttering-sounding Hungarian 'didi' (slang for breasts) and 'dadog' (stutter, in the coinage, 'circum-stutter'), in a move that enhances the Coda's vulgar *double entendre* and sets in motion a disseminative unpacking of meanings, including a circum-groping of breasts at heart's content. In the second phrase, in place of the blackface lingo a few multilingual portmanteaux feature: 'massa Pat' is styled up into *Piás VII* (slang for 'boozer,' from *pia*), a kind of sots' pope. Szentkuthy also fashions an extra link to the words of the liturgy — *vere dignum et justum est* ("It is truly meet and just") —, repeating Father Conmee's memoriter in "Wandering Rocks" to help remember Dignam's surname. Instead of the racial slur 'darkies,' Pat is pronounced the most decent skin in the *nacionálgaleri* — a play on the National Gallery and the slang word *galeri*, gang. What for the English reader is a matter of internal translation between accents comes to the Hungarian audience in the form of interlingual fireworks. With some sleight of hand one may see this, and many other examples scattered throughout the Hungarian *Ulysses*, as the applying of the kaleidoscope method to translation, so that by hazard and accident, multidirectional, polyguous meaning and Gargantuan linguistic humor may result.

* * *

If Szentkuthy's *Prae* were only a witty exercise in imploding the novel form, leaving few conventions untouched, it would at best be of academic interest and could be neatly summed up in a few theoretical precepts. What makes Szentkuthy a writer's writer though is his capacity of generating images of a strikingly unexpected, granular, at once hyperrealistic and surreal quality

— images that jolt the reader in the way an André Kertész distortion photograph reveals to the viewer something unsuspected in however banal an object. The way he describes the progression of the clockhands on a grandfather clock during a time of tedious waiting, or the bodily sensations of the small hours in a hygienically unhomely hotel room, invite comparisons to that mode of vision described by Breton, where "the real and the imagined, past and future, the communicable and the incommunicable, high and low, cease to be perceived as contradictions."[26] Virtually on every page images abound — light rays stretching like clothes strings, champagne-filled glasses appearing as cone-shaped tents made of refrigerated light — that linger in the mind long after digesting one outré philosophical scheme or another thrown up from Touqué & Co.'s laboratory of ideas. These images require a slow, long-exposure reading that they will repay. In one of the book's many potential unfurlings, Leatrice remembers the previous day's champagne glasses, and their superinscribed images seen or dreamt in different moments constitute a veritable "space-Proust" writing at a micro level. Szentkuthy's is a text that can startle at every bend of the phrase, and his kaleidoscopic shaking together of images evinces a radicalism of vision that can at times be grating and which never ceases to surprise:

> The noise of the morning was probably the noise of possibilities; the humming of a thousand start-lines folded back into the womb, and when the bar owner addressed her in a tone of half phlegm and half naïve pathos, "A great morning we're having," at first she barely heard it. She saw large glasses in three kinds of 'developments':

26. André Breton, "Second Manifesto of Surrealism," in *Manifestœs of Surrealism*, tr. Richard Seaver and Helen R. Lane (Ann Arbor: University of Michigan Press, 1969) 123.

her memory stored exact copies, the way they had been the previous night on the table; then she fell asleep from too much champagne and they surrounded her in her dream like conic, transparent tents made of refrigerated light; and lastly, from the dawn's light crossing her dreams, a third variation was born. She felt that the morning's beauty was in these two things: the music-pastiche brought to her ears from here and there like a straying ray-bill, and the dream-figments hung out to dry on the slender ray's strings. Night is the realm of discipline, of classical stifling, where palpation reigns; feeling about reduces the body to a few leaden, clumsy gestures and the dreams, too, revolve in the same place, in the down-at-heel laboratory of the brain. (*Prae II*, 818)

Acknowledgments

THE TRANSLATOR AND THE PRESS EXTEND THEIR GRATITUDE TO:

Maria Tompa, for answering a barrage of continuous queries, all of which aided in the clarification of many thorny parts of this monster of a text;

classical scholars Péter Somfai & Ábel Tamás for elucidating the Latin passages;

Pierre Senges and Armağan Ekici for helping with some of the obscure references;

and to David Van Dusen & Alexander Faludy for tending to a church-related query.

COLOPHON

PRAE
was handset in InDesign CC

The text font is *Adobe Jenson Pro*.

Book design & typesetting: Alessandro Segalini
Image credit: Opening spread based on a drawing by László Nagy;
maze image by István Orosz.

The book title is a CMP exclusive digital recut in Fontlab
from the original types used in 1934.

Cover design: CMP

PRAE
is published by Contra Mundum Press.

Contra Mundum Press   New York · London · Melbourne

CONTRA MUNDUM PRESS

Dedicated to the value & the indispensable importance of the individual voice, to works that test the boundaries of thought & experience.

The primary aim of Contra Mundum is to publish translations of writers who in their use of form and style are *à rebours*, or who deviate significantly from more programmatic & spurious forms of experimentation. Such writing attests to the volatile nature of modernism. Our preference is for works that have not yet been translated into English, are out of print, or are poorly translated, for writers whose thinking & æsthetics are in opposition to timely or mainstream currents of thought, value systems, or moralities. We also reprint obscure and out-of-print works we consider significant but which have been forgotten, neglected, or overshadowed.

There are many works of fundamental significance to *Weltliteratur* (*& Weltkultur*) that still remain in relative oblivion, works that alter and disrupt standard circuits of thought — these warrant being encountered by the world at large. It is our aim to render them more visible.

For the complete list of forthcoming publications, please visit our website. To be added to our mailing list, send your name and email address to: info@contramundum.net

Contra Mundum Press
P.O. Box 1326
New York, NY 10276
USA

OTHER CONTRA MUNDUM PRESS TITLES

2012 *Gilgamesh*
Ghérasim Luca, *Self-Shadowing Prey*
Rainer J. Hanshe, *The Abdication*
Walter Jackson Bate, *Negative Capability*
Miklós Szentkuthy, *Marginalia on Casanova*
Fernando Pessoa, *Philosophical Essays*
2013 Elio Petri, *Writings on Cinema & Life*
Friedrich Nietzsche, *The Greek Music Drama*
Richard Foreman, *Plays with Films*
Louis-Auguste Blanqui, *Eternity by the Stars*
Miklós Szentkuthy, *Towards the One & Only Metaphor*
Josef Winkler, *When the Time Comes*
2014 William Wordsworth, *Fragments*
Josef Winkler, *Natura Morta*
Fernando Pessoa, *The Transformation Book*
Emilio Villa, *The Selected Poetry of Emilio Villa*
Robert Kelly, *A Voice Full of Cities*
Pier Paolo Pasolini, *The Divine Mimesis*
Miklós Szentkuthy, *Prae, Vol. 1*
2015 Federico Fellini, *Making a Film*
Robert Musil, *Thought Flights*
Sándor Tar, *Our Street*
Lorand Gaspar, *Earth Absolute*
Josef Winkler, *The Graveyard of Bitter Oranges*
Ferit Edgü, *Noone*
Jean-Jacques Rousseau, *Narcissus*
Ahmad Shamlu, *Born Upon the Dark Spear*
2016 Jean-Luc Godard, *Phrases*
Otto Dix, *Letters, Vol. 1*
Maura Del Serra, *Ladder of Oaths*
Pierre Senges, *The Major Refutation*
Charles Baudelaire, *My Heart Laid Bare & Other Texts*

2017   Joseph Kessel, *Army of Shadows*
      Rainer J. Hanshe & Federico Gori, *Shattering the Muses*
      Gérard Depardieu, *Innocent*
      Claude Mouchard, *Entangled — Papers! — Notes*
2018   Miklós Szentkuthy, *Black Renaissance*
      Adonis & Pierre Joris, *Conversations in the Pyrenees*
2019   Charles Baudelaire, *Belgium Stripped Bare*
      Robert Musil, *Unions*
      Iceberg Slim, *Night Train to Sugar Hill*
      Marquis de Sade, *Aline & Valcour*
2020   *A City Full of Voices: Essays on the Work of Robert Kelly*
      Rédoine Faïd, *Outlaw*
      Carmelo Bene, *I Appeared to the Madonna*
      Paul Celan, *Microliths They Are, Little Stones*
      Zsuzsa Selyem, *It's Raining in Moscow*
      Bérengère Viennot, *Trumpspeak*
      Robert Musil, *Theater Symptoms*
      Dejan Lukić, *The Oyster* (AGRODOLCE SERIES)
      Miklós Szentkuthy, *Chapter on Love*
2021   Charles Baudelaire, *Paris Spleen*
      Marguerite Duras, *The Darkroom*
      Andrew Dickos, *Honor Among Thieves*
      Pierre Senges, *Ahab (Sequels)*
      Carmelo Bene, *Our Lady of the Turks*
      Fernando Pessoa, *Writings on Art & Poetical Theory*

SOME FORTHCOMING TITLES

Ugo Tognazzi, *The Injester* (AGRODOLCE SERIES)
Blixa Bargeld, *Europe Crosswise: A Litany*
Robert Musil, *Literature & Politics*

THE FUTURE OF KULCHUR
A PATRONAGE PROJECT

LEND CONTRA MUNDUM PRESS (CMP) YOUR SUPPORT

With bookstores and presses around the world struggling to survive, and many actually closing, we are forming this patronage project as a means for establishing a continuous & stable foundation to safeguard our longevity. Through this patronage project we would be able to remain free of having to rely upon government support &/or other official funding bodies, not to speak of their timelines & impositions. It would also free CMP from suffering the vagaries of the publishing industry, as well as the risk of submitting to commercial pressures in order to persist, thereby potentially compromising the integrity of our catalog.

CAN YOU SACRIFICE $10 A WEEK FOR KULCHUR?

For the equivalent of merely 2–3 coffees a week, you can help sustain CMP and contribute to the future of kulchur. To participate in our patronage program we are asking individuals to donate $500 per year, which amounts to $42/month, or $10/week. Larger donations are of course welcome and beneficial. All donations are tax-deductible through our fiscal sponsor Fractured Atlas. If preferred, donations can be made in two installments. We are seeking a minimum of 300 patrons per year and would like for them to commit to giving the above amount for a period of three years.

WHAT WE OFFER

Part tax-deductible donation, part exchange, for your contribution you will receive every CMP book published during the patronage period as well as 20 books from our back catalog. When possible, signed or limited editions of books will be offered as well.

WHAT WILL CMP DO WITH YOUR CONTRIBUTIONS?

Your contribution will help with basic general operating expenses, yearly production expenses (book printing, warehouse & catalog fees, etc.), advertising & outreach, and editorial, proofreading, translation, typography, design and copyright fees. Funds may also be used for participating in book fairs and staging events. Additionally, we hope to rebuild the *Hyperion* section of the website in order to modernize it.

From Pericles to Mæcenas & the Renaissance patrons, it is the magnanimity of such individuals that have helped the arts to flourish. Be a part of helping your kulchur flourish; be a part of history.

HOW

To lend your support & become a patron, please visit the subscription page of our website: contramundum.net/subscription

For any questions, write us at: info@contramundum.net

SZEN
TKU
TH
Y